MEASURES OF P(___

Also by Domhnall Mitchell—
Emily Dickinson: Monarch of Perception

MEASURES OF POSSIBILITY

Emily Dickinson's Manuscripts

Domhnall Mitchell

UNIVERSITY OF MASSACHUSETTS PRESS

Amherst and Boston

Printed in the United States of America

LC 2005016188
ISBN 1-55849-456-1 (library cloth ed.); 1-55849-462-6 (paper)

Designed by Dennis Anderson
Set in Janson Text with Centaur display typography
by Binghamton Valley Composition
Printed and bound by The Maple-Vail Book Manufacturing Group

Library of Congress Cataloging-in-Publication Data

Mitchell, Domhnall, 1962–
Measures of possibility : Emily Dickinson's manuscripts / Domhnall Mitchell.
p. cm.
Includes bibliographical references and index.
ISBN 1-55849-456-1 (library cloth : alk. paper) —ISBN 1-55849-462-6 (pbk. : alk. paper)
1. Dickinson, Emily, 1830–1886—Criticism, Textual.
2. Dickinson, Emily, 1830–1886—Manuscripts. 3. Manuscripts, American—Editing.
4. Poetry—Editing. I. Title.

PS1541.Z5M583 2005
811'.4—dc22
2005016188

British Library Cataloguing in Publication data are available.

Cover art: Amherst College Archives and Special Collections,
Emily Dickinson Collection, A 499a.
Poetry text reprinted by permission of the publishers and the Trustees of Amherst College
from *The Manuscript Books of Emily Dickinson: A Facsimile Edition*, Ralph W.
Franklin, ed., Cambridge, Mass.: The Belknap Press of Harvard University Press,
Copyright © 1981 by the President and Fellows of Harvard College.

Til Patrick Mitchell Utne og Lise Utne

Dó Daniel agus Kathleen Johnston nach maireann; Róisín Conlon,
Elizabeth agus Jimmy McKenna, Dan Johnston, Bobby agus Ruth Johnston,
Séamus agus Brid Mac Seáin, Caitlin agus Seosamh Misteáil, Séan agus Máire
Mac Seáin, Liam agus Cristín Ó Bruadar, agus Pilib MacMathúna;
Ní bheidh a léitheid arís ann. Dó Kate Blaney, Theresa agus Pat McCann agus
Nell Long. Agus i gcuimhne Monica Johnston, Frank Johnston,
Jimmy Conlon, Felix Blaney, Ed Long, agus Peggy Mullaney:
Go ndéana Dia trócaire ar a nanam.

To Jeremy Hawthorn and Daniel Lombardo

Contents

ACKNOWLEDGMENTS

I AM GRATEFUL first to Houghton Library of Harvard College Library, Harvard University, for a fellowship in 2000, and to Amherst College, for the Copeland Fellowship in 2002, which made the greater part of the research for this book possible. My particular thanks to Cristanne Miller for supporting my application for the former, and to Karen Sanchez-Eppler and Kevin Sweeney, at Amherst College, for recommending me for the latter. Dawn Behne and Jeremy Hawthorn, former heads of department at the former Department of English (now the Department of Modern Foreign Languages) at the Norwegian University of Science and Technology in Trondheim deserve special mention for their flexibility in allowing me to barter extended research leave for additional teaching in 2001–2002. I am especially thankful and indebted to the staff of Archives and Special Collections, Frost Library at Amherst College—Daria D'Arienzo, Margaret R. Dakin, John Lancaster, Peter Nelson, Barbara Trippel Simmons, and Marian Walker; to Giuseppe Bisaccia, Eugene Zepp, and Roberta Zonghi and the staff at the Galatea Room of the Boston Public Library, Rare Books and Manuscripts Division; to the staff of the Houghton Library of Harvard College Library—Denison Beach, Philip Capernaros, Elizabeth Falsey, Tom Ford, Susan Halpert, Rachel Howarth, Leslie Morris, Sylvia Parsons, Jenny Rathbun, William P. Stoneman, Emily Walhout, Jozef Zajac, and the late Robert Abrams; and to the staff of Special Collections at the Jones Library in Amherst—Kate Boyle, Tevis Kimball, and Barbara Willis. Without them, this book would not have been possible; writing it was certainly made more enjoyable because of their good humor, professionalism, and warmth.

My former wife, Lise Utne, and son, Patrick Mitchell Utne, accompanied me to Amherst: Patrick attended his first school at Wildwood, and would like to thank his teachers Adrienne Goldman and Mrs. Hanks, Rebecca Keenan and Therese Daneke, and his fellow classmates from K1 2001/2002, especially Lucas (and parents Kelly and Erwin), Maya (and Kris), Isabel (and Joe), Georgia (and Yanik). Lise would like to thank Linda Barca, Kate Boyle, Wolf Krakowski, Claudia Lewis, Dan Lombardo, Lynn Mazar, and Catherine Rojas Olavarria. In Amherst itself Lise, Patrick, and I owe many and major debts of gratitude, in particular to Win and Betty Bernhard for their kindness and hospitality during and since 2001–2002, and for many occasions in Nancy Jane's and at their home in South Amherst. I am particularly and personally grateful to Cindy Dickinson and Jane Wald, of the Emily Dickinson Museum, for answering questions and for dinner; to Sherrill Harbison for renting her beautiful home in Taylor Street to us; to Dossie Kissam for helping to commemorate a lost friend; to Polly Longsworth for coffee and suggestions; to Peggy O'Brien for coffee and advice about relationships and classical music; to Ruth Owen Jones for lifts to and from Cambridge and for a wonderful lunch at her home in Amity Street; to Kate Boyle for lunches and long talks on the Common; and to the guides at the (former) Dickinson Homestead for their criticism and support. I would also like to acknowledge the staff of Antonio's Pizza on North Pleasant Street for the best slices in Massachusetts. Alfred and Nellie Habegger were kind enough to stay with us at Taylor Street, and Al made many generous contributions to the writing of this book. Stefann Müller and Heike Müller-Sedlaczek, Dougie MacShane, and Claudia Lewis, Zack Marti, Nadia, and Eaden deserve special mention for their friendship and kindness.

Outside Amherst, Jeremy Hawthorn drew my attention to useful articles and writers, and was constantly willing to read and respond to materials in depth and at short notice. Paul Goring and Ruth Sherry offered further support and advice, as did Bjørg Hawthorn. I am also indebted to Daniel Lombardo of Westhampton for his support, his oral glossary of Sicilian language and culture during Monday-night episodes of *The Sopranos*, and for a memorable introduction to live baseball at Fenway Park on Friday, 24 May 2002, during which the Red Sox beat the Yankees 9–8, scoring the winning run in the eleventh inning of an emotionally exhausting game. And to Karen Banta many thanks for the gift of her Toyota station wagon, which is still sorely missed, and her continued hospitality in Westhampton and Cape Cod. My thanks also to Bruce Wilcox and Carol Betsch of the University of Massachusetts Press for their work with this book, to Nancy J. Raynor for her wonderful copyediting, and to Mary Bellino for her indexing and additional proofreading. Needless to say, any errors are entirely the responsibility of the abovementioned.

Ralph W. Franklin, Cambridge, Mass.: The Belknap Press of Harvard University Press, Copyright © 1998, 1999 by the President and Fellows of Harvard College. Dickinson's letters are reprinted by permission of the publishers from *The Letters of Emily Dickinson*, ed. Thomas H. Johnson and Theodora Ward, Cambridge, Mass.: The Belknap Press of Harvard University Press, Copyright © 1958, 1986 by the President and Fellows of Harvard College.

By permission of Archives and Special Collections, Amherst College Library, Dickinson manuscripts A 20; A 21; A 34; A 41; A 42; A 82-7/8; A 85-3/4; A 86-7/8; A 88-13/14; A 91-3/4; A 94-1/2; A 115; A 130; A 132; A 133; A 157; A 160; A 175b; A 179; A 182; A 184; A 186; A 193; A 201; A 202; A 210; A 211; A 222; A 229; A 236; A 238; A 249; A 277; A 278; A 309; A 310; A 315; A 316; A 317; A 339; A 343; A 351/A 352; A 357; A 359; A 364; A 366; A 367; A 370; A 373; A 388; A 391; A 398; A 401; A 416; A 432; A 439; A 440; A 450; A 468; A 498; A 499; A 514; A 531; A 635; A 636; A 638; A 645; A 646; A 655; A 660; A 668; A 671; A 674; A 675; A 677; A 678; A 679; A 680; A 681; A 684; A 685; A 686; A 687; A 688; A 689; A 691; A 692; A 697; A 698; A 703; A 704; A 706; A 707; A 709; A 713; A 730; A 734; A 736; A 738; A 739; A 740; A 741; A 749; A 767; A 769; A 774; A 776; A 777; A 782; A 785; A 796; A 797; A 798; A 799; A 806; A 819; A 827; A 828; A 829; A 830; A 853; A 890; Ms D56 7.

By permission of the Boston Public Library/Rare Books Department, Courtesy of the Trustees, Dickinson manuscripts Ms Am 1093 no. 87, and Ms Am 1093 nos. 111 and 126.

By permission of the Houghton Library, Harvard University, Dickinson manuscripts Ms Am 1118.2 (35a), (46), (59), © The President and Fellows of Harvard College.

By permission of the Houghton Library, Harvard University, Dickinson manuscripts Ms Am 1118.3 (61), (68), (74), (123), (175), (180), (205), (230), (244), (263), (274), (294), (312), (315), (333), (335), (338), (339), (346), (350), (356), (358), (361), © The President and Fellows of Harvard College.

By permission of the Houghton Library, Harvard University, Dickinson Manuscripts Ms Am 1118.4 (L1), (L6), (L8), (L16), (L19), (L50), © The President and Fellows of Harvard College.

By permission of the Houghton Library, Harvard University, Ms Am 1118.5 (B20), (B22), (B23), (B31), (B32), (B33), (B44), (B50), (B54), (B55), (B62), (B66), (B67), (B73), (B79), (B88), (B90), (B98), (B106), (B119), (B123), (B125), (B131), (B139), (B150), (B162), (B175), (B184), (B186), (B193), © The President and Fellows of Harvard College.

By permission of the Jones Library, Amherst, Inc., Amherst, Mass., Emily Dickinson manuscript original of L190, *The Letters of Emily Dickinson*, ed. Thomas H. Johnson and Theodora Ward (Cambridge: Harvard University Press, Belknap Press, 1958), 2:335–36.

By permission of the Mortimer Rare Book Room, Smith College, North-ampton, Mass., Emily Dickinson manuscript originals of L221 (*Letters*, 2:364) and L336 (*Letters*, 2:465).

By permission of Archives and Special Collections, Amherst College Li-brary, Pharmacist Henry Adams Advertisement (Dickinson Manuscript A811 [verso], ED Collection Box 5); Susan Dickinson "letters to Mrs. Todd [and Mrs. Wilder]" (Amherst manuscript 791–1c); Helen Fiske Jackson to Rebecca Snell (7 October 1841); Otis Lord caricatures (Amherst manuscript A761a-z); and Miscellaneous Manuscripts: Harriet Beecher Stowe to Mary Ann (Cock-ell) Milman (1852).

By permission of the Houghton Library, Harvard University, Abigail May Alcott, Ms Am 1817.2 (15); Catherine Scott Turner Anthon, bMS Am 1118.95 (box 9); Lavinia Dickinson, Amy Lowell Collection; Susan Huntington Dickinson, Ms Am 1118.95 (box 9); Andrew Duncan, Ms Am 1838.2 (3); Annie Fields, Ms Am 1679; Sarah S. Hammond, MS Am 1609; Mary Landis Hampson, bMs Am Box 1923; Sarah Orne Jewett, Ms Am 1743.23 (1), (2), Ms Am 1743.26 (1); Fanny Kemble (Ms Am 1639); Helen S. Mitchell, bMS Am 1923 (7); Mary W. Mitchell (bMs Am 1280.226 (3853); Adelaide Proctor, Ms Am 1838.2 (7); Elizabeth Sedgwick, Ms Am 1670.1; Richard Whately, Ms Am 1838.2; William Wordsworth, Ms Am 1838.2 (12), Lowell autograph.

By permission of the Jones Library, Inc., Amherst, Mass., Helen Hunt Jackson, letter of 4 October 1841, in Mss. Coll., Helen Hunt Jackson Letters (1840–45); Martha Dickinson Bianchi, Last Will and Testament, Amherst, Mass., 15 November 1938, (copy); "Roper Rifle Co." folder; General Services Administration of the National Archives and Records, Washington, D.C., to Mr. Charles Green, librarian of the Jones Library, 28 January 1955, in "Am-herst Postmasters" folder; letter from Seth Nims, microfilm; "Amherst Post Office, List of box-holders, 1861;" assorted envelopes from "Envelopes and Stamps" folder A; assorted commercial materials from "Advertisements, Mis-cellaneous" folder; letter from Caleb H. Rice to Uriel Montague, 19 March 1846, in "Montague, Uriel, Correspondence"; calling card from Mrs. Herbert T. Cowles, in "E. D., Todd, Mabel Loomis, Miscellaneous Collection"; Emily Dickinson, Last Will and Testament, photostat; letter of 10 October 1960 from William McCarthy Jr.; Sarah Gates, Kate P. Kingman, and H. C. Pease, autographs, in "Autograph Albums," Clifton Johnson Collection.

By permission of the Mortimer Rare Book Room, Smith College, North-ampton, Mass., Margie R. Dodge, Journal (1885–86); Amanda M. Corey Ed-mond, "Journal of a Tour across the Atlantic, and through England, Scotland, Ireland, France, Germany & Belgium" (1844); Atossa Frost Stone, Manu-script Journal (1817–28).

By permission of the William Allan Neilson Library, Smith College, letter of Lucretia Peabody Hale to Edward Everett Hale (11 June 1855); letter of Susan Hale to Lucretia Peabody Hale (9, 19 June 1859, 19 June 1860 and 3 July 1863); Hale Family Papers, Sophia Smith Collection, Smith College, Northampton, Mass.

A Note on Measurement

In a letter to Elizabeth Holland, one of only a few women she addressed as "Sweet Sister," Emily Dickinson pronounced: "I measure by Fathoms, Numbers past away."[1] Something of the same attitude to numbers governs the spirit with which measurements are taken and used in this book. *Measures of Possibility* was begun in 1996–97, during a year of research leave spent in Amherst, Cambridge, and Boston, Massachusetts, when I first became interested in spatial patterns corresponding to metric line endings, paragraph endings, and generic markers in Dickinson's writing. At the time, reporting these patterns in general terms ("at this stage, the writing does not reach the right-hand margin of the page as it does in previous and subsequent lines") seemed too crude (it allowed no way of distinguishing between slight and substantial spaces, for instance), and it failed to provide a reader who had no immediate access to the originals with the kinds of information that would allow her or him to make informed and independent decisions about what the interaction between handwriting, space, margins, and paper might signify. It was for this reason that I decided to include measurements, in centimeters and millimeters, of the lines and spaces under consideration. Unless otherwise stated, all measurements are of original manuscripts, and they are taken with an Accu-SpecII transparent metric scale—chosen in part because it is a professional tool, but not least because it is extremely lightweight, and therefore unlikely to harm the original. Extreme care was taken in lowering the scale onto the surface of the autograph poems, letters, drafts, and fragments, and at no stage was any pressure applied to the scale, even when measuring the many originals which had at some stage been folded (during manufacture, or subsequently by hand), and which consequently did not lie fully flat. The accuracy of the measurements is therefore relative to the fragility and shape of the original materials, the nature of the handwriting—the size and shape of which can vary over time, and even within specific documents—and the distance between a sequence of handwriting and the edge of a page or between a sequence of writing and the line above or below it. Although certain allowances must be made because of these factors, I am nevertheless satisfied that an accurate impression of the totality of relationships between the length of a row of handwriting, marginal and end spaces, and paper size is reliably and consistently represented within each manuscript description.

1. L882, early 1884. In *The Letters of Emily Dickinson*, ed. Thomas H. Johnson and Theodora Ward (Cambridge: Harvard University Press, Belknap Press, 1958), 3:811.

MEASURES OF POSSIBILITY

Prologue

Emily Has Left the Building

Even the most perfect reproduction of a work of art is lacking in one element: its presence in time and space, its unique existence at the place where it happens to be.

Walter Benjamin, "The Work of Art in the Age of Mechanical Reproduction"

HISTORY MOVES in mysterious ways. In 2001 it was announced that work was under way to convert part of the Homestead, birthplace of Emily Dickinson, that most anticommercial and publicity-hostile of nineteenth-century writers, "to a visitor reception area that will include a gift shop and restroom."[1] At the same time, it was reported that important renovations were being made to the Evergreens next door, former home of Emily Dickinson's brother Austin and her most important correspondent, Susan Gilbert Dickinson. The Evergreens had almost been lost, for at one stage Susan's daughter Martha Dickinson Bianchi decreed in her will that "for sentimental reasons I do not want my dwelling house occupied by anyone else, other than as specified above [by Alfred Leete Hampson], and when the property is no longer desired for occupancy by those mentioned above, and the owner desires to sell said real estate, the said house shall be razed before the purchaser secures a good title to said land. To satisfy this condition it is not sufficient that the house be removed and placed upon some other land. It is my will that the house be taken down to the cellar."[2] As Greg Farmer pointed out, Bianchi was concerned that the family home "might be converted to a teahouse, a student residence, or a fraternity."[3] And her reasons for opposing such a change of ownership are the same factors that make the Evergreens a more interesting structure than the Homestead—at least from the viewpoint of material history: so many of the house's contents, personal effects, and interiors remained either intact or salvageable.[4] For those who were fortunate enough to be given access before the process of restoration was fully completed, there was a feeling that the house had only very recently, and hurriedly, been abandoned.

There are interesting parallels with the poetry of Bianchi's aunt, Emily Dickinson, whose autographs are now reproduced in a variety of media. Part of their appeal at this point in the history of Dickinson's publication by others

I

is that they seem to bring us as close to the source as is physically possible.[5] The vocabulary used to describe them attests to this: readers report "the sense that they are actually holding the manuscripts themselves" and "testify to the near sensate experience of viewing photographic representations of the manuscripts in color and in close-up."[6] In addition, Dickinson is often referred to by her first name, as if she were personally known to the reader.[7] J. Hillis Miller, writing about Proust, provides some insights into the dimension of intimacy: "A desire to know and possess, to know by possessing or possess by knowing, a desire that might be called an unassuageable, concupiscent curiosity, leads the lover to substitute by a species of metonymy things near to the central object of desire, in ever-receding degrees of proximity, for the beloved herself or himself. Freud called these substitutes 'fetishes.' If the lover can possess the substitutes, he or she may by indirection come to know and possess the central object of desire they replace."[8] A fine line exists between attempting to know and attempting to control: the former seems to me an absolutely reasonable activity, and as David Higdon points out about Joseph Conrad, there "is an undeniable mystique to the holograph manuscript of any author, perhaps because one intuits that he has come close to touching actual creativity."[9] Especially those Dickinson texts that appear to be unfinished, which show words that are crossed out and written at angles, seem—like the Evergreens—to have been left just moments before. They bear the marks of intense presence—not of completed works, but of the artist working. Photographic and electronic reproductions, like guided tours, give an appearance of proximity to authenticity: domestic and imaginary interiors are seen as they once were and not through the eyes of others.

At the same time, we need to remind ourselves that getting close to the domestic and imaginative spaces once occupied by them is an activity that Dickinson and Bianchi never explicitly approved. Indeed, it was rumored (by Bianchi herself) that Dickinson instructed the family servant, Irishwoman Margaret Maher, to burn her papers after her death (though these may have been working papers or partial drafts, the so-called scraps and fragments that have become a primary object of recent study and estimation).[10] And "Dickinson's sister, Lavinia, destroyed most of her sister's correspondence immediately after her death, believing this to be her sister's wish."[11] Though no one suspects Dickinson of having wanted the poems placed in a locked box in her mahogany bedroom bureau to have been similarly immolated, their double enclosure coincides with her practice, while alive, of vigilantly and vigorously controlling the circumstances by which her poems were circulated.[12] Of nearly two thousand lyrics, only ten were ever published in the conventional sense, though many more were circulated privately (usually singly, and mostly to close friends and to family).[13] Like visitors to the Homestead Gift Shop and to the Evergreens, then, viewers of Dickinson's manuscripts occupy an ambivalent or uncertain position—we are at once privileged witnesses and uninvited guests.[14]

How do we organize and present once private and carefully regulated spaces for public consumption while preserving the integrity and significance of the appearances they once had? For observers may see the same papers and sites as the Dickinson family, but we do not see them from the same place in time. Contemporary readers come from a point in literary history that is different and distant from the point at which these documents emerged. Emily Dickinson wrote *before* e. e. cummings, T. S. Eliot, H. D., D. H. Lawrence, Marianne Moore, Ezra Pound, and William Carlos Williams, but she is read long *after* them. The impact of modernist (and, subsequently, postmodernist) experiments with poetic form may be understood in part as a move away from regular meter and toward its organization according to other stylistic criteria. In the twentieth century, inherited and traditional patterns of verse were often discarded in favor of innovative and individual designs. In addition, there was a breaking down of the distinctions between poetry and prose—or, rather, a privileging of loosely formatted poetry over poetry formatted as verse. I mention these commonplaces because it is important to approach Dickinson's documents with some degree of self-consciousness—for what is our own role in the attempted reconstruction of her meanings? Do Dickinson's autographs anticipate the attention given to the meaningful potential of writing's graphic dimension in modernist writers, or does modernist writing create a lens through which such an image of Dickinson is projected? Does the attention paid to manuscripts mean that "the work can now, more than a hundred years later, finally speak for itself," or is this to confuse contemporary taste with the author's?[15] What does it mean when we apply aesthetic judgments derived from experimentation with the possibilities of visual form in the layout of printed poetry to the appearance of a handwritten worksheet or an autograph letter to a friend or Amherst neighbor?

To take a specific example: among the Dickinson worksheets that are stored at the Special Collections Room of the Frost Library at Amherst College is a scrap of blue-lined stationery, on which the following draft was originally written in pencil:[16]

> Flowers are
> so enticing
> I fear that
> they are
> sins – like
> gambling

or apos-

tasy –

Because Dickinson grew flowers in her bedroom and conservatory and frequently commented on them in her correspondence, this tiny fragment may have been intended to accompany the gift of a real flower to, or to acknowledge a floral gift from, a friend, relative, or neighbor. It may have been written in anticipation of one or both, or intended for inclusion in a longer and more general letter.

But what happens if I think of publishing this document? What are the most appropriate media of reproduction and distribution? To take a fairly basic starting point: am I to understand that the message above demonstrates a fully considered and integral formal design, or can it legitimately be regularized as prose? In the case of other writers, the graphic dimensions of a note to a neighbor, friend, or relation might be understood as functions of its informality. More generally, manuscripts of letters and poems are usually understood by their recipients as conforming in some way or another to certain genres; how the genre is embodied in a handwritten document may not necessarily alter that recognition. Although Dickinson fits approximately two or three words into the lateral space of the paper she wrote on, in other words, no evidence exists that any of her correspondents ever thought of this as an attempt at blurring the lines between poetry and prose: poetry was recognized as poetry, prose as prose (which is not the same as saying that the latter was seen as less literary or compelling). But, increasingly, some Dickinson critics see her nonpublication as a choice made in order to protect a much more sophisticated and flexible textual and generic medium than conventional culture and type could have accommodated. For these critics, there is a sense in which her manuscripts can be seen as "published" and final versions—especially those manuscripts that were circulated in letters or gathered in autograph miscellanies. The irony of standard editions of Dickinson's poetry, according to this argument, is that the material details of such a medium are lost in any conversion from manuscript to print—which is precisely why Dickinson refused to publish in the first place.[17]

For instance, the print translation I have offered attempts as much as possible to be faithful to Dickinson's own arrangement of lines and words in a way that is inflected by recent theories and practices of editing her. But in their three-volume *Letters of Emily Dickinson* (1958), Thomas Johnson and Theodora Ward offer a very different version:

Flowers are so enticing I fear that they are sins – like gambling
　　or apostasy.[18]

Given the possibility that this was an unsent draft for an informal note addressed potentially to anyone whom Dickinson had (or might have) sent flowers to or received flowers from, Johnson and Ward's rearrangement may not seem unreasonable. Nevertheless, a great deal of recent critical energy has been spent on the issue of whether Dickinson's letters can be isolated as conveniently from her lyrics as the separate editions of her correspondence and poetry might lead us to assume. Prose fragments differ materially from their presentation in previous editions of the correspondence, and some argue that not acknowledging the difference can amount to serious misrepresentation. What these critics would claim is that any distinction between Dickinson's prose and her poetry is an editorial imposition that does not consistently exist in fact. So what Johnson calls a "prose fragment" may be a poetic fragment: instead of one sentence, eight lines slow down our reading and force us to give more weight of attention to individual words and lines. Even the splitting of "apostasy," or so the argument would have it, may be seen as significant; in this case, the division might correspond to a kind of fear on the part of the speaker to confront the truth of her addiction and its consequences for her immortal soul. Extending the word over two lines has the effect of delaying the knowledge of her sinfulness. Indeed, if one plays the impossible game of pretending that these lines constituted an undiscovered work by Jean Toomer or D. H. Lawrence, then such an argument would have been accepted almost without question.

Johnson and Ward supposed that this fragment was prose, then, but there is some evidence for a different assumption.

> Flowers are so enticing
> I fear that they are sins –
> [L]ike gambling or apostasy –

As this arrangement shows, what Dickinson's editors have previously identified as prose fragments occasionally demonstrate a degree of metrical regularity; in my reconstruction, the note reads as two lines of iambic trimeter (with a common trochaic inversion in the opening foot) and one of tetrameter. Read this way, the meter and half rhyme (*aab?*) create an effect equivalent to aposiopesis: the final line (if it existed; the writing could amount to a complete tercet or to a sequence of prose) is not supplied, but the prosodic organization leads us to anticipate it and to speculate as to its contents. Of course, the appearance of Dickinson's note does not correspond to the standard physical, stanzaic layout of most nineteenth-century poetry, and the partial rhyme I have described seems more oblique in the autograph original. In addition, the capital letters with which Dickinson and other nineteenth-century writers identified the beginning of a verse (a poetic line) are missing from this draft. And the rhyming couplets—if they are rhyming couplets—are proportionately unusual though by no means unprecedented in Dickinson's work. One wonders, then, if the writer herself thought of this fragment as material for a poem or a letter, or if it was somehow meant to result in the suspension or interrogation of such boundaries.[19]

Ralph W. Franklin argues that the critic is often faced with giving up "the semi-final drafts to an eternal limbo," and he goes on to sum up the difficulty of producing a finalized text when Dickinson herself offered no indication as to how to do so: "We lack, then, authorial final intention throughout the poems of Emily Dickinson. If we were to read the poems as she intended them, we could not progress beyond a full variorum edition, or more strictly, not beyond the manuscripts."[20] Such uncertainties can enable as much as they confound.[21] There is a sense in which Dickinson's failure, or decision not, to specify exactly how she wanted her works to be presented has been historically liberating: editors have been free to represent her "intentions" without authorial interference, though often invoking her name in the process.[22] Past editions of Dickinson's writings necessarily overlap in terms of contents, but they present poems in often very different ways, thus promoting divergent strategies of reading, at both the collective and individual levels. The first wave of editors, Mabel Loomis Todd and Thomas Wentworth Higginson (during the 1890s), grouped the poems according to themes (love, nature, time and eternity) and often regularized (among other things) punctuation, capitalization, rhyme, and spelling. Todd's 1894 edition of Dickinson's letters assumed a separation of Dickinson's lyrical and epistolary productions which recent critics have contested.[23] During the 1920s and 1930s, Martha Dickinson Bianchi and Millicent Todd Bingham often included poems in what they perceived to be their biographical contexts. Thomas Johnson (1955) and Ralph Franklin (1998) offered what are essentially New Critical editions: the poems are published in chronological order, numbered, and printed in neat stanzas.[24] Franklin (1981) presented photographic reproductions of the poems grouped together as fascicles and sets (manuscript anthologies collated by Dickinson herself; fascicles are sewn together, sets are not). Ellen Hart and Martha Nell Smith (1998) reproduce "letter-poems" sent to Susan Dickinson, preserving the original line breaks, blank spaces, marks, crosses, and dashes. Implicit in a mode of presentation or editorial apparatus is a framework of interpretation: to include Dickinson's letters and poems together as correspondence to a particular individual is to suggest that the meaning of those texts is somehow bound up with the relationship between them. Alternatively, any chronological presentation of the poems assumes at some level that this is how Dickinson experienced the progression of her own work. Intention does not necessarily enter into such textual systems of organization, however. When Franklin edited *The Manuscript Books of Emily Dickinson*, he did not argue that poems had to be read in the context of their fascicle sequence, though other critics have, separately, come to that conclusion.[25]

The slip of paper on which Dickinson wrote "Flowers are so enticing" is small and narrow (approximately 4 x 10 cm), and one may infer from this that Dickinson deliberately cut or tore paper into smaller sections in the knowledge that they would better fit her habits of composition. In other words, the size of the paper is connected to the space in which it was carried, stored, sent, or held—the pocket of a dress, skirt, or apron; a workbox; an envelope; or a hand, to take some obvious examples. It might even be related to where she placed the paper when writing: did she scribble while the page was balanced on her leg, flattened on a windowsill, or at the margins of a kitchen table covered in rising dough and flour?[26] In short, it is possible to imagine a scenario where Dickinson carried blank slips of paper in case a phrase or image came to her while she was performing some other task—indoors or out, in the kitchen, garden, or conservatory. Or it may be that the scale was determined by reasons of economy or imaginative procedure. If this is a draft, then it tells us that Dickinson used smaller bits of paper because inspiration occasionally came to her in short sequences, to be jotted down as and when they arrived; short bursts of the imagination do not need to be written on large sheets. For full pages would be distracting: the evidence seems to suggest that Dickinson stored lines and images separately for combination or revision elsewhere (though if she eventually transferred this example of writing onto a larger sheet, she could still have retained the lineation, of course).

Nevertheless, a major discrepancy in works of criticism promoting manuscripts as the principal site of Dickinson's creative enterprise is that they do not attempt to record or represent the relationship between the extent of the writing and the page that is written on. This is important, because a substantial difference exists between the two "editions" that follow:

Flowers are	Flowers are
so enticing	so enticing
I fear that	I fear that
they are	they are
sins – like	sins – like
gambling	gambling
or apos-	or apos-
tasy –	tasy –

Because the first version is situated within blank space, it suggests that the lineation is motivated or deliberate—like poetry, which does not reach the physical margins of the page because its lines are governed by some principle of organization or presentation that is aesthetic and semantically charged. The second version gives an impression of the totality of relationships between words, lines (or rows), and paper. This version does not absolutely preclude the possibility that the alignment on the page was deliberate—but it allows us at least to consider that the layout may in part have been a consequence of the dimensions of the writing surface. It was the contours of the paper, and not the mind, which helped shape the physical topography of the writing. Thus, when Johnson and Ward presented their edition of the note as a line of prose, it is possible to argue that they were influenced by their perception of the material boundaries of the paper and not by (or not only by) the ideological or literary-theoretical limitations of New Criticism.

To take another example, Dickinson's letter of 11 January 1850, to her uncle, Joel Warren Norcross ("Dearest of all dear uncles"), concludes with three paragraphs that are all inscribed vertically on the left-edge margins of three pages of the autograph original.[27] One might safely conclude that such an inscription is, first, a side effect of Dickinson's having run out of space and, second, a characteristic of its informal epistolary production, where the appearance of the letter or note is less significant than (say) its phatic function, contents, or style. Yet, one of the consequences of the manuscript approach is that readers are more than ever attuned to all of the physical details of a Dickinson autograph. Thus, Melanie Hubbard has stated that "the reader must literally turn the page—must switch from reading down the vertical axis to reading along the horizontal axis."[28] Although Hubbard's comments are related to a specific example (rather than to drafts in their entirety), her work can be applied as a methodology to many more of Dickinson's manuscripts. Indeed, at the 1999 conference of the Emily Dickinson International Society, it was suggested that vertical inscription in a manuscript poem or letter should be reproduced as vertical inscription in a print transcription, as one must always allow for the possibility that this was an integral part of the letter or poem's communicative apparatus.

Hubbard's argument has massive implications, because, after her death in 1886, Dickinson left behind not only some eight hundred poems gathered together into neatly sewn fascicles and unthreaded sets but also hundreds more of apparently miscellaneous segments of writing scribbled on scraps of paper. Johnson and Ward classified many of these workshop scraps as "prose fragments" or drafts; Hubbard contests this definition and argues instead that many of them were compositional units whose significance was embedded in the materials on which they were inscribed.[29] One wonders, then, what we are

to make of this, the discarded rough draft of a note in pencil from Dickinson
to her nephew Ned; Johnson and Ward thought of it as an earlier version of
L988, dated June 1885.[30]

We do not   think

enough of   the

Dead ⟨That⟩ as   Exhili   none

rants –   they are

not ⟨they⟩dissuaders |

but   Lures

Keepers of   that   existed

great ⟨still⟩   Romance

still   to   us   fore

closed   –   while   have   away

we   Envy ⟨exist⟩   their

wisdom   ⟨is⟩   we de

⟨a⟩   lament

Coveting their   wis   they   take

dom we ⟨daring⟩ ⟨trust so⟩   lament

their   silence

Grace   is   still

a secret –   that   can

Do the frequent line breaks and end spaces make this a poem?[31] Assuming (for
the sake of argument) that the answer is yes (which is also to assume that the
author would have approved our reading this draft in the first place), can we
then further assume that the horizontal and vertical arrangement of the writ-
ing is a considered one? Johnson and Ward thought not, transcribing the same
lines (which they identify as Prose Fragment 50) in this way:[32]

We do not think enough of the Dead as exhilirants – they are not dis-
suaders but Lures – Keepers of that great Romance still to us foreclosed
– while coveting (we envy) their wisdom we lament their silence. Grace
is still a secret. That they have existed none can take away. That they
still exist is a trust so daring we thank thee that thou hast hid these things
from us and hast revealed them to them. The power and the glory are
the post mortuary gifts.[33]

To take the example of a poem: what follows is as close as a limited knowl-
edge of word processing and print technology will allow me to approximate
the appearance of a Dickinson autograph lyric.

silence you – (inverted)
But it can (inverted)

That sacred
Closet when
you sweep –
Entitled "Memory" –
Select a
reverential Broom –   *itself,* (rotated)
And do it
silently –

'Twill be a Labor
of surprise –
Besides Identity
Of other Interlocutors
A probability –

August the Dust   *sede* (rotated)
of that Domain –
Unchallenged –
let it lie –
You cannot super-

In the standard print versions of this poem, two- and three-word sequences
are joined together ("August the Dust of that Domain"), and a first stanza of
eight rows of writing is shortened to four lines.[34] But perhaps the most serious
loss, it might be claimed, takes place when Dickinson's editors shift the mode
of inscription and presentation from handwriting to normative typographic
practice. While Dickinson's autograph features multidirectional writing

where the letters tilt left to right with an energy that might be seen as corresponding to the movement of the broom, the edited version is uniform: the lines are horizontal and the stanzas consistently spaced and shaped.

For some critics, part of the effectiveness of "That sacred Closet" lies in its manuscript design. The experience of reading the poem is fairly conventional until near the end, when the reader is forced to follow the script up the right-hand margin and then to turn the page upside down before being confronted with the final line(s): "But it can / silence you."[35] According to the argument of the manuscript school (as I understand it), the material arrangement of the last words (from "supersede" onward) creates a suspension, a postponement, of meaning: as we swivel the page, the closing phrase is anticipated but also delayed before striking home with additional force. The reversal of the writing is a tactic, then: the message delivered at the close is made all the more chilling by the physical deferral enabled by the shift in the direction of the handwriting.

But to take such a view is not necessarily to suspend critical judgment or intervention: it is to privilege one aspect of the manuscript's particulars (the direction of its last seven words) over the logic of its other aspects (its pattern of rhythm and rhyme, for instance, which is no less material, or the fact that the majority of the poem is written horizontally). That the manuscripts themselves offer the best indications as to the possible significance and integrity of their own appearance is undeniable; but what kinds of signals does this one provide about itself? Are there consistent features and anomalous ones? What things strike us as being unusual or different within the pattern of inscription suggested by the poem itself?

Postponing discussion of the writing on the margins and at the head of the poem, perhaps the first thing one notices about "That sacred Closet" is the relationship of upper- and lowercase letters. In the first stanza, the words "That," "Closet," "Entitled," "Memory," "Select," "Broom," and "And" are capitalized. If I group these words according to possible patterns, I see that "Closet," "Memory," and "Broom" are nouns, "Entitled" and "Select" are verbal forms, while "That" and "And" are (among other things) different kinds of conjunction. In short, no obvious pattern of grammatical or even semantic similarity governs the capitalization of these words. But "That," "Closet," "Entitled," "Select," and "And" all coincide physically with the beginning of a row of writing, so one might respond to the prompting of the manuscript by visualizing the first stanza of the poem in this way:

> That sacred
> Closet when you sweep –
> Entitled "Memory" –

> Select a reverential Broom –
> And do it silently –

It seems to me that there is still an apparent discrepancy here: "Memory" and "Broom" are assigned capitals even though neither coincides with the start of a line in the autograph original. Both are nouns, as is "Closet," and one knows from Dickinson's other poems that she often assigned capitals to nouns to free them from their literal or conventionally assigned definitions. If I revise my intimations about the stanza with this information in mind, I produce the following:

> That sacred Closet when you sweep –
> Entitled "Memory" –
> Select a reverential Broom –
> And do it silently –

At least for this stanza, I have a working model of Dickinson's practices that seems consistent with the material evidence of the original. Moreover, the lines observe metrical consistency, though they were not reconstructed with such consistency in mind. The poem's meter (iambic tetrameter and trimeter) and rhyme scheme (*abcb*) act independently to corroborate my surmises, however: attending only to the pattern of upper- and lowercase letters in the autograph, I arrived at a layout that coincided with a definite structure of rhythm and rhyme. Clearly, the unsolicited emergence of rhyme and meter in my adaptation of this lyric suggests that there are poetic conventions which are not immediately apparent in the physical draft but which can nonetheless be detected as operating within it.

  This is how the poem is represented (as Fr1385) in the standard three-volume variorum edition of Dickinson's poems:[36]

> That sacred Closet when you sweep –
> Entitled "Memory" –
> Select a reverential Broom –
> And do it silently –
>
> 'Twill be a Labor of surprise –
> Besides Identity
> Of other Interlocutors
> A probability –

August the Dust of that Domain –
Unchallenged – let it lie –
You cannot supersede itself,
But it can silence you.

Although manuscript critics would be justified in claiming that this version lessens the presentational options contained within (but not by) the handwritten original, it is still clear that this way of inscribing the poem seems consistent with most aspects of its draft appearance. Indeed, there is a strong argument for saying that this rendering of the poem conforms in every detail to both the visible *and* (initially) invisible laws that may be said to regulate its shape. Granted, viewing a digitized image of the autograph poem on a computer screen at the start of the twenty-first century may seem superior to the printed version in the technology used to reproduce it. But if we take into account all the information conveyed by the manuscript, the standard printed version is at least equal to the digitized image in reconstructing how readers of the *nineteenth century*, including Dickinson and her correspondents, would have understood the logic of its appearances.[37]

"That sacred Closet when you sweep" is the last of a total of fifteen poems enclosed within Set 14, as it is designated in Franklin's *Manuscript Books of Emily Dickinson*: according to his estimate, these poems were composed between 1873 and 1877 and were inscribed on ten leaves of grayish white stationery with a blue rule, embossed "C. V. Mills" above a capitol with Congress below it.[38] In his variorum edition of the poems, Franklin assigns a new number to the poem, Fr1385 (formerly J1273) and estimates the date of its composition to have been around 1875. This information is useful for two reasons. First, it establishes the poem as having been written well into the period (about 1870) when most manuscript critics believe that Dickinson was at her most graphically experimental. Second, the poem's placement with fourteen others provides us with an aggregate of material details that may serve as useful data for the reader seeking information about how best to represent manuscript lyrics in other textual and electronic environments.

If, as I did, one comes to this set expecting evidence of a visually innovative and transgressive imagination, one is surprised by the general neatness of the handwriting and the relative consistency in layout. Most poems begin approximately three to three and one-half centimeters from the top of the page, as "That sacred Closet" does. Most come to within half a centimeter of the right-hand edge of the paper, as "That sacred Closet" does. Most leave a noticeably increased space between the end of a word and the paper's edge in order to indicate that the word belongs to the line that precedes it, as "That sacred

Closet" does. (As I argue elsewhere, Dickinson consistently reverses the prac-
tice of indenting a line to indicate nonintegral separation: she prefers to leave
space *after* a word, not *before*.) But none of the other lyrics have the upside-
down and marginal inscription that characterizes "That sacred Closet." With-
out denying the validity and value of other attempts to explain the purpose of
such chirographic deviation, I offer the following scenario for consideration:
there are fifteen poems in this set, written on ten sheets of paper. Since they
are not folded, these ten sheets provide twenty sides of paper, and the first
fourteen poems in the set occupy nineteen of these writing surfaces. Most of
the pages have seventeen or eighteen rows of script; the first poem has seven-
teen rows on one side of the sheet and fifteen on the other (plus two variant
rows). On only one other page are there twenty rows: this is on the side of a
sheet that includes the third and fourth stanzas of Fr1382, "Not any more to
be lacked," together with three rows of variants. Thus in this set at least,
Dickinson took approximately seventeen or eighteen rows of writing to ap-
proach the end of a page, at which time she would continue the poem overleaf
(if necessary). But when she came to record Fr1385, only one side of a leaf
remained, so that after eighteen rows, there was nowhere else to write except
in the right and top margins. And unlike the other page where she fits twenty
rows of writing, this one included two stanza breaks (represented by blank
interlinear spaces), lessening the area available to work in. So there is at least
the possibility that, on this last side of the last sheet of paper, Dickinson ran
out of room when inscribing the last six and one-half words (or two and one-
half rows) of the last poem she wanted to include in this set. The vertical and
upside-down inscription of these words may not be premeditated, but an ac-
cidental and nonsignificant side effect of the total physical relation of words,
lines, stanza breaks, and paper space.

  In the absence of the author's own wishes (either expressed or unambigu-
ously implied), any attempt to do justice to such materials must rely on com-
bining a close observation of the materials themselves with a knowledge of
nineteenth-century handwriting practices generally. For example, the last
page of an otherwise uniform letter dated 31 December 1855 from Julia K.
Field to her mother, written on ruled paper, first employs horizontal hand-
writing and then overlays this with vertical script. Such instances of cross-
writing or cross-hatching are by no means unusual in the nineteenth century:
the last page of a letter from Camilla Wergeland (later Collett) to Jonas Col-
lett, dated 24 May 1840, is written in the same way.[39] Closer to home, the
Oxford English Dictionary quotes Mrs. Carlyle in 1850 referring to a letter with
"two little sheets all crossed," and there is also the following exchange from
Jane Austen's *Emma*: "I really must, in justice to Jane, apologise for her writing
so short a letter – only two pages you see – hardly two – and in general she

fills the whole paper and crosses half. My mother often wonders that I can make it out so well. She often says, when the letter is first opened, 'Well, Hetty, now I think you will be put to it to make out all that chequer-work.' "[40]

Variation in the direction of lettering in autograph correspondence, and insertion in the left, right, top, and bottom margins, were widespread and casual phenomena in the nineteenth century.[41] Consider the following detail, from a letter by Abby Wood Bliss (at an early stage of her life, one of Dickinson's closest friends) to the Reverend Daniel Bliss, dated Amherst, 1 January 1874. It begins, "My Dearest love – A Happy New Year to you."[42]

Again, Jane Austen's letters are full of instances where there is writing upside down on the page, and yet this has no significance.[43] Similarly, a letter to the young Helen Fiske (later Hunt Jackson) from her mother finishes with lines written vertically along the left-hand margin and across the place and time of the letter's heading on the opening page.[44] Crucially, another letter from the same writer to Rebecca Snell (dated Thursday, 7 October 1841) opens with an instruction above the salutation: "Read overhead first," meaning that the lines written vertically above the date had to be read *before* the rest of the letter because the convention was to read such passages last (as overflow

that did not fit into the space available on the final page).[45] Writing from
Madison in May 1861, Byron Hartley Williams also resorts to vertical script
along the left-hand margin when he runs out of available space. Julia K. Field
sends another letter to her mother in March 1861 where she writes horizon-
tally but upside-down above the heading on the first page. On lined paper,
Ruth Payne Burgess writes a letter in which she switches to vertical script
above her opening address, "Home March 20th, 1889 / My dear Daughter."[46]
An early draft of Matthew Arnold's "Dover Beach" proceeds normally down
the page for twenty lines, until the author runs out of room and pens the next
eight lines (there are a total of only 28 in this version) vertically on the right-
hand side of the paper.[47] All these examples suggest a rule that also applies to
Dickinson's manuscripts: the multidirectionality of the handwriting is a non-
significant component of a letter or poem's appearance.

The task of attempting to reconstruct the significance of the spaces Dick-
inson wrote *upon* is somewhat similar to the task of identifying the space that
she wrote *in*. In the *Emily Dickinson International Society Bulletin*, Kristin Her-
ron described the research she carried out for a Historic Furnishings Report
(HFR) on Dickinson's bedroom, as well as the methodology behind it: "More
than just a guide to decoration, a historic furnishings report provides an anal-
ysis of objects and primary and secondary sources, while contextualizing
choices in the placement of objects. Context is provided not only through
secondary sources but also through information from the people who lived in
or visited the Homestead (from letters, memoirs, or oral communications)."[48]
As Herron goes on to admit, direct contextual evidence is scarce—Dickinson
wrote *in* her bedroom, but rarely *about* it. And there are no contemporaneous
pictorial records or probate inventories. Instead, current representations of
Dickinson's bedroom rely on her niece's limited recollections, as well as on
"period sources, including trade catalogs, probate inventories from New En-
gland households of the same era, and prescriptive literature (i.e., home dec-
orating advice)." As the report concludes, "we may never know what the room
really looked like during the poet's tenure in the space."[49] By extension, more
than a century after her death, the challenge of seeing Dickinson's writing
spaces *as they might have appeared to her*, and not as we want them to appear, is
still considerable. Given that she chose not to publish in the conventional
sense and left no explicit instructions as to how (or even if) her autographs
were to be assembled, presented, and distributed, our interpretations can
never easily be authenticated; certainly, they may never be definitive. But that
does not mean that authoritative versions cannot or should not be attempted,
that some versions are not more convincing and useful than others, or that the
project itself is not legitimate and worthwhile.

In the first chapter of this book, then, I will briefly consider what kinds of contexts—biographical, cultural, editorial, and epistolary—have been found useful in reproducing Dickinson's practices and attempt to evaluate their value. Are the physical appearances of Dickinson's drafts related to economies of scale, or were they meant to influence the meaning of the poem? For many critics, the endless appeal of Dickinson's work lies precisely in its ability to provoke such questions while refusing to provide definite answers to them. But again and again, one runs up against the problem of intention in Dickinson's works; again and again, intention in Dickinson is irrevocably bound up with issues of manuscript status and appearance, as well as genre. If we understand "Flowers are so enticing" as a draft note or as material for a letter, does the lineation matter? Is our apprehension of its poetic status related to something intrinsic and deliberate (the quality of the language, the appearance of meter and rhyme) or extrinsic and accidental (a side effect of the size of the paper on which it is written)? How did Dickinson want us to respond to this writing (if at all), and are her wishes fully recoverable or only to be conjectured about? Does a text have to be deliberate for us to accept the integrity of its graphic appearance? Intention is most often understood as fallaciously equivalent to authorial meaning—not what the text signifies but what the writer wanted it to signify, as well as her or his design or goal in writing in the first place. But what if the text can be understood as demonstrating patterns of inscription that point to a conventional, extralinguistic principle of organization? Can we then largely dispense with manuscripts and rely on printed editions? Are Dickinson's original texts fully deliberate and ongoing exercises in aesthetic process that demand attention to their every graphic detail? Or are there circumstances and procedures external to the manuscript page which explain the logic, and coincide with the details, of such appearances and that justify recourse to their printed equivalents? What criteria are available to us in attempting to locate editions of Dickinson's poetry and letters that respect the author's practices and can be relied on as sufficiently authoritative for most critical and pedagogical purposes? These concerns touch on practical and literary-theoretical issues of textual editing, genre, and understanding which form the basis of this book. They are central to approaching a place Dickinson once famously defined (in Fr320) as "Where the Meanings, are."

CHAPTER ONE

Packaging Emily
Dickinson in Books

The question is: How many competing versions do you want?

Melinda T. Koyanis, Director of Intellectual Property,
Harvard University Press

IN THE FALL of 1994, Phillip Stambovsky, English Department chair and professor at Albertus Magnus College, requested permission from Harvard University Press to publish a selected edition of two hundred Dickinson poems that he had transcribed himself directly from her autographs, complete with original line breaks, irregular dashes, word variants and divisions.[1] The book, then at the final review stage with the University of North Carolina Press, was provisionally titled "Poetic Work of Emily Dickinson: A Reader's Text," and it was designed for use in introductory (undergraduate-level) classes on poetry and for a general readership. Stambovsky was one of a growing number of talented readers who had turned their attention to Dickinson's manuscripts in dissatisfaction with what they perceived to be the continued and textually unsanctioned regularization and misrepresentation of Dickinson's poems by print editors. Many of these critics now work from the assumption that autograph poems have primacy over their printed versions, and it has been alleged that to read Dickinson in any standard typographic edition is effectively to read her in translation, at one remove from her actual practices. Specifically, it has been claimed that line arrangements, the shapes of words and letters, and the particular angles of dashes are all potentially integral to any given poem's meaning, making a graphic contribution to its contents.[2]

Despite this, Stambovsky's book was never published; his request to Harvard University Press was turned down flat, and the University of North Carolina Press did not pursue the book, presumably on the grounds that it could not afford to mount a costly and time-consuming legal challenge to Harvard's right to control Dickinson materials.[3] In a letter, a Harvard University Press spokesperson justified its refusal on the following grounds: "It is our position that authorizing such an anthology based on one person's variant typographic interpretation of the poetry, aimed at a general reader, was not in the best interest of preserving or presenting the integrity of the Dickinson work."[4] And in a letter from October 1994 to Stambovsky, Harvard further opined that it was "in the best interest of overall integrity in presenting the work of Emily Dickinson to hold off on licensing other editions or compilations until the completion of the new variorum text."[5]

These opinions are not necessarily mutually reconcilable: the first (in tandem with the epigraph to this chapter) seems to offer an absolute ethical position—too many texts offering differently formatted versions of the poetry and aimed at a general readership will only result in confusion. Melinda T. Koyanis, then copyright and permissions officer for Harvard University Press, solidified this impression when she claimed that they responded negatively to "proposals that involve selection of variants on aesthetic grounds, allowing for combining and recombining, to make versions of new poems, [because they] add yet another level of complexity and fragmentation."[6] But the second position appears to be more relative (and therefore potentially undercuts the argument of the first, which would have to be universally applied to be valid): Harvard University Press did not want to contribute to a proliferation of Dickinson editions until such time as Ralph Franklin's *Poems of Emily Dickinson* was published—by the press—in 1998. And they were as good as their word: Ellen Louise Hart and Martha Nell Smith's *Open Me Carefully: Emily Dickinson's Intimate Letters to Susan Huntington Dickinson* (1998), which was also transcribed with the goal of preserving and presenting the autograph alignment and punctuation, was published with their permission.[7] It would be interesting to see what, if anything, would happen if Stambovsky reapplied for permission to realize his book today.

Issues of copyright aside, the exchange between the representatives of Harvard University Press and Phillip Stambovsky provoke a number of interesting questions. The one that has most relevance to my concerns in this book is the matter of local, formal presentation: which one of the following most closely approximates Dickinson's autograph procedures?

He touched me, so I live to know   +
That such a day, permitted so,
I groped opon his breast –
	349 *He touched me, so I live to know*
	
	MANUSCRIPT: About summer 1862, in Fascicle 17 (A 85-3/4).
	
	A He touched me, so I live to know F17.3
	          That such a day, permitted so,
	          I groped opon his breast –

The first of these images attempts to represent one of Dickinson's autographs (A 85-3/4), the third poem in the seventeenth of her fascicles (hand-sewn and

self-assembled manuscript anthologies); the second is a (partial) reproduction
of the same document as it appears in Ralph Franklin's *Poems of Emily Dickin-
son*.[8] If we are to believe Harvard University Press, the second of these is the
more accurate and authoritative *edition*; the first, though actually more faithful
to the handwritten poem on the page, is an *interpretation* based on aesthetic
and not textual or editorial considerations. But for a number of leading con-
temporary critics, the opposite is the case: Franklin's version is a translation
formatted according to the conventions of the printed book and informed by
New Critical principles of stanzaic and metric organization. In their view,
what he construes as a tercet would be a five-line stanza that relates to the
tercet as a base from which to improvise, in much the same way that a jazz
musician will use an inherited melody—and its scale and rhythmic structure—
as the ground from which to launch individualistic sequences of creative ex-
pression which often depart significantly from that structure and return to it
again.

The present phase of Dickinson's historical reception has seen an increas-
ing acceptance of the idea that the layout of a Dickinson autograph is delib-
erate or motivated: at the very least, it is hers, and not that of her editors. So
the fact that "to know" and "so" are visually isolated is conscious; it disrupts
the metrical regularity of the line and acts as a form of emphasis. Such an
argument seems feasible, interesting, and even (in a postmodern age) attrac-
tive, but it has several problems (none of which may be regarded as definitive).
First, Dickinson already had two forms of graphic emphasis (underlining and
capitalization), and one wonders how this additional system meshes with
those. Second, this contention presupposes a greater degree of regularity to
Dickinson's meter than is always immediately apparent; note here, for exam-
ple, how Dickinson switches from two lines of iambic tetrameter (or four
beats) to a third of trimeter (or three beats) and at the same time interrupts
the progress of the rhyming couplet. The effect is strikingly disruptive—and
the rest of the poem plays very complex games with meter, rhyme, and stanza
length (altering from three to six lines, for instance, and having the third and
sixth lines coincide sonically to provide a kind of counterpoint).

The sophistication of Dickinson's play with rhyme and rhythm seems ar-
chitectural to me—it is a structured polyphony. Emphasizing the visual places
a disproportionate semantic weight on local areas; it also seems latent with
contradictions. For example, if the visual layout is deliberate, why does Dick-
inson begin rows one, three, and five with capital letters, but not rows two and
four? One accepts that "I" must be capitalized as the first-person pronoun,
and "He" because it is the start of a grammatical unit, but what about "That"?
And what of other instances of similarly innocuous words in the rest of the
poem—words such as "And," "As," "Or," and "To"? These words are not
usually important enough to receive special attention, but they all coincide

with the beginning of metrical lines, which in the nineteenth century were marked with uppercase letters. By extension, if Dickinson marked lines off from each other at the start with initial capitals, why are rows two and four not marked this way? The answer, I suspect, is that they are not meant to be separate lines: they are continuations of the portions of writing immediately above them, and their tie to those portions is signaled in part by their not having initial capitals.[9]

The difficulty for most readers who are not trained textual scholars (and I include myself in that number) is how to evaluate the merits of these opposing arguments. The question is an urgent and important one, because—pace Harvard—Stambovsky's arguments effectively cast doubt on the accuracy of even standard editions of Dickinson's work, editions which provide most readers with an entry point to her work and which most professionals use in their teaching and interpretive research. There is an ethical and a practical dimension to these questions, then, for the fear of textual proliferation voiced by the representatives of Harvard University Press in 1994 is a market reality today: the bookshops in Dickinson's hometown (of Amherst, Massachusetts) alone stock more than ten separate editions of her poetry and letters, and as a teacher one has to recommend to students what one believes to be the most reliable edition. In addition to the two standard three-volume hardback variorum texts—published in 1955 (edited by Thomas H. Johnson) and 1998 (edited by Ralph W. Franklin), both by Harvard University Press, there are the two single-volume reader's editions derived from these—the 1960 *Complete Poems of Emily Dickinson* (edited by Johnson) and the 1999 *Poems of Emily Dickinson: Reading Edition* (edited by Franklin).[10] These are expensive: as of 2004 the three-volume Franklin runs to $130, and the one-volume reader's edition to $29.95, while the one-volume Johnson retails at $35 (hardcover) and $19.95 (paperback). Franklin's 1981 hardcover two-volume edition of *The Manuscript Books of Emily Dickinson* (which provides facsimiles of some eight hundred Dickinson autograph poems in the estimated order of their original collation) costs $210.[11] Cheaper alternatives include Johnson's *Final Harvest: Emily Dickinson's Poems* ($14.95, paperback); Peter Washington's *Dickinson: Poems* ($12.50); *The Selected Poems of Emily Dickinson* ($14.95) and *The Selected Poems of Emily Dickinson: Introduction by Billy Collins* ($9.95).[12] The standard one-volume hardcover reprint of Johnson and Theodora Ward's three-volume *Letters of Emily Dickinson* (1958) retails at $105: the *Selected Letters* costs $19.50.[13] More-recent and experimental editions include Marta L. Werner's 1995 *Emily Dickinson's Open Folios: Scenes of Reading, Surfaces of Writing* ($65) and Ellen Hart and Martha Nell Smith's *Open Me Carefully: Emily Dickinson's Intimate Letters to Susan Huntington Dickinson* ($19.95).

Poems are not breakfast cereals—the original may be the best, as Stambovsky and others have argued, but the best is not easily available, ensconced as Dickinson's manuscripts are in the libraries of Amherst, Boston, Cambridge, New Haven, New York, and Northampton (not to mention those which are privately owned). In addition, the originals are often fragile or in danger of becoming more faded through exposure to light or skin oils; readers are not ordinarily given access to them. Editions based on the originals, such as Franklin's two-volume *Manuscript Books of Emily Dickinson* (1981) and the on-line (and ongoing) Dickinson Electronic Archives (DEA), are clearly the next best thing, in that they provide photographic and electronic reproductions, enabling viewers to see Dickinson's handwriting and lineation.[14] Even these superb scholarly initiatives have their shortcomings, however: the Franklin edition is prohibitively expensive, and accessing the Dickinson Electronic Archives depends (in 2002, at least) on having the requisite electronic hardware and software, as well as the right password and user-name (though these are problems that market demand may lessen or make disappear, and the editors of the DEA generously and routinely make their user-name and password available on a variety of Dickinson e-mail discussion groups).

Other difficulties are less easily negotiated. It is not always possible to make watermarks and embossments fully visible, colors may be distorted, the size of the paper may be altered, and the differences between pen and pencil or between words written on the same surface at different times cannot always be distinguished. In addition, Dickinson's handwriting is not uniformly legi-ble: uppercase letters are easy to confuse with lowercase ones (to take one example), which is important given that Dickinson assigned capitals to words for symbolic purposes but also (and separately) signaled the beginning of metrical lines in the same way. Textual notes can compensate for such limita-tions and difficulties, but even the most literal of descriptions can stray into the arena of interpretation—for instance, by promoting a blank space as being rhetorically significant while omitting to mention that it coincides with and may therefore have been enforced by the raised edges of an embossment on a leaf of stationery, causing the writer to move her hand further from the edge of the paper than elsewhere on the page. And if even the least intrusive of modern technologies of textual reproduction and the most diplomatic or lit-eral of transcriptions and notes still involve interpretive alignments of one kind or another, might Dickinson not be equally served by publishing clearly legible and affordable print versions of her poems?[15]

It is this question, among others, which I seek to address in this book. For the problem with print editions is that they are seen as multiplying the textual area that has to be converted to type and thus increasing the opportunities for contamination or misrepresentation. Electronic editions are regarded as being superior in this respect; in theory, they can keep textual commentaries to a minimum, and although in practice the transcriptions they offer do function as interpretations of what is copied (by deciding that a letter is minuscule or not or by drawing attention to a dash), they appear to make fewer interventions by refusing, for example, to alter the lineation of the original. There are good, practical reasons for such a refusal: print transcriptions that follow the layout of the original are easier to read when placed side by side with the original than with the standardized versions. But in new editions of Dickinson's work that use diplomatic transcription, such as Hart and Smith's *Open Me Carefully*, the images disappear and the printed versions *still* retain the lineation of the autograph, thus suggesting that a manuscript layout is deliberate. The editorial mediation seems minimal but is only less obvious: choices are still being made on Dickinson's behalf.

To take one example, in the first section of *Open Me Carefully*, the editors ignore a series of blank spaces in a letter to Susan Dickinson dated 15 January 1854, to which they assign the number 18.[16] The original paper is embossed, with an oval pattern of laurel leaves enclosing a crown shape and the word "BATH."[17] Because the sheet of paper was folded during the manufacturing process *before* the embossment was applied, there are raised edges on the pages on which the letter is written. The result is that, at the top of the second and third pages, there are intervals of space (at the right edge for the second page and at the left for the third; the vertical line represents the fold):

though I kept resolving to be as brave		morning sermon. Now Susie, you and I, ad-
as Turks, and bold as Polar Bears, it		mire Mr Warner, so my felicity, when he
did'nt help me any. After the opening prayer		arose to preach, I need not say to you.

Hart and Smith, like Johnson and Ward before them, rightly decide that because these spaces were most likely to have been caused by Dickinson's reluctance to write in ink on the raised edges of the embossment, they are not to be regarded as significant. Thus, the spaces are not represented in the printed text. But in their version of "The Frost of Death was on the Pane," Hart and Smith include instances of similarly produced gaps *as spaces*, thus raising them to the level of potential significance.[18]

> Our passive Flower
> we held to Sea –
>   To Mountain,
> To the Sun –
> Yet even on his
> Scarlet shelf
> To crawl the
> Frost begun –

Such an isolated indent seems intriguing, but even a cursory glance at the manuscript reveals that it, too, was caused by a physical characteristic of the paper on which the poem is written. Although Hart and Smith are ostensibly committed to recording the physical details of the manuscript, they neglect to mention that "To Mountain" is the first piece of writing on the second page of the autograph. (Franklin includes this information in the notes immediately below the poem.) That it follows a page break in part explains why it is preceded by an interval of space, for in the upper left-hand corner is an embossed stamp (in an oval, pebbled frame with the word "PARIS"). Again, the editorial apparatus mentions the embossment but not its exact position on the page, thus preventing the reader with no access to the manuscripts from evaluating the status of the space in their version. Since Dickinson could not, or chose not to, write on the raised edges of this mark, she moved her pen further into the page than was customary. Franklin makes no reference to these gaps, without compromising Dickinson's procedures. But despite setting out to reproduce as much of the manuscript as possible, Hart and Smith effectively transform incidental aspects of its surface material into visual signs. For as it stands, the blank space in their printed version of the text amounts to a misrepresentation. There is no equivalent spatial pause in the original; there is a mark that is not distinctly visible in either photographic or electronic reproductions.

Exactly the same relation of a space being imposed on a quite different material phenomenon in a handwritten original may be detected in different versions of "The Wind begun to knead the Grass."[19] Rows fourteen and twenty-seven are indented in *Open Me Carefully*:

> The Wagons
> quickened on the Streets
>
> ....
>
> And then as if
> the Hands

In this instance, the writing covers two separate sheets: the first a half sheet, where the poem begins and proceeds up to "Road –," and the second a full sheet that has been folded during manufacture to make a bifolium. On the outer page of this second sheet, Dickinson writes from "The Wagons" to "Rain"; on the inner page, right, she places the rest of the poem, from "And then" to "Tree –." (Hart and Smith fail to include the final dash, as they also do after "Streets," though they are correct not to include dashes after "nests," "hold," and "Sky," as Franklin does.) But again, all these pages are embossed with the oval stamp bearing the legend "PARIS." It is the raised edges of this stamp that, in each instance, causes Dickinson to move slightly further into the beginning of pages two and three than normal. In these examples, the spacing is not an element of the poem's formal apparatus.

What haunts many Dickinson readers is, to continue the previous metaphor of the breakfast cereal, that the packaging (*Collected Poems*) misrepresents the contents (which were not sanctioned by Dickinson and often distort—or seriously deflect—the rationale of their appearances: Peter Siegenthaler's *Emily Dickinson: Collected Poems* and Gregory Aaron's *Emily Dickinson: Selected Poems*, to take two current examples, are based on the textually suspect Mabel Loomis Todd and Thomas Wentworth Higginson editions of 1890, 1891, and 1896). Ample historical precedent exists for such concern: the early editions of Dickinson's poetry, though the most proximate to her in terms of time, are also the least reliable, the most distant from the particularities of her practice. For example: consider the earliest *surviving* adaptation (designated Fr1096B in the 1998 Franklin *Poems of Emily Dickinson*) of a poem known as "A narrow fellow in the grass," the first—now lost—version of which is thought to have been composed around 1865; it looks approximately like this:[20]

> A narrow Fellow in
> the Grass
> Occasionally rides –
> You may have met Him –
> did you not
> His notice sudden is –

In *Poems: Second Series* (edited by Todd and Higginson in 1891), the poem was represented thus:[21]

> A NARROW fellow in the grass
>   Occasionally rides ;
> You may have met him,—did you not,
> His notice sudden is.

What might have been, like 1096B, a six-line original was altered to a standard quatrain: three capitals were amended to lowercase letters, and Dickinson's sustained use of the dash was replaced with a semicolon, two commas, an em dash, and a period. In addition, the poem was assigned a title ("The Snake"), which Dickinson did not supply herself.

Such errors continue to enjoy an existence (and therefore a sphere of influence) beyond the decade or two of their immediate publication. If I enter "A

narrow fellow in the grass" as a query on a standard search engine (such as
<www.google.com>), the first answer I get is the excellent Representative
Poetry site at the University of Toronto, which carries with it a considerable
authority by virtue of its association with an institution of higher learning and
its informative apparatus of editorial notes. Its introductory page on Emily
Dickinson lists the edition used as a scholarly facsimile dating from the first
posthumous editions of 1890, 1891, and 1896, and it provides the observation
that some of these versions differ from the originals but that "any substantial
variation from the existing manuscripts is noted here." The poem presently
under discussion is listed as "The Snake (A narrow fellow in the grass)," whose
first lines are given as follows:[22]

> A narrow fellow in the grass
> Occasionally rides;
> You may have met him,--did you not,
> His notice sudden is.

In the comments that accompany the poem, we are told that the existing
manuscript version of the poem has "boy" instead of "child" in line eleven,
which is tantamount to saying that the first four lines are substantially correct.
Thus, the changes in titling, lineation, capitalization, and punctuation that we
observed previously are made invisible, and a suspect edition from the 1890s
continues to have an unwarranted and unnecessary impact more than a cen-
tury after its first appearance.[23] In addition, readers are given the impression
that the original manuscript of the poem still exists (and can be viewed in
Franklin's 1981 *Manuscript Books*), when there are two extant versions, neither
of which can with absolute certainty be equated in their entirety with the
presumed original, the current whereabouts of which is unknown.

Nevertheless, the editions of Emily Dickinson's poetry that appeared dur-
ing the 1890s at least had a rationale that their further dissemination in the
twenty-first century lacks: Todd and Higginson believed that the manuscript
poems had to be modified to make them legible and more palatable to pre-
vailing fin de siècle literary taste, and would have implicitly assumed Dickin-
son's acceptance of the necessity for such adjustments, or the right of editors
to implement them.[24] (Wordsworth, famously, left the punctuation of the
second edition of *Lyrical Ballads* to Humphry Davy, and Robert Browning
often ceded decisions about the punctuating of his poems to his publishers.[25]
Witness, too, "the composition of *Isabella*, in which Keats is responsible for
most of the text, but his friend Richard Woodhouse and the publisher John
Taylor responsible for the title and the punctuation"; Byron, Coleridge, and
Shelley engaged in similar collaboration.)[26] The policy seems to have worked,

though only just: a feature of Dickinson's posthumous reception in the nine-teenth century was that again and again readers returned, often defensively, to alleged deficiencies of grammar, meter, and rhyme. "Literary form," wrote one of the kinder critics, "she regarded little." She "had her own standard of rhythm, or perhaps we should say of music."[27] The question is, do present-day attempts at reproducing the poems in hypertext markup language or print facsimile escape the influence of contemporary judgments with regard to po-etic form? Where one of the nineteenth-century reviewers had nervously ac-knowledged that Dickinson's poetry was "cast in no conventional mode," re-viewers of the 1998 variorum responded with disappointment to its perceived uniformity: the subtitle of the lead essay in a journal collection released to coincide with and evaluate its publication read "Is That All There Is?"[28] In slightly over a hundred years, then, critics have moved from finding too little formal conformity in editions of Dickinson's poetry to finding too much, and one might ask why.[29] Part of the answer lies outside the text—in the twentieth-century shift from the formal paradigms of meter and rhyme to those of free verse and in the graphic innovations of such poets as Bishop, cummings, H. D., Eliot, Lawrence, Moore, and Pound.[30] Historically, the intervention of the 1960s and 1970s (with its student movement, civil rights, and feminism) has had a profound—and often positive—effect on literary studies; reader-response theory and criticism, for instance, are but two exam-ples of how ideological movements carry over into the sphere of teaching and interpretation.[31] The move to wrest authority away from a single, white, male power base also has its corollary in Dickinson studies: readers are no longer content simply to accept Dickinson's life and writings as these have been handed down to them by Thomas H. Johnson, Richard Sewall, and Ralph W. Franklin. The end of the 1970s and the early 1980s saw the rise of academic interest in popular and material culture—in the study of advertising, for in-stance—which in turn led to an interest in Dickinson's draft compositions; these are often written on (among other things) the back of advertising flyers, pamphlets, and commercial wrappers. The version of a poem sent to Susan Dickinson in 1859 (Fr125A, "A poor torn heart") has even been described as a mixed-media event.[32]

But just as important are the technological advances in the media and man-ufacture of text reproduction that facilitated the appearance of *The Manuscript Books of Emily Dickinson*, edited by Franklin, which was made up of photo-graphic facsimiles of over eight hundred Dickinson autographs. Franklin's edition opened up at least two major trajectories in Dickinson scholarship that are still being explored and charted today. First, a general readership was able to see for the first time Dickinson's poems arranged and combined in the order that she herself appeared to have ordained. For after her death, Dickinson's sister Lavinia discovered forty of her bound fascicles or hand-sewn booklets, each containing on average nineteen to twenty poems.[33] To some scholars, poems collected in fascicles exist in an imagistic, narrative, or thematic relationship to each other, whereas others (including Franklin himself) see their collation as an accident of their all having been completed around the same time. But since standard print editions disarranged the order of the fascicles and reorganized the poems according to a chronology of first composition identified by characteristics of the handwriting, a potential conflict emerged between editorially imposed and fascicle-derived sequences.[34] Does a poem derive its meaning from its placement relative to other poems in a fascicle, or more extensively from the placement of the fascicle relative to other fascicles? Are fascicles purposive literary events (selections of poetry) or administrative and archival ones (records of poems filed away as complete at around the same time)? Such questions remain unresolved and to some extent unsolvable; I will return to them later in this book.

The second consequence of Franklin's *Manuscript Books* was that many more readers were able to see Dickinson's originals than previously, when they were available primarily to scholars only at Amherst and Cambridge, Massachusetts. As Stambovsky and others have pointed out, Dickinson manuscripts look very different from their typographic equivalents; even Franklin noted that they "resist translation into the conventions of print. Formal features like her unusual punctuation and capitalization, line and stanza divisions, and display of alternate readings are a source of continuing critical concern." Like the early reviewers and editors, Franklin believed such anomalies often resulted from Dickinson's having "left her manuscripts unprepared for print."[35] He concurred substantially with the methodology of Johnson's standard edition of 1955, which reformatted the manuscripts and presented lyrics that consistently adhered to fairly traditional formal structures such as the quatrain and the metrically defined line. But for more-recent editors, readers, and theorists, Franklin's 1981 edition suggested a radically different possibility (which he himself did not support)—that Dickinson experimented visually with stanza shapes, line length, word division, word cancellations, the angle and length of dashes, the use of blank spacing, and even the formation of alphabetic characters.

After 1981, then, several decades of critical consensus about what constituted a book of Dickinson's poetry or even a Dickinson poem began to evaporate. This dissipation of certainty has been accelerated by other developments—not the least of them improvements to the electronic media of communication (computer, telephone, television, and video)—that have brought about a contemporary age of information whose emphasis is on the visual (even cell phones now offer text and picture transmission). These developments are neither better nor worse than what has gone before; they are simply different, other, and we should factor an awareness of that difference into our evaluation of a Dickinson poem reproduced as a photographic image or as a sequence of bytes on a computer monitor. Indeed, a number of questions emerged in 1981 which continue to exercise Dickinson scholars and readers and which underpin the writing of this book. What happens when a writer whose paradigm of literary production and reception was the codex, the (handwritten or printed) book made up of pages made of paper, is published on a screen? Do Dickinson's manuscripts look the way they do because she neglected to publish, or did she refuse to publish in order to protect and preserve the integrity of her manuscripts?[36] Did Dickinson reject the equation of books with print by producing her own handwritten and assembled miscellanies and by circulating poems in her correspondence?[37] Is the technology of representation only now starting to catch up with Dickinson, or do the existence and popularity of electronic media in conjunction with paradigms of poetic form which differ from those of the nineteenth century demand that a different set of Dickinson materials—specifically, unfinished drafts and fragments—become the object of scholarly attention? Do advances in the technology of electronic reproduction and distribution, in combination with changes in how we define (or refuse to define) poetry, necessitate the suppression of unfashionably conventional aspects of her lyric practice, such as meter and rhyme? Is Dickinson a poet of the finished product who never got to supervise the final stage of her productions, or is she a poet of process, who rejected the idea of finality in writing, including the finality of print? Is it the case that the current emphasis on Dickinson's handwritten originals means that "the work can now, more than hundred years later, finally speak for itself," or is this a species of ventriloquism, whereby we project our voices back into the nineteenth century and confuse them with our own?[38] Because Dickinson left no explicit statements about which methods of poetic display, assemblage, and transmission (if any) she authorized for the future, the answers to these and other questions must remain sought after but perhaps never arrived at. But because different editions present radically different images of the poems (through different technologies of representation), what seems certain is that the edition one reads will have decisive consequences for the kinds of answers one is capable of producing. And as Roger Chartier reminds us, a text "is invested with a new meaning and status when the mechanisms that make it available to interpretation change."[39]

I

Determining the accuracy of textual reproductions of Emily Dickinson's autograph writings can at least partially be attempted by focusing on a particular document and the history of its configurations. Such a historical overview serves as a useful beginning in any effort to evaluate the theoretical and practical parameters of debates about the actual conditions of the Dickinson canon, but is also a valuable reminder of the culture-boundedness of editorial formulations of that canon, both past and present. This scrutiny helps to introduce a climate of defamiliarization and skepticism, an acute self-consciousness, that is necessary for looking more closely at poems and letters written in Dickinson's own hand, and it will, hopefully, enable readers to make informed judgments as to the status of their appearance. Thus, this chapter will be divided into four main sections, each corresponding to a different phase of a single document's transmission and transformations. The text chosen for discussion is the much-anthologized "A narrow fellow in the grass," numbered Fr1096 in the most recent variorum. Ostensibly the story of a young speaker who mistakes a snake for a discarded whiplash, as well as the memory of that frightening encounter in later years, it typifies the kinds of indeterminacy associated with the very best of Dickinson's writings. Particularly fascinating is the concluding image of "Zero at the Bone"; the phrase revises and unsettles all that precedes it. At one level, it suggests the extreme coldness associated with shock or terror. At another, it suggests clarity—with zero as the lens, the perspective, with and from which things are retroactively understood. But exactly *what* is seen remains uncertain: if theological, the meeting with the snake echoes the seduction by the serpent, so that the speaker returns to a primal, original scene that continues to haunt and define the present. In such a reading, the snake is a reminder of shame and guilt, a cue to one's sinful state in a postlapsarian world. On the other hand, the encounter might represent the contamination of the natural by religious discourse: the speaker is unable to respond neutrally to the snake because its appearance is already inflected by its association with the myth of the Fall. By extension, the speaker's reduction to nothingness has clear similarities with Romantic theories of the sublime; interestingly, there is no indication of the countermovement toward belief that often accompanies such moments in other nineteenth-century literature.[40] Of course, very different readings are also possible. If sexual, "Zero at the Bone" can be seen as referring to the vaginal mouth and to an epiphanic instant where the speaker fails to respond to the snake's phallicism and thus senses for the first time an alternative sexual proclivity. But, typically, the opposite can also be asserted, with zero seen not as the absence of a response but as its instigation (from zero to one and onward).

"A narrow fellow in the grass" exists in a number of editions, to which I attend in roughly chronological order in this chapter. The first, Dickinson's own (now lost), is believed to have been sent to her sister-in-law, Susan Dickinson, who may then have passed it on to Samuel Bowles, editor of the *Spring-*

field Daily Republican, where it appeared (anonymously) as "The Snake" on 14 February 1866. A subsequent—and still extant—fair copy, Fr1096B, dates to around the same period and was collected in Set 6C (a set being the term for an unbound manuscript miscellany). A third version, Fr1096C, was sent in a note to Susan Dickinson during the autumn of 1872. I discuss these versions in the next section of this chapter, considering the most significant phases of the text's posthumous career in three subsequent sections.[41] "A narrow fellow in the grass" was included (again as "The Snake") in *Poems by Emily Dickinson*, *Second Series*, edited by Thomas Wentworth Higginson and Mabel Loomis Todd: this I discuss in the 1890s section. During the 1950s, it was released twice: first in Thomas H. Johnson's three-volume variorum edition of *The Poems of Emily Dickinson* (1955), and then in Johnson and Theodora Ward's three-volume *Letters of Emily Dickinson* (1958).[42] More recently, it was published twice in the same year: in *The Poems of Emily Dickinson* (1998), edited by Ralph W. Franklin, and in Ellen Hart and Martha Nell Smith's *Open Me Carefully: Emily Dickinson's Intimate Letters to Susan Huntington Dickinson* (1998).[43] Each edition reproduces the same document in subtle but significantly different ways, and the various modes of presentation it occasions help bring to light more general disagreements about the theory and methodology of editing literary manuscripts.

II

Reproduced here are the first four lines of "A narrow fellow in the grass" as printed in the *Springfield Daily Republican*:

THE SNAKE

A narrow fellow in the grass
Occasionally rides;
You may have met him—did you not?
His notice instant is,

The publication is a fairly infamous one, because Dickinson was unhappy about changes that were made to the punctuation and protested them to Higginson: "Lest you meet my Snake and suppose I deceive it was robbed of me –

defeated too of the third line by the punctuation. The third and fourth were one."[44] Critics (reasonably) share Dickinson's indignant tone in discussing this passage: Tom Paulin writes that her withdrawal from print "was partly caused by a wish never to see them subordinated to male editorial control."[45] The protest is justified, but (like many apologias) overstated, for Dickinson does not object to the rearrangement in its entirety but to a specific change at a particular point that altered the semantic trajectory of two lines. She does not distance herself from the title assigned by the newspaper, the discarded capitals, or the altered punctuation. In fact, it appears from her rebuttal that Dickinson may have ignored as many as seven changes before reacting to the imposition of the question mark: the title, three capitals ("Fellow," "Grass," "Him"), two line breaks ("in / the Grass" and "have met Him / did you not"), and one change to the punctuation ("Occasionally rides – ").[46] In addition, her motivation for writing to Higginson seems to have been the fear that he would think her dishonest: although she had earlier told him that she did not want to publish, there now appeared a poem (or a style) that he was sufficiently familiar with to judge as hers. The lesson to be extracted from these comments is more ambiguous than critics have always acknowledged; at the very least, they foreground issues of ideology (moral reputation, honesty, privacy, and propriety) as much as—if not more than—they do a preoccupation with textual matters.

From a contemporary editorial standpoint, what fascinates is that Dickinson does *not* object to the lineation: she refers to the "third and fourth" lines, whereas in her extant manuscripts these take up (in chronological order) three and four rows of space.[47] As we saw earlier, "A narrow fellow in the grass" exists in three fair copies made by the poet herself, the first of which is thought to be lost. The earliest surviving manuscript (1096B) with the cluster of lines disputed by Dickinson is estimated as having been recorded around 1865 and was collected in a booklet of the poet's own making:[48]

> A narrow Fellow in
> the Grass
> Occasionally rides –
> You may have met Him –
> did you not
> His notice sudden is –

Finally, a later version (1096C), transcribed around 1872, was again sent to Susan (perhaps to replace the first one or to clear up any misunderstanding about the punctuation):[49]

> A narrow Fellow
> in the Grass
> Occasionally rides –
> You may have
> met him?
> Did you not
> His notice instant is –

Apart from the variant ("instant" for "sudden") the differences between the autographs appear to be fairly minor. Some of the rows split in slightly different places ("have met Him – /" and "have / met him"), and there is an exchange of capitals at one point ("Him – / did" and "him? / Did," enforced by the altered punctuation). The "fourth" line referred to by Dickinson also commences at slightly different places in the manuscripts—the sixth row in version B, and the seventh in C. Granted, Dickinson's comments in the letter to Higginson refer to the published version of the poem; even so, she does not contest the *Republican*'s lineation but the *punctuation*, which robbed of her an important enjambment. This suggests that the lineation in this particular manuscript is not to be understood as deliberate or literal: rows four, five, and six in version B and rows four, five, six, and seven in version C are both two *metrical* lines of poetry.[50]

Dickinson's apparent acceptance of the newspaper's lineation is significant precisely because some modern editors and theorists have argued that the line arrangements, the spacing, and even the shape and extent of the handwriting in the originals exist as fully integral and meaningful aspects of their formal design. To take the 1865 example (1096B), one notices that it is inscribed over six rows rather than four: how is one to judge if this arrangement was deliberate? One answer is that there is no answer; Dickinson left no explicit instructions on how, or even if, her autographs were meant to be read. But a number of strictly physical or material features do provide us with a series of signposts that lead in the direction of a possible set of guidelines for understanding the significance of the layout of this manuscript. The first of these is the assignment of upper- and lowercase letters: it seems incongruous that "A," "Occasionally," "You," and "His" begin with capitals but not "the" and "did." But if one keeps in mind that nineteenth-century writers habitually allotted capitals to the beginning of a poetic line, then the apparent discrepancy in Dickinson's original disappears. For the uppercase letters in "A," "Occasionally," "You" and "His" are line-initial phenomena, whereas the lowercase letters in "the" and "did" indicate that those words are not line-initial and therefore probably not separate or integral—they are continuations of the preceding line.

In addition, the poem is recorded on ruled paper that is 20.4 cm high and 12.5 cm wide. The space between where a row of writing begins and the left edge of the paper measures approximately 1.0 cm. But the spaces between the end of a row and the right edge of the paper are not so regular:[51]

> A narrow Fellow in [1.4 cm]
> the Grass [7.4 cm]
> Occasionally rides – [3.2 cm]
> You may have met Him – [0.1 cm]
> did you not [5.0 cm]
> His notice sudden is – [1.2 cm]

What intrigues and even haunts many readers about this and many other handwritten documents is the lineation: instead of the uniform quatrains of the printed editions, the originals appear to anticipate modernist relationships between print and space. Or, at the very least, the originals *are* the originals: in the absence of permission or instructions to the contrary, the argument tends to run, we ought to respect the only arrangements authorized by the artist herself (if only because they are associated physically with her presence). Yet the logic of the uppercase letters complicates any reproduction of the above portion of the manuscript which arranges it as six rather than four lines, for the consignment of line-initial capitals seems to indicate that there are six physical *rows* of writing but only four *lines*. The spacing in the right margins independently confirms this: three rows of writing leave less than 1.5 cm of space, while the other three vary in length from 3.2 to 7.4 cm. What that pattern tells us is that such large intervals of final space tend to be line-end phenomena: they are blank precisely because they correspond to and mark the close of a metrical line.[52]

Example: Rows 1 and 2
A [capital = line beginning] narrow Fellow in [nonsignificant space of 1.4 cm]
the [no capital = no separate line] Grass [significant space of 7.4 cm = end of line]
=
A narrow Fellow in the Grass

And if we act on the formula provided by these material codes and conventions, we come up with a way of understanding the logic of this first stanza which matches exactly its equivalent in Franklin's print edition:

A narrow Fellow in the Grass
Occasionally rides –
You may have met Him – did you not
His notice sudden is –

Another phenomenon of the autograph that print stands accused of failing to reproduce is Dickinson's lettering, and again this erasure troubles some readers. "A narrow fellow in the grass" is typical of others in that it has an orthographic feature which appears in isolation to be unusual and therefore potentially significant. The uppercase Z in the poem's closing phrase, "Zero at the Bone," is tilted at an angle that draws attention to itself, raising the possibility that Dickinson might have playfully wanted to suggest the zigzag motion of a snake through grass or perhaps the design on its skin.[53] But in two other poems from approximately the same time period, which have nothing to do with snakes, Dickinson inscribed the Z in the same way. Both "It bloomed and dropt, a Single Noon" (Fr843) and " 'Twas awkward, but it fitted me" (Fr900) have uppercase initial letters (in "Zones" and "Zone," respectively) that provide a context by which to measure the feasibility of such claims about aspects of Dickinson's handwriting.[54] In this instance, the broader evidence makes it unlikely that there was any degree of deliberation or will behind the inscription of the Z. The more general conclusion to be drawn is that assigning a semantic weight to specific autograph characters in single poems is methodologically unsound; such assertions should be made only after being routinely checked against more samples of Dickinson's lettering.[55]

In this case, at least, an edition of this poem that reproduced or otherwise drew attention to the minutiae of its original would not yield a neutral or uncorrupted text. Indeed, such a version would raise many new problems. For if the manuscript lineation and spacing is salient, then the blank space that follows "not" in versions B and C would force the reader into the same kind of brief delay as did the very punctuation that Dickinson objected to in the *Republican*.[56]

So far, in my consideration of the poem I have concentrated on the local level of formal presentation. But equally important is the aspect of selective or sequential presentation. Version B of "A narrow fellow in the grass" was included in one of the unbound manuscript miscellanies Dickinson left behind after her death, the only collections or anthologies (outside the correspondence) that she supervised and collated (and presumably approved) herself. Understanding the poem, one might argue, requires our being aware of its place in a larger sequence, and if this is the case, any arrangement other than Dickinson's own will change and possibly distort the significance of individual poems.[57] In Set 6C (believed to have been assembled in 1865), Fr1096B, "A narrow Fellow in the Grass," is the ninth of twenty-two poems, preceded by Fr1094A, "We outgrow love like other things," and Fr1095A, "When I have seen the Sun emerge," and followed by Fr1097A, "Ashes denote that fire was."[58] In the *Republican*, it was printed singly in the sixth column of the front page, sandwiched between lines of various thickness and a list of "Pamphlets & Magazines" (above) and an article on "how to use chloroform" (below). In the posthumous *Poems by Emily Dickinson*, Second Series (1891), edited by Higginson and Todd, yet another principle of organization was applied; the book was divided into four imposed themes: life, love, nature, and time and eternity. Entitled "The Snake," "A narrow fellow in the grass" was poem 24 in the third of these sections, preceded by 23, "A bird came down the walk," and followed by 25, "The mushroom is the elf of plants."[59] The poem's placement under the general heading of "nature" *and* within a progression of lyrics distinct from that of the fascicles encourages us to read the encounter with the snake as natural and descriptive rather than (say) a rite of passage inflected with religious or sexual overtones.

Later editions of the poem alter the immediate cycle in which it had originally appeared in similar though less obvious ways—by adopting a chronological progression, for instance, as in the 1955 variorum. There "A narrow fellow in the grass" became J986, was preceded by J985, "The missing all prevented me" (now Fr995), and followed by J987, "The leaves like women interchange" (now Fr1098B), and J988, "The definition of beauty is" (now Fr797B, a poem Franklin places in Set 6A). In Johnson, the order of Set 6C is so changed that only fourteen of the original twenty-two exist in any kind of sequence, though only in pairs and triplets and not in proper succession (they line up separately as 813, 828, 850, 855–56, 887–88, 930, 948, 986–87, 1063, 1071, 1077–79, 1084–85, 1098–1100, and 1104). Given such a radical dislocation, it is clearly within the bounds of possibility that the disorientation Joyce Carol Oates reported after reading the collected poems sequentially may have been a side effect of the edition that she used (the Johnson) and not necessarily an integral condition of the poetry.[60] And one also wonders if the celebrated indeterminacy of many Dickinson lyrics is in part an effect of the Johnson and Franklin one-volume reading editions: suspended in blank space, separated from other contacts and contexts, the poems are freed promiscuously to seek but never to secure relationships of their own.[61] This is especially true in anthologies: the *Norton Anthology of American Literature* precedes "A narrow fellow in the grass" (J986, Fr1096) with "A man may make a remark" (J952, Fr913) and "It bloomed and dropt, a single noon" (J978, Fr843), then follows with "Further in summer than the birds" (J1068, Fr895).[62] In the *Heath Anthology of American Literature* (for which Ellen Hart is one of the two editors), it is headed by

"The missing all prevented me" (J985, Fr995) and followed by "Perception of an object costs" (J1071, Fr1103).[63]

An obvious question, then, must be to what extent the creation of alternative contexts helps either to augment or to compromise the indeterminacy that many readers cherish in Dickinson's poems. In Hart and Smith's *Open Me Carefully*, the fascicle and chronology paradigms are displaced by an alternative sequence of poems and letters sent to single correspondents—in this case, to Susan Dickinson. The distinction is important: for Johnson and later Franklin (1998), "A narrow fellow in the grass" is numbered according to (their reconstruction of) its temporal relation to other poems and other versions of the same poem. For Hart and Smith, it is number 147 out of 254 letters, poems, and notes sent to Susan: the opening ("My Sue – / Loo and / Fanny / will come / tonight") is therefore a significant and perhaps even primary aspect of its meaning. The danger with such an approach is that the poem may become subsumed by its placement in a larger narrative; the lyric becomes important for its value (in this instance) as a token of literary enterprise and love shared between two women.[64] Or, to put it another way, Hart and Smith promote one textual axis (that of the correspondence) over another (that of the fascicles). As a consequence, "A narrow fellow in the grass" becomes disengaged from its fascicular surroundings and placed between versions of "I bet with every Wind that blew" (Fr1167) and "Who were 'the Father and the Son'" (Fr1280), though there is no unambiguous evidence that Susan received either during Dickinson's lifetime.[65]

Anthologies and compilations are merely extreme examples of the ways in which many editions of Dickinson's poetry realign relationships between individual poems and therefore impose structures of interpretation on what we read. Nonetheless, that Dickinson was happy to send individual poems from fascicles to correspondents seems to allow for the possibility that they could survive on their own as autonomous aesthetic objects. (In the case of Set 6C, Susan Dickinson received seven of the twenty-two, Higginson one, and Josiah Holland another.) And no record exists of her having distributed entire fascicles to her friends—not even to Susan, who lived next door and otherwise received close to three hundred notes of one kind or another.[66] All indications suggest that Dickinson's preferred form of circulation during her lifetime was to enclose poems singly, or in small clusters of three and four, in letters or as freestanding notes, which would appear to weaken any arguments for the fascicles as integral and deliberate selections. At the same time, the logic of the fascicles seems to suggest that poems which were sent to individual correspondents do not have to be read within the context of her friendship with historically specific personalities to be fully understood.[67] Dickinson appears to have operated with the assumption that her poems had a critical mass of their own: they were not satellites whose significance depended primarily on their relation to other centers of gravity—biographical or thematic. Her own usage confirms this: versions of Fr1641 (the elegiac "Though the great waters sleep") enclosed in separate letters made it seem to refer to the deaths of Samuel Bowles (Fr1641D), her own father and her nephew Gilbert (Fr1641E), Otis Lord (Fr1641F), and Edward Tuckerman (Fr1641G). (No version was included in a fascicle or set because, by 1884, Dickinson had ceased to collate her poems in this way.) Each letter seems to form a defining context of origination, but a misleading one: the poem may have been occasioned by one of these deaths, or by none of them. Its applicability certainly transcends them all.

III

On 8 October 1890, John Wilson and Son of Cambridge, Massachusetts, printed five hundred copies of *Poems by Emily Dickinson*, edited by Mabel Loomis Todd and Thomas Higginson; the books were published in November of the same year by Roberts Brothers of Boston.[68] Its three-piece binding, consisting of a medium gray cloth spine that extended to meet white cloth on the front and back boards, joined by a silver-stamped wavy vertical rule, was supplemented by ornate writing in silver and a large (8.7 cm high) design of Indian pipes.[69] A similar but smaller (1.7 cm) Indian pipes ornament was repeated in gilt on the spine of the book and functioned both as a decorative promotional emblem and as a preemptive device for helping to shape responses to the book's contents. For the choice of the Indian pipes was something more than a question of formatting, an aesthetic choice—it also served as a key element in the book's overall editorial strategy and apparatus.[70] At one level, it looks forward to the verbal image in the Preface, where Higginson described Dickinson's verses as "in most cases like poetry plucked up by the roots; we have them with earth, stones and dew adhering, and must accept them as they are."[71] At another level, it looks back, drawing for its significance on Thomas Gray's lines "Full many a flow'r is born to blush unseen, / And waste its sweetness on the desert air" and perhaps also to Wordsworth's image of a "A violet by a mossy stone / Half hidden from the eye!"[72] In other words, the floral design promotes the idea of a poet who remained relatively unknown during her own lifetime and whose poetry was seen as existing in a "natural" state—being formally raw and sometimes crude, but (so the argument went) containing "profound insight[s] into nature and thought."[73] Finally, the design suggests the arrival of a "native" American talent: the Indian pipes are at once an indigenous subject matter and an indigenous response to and representation of that subject. Thus, Higginson and Todd were able to situate their discussion of Dickinson's natural power and related lack of finish within larger nineteenth-century cultural debates about the merits and defects of the literature of the United States. Within America at least, they anticipated and partially disarmed potentially negative responses to her formal innovations by framing her within a native and natural discourse.[74] Alexander Young, in the *Critic*, is often seen as taking his cue from Higginson when he wrote that "the rough diamonds in the collection have a value beyond that of many polished gems of poetry."[75] Such a formula of compensation, by which verbal contents made up for technical deficiency, became something of a leitmotif in early reviews and was clearly prompted by Todd and Higginson's editorial and promotional strategies.[76]

Poems by Emily Dickinson, Second Series (1891), again featured the Indian pipes design on the front board: the design, lettering, and straight border between the half green and white cloth were all gilt, as were the smaller Indian pipes ornament and lettering on the spine. And again the poems were organized according to the categories of Life, Love, Nature, and Time & Eternity, with "A narrow fellow in the grass" placed in the third of these and beginning thus:[77]

> A   NARROW fellow in the grass
>   Occasionally rides ;
> You may have met him, — did you not,
> His notice sudden is.

Todd and Higginson's insertion of the comma at the end of the third line does not quite prevent the run-on that Dickinson so rightly and passionately argued for in her letter of 1866, though given what Higginson knew about the poem's misrepresentation, the change seems unnecessary.[78] Again, the poem is assigned a title ("The Snake"), and though nothing indicates that Dickinson approved of titles in this particular instance or in principle, she did not contest the *Republican*'s label and may therefore have been inferred (erroneously but understandably) as having accepted its designation.[79] But these are modern judgments. The critical disquiet about Dickinson's allegedly errant form suggests that Todd and Higginson's emendations, however distorting, egregious, and unsanctioned, may have been a necessary stage in preparing a nineteenth-century readership for such an unconventional voice; they certainly have their dignity as such. Yet, sixty years later, in the heyday of New Criticism's insistence on the lyric as a fully autonomous aesthetic territory, a different age required a different set of editorial procedures and products.

IV

In 1955 Harvard University Press published the comprehensive *Poems of Emily Dickinson*, including variant readings critically compared with all known manuscripts. Its sober cover proclaimed an academic rather than a promotional intent: Dickinson's earlier editors had succeeded in securing a reputation for her, and now Harvard was going to give her its imprimatur. Though there were no designs front or back, which were bound in dark gray buckram, the publisher's regal gold-stamped lion on the spine functioned as a visual seal of prestige, approval, and authority.

The editorial machinery of the 1955 variorum was scholarly rather than speculative, and it deservedly became the standard edition. Like the 1,774 other poems, "A narrow fellow in the grass" could be referred to by its first line or by the number Johnson assigned it (986) in his reconstructed chronology of the overall lyrical production—no verbal titles were imposed. Johnson included both extant versions of the poem, privileging the earlier one; the later is relegated to the editorial notes and is printed in smaller type, along with an invitation to Sue that preceded it ("Loo and Fanny will come tonight, but need that make a difference? Space is as the Presence").

A narrow Fellow in the Grass
Occasionally rides –
You may have met Him – did you not
His notice sudden is – [1866 version]

A narrow Fellow in the Grass
Occasionally rides –
You may have met him? Did you not
His notice instant is – [1872 version]

In 1960, Johnson produced a reader's edition of the variorum, *The Complete Poems of Emily Dickinson*, in which one version of each of the 1,775 poems was chosen; again, the earlier edition of "A narrow fellow" was selected. Each poem in the reader's edition was printed in neat stanzas without editorial commentary; suspended in blank space, one discrete verbal icon after another, the poems seemed like and were an advertisement for New Critical theories of lyrical autonomy. Todd and Higginson editions presented their selections of poems, organized thematically, and often adapted in terms of grammar, meter, punctuation, rhyme, spelling, syntax, visual appearance, and word choice. Johnson comprehensively listed all the manuscript variants available to him, listed in chronological order (based on estimated changes to the poet's handwriting) and with no consistent alterations to anything other than their visual appearance.

In 1894, a selection of Emily Dickinson's letters had been published, discrete from the poems, under the editorial stewardship of Mabel Loomis Todd. In 1958, Johnson and Theodora Ward's *Letters of Emily Dickinson* reinforced that generic distinction when it appeared subsequently to and separately from the earlier *Poems of Emily Dickinson* (1955). Nevertheless, in some instances the same text was classified as *both* a poem and a letter (or part of a letter). The later version of "A narrow fellow in the grass" provides such an overlap: it appeared first in the variorum *Poems* and three years later in the *Letters* (as L378, to Susan Dickinson, dated autumn 1872).[80]

> My Sue,
> Loo and Fanny will come tonight, but need that make a difference?
> Space is as the Presence –
>
> A narrow Fellow in the Grass
> Occasionally rides –
> You may have met him? Did you not
> His notice instant is –

Johnson and Ward divided this text into different segments: a salutation, two consecutive paragraphs of prose, a six-quatrain poem, and a signature. For the next thirty years or so, their edition would remain the standard one, but by the end of the 1990s, both it and the variorum *Poems* had come to be regarded with increasing skepticism by a new generation of younger theorists and critics who were not convinced that Dickinson had sanctioned the kinds of generic divisions observed by her historical editors.

V

In 1998, Harvard University Press published its new three-volume *Poems of Emily Dickinson*, variorum edition. Its design aligned it with both the 1890 series and the 1955 variorum: it had a light spine meeting a darker gray-green on the front and back boards (echoing the 1890 edition) but no image on the front (like the 1955). Again like the 1955, the 1998 had "THE POEMS OF *Emily Dickinson*" inscribed on the spine against a dark blue background with an ornamental design above and below it; but it omitted the image of the lion, featured silver rather than gilt for the lettering, and separated Franklin's name visually from Dickinson's via its printing in small capitals against a narrower dark blue band.[81] Like Johnson too, Franklin inserted each poem in the order of his revised chronology of her total lyrical output, assigned numbers to the poems (and otherwise titled them by their first lines only), and kept them separate from the letters. In November of the same year, Paris Press released *Open Me Carefully: Emily Dickinson's Intimate Letters to Susan Huntington Dickinson*. Edited by Ellen Louise Hart and Martha Nell Smith, it featured a cover photograph of Imogen Cunningham's *Calla 2, about 1925*. Again, the design functioned as an ornamental device and as a statement of editorial intent. Clearly, it aligns Dickinson with both public and private female aesthetic traditions—not only with Cunningham and Georgia O'Keefe, but also with the nineteenth-century cultural practice whereby women grew and presented flowers to each other as gifts, as tokens of affection, and as comments on personal events and experiences. An early working title for *Open Me Carefully* had been *The Book of Emily and Susan Dickinson*, which shows that Hart and Smith thought of this correspondence as challenging theories of the printed "book" and displacing the institutional paradigm of writer and audience with one of writer and reader. And in isolating Dickinson's letters to Susan from the other correspondence, Hart and Smith questioned the standard assumption that publication of a poet's letters in one complete edition was always useful or desirable.

Perhaps the main difference between the two editions, however, was in the formatting of the poems. Where Franklin (like Johnson before him) employs standard verse paragraphing, Hart and Smith claimed to have more rigorously followed the lineation, spacing, and varied dashes of the handwritten originals. Where Franklin (like Johnson and Ward, and like Todd before him) distinguished between letters and poems, Hart and Smith refused to do so unless there was clear material evidence to that effect. Thus the four lines we looked at earlier are identified by Franklin as part of the poem "A narrow fellow in the grass" that he numbers 1096C, and by Hart and Smith as part of the document they index as "My Sue" and number 147:[82]

> My Sue –
> Loo and
> Fanny will come
> tonight, but need
> that make a
> difference?
> Space is as the
> Presence –
>
> A narrow Fellow
> in the Grass
> Occasionally rides –

You may have
met him?
Did you not
His notice instant is –

Again, however, this transcript is problematic. In the first part of their book, Hart and Smith choose to represent paragraph spaces vertically, rather than through the more conventional initial indentation. But they fail to do so here: their account of the writing flattens its details, so that it is impossible to see (for example) that there are horizontal spaces of 4.5 cm and 5.7 cm (out of a possible 10.7 cm in paper width) after "difference?" and "Presence – " which quite clearly mark paragraph endings. The problem with such an editorial procedure is that it conflates two separate forms of spatial boundary in Dickinson's autographs: the vertical (which she used between stanzas of poetry and to divide a passage of prose from a passage of poetry) and the horizontal (which she used to signal paragraph endings and the limits of a metrically defined line). In *Open Me Carefully*, these become one, and the results are misleading.

For Hart and Smith, though, redefining "A narrow Fellow" as "My Sue" is not simply (or even) to personalize its significance but also to challenge the validity of standard generic distinctions. For them, "My Sue" is neither a poem included in a letter nor a letter attached to a poem—it is a letter-poem: "The letter-poem, a category that includes signed poems and letters with poems or with lines of poetry, will be seen here as a distinct and important Dickinson genre. Johnson arranged lines in letters to separate poems and make them look the way we might expect poems to look. We do not do this here. Neither do we divide the correspondence into 'Poems to Susan' and 'Letters to Susan.' Instead, we follow Dickinson's commingling techniques, mindful that conventional notions of genre can limit our understanding of Dickinson's writing practices."[83] Yet, the evidence of the manuscript complicates that assertion. First, Dickinson introduces a vertical space after the word "Presence – ," and that gap (about 1.6 cm, double the average length elsewhere) is unusual, for Dickinson does not normally indicate *prose* paragraph breaks in this way. As a general rule in autograph letters, Dickinson avoids indentation at the beginning of a new paragraph: she leaves space at the end of the previous one. Vertical markers such as this one are more commonly employed to mark division between poetic stanzas, or, as here, to record a change of genre. Second, the register shifts (mediated by the lovely "Space is as the Presence") between the everyday inquiry at the start and the cluster of lines beginning "A narrow fellow in the grass," where there is increased attention to words as sounds, evidenced by the sequence of sibilants in "Grass," "Occasionally," "rides," "His," "notice," and "is." Finally, there is the unmistakable emergence of metrical pattern in the poem, where there was rhythm in the prose: the lines correspond to common meter (or measure) or to alternating lines of iambic tetrameter and trimeter, rhyming (very loosely in this instance) *abcb*.[84] Indeed, the rhyme pattern of the poem as a whole is crucial, for in the nineteenth century, rhyme is a structurally predictable device that accompanies and helps define the meter (each rhyme coinciding in this case with the shorter line). Interestingly, James Guthrie's argument, that the poem "demonstrates the way Dickinson used rhyme to achieve a crescendo," would be invalidated by any edition of the poem that follows the manuscript lineation, for the rhyme is dissipated in such arrangements.[85] This is not reason in itself to dismiss the validity of such editions (or the motives behind them), but it does show how closely critical arguments are bound up with textual issues.

Thus, when Johnson and Ward distinguished between the first part of the note as a line of prose and the second part as poetry, they were clearly influenced by the sum total of these different material elements (space, meter, rhyme, and so forth), and not only (if at all) by the literary-theoretical limitations of New Criticism. In addition, the Hart and Smith version, situated within blank space, suggests that the lineation is motivated or deliberate: because it does not reach the physical margins of the page, it must be governed by some principle of organization or presentation which is visual and meaningful. Another version, with the edges of the paper charted in relation to the writing, would give a better impression of the total configuration of words, rows, spaces, and paper boundaries. Such a template would allow us at least to consider the possibility that the layout was a consequence of the physical dimensions of the writing surface in combination with metrical codes and not necessarily an integral visual design. It would further enable us to see that the "diplomatic transcriptions" which aim to reflect Dickinson's originals as closely as possible may not do proper justice to the significance of their aggregate details. For the logic of the material signs in the originals—of page size; dimensions of handwriting; distribution of capitals, rows, and marginal spaces—suggests that they were scripts for performances very different from those recorded in *Open Me Carefully* or those transcribed online at the Dickinson Electronic Archives site.

In bibliographic terms, electronic media of reproduction are a fairly recent development. For anyone with access to the necessary computer hardware and software, copies of many of Dickinson's handwritten originals are now freely available. Thus, at the Jones Library at Amherst, I can sign up for a free half-hour session on the Internet and go to the Dickinson Electronic Archives site, enter the password and user-name that takes me into Dickinson Correspondences, and then click on the number (HB 193) that corresponds to the document currently under discussion, sent by Dickinson to Susan.[86] The "diplomatic transcription" made available beside the image raises some questions, however. For instance, the editors choose to represent the dash that follows the words "on," "Acre," and "Corn" as being longer, lower, and straighter than they appear to be in the autograph. The printed dashes measure from 8 to 9 mm and follow the final words almost immediately: the autograph dashes are (respectively) 1 cm, 7 mm, and 5 mm and are preceded by corresponding spaces of 1 cm, 6 mm, and 2 mm. At the same time, the printed phrase "cool for Corn" (to take a single example) measures about 3.3 cm on the screen; the original takes up 11 cm ("further on" measures 7.5 cm, and "Boggy corn," 10.4 cm).[87] In other words, the online typographic image that corresponds to the original "cool for Corn" and which is meant to be as non-altering as possible, shifts the relationship of dash to written sequence from 5 mm out of 11 cm to 8 mm out of 3.3 cm (or from 4.5 percent to 24 percent). To change the prominence of the dash is to distort its potential significance in each of these instances; until "on," the printed dashes had been similarly regular, and the departure from such uniformity implies the need for a concomitant shift in the level of attention that is disproportionate to the physical scale of the original. Indeed, the transcript is full of silent (or in this case invisible) editorial choices, despite its apparent nonintrusiveness: the editors write "My Sue" when Dickinson wrote something closer to "My Sᴜᴇ," for example. Throughout the original communication, Dickinson alternates between two different versions of the same sign: a closed and an open version of the lowercase *e* (which I will discuss in greater detail elsewhere).[88] Given that the material and visual aspects of her artifacts are a motivating factor in the existence of the Dickinson Electronic Archives site, one would have thought that such deviations were noteworthy; that they are not suggests the editors' belief that some aspects of Dickinson's handwriting and graphic presentation are significant, whereas others are not.[89] Also here, then, one sees that even editions of the poem that attempt (genuinely and thoughtfully) to be as faithful to the autograph as possible move away from her actual practices and stray into the arena of interpretative choice. For how else can one explain the fact that where Dickinson uses two types of *d*, her editors use only one? Or that where Dickinson joins the ascenders of both *t* shapes with an extended cross-stroke in "tighter," "instant," and "Without," her editors do not?[90] Of course, verbal transcriptions that accompany the visual image of the artifact are necessary and useful, because the handwriting is often difficult to decipher. But it is a mistake to believe that a literal transcription is somehow closer to the spirit of the original than any other verbal representation: deciding to copy three rows of writing in the physical manuscript ("You may have / met him? / Did you not") as three lines in a transcript or letter-poem amounts to an interpretation

(Dickinson wanted it this way), not the suspension or abnegation of editorial choice it might aspire to (Dickinson left it this way). Such arrangements may amount to at least as much of a distortion of Dickinson's practices as those of 1890, 1891, and 1896, especially if (as I will argue) Dickinson thought of the *three rows* of writing just alluded to as *one line* of verbal text.

As G. Thomas Tanselle writes, "the originals will always be of value as the ultimate authority for settling the questions that reproductions inevitably raise."[91] Electronic editions make the truth of that statement less obvious, as they offer images of the manuscript accompanied by print translations that seem to correspond, word for word, row for row, stroke for stroke, with what is visible. But what if the design on the page is regulated by other factors, as Thomas Johnson once speculated? "People are subject to moods which handwriting reflects. You write one way when you are rested, or another when you are in haste. The size of letters may vary with the size of the sheet written on, depending on how much you wish to say in a given space. The form and shape of the letters depend also upon the implement you use, as well as the quality of the stationery. A sharp, stiff pen gives results very different from those formed by a stubby pencil. A glossy ledger sheet permits a movement of arm, hand and fingers that rough, resistant linen will not allow. Absorbent foolscap is something different still."[92] Johnson fails to mention writing surfaces and locations: the table used to place the paper on, and whether it was upstairs in the bedroom or downstairs in the dining room, or the kitchen, or even the cellar. Nor is the time of year or day alluded to: what difference would it make to write in winter or summer, by day or in the evening? What difference too would it make to write from April to November 1864 and then again in 1865, during the long periods of Dickinson's eye treatment in Cambridge, when she was away from home and had been instructed to use only a pencil, and to avoid bright sunlight? But Johnson does speculate on a relationship between the eye problem, Dickinson's general state of health, and the abrupt change to her handwriting in 1878 (when the letters unlink and are almost exclusively written in pencil): "By 1867 her writing certainly has increased in size and the letters within words are broken to a point that one reckons, not in terms of linked words or syllables, but in terms of those that are unlinked, so general has become the separation of letters. The process was so steadily continuous that by 1875 only an occasional *of*, *th*, or *Mr.* remained fastened. She was still writing most of her letters by ink, however. In this year the size of the letters she formed with her pen reached a maximum. By 1878 she evidently found it necessary to forego ink altogether, and no part of any word is linked after that year. But the size of letter decreased when she used pencil."[93] Factors such as paper size and texture, implement (pen, blunt or sharp pencil) and place (kitchen or bedroom) of inscription, time of year and day (winter and spring, night and day), the physical health and the emotional disposition of the writer, the level of energy or fatigue, the assumed competence of the reader, the cultural and social environment, and much more are not represented in electronic editions. Hypertext markup language appears to bring us closer and with less mediation to the site of composition than do other technologies of reproduction, but it raises its own kinds of problems, as we shall see. The truth is that only the original is the original; everything else is a copy. Everything.[94]

VI

Replying to Harvard University Press's rejection of his request for permission to edit his own text of Dickinson's poetry, Phillip Stambovsky reacted with understandable dismay: "Who are they to stop that debate?" He continued; "To me, this is almost a freedom-of-speech issue."[95] But the issue of free speech cuts both ways. If Dickinson's originals contain expressive devices which are attenuated in standard editions and do not always appear in electronic or photographic reproductions, and if these devices convey subtly differentiated meanings to the reader (meanings that can reflect but also contradict verbal contents), then the danger exists that the manuscripts, and only the manuscripts, will become the ultimate determinants of meaning in Dickinson scholarship. At least in theory, and sometimes in practice, any scholar who has had access to a Dickinson autograph can cast doubt on an interpretation derived from reading a standard edition by claiming that the original layout denies it.[96] As I reported at the beginning of this chapter, Dickinson's manuscripts are scattered all over the United States, and if they become the primary objects of future discussion, then potentially this reduces the number of people with the competence necessary to participate in such a discussion to those who have had or continue to enjoy regular exposure to a large proportion of the handwritten originals. But even at Amherst College or Harvard's Houghton Library, readers are not automatically furnished with the originals: they are given photostats, and if they then need to consult an original, they ask the curator for permission to do so. Requests are granted only if there is sufficient scholarly justification to outweigh the need to protect the manuscript.

There is an ethical dimension to these issues, for as educators we have a moral responsibility to guide general readers toward the best possible text, in the knowledge that editions have a profound impact on the reception and understanding of Dickinson's work; editors are obliged to do no less. At one level, this is an extreme example of the ethical commitment that all reading demands, as J. Hillis Miller puts it: "Reading [a] work makes me in one way or another responsible for it—responsible to teach it or to write about it, to account for it, to explain it to others, to pass judgment on it, even if I keep that judgment to myself. Such a responsibility can never be completely ful-filled, though that does not make it any less exigent."[97] As we have seen, Harvard University Press feels itself charged, as copyright owners of the Dick-inson poems and letters, with a duty toward the author and her readers to represent her works as accurately as possible. At the same time, Ellen Hart, Martha Nell Smith, and Phillip Stambovsky are equally serious and genuine in their desire to inform students and a wider readership of differences be-tween Dickinson's autographs and their historical representation in print—differences that, in their view, amount to a continuing misrepresentation. In such a landscape of disagreement, with conflicting directions as to where the poems lie, where do Dickinson's readers go, and how are they to get there? Is consensus a desirable or necessary goal for the facilitation of further interpre-tation, and if so, what are the criteria by which such a consensus might be arrived at? Are we morally obliged to represent an author's wishes as faithfully as possible in each and every edition of her work, particularly when the evi-dence as to her wishes may be conflicting or indeterminate? Are we further obliged to attempt to assess the significance of a cultural product's appear-ances within the terms of the cultural era in which it was produced?

"An editor establishes a text on which others will base their work," writes Ellen Hart, "and, therefore, has the responsibilities of returning to original documents, staying informed about current trends in editing, and keeping to standards of accuracy. In my view, editing is a science, and sloppy scholarship is misconduct."[98] To what degree should editors assume responsibility for any misunderstandings that they help to transmit? To take a single instance, an electronically published essay, which is gathered under the auspices of the Dickinson Electronic Archives (but not written by the DEA editors), evaluates and dismisses Franklin's claim that lineation in Dickinson's manuscripts is often enforced by material factors. The authors answer: "The poem 'Title divine, is mine,' for instance, exists in two known variants that are not lineated according to available space, but rather lineated according to Emily's own desires and possibly her audience."[99] The first part of this statement (up to and including the word "variants") is almost correct: there *are* two variants of a Dickinson poem that have the words "Title divine is mine" in the first line. But they are differently punctuated (and since the article focuses on the neg-ative consequences of suppressing Dickinson's punctuation, conflating these would appear to represent an inconsistency): one begins "Title divine – is mine!" and the other "Title divine, is mine."[100] The rest of the statement is far from being unambiguously confirmed by the evidence of the original, however (in the second version, for example, the *y* and downwardly sloping dash that close the word "Melody" are written *below* the *d* because Dickinson ran out of space).[101] The first version (A 678) is written in ink on one sheet of nonruled paper that has been folded to create two pages and is embossed "PARIS" on the upper-left corner of the first and third pages:[102]

Title divine – is mine! The Wife – without the Sign! Acute Degree – conferred on me – Empress of Calvary! Royal – all but the Crown! Betrothed – without the swoon God sends us Women – When you – hold – Garnet to Garnet – Gold – to Gold – Born – Bridalled –	– Shrouded – In a Day – "My Husband " – women say – Stroking the Melody – Is this – the way? Heres – what I had to "tell you" – You will tell no other? Honor – is it's own pawn –

We return again to the problem of blank spaces: Dickinson writes on the first and third pages of this bifolium, which means that she has to negotiate the embossment at the upper left-hand corner of both pages.[103] In the first instance, she avoids the raised edges of the "PARIS" name by beginning just below it; in the second instance, she misses it by moving about 1.9 cm horizontally into the page before continuing the incomplete line from the first page. A diplomatic edition would presumably leave a blank space before "Shrouded"; amend it and provide an explanatory footnote; or simply ignore it as an accidental and incidental feature of the paper on which the poem is written. The first solution would amount to a distortion, of course (there is no blank space before "Shrouded"), whereas the second and third would represent editorial choices (which means that diplomatic transcriptions no less than standard ones often involve invisible editorial choices, such that one wonders, at what stage and with which criteria is it permitted to distinguish accidentals from substantives, especially given the premise that every aspect of a handwritten original can make a potential contribution to a poem's meaning and should not be therefore suppressed?).[104]

The paper in question measures approximately 10.1 cm across and 15.9 cm down; the first row of writing reaches to within 0.3 cm of the right edge of the paper. The second row of writing similarly extends to within 0.6 cm of the right edge of the paper. The third is followed by a gap of 7.6 cm, however, which is to say that approximately 75 percent of the paper available at that horizontal section is unused.[105] This pattern is repeated in the fifth row: after (the dash that follows) "me," there is a gap of 6.6 cm (approximately 65 percent of the surface available at that point). Dickinson's nonusage of the total space available to her at those positions would indicate that either she wants to isolate words or phrases for dramatic effect or those words and phrases are segregated from the preceding rows of writing because of material limitations (she had only 0.6 mm and 0.5 mm of space in which to write, respectively, "Sign!" and "on me –"). In circumstances where she was unable to complete a metrical unit for reasons of material extent, Dickinson moved down the page, recorded what remained of the line, and then moved down the page again to the next row of space to begin a new line of verse. Such a conclusion is strongly and conveniently supported by the (proportionately uncommon) *aabb* rhyme scheme: the rhyme marks the end of each separate metrical sequence, and in these cases two of the rhymes are followed by blank spaces, confirming the impression that such spaces in themselves often coincide with and define the boundary of metrically defined units. Thus, far from capriciously ignoring autograph turnovers in order to make lines conform to a quite different mental template of lyric structure, Franklin's presentation of these same rows of writing arise from and fully comply with the total aggregate of its material particulars.

> Title divine – is mine!
> The Wife – without the Sign!
> Acute Degree – conferred on me –
> Empress of Calvary!

Moreover, after the poem closes (on the third page, with "Is *this* – the way?"), Dickinson leaves a substantial and, for this document, an unprecedented amount (2.5 cm) of vertical space, which coincides with and signals a shift from poetry to prose. And this brings us back full circle to Hart and Smith's earlier rebuttal of the historical division of Dickinson's writing into separate genres, which they see as an editorial imposition on more diffuse autograph realities. That Dickinson makes a generic distinction in one autograph is not in itself proof that she observed such proprieties universally (a matter I return to in a later chapter), but it does perhaps suggest that such distinctions *are* often a matter of convention—that is, they exist as systems of codes which work because other readers have previous knowledge of their existence and regulate their responses to any given text accordingly. Levels of assumed competence exist in the reading and writing of autographs which may be extralinguistic, unstated but nevertheless demonstrably present, such as the notion that a line of verse begins with a capital and ends with a rhyming word (or a nonrhyming word within a pattern of rhyming and nonrhyming elements, such as an *abcb* scheme). This kind of knowledge is tacit, socially organized, and relative to the age of the writing, which means that it may not always be obvious to later commentators and readers who are accustomed to very different principles of lyric expression, organization, and presentation.

Although critics have focused a great deal on specific moments of Dickinson's handwritten originals, such as certain letters within a particular poem, they have failed to ground their observations in a more comprehensive review of similar lettering across the manuscripts generally. Just as important, less attention has been paid to script in the *theoretical* sense—to the idea that "familiar events such as, for example, 'eating out' commonly involve a script, or a skeletal outline of what it is normal to report. Thus (unless there are exceptional reasons so to do), when reporting on a meal out one will typically assume that there was a waiter (and so not mention the fact), and will not normally give a description of the protagonists' eating processes."[106] In other words, some of the information that explains why a text looks the way it does will not be supplied because a meaning will not have occurred to the writer, or a certain detail will not be thought of as meaningful, or the meaning (or lack of meaning) will be thought of as being obvious. Therefore, instructions to the effect that a word division or the shape of a letter or a blank space is not deliberate will not be stated because it will simply be assumed as a given; by extension, educated and middle-class readers who subscribe to the idea that poetry is important will not need to be told when a poem begins on the page (in the middle of a letter) or that it is organized metrically.[107] If something is out of the ordinary about a manuscript (such as visual stylization or the suspension of generic boundaries), one would expect the writer to draw attention to this—especially if the writer had already experienced misunderstanding with those of her poems which had been published previously (and apparently against her wishes) in newspapers. Consequently, understanding what the appearance of a given manuscript may signify involves a familiarity with the entire scene of writing: not just the author at her table but also the myriad and shared (social, cultural, material) circumstances prevailing at the time of composition.[108] (It is interesting, for example, that manuscript critics are happy to cite the presence of a coffee stain on a piece of paper but neglect to find out how the coffee got there and where it came from. Nor are they interested in investigating the conditions of coffee production, distribution, purchase, display, preparation, and consumption and what relation these might have to the poem's meaning. For instance, if I insist on reading a coffee mark as a sign of a radical new textual production that is at odds with market-driven and print-dominated practices, how does my view of Dickinson's liberalism coincide with the chain of exploitation that brought the coffee to her writing table in the first place? For that matter, where did the writing table Dickinson used, as well as her paper, pen, and pencil, originate? In all the arguments about the inside and outside of a text, why is it assumed that the text stops on the page?)

Many aspects of cultural practice are conventional, public, shared, or superpersonal, however originally deployed they might be. "You ask me what my flowers said," Emily Dickinson once mused, before continuing, "then they were disobedient – I gave them messages."[109] And to Emily Fowler Ford she said, "They are small, but *so* full of meaning, if they only mean the *half* of what I bid them."[110] Clearly, flowers themselves are incapable of direct speech— but can carry and deliver a set of messages that are made available to addresser and addressee by their location in a culture which is familiar with the cluster of conventional associations assigned to the flower over a period of time. Dominic Strinati writes: "How can we know that a bunch of roses signifies passion unless we also know the intention of the sender and the reaction of the receiver, and the kind of relationship they are involved in? If they are lovers and accept the conventions of giving and receiving flowers as an aspect of romantic, sexual love, then we might accept . . . [this] interpretation. But if we do this, we do so on the basis not of the sign but of the social relationships in which we can locate the sign."[111] Contexts provide us with valuable and necessary information, and we therefore need to "read between the gaps between the words too, and [to] supplement them with a complex of insight and information that come from outside the text."[112] We may no longer have (and in Dickinson's case may never have had) access to the motives behind a choice of genre, to any private or subjective set of associations that the genre may have contained for the writer, but we can, and do, understand most of its public dimensions. And one of the ways that we can try to recover the field of meaning of a text is by recovering the conventions that applied during Dickinson's day. Of course, not all the conventions are equally relevant or applicable; they may never be decisive. Most poets used titles in the nineteenth century, for example, whereas Dickinson almost never did. Knowing that most writers in the nineteenth century expected titles cannot supersede the knowledge of Dickinson's not having used them, or somehow make it redundant. Even if we suspect that, given the right circumstances, Dickinson may have assumed the necessity of choosing titles for her work or having them chosen for her, the vast majority of her autograph poetry proves that she did not do so. It would therefore be presumptuous at best and criminal at worst to argue from the position of likelihood that we can impose titles on her poems.

But when the historical evidence coincides with an aspect of Dickinson's usage, then we are obliged to consider the possibility of its relevance. Such evidence may not be conclusive or determinate: in the postmodern era it may not even be convenient. But it cannot be denied. In Dickinson's case, we have not words but the inscription of words and lines—their placement on the page, their shapes, their division, the angle and direction of their inscription. To attempt to understand the range of potential meanings these might have, we need further to understand some of the conventions that arise from poetry and letters written by hand. In other words, we need to look at the manuscripts themselves, to observe what kinds of phenomena they exhibit and to see if these phenomena exist independently of each other or as patterns that suggest a set of conventions, a guiding practice. There are limits to what we can know about Dickinson, but attempting to see what she may have meant by her habits of inscription involves something slightly more sophisticated than trying to imagine exactly what the writer was thinking about during the process of inspiration and composition. At the same time, it must go beyond the aura of authenticity that comes from physical proximity to the author's historical person—the assumption that, because the author touched or wrote something, everything about that object must in some way be authoritative.

In this book I attempt to assess the feasibility of claims about aspects of Dickinson's attention to what had previously been thought of as the accidentals of manuscript production: the size and shape of paper, the physical direction and placement of the writing, patterns of spacing between letters and lines, and habits of chirographic inscription. One surely cannot deny individual readers the right to take pleasure in the interpretative possibilities afforded by Dickinson's manuscripts and to share this pleasure with others. But editors, teachers, and historical scholars have responsibilities to people other than themselves, and these may occasionally conflict with the idea of the autograph as a site of interpretive display. For instance, if one subscribes to the argument that the inscription of a particular letter (such as an uppercase *W*) in a single poem makes a significant contribution to that moment of its contents, it seems obvious that one would want to correlate such an impression with other samples of the same letter in other poems to see if they are the same or significantly different and whether the similarity or difference can be related to differences or similarities in their semantic environments. By extension, if one does believe that lettering (its shape and extent) matters, what difference does it make that the first capital *W* in "Title divine – is mine!" is pointed while the second and third are rounded; that some of the lowercase *e* shapes are open while others are closed (and sometimes in the same word, as in "Betrothed"); or that there are two kinds of lowercase *d* (one made with a single stroke, the other with two)?[113] Dickinson's multiple ways of writing the same letter have implications beyond the immediate confines of their inscription: they strongly suggest the absence of any sustained purpose or premeditation behind the vagaries of her handwriting and the lack of any impropriety in standardizing such letters in type.

Attempting to gesture in the direction of likelihood or plausibility in responding to the manuscripts, one requires some hypothesis of objectivity, some means of testing insights, that goes beyond the principles of individual pleasure or of postmodernist possibility.[114] And by contextualizing Dickinson's manuscripts, as I have begun to attempt in the discussion above, one finds evidence that complicates and potentially contradicts the conclusions drawn by manuscript scholars. (At the same time, this opposition need not be universal: erroneous use of specific examples of manuscript practice does not mean that the *larger* points of manuscript criticism and theory can be ignored or declared to be invalid.) Rigorous and sustained cross-referencing provides us with a set of procedures, a critical apparatus, by which to measure the extent to which contemporary critical approaches to Dickinson's autograph procedures can accurately be formulated as corresponding to the poet's own purposes. The book which follows, then, is built on the assumption that contextualization is one method of attempting to move beyond the subjective and that doing so is desirable. But to achieve historical perspective, one has to take into account the various levels of Dickinson's work, both poetic and epistolary, as well as manuscript practices generally in the nineteenth century—both literary and nonliterary.

Two fair copies of "Title divine is mine!" (as Franklin titles it) were sent to recipients in 1861 and 1865—the earlier to Samuel Bowles, the later to Susan Dickinson.[115] As the first moves towards attempting to provide what social anthropologists call a "thick description" of Dickinson's manuscript practices which may be of use to readers who have not had frequent access to the originals, as well as to professionals more familiar with the theoretical debates (and disputes) about them, in the next two chapters I focus exclusively and in detail on separate and substantial bodies of work: handwritten poems and letters known to have been sent to Susan Dickinson (chapter 2) and to Samuel Bowles (chapter 3). The reason for organizing the chapters in this way relates to matters of convenience, reliability, and extent: each corpus of work is large and generically inclusive but simultaneously limited and controllable. Together, they help point us toward an understanding of the principles that regulate the visual appearances of Dickinson's manuscripts.

CHAPTER TWO

Getting Nearer, Knowing Less

Emily Dickinson's Correspondence with Susan Gilbert Dickinson

TRADITIONALLY, such characteristics of Emily Dickinson's handwritten literary documents as words that were canceled, divided over two lines, or written vertically in the margins have been regarded by her editors as incidental and nonsignificant aspects of manuscript production. More recently, however, many of these features of Dickinson's autographs (and others) have come to be seen as potentially motivated graphic elements of the artifact's formal structure.[1] A convenient way to test the accuracy or value of such premises is to focus on the attributes of a restricted but representative body of work, and none is more suitable for such study than those documents sent by Dickinson to her sister-in-law Susan Huntington Gilbert Dickinson. Although estimates vary, the most conservative figures suggest that as many as one hundred and fifty of the approximately eleven hundred letters written by Dickinson to ninety-nine correspondents went to her sister-in-law, and the majority of these manuscripts are in the possession of the Houghton Library at Harvard University. The correspondence was carried on with few interruptions from late February 1851, when the poet was in her early twenties, to 1886, the year of her death, and is therefore comprehensive.[2] Finally, this corpus combines poems and letters, and one can thus compare patterns in both to see if there is common ground and what conclusions, if any, can be drawn. Considering both genres of Dickinson's creative output attempts also to meet the challenge of Ralph W. Franklin, who has argued that "any special theory of Dickinson's mechanics will have to fit both poems and letters."[3]

I

By any numerical account, Susan Gilbert Dickinson was Emily Dickinson's most important and constant addressee: she received approximately 153 letters (according to Johnson's estimate) and 252 poems (according to Franklin).[4] Unlike her correspondence with Bowles, the correspondence with Susan seems not to have been suspended for any major period of time after 1851, when it began: there is only a two-year gap in poems *and* letters sent, immediately subsequent to 1855.[5] The allocation of poems is greater than that of letters; Johnson thinks that 17 letters were sent between 1859 and 1866, for instance, while 21 poems were forwarded in 1859 alone.[6] And the distribution of poems seems to follow, approximately and proportionately, the same patterns as the overall literary production: 18 out of 227 (7.9 percent) in 1862; 29 out of 295 (9.8 percent) in 1863; and 27 out of 229 (11.8 percent) in 1865.[7] After that, there is a sharp fall to 5 poems in 1866, never rising above 8 in any subsequent year—but in 1866, Dickinson finished only 10 poems in total, and the number of those sent to Susan is therefore substantial.[8] The falloff is part of a larger and quite dramatic deceleration of lyric energies and cannot be said to reflect any sort of personal disengagement. In the early 1870s, the ratio of poems composed and poems sent to Susan remained quite high: 8 out of 48 in 1871 (16.6 percent); 7 out of 35 in 1872 (20 percent); and 7 out of 38 in 1873 (approximately 18 percent).[9] Only in 1876 did someone else receive more than Susan Dickinson: Higginson was sent 17 in that year, and Susan 4 (which was still a reasonably customary 13 percent).

The purpose of this chapter is not to assess the nature of Dickinson's relationship with Susan Dickinson so much as to focus on the physical features of the unsurpassed group of materials the relationship occasioned.[10] The body of writings is the most fully comprehensive available to us, in terms of both genre and temporal extent; just as important, there is clear and unambiguous evidence that Susan Dickinson worked on a posthumous edition of Dickinson's poems, and her procedures of selection and transcription provide valuable insights as to how a uniquely positioned and sympathetic nineteenth-century reader understood the nature of the manuscript materials in her possession. As Ellen Hart and Martha Nell Smith have argued, Susan Dickinson's judgment was "informed by decades of her creative work with Emily."[11]

The first extant letter sent to Susan Gilbert (dated December 1850 by Johnson and late February 1851 by Alfred Habegger) is fairly unremarkable, except inasmuch as it signals simultaneously the beginnings of Dickinson's deep affection for Susan and a slight tentativeness about how welcome such affection might have been:[12]

> Thursday noon.
> Were it not for the *weather* Susie –
> *my* little, unwelcome face would come
> peering in today – I should steal a kiss
> from the sister – the darling Rover re-

turned – Thank the wintry wind my
dear one, that spares such daring in-
trusion! *Dear* Susie – *happy* Susie – I rejoice
in all *your* joy – sustained by that dear
sister you will never again be lonely.
Dont forget all the little friends who
have tried so hard to *be* sisters, when
indeed you *were* alone!
You do not hear the wind blow on this
inclement day, when the *world* is shrug-
ging it's shoulders; your little "Columbarium [page break]
is lined with warmth and softness,"
there is no "silence" there – so you differ from
bonnie "Alice." I *miss one* angel face in
the little world of sisters – dear Mary –
sainted Mary – Remember lonely one – tho'
she comes not to us, *we* shall return to
her! My love to *both* your sisters – and
I want so much to see Matty.
      Very aff yours, Emily

There is much that is characteristic here: Dickinson's self-appointed and gen-
erous role as the voice of consolation in the aftermath of death, and her
preoccupation with home and sisterly friendship as mutually supporting en-
vironments of tranquillity and trust. Dickinson's delicate health would have
prevented her from venturing outdoors in inclement weather, but one notes
here as elsewhere that epistolary reassurances of continued friendship often
softened the blow of a failed visit. Finally, one silently applauds the beautiful
inversion of the final lines, with its subtle implications of abandonment: the
dead may not return to visit the living, but the living shall continue to keep
faith and remember the dead. (Alternatively, "*we* shall return to *her*" may also
mean that the living will eventually join her in death. Fr41, "I often passed the
Village," seems to be spoken by Mary, who died "Earlier . . . Than the rest"
and who waits for "Dollie," her sister Sue).[13] The message is one of comfort,
of family bonds that cannot be broken, but it also cleverly gestures toward a
reversal of the phenomenon known as "survivor's guilt": here it is the dead,
not their living relatives, who no longer fulfill emotional obligations. It is an
idea that Dickinson was to develop and play on extensively in her poetry—the
soul's arrogant indifference to and betrayal of the world it leaves behind.

    But already in 1850, in a letter that is reasonably conventional in its con-
tents and formatting, we notice inconsistencies in the inscription of the

dashes. In the sequence "sisters – dear Mary – *sainted* Mary – Remember lonely one –," the first dash is fairly horizontal and slightly squiggly; the second is short, slightly curved, angled, and below the line of writing; the third is straight and on the line, and the fourth is straight and below the line. And "*both* your sisters" is followed by a dash that is sharply angled, short, and below the line of writing. Much has been made of distinctions between dashes in Dickinson's writing, but their idiosyncratic appearance at such an *early* stage of the work strongly suggests that the continued vagaries of their direction, extent, and placement in the *later* work represents a sustained habit of the handwriting and not a deliberate rhetorical procedure.[14]

The theory that Dickinson's dashes might represent "an attempt to create a new system of musical notation for reading her verse" was proposed as early as 1960 by Charles Anderson in *Emily Dickinson's Poetry: Stairway of Surprise* and then further and more fully explored in a 1963 article by Edith Perry Stamm.[15] Stamm contended, rightly, that punctuation marks represented uniformly as dashes in the Johnson edition were often quite different from each other in the originals, but she then went on to argue, somewhat more controversially, that the differences amounted to careful distinctions. She identified Dickinson's punctuation as comprising the period, the question mark, and the exclamation point, as well as five others:

> [A] horizontal dash (–) ("irregular" because it is obviously not intended as the grammatical break or turn of thought), which may be as short as a period, or standard length, or "extra-long"; an angular slant (/), which Johnson transcribes as a comma, but which does not have the usual curve to it, and as a comma is often grammatically senseless; and a "reverse" slant (\), which is the exact reverse of the comma as transcribed by Johnson. These three marks will appear above, at, or below the writing line (at least in the fair copies, where such relative positions are discernible). Occasionally, but rarely, a "dividing vertical" (|) appears in the middle of a line, and a half-moon mark at a line's end.[16]

Stamm's description was accurate and interesting, and she went on to claim that these signs corresponded to inflectional notations inherited from elocutionary and rhetorical texts, professing that they were therefore meant to direct the oral performance of Dickinson's poetry. Stamm did seem to elide slight but significant differences, however: Dickinson's dashes are usually *after words*, while rhetorical readers assign their inflections *above syllables* in words, for example.[17] And if the dashes corresponded to a system of word articulation, does that mean that Dickinson's poems are entirely bereft of punctuation? Is a guide to pronunciation of single elements within single words able to function simultaneously as a guide to the emphasis of words within sentences?[18]

Still, Stamm's thesis was exciting and impressive, based as it was on familiarity with the autographs and with relevant cultural history, though it was immediately opposed by Theodora Ward, coeditor of *Letters*, in the next edition of the *Saturday Review*.[19] Her counterargument was that "marks of this kind" were used in *both* poems and letters and that their appearance in the latter made it unlikely that their inclusion in the former were as "indications for rhetorical rendering." Commenting on a letter to Higginson that included no less than twenty-eight dashes, Ward felt it "hard to imagine Emily urgently asking for help and at the same time dictating to her correspondent how to read her letter to an audience."[20] And indeed Stamm's perceptive remarks about the capricious positioning of the marks ("above, at, or below the writing line") suggests an inconsistency that potentially complicates the thesis that the dashes were systematic; for if one procedure (placement) was insignificantly variable, why not the other?[21]

In addition, critics who have ascribed a range of meaning to Dickinson's variegated dashes fail to take into account the similar variation in dashes elsewhere in her writing. To take some random examples: the dash that follows the address "Prof Tuckerman" on a scrap of torn paper at Amherst College rises sharply (at about a forty-degree angle) from lower left to upper right and is about 0.2 mm long.[22] But the envelope addressed to "Dr J. G. Holland / Springfield / Mass –" finishes with a dash that angles downward, from upper left to lower right (and is somewhere between 30 and 40 degrees).[23] The dash on one envelope addressed "Mrs Todd –" again rises sharply from lower left to upper right; a second begins and ends at roughly the same horizontal level but curves (slightly up, then down) in between; and a third also curves, but downward.[24] An envelope addressed to "Mr Chickeríng'" and dating to late 1882 has three dashes of about the same length (0.5 mm, 0.6 mm, and 0.4 mm): the first two of these are above the first and second *i*'s in his surname and are clearly meant to represent dots; the third is after the name and corresponds to a dash (though it is angled in the same way as the symbols above the *i*'s, and may therefore represent a period).[25]

Thus, Dickinson's inscription of the dash changed according to inclination and time, and it is often difficult to distinguish from her comma, dot, and period. By extension, then, attention to changes in Dickinson's dashes needs to be contextualized through comparison with inconsistencies in her handwriting generally, a point I will come back to during the course of this book. To take a single example of an extensive phenomenon: Dickinson fluctuates in the way that she records dots above the letter *i*. For instance, in A 34, the manuscript of a letter to Sarah Tuckerman dating to 1878, the marks above the *i* in "is" (at the end of the first page) and "inundation" measure about 0.3 mm; in the Dickinson surname, the first *i* is 0.5 mm long, and the second,

0.3mm. The two strokes in "insuring" are 0.2 mm, while the word "climb" features an *i* that is dotted normally.[26] Dickinson was not the only one to inscribe words (most famously, "opon" for "upon" and "it's" for "its") or letters (*i* with a superior dash rather than a dot) in a variety of ways. In Atossa Frost Stone's Manuscript Journal (1817–28), the letter *i* is dotted with small vertical strokes. Solomon B. Ingram's Diary (of October 1827) uses a short, backward-slanting slash (`) in place of the dot above the *i*. Elizabeth Barrett Browning signs her name in October 1856 with a slight dash above the *i* in her surname and an equivalently angled dash after it. And Kathleen Coburn reports that "Coleridge frequently (not always) writes as possessive of *it*, *it's*, the spelling now reserved for a contraction of *it is*, but sometimes he wrote *its*'. And when he wrote 'Wordsworth's coat,' let us say, where I had a normal *'s*, my reader could demonstrate with a compass and a ruler set to true north, that the apostrophe was east (or to the right) and not west (or the left) of the final *s*."[27] Though recognizably hers in most respects, Dickinson's hand is nonetheless no different from those of other nineteenth-century writers in its idiosyncrasies: the difference is that her anomalies have been raised by some commentators to the status of consciously deployed elements of a graphic vocabulary.

Again, if there are discrepancies in the way that words, alphabetic characters, and punctuation marks are written, to what degree should that inconsistency influence our understanding of similar diversity in the writing of the dash?[28] One wonders also if the attention paid to Dickinson's dashes makes them unique to her when they were quite common and casually applied substitutes for other forms of punctuation in the nineteenth century. Sydney Smith used dashes of every kind of length and direction for punctuation, and Robert Browning's autographs have two dots that "are often indistinguishable from comma-dash or period-dash."[29] John Clare's letters were punctuated almost exclusively by dashes. In Jane Carlyle's letters, dashes often "take the place of all other punctuation."[30]

First in an article of 1965 and then in her impeccably researched *The Voice of the Poet*, Brita Lindberg-Seyersted showed inconsistencies in the application of the dashes as Stamm understood them: allegedly "solemn" tones were given to commonplace elements, and vice versa.[31] She carefully described Dickinson's range of punctuation marks, showing that commas and dashes were often interchangeable and that during revision there were frequently minor differences in the punctuation of a poem. She usefully summed up her arguments: "This indicates that the pointing applied by the poet was not a consistent system; it was a conscious, but impressionistic method of stressing, of arranging the rhythmical units of her verse; sometimes the adding of meaning to the linguistic units; and, it was a creation of the moment, seldom deliberated."[32]

Famously, Lindberg-Seyersted pointed out that the dashes in Dickinson's handwritten recipe for gingerbread were also "rhetorically" punctuated. Of course, the argument could have backfired: are gingerbread recipes, then, rhythmically punctuated?[33] But the observation still has relevance and force if one understands dashes and commas primarily as integers in a flexible and informal system of punctuation, enforcing gaps or pauses between units that, for whatever reason, Dickinson thought of as separate. For the remainder of this book, therefore, I will treat Dickinson's dashes as casually anomalous versions of the same sign.[34]

The second point to make about this early manuscript relates to the frequency of word divisions, both here and in the writing generally. Much recent critical energy has been expounded on such splitting in Dickinson's poems. Until Franklin's editions (of 1981 and 1998), these were invisible to most readers, but because it has subsequently come to be felt that many of these were visual puns, their erasure in printed texts confirmed the more general suspicion that conventional publication was not sensitive enough to her practices. To take a few examples: in "She sweeps with many-colored Brooms" (Fr318B), there is a split on the second (autograph) page.[35]

> And still she
> plies Her spotted
> thrift
> And still the
> scene prevails
> Till Dusk ob-
> structs the Diligence –
> Or Contemplation fails.

This is typical of many such instances: Dickinson runs out of space, but the break is felicitous in the sense that it seems to mirror formally or visually the experience it describes. Since obstruction places a barrier or impediment in the way of progress, the argument might go, Dickinson enacts this by splitting the word and thus preventing us from immediately arriving at its meaning. In an earlier poem, "The One who could repeat the Summer day" (Fr549A), Dickinson splits "repro- / duce" in the first (autograph) page, suggesting the difficulty of accurately representing nature in art.[36] Now, one might have several reservations about these: punning invokes several meanings at once (not always obviously), whereas this kind of pun is more mimetic—the shoring up of a single meaning rather than a proliferation. And there is also the question of readerly competence: how much is a middle-class nineteenth-century white woman or man in Amherst or Massachusetts generally likely to have taken this delay in the furnishing of the handwritten word as a self-conscious meditation on the role of language in the production and postponement of meaning? By extension, given that most of her readers would have encountered such word breaks before (passively in the correspondence of others, actively in the composition of their own letters), would they not have normalized them, converting them from graphic experiments into nonsignificant elements of Dickinson's writing?[37]

It seems to me that this is the heart of the matter: to what degree might word breaks in Dickinson's manuscript poems be said to differ significantly from common practice, both her own and that of others? One way of attempting to answer that question is to look at Dickinson's usage in her writing as a whole, including letters. For if there are similarities between the physical placement and proportional frequency of word division in the epistolary handwriting, the implication is either that it is similarly routine in the poems or that it is not routine in the poems or the letters. And if it were not routine, one would think that Dickinson would have made an explicit reference to its motivated aspect in at least one of her many thousands of letters. For there is overlapping between the poems and the letters sent to Susan Dickinson, right from the beginning. In the first page of Dickinson's first letter to Susan, number 38 as Johnson and Ward identify it, there are three word splits: in rows 4 ("re- / turned"), 6 ("in- / trusion"), and 14 ("shrug- / ging").[38] In L56 there are three on the first and two on the fourth (autograph) page: in rows 13 ("her- / self"), 19 ("pat-/ ter"), and 22 ("ear- / nestly); and in rows 2 ("en- / courage") and 3 ("mis- / takes").[39] In L70, there is one on the first page and one on the second: in row 2 ("on- / ly") and row 17 ("de- / luded").[40] In L73, there are splits in the first and second pages: in rows 5 ("dear- / ly"), 9 ("a- / shamed"), and 16 ("al- / ways"); and in rows 2 ("grow- / ing"), 7 ("sympa- / thy"), 21 ("some- / times"), and 25 ("prom- / ise").[41] L74 has four: in rows 5 ("with- / in") and 10 ("wan- / der") of the first page; row 6 ("per- / haps") of page two; and row 5 ("treas- / ure") of page three.[42] L77 has five: in rows 1 ("rath- / er"), 17 ("sab- / bath"), and 20 ("feel- / ings") of page one; and rows 23 ("be- / sides") and 26 ("a- / bout") of page two.[43] In L85, "no- / body," "some- / one," "per- / haps," "for- / give," and "un- / ceasingly" are split (in rows 5 of the first page, 5 and 9 of the third page, and 16 and 23 of the fourth page).[44] In L88, "sing- / ing," "be- / cause," "fire- / side," "fret- / ful," "no- / body," and "dear- / est" are divided (in rows 16 and 17 of the first page, 12, 21, and 24 of the second page, and 27 of the third page).[45] In L92, "ech- / oed," "smi- / ling," "fra- / grant," and "sun- / set" are broken (in rows 14 and 15 of the first page, 1 of the second page, and 11 of the fourth page).[46] In L93, "some- / times," "be- / fore," and "hav- / nt" are split (in rows 5 and 9 of the third page and 13 of the fourth).[47] In L94, "be- / come," "an- / guish," "lan- /

guage," "faith- / ful," "coun- / trie," and "some- / time" are split (in row 8 of the first page, 1 and 11 of the second page, and 12, 16, and 18 of the third page; "remem- / brance" is also split, by the break between pages one and two).[48] In L96, "fancy- / ing," "ma- / king," "wel- / come," "con- / clusion," and "dis- / dain" are split (in row 15 of the second page, 14 and 21 of the third page, and 2 and 22 of the fourth).[49] In L97, "yester- / day" and "throw- / ing" are broken (in row 3 of the first page and 14 of the second; the latter is also split by the break between pages two and three).[50] Thus, in a three-year period comprising about forty-nine pages of writing, there were approximately fifty-nine instances of word division. Of course, factors such as page size, extent of writing, ratio of words per row, ratio of rows per line, and the frequency of paragraph markers have not been taken into account, so that the numbers have little statistical currency. But what is significant is not so much the average of one word division to every page, but the knowledge that such division was a common and routine characteristic of Dickinson's handwriting from 1850 through 1853. And this implies that instances of word division in handwritten poems of the same period were part of the same physical landscape and therefore without deliberate meaning.

Nonetheless, it is particularly later in Dickinson's career that such features have been ascribed an expressive potential. During the 1860s, according to Johnson, there are approximately twenty-five letters to Susan but (by my estimate) only two instances of word division.[51] In L288, "Neigh- / bor" is split (on row 8 of the second autograph page), and in L333, "ambi- / tious" is split (on row 8 of the third page).[52] So there is a marked reduction in such occurrences, partly because Dickinson is writing shorter notes to Susan (who, after 1856, lives next door in the Evergreens) and partly because she has fewer words per line (her handwriting has changed). To take one example, in 1852, Dickinson fitted 314 words into the first autograph page of a February letter to Susan; in September 1864, the first page of a letter from Cambridge has 45 words.[53]

From 1860 to 1869, Franklin estimates there to have been 137 poems sent by Dickinson to Susan, and during this time there are ten word breaks.[54] Superficially, then, little difference exists between letters and poems: in the former, one has a single word break every 12.5 letters; in the latter, there is a word break every 13.7 poems. In the 1863 "Bloom opon the / Mountain – stated," there are splits on row 4 of the second autograph page and row 5 of the third; "dis- / appear" and "expand- / ing."[55] Both instances are potentially meaningful: splitting the first enacts the process of disappearance, and dividing the second mirrors the experience of expansion. Immediately following the second segment of the words, however, are significant spaces: 5.3 cm after the first and 6.1 cm after the second. For most manuscript critics, such spacing is strategic—it provides emphasis. In these instances, it seems strange that

Dickinson would have wanted to draw attention to two half-words, unless she was trying to give the reader extra time to savor the graphic puns: in other words, physical gaps would draw attention to the visual experimentation. Yet again we come to a "crux," the term used by textual scholars to refer to documents and passages about which there is an element of the undecidable. For both words coincide with the end of a metrical line, which suggests that the spacing may be related to dynamics of sound, not sight. One wonders, too, why Dickinson would want to pun on "dis- / appear" but not "fading," or why "expanding" (written with a small *e*) is deemed more significant (by this theory of semantic evaluation) than "Culminate." And does the increase in word division indicate a greater degree of will behind the arrangement of words on the page, or is it an effect of genre? That is, when recording poetry, Dickinson was conscious of having a fixed number of accents per metrical line, whereas in prose she had no such constraints—how much might this have influenced her physical writing?

Perhaps the most interesting word split occurs in "Risk is the Hair that holds the Tun" (Fr1253A), which is written on the inside of an envelope addressed by Lavinia Dickinson to Dr. Edmund M. Pease.[56] The flap end has been placed to the left, and Dickinson writes most of the poem on that side, switching sides after "The 'foolish Tun' the [page break] Critics say." On this side of the envelope, the paper is not flat and integral, but is formed by two interlocking sections, as shown below.

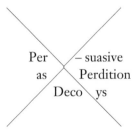

These leave edges that Dickinson has to negotiate, and she does so by splitting certain words and phrases physically: "Deco [edge] ys"; "Tr [edge] aveller"; and "mo [edge] unts." The splits between the verbal components of "Decoys," "Traveller," and "mounts" are (respectively) 0.6 cm, 0.3 cm, and 0.45 cm.[57] But the gap between the first and second parts of the word "Per [edge] – suasive" is 1.25 cm, twice as much as for "Decoys." Where the other spaces are sufficiently minimal for them not to be mistaken for deliberate, the breadth of interval in "Persuasive" causes Dickinson to use a dash, indicating that the word is not intended to be split, but is one unit. Now, the crucial point is that Dickinson uses exactly the same procedure for words that are divided physically because she comes to the end of a line and no longer has enough room to complete the word: she inserts a dash to signal that the division is physical and incidental and not grammatical or intentional. And such a procedure is not hers alone; it is inherited and entirely conventional.

In another example, "One need not be a chamber – to be Haunted" (Fr407A), but not the version sent to Susan, the word "Apart- / ment" is split. It is a great example of the potentiality of such instances: it seems again to enact the very experience it describes. But in L874, Dickinson writes: "Thank Sister / with love, and / reserve an Apart- / ment for two / Cocks in the / Cocks / Thanksgiving plan- / ning."[58] Reading the first example in the light of the second, one becomes more skeptical about the degree to which it might have been willed. And such skepticism is furthered by examples of word division in poems that seem to contradict the meaning: in "The Soul's superior instants" (Fr630A), "as- / cended" is split on the seventh row, so that it descends physically even as it describes the soul's upward movement. In another poem, this might be comic or ironic, but not here, where the speaker announces a sense of her election, of being one of the few chosen ones—and of managing also to rise above her own sense of superiority.[59] (In another poem, Fr796A, which was not the version sent to Susan, "quick- / ened" is separated, with the result that a word describing an increase of pace is slowed down by its inscription.)[60] But the opposition (between verbal and visual meaning) only exists if one takes seriously the notion that such aspects of a word's material inscription are deliberate. And such a thesis is so problematic, so riddled with contradictions, that it cannot be taken seriously.

II

A one-page note to Susan, dated October 1860, usefully illustrates a variety of techniques for recording paragraphs in letters, techniques that differ from standard practice:[61]

> Dear Sue –
>   You cant think
> how much I thank you
> for the Box –
> Wont you put the things
> in *this* one – it is'nt
> half so pretty, you know,
> but it's such a bother
> to tip one's duds out –
>   Thank Sue, *so* much.
>   Emily.

There is a conventional (initial) indentation after the opening salutation, followed by a typically Dickinsonian paragraph marker in the fourth row, where there is a 5.5 cm gap after "Box –." Johnson neglects to begin a new paragraph, though there is no reason why he should have: a refusal to exploit all the space available after a word and before the right edge of the paper is unambiguously equivalent—in Dickinson's letters—to the close of a paragraph. (In addition, Dickinson switches referent from a box to another unknown object.) Finally, there is a slight and (for the correspondence) unusual indentation of 1.5 cm in the penultimate row, which may have been enforced by there being insufficient space (horizontally) at the end of the previous line and (vertically) to the end of the page for the more familiar paragraph marker.

A one-page note from the following year shows some of the features that distinguish Dickinson's poetry from her prose, at least during this period:[62]

> Could *I* – then –
> shut the door –
> Lest *my* beseeching
> face – at last –
> Rejected – be – of *Her*?

This passage does not make sense, grammatically, as prose (though Bianchi published it as such in 1932); the assignment of capitals to "Lest" and "Rejected" would suggest, if read thus, that they were separate sentences, which would be very odd (Could *I* – then – shut the door. Lest *my* beseeching face – at last. Rejected – be – of *Her*?).[63] Instead, such capitals correspond to the beginning of poetic lines, which Dickinson (like most nineteenth-century writers in meter) signaled with uppercase letters. So the five rows of writing above are in fact equivalent to the following:

> Could *I* – then – shut the door –
> Lest *my* beseeching face – at last –
> Rejected – be – of *Her*?

Chances are, then, that these constitute a tercet (or alternatively the second, third, and fourth lines of an incomplete stanza in short meter, with alternate lines of four and three beats and a rhyme scheme of *abcb*).

If we look at the first page (recto only) of a poem meant for Susan, but probably not sent, with the right edge of the paper sufficiently clear to make measurements possible, the conclusions are much the same.[64] For the sake of convenience, I have included some measurements with my transcription: the sign "↑" indicates a vertical space (in centimeters, unless otherwise noted), while "↔" is the horizontal gap between the last mark in a line and the right side of the paper. Unless otherwise indicated, the gap in both cases is about one centimeter (remember that Dollie is a pet name for Susan Dickinson):

> *Excuse* me – Dollie –
> [↑ 1.5]
> The Love a Child can
> show – below – [↔ 5.8]
> Is but a Filament – I
> know – [↔ 8.3]
> Of that Diviner – Thing – [↔ 0.6]
> That faints opon the face
> of Noon – [↔ 7.2]
> And smites the Tinder [↔ 0.5]
> in the Sun – [↔ 5.1]
> And hinders – Gabriel's Wing! [↔ 0.2]
> [↑ 1.5]
> 'Tis This – in Music –
> hints – and sways – [↔ 2.3]
> And far abroad – on [page break]

This is how Franklin arranges this excerpt of the poem variant, which he identifies as Fr285A:[65]

> The Love a Child can show – below –
> Is but a Filament – I know –
> Of that Diviner – Thing –
> That faints opon the face of Noon –
> And smites the Tinder in the Sun –
> And hinders – Gabriel's Wing!
>
> 'Tis This – in Music – hints – and sways –
> And far abroad – on

Franklin includes the address ("*Excuse* me – Dollie –") in his notes on the poem and also records the placement of line and page breaks (after "can," "I," "on," etc.). Again, this seems defensible on the grounds of spatial patterning. There is a greater vertical gap between "*Excuse* me – Dollie" and "The Love a Child" parts of the manuscript, and again between "Gabriel's Wing!" and " 'Tis this," than otherwise between lines: the second of these gaps certainly confirms the presence of stanzaic division. And the pattern of blank spaces among the lines surely suggests (for instance) that Franklin was right to feel that "The Love a Child can / show – below –" was meant to be one unit, "The Love a Child can show – below –."

This is not to say that the manuscript cannot be read and reproduced in other ways, with its alignment regarded as having been arranged with some aesthetic and semantic purpose. Such an approach would understand (for instance) "The Love a Child can / show – below" as a kind of visual pun, with the "second" part of the sequence visually enacting the concept of beneathness. One could go through the entire poem looking for similar effects, such as the deliberate isolation of the verb "know" throwing doubt on the degree of knowledge, or the dramatic heightening that accompanies "of Noon" being assigned a line of its own. But voices of doubt interpose themselves at this point: would the foregrounding not work better if "Noon" alone were cut off, given that the preposition seems to dangle loosely, lessening and diluting the presumed purpose? And what is the idea behind a deliberate segregation of "in the Sun"? Are we supposed to stumble across this like Fishian readers, surprised by the Sun's appearance in a place we expected some other sequence (in the Fire)? And while we are in a visual mood, why not divide "And hinders – Gabriel's Wing" into two so that the phrase is literally impeded by the line sequencing ("And hinders – / Gabriel's Wing")? Surely an imagination so attuned to the possibilities of graphic inscription would not have missed such an opportunity. And if she did miss it, does this mean that Dickinson was inconsistent or just that the deliberate aspects of her line division are informed primarily by metrical and not visual conventions?

Franklin's transcription also separates the address ("*Excuse* me – Dollie –") from the poem, as indeed he subsequently does with the signature (Dickinson ended the poem and then signed it "Emily."). Such an intervention implies that the poem remains, in a sense, different from its performance within the letter, and indeed the variorum edition also presents another variant of the poem that was included in Fascicle 35 in 1863. One of the major arguments of the manuscript school is that the address and signature are not detachable from the poem but transform it from being a self-contained aesthetic object into a communicative act that derives some of its meanings from the network of relations between identifiable historical individuals. So, the original of Fr285A is not a poem enclosed within an epistolary frame but a "letter-poem." If one accepts this argument, then the irony is that decisions to separate poems and letters in instances where it is alleged that there was no division replicate precisely the kinds of editorial procedures that prevented Dickinson from publishing in the first place.[66]

But Franklin's supposition that a poem *can* to some extent remain separate from its material performances is supported by Dickinson's inclusion of a variant of this poem, Fr285B, in Fascicle 35, where it was the nineteenth in a sequence of twenty-five.[67] For ease of comparison, I have supplied only the first stanza:

> The Love a Life can show
> Below
> Is but a filament, I know,
> Of that diviner thing
> That faints opon the face
> of Noon –
> And smites the Tinder
> in the Sun –
> And hinders Gabriel's Wing –

Dickinson's recording of the poem independent of any address implies that it was not irrevocably linked in her mind with Susan—in fact, the revisions show Dickinson moving away from familial specificity ("Child" is replaced with the more universally applicable "Life"). In other words, the poem is made autonomous, independent of its first epistolary context—or of any originating circumstances.[68] Moreover, one can argue that the poem is not necessarily fully coincidental with every detail of its own material appearances, which is why "can / show – below –" in A becomes "can show / Below" in B; "I / know –" in A becomes "I know," in B; and so forth. Here, *the metrical integrity of the unit is preserved*: in both versions, the blank space after the word "below" is retained to indicate that it belongs together with the sequence "the Love a Child/Life can show." There is physical variation ("can / show"; "can show"), but also metrical consistency (iambic tetrameter). And this is significant because it suggests that when we attempt to transcribe the poem, we need to attend to patterns that may operate irrespective of, or in combination with, a line's inscription on a particular page.

III

A note sent to Susan Dickinson in 1865, written in pencil on a single page, looks like this:[69]

> So set it's Sun in
> Thee
> What Day be dark
> to me –
> What Distance – far –
> So I the ships

> may see
> That touch – how
> seldomly –
> Thy Shore?
>
> >   Emily

Following "Thee" (7.2 cm), "me" (5.1 cm), "see" (5.5 cm), and "seldomly" (5.7 cm) are the amounts of space that correspond to either paragraph conclusions or line-end phenomena. We can rule out the notion that these spaces separate one paragraph from another; otherwise we would have to accept that there is no connection between "That touch – how seldomly" and "Thy Shore?" The other possibility, of course, is that Dickinson deployed such spacing as a form of emphasis; but if so, one wonders why the sequence "in Thee" is divided between the preposition and the pronoun, whereas "to me" is isolated as one unit (with preposition and pronoun joined). In other words, if we accept the hypothesis of prominence being achieved through physical segregation, one also has to accept that the procedure is so regularly but inconsistently applied as to be meaningless. Or put another way, if highlighting is the desired effect, then we have to spend a proportionately greater amount of time focusing on "Thee," "to me," "may see," and "seldomly" than on the phrases that precede them. In addition, the argument that manuscript line endings are deliberate carries with it the implication that "in," "Thee," "dark," "me," "far," "ships," "see," "how," "seldomly," and "Shore" represent a rhyme scheme of *xaxabxabab* (as opposed to the *aabaab* of the "regularized" version). It is not so much that the dispersed rhyme scheme is unthinkable as that it fails to comply with Dickinson's practice more generally. One quickly runs into the territory of the absurd by taking seriously the proposition that the manuscript design is to be reproduced literally, whereas a metrical layout results in a stanza that coincides in every detail with the physical coordinates of the original. Dickinson's autographs are maps rather than photographs: their lines and spaces *do* represent the contours of meter and rhyme but do *not* always describe physical expanse and material boundaries. Thus, the large space that follows "So set it's Sun in / Thee" indicates that the last element belongs to the first and that the two rows of writing constitute one line of verse. Nineteenth-century readers understood this; in a note to Gertrude Vanderbilt, Susan Dickinson added and elided punctuation but ignored original line division in her transcription of these same lines:

> So set it's Sun in Thee
> What Day be Dark to me,
> What Distance, far,

> So I the Ships may see,
> That touch how seldomly
> Thy Shore?
>
> > Emily

The substitution of commas for dashes in the third line may be acceptable given that the two are difficult to distinguish and fairly interchangeable in Dickinson's work. But in the original, there are clear punctuation marks (dash or comma) on either side of "how seldomly," but no such mark after "see": these are Susan Dickinson's decisions, and hers alone. Finally, another version of the same lines, by Martha Dickinson Bianchi, seems to confirm the idea that the manuscript above was equivalent to the poem below in terms of its line arrangement (the punctuation and capitalization are another matter).[70]

CXXX.

> So set its sun in thee,
> What day is dark to me—
> What distance far,
> So I the ships may see
> That touch how seldomly
> Thy shore?

Another document, dated by Franklin to around 1865, shows Dickinson formatting the poem in her customary manner.[71]

> Rare to the Rare –
> Her sovreign People
> Nature knows as
> well
> And is as fond
> of signifying
> As if fallible –
>
> > Emily –

To digress, the script presents much that is intriguing, not least the casual switch between different ways of inscribing the lowercase *e*—a regular, closed form, and a small, open alternative that is like a capital (almost a Σ).[72] As I have suggested before, if one of the characteristics of Dickinson's script is a nonsignificant irregularity in the writing of particular letters, often in the same document, we ought to be cautious about pronouncing other variations (such as in the dashes) as willed features of a manuscript art. (Nor was Dickinson unique in the freedom with which she inscribed the same alphabetic character. A letter from Lucretia Peabody Hale to Edward Everett Hale, dated 11 June 1855, includes a portion written by her brother Charlie, in which he relates that the "roadway which is undEr the railroad is enclosed, and is as firm and as solid in appearance as any truss bridge." He then promises to return "in the day-time + Examine the work morE particularly.")[73]

Written in pencil on unruled paper, measuring approximately 9.8 × 15 cm, and embossed "PARIS" within a horizontal oval in the upper-left corner, the note is folded in thirds. The spaces after "well" and "signifying" come to 6.7 cm and 3 cm, respectively, and they are domain-end phenomena—that is, they coincide with and mark the close of a metrical line. (Elsewhere, the spaces are 0.3 cm, 1.2 cm, 1.2 cm, and 1.1 cm, after "Rare –," "People," "as," and "fond." Intriguingly, the spaces *before* the first "Rare, "well," and "of" are the largest in the sequence: 1 cm, 0.9 cm and 0.8 cm, respectively. In this message at least, Dickinson seems to have moved slightly more into the page when writing her prose address and runover lines.) When combined with the knowledge that capital letters often correspond to domain-initial phenomena, signaling the commencement of a metrical sequence, one sees that what Dickinson wrote actually signifies the following:[74]

> Her sovereign People
> Nature knows as well
> And is as fond of signifying
> As if fallible –

And yet, this stanza is much less obviously regular in meter than a brief communication sent to Susan in 1869:[75]

> The things of
> which we want
> the proof are those
> we knew before –

This sequence is indisputably metrical: it bears comparison with the opening lines of Fr1279, "The Things we thought that we should do / We other Things have done" (and may well have been a discarded remnant of its earlier composition).[76] And that perception of iambic regularity (equivalent to Dickinson's use of common meter—or, alternatively, *Eights and Sixes*) led editor William Shurr to excavate it as a "fourteener epigram" he then numbered 56:[77]

> The things of which we want the proof
> are those we knew before –

But Shurr recognized (and to his eternal credit made no attempt to alter) the lack of the capital at the beginning of the second line. Metrical or not, Dickinson chose not to render this as a poem—or to render it differently from the ways that she did previously and subsequently to Susan, marking the start of a metrical unit with a capital letter. And it is misleading to compensate for this by saying, as some scholars have done, that the writing "is centered on the page," as if it were arranged like a poem.[78] Writing in pencil on paper measuring approximately 12.6 cm across and 6.8 cm down (with one horizontal and one vertical edge carefully torn, showing that the paper was once part of a larger original), Dickinson nonetheless ran out of room immediately on the first row of writing. For after "of," only 2.6 cm of space remained, and the next word in the sequence, "which," measured approximately 3 cm. What makes this document a note and its predecessor a poem (if anything) are Dickinson's own practices: the assigning of uppercase letters and blank spaces is hers, which therefore obligates to note that the distinction is made, even if we then choose to disregard it. This much is also true for another message dated (by Franklin) to 1869:[79]

> Best Witchcraft
> is Geometry
> To a magician's
> eye –
>   Emily

Rows 1 and 3 come to within less than half a centimeter of the paper's right edge (about 0.1 cm and 0.4 cm, respectively). Rows 2 and 4 are trailed by intervals of 1.7 cm and 5.6 cm, respectively. What best explains the difference between odd and even rows, once more, is that the spaces indicate the close of metrical sequences; indeed, in another version of the same item, Dickinson writes:[80]

> Best Witchcraft is
> Geometry
> To the magician's mind –

Are these discrepancies miniature experiments in line placement (to place "is" on the first line or the second; to assign "eye" its own line or subsume its variant within a slightly more extended sequence), or are they physically different versions of what is essentially the same two-line object?

> Best Witchcraft is Geometry
> To a magician's eye –

In favoring the second of the two possible answers to my previous question, one is swayed not by meter or rhyme alone (for the concordance of "Geometry" and "eye" might arguably be nebulous, though it seems to me a typically Dickinsonian slant rhyme of two different long vowels), but also by the inner relation of the opening equation. For where the two-line version preserves the opening equivalence (witchcraft = geometry), the four-row one disrupts it, increasing the emphasis on, and significance of, "Geometry" by virtue of its isolation. And the visual isolation works further to delay the movement of the lines: the pause after "Geometry," minimal in the two-line version, becomes pronounced and salient, almost end-stopped, in the four-row. A shift occurs in the center of balance in the poem: in the two-line version, the comparison reads fluidly and is sufficiently original for the weight of interest to be distributed equally along its constituent parts; in the four-row, the emphasis on "Geometry" makes the single word proportionately more important than the metaphorical contract (the equation "Best witchcraft = Geometry") it was meant to fulfill (and which the "edited" version, not the diplomatic transcript, best preserves).

Among the more interesting of the notes Dickinson sent next door to Susan are her celebrations of the latter's birthday: in December 1880, she sent Fr1541, "Birthday of but a single pang," and in 1870, the following:[81]

> Lest any doubt
> that we are glad
> that they were born
> Today
> Whose having lived
> is held by us
> in noble Holiday
> Without the date,
> like Consciousness
> or Immortality –
> 　　　　　Emily –

Written in pencil on a leaf of notepaper, the poem is unusual for Dickinson: it represents three lines of seven beats (or fourteen syllables), rhyming *aaa*.

> Lest any doubt that we are glad that they were born Today
> Whose having lived is held by us in noble Holiday
> Without the date, like Consciousness or Immortality –

The manuscript version would otherwise embody lines of iambic dimeter, monometer, and trimeter, rhyming *xxxaxbaxba*; such variations in any other lyric would suggest precisely the kinds of uncertainty and doubt that the poem professes to deny. The point of the repeated rhyme (*aaa*) and extended meter is exactly the opposite: a tripping rhythm and happy sonorities convey a light and positive tone at the same time as the message becomes progressively more abstract—and flattering (Today, Holiday, Immortality). To insist that the autograph copy more accurately reflects Dickinson's wishes with respect to her sister-in-law is to confuse what is essentially a greeting card with a post-modernist exercise in irony. Instead, it is typical of many of Dickinson's messages to Susan Dickinson; it denies indifference (which suggests that such a charge may have been in the air at times—and it is interesting that the poem cleverly avoids the second-person singular in this respect) and eulogizes munificently: Dickinson claims that her praise is constant and not annual or occasional. There are slight echoes of courtly love here, and one is struck at times by the formal, odelike character of many of these notes: "I must wait a few Days before seeing you – You are too momentous. But remember it is idolatry, not indifference," for example. Or "Susan is a vast and sweet Sister, and Emily hopes to deserve her, but not now."[82] Not even Susan was exempt from being turned away at times, and the hyperbole of Dickinson's reassurances and praise fascinates—there is joy in knowing Susan, but also a discourse that is simultaneously loving and distant. Intimate is probably the wrong word for it; "idolatry" seems closer.[83]

Another interesting aspect of the poem's material rendering is the habit of linking plural, lowercase *t*'s with a single long cross-stroke (in this poem, "that," twice, and "without" are written this way, though in "without" the stroke is at a slant and does not bifurcate the first ascender).[84] Dickinson's handwriting has attracted increasing levels of scrutiny and speculation since the publication of Franklin's *Manuscript Books* (1981). In their introduction to *Open Me Carefully*, for example, Hart and Smith comment on her "calligraphic orthography (unusually shaped 'S's,' extravagantly crossed 'T's,' etc.)" and then point out such instances in their notes to a few messages.[85] Thus, in the commentary on one document the underlinings are described as being "very wavy, calling attention to themselves," though one would have thought that underlining was meant to bring attention to itself, that being precisely its purpose or function in the first place.[86] Other letters that are singled out include *F* ("crossed with flourish"), *Y* ("written with flourish"), *L* ("noticeably large"), and *T* ("crossed extravagantly" and written with "an extraordinary flair").[87] Though the editors do not say so directly, there are hints here of the kinds of comments made, separately and previously, by Smith and others: that alphabetic characters and words are crafted in such a way visually to support or give emphasis to (or even to undermine) what was being conveyed. One is reminded of what Ruth Miller said in the wake of debates about the placement and direction of the dash; that such an "analysis rests on the assumption that Emily Dickinson was so highly meticulous a craftsman that her handwriting was more deliberate than her choice of words."[88]

Isolating certain alphabetic characters for commentary suggests that they have a more than decorative status: it complies with the observation that such letters (mainly consonants, it seems) "help to convey meaning."[89] Observing that letters are written ornamentally is hardly inappropriate, but extracting a general procedure of premeditated design from a few examples is a risky practice; certainly, the examples given seem less convincingly graphic when correlated with wider clusters of inscription. In addition, the interpretation appears to be inconsistently applied. For instance, moments occur in many autographs when a word will be repeated on the same page but take up different amounts of space: are we, then, to proceed as if the largest instance was the most significant? And what does it mean that the letter *t* is almost invariably written with a flourish when there are two or more instances of it in the same word? For claims about the "stunning flourish that crosses both *T*'s" in the word "Tonight" and is related to the "seductive . . . calligraphy" of the "Wild Nights" autograph where it appears, must be judged against the exceeding commonality of such strokes in Dickinson's poems *and* letters.[90] In 1852, such features can routinely be observed in the horizontal stroke across the ascender of the lowercase *t* (thinks, letter, storm, bitterly, than), the capital *F* (Forgive), but especially in words that have two minuscule *t*'s (thoughts).[91] In 1853, the practice of one stroke joining two ascenders continues, as in "together" and "thought" in L102 and "thought" in L103.[92] In 1854, Dickinson extends the stroke from the initial to just above the penultimate letter in "Father" and crosses from the first to the fourth letter in "Thanksgiving" in L176.[93] The habit continues up to (and beyond) December 1861, the estimated date of composition for "Wild Nights." In L243, to Edward S. Dwight, she joins the initial and ultimate letters in "thought" and (most significant) "tonight."[94] In an 1862 poem addressed to Susan Dickinson, she joined the first and last letters when writing "Your – Riches – taught me – poverty."[95] In 1865 (the date is conjectural), Dickinson was still linking the first and last letters of "Tonight," as in L303.[96] In 1867, she joins the initial and ultimate *t* of the word "without" twice on the first page of "The largest Fire ever known."[97] She continued to connect *t*'s in two draft poems of 1870, written on the inside of separate envelopes, where "straighter" and "intimate" are thus inscribed; in the same year, she linked the first, second, and last *t*'s of "Strategist" with one continuous stroke in "The Suburbs of a Secret."[98] In the 1872 manuscript of "A narrow Fellow in the Grass," included in a letter to Susan, Dickinson uses an extended stroke in "transport" and "tighter."[99] In 1877, she joined both *t*'s of the words "states," "that" (four times), and "constant" in "She laid her docile Crescent down" (Fr1453B); in 1879, she joined the first and last letters of "that" in the second (autograph) page of "Those not live yet" (Fr1486A); in 1882, in a letter to Joseph K. Chickering, Dickinson writes "thought" and joins the first *t* to the second by a horizontal stroke of the pencil, as she did with "Tonight" in the poem, and in another letter she writes "substantiate" with a cross-stroke that measures no less than 4.8 cm; in 1883, she joined the *t*'s in "that" in L853 and in "temerity" in "No Brigadier throughout the year" (Fr1596B).[100] Taken together, then, the accumulated force of these examples suggests a calligraphic habit in her writing (where there is more than one *t*, they are joined by a cross-stroke), not necessarily a semantic effect.[101]

This habit of joining *t*'s is not exclusive to Dickinson's writing but reflects wider practices. Edward Dickinson's 1 January 1860 entry in his account books includes (under the section for "Doubtful & unproductive" property) the description "Watertown Lot" in which the stroke begins at the first *t*, goes through the second, and closes at the uppercase *L*.[102] And one need not confine oneself to the Dickinson family: David Mack, in a letter dated 5 March 1839, starts the horizontal stroke above the word "proprietors" slightly before the first *p* and ends it just after the final *s*. Elsewhere, Mack uses the *t* as an opportunity for drawing a line above and between the words "justify it" and above "others," "there," "affected," and "petition" (to take a few examples). A letter to Clifton Johnson, dated 3 December 1884, has many similar examples, as do Julia Field's letters to her mother, including those dated "Smithfield, Dec. 31./55." and "Montpelier March 4, 1861."[103] In a letter of 4 December 1843 to a recipient in Wilbraham, Massachusetts, Hershel Aldridge of Pelham employs a single cross-stroke to intersect the ascenders of the *t*'s in "that" and "settlement."[104] In the "Journal of Frazar Stearns, Commencing Oct 14th 1859," there is consistent evidence that each time he wrote a *t*, he elongated the cross-stroke.[105] In his "Diary" entry for 1 July 1865, Martin C. Thayer writes: "Sunday. Started for Greenboro . . . Started for Danville . . . Started from Danville." In each instance, both ascenders in the verb are intersected by a single stroke.[106] In Margie Dodge's handwritten "Journal" (1885–86), "interest," "representative," "station," and "that" are all written in such a way that the ascenders of the letter *t* are crossed and linked by one stroke.[107] Again, the cumulative import of these instances would appear to be that what contemporary critics see as integral and intentional *aesthetic* effects in Dickinson were just as likely to have been common features in nineteenth-century handwriting generally. Such marks may well have been decorative and ornamental— executed because they were visually pleasing—but this does not mean that they had any content, purpose, or function beyond that.

IV

About September 1871, Dickinson wrote to Susan while the latter was visiting her sister Martha in Geneva, New York.[108] What interests me here is not the letter as a whole, admirable though it is, but the third and fourth manuscript pages:

The Novel "out,"
pathetic worth
attaches to the
Shelf.
Nothing has gone
but Summer, or
no one that you
knew.
The Forests
are at Home –
the Mountains intimate at
Night and arrogant
at Noon, and
lonesome Fluency [page break]
abroad, like
suspending Music.
Of so divine
a Loss
We enter but
the Gain,
Indemnity for
Loneliness
That such a
Bliss has been.
Tell Neddie
that we miss
him and cherish
"Captain Jinks."
Tell Mattie
that "Tim's Dog [page break]

Reading the letter, there seems to be an oblique hint in the use of the word "Music" of the poetry that immediately follows, and the words from "Of so divine" to "Bliss has been" impress themselves on the mind as verse, partly because of the rhyme ("Loss" and "Loneliness" indicate a familiar *abcb* structure) and partly because of the meter (a regular iambic pattern of trimeter, trimeter, tetrameter, and trimeter). The architecture of the poem asserts itself: one notes that the strongly stressed "Loss" and "Gain" are correctly brought into a closer and more dramatically oppositional alignment by the so-called edited version (where these, quite properly, are line endings); in a diplomatic transcription, such a neat antithesis becomes attenuated.

The switch from a speaking to a singing or lyric mode is confirmed independently by the alteration in the writing's spatial patterns that coincide with the beginning of the poem. There are substantial intervals of space subsequent to "Loss" (6 cm), "Gain" (4.5 cm), and "Loneliness" (4.2 cm), which would normally correspond to paragraph endings in a more straightforward letter. (After the words "power" and "mean" in the opening of the letter, there are spaces of 4.5 and 6.6 cm, respectively, though it is clear that there is sufficient room for the words which follow them, "The" and "To." These, then, are paragraph markers.) But these spaces are clearly not the same as paragraph markers; for why would Dickinson begin a new paragraph after a word followed by a comma ("Gain") or after a phrase that clearly links with another ("Loneliness / That such a Bliss has been")? And it is clear, too, that Dickinson could have fit "We" (and even "enter") into the 6 cm of space subsequent to "Loss"; what prevented her from doing so were imperatives associated with poetry (matching and limiting sequences of words to predetermined quantities of syllables or stresses) and not prose. In addition, subtle changes occur in the poetry section of the writing, such as the grammatically redundant assigning of capitals to words with little semantic weight (the first personal plural, "We," and the demonstrative pronoun, "That"), for instance. These make sense only as indications of a new metrical unit. One also notes the substantial increase in the number of end-domain spaces (3 in 8 lines, from "Of" to "been," an average of 1 every 2.6 lines, whereas in the rest of the letter there had been 11 in 47 lines, or 1 every 4.2 lines).[109] Such a cluster of tendencies with the same related explanation add up to compelling evidence that Dickinson continued to distinguish between poetry and prose in letters to Susan, even as late as 1871.

V

Jumping forward five years, to about 1876, one finds another communication that seems, again, to distinguish between epistolary and lyric modes of discourse.[110]

> Sue – this
> is the last
> flower –
>
> To wane
> without
> disparagement
> In a dissembling
> hue
> That will not
> let the Eye
> decide
> If it abide
> or no
> is Sunset's –
> perhaps – only.
>   Emily

There are very clear intervals between the opening statement (explaining an enclosure) and the poem: a horizontal space of 5.7 cm after "flower" (equivalent to a paragraph break) and a vertical space of 1.5 cm (equivalent to a generic boundary or a stanzaic division). Nevertheless, the spacing afterward is unusual, mainly because the word "without" will not fit into what space remains after "wane" (2.8 cm), and "disparagement" will not fit after "without" (4.2 cm). That both words are written in lowercase letters indicates that they are not line-initial. Other spaces cannot be explained as having been determined by material factors; "hue" is followed by 8.7 cm, for instance, though such an intermission would easily accommodate the "That" which begins the next line. Like "decide" (followed by 5 cm and on the next line by "If") and "no" (followed by 6.2 cm and on the next line by "is"), these spaces are physically and grammatically unnecessary: they are imposed by the regulatory measures of poetry and not the material margins of prose. By extension, "In," "That," and "If" are assigned capitals that do not indicate punctuation or semantic weight; evidently, such uppercase letters correspond to the start of metrical lines. Had Dickinson wished to produce a poetically lineated prose (a writing the extent of whose lines were guided by alternative forms of visual, semantic, or nonregular stylization), then such capitalization would have been redundant. Dickinson's continuing use of nineteenth-century conventions for marking the commencement of a metrical line shows that the rows in her manuscripts were not autonomous and that the templates for her poetry were still meter-driven rather than graphic.

Perhaps the crucial area of uncertainty in this letter is the switch at the end from poetry to prose. Whereas Dickinson clearly made known the generic shift at the start by using a vertical break, she does not appear to have made such an announcement at the end—or did she? Once more, there is the kind of horizontal space (6.2 cm after "no") that is equivalent to a paragraph break or line ending; in either case, the next word would have begun with a capital. Instead, the next line begins with a word that is written entirely in lowercase, indicating continuity of thought, at the same time as the space previous to this records the cessation of one genre and the commencement of another. (Crucially, in another version sent to Higginson, Dickinson once more left space— this time 5.7 cm—after "no.")[111] The phrase "is Sunset's only" was clearly meant to help Susan understand that the quatrain was about fading light, but it is not an essential part of that quatrain. Rather than seeing Dickinson experimenting with genres, such habits of inscription seem to indicate that their separation was a matter of convention or habit to her; she *could and did* include the two on a single page, but she did not suspend the separate conventions associated with their organization. In the end, the casual and routine combination of the two genres may be no more unusual than a letter in English that makes occasional use of Latin or French phrases: the change need not be announced, but it hardly amounts to an interrogation of linguistic transparency either.

VI

The title of this chapter is taken from a memorable note to Susan Dickinson that dates from 1877.[112]

> But Susan is
> a stranger yet –
> The ones who
> cite her most
> Have never scaled
> her Haunted House
> Nor compromised
> her Ghost –
>
> To pity those who
> know her not
> Is helped by the
> regret
> That those who
> know her know

> her less
> The nearer her
> they get –
>
>   Emily –

Again, there is much here that is typical of the correspondence with Susan Dickinson: the precise praise; the association of Susan with nature; and Dickinson's sense that although she had been her friend for over twenty years, Susan continued to mystify her in many ways. The latter is something of a leitmotif in Dickinson's description of their relationship: in Fr5, "One Sister have I in our house," the speaker observes that Susan "did not sing as we did" and that she was "Herself to her a music." That combined sense of self-enclosure and self-reliance was part of Susan's fascination for Dickinson: there were always depths to her that could never be plumbed. And it is clear that the "I" in that poem is the more active, the more needy one in the relationship: we are told that "I held her hand the tighter," but nothing about an affirming, responding squeeze.[113] What is extraordinary is that the feelings of 1858 (when Fr5 is thought to have been written) continued to be experienced almost twenty years later, in 1877. And Dickinson was still commenting on those mysteries in 1882: "With the Exception of Shakespeare, you have told me of more knowledge than any one living – To say that sincerely is strange praise."[114] In the poem above, mention of the "Ghost" returns us to the final description in Fr5 of Susan as "this single star:" both images suggest brilliance, exoticism, but also distance and an otherworldly self-sufficiency.

But the vertical spaces that occur in this document are not common features of Dickinson's prose; most often, they signal a break between stanzas.[115] By extension, the distribution of capitals and end spaces cannot be understood in terms of prose—one does not assign capitals to medial phrases, and one does not begin new paragraphs in the middle of a thought. Once again, the *physical* attributes of this communication make it clear that Dickinson thought of it as a poem. That it was sent and refers to a historical individual and had personal significance for both writer and reader is another matter, one I will discuss in a subsequent chapter.

VII

Perhaps one of the most touching documents from the entire correspondence with Susan Dickinson (and I am by no means the first to have recognized it), as well as compelling evidence of Dickinson's generous compassion at a time of great personal suffering, is the beautiful letter of consolation sent to Susan shortly after the death of her son Gilbert on 5 October 1883:[116]

Dear Sue –
     The Vision
of Immortal
Life has been
fulfilled –
How simply at
the last the
Fathom comes!
The Passenger
and not the
Sea, we find
surprises us –
Gilbert rejoiced
in Secrets –
His Life was
panting with them –
With what menace [page break]
of Light he cried
"Dont tell, Aunt
Emily"! Now my
ascended Playmate
must instruct *me*.
Show us, prattling
Preceptor, but the
way to thee!
He knew no
niggard moment –
His Life was
full of Boon –
The Playthings of
the Dervish were
not so wild
as his –
No Crescent was
this Creature – [page break]
He traveled from
the Full –
Such soar, but
never set –
I see him in

the Star, and
meet his sweet
velocity in every-
thing that flies –
His Life was
like the Bugle,
which winds
itself away,
his elegy an
Echo – his Requiem
Ecstasy –
Dawn and
Meridian in one. [page break]
Wherefore would
he wait, wronged
only of Night,
which he left
for us –
Without a spec-
ulation, our
little Ajax
spans the whole –
Pass to thy
Rendezvous of
Light,
Pangless except
for us –
Who slowly ford
the Mystery
Which thou hast
leaped across!

Emily –

There are two word splits here, but it seems almost unthinkable that Dickinson would introduce deliberate visual puns in a communication such as this—not least because Susan, devastated by her loss, would not have been at her most receptive to graphic experiments. If we take the blank spaces in the writing as interludes of some kind (without speculating as to their nature), it is possible to arrange the autograph according to the following groupings:

Dear Sue –

[initial indent] The Vision of Immortal Life has been fulfilled – [6.6 cm]

How simply at the last the Fathom comes! The Passenger and not the Sea, we find surprises us – [3 cm]

Gilbert rejoiced in Secrets – His life was panting with them – With what menace of Light he cried "Dont tell, Aunt Emily"! Now my ascended Playmate must instruct *me*. Show us, prattling Preceptor, but the way to thee! He knew no niggard moment – His Life was full of Boon – The Playthings of the Dervish were not so wild as his – [5.7 cm]

No Crescent was this Creature – [page break]

He traveled from the Full – [6.4 cm]

Such soar, but never set – [3.9 cm]

I see him in the Star, and meet his sweet velocity in everything that flies – His Life was like the Bugle, which winds itself away, his elegy an Echo – his Requiem Ecstasy – [7 cm][117]

Dawn and Meridian in one. [page break]

Wherefore would he wait, wronged only of Night, which he left for us – [6.2 cm]

Without a speculation, our little Ajax spans the whole – Pass to thy Rendezvous of Light, [8.2 cm]

Pangless except for us – [6.3 cm]

Who slowly ford the Mystery [4.6 cm]

Which thou hast leaped across!

[initial space] Emily –

Clearly, blank spaces in the message correspond mostly to paragraph endings, but it is only toward the end of the document that we get short verbal sequences that are successively separated, and these correspond to the quatrain identified by Franklin as Fr1624. There is a shift in the mode of address from consoling Susan, identifying with her pain, and referring to Gilbert in the third person ("Wherefore would *he* wait, wronged only of Night, which *he* left for us – Without a speculation, our little *Ajax* spans the whole"; emphasis added), to a direct encomium using the second person ("Pass to *thy* Rendezvous of Light;" "Which *thou* hast leaped across"; emphasis added). Yet, there are other passages in the message that are poetic:

No Crescent was
this Creature – [page break]

He traveled from
the Full – [6.4 cm]
Such soar, but
never set – [3.9 cm]

Such a sequence observes the kinds of tendencies—material and accentual or syllabic—that are associated elsewhere in Dickinson's work with lyric inscription: capitals, an increased frequency in end-domain phenomena (the blank spaces in rows 4 and 6 of the excerpt) and regular meter. Nevertheless, Franklin, and Johnson and Ward, did not recognize this as poetry, presumably on the grounds that it did not rhyme and did not constitute a complete stanza (of four lines).[118] The difficulty in identifying whether this is one or the other is not a matter of rhythm or linguistic density, however, for as I argue in a subsequent chapter on genre, style or linguistic register alone cannot be used as a criterion for distinguishing between a Dickinson letter and a poem, or between a portion of a letter and a portion of poetry. Rather, what separates the two are differences in the physical characteristics of their inscription, reflecting the influence of one or another set of principles of organization—and in this instance, they could be interpreted as reflecting either. One sympathizes with any editor confronted with the necessity of having to choose how to present these lines in print: they could be either or both.

Does that mean that Dickinson was consciously experimenting with the production of a new generic hybrid, a mode of writing which grafted together elements of prose and poetry? In tentatively proposing a negative answer to such questions, one takes into account the document as a whole, which is certainly profound and figuratively complex but clearly ends with an epitaph that differs in its material aspects from the remainder of the writing. And one notes, too, that there are other verbal cycles in the message that are similarly poetic but not visually encoded as such:

He knew no
niggard moment –
His Life was
full of Boon –
The Playthings of
the Dervish were
not so wild
as his –

Or:

> His Life was
> like the Bugle,
> which winds
> itself away,
> his elegy an
> Echo – his Requiem
> Ecstasy –

The first of these begins metrically and could be construed as a quatrain (with no rhyme, and a slightly awkward switch from iambic to trochaic meter in the last line); the second is a perfectly acceptable instance of a four-line stanza written in iambic trimeter and rhyming (very approximately *abcb*). But because Dickinson did not use capitals where the metrical units began, as she very clearly did in the final lines, it seems that she did not want these clusters acknowledged formally as poetry. Now, the very argument that manuscript critics embrace is this: Dickinson refused to separate poetry from prose in her late writing. But one then wonders why she would have continued the traditional habits of poetic inscription (capitalized line beginnings, meter, rhyme, stanzaic organization) alongside such alleged elisions of genre—unless she continued to distinguish between the two in her own mind? For most of this document, the distinction is clear: in the one sequence that remains (to my mind) problematic, it is the presence of conventional signals and not their suspension that creates the difficulty.

VIII

The following year, in 1884, Dickinson sent another of her impressive gestures of reassurance and support.[119]

> Wish I had
> something vital
> for Susan, but
> Susan feeds
> herself –
> Banquets have
> no Seed, or
> Beggars would
> sow them –
> Declaiming Waters

none may dread –
But Waters
that are still
Are so for
that most fatal [page break]
cause
In Nature – they
are full –

Emily –

Comparing the first five rows of writing with the last five reveals important similarities and differences: the first five have two words that begin with capital letters (both necessary because one, Susan, is a proper name and one, Wish, starts a sentence), while the last five also have two (neither of which is explicable grammatically or semantically). And though there are similar material interludes after "herself –" and "cause," the first clearly accompanies a paragraph break (or at least the end of a sentence, a semantic unit of some kind), whereas the second does not—it introduces an idea that is only fully explained in the next passage of writing. Had Dickinson been uninterested in observing generic differences, she would not have made such distinctions. That she did may not unequivocally support Johnson and Franklin in indenting a section of this document as poetry, but it does prove that the basis of their decision was physical and authorial and not the result of prior assumptions that were imposed onto very different autograph realities.

A less clear-cut example derives from the same period of time.[120]

Morning
might come
by Accident –
Sister –
Night comes
by Event –
To believe the
final line of
the Card would
foreclose Faith –
Faith is *Doubt.*

Sister –
Show me
Eternity, and [page break]

> I will show
> you Memory –
> Both in one
> package lain
> And lifted
> back again –
>
> Be Sue, while
> I am Emily –
> Be next, what
> you have ever
> been, Infinity –

Like the previously quoted communication, the first section exhibits the material tendencies of prose, the second of poetry. There is nothing grammatically anomalous about the opening sequence; it has no capitals where capitals are not called for, whereas the second has one ("And lifted back again"). The first section has clear paragraph breaks after "Sister" (6.6 cm) and "Event" (4 cm). It is not that the first lines are non-lyrical: one sequence, "Morning might come by Accident" scans as well as any other line on the page, and "Night comes by Event" rhymes with it. The insertion of the "Sister" breaks up the incipient meter, however, and "To believe the final line of the Card would foreclose Faith" does not scan, as Alfred Habegger rightly points out.[121] Again, to insist on the distinction is not to believe that meter is always required for language to be defined as poetry; it is not even to presume that Dickinson herself insisted on that difference. In this instance, Dickinson's assignation of an uppercase letter to the conjunction ("And lifted back again") when the ordinary rules of grammar in prose did not demand it shows her behaving as if this passage were poetry. And we should, I am persuaded, do her the honor of respecting her wishes in this instance.

If—and it is a big if—one accepts that the first part of this note is prose and the second is poetry, where does that leave the third ("Be Sue, while I am Emily")?

> Show me Eternity, and I will show you Memory
> Both in one package lain
> And lifted back again –
>
> Be Sue, while I am Emily –
> Be next, what you have ever been, Infinity –

Johnson and Ward printed these lines—wrongly, in my view—as a five-line poem with no break between lines 3 and 4, overlooking the proportionately larger interval of vertical space after "again" that corresponds either to an end-of-stanza or end-of-poem marker (Johnson did not include the lines in the *Poems* of 1955, however). Franklin, on the other hand, does not include the prose part of the document, and therefore, like Johnson and Ward, assumes that these lines are *all* poetry.[122] Presumably, he was persuaded—again like Johnson and Ward—that "Emily" and "Infinity" constituted a rhyming couplet that closed the auditory circle first opened by "Eternity" and "Memory." And "Be Sue, while I am Emily" does scan, though that need not be conclusive (in 1884, it may have been unusual for Dickinson to think in language that did *not* scan).

It seems to me that the crucial factor is whether we regard the second "Sister" as a signature or an additional address. Johnson (1958) and Franklin (1998) define it as a signature, Hart and Smith (1998) as an address. Both arguments have their merits: Hart and Smith because there is an unusually large gap from the "Faith is *Doubt*" to "Sister" (1.3 cm), but only 0.9 cm to the top of the *m* in "Show me." Physically, "Sister" seems to belong to the second sequence of writing—the poem—and would therefore represent an integral part of it. The complicating factor is the indentation of the word: Dickinson's most common mode of address places the name at the left margin, while the most common position for signatures is toward the right margin. In addition, the previous note to Susan ("That any Flower should") is also signed "Sister," and the signature there is toward the right-hand margin in addition to being 1.5 cm beneath the final phrase, "Past of Peace."[123] In other words, the placement of "Sister" in "Morning might come by accident" is consistent with horizontal and vertical patterns of placement associated with signatures and not addresses. The point is minor but crucial nonetheless: it shows that as late as 1884 Dickinson continued routinely to distinguish between passages of prose and poetry. For the signature marks the end of the letter: what happens immediately afterwards is not only an epistolary event, but a lyrical one.

IX

A central document in the thesis that Emily Dickinson shared her ambitions with Susan is a communication dated (by Franklin) to March 1853, when the latter was in Manchester, New Hampshire. One of the first notes to Susan, it draws a clear visual distinction between prose (the first line of writing) and the poetry that follows:[124]

<u>Write! Comrade, write!</u>
On this wondrous sea
Sailing silently,
Ho! Pilot, ho!
Knowest thou the shore
Where no breakers roar –
Where the storm is oer?

––––––––––

In the peaceful west
Many the sails at rest –
The anchors fast –
Thither I pilot <u>thee</u> –
Land Ho! Eternity!
Ashore at last!

      Emilie –

It was Thomas Johnson and Theodora Ward who first misleadingly suggested that Dickinson "had begun writing poetry and was probably encouraging Sue to do the same."[125] And other scholars have drawn attention to Susan's having transcribed the poem twice (presumably on the grounds that this is evidence of its significance in the history of literary relations between the two, as well as proof of the collaborative nature of those relations).[126] In the fascicle version, though, Dickinson did not record this aspect of the poem's first distribution; its biographical potential does not seem to have been a significant element of its composition when retrospectively considered for storage:[127]

––––––––––

On this wondrous sea – sailing silently –
Ho! Pilot! Ho!
Knowest thou the shore
Where no breakers roar –
Where the storm is o'er?

In the silent west
Many – the sails at rest –
The anchors fast.
Thither I pilot thee –
Land! Ho! Eternity!
Ashore at last!

––––––––––

And although Susan Dickinson *did* make two transcripts of this poem, both were inaccurate in different ways. This is the first of her efforts:[128]

> Wait Comrade Wait!
> On this wondrous sea
> Sailing silently
> Ho! Pilot ho!
> Knowest thou the shore
> Where no breakers roar
> Where the storm is o'er?
>
> ———
>
> In the peaceful West
> Many the sails at rest
> The anchors fast
> Thither I pilot thee
> Land Ho! Eternity
> Ashore at last E.
>   1848 –

If the injunction to write was an attempt at encouraging Susan Dickinson to be a poet, then the irony is that the recipient seems to have misunderstood: she records "Wait" for "Write" and seems to have believed that "Wait Comrade Wait!" was a part of the poem. In her second attempt she performs an even more radical amputation, beginning with the third (or, depending on the version, the second) line, possibly because the first lines were forgotten (if transcribed from memory) or because she was attempting to bring the poem into alignment with Goethe's "Kennst Du Das Land," from *Wilhelm Meister*:[129]

> Ho Pilot ho!
> Know'st thou the shore
> Where no breakers roar
> Where the storm is o'er?
>
> In the peaceful West
> Many the sails at rest
> The anchors fast –
> Thither I pilot thee
> Land ho! Eternity!
>   Ashore at last!
>   Emily

Another of the early poems sent to Susan Dickinson (in 1859) was Fr123A,
"Besides the autumn poets sing":[130]

> Besides the autumn poets sing
> A few prosaic days
> A little this side of the snow
> And that side of the Haze.
> A few incisive mornings –
> A few ascetic eves –
> Gone – Mr Bryant's "Golden Rod"
> And Mr Thom'son's "Sheaves" –
> Still, is the bustle in the brook,
> Sealed, are the spicy valves.
> Mesmeric fingers softly touch
> The eyes of many Elves –
>
> Perhaps a squirrel may remain
> My sentiments to share –
> Grant me Oh Lord a
> sunny mind –
> Thy windy will to bear!
>
> > > Emilie –

Below I give Susan Dickinson's version, which she revised by hand after her
son, Ned, had first typed out a copy: their amendments are indicated by square
brackets. (For example: Susan and Ned changed "Besides" to "Beside," and to
indicate that this change was made, I write "Beside[ ]," thus marking a deletion
or other emendation.)

> [Afterward]
>
> Beside[ ] the autumn[,] poets sing[,]
> A few prosaic days[,]
> A little this side of the snow[,]
> And that side of the Haze.
> A few incisive mornings[,]
> A few ascetic eves[,]
> Gone [ ] Mr[.] Bryant[ ]s [ ]Golden Rod[ ][,]
> And Mr[.] Thom[ ]son's [ ]Sheaves[ ][.]

Still[ ] is the bustle in the brook,
Sealed[ ] are the spicy valves[,]
Mesmeric fingers softly touch
The eyes of [merry] [e]lves[.]

Perhaps a [squirrel] may remain
My sentiments to share –
Grant me Oh Lord a sunny mind[,]
Thy windy will to bear[.]

[Emily Dickinson]

It is Susan who adds a title in her own handwriting, reconstructs line 15 as a single entity (by not observing its arrangement over two rows), changes "many Elves" to "merry elves" (though Ned had first typed "many"), and removes the line underscoring "squirrel" in the original. Of course, this presupposes that she used the version sent to her in 1859 and not the fascicle copy, which is arranged as four quatrains and has no line division (though the final quatrain moves to a different page after "Elves"). It also presupposes that my transcript of the autograph at Amherst College is correct, though some of its features are ambiguous ("mornings" and "eves" could be "Mornings" and "Eves," for example). So, in saying that as many as thirty-one changes may have been made to the original (including the addition of a title), one should keep in mind that some of these are more debatable than others. Nevertheless, the point of the exercise is not to criticize Susan's version so much as to suggest that there were many aspects of this original (and others) that she chose to represent differently or simply misread. In short, it is wishful thinking to believe that Susan Dickinson would have made a better editor than Mabel Todd (whom she is favorably contrasted with) and Thomas Higginson at the level of local presentation—that is, in terms of overall sensitivity and fidelity to the aggregate of precise material details embodied in the manuscripts. (Whether she would have made a better editor in terms of *which* poems, letters, and drawings she might have included is another matter entirely—and one I return to at the end of this book.)

A more positive way of understanding Susan Dickinson's take on her sister-in-law's lineation in the autographs is to say that she knew that those arrangements were not deliberate.[131] One of the most useful examples of Susan Dickinson's understanding of Dickinson's line arrangement is "The Face we choose to miss," which has Susan's transcription on the reverse of Dickinson's original (the two are presented here side by side):[132]

The Face we	The face we
choose to miss –	choose to miss
Be it but for	Be it but for
a Day	a day
As absent as	As absent as
a Hundred	A hundred years
Years,	When it has
When it has rode	rode away –
away –	Emily.

Susan indents run-on lines according to nineteenth-century conventions of print, positioning the words from the first line that do not fit into the space allotted them on a row of their own, but at a farther remove from the left margin and in lowercase to show that they do not constitute a separate line. Where Dickinson indents from the right margin of such sequences, Susan indents from the left: "choose to miss" and "a Day" both correspond this way. Susan seems to have interpreted the "a" before "Hundred Years" as capitalized and therefore assigns it a line of its own, while continuing to recognize that "Years" was not meant to be deliberately segregated. And where Dickinson fits more of the phrase "When it has rode away" into the first space than Susan does, the latter is clearly aware that the sequence is integral and not to be transcribed over two lines.

X

The numbers speak for themselves, or should be allowed to do so: Susan Dickinson was clearly Emily Dickinson's most important and long-term correspondent and the recipient of more poems than any other individual. What is not clear is that Dickinson and her sister-in-law shared a poetry workshop and that they each found the other's work to be inspiring. This is not to say that such a workshop could not have existed in theory or that it did not exist in practice; it is simply to say that the surviving historical evidence no longer unequivocally supports such an assertion. But even though there is only one absolutely indisputable instance of collaboration (an exchange of letters on "Safe in their Alabaster Chambers"), Ellen Hart and Martha Nell Smith incorporate a number of working drafts in *Open Me Carefully*, on the assumption that they had been sent to Susan.[133] These include Fr1129 ("I fit for them"), Fr1137 ("Too cold is this"), Fr1280A ("Who were 'the Father and the Son'"), Fr1365 ("Crisis is sweet and yet the Heart"), Fr1423A ("The inundation of the Spring"), and Fr1510 ("The Devil – had he fidelity"). This claim is bold and original: Franklin either fails to mention Susan Dickinson in association with these documents or identifies them as having been given to her by Lavinia *after* her sister's death, in preparation for a posthumous volume.[134] Two other drafts are included on the strength of comments made by Bianchi: Fr1131A, "A Diamond on the Hand," and Fr1354A, "Two lengths has every day." In *Emily Dickinson Face to Face*, Bianchi had published a photograph of the working draft of the poem's second stanza, with the caption "written on the flap of an envelope and sent to 'Sister Sue.' "[135] But Bianchi may have confused the poem with its partial artifact: Franklin argues that Susan did receive Fr1354, but as a three-stanza fair copy (version B rather than A: the envelope scrap on which A was written, according to Franklin, passed into Susan's hands after Dickinson's death).[136]

In other words, the provenance of these manuscripts is uncertain; or to put it another way, even in instances where there is evidence that Susan did receive a particular lyric ("Two lengths has every day"), it is not always clear which physical version she looked at (Fr1354A or Fr1354B). The distinction is an important one, because the implications of regular discussion of draft materials go beyond the boundaries of Dickinson's friendship with Susan. They suggest that Dickinson had a privileged audience, a trusted and intimate reader, for works that would otherwise have been considered unfinished, which supports the contention that Dickinson publicized a radically different kind of poetry to Susan than she did to others. To summarize, some critics have felt that poems previously categorized as unfinished drafts or fragments are in fact finished—or, they at least reject the idea of externally imposed directions in choosing between variant words. The weakness of this argument has been that no record existed of Dickinson sending such documents to her correspondents; though they do not say so directly, Hart and Smith implicitly refute such an objection by including draft poems in their edition of the correspondence. To take two examples; the principal *material* argument for including LP199 (Fr1365, "Crisis is sweet and yet the Heart") and LP200 (Fr1423, "The inundation of the Spring") seems to have been that they were folded, the first in thirds (standard procedure for letters) and the second in half.[137] Both poems were also included in Bianchi's *Single Hound*, which seems to have clinched the argument for inclusion in each case: in her preface, Bianchi wrote that each of the poems incorporated in that volume were "folded over, addressed merely 'Sue,' and sent by the first available hand."[138] Certainly, the paper in both cases—blue-ruled without embossments in the first instance, brown scrap in the second—is not decisively linked to Susan Dickinson; there are no pinholes, paste marks, or instances of Susan's handwriting (additional identifying characteristics that Hart and Smith cite elsewhere as evidence of transmission). Those features would not necessarily be sufficiently compelling in themselves, but their absence makes the suggestion of creative reciprocity rather tenuous.[139]

For folds do not in themselves constitute proof of a document having been sent. Written in pencil on an elongated band of wrapping paper, for example, a rough copy from 1883 measures 29.8 cm at the top, 27.9 cm at the bottom, and 5.5 cm in height; it is folded in five places.[140] Two of the folds seem primary, either through pressing, usage, or manufacture: the two that are most prominent give the impression that the paper was folded into thirds. The two outermost folds, which are the slightest, may indicate a further, subsidiary folding, but not an emphatic one. This sliver of paper has traditionally been associated with Otis Lord, though it was clearly never sent: the point is that although an unsent rough working copy, it was *still folded*. At times, the folded fragment was tiny; in the case of A 359, measuring 5.7 cm wide and 7.7 cm high, there are two folds, one that seems a residue of manufacture and the other introduced probably by Dickinson herself (with the result that the paper could be divided into thirds).[141]

Still as the
Stern
Profile of a
Tree against
a winter sky
  sunset sky –
  evening –

I never heard
you call anything
beautiful before.
It remained
with me

Again, it seems clear that this draft (also associated with Otis Lord) was not sent and that it was intended as part of a longer whole. Too, the draft is folded. About 1880, Dickinson used the inside of a Western Union telegram envelope to record (in pencil) two rough drafts of poems (Fr1518, "Glass was the Street – in Tinsel Peril," and Fr1519, "It came his turn to beg"), with variants; the paper is folded in quarters.[142] The envelope is addressed to "Vinnie Dickenson [*sic*] / Care Judge Lord." A 734 ("My lovely Salem smiles at me") and A 736

("Ned and I were talking"), both fair copy drafts written in pencil, are divided into thirds; internal evidence associates them with Lord, though it seems unlikely that they were sent.[143] A 738 and A 739, both portions of larger fair copy drafts written in pencil, are divided in half.[144] The accumulated evidence of worksheets such as these and others suggests that folding is not a reliable indication that materials were sent.[145] Dickinson often folded papers on which she was in the process of composing—perhaps to fit into a dress pocket (as she went about other daily tasks) rather than an envelope, perhaps for reasons of privacy, or perhaps to facilitate storage in a workbox or drawer.[146]

For a long time, Susan Dickinson was unfairly ostracized by a critical and biographical strain in Dickinson scholarship that can be traced back to contemporaneous persons who had reason to be hostile to her. But in revising estimates of the nature of her importance to Emily Dickinson, groundbreaking critics may have strayed slightly too far in the other direction.[147] Even the emphasis on Susan's identification of the "letter-poem" as a "distinct and important Dickinson genre" seems like a miscalculation.[148] For despite her indisputable centrality during the poet's lifetime, Susan Dickinson found herself increasingly marginalized and humiliated after Dickinson's death in 1886.[149] First, two volumes of the poetry were coedited by Mabel Loomis Todd, her husband's mistress, and published (apparently without her knowledge); then a two-volume edition of the letters appeared, edited by Todd alone, without the inclusion of any of those sent to Susan.[150] The letter-poem taxonomy is therefore a way of reclaiming some center ground: Susan was saying that, as letters, many of the poems had already *been* published, and most of those by Dickinson to her. And Susan was further letting it be known that, since the poems *were* sent to her, she had some rights of ownership in them— imaginative and personal, if not legal. She was therefore fighting to establish prior rights in the matter of Dickinson's literary estate, for she had an emotional, historical, and geographic proximity to Dickinson's genius which gave her a kind of primacy and legitimacy that none of Dickinson's other editors could claim. The use of the term "letter-poems" therefore relates to issues of biography and literary rights more than genre; already in the 1890s, Dickinson's literary reputation was a site over which there were competing claims of ownership. Susan was arguing—rightly—that she should have been given her considerable due and that she deserved a place in her sister-in-law's future reception.[151] But it is difficult to gauge accurately the exact nature of that debt, for much remains unknown—and unknowable—about it: letters were destroyed on behalf of both.[152] In the end, a remark by Martha Dickinson Bianchi provides a convenient epitaph for their relationship as it is seen by posterity: "It should have been my mother's task to record the life of the Emily Dickinson she knew, and that this was not done by her must remain a lasting regret to the friends of both."[153]

CHAPTER THREE

"Because I could not say it –
I fixed it in the Verse"

Dickinson and Samuel Bowles

SAMUEL AND MARY (Schermerhorn) Bowles received their first, joint, Dickinson letter in 1859, when Emily was twenty-eight, Samuel thirty-three, and Mary thirty-two.[1] She wrote separately to them after that—about thirty-five letters in all to Bowles, and sixteen to Mary—thus adhering to her own rule that a shared letter was little better than no letter at all.[2] Bowles often covered Amherst College's commencement proceedings for the *Springfield Daily Republican*, a newspaper that he inherited after his father's death and of which he was the chief editor and correspondent.[3] According to Susan Dickinson's recollection, in "Annals of the Evergreens," she and Austin made his acquaintance when he came to Amherst in June 1858 "to report the result of some agricultural experiments on an estate" owned by Levi C. Cowles.[4] Bowles dined with the young couple and was named (by Susan Dickinson) as one of their first visitors; he shared their interest in agriculture, art, and politics and wrote to them often (his letters to them are among the Dickinson papers at Harvard: only one of his letters to Emily Dickinson survives).[5] Although biographers and critics have speculated as to the nature of Dickinson's attraction to Bowles, it should be kept in mind that they corresponded much more than they met, that there were significant gaps in the correspondence, and that their initial friendship was a minor part of a larger circle of friends which included Dickinson's brother and sister-in-law at its core (and, very occasionally, her father Edward at its fringes).[6] In his letters to Austin and Susan Dickinson (of which there are slightly over 160), Bowles seldom refers to Emily, and when he does, often tangentially and out of courtesy: "Thank Emily & Vinnie, with my love, for their little pleasant notes" is a typical example.[7] Austin and Susan Dickinson were his main—perhaps his best—friends, then, and the Evergreens his favored destination; Emily Dickinson was a part of that emotional network, but as a constituent and not a primary element.

One of his favorite resorts was the house of his friend Austin Dickinson
at Amherst. It was a place where he was perfectly at home; he was on
terms of brotherly intimacy with Mr. and Mrs. Dickinson, and the chil-
dren knew him as "Uncle Sam." Here he would occasionally come to
spend a Sunday, often driving up through the beautiful mountain gap;
sometimes arriving unannounced, sometimes telegraphing his advent,
with a petition for some favorite dish. He was glad to give himself up to
lazy enjoyment; now talking on every subject except his newspaper, now
picking up the last new book, now lying silent on the lounge. On some
of these visits, Dr. David P. Smith was his companion, and under their
mutual incitement the talk was very bright. Sometimes on his return
home he would write back, "You gave me too rich food, – the talk was
too stimulating." But at other times he would sink into easy idleness. In
such a mood once as he lay on the piazza with the apple – blossoms
blowing over him, – "This," he said, "I guess, is as near Heaven as we
get in this life!"[8]

The epistolary relationship with Bowles covered almost twenty years from
beginning to end, albeit with a significant hiatus from 1863 to 1874 (though
poems were sent up to 1865 and again after 1870).[9] Although there are inti-
mations of her reclusiveness from time to time, Dickinson's letters to him
often celebrate a *shared* friendship and her social niche as the satirist and wit
of the company.[10] (At times, this went too far; in L223, she apologized to
Bowles for having poked fun at women who were socially active.)[11] One, L256,
is apparently undertaken on behalf of Susan and Austin, asking Bowles for
information that would help Susan pick out a going-away present and urging
him to write to Austin just after his friend and former classmate Frazar Stearns
had been killed in the Civil War.[12] Still another (L284) is written for her
mother, who was sending a gift of apples.[13] (The Dickinsons had a small
orchard, and Bowles seems to have received apples at least twice from Mrs.
Dickinson—in an 1861 letter to his wife he acknowledges the receipt of "a
fine basket full of big apples, which are a great treat for me.")[14] The writing of
letters was an important and acknowledged part of Dickinson's function
within her family, then, and her correspondence with Bowles was not gov-
erned by personal imperatives alone.

Indeed, in many letters Dickinson identifies her friendship with Bowles as
one she shared with others: in L259, written in March or early April 1862, she
describes the aftermath of a welcoming party (comprising herself, Susan, and
Lavinia) whose principal guest (Bowles) failed to show up:[15]

We cannot *count* – our tears – for this – because they drop so fast – and
the Black eye – and the Blue eye – and a Brown – I know – hold their

lashes full – Part – will go to see you – I cannot tell how many – now –
It's too hard – to plan – yet – and Susan's little "Flask" – *poor* Susan –
who doted so on putting it in your own hand –

This sentimental portrait of three intelligent women reduced to tears by the
nonappearance of a man is at least in part a camp performance. Perhaps Dick-
inson was taking revenge for having to be the passive spectator of a male
drama of canceled arrival by providing an exaggerated account of the results
of this postponement. Perhaps she meant to reassure him of his importance
to the Dickinson women collectively, while creating a scenario that would
encourage him to complete his planned trip, which he did on 5 April. At the
end of the letter, she moves from the plural to the singular, and writes "I must
do my Goodnight, in *crayon* – I *meant* to – in Red," suggesting that he has
missed a kiss from her lips because of not being in Amherst. Presumably, she
meant to contribute further to motivating his return, but "Good night" is a
fairly common leave-taking in her letters to Bowles.[16] Readers interested in
detecting an erotic content to the letters should keep in mind that the many
"goodnights" were at least in part a side effect of their being written late in
the evening, and often while everyone else was asleep (Susan Dickinson men-
tions her sister-in-law sitting "up late at night long after her family had re-
tired").[17] Bowles himself was not a good sleeper, and the reading and writing
of personal correspondence was something he, too, left to the late hours.
Indeed, the correspondence confirms the impressions we have of Dickinson's
habits as a writer, for the letters are often set at night or during the evening.
L247 invites Bowles to "look out tonight," as she does, to see that the "Moon
rides like a Girl." L189 (the first, joint, letter) mentions that "it is almost nine
o'clock," while another finishes with the postscript, "Vinnie halloos from the
world of nightcaps."[18] This postscript confirms again the family's knowledge
that Dickinson wrote well into the night, though they may not have been fully
aware of what she wrote or how much. But it also suggests that a degree of
insomnia, or at the least nocturnal isolation, was a condition which Bowles
and Dickinson shared and which enabled a measure of identification between
them.

Unlike Dickinson's letters to her sister-in-law Susan, however, which re-
mained constant from 1850 onward, a substantial and significant gap occurs
in the correspondence with Samuel Bowles (a gap that may, of course, have
arisen accidentally because of the loss of letters and poems we do not know
about). According to Habegger's revised dating, Dickinson sent twenty-six
letters between 1859 and 1863, fully twenty-one of those during the years
1861 and 1862.[19] But from 1863 through 1869 there are no letters at all; in
1870 there was one (that was not sent); and then there followed three more

years of silence until 1874, when she wrote three times.[20] There is a broadly similar pattern between the ratio of letters to years and poems to years—with approximately forty poems being sent in total, the fourth largest after Susan Dickinson (252), Thomas Wentworth Higginson (103), and Louise and Frances Norcross (71). The poems are either sent separately or embedded within the text of the letters themselves, and most are believed (by Franklin and Johnson) to have been sent in the first half of the 1860s, with seventeen in 1861, seven in 1862, three in 1863, two in 1864 (though one is of uncertain provenance), and one in 1865. According to Johnson and Franklin both, the poems were resumed in 1870, when Bowles received one or possibly two; there was one other in 1874 and three in 1877, when Bowles was seriously ill (he had his final stroke in December of that year). If Johnson and Franklin are correct, Dickinson sent most poems in 1861 and most letters in 1862; whether this shift in genre is truly significant (a conscious change on Dickinson's part) or accidental (a side effect of inaccurate dating) is difficult to ascertain. Perhaps it is sufficient to note that, during a two-year period, Bowles was an intensely important member of Dickinson's extended literary/epistolary audience, after which she did not write at all (for six years) and then only occasionally. Again, attributing personal significance to this pattern (an increased level of emotional or intellectual attraction followed by a period of diminished interest) needs to be tempered by the knowledge that there was a surge in textual production generally during the same years, followed by a similar falling away of primary creative energies.[21] Nonetheless, Himelhoch and Patterson's summary of 1862 seems an accurate one:

> In late April or early May Emily wrote somewhat emotionally to comfort Mary Bowles (L262), and in June and again in August she wrote warmly emotional letters to Bowles in Europe (L266 and L272), but she had already turned to a new friend, T. W. Higginson, for the reassurance, the emotional support, that she had sought in Bowles the preceding winter. When he returned from Europe and came to Amherst about mid-November, she refused to see him (L276). He wrote to ask whether she had forgotten him, and she replied with an affectionate but somewhat distant letter enclosing poems. The period of her intense need of him was now apparently over (L277).[22]

Certainly, the register of the letters from Dickinson to Bowles changes over the period of their correspondence: in addition to several lighthearted examples of a kind of epistolary comedy of manners, Dickinson sent him a poem with a brief introduction in 1860, using the image of the sea that so attracted her imagination.[23]

I cant explain it, Mr Bowles –

Two swimmers wrestled on the spar
Until the morning sun –
When One turned, smiling, to the land –
Oh God! the other One!
The stray ships – passing, spied a face
Opon the waters borne,
With eyes, in death, still begging – raised,
And hands – beseeching – thrown!

It is always tempting to read poetry, especially lyric poetry, as an autobiographical exercise, and in this case the two swimmers might be said to correspond in some way to Dickinson and Bowles. If that is the case (and perhaps the safest way to approach this is to say that, in the context of the correspondence, the poem *may* refer to them but that it has other potential poles of reference), then it seems difficult to say which is which, or even what kind of experience is being referred to. The imagery of struggling or drowning at sea is very similar to that of the poem included within the text of L249, "[Sh]ould you but fail [at] – Sea –" and is the first in a series of musings on aspects of belief and doubt which include " 'Faith' is a fine invention" (Fr202) and "Through the strait pass of suffering" (Fr187, a favorite of Susan Dickinson). In matters of faith, Dickinson felt more experienced and perhaps even more able than Bowles: although she often adopts *social* postures of self-deprecation, she is a spiritual or cultural "*Queen*" in L249 and then writes of an "Empress" in L250 (which begins with Fr194, "Title divine – is mine!"). Clearly, these last two letters suggest the kind of urgency that often accompanies the desire to persuade. Dickinson is either responding to, or anticipating, Bowles's questions (about her behavior/life/belief/writing), or she is trying to effect a change in his attitude to her (he may have underestimated her, become more curious about her, or paid her the wrong kind of attention).

Nevertheless, one needs to draw back slightly from the framework of the Bowles-Dickinson friendship to see that such images were not specific to them as individuals but were part of Dickinson's evolving literary vocabulary. In other words, their significance is not tied to the context of the historical and personal relationship in which they are occasionally performed, but have a potential horizon of reference which transcends that particular relationship. Here is a letter to Mary Bowles, for instance, in which the sea imagery also occurs:

Don't cry, dear Mary. Let us do that for you, because you are too tired now. We don't know how dark it is, but if you are at sea, perhaps when we say that we are there, you won't be as afraid.

The waves are very big, but every one that covers you, covers us, too.

Dear Mary, you can't see us, but we are close at your side. May we comfort you?[24]

Another letter to Susan uses the same imagery:

You must let me go first, Sue, because I live in the Sea always and know the Road.

I would have drowned twice to save you sinking, dear, If I could only have covered your Eyes so you would'nt have seen the Water.[25]

And here is an excerpt from a letter to the Hollands, in September 1859, about the imminent death of her aunt Lavinia:

Mother's favorite sister is sick, and mother will have to bid her good-night. It brings mists to us all; – the aunt whom Vinnie visits, with whom she spent, I fear, her last inland Christmas. Does God take care of those at sea?[26]

It takes very little manipulation to associate the sea with a place of danger in nineteenth-century Massachusetts, especially at a time when much of the state's economic and political significance derived from its maritime traditions and when the newspapers were full of stories about ship journeys and ship-wrecks. Such significance is increased, made naturally figurative, for people living inland, as Dickinson did. Characteristically, too, Dickinson appropri-ates imagery associated with masculine commerce and adventure to show women confronting and trying to cope with dangers of equal magnitude. And her letters to Bowles, delicate and solicitous, correct the impression of a poetic sensibility attuned only to its own concerns. What is significant for the present purpose, however, is that the broad use of such imagery counteracts our ten-dency to read the "sea" as a private reference point for Bowles and Dickinson; in reality, it has a much wider reach.

Reading through the correspondence as a whole, one has the sense that Dickinson never quite went further than the parameters enacted by the dual address of L205 (in early April 1859), where she writes "Friend" and then "Sir."[27] Though this is playful (part of the comedy of manners mentioned before), it usefully illustrates two competing impulses: one toward intimacy, confidentiality; the other toward formality, distance (and humor, it should be said, can be manipulated in such a way as to create and perpetuate a barrier to further intimacy). She also developed silence as a literary strategy in these letters: "I skipped a page – tonight – because I come so often – now – I might have tired you. *That* page is fullest – tho'."[28] There are parallels with Fr277C, "Going to Him! Happy letter!" (formerly thought to have been sent to Bowles), which includes the line, "Tell Him the page I did'nt write."[29] More often than not, of course, the refusal to speak is as semantically charged as the words on the page (if not more so). But there were limits to what Dickinson was prepared to tell Bowles, at least in a letter (a poem is another matter, as we shall see later). Silence may correspond to social imperatives, of course: *The Young Lady's Own Book* (1841) claimed that a "lady neither writes nor speaks to a gentleman as she would to one of her own sex."[30] But it may also be that Dickinson chose from time to time not to speak directly or at all about her real concerns because she was too shy, because she thought she might be misunderstood, because the expression of such feelings would have been too painful—or because the friendship was not sufficiently intimate. (Nonetheless, relations between intelligent single women and married men generally were favorable at that time; by Theodora Ward's account, women of this type "simply lived above suspicion," while married men could be addressed without compromise, because they were legally and morally attached to another woman.)[31]

According to Judith Farr, one of the reasons Bowles "appealed to Dickinson [was] because he understood pain and had suffered it in many forms, emotional and physical."[32] Many of her letters inquire about his health or offer comfort during periods of sickness or after one of the three miscarriages suffered by Mary. It may also be that Dickinson felt that he could understand her better than most men because he suffered from depression, a "nervous malady" that was more commonly associated with housebound middle-class women of the nineteenth century.[33] Whatever the nature of her interest, at times they seem to echo each other in different contexts: Dickinson's claim that "Jerusalem must be like Sue's Drawing Room, when we are talking and laughing there, and you and Mrs Bowles are by," is very like the references to the Evergreens as "heaven" attributed to Bowles in Merriam's biography.[34] Of course, there are sociological reasons for this: the middle years of the nineteenth century saw a gradual consolidation of the home as a sacred territory, a paradise on earth. For men in particular, home was supposed to be a refuge. For women like Susan Dickinson, it was an arena for the display of good taste and artistic judgment. For Dickinson, however, home *competed* with and outranked heaven as much as it sought to mirror it.

There have been claims that Bowles was one of Dickinson's disappointments in love, though Himelhoch and Patterson's dating of the first letter (1859) should have prevented further discussion of Bowles as a candidate for that permanent vacancy known as "Master" (the unknown figure Dickinson first drafted letters to in 1858).[35] Certainly, the contents of the poems and letters do not in themselves absolutely contradict the supposition of dependency or attraction, but they do not support it either. In L223, Dickinson adopts many of the diminutive personae she occasionally used in writing men; she is a "little friend" who "misbehaved" and now seeks forgiveness. She is also "Bob o' Lincoln" (as mentioned previously, a pun on the bobolink also referred to in L189), which is part of her repertoire of self-referring bird images, meant at times to disarm men (by making the writer seem small and nonthreatening and in need of protection/understanding).[36] More often than not, however, Dickinson addressed Bowles as either "friend" or "Mr Bowles," and the consistent use of those terms seems to specify the boundaries of the relationship (they define the outer limits of formality and friendship, beyond which Dickinson does not wish to travel).[37] And as Himelhoch and Patterson point out, so "lively and so warm are her letters of apology [for missed visits] that one tends to forget how suspiciously numerous they are."[38]

I

The remark about heaven attributed to Bowles in Merriam's biography is echoed in the first letter to Samuel and Mary Bowles. I quote the opening two pages of the manuscript separately because they establish some precedents for the contents of the subsequent correspondence and because they provide a template of physical or material patterns that are fairly typical of the late 1850s and early 1860s. The letter is written in the emotional aftermath of a visit, and in it, like in many others, Dickinson meditates on the relationship between friendship and loss:

> Dear Friends.
>   I am sorry
> you came, because you
> went away.
> Hereafter, I will pick
> no Rose, lest it fade
> or prick me.
> I would like to have
> you dwell here.
> Though it is almost
> nine o'clock, the skies
> are gay and yellow,
> and there's a purple [page break][39]

The first two paragraphs are ludic, of course, but a familiar enough refrain from both poems and letters to have a degree of seriousness to them.[40] For Dickinson, the visit of a close friend was always a double-edged affair because it provoked emotional extremes: the excitement of personal contact, and the "Freight" of "Emptiness" that followed departure, when Dickinson experienced, at some level, a lowness of spirits or, perhaps, a premonition of terminal loss.[41] Again, at a time when mortality rates were higher and life expectancy was generally shorter than today (especially for women), it is understandable that Dickinson would reflect on death every time her friends left her (and some of her friends did die young). "My friends are my 'estate,' " she writes, and the cleverness of the phrase obscures the historical truth of its saying for a nineteenth-century woman who had no property or independent economical means: because social networks and obligations were seen as being part of a woman's sphere, Dickinson defines her value in terms of the friends she has. They are "gold" in one letter, "gems" in two others.[42] When she is trying to persuade Bowles to take his time in recovering from illness, she gently reminds him that economic considerations are not that important: his wealth is that he has "Estates of Lives." In 1874, this remained a theme of her letters to him—necessarily so because Bowles lived in Springfield, not Amherst, traveled often, and sometimes went abroad: "Come always, dear friend," she writes, "but refrain from going."[43]

The reference to "Jasper" (on the third page of this two-sheet letter) suggests that Bowles and Dickinson often discussed the Bible and occasional literary affinities (also shared by Susan Dickinson).[44] Alfred Habegger suggests that the reference is to Revelations 21, at least as Elizabeth Barrett Browning covered it in *Aurora Leigh*.[45] Dickinson's letters to Bowles are sprinkled liberally with such literary and scriptural references. In L241, she refers to him as "[Dick] Swiveller" and signs off as the "Marchioness." (Both are characters from Dickens's *The Old Curiosity Shop*; they marry at the end of the novel.) Although an oblique biographical inference may be drawn from the allusion, Dickinson is working very hard in the letter to explain her nonappearance during one of his visits. Her point is not that they will marry but that he can depend on her continuing sympathy, though the use of the fictional names suggests that their future will be in a world of letters, not necessarily in "real" life.[46] Other literary references are to *All's Well That Ends Well* (in L242); Byron's "The Prisoner of Chillon" (L249); Henry Howard (L275); the Brontë sisters (L299); and Browning's *Dramatis Personae* (L300).[47] In L205, she refers to the "Quick and the Dead," a phrase taken from the Nicene Creed.[48] In L241, the tone is slightly different; she writes "I pray for your sweet health – to 'Alla'," and the Arabic name fits in with the kind of skeptical irreverence that Dickinson displayed when she told Higginson (in L261) that her family addressed "an Eclipse, every morning."[49]

The physical attributes of the holograph letter quoted above are as standard for this part of the correspondence as are the literary and biblical references. Dickinson indents the first line after the salutation (positioning it 3.2 cm into the page, as opposed to 1 cm or less elsewhere). She employs clear end spacing after "away" and "me" (4.6 cm and 3.6 cm) to indicate the close of a paragraph. Most of the other spaces on the right side of the page are small (1.3 cm, 0.8 cm, 0.4 cm, and 0.8 cm for rows 1, 2, 4, and 5, for instance). The 1.9 cm of space after "here" is judged to be insignificant because the following word ("Though") takes up approximately 2.7 cm of space and clearly would not fit into the preceding line.

This is the second page:

> craft or so, in
> which a friend could
> sail. Tonight looks
> like "Jerusalem."
> I think Jerusalem
> must be like Sue's
> Drawing Room, when
> we are talking and
> laughing there, and
> you and Mrs Bowles
> are by. I hope we
> may all behave so
> as to reach Jerusalem.
> How are your Hearts
> today? Ours are pretty [page break]

This is the first page where the embossment ("PARIS") makes a noticeable impact on the layout: because it appears, reversed, on the top right of the paper, it hinders the writing and causes Dickinson to leave an interval of 2.8 cm after the first row. Such a space seems visually incongruous and therefore potentially significant—equivalent to a dramatic pause during a reading. But, here, it is clearly related to the topography of the paper on which it is inscribed and is therefore not an integral part of the poem's semantic apparatus.

Another striking feature is the manner in which the quotation marks surrounding the first instance of "Jerusalem" are inscribed. Both slant in the same direction (from upper left to lower right), instead of the first slanting in one direction (`) and the last in another ('').[50] The inscription is significant only because it is unusual, and in poetry, anything out of the ordinary draws attention to itself and quickly gains the status of a sign or rhetorical code of some kind.[51] In Dickinson's manuscripts, punctuation and orthography occasionally deviate—in the case of the dash, for example—from standard inscription and therefore suggest a degree of will or deliberateness behind them. In this instance, however, the quotation marks are the same as many other quotation marks elsewhere in Dickinson's holographs: they are uncommon by conventional standards, but not by hers.[52] By extension, although some aspects of Dickinson's handwriting may appear to deviate from standard usage, this idiosyncrasy is not necessarily a formal device designed to shape the reader's response to a word, phrase, or image in a particular way. In short, it is the assignation of the quotation marks that is significant (they suggest distance); the manner of their inscription is not.

Nevertheless, a great deal of editorial and interpretative attention has been focused on the meaningful potential of Dickinson's handwritten characters. Commenting on "Wild nights – Wild nights!" (Fr269), Martha Nell Smith refers to its "extraordinary, somewhat seductive, calligraphy—the wide-mouthed *W*, the triangular *T* at the beginning of the sixth line, and the stunning flourish that crosses both *T*'s in Tonight."[53] As I noted in the previous chapter on letters and poems sent to Susan Dickinson, Smith's comments have sometimes been misinterpreted as sanctioning a critical approach that assigns meaning to the inscription of particular alphabetic characters. It has also been suggested that communications to Susan Dickinson and Samuel Bowles differ in the degree of their formality: documents received by Bowles are thought to be less casual, which might have implications for the ways in which particular alphabetic characters are inscribed. It is therefore useful to observe that in the Bowles correspondence there are many examples of "wide-mouthed" *W*'s (for instance in "A feather from the Whippowil," or at the start of L256) and *T*'s that are crossed with a similarly "stunning flourish."[54] "Nature, and God, I neither knew" is a good example of the latter: the *t*'s in "startled" (row 5), "identity" (row 7), "that" (row 9), and "interest" (row 12) are all written with such flourishes. In the letter beginning, "Dear Mr Bowles. I got the little pamphlet," "petite" and "tastes" (on the third page) are similarly inscribed. In the note "Dear Mr Bowles. Thank you," "thought" has two ascenders that are joined by a single stroke of the pen. In "Perhaps you thought I didn't care," "thought" and (twice) "that" (on rows 1, 12, and 13 of the first page) and "that" (row 7 of the second) all have double ascenders that are joined by one stroke. In "The Drop, that wrestles in the Sea," "that" and "Amphitrite" (on the first page) have similar conjoining marks. In the letter beginning "Dear friend. Are you willing?" she inscribes "tonight" (on the third page) and

"Tonight" (on the fourth) in this way: there are two instances of "that" on the fourth page that are similarly inscribed (with a single horizontal stroke). In the poem "Title divine – is mine" sent to Bowles in 1861, "without" (twice) and "betrothed" (on the first page) are written with singly linked double ascenders. In "Dear friend If you doubted my snow," "thought" and "strait" (in rows 11 and 14 of the first page) are singly crossed, as are "Temptation," "stately," "troth," and "Expectation" (in rows 2, 4, 11, and 12 of the second page). The letter beginning "Dear friend. Will you be kind to *Austin*" features a "without" (row 13, first page) and "entreat" and "that" (rows 3 and 13, second page) with crossed ascenders. "Dear friend. The Hearts in Amherst – ache" has "thought" (row 5, first page), "tight" (row 3, second page), "thought," "throat," and "that" (rows 1 and 12, twice, on the fourth page) that have horizontal strokes joining the first and second ascender. And in "Dear Mr Bowles. I cant thank you any more," "thoughtful" is crossed with a stroke that takes up almost the same length as the word itself. Finally, "Dear friend. Vinnie accidentally mentioned that you hesitated" has "that" (twice on the first page) and "extent" (on the third) that are identically crossed.[55] The list is not fully comprehensive but it is typical, and the widespread evidence of such examples in the documents associated with both Bowles and Susan Dickinson strongly suggests that they represent rhetorical signs less than a habit of the handwriting and that they are not, therefore, essential elements of a vocabulary of graphic forms.

The inconsistency or variation with which Dickinson sometimes wrote exactly the same linguistic components in different ways has to be factored into the overall assessment of the potential contributions her handwritten letters can make to our understanding. For instance, in the sequence "Dear friend. / It was so / delicious to / see you – / a Peach / before the time," the minuscule, closed e in "friend" and "see" differs from the more open e in "Dear" and "Peach" (which looks more like a small capital). The open, capital-like E instead of e is repeated at the end of the word "caprice" in the same communication, and in writing "permanence," Dickinson used regular closed e's twice and then a small open E at the end.[56] In another letter, she says that Bowles has "the most / triumphant Face / out of / Paradise – / probably because"; here, the last word has *two* kinds of e inscription: first e and then E. In the same letter, Dickinson includes the poem "Ourselves – we do inter" and records two types of the same letter in the sequence "once achieves" (E, e, e).[57] Nor is this kind of feature confined to the correspondence with Bowles (and therefore a possible side effect of her personal relationship with him; it is not even a feature confined to Dickinson's work).[58] In a draft of "Fame is the one that does not stay," the phrase "Electrical the embryo" includes both types of small e (the capital-like version in the second E of "Electrical" and the more common *e* at the end of "the").[59] And in the phrase "The Prince of Honey and the Prince of Sting," from a pencil draft written on a fragment of paper measuring 12.7 × 2.9 cm, Dickinson assigns an open *e* to the end of the first "Prince" and a closed, or looped, one to the second.[60] One could also look at lowercase instances of the letter *d* in Dickinson's writing: in a draft of "Facts by our side are never sudden," written in pencil on blue-lined paper that is carefully torn at the right edge and cut with scissors at the bottom, there are two versions of the same alphabetic character. One is inscribed with a single stroke, with the ascender bending or curving back to the left; the other has a straighter ascender that slants slightly to the right. With the second example, the round body is sometimes joined at its top to the ascender and sometimes not: the ascender is formed by the pencil traveling upward, then down again, with a slight loop at the bottom, pointing to the right. Thus, the word "sudden" in row 2 of the autograph has two *d* shapes where the ascender bends back to the left, but "around" in row 4 ends with a right-leaning ascender.[61] These forms are then used interchangeably for the rest of the manuscript, but not in any systematic way. More generally, the inconsistency with which Dickinson wrote the same letters in the same documents suggests that similar deviation in the inscription of dashes need not constitute evidence of subtle distinction or semantically pointed differentiation.

By extension, Smith's additional opinion that Dickinson's "lines [do not] accidentally spill over" suggests a degree of will to manuscript lineation as well as to features such as word splits. But the evidence of the letters makes such an assertion difficult to support.[62] In the letter beginning "Dear friend. / How hard to / thank you," there are word splits on the second and third pages of the manuscript: "ob- / noxious" spills from row 3 to 4, and "tight- / ening" from row 10 to 11 (on pages 2 and 3 respectively). In "Dear friend. / Will you be / kind to *Austin* – again?," the word "disap- / pointed" crosses over from row 9 to row 10 on the first page of the holograph. In "Dear friend. / Had We / the Art / like You," "Congrat- / ulate" occupies the final and initial portions of rows 2 and 3 of the second page. And in the autograph letter beginning "Perhaps you thought / I did'nt [*sic*] care," "some- / thing" is begun on the last row of the second page and completed on the first of the third.[63] Poems to Bowles also contain instances of such word division, as in Fr608A, where "justifi- / ed" takes up rows 7 and 8 of the unruled manuscript page on which it is inscribed. The fewer instances of division in the poems than in the letters should not surprise us, as poems contain many more short lines that fit between the edges of the page, whereas prose lines are not often completed in a single horizontal space. The word "justified" is a typical exception, because it is part of a longer metrical sequence (tetrameter, in this case), is made up of three syllables (two of them stressed) at the end of a line, and is therefore more likely to be inscribed over two rows of space. Generally speaking, however, such division is rare in this corpus.[64] In poems and letters to Susan, as we have seen, there are many more. If the correspondence with Susan is characterized by a greater degree of casualness and confidentiality than is the Bowles correspondence, then word division might be seen as an indicator of that informality, in which case it is unlikely to represent a key element in a new visual poetics. And the similarity in word-division distribution between letters and poems would appear to strengthen the case for not regarding such things as key properties of Dickinson's formal apparatus.

The same can be said of dashes in the manuscripts. As we have seen, a great deal of attention has been paid to this phenomenon—and rightly so, as scholars puzzle over what previous generations might have overlooked or not taken seriously in the originals. Certainly, one recognizes as fully legitimate the anxiety and frustration of critics who note the inconsistency with which commas and dashes are inscribed in the autographs and their paraded regularization in the printed edition of the letters. Take the following example, which Johnson numbers L272:[65]

> Dear Mr Bowles.
> Vinnie is trading with a Tin peddler – buying Water pots for me to sprinkle Geraniums with – when you get Home, next Winter, and Vinnie and Sue, have gone to the War.
> Summer a'nt so long as it was, when we stood looking at it, before you went away, and when I finish August, we'll hop the Autumn, very soon – and then 'twill be Yourself. I dont know how many will be glad to see you, because I never saw your whole friends, but I have heard, that in large Cities – noted persons chose you.

Here is how the letter appears in a slightly more diplomatic form (the rows are numbered for subsequent reference):[66]

1. Dear Mr Bowles,
2. Vinnie is trading
3. with a Tin peddler – buying
4. Water pots for me to sprinkle
5. Geraniums with – when you
6. get Home, next Winter –
7. and Vinnie and Sue, have
8. gone to the War –
9. Summer a'nt so long as it
10. was, when we stood looking
11. at it – before you went away –
12. And when I finish August –
13. We'll hop the Autumn, very

14. soon – and then 'twill be
15. Yourself. I dont know how
16. many will be glad to see
17. you – because I never saw your [page break]
18. whole friends, but I have
19. heard, that in large Cities –
20. noted persons chose you.

Written in ink on very light, pale blue, transatlantic paper (Bowles was in Europe at the time), measuring approximately 13.5 × 20.9 cm, and made of one sheet folded to make two leaves, the letter dates from August 1862.[67] In the Johnson and Ward edition, the distinction between commas and dashes seems effortless and clear, but in the original, they are more difficult to separate. Consider "next Winter," which is bordered by commas in Johnson and Ward's version; in the original, the first punctuation mark looks like (and is) a comma, but the second one is its mirror image—similar, but reversed, so that it slopes in the opposite direction. Are these the same punctuation mark? (And is Dickinson's inconsistent practice with regard to quotation marks similar to her formation of commas?) Johnson and Ward also enclose the phrase "before you went away" in commas; in the original, the first mark is short, flat, horizontal, and below the line of writing, while the second is level with the line but angled downwards in the opposite direction of a comma (that is to say, it is angled ، rather than ,). Again, the sign which Johnson and Ward represent as a comma and which follows "August" (in row 12) slants at an acute angle and *away* from the writing, rather than toward it as commas conventionally do; it also begins slightly below the line of writing. The mark that follows "you" (in row 17) runs in a similar direction and is the reverse of conventional commas.

Johnson and Ward's procedure seems to have been to represent flat and extended horizontal strokes as dashes, and anything angled as a comma. The placement of the sign relative to the line of writing does not seem to have been regarded as decisive either: the dash in row 5, for instance, is level with the line, whereas the one in row 3 is slightly above it, yet both are represented as being the same. (And in a subsequent page, Johnson and Ward insert a dash in the sequence "We reckon – your coming," when the mark is an imperfection of the paper; it is situated 6.6 cm below the top of the page and 6.6 cm below the top of the next page too.) One's instinct in such matters is to represent marks slanting at opposite angles to standard commas as dashes, despite acknowledging the supremely debatable nature of any such decision. Yet my remarks are not intended to discredit Johnson and Ward but to show that Dickinson's inscription of punctuation marks was often quite volatile in its placement, duration, and direction. And such volatility in *letters*, where readers would not have been on the lookout for graphic experiments in the production of rhetorical signs (especially unannounced ones), suggests that the similar variety of inscription in *poems* need not be regarded as significant.

II

In the correspondence, one can often see Dickinson working from real life but improvising on it for her own purposes, as with the references to cups and to wine which run throughout her letters to Bowles. She finishes her first letter with "Vinnie's love brims mine"; another is accompanied by the promise of a bottle of wine as a present.[68] Dickinson knew that Bowles appreciated fine wines, and there is an argument for saying that the cup images reflect a pro-foundly social aspect of her consciousness which is often missing from critical accounts: it celebrates and re-creates conviviality, the joining together of friends, and demonstrates her adherence to the culture of gifts that had arisen around this time. Samuel Bowles was a Unitarian (as was Mary); there is a sense sometimes that the cup imagery Dickinson employs has a humorous, quasi-sacrilegious purpose. It derives much of its meaning, in other words, from an intersection of secular and parodic associations. In one of the first letters sent to Bowles, separately reconstructed by Johnson as (the poem) J16, Dickinson begins "I would distil a cup, and bear to all my friends." By January 1862 she begins a letter like this:

> Dear friend.
>   Are you
> willing? I am so
> far from Land –
> To offer *you* the
> cup – it might some
> Sabbath come *my*
> turn – Of wine how
> solemn – full![69]

Clearly, the symbol of the cup does not remain static in her correspondence but acquires an increasingly complex range of associations. And religious mat-ters were a topic of conversation, as the following suggests:[70]

> Dear Mr Bowles.
>   Thank you.
> "Faith" is a fine invention

When Gentlemen can *see* –
But *Microscopes* are prudent
In an Emergency.

You spoke of the "East."
I have thought about it
this winter.
Dont you think you and I
should be shrewder, to take
the *Mountain Road?*
That *Bareheaded life* – under
the Grass – worries one like
a Wasp –
The Rose is for Mary –

                                        Emily –

The "Thank you" is a wonderful piece of understatement: it would seem as if Bowles had encouraged her in some way, perhaps in the face of illness (in his letters to Susan and Austin Dickinson, "faith" appears to be synonymous with "optimism"). Or he may have attempted to answer Dickinson's doubts by urging her to have faith, to trust in God, or reported the advice given to him by a third person for problems of belief which they both shared. In any case, Dickinson playfully suggests that evidence of some kind is required before a fuller commitment to hope or to the tenets of Christianity can be accepted. Her rejoinder suggests that she was less likely than Bowles to be convinced by externally generated positive answers to the great questions of life and death.

Intriguingly (and exasperatingly for some recent critics), Johnson prints rows 3 through 6 of this document twice: once, differently indented, as a portion of a letter (L220) and once as a poem (J185).[71] Franklin explains that the same lines "were incorporated into a letter to Samuel Bowles that begins by expressing gratitude," and he too indents them differently from the prose. Both operate with the assumption that prose and poetry can be distinguished in the text, an assumption that is often questioned in recent articles on editing Dickinson.

Nevertheless, there is a distinction, and it is Dickinson and not her editors who makes it. It is not initially obvious from the purely physical arrangement of the text, because Dickinson is left with less than a centimeter of room following "Thank you," and the normal end space that signals the subsequent beginning of a new paragraph is therefore missing. But after "Emergency" in row 6, there is an interval of 3.4 cm, which is the kind of space that normally corresponds to the end of a paragraph. What follows, however, is a vertical space which is not repeated elsewhere in the letter and which is not character-istic of Dickinson's procedures for marking *prose* paragraphs. It *is* typical of the kinds of space that she inserts vertically between stanzas of poetry, though, and its appearance corresponds to the closure of a poetic sequence. This is confirmed by the pattern of blank spaces in other places on the page—for example, after "winter" (6.9 cm), "*Road?*" (3.4 cm), and "Wasp" (8.3 cm)—where Dickinson does not assign additional vertical gaps to separate the par-agraphs. Perhaps the most crucial difference is after "*Road?*" in that it has approximately the same ensuing break as "Emergency," and yet only the latter is followed by the appearance of a material code associated with the inscription of lyric writing.

In addition, there are distinct procedures of capital assignation in operation between rows 3 to 6, and between rows 7 and 16. If rows 3 through 4 had been prose, "When" would not have been given an initial uppercase letter. Had rows 8 through 15 been poetry, then "this," "should," "the," "the," and "a" would not have begun in lowercase. (Indeed, the entire poem could easily have been written as prose, as it forms a single complete sentence: "Faith" is a fine invention when Gentlemen can *see*—but *Microscopes* are prudent in an Emergency.) Clearly, Dickinson thought of this as a letter with a passage of poetry, because she inscribed the genres differently. True, she does not oth-erwise announce the change, but such casualness is historical and personal rather than an experimentation with generic assimilation: educated and middle-class nineteenth-century friends did not expect or require that generic differences be pointed out to them, because they were competent enough to tell the difference; because most of them knew that Dickinson wrote poetry; and because, in a familiar letter, such observances were unnecessary.

Another example of a text that Dickinson's editors have identified as trans-generic is a note to Bowles from February 1861 which is included in Johnson and Ward's *Letters*, Johnson's *Poems*, and Franklin's *Poems*; Johnson and Franklin separate the prose from the poetry. Written in ink on one sheet of paper folded to make two leaves, measuring 10.1 × 16 cm, and embossed "PARIS" on the upper left-hand corner of the first leaf, the text begins as a letter, describing Dickinson, Lavinia, and Susan as the sole members of a society whose purpose is discussing Bowles:[72]

> Dear friend.
> You remember
> the little "Meeting" –
> we held for you – last
> spring? We met
> again – Saturday –

'Twas May – when we
"adjourned" – but then
Adjourns – are all –
The meetings wore
alike – Mr Bowles –
The Topic – did not
tire us – so we chose
no new – We voted [page break]

One sees here Dickinson's playful transformation of the everyday—a conversation between the three sisters in which Bowles was mentioned—into something that oscillates between flirtatious and official discourses ("Topic," "adjourns," and "voted" all suggest a town or parish meeting). In other letters, the idiom is inflected with a mock-sacredness (one closes by informing him that "We pray for you – every night – a homely shrine – our knee").[73] Typically for Dickinson, however, the lines may be read in different ways: on one level, they are comic, parodying the nineteenth-century division of the genders (for though at "home," these women have official "business"), but on another they make it clear that Bowles is a favorite topic of discussion and someone worth remembering. Though she is engaging in the lighthearted form of self-deprecation that might have been expected of educated middle-class women of the nineteenth century in Massachusetts, she is also protecting herself against writing something that might be construed as inappropriate or embarrassing. For instance, Dickinson emphasizes that all three women share this admiration for him, and there is no reason to disbelieve this, though it is she who does the writing and creates the imagery. In other words, she manages to express some degree of affection or admiration for Bowles without making it more serious or personal than it needs to be. In fact, this comes to be something of a strategy on Dickinson's part. In L300 (dated soon after 8 June 1861), she begins by referring to hearts (her own and Bowles's), then switches direction by introducing Austin's report of his ill health.[74] From that point onward, she is able to enmesh her feelings ostensibly with those of her brother: instead of "I," it is "us" and "we," then "I" again, "we," "I," and "We." It is tempting to see such oscillation between pronouns as deliberate, even if the motives are uncertain: are they there to mask or to legitimate the source of the very strong feelings that are being expressed? Or is she not so much *masking* as *clarifying* or *contextualizing* her feelings so that Bowles does not mistake them for being anything other than expressions of compassion and concern? Although some critics (most recently Judith Farr in *The Passion of Emily Dickinson*) privatize these letters as covert or disguised communications of love, there is no reason why they should not be seen as very precisely and consistently differentiating Dickinson's emotions from those of romantic attraction.

Dickinson may have wanted to hide her feelings because she was afraid that Mary Bowles would misunderstand the nature of those feelings. A number of biographers have stereotyped Mary as the typically inferior and jealous wife of a brilliant man. They do not appear to take into account the possibility that she may have had reasons for being envious. Any insecurity she may have felt, so the argument runs, would have been naturally exacerbated by her almost continuous pregnancies (ten in all), her sickness (she had chronic asthma), as well as the realization of her husband's fondness, and need, for the company and admiration of other women. Even Dickinson recognizes this when she several times imagines herself as part of a group of Bowles's female admirers. But the letters to Mary very openly express admiration and affection for Samuel, so that it would seem incongruous that she would want to be at once candid and dissembling to the same person (though the history of human behavior would not rule out such incongruity).

In terms of this manuscript's material appearances, however, there is little to remark on—no unusual spacing and therefore no paragraphs or generic shifts. A standard indent follows the salutation, and the quotation marks are fairly uniform in their slant from upper left to lower right. On the second page (beginning "to remember you –" and closing with "Morning") there are two end spaces, at the close of the first and last rows. The first measures 2.3 cm, is enforced by the raised edges of the reversed embossment in the upper right corner of the paper, and is nonsignificant. The last, measuring 4.4 cm, is not produced by any anomalies in the paper and signals the end of a paragraph (which coincides with the page break).

On the third page (A 677a), there is an initial indent of 2 cm in the upper left corner, caused by the repeated embossment; again, it is a by-product of the paper and is not significant.[75] A 3 cm blank space after "sleigh" in row 6 signals the close of a paragraph. But it is on the fourth page that the spaces increase, at least in comparison with the previous pages (pages 3 and 4 follow):[76]

> We hope – it is
> a tri-Hope – composed
> of Vinnie's – Sue's – and
> mine – that you took
> no more pain – riding
> in the sleigh –
> We hope our joy to
> see you – gave of it's

own degree – to you –
We pray for your new
health – the prayer that
goes not down – when
they shut the church –
We offer you our cups –
stintless – as to the
Bee – the Lily, her new [page break]
Liquors – Would you
like Summer? Taste of
our's – Spices? Buy – here!
Ill! We have Berries,
for the parching!
Weary! Furloughs of
Down!
Perplexed! Estates of
Violet – Trouble ne'er
looked on!
Captive! We bring
Reprieve of Roses!
Fainting! Flasks of Air!
Even for Death – A
Fairy medicine –
But, which is it – Sir? Emily

The closing space after "Liquors – Would you" coincides with the reversed embossment and is clearly nonsignificant. But then other spaces appear which are unusual within the context established elsewhere in the document by the relationship of rows of writing to the right edge of the paper. Right marginal end spaces are quite rare in this text: not counting embossments, there is one on the second page, one on the third, but four on the last, which is where the poem "Would you like Summer" begins. These occur after "Down!" (7.3 cm), "on!" (5.5 cm), "Roses!" (2 cm), and "medicine" (3.7 cm), but none correspond to a paragraph break, as those on the previous pages all do. In addition, there is an increase in the use of capitals from a total of thirteen on the first page (approximately one per row) to twenty-nine on the last (approximately two per row). But whereas most of the capitals on the first are grammatically necessary (because they mark the start of the letter, the start of a sentence, a season, day of the week, month, title, and surname), many of those on the last page are not: the capitalization signals the presence of a different set of imperatives or codes at this point. Still, Dickinson does not signal the alteration from prose to poetry in any obvious way: the change occurs in medias res, as it were, over one row of writing (the first on the page). It is only the accelerated use of nonfunctional capitals and the greater prominence of end spaces that hint at such a shift. After "Down!," Bowles would have been certain that he was reading poetry, and rereading the manuscript, he may well have intuited where the switch took place.

So this text does not initially demarcate where the epistolary prose ends and the poem begins. One may conjecture as to why: most likely it is because only a single page remained on which to inscribe the poem, a space that was further reduced by the raised edge of the reversed embossment in the upper right-hand corner (where there is an interval of 2.2 cm; even the signature on the same level as the last line of the letter shows that she was pushed for space, for elsewhere Dickinson signed her name *below* the final line of a letter). Dickinson may have begun by feeling that she did not have sufficient room to insert the normal vertical space with which she distinguished poetry and prose in other manuscripts; similarly, she could not leave vacant intervals at the close of a metrical line, as she does elsewhere. It is only after "Down!" that she seems to have realized that there was more space available than she had first estimated, and she then resumes the normal patterns of increased spacing associated with the transcription of poems in holographs.

III

Written in pencil on unruled paper measuring 9.9 × 15.5 cm, and embossed with a circular motif containing the word "PARIS," a note that Franklin dates to 1864 has no opening address but is signed.[77]

> Nature, and God, I
> neither knew
> Yet both, so well
> knew me
> They startled – like
> Executors
> Of an identity –
> Yet neither – told –
> that I could learn –
> My secret, as secure
> As Herschel's private
> interest, [page break]
> [blank page]
> Or Mercury's
> Affair –
>
>   Emily –

This document contains many aspects of the handwriting that are especially worth looking at. To begin with, there is further evidence that Dickinson regularly and casually crossed two *t*'s in the same word with a single horizontal or slanting line: this is the case in "startled," "identity," "that," and "interest." Such accidentals are mentioned precisely because in isolated instances meanings can be attributed to them that a wider acquaintance with orthographic practice firmly disavows. In addition, one notes that the "dot" above the *i* in "interest" as well as the comma that follows it are very similar: both slant at an angle of about fifteen degrees and are similar in length (0.25 cm and 0.3 cm, respectively). The pattern is repeated in the signature: the "dot" (actually a dash) in "Emily" and the dash that follows it are, again, angled at approximately fifteen degrees, although the dot is slightly longer (0.45 cm, as opposed to the 0.3 cm of the dash). All four signs slope from lower left to upper right, and telling them apart is quite difficult. The pattern of inscription is similar elsewhere, and one then wonders what impact the failure to draw clear distinctions between quite different signs might have on debate about the dashes in Dickinson scholarship. For such debate sees consistency and careful deliberation in manuscripts that otherwise demonstrate volatility and casualness in their recording of punctuation marks or secondary signs.

Once again, there are the kind of regular end spaces used to mark the close of a paragraph in prose sequences and the close of a metrical line in lyric ones. They occur after "knew" (4.1 cm), "me" (5.4 cm), "Executors" (5.7 cm), and "interest" (5.2 cm), and although they could be construed as visual signals corresponding to emphasis, they coincide with (in each instance) and make more sense as codes for the end of a metrical line. In combination with the distribution of lower- and uppercase letters (signifying the start or continuation of a metrical phrase), such an aggregate of codes strongly suggests that the layout of this manuscript was regulated by metrical principles, not graphic ones. In other words, what we see above in actuality represents the following:

> Nature, and God, I neither knew
> Yet both, so well knew me
> They startled – like Executors
> Of an identity –
> Yet neither – told – that I could learn –
> My secret, as secure
> As Herschel's private interest,
> Or Mercury's Affair –
>
>   Emily –

But what of the signature: is this an integral part of the poem's meaning? The answer may be inferred in part from Dickinson's having collected a variant of the same lyric in Set 5; too, she made no reference to Bowles in the transcript. In short, the signature is a local aspect of the poem's epistolary circulation and is not a necessary part of its meaning. Or, to be more specific; knowing that the poem was sent to Bowles is valuable in a larger sense because it makes us aware that Dickinson distributed many poems in letters, that an extensive and important network of people knew that she wrote poetry, and that she was comfortable sending poems out to certain readers. Although there may be significance to the fact that Bowles was sent this poem (or poem X and Y rather than Z), it does not follow that the poem was written *for* or *about* him: such knowledge may make an interesting contribution to our understanding of their relationship, but not of this particular poem.[78]

Of the forty poems thought to have been sent to Bowles, at least twenty-three were included in fascicles or sets.[79] In some instances, a cluster of poems that had been sent separately to Bowles were included in single fascicles: versions of poems 202, 208, and 253 (in Fascicle 10); versions of poems 226, 227, 230, and 237 (in Fascicle 9). And yet Dickinson made no attempt to draw Bowles's attention to any relationship between these. Nor, in the fascicles, did she indicate in any way that these poems were connected to or occasioned by her relationship with Bowles. In other words, even if she sent poems to Bowles (or to Susan Dickinson, for that matter), Dickinson did not collate these in an album of their own; she also did not distribute the booklets in which many of these poems were ultimately placed.[80] The point is that the fascicles and correspondence are not mutually supportive archives, and we should therefore be wary of interpretations that are anchored only or mainly in one or the other.

IV

Dickinson's 1865 note to Bowles gains an extra poignancy by being the only poem that we know of for that year—and the last one sent until 1870.[81]

> Before He comes,
> We weigh the
> Time,
> 'Tis Heavy, and
> 'tis Light –
> When He departs,
> An Emptiness
> Is the superior
> Freight –
>   Emily –

The theme is a familiar one, which I have referred to previously: visits are eagerly anticipated but leave a sometimes painful aftermath of listlessness and vacancy. Franklin reproduces the poem as four lines, which is certainly justified by the meter (alternating lines of iambic tetrameter and trimeter) and rhyme (*abcb*). The spacing does not contradict his arrangement either: there are intervals of room after "Time" (6.3 cm), "Light" (3 cm), "Emptiness" (2 cm), and "Freight" (3.5 cm). But the pattern of capitals suggests a different possibility, one that Mabel Loomis Todd and Martha Dickinson Bianchi were more convinced of and by: they (separately) reproduce the poem as six lines.[82]

> Before He comes,
> We weigh the Time,
> 'Tis Heavy, and 'tis Light –
> When He departs,
> An Emptiness
> Is the superior Freight –

Dickinson's manuscripts do not always resolve all the textual uncertainties associated with them: from a purely material standpoint, both the quatrain and the sestet would appear to be equally legitimate and accurate representations of the original. Normally, the fascicle version would clear up the mystery (as it appears to have done, decisively, for Franklin); in this case, Set 7 is not conclusive.[83]

> Before He comes
> We weigh the Time,
> 'Tis Heavy and 'tis Light.
> When He depart, an
> Emptiness
> Is the prevailing Freight –

The crucial factor, it seems to me, is the "an" at the close of the fourth row (written in lowercase), and the considerable end space that follows "Emptiness" (approximately 7.1 cm). Taken together, these would normally signify a noninitial status for "an" and an end-domain status for "Emptiness." In other words, "an Emptiness" would not constitute a separate and integral metrical unit, but the concluding elements of the line beginning "When he depart." And if that is the case, then the stanzaic structure would require rows 1 and 2 to be similarly joined (to form a symmetrical pattern of iambic tetrameter in lines 1 and 3).

> Before He comes We weigh the Time,
> 'Tis Heavy, and 'tis Light.
> When He depart, an Emptiness
> Is the prevailing Freight –

Franklin's arrangement of the first variant would appear to have been informed by the example of the Set variant. But a six-line variant cannot absolutely be dismissed as a reasonable possibility: Dickinson may have experimented with the structure, and her later composition could very well have been decisively shaped by the lack of paper at her disposal.

V

Some readers have seen Dickinson as often negotiating between very strong impulses in her relationship to Bowles. Yet, those times when she failed to see him testify not so much to a failure of nerve or the *fear* of such a failure as to an occasional struggle between her desire to see friends and some other imperative that overrode such a desire at particular times. A useful corrective may be to hypothesize that Dickinson often could not bring herself to meet Bowles because he was not important enough to enable her to overcome whatever principles or problems she may have had about meeting people generally. Or, to put it another way, Dickinson was often sufficiently busy with her own career as a writer not to have time to meet people every time they dropped in for a visit—especially when she was not the sole occasion for the visit. In the following poem, written in 1870 when Samuel and Mary Bowles were on a call, there is the familiar mechanism of praising Bowles indirectly but being unable or unwilling to express her own "affection" for him in a social setting:[84]

> He is alive, this
> morning –
> He is alive – and
> awake –
> Birds are resuming
> for Him –
> Blossoms – dress
> for His sake –
> Bees – to their
> Loaves of Honey
> Add an Amber
> Crumb

> Him – to regale [page break]
>   Me – Only –
> Motion, and
> am dumb.
> Emily

The period between "dumb" and "Emily" prevents our reading the poem unproblematically as a piece of lyric autobiography. Nevertheless, the signature at the end and the use of the present tense (suggesting an *actual* personality whose presence is being experienced and reported almost simultaneously, *now* at it were) do hint in this instance at a set of personal or biographical circumstances about which we can only guess at (and that the poem was not included in a fascicle or set implies that its private aspects made Dickinson think that it would not survive the time and place of its saying). One notes the repetition—of "He is alive" (twice), "Him" (twice), and "His" (once)—which conveys a strong sense of *quidditas*, of insistent "hereness," and the sudden bluntness and starkness of the last six words (which coincide with the introduction of "Me"). A chorus of praise (which is predominantly, and conventionally, female: blossoms dress for him and bees bring cakes with extra sweetness) is followed by the speaker's stricken silence, and one wonders why. But similarities exist between the speaker's stance and Dickinson's earlier refusal to make a declaration of Christian faith, either at Mount Holyoke or afterward in letters to friends; this poem may therefore not be about Bowles, or about Bowles only, but about the speaker's relationship to creation and the idea of a creator. Nevertheless, the poem's origin as a note to Bowles which was never sent gives a strong impression of him as a center of gravity in the speaker's universe, but not one that she could bring herself to pay homage to.[85] The price she paid for such reluctance appears to have been a kind of silencing—whether imposed or self-inflicted remains unknown.

VI

The last extant element of the correspondence was prompted by a visit in 1877 that Dickinson had declined to attend, whereupon Bowles is said to have called upstairs, "Emily, you damned rascal! No more of this nonsense! I've traveled all the way from Springfield to see you. Come down at once!"[86] The episode was first reported by Gertrude M. Graves in a 1930s interview for the *Boston Globe*, "A Cousin's Memories of Emily Dickinson: Boston Woman Also Recalls Visit of the Poetess' Sister, Lavinia."[87]

Dear friend.
Vinnie
accidentally
mentioned that
you hesitated
between the
"Theophilus"
and the
"Junius."
Would you
confer so
sweet a
favor as to
accept that [page break]
too, when
you come
again?
I went to the
Room as soon
as you left,
to confirm
your presence –
recalling the
Psalmist's
sonnet to
God, beginning

I have no
Life but this –
To lead it
here – [page break]
Nor any Death –
but lest
Dispelled from
there –
Nor tie to
Earths to
come,
Nor Action
new

Except through
this Extent
The love of
you.
It is strange
that the
most intangible [page break]
thing is the
most adhesive.

Your "Rascal."

I washed
the Adjective.

Written on paper measuring 12.6 × 20.4 cm (and with its envelope still ex-
tant), the document is typical of Dickinson's later years, with only one or two
words comprising each row of writing. (The words themselves are proportion-
ately larger than the writing of earlier decades.) There is an initial indent of
6.5 cm preceding "Vinnie," and an end space of 6.1 cm following "Junius"
(and marking the end of a paragraph).[88] On the second leaf, there is a space of
5.8 cm after "again?" and then a vertical space of 1.2 cm after "beginning." So
there are clear textual and material indications of a shift in genre: Dickinson
introduces the poem playfully, referring to it as "the Psalmist's sonnet to God,
beginning," and then creates an extra division of space. In addition, the visual
pattern of spacing alters with the commencement of the poem: there is a
marked increase in the use of end spaces, which corresponds to a switch from
epistolary to lyrical conventions. For such spaces are not equivalent to para-
graph markers, but correspond to the completion of metrical sequences.[89]

I have no
Life but this –
To lead it
here – [6 cm]
Nor any Death –
but lest [4.7 cm]
Dispelled from
there – [6 cm]
Nor tie to
Earths to
come, [6.4 cm]

Nor Action
new [8.6 cm]
Except through
this Extent
The love of
you.
[7.6 cm, followed by a greater-than-normal
vertical space of 1.2 cm before the letter resumes]

Where end spaces were previously intermittent and fairly random in the prose section of the letter, they coalesce and form a relatively continuous pattern (appearing about once every three rows). Nothing better illustrates Dickinson's observance of generic distinctions than this letter, then, where there is a clear verbal bridge supplementing the visual transition (an increased vertical space) from prose to poetry, and where the spatial patterns alter from one genre to the other. And it is consistent with earlier stages of the correspondence—for example, in 1861, when Dickinson did something similar, first introducing the poem verbally and then leaving a gap between the introduction and the poem:[90]

Dear friend
        If you
doubted my Snow –
for a moment – you
never will – again –
I know –
Because I could not
say it – I fixed it
in the Verse – for
you to read – when
your thought wavers,
for such a foot as
mine –
Through the strait pass
of suffering – [page break]
[blank space]
The Martyrs – even – trod.
Their feet – opon Temptation –
Their faces – opon God –
        A stately – shriven –
Company –
Convulsion – playing round –

Harmless – as streaks
of meteor –
Opon a Planet's Bond –
    Their faith –
the everlasting troth –
Their expectation – fair –
The Needle – to the North
Degree –
Wades – so – thro' polar Air!

Some features of the holograph are unusual—the initial indentation that co-
incides with the commencement of a new stanza, for example, in rows 4 and
10 of the second page (situated respectively 1.4 and 2.5 cm in from the left
edge of the paper, where much of the other spacing on that side measures
around 0.4 cm only). Such indentation is highly uncommon in Dickinson's
prose: one sees it immediately after a salutation, normally, as here on the first
page ("If you," for instance, is 4.5 cm into the page). But Dickinson's usual
procedure for signaling a shift of paragraph is to leave space at the end of one
she has just completed, as she does here: there are intervals of 6.3 cm after
"know" and 7 cm after "mine" (in rows 6 and 13 of the first page: "Dear friend"
is counted as the first row). Intriguingly, the ratio of blank spaces per rows of
writing increases after the prose introduction: from one in six to approxi-
mately one in four, none of which coincide with a clear paragraph ending and
only the second of which appears to mark a grammatical pause. Not only do
the visual patterns of the inscription point toward the generic change but
Dickinson also makes an explicit distinction between "saying" (speaking, con-
versation, correspondence) and "verse" (which has a permanence and solidity
that speech lacks). Such a remark echoes the distinction Dickinson makes
elsewhere between poetry and prose and strongly suggests the propriety of
operating with similar distinctions in editions of her writing. And it is precisely
the nature of generic differences that I attend to in the next chapter.

CHAPTER FOUR

"The Way I read a Letter's – this"
Dickinson and Genre

When is a letter a poem? When is a poem a letter?

—Marta L. Werner, *Emily Dickinson's Open Folios*

LETTER, n. [L. litera.] 2. A written or printed message; an epistle; a communication made by visible characters from one person to another at a distance. The style of letters ought to be free, easy and natural. PO'EM, n. [L. poema; Gr. to make, to compose songs.] 1. A metrical composition; a composition in which the verses consist of certain measures, whether in blank verse or in rhyme; as the poems of Homer or of Milton; opposed to prose.

—Noah Webster, *American Dictionary of the English Language*

WHEN THE first post office established in Amherst by the United States government opened for business on 1 January 1806, it was located in a room of James Watson's dwelling house, with mail arriving by stagecoach once a week (later, with the establishment of Amherst College, there were three weekly mails from Boston alone).[1] Watson was the first of thirteen postmasters to be appointed in Amherst during the course of the nineteenth century; some of them (like Samuel C. Carter, Orson G. Couch, and Seth Nims—Dickinson anxiously alluded to the latter in a letter of 1847) served more than once, though not always for consecutive terms.[2] Ironically, one of the longest incumbents was Hezekiah Wright Strong (from 20 April 1825 to 29 March 1842); as Alfred Habegger notes, Strong avoided paying a debt of thirty-eight hundred dollars to Samuel Fowler Dickinson in August 1824 and then "snagged the Amherst postmastership that Samuel coveted for himself [and later for his son Edward]. Outraged at his debtor's coup, Samuel whipped off a letter of protest to the postmaster general that disclosed Strong's shaky finances and presented his own superior qualifications."[3] The petition failed; on Strong's appointment less than a year later, the post office was relocated to his home, "a room being built on the west side of the house for office use."[4] On 15 March 1842, Seth Nims lobbied to have Strong removed, on the grounds that "he allowed persons to sit in the office and read papers that came through the mails directed to other parties, and that the papers were not always returned to the boxes where they belonged."[5] Though he did not take over immediately, Nims does not seem to have been an improvement, at least in Dickinson's eyes: writing on 1 July 1853 (less than a month after Nims's second term of office had begun), she informs Austin that some "of the letters you've sent us we have received, and thank you for affectionately – Some, we have not received, but thank you for the memory, of which the emblem perished."[6] It was clear that messages *to* Austin had also gone missing, as well as communications between him and Susan Gilbert: the "new Postmaster" is not named but obliquely held culpable. At that time, mail was not delivered to private addresses (unless carried by family, friends, or servants). Most of the principal families in Amherst had their own boxes, which they rented in the post office building; the Honorable Edward Dickinson's was (at least in 1861) number 177.[7]

The reference to "letters" written by Austin is typical of Dickinson's use of the term: the object referred to is much less contentious than the people whose job it was to deliver it. What strikes one reading the entry for "letter" in Cynthia MacKenzie's *Concordance to the Letters of Emily Dickinson* is how unproblematic most of the references to "letter" are: Dickinson answers them, anticipates them, asks for them, burns them, carries them, demands them, encloses them, enjoys them, gets them, goes without them, imagines them, looks for them, peruses them, reads them, receives them, refers to them, reports them, seeks them, sends them, signs them, thinks about them, and welcomes them.[8] There are 397 references to "letter," "letters," and "letter's," in the (Johnson and Ward edition of the) correspondence, but the object referred to never seems in doubt. It is mostly in poems that Dickinson reflects on letters—fifteen times in fourteen poems, though even here the referent "letter" does not seem as slippery as the relations between the people it links: there is never any great distance between the signifier and signified of "letter," between the word and the object to which the word refers. For Dickinson, "letters" do not appear to have been a problematic category.

For Dickinson's archivists and editors, the definition of a letter has not proved difficult either, until recently. As I discussed in chapter 1, a two-volume edition of Emily Dickinson's letters was published, in isolation from the poems, in 1894. In 1958, Thomas H. Johnson and Theodora Ward's three-volume edition of the *Letters of Emily Dickinson* reinforced the generic distinction when it appeared subsequently to and separately from Johnson's three-volume variorum edition of *The Poems of Emily Dickinson* (1955). The Emily Dickinson Collection at the Jones Library, Amherst, houses twenty-one manuscripts, but lists them independently of each other as four poems and seventeen letters.[9] The Special Collections of the Frost Library at Amherst College divides its manuscripts into fascicles, unbound poems and fragments, and letters and prose fragments.[10] The Houghton Library of Harvard University similarly organizes its collection of Dickinson manuscripts according to whether they are letters or poems. But as the questions that I raise in this chapter indicate, the status of such manuscripts is not as easy to fix as their discrete and utilitarian categorization by archivists and librarians might suggest.

<h1 style="text-align:center">I</h1>

These musings are prompted by historical divergences in the editorial classification of Dickinson's manuscripts, all of which proceed from close observation of the originals. As I have discussed, versions of "A narrow fellow in the grass" appeared both in Johnson's *Poems of Emily Dickinson* (as J986) and in Johnson and Ward's *Letters of Emily Dickinson* (as L378, to Susan Dickinson).[11] More recently, it was published twice in the same year: in *The Poems of Emily Dickinson* (1998), edited by Ralph W. Franklin, and in Ellen Hart and Martha Nell Smith's *Open Me Carefully: Emily Dickinson's Intimate Letters to Susan Huntington Dickinson* (1998). Although such overlapping need not be regarded as problematic, it has led some critics to question if traditional divisions between letters and poems are helpful or even sanctioned by Dickinson's work. Nevertheless, the reversion of many contemporary readers to the manuscripts in an attempt to formulate a less mediated and more precise description of the writer's actual practices has so far failed to produce a consensus as to what those practices actually consist of or their status.

As a further example, one might cite a verbal sequence identified by Johnson and Ward as letter 972, which they believed to have been sent to Higginson in February 1885:

Dear friend –

It is long since I asked and received your consent to accept the Book, should it be, and the ratification at last comes, a pleasure I feared to hope –

Biography first convinces us of the fleeing of the Biographied –

> Pass to thy Rendezvous of Light,
> Pangless except for us –
> Who slowly ford the Mystery
> Which thou hast leaped across!
>   Your Scholar –

In 1993, William Shurr edited the *New Poems of Emily Dickinson*; in his view, the second paragraph of this document belonged to the category of the epigram, a genre "never before identified" in Dickinson's writing. As a result, he reformatted the sequence thus and assigned it the number 196:[12]

> Biography first convinces us
> of the fleeing of the Biographied –

According to Ellen Hart, however, these are lines of prose, not poetry.[13] Even so, she argues forcefully that in the original manuscript sequence, Dickinson makes use of devices that are traditionally defined as poetic—that is, the careful deployment of words across lines in order to suggest or support meaning. She follows the autograph in her reproduction of the phrase:

> Biography first
> convinces us
> of the fleeing
> of the Biogra-
> phied –

Hart goes on to specify the intention behind the effect: "Furthermore, the divided 'Biogra- /phied,' mimicking the fleeing, suggests 'Biogra-fleed.' " But although she leans toward seeing the pun as a consciously applied part of an extensive graphic vocabulary, one wonders if it might not be an accident of space (running out of room) or—if a pun—an instinctive and spontaneous division made at that point in the writing, with no larger implications. For example, in an 1862 letter to Bowles, Dickinson claims to have "skipped a page – tonight" because she wrote so often and did not want to tire him, but that "page is fullest," she goes on to explain.[14] But leaving the second page of a four-page bifolium blank was a common occurrence in Dickinson's letters. In L252, from the same period of the year and to the same recipient, Dickinson leaves the second page blank, without making any reference to doing so.[15] A short note (L505) to Bowles that had been dated by Johnson and Ward to about 1877 also has a blank second page, as does A 688 (Fr600B), "Her – 'last Poems,' " previously associated with Bowles but probably retained by Dickinson for her own purposes. (Some of the letters and poems sent to Susan Dickinson have the same feature.) The point is that a single example of such phenomena in one letter may amount to a moment of local opportunism and not a full-scale poetic strategy.

In the specific case of "biographied" equaling "biografleed," one concedes the possibility of the pun in theory, but in practice its playfulness seems contrary to the tone of what precedes and (in particular) immediately follows it: part of a poem previously sent to Susan Dickinson in reference to the death of her son Gilbert, a loss that devastated both Dickinson women and coincided with the terminal decline of the poet's own health.[16] This is not a punning letter, generally, and one would think that, in order to make such a graphic event visible and successful, Dickinson would have had to prepare the reader for it in some way (either within the context of the letter or in the correspondence more generally). Then again, this is perhaps a question of evaluative, and not critical, judgment—a matter of taste: for as puns go, this one seems feeble. Or to put it another way, the phrase *in its entirety* is memorable and thought provoking; the pun (if it is a pun) cheapens and falsifies it. Indeed, many of the meanings attributed to Dickinson's visual layout strike one as being less witty or profound than slight and obvious.

Whatever the merits or defects of the various arguments and modes of presentation, even this brief exchange shows how readers can find themselves subject to criticism for not using autograph-based layouts, even if those readers have no interest in manuscript study or are pursuing interpretations that are not dependent on knowledge of the originals. At least potentially, the current climate of engagement with Dickinson's lyrics does more than focus attention on the status of the manuscripts—it creates a situation whereby they become the sine qua non of interpretive debate. For being able to disagree with Hart's reading depends to some degree on knowing the relation of the handwritten words to the material extent of the paper; without such information, the grounds on which to base a decision as to the plausibility of interpretations such as Hart's become significantly diminished, if they do not disappear entirely.

But if manuscripts are not readily available, what then? Of the available editions, Franklin (1998) includes information about line breaks and therefore allows speculation as to their potential significance, while in their ground breaking *Open Me Carefully* (1998), Hart and Smith print versions of communications to Susan Dickinson exactly as they are originally lineated and without indenting "prose" differently from "poetry."[17] Arguing that readers and editors should adopt a policy of "diplomatic transcription," retaining Dickinson's lineation as much as possible, and suspending judgments about generic status, they put into practice an earlier declaration by Hart which has become a central methodological statement of the manuscript school of Dickinson criticism: "An outcome of new print translations will be a view of Dickinson as less cryptic, more systematic and accessible than she is sometimes seen to be, an artist whose capitalization, punctuation, and line breaks are not 'eccentricities,' 'accidents,' or 'habits of handwriting,' but visual strategies, symbols used in combination with each other to indicate emphasis and accent, to create and explain her meaning." Thus, if we return to Dickinson's autograph letter and attempt a more descriptive or less intrusive transcription based on the guidelines established by Hart's arguments, as well as the practices of Hart and Smith, one emerges with the following:

> Dear friend –
> It is
> long since
> I asked and
> received your
> consent to
> accept the
> Book, should
> it be, and
> the ratification
> at last comes,
> a pleasure
> I feared to
> hope –
> Biography first
> convinces us
> of the fleeing
> of the Biogra-
> phied.
> Pass to thy
> Rendezvous of
> Light,
> Pangless except
> for us –
> Who slowly
> ford the
> Mystery
> Which thou
> hast leaped
> across!
>
> Your Scholar –

The issues raised by these competing versions are nicely encapsulated by the sequence beginning with "Biography" and ending with "Biogra- / phied." Is this a prose paragraph (Johnson and Ward), poetry formatted as prose (Shurr), or a combination of the two (Hart)? One sees here why issues of presentation are so often bound up with issues of genre: if the portion of the text currently under discussion is prose, for instance, then Johnson and Ward would have some degree of justification in separating it graphically—and thus generically— from the poem that follows it (which they indent differently in *Letters*). If this is writing that moves fluidly from one genre to another, which merges the best qualities of lyric poetry and epistolary prose and refuses the necessity of choosing between them, then editors have no justification for making any visual (and textual) distinction between one portion of the writing and another.

On the surface, at least, the version above seems closest to Dickinson's own practices, and to Hart's reproduction of a part of it, and simultaneously far removed from (in order of accuracy) the edited constructions of Johnson and Ward and of Shurr. Despite this, Hart's assignation of meaning to physical features is problematic in its inconsistency. She opposes the idea that there are minor aspects of the text's inscription but nevertheless continues to make assumptions about what is and isn't accidental in the original.[18] Here is another version of the full text under discussion, this time with the physical margins of the page included:

Dear friend –	of the Biogra–
It is	phied.
long since	Pass to thy
I asked and	Rendezvous of
received your	Light,
consent to	Pangless except
accept the	for us –
Book, should	Who slowly
it be, and	ford the
the ratification	Mystery
at last comes,	Which thou
a pleasure	hast leaped
I feared to	across!
hope –	Your Scholar –
Biography first	
convinces us	
of the fleeing	

Although Hart appears to insist on preserving the material integrity of the manuscript in her transcription she does not mention or map the detail of the page turnover, presumably (and rightly) on the grounds that it is insignificant.[19] Dickinson's verbal sequence is nevertheless different from Hart's "diplomatic transcription": Hart charts the words almost exactly as they appear *in* the manuscript but not *on* or *within* it, and therefore her version does not afford readers a fully comprehensive and reliable text with which to attempt accurately to evaluate the conclusions she draws from it. Naturally, one does not contest Hart's choice about the page break: that the remainder of the letter continues on the inside of the folded piece of notepaper at the point after "fleeing" seems of little consequence. Yet, one *can* construct a significance for the page division: it visually mimics the inaccessibility of the "biographied." Dickinson (so the argument might go) twice postpones "biographied" (first by the page interval, second by the word split) in ways that echo and contribute to the sense. For this to be true, however, I have to accept that Dickinson arranged the letter in such a way that the first side would end with the verb "fleeing," and that "phied" is a pun on "fleed" (itself a substitute for "fled"). More than anything else, though, I have to presume that any and every detail of a text's physical inscription is potentially *intentional* (at least on the basis that the antonym of accidental is intentional: later, I will deal more fully with the theoretical aspects of intentionalism as a critical approach). And far from seeing language released into the custody of the reader, it seems to me that if what Hart says is true, it shows Dickinson trying to *impose* her preferred reading, rather than releasing it to the multiple desires of her audience. If one accepts the argument of a willed dimension to the layout of the writing, Dickinson would not simply be expressing an opinion but insisting on its veracity: "Biography first convinces us of the fleeing (at which point there is a graphic pun equivalent to the act of flight) of the Biogra- (at which point there is another graphic pun equivalent to the act of flight) phied." What Hart does here is to increase the degree of *motivation* or *positioning* in the splitting of the word: the division is not arbitrary, a convention of size or scale, but is meant to resemble or imitate the action it describes.

Whether or not one agrees with the conclusion that these effects *are* accidental, it seems incontrovertible that Hart herself makes silent choices about what is and is not deliberate in a manuscript, which is contrary to her stated methodology. Indeed, if the point of diplomatic transcriptions is to make Dickinson "less cryptic, more systematic and accessible," then such arrangements are demonstrably counterproductive. For if breaking a word in half or isolating it on a line of its own is a visual strategy designed to create or support meaning, the reader is obliged to consider the poem's autograph layout as an extra dimension, and even as the ultimate arbitrator, of its significance. Thus, we no longer read "I feared to hope" but "I feared to / hope"; we must puzzle, too, at the segregation of words such as "Light," Mystery," and "across." It does not automatically follow that diplomacy of transcription would have the effect of decreasing the levels of difficulty associated with Dickinson's poetry; rather, it would appear to make her seem more arbitrary. Why "I feared to / hope" instead of "I / feared to hope," "I feared / to hope," or "I feared to hope," for example? Not only do we have to guess at a poem's meaning, but we are also obliged to take the lineation seriously and to second-guess its effects (thus, in the case of "I feared to hope," increasing its complexity three or four times over).

II

In his introduction to *New Poems of Emily Dickinson*, William Shurr admitted that many of the pieces he presented as poems were originally formatted as prose—that is, no graphic signals (such as indentation, capitalization, the deployment of blank spaces) appeared to separate them from their epistolary surroundings. His justification for the visual and generic realignment was metrical: for Shurr, poems and poetic fragments can be detected because they broadcast rhythmical pulses that are more regular than those of prose. The reason for Shurr's edition coming into being in the first place was his claim that Dickinson's editors had failed to identify metrical sequences within the correspondence. Therefore, if we attempt to separate poems from prose on the basis of meter (or even linguistic density) alone, we soon run into problems; the letters are full of passages that correspond to one kind of rhythm or another. Of course, one can sift further: since Dickinson almost invariably used rhyme in her poetry, that technique may be an additional criterion by which to attempt generic classifications. But then we come up against the following:

> Your sorrow was in Winter – one of our's in June and the other, November, and my Clergyman passed from Earth in spring, but sorrow brings it's own chill. Seasons do not warm it. You said with loved timidity in asking me to your dear Home, you would "try not to make it unpleasant." So delicate a diffidence, how beautiful to see! I do not think a Girl extant has so divine a modesty.
>
> You even call me to your Breast with apology! Of what must my poor Heart be made?
>
> That the one for whom Modesty is felt, himself should feel it sweetest and ask his own with such a grace, is beloved reproach.

This incomplete fair copy, thought by Johnson and Ward to have been intended for Otis Lord, is included in the correspondence as L790.[20] But Shurr identifies a portion of it as a poem that he numbers 304.

> So delicate a diffidence,
> how beautiful to see!
> I do not think a Girl extant
> has so divine a modesty.

Again, one concedes the possibility: the lines are fairly regular (trimeter and tetrameter, though with a slight faltering in the final line), the rhyme is a familiar one (*abcb*), and the quatrain is easily recognizable as a type (of common meter). One wonders, though, about the next paragraph, which can be reformatted thus:

> You even call me to your Breast
> with apology!
> Of what must my poor Heart be made?

The first line is iambic tetrameter, the second a catalectic trochaic trimeter, the third (a very contrived) iambic tetrameter. Even the middle rhyme corresponds to the previous sonic echo of "see" and "modesty." Admittedly, the rhythm falls apart at this stage of the letter—in terms of metrical predictability, at least—but need that matter? Dickinson also writes in tercets elsewhere, so why not here?

Perhaps the most serious objection to Shurr's excavations at the local level has to do with his overlooking the significance of the lowercase letters on "how" and "has." For it is clear from the manuscripts in general that Dickinson conformed to the nineteenth-century practice of assigning capitals to the beginning of lines of poetry; that she did not do so here implies that Dickinson herself was not interested in having this cluster of lines recognized as poetry. That does not rule out the possibility that they might have *begun* as lines of poetry, and it would not have prevented Lord (if he ever received a letter based on this draft) from recognizing meter and rhyme when it occurred. But it does suggest that Dickinson herself had no wish to isolate these lines as poetry (as she often does elsewhere), and we should therefore do her the honor of respecting her wishes in this matter.

Nevertheless, it should be pointed out that neither Johnson and Ward's nor Shurr's version of the letter faithfully represents its manuscript appearance. Of her present editors, Marta Werner best approximates the original in her book *Emily Dickinson's Open Folios* (though I should mention that Werner adds the punctuation by hand, that her spacing is less regularized than in what follows, and that she does not note page breaks because her versions are arranged side by side with facsimiles of the original):[21]

Your sorrow was
in Winter – one
of our's in June [page break]
and the other,
November, and
my Clergyman passed
from Earth in
Spring, but Sorrow
brings it's own
Chill – Seasons do
not warm it –
You said with
loved timidity
in asking me
to your dear
Home, you would
"try not to make
it unpleasant –"
So delicate a
diffidence, how
beautiful to see! [page break]
I do not think
a Girl Extant
has so divine
a Modesty –
You even call
me to your Breast
with apology!
Of what must
my poor Heart
be made?
That the one
for whom Modesty
is felt, himself
should feel it
sweetest and ask
his own with
such a grace,
is beloved reproach –

Werner is the most gifted and textually oriented of Dickinson's more current archivists, and she is also the most precise:

> In "Open Folios" the drafts and fragments serve primarily as a point of entry into a late, brief, scene of Dickinson's writing. Left unfinished at the time of her death, they are not so much Dickinson "autographs" as symptoms of the processes of composition that can never be said to achieve closure, or the materials for a biography of *style*. Many of the drafts and fragments appear to have begun as letters and later turned into working papers; others are more clearly poem drafts, traces of which will almost certainly reappear in other contexts. The transcription of each material document completely and without regard for traditional generic categories, a practice that runs counter to all previous editorial treatments of these materials, reveals a number of hitherto unknown texts and challenges us to discover or invent a terminology to describe their forms.[22]

There is much that is fine about this passage, not least the careful delimitation of a time period ("late, brief") and the recognition that difficulties of classification are partly related to the status of these documents: the term "draft" suggests a different kind of text, a stage on the way to becoming a poem or a letter, but nonetheless an object in its own right. Werner coins the phrase "biography of style" to suggest that her interest is in accurately representing the different stages in the process of arriving, rather than in what (if anything) is arrived at.

Nonetheless, like Hart and Smith (with whom she is often, but not always accurately, associated), her book does suggest a tentative procedure for transcribing documents such as the one presently under discussion, and in this specific instance, it does raise some problems. Some of these are minor: Werner assigns capitals where Johnson and Ward do not, for example, but these are matters that are difficult to reach universal agreement on, and the differences are therefore legitimate. And some of the problems, one surmises, had to do with the limitations of word processing technology and print reproduction at the time Werner's book was published; thus words (for example) are typed but punctuation marks are written by hand. Nonetheless, this mixture of manual and machine-applied writing hints at a potential contradiction in any typographic version of a manuscript. For the choice of type for the words suggests that their appearance (or the appearance of the alphabetic characters that constitute the words) is relatively unimportant. Or put another way, the decision to write punctuation marks by hand has the effect of isolating them and suggesting that they are visually (and semantically) more significant or distinctive than what Werner memorably identifies as "Dickinson's late performance script."[23] By extension, one suspects that the tension at the heart of any attempt at representing manuscripts as closely as possible in print is that the motivation behind doing so in the first place is a perception that almost any physical aspect of the original is potentially significant. Thus, the concern with even a diplomatic transcription such as Warner's is (to paraphrase Browning) that print cannot hope to reproduce the faint subtleties behind each stroke of the pen or pencil. As soon as one transcribes any manuscript into type, one risks compromising some aspects of its procedures or (as in the example above) prioritizing one over another. One therefore sees why such an immensely talented generation of readers as Werner, Smith, and Hart increasingly works with electronic editions of the poems that reproduce the manuscripts visually. Nevertheless, the occasional difficulty or illegibility of some aspects of particular originals means that print "translations" of the works often accompany such images, and these mediate and influence our understanding of the status of the images they accompany. Even cataloguing poems as manuscript images pushes us in the direction of seeing them as visual objects rather than, say, aural ones.[24]

Issues of presentation aside, I commented earlier that one of the many things that I find admirable about Werner's theoretical meditations is that her reluctance to use traditional generic categories derives from the recognition that many of these drafts occupy an intermediate or uncertain position: *as drafts*, they have not yet been designated as either poems or letters, though Werner is happy to acknowledge that they may become either. It seems to me that this approach differs from what Hart and Smith do, which is to reject traditional or inherited generic categories and to employ another of their own (or, more accurate, of Susan Dickinson's) making. Take, for example, the quotation we have previously looked at in the first chapter: "The letter-poem, a category that includes signed poems and letters with poems or with lines of poetry, will be seen here as a distinct and important Dickinson genre. Johnson arranged lines in letters to separate poems and make them look the way we might expect poems to look. We do not do this here. Neither do we divide the correspondence into 'Poems to Susan' and 'Letters to Susan.' Instead, we follow Dickinson's commingling techniques, mindful that conventional notions of genre can limit our understanding of Dickinson's writing practices."[25] Hart and Smith seem to have replaced two genres (which are actually subgenres, letters and lyrics traditionally being grouped under prose and poetry) with a kind of super-genre or anti-genre—but one that they still define as "a distinct and important Dickinson genre." In other words, it seems as if the letter-poem is as an identifiable type of discourse with recognizable properties. Yet, in many of the notes that accompany their edition of letters and poems sent to Susan Dickinson, Hart and Smith are inconsistent about Dickinson's suspension of epistolary and lyric distinctions. For instance, in their comments on LP147 (traditionally known as "A narrow fellow in the grass"), they write: "The poem that Emily includes here was printed in the *Springfield Daily Republican* on February 14, 1866. It is possible that Emily now sends Susan the poem to replace the copy that Susan sent to the newspaper. From this letter-poem, it is clear that the two women are seeing each other face-to-face."[26] The document in question is dated by Hart and Smith to about 1870, which is well into the period in which they place Dickinson's generic experimentation. Nonetheless, there seems to be some confusion here, if only by the editorial standards proposed by Hart and Smith. To begin with, they conflate the 1866 variant of "A narrow fellow" with the 1875 copy sent to Susan, even though no manuscript exists for the first version, and slight differences exist between Susan's version and another recorded around the same time.[27] According to Hart and Smith's arguments (as I understand them), the two copies amount to two separate poems, hence such material differences: to identify them as the same work presupposes that there is an abstract template for the poem which remains fairly stable even though its physical and verbal performances differ. And the editors are twice able to identify a poem that is discrete from the letter (the "poem that Emily includes here"; "Emily now sends Susan the poem") before switching to their favored term, "letter-poem." The fact that they can refer to a poem within the letter suggests that in practice one can be distinguished quite easily from the other.

And this is the case: as we have seen from the previous two chapters, it *is* possible to distinguish between genres in many of Dickinson's manuscripts without resorting solely to conventions of content (or subject matter) and style.[28] It is primarily the *physical* structure that is often decisive in this respect; changes in the visual layout of the writing on the page will often accompany a shift in genre, and such changes are consistently detectable in Dickinson's work. To take simple examples, in two short notes to Samuel Bowles that were thought to have been sent in 1862 and 1863, one is formatted as a letter, and one as a poem.[29]

> Dear friend
>   I cannot
> see you. You will
> not less believe me.
> That you return
> to us alive, is
> better than a Summer.
> And more to hear ˎ
> your voice below, than

News of any Bird.
   Emily.

So glad we are – a
Stranger'd deem
'Twas sorry, that we were –
For where the Holiday
should be
There publishes a Tear –
Nor how Ourselves be justi-
fied –
Since Grief and Joy are done
So similar – An Optizan
Could not decide between –
   Emily

Whereas the writing in the first document goes from one margin to the other, the second has many spaces that could have been used but were not. The reasons for that may relate to physical extent: the first document is written (in pencil) on unruled paper that is 9.9 cm wide; the second is written (in pen) on unruled paper that is 11.8 cm wide. Nevertheless, there are similarities: after "Summer" in the first and "were" in the second, there are sharply angled and brief marks below the line of writing, which are inscribed thus because of lack of space. And the word "justified" is divided because it, too, reaches the edge of the paper before it is fully completed. In short, the spaces that accompany the second of the two documents are not solely explicable in terms of differences in the breadth of the two pieces of paper on which they are written. To begin with, such spaces are quite substantial: 4.4 cm after "deem," 7.3 cm after "be," and 9.2 cm after "fied." There are no grammatical justifications for their occurrence—two of them at least are not preceded by the period or dash that might mark the end of a prose sentence or paragraph, for instance. And "be" and "fied" are written with lowercase initial letters, demonstrating that the spaces that follow them are indicators of a different kind of closure from prose. No matter how we choose to understand these three spaces, they cannot be explained in terms of prose or epistolary conventions, and such formatting means that Bowles would therefore have been very sure that he was reading a poem, even if it was not otherwise signaled verbally.[30]

A word of warning, however: the draft messages to Lord, along with "nearly five hundred new poems" and fragments of poems excavated from Dickinson's correspondence by William Shurr, show that a writer such as Dickinson, once she reached her maturity, would not necessarily have found it easy to be

prosaic—to write the kinds of gossipy, chatty, transparent messages that con-
vention has (wrongly) associated with letters.[31] Webster's 1828 *American
Dictionary of the English Language* urged that a letter "ought to be free, easy
and natural," but if one's instinct or practice is to think and write figuratively
or metrically, then *not* to do so would be restricting, unnatural, and difficult.
Questions of style are not easy to separate from social or ideological concerns.
True, Webster's definition matches Jane Austen's comments in a letter to
Cassandra, dated 3 January 1801, in which she claims to "have now attained
the true art of letter-writing, which we are always told, is to express on paper
exactly what one would say to the same person by word of mouth."[32] But the
idea that letters should be "free, easy and natural" relates to standards of
decorum and propriety that are not straightforwardly descriptive or formal.
Austen reports (in the same excerpt) being "always told" to write in a certain
way, and the telling is related to moral instruction and discipline: letters have
to be plain because ambiguity can compromise the intentions, and by exten-
sion the integrity or social standing, of the sender. Letters are private docu-
ments that are addressed outside the self (unlike diaries and journals) and that
circulate publicly; by their very nature, they occupy an ambiguous position
between the inner and the outer. Eighteenth- and nineteenth-century conduct
books and materials therefore caution letter writers about the dangers of being
misunderstood.

And as Dickinson grew older, her letters began increasingly to demonstrate
those densities of language for which her poems are famous. To Mrs. Abigail
Cooper, for example, she writes in 1876, "The Founders of Honey have no
Names –."[33] There is no signature and probably no need for one, because the
sender would be identified through the handwriting and style. There is no
personal address ("Dear Abigail"), and again no need for it, since the outside
fold of the note was addressed with the woman's name and the message itself
would likely have been delivered personally (by a servant or friend), thus
enabling an unproblematic identification of both the sender and the intended
recipient. Such notes conveniently illustrate the ambiguous status that infor-
mal letters can attain: they are personal and yet contain little or no private
information; they are often social or occasional and yet presuppose some de-
gree of familiarity. Perhaps just as important, such letters form part of an
exchange culture, and much of their meaning is therefore conventional. The
gift is both personal and related to practices within very specific social strata
where one establishes a sense of belonging and status by giving things away.
Part of the procedure of gift exchange was that short notes should accompany
presents (in the case of the Cooper note, this was probably a bouquet of
flowers: flowers carry pollen, which bees convert to honey, thus the flower is

the source, the founder, of honey). Because of their brevity, such notes tend to concision and complexity of meaning, precisely the sort of qualities that are traditionally associated with poetry. The language of notes therefore approximates the status of a verbal object: it exists to be memorable, almost as a gift in itself. Demetrius, for example, makes a very similar point: "Artemon, the editor of Aristotle's letters, says that dialogue and letters should be written in the same manner, since a letter may be regarded as one of the two sides of a dialogue. His comment has some truth perhaps, but not the whole truth. A letter should be slightly more elaborately written than a dialogue, because the latter aims at an effect of improvisation but the former is of its very nature written and is sent as a sort of gift."[34]

The size of the letter is another factor to be kept in mind with regard to style. Dickinson's early letters were often quite expansive: L177, to Susan Dickinson in 1855, is written in ink on lined paper (measuring 12.8 × 21.6 cm), embossed "SUPERFINE LAID PAPER," and has 99 words in an opening paragraph of fifteen lines.[35] A letter to Joseph Sweetser, L190, is written in ink on lined paper (measuring 12.3 × 18.6 cm) and has about 345 words spread over four pages (about 86 words per page).[36] Again to Susan Dickinson and dated about 1865, L310 consists of only 10 words (not including the signature):[37]

> Are you sure
> we are making
> the most of it ?
> Emily –

The writing is represented here without margins because it is almost exactly centered lengthwise on a page that measures 17.8 cm in height (and such centering elsewhere is often erroneously interpreted by modern readers as an indication of poetic status). The breadth is 11.1 cm, and the first row of writing begins approximately 2.4 cm from the left edge of the paper, with the second 1.1 cm from the edge. The note is written in pencil on ruled notebook paper that is folded in quarters; Johnson thought that its exuberance allowed it to be dated to after Dickinson's return in October 1865 from treatment in Cambridge for eye trouble. To what extent Dickinson's visual impairment might have affected the arrangement of the words on the page or the brevity of the message is impossible to say, but one notes that the ratio of words per line has been reduced by exactly half, from 6.6 in L177 to 3.3 in L310. The percentages are less important than the trend that they suggest, continued in another note to Susan Dickinson from 1873 (the page is only partially reproduced in what follows):[38]

> Sister
>   Our parting
> was   somewhat
> interspersed and
> I cannot con-
> clude   which
> went.
> I   shall   be
> cautious not to
> so   as   to miss
> no one.

This letter (not counting the salutation) has about 2.4 words per line, a slightly misleading statistic because it includes two paragraph breaks (not one, as Johnson and Ward represent it), though the third page (which has only one paragraph break) has 48 words over eighteen rows of writing, or 2.6 words per line. Still, the tendency in Dickinson's letters is for words—and the spaces between them—to grow larger and the number of words per line to lessen; this trend is confirmed by another document, again to Susan Dickinson, dating from about 1878:[39]

> Sue – to   be
> lovely   as   you
> is   a   touching
> contest,   though
> like   the   Siege
> of Eden, impracticable.
> Eden   never
> capitulates –
>   Emily –

The gaps between words (though they are not literally represented here) vary from 1.3 cm ("like / the," "of / Eden") through 2 cm ("is / a," "the / Siege"), 2.3 cm ("a / touching," "Eden / never"), and 2.5 cm ("to / be). Spaces from the margin of the writing to the right edge of the paper range from 2.9 cm (after "never") and 3 cm (after "be") to 4.5 cm (from the punctuation mark after "capitulates"). There are 20 words spread over eight rows of writing (not including the signature), or 2.5 words per row. The same is true of L869, to

Susan Dickinson and dated to about 1883: it has 18 words spread over nine rows of writing, or 2 words per row.[40]

Nor is Susan Dickinson the only one who received such short notes; the 1876 note to Abigail Cooper referred to previously is written on a small scrap of paper (measuring 12.8 cm in width by 20.5 cm in height), with only two words to the line:[41]

> The Founders
> of Honey
> have no
> Names –

The increase in the size of the lettering and the reduction in the ratio of words per line creates a kind of optical and generic illusion: this note *looks* like a lyric in the sense that it is brief and has many fewer words per line than one would normally expect in a letter. At the same time, the note's overall brevity results in a greater amount of semantic weight being placed on a smaller area of language; it becomes more compressed, figurative, and dense with meaning. The result is quasi-sibylline, so it is therefore understandable that some readers have responded by describing such notes as "letter-poems." But such an effect is at least partly caused by succinct expression, in combination with the scarcity of words per line: a late-1880 note to Mrs. Henry Hills, for example, says only that "The little Annual Creatures solicit your regard," a statement that is similarly brief and does not quite approach the status of poetry but is hardly a utilitarian use of language either.

Nevertheless, in the case of many documents such as "Flowers – are so enticing" (which I considered in the prologue to this book), an extreme splitting of generic categories cannot be sustained on the basis of subject matter or style alone. "Flowers – are so enticing" contains elements that have traditionally been defined as identifying characteristics of poetry, including meter and (possibly) rhyme. It is playful, in that Dickinson is clearly mocking the idea that the love of flowers, like the love of earthly things, could be the cause of damnation or even condemnation (a useful reminder that this New England "Queen," unlike the Victoria of stereotype, was often amused and amusing). In addition, the note largely consists of an unusual double simile: flowers are like gambling and (or alternatively) apostasy. One can expand from this to say that, at one level, "Flowers – are so enticing" challenges extreme distinctions between the ideals of transparency and non-transparency which are associated with epistolary and lyrical discourse, and between concepts of the complete and incomplete in literary texts.

But whose definitions are these? Is it possible that claims made on behalf of Dickinson's generic experiments depend, paradoxically and often confusingly, on the assumption of a far more dramatic and absolute distinction between the two categories than Dickinson herself operated with? For it is only in their most extreme forms that letters and poetry are kept separate from each other. Given the etymological associations between letters and literature (in Latin, *litterae* and *litteratura*), the idea that letters could be held absolutely separate from other literary productions is a strange one: the tradition of the verse-epistle, a "poem addressed to a friend, lover or patron, and written in a familiar style," certainly complicates this idea.[42] A letter from Jane Austen to her brother Frank, dated 26 July 1809 and congratulating him and Mary on the safe delivery of their second child, is written entirely in couplets; Oliver Wendell Holmes's "A Familiar Letter" of 1876 is also in verse (though unlike Austen's, it was meant to be printed.)[43] In Dickinson's case, portions of letters, notes, and poems seem to have had shared resources or origins, as Werner points out in her comments on the Lord materials.[44] Brita Lindberg-Seyersted makes the same point: "A perusal of Emily Dickinson's later poems and letters would indicate that the *occasion* itself seldom or never prompted the initial composition of the poems; the first drafts of poems, unfinished or fragmentary, probably already existed in the poet's scrap basket; a special event, or the need to reply to a friend's note, then afforded the necessary impetus for a decision on the final form of the fragmentary lines. Significantly she never sent rough or even semi-final drafts to her correspondents. Often the poem does not actually fit the context of the letter; it seems rather different from the prosaic framework, and more fraught with meaning."[45] The use of prose fragments from the basket, which included hundreds of other phrases and scraps of writing, partly explains the style of some documents that seem to include apparently unrelated and oblique elements. There is something oracular about these phrases, which because they are compact and concise, often read like proverbs. This is a small list of examples:

> Life is the finest secret. (L354, 2:482)
> To shut our eyes is Travel. (L354)
> Each expiring Secret leaves an Heir[.] (L359, 2:485)
> No bird resumes its egg. (L379, 2:499)
> [T]he imperceptible has no external Face. (L391, 2:508)

To formulate a proverb is to compose a truth that appears to be not of your own making, which makes it more powerful (it does not issue from a single source) and also more oblique (what it says may not be identified exclusively with your own feelings on the subject). Keep in mind also that the speaker of

"This is my letter to the World" (Fr519) claims that she is the bearer, and not the originator, of the news from nature and that the reader should think kindly of her not because of any personal worth of her own but because of the value of the materials she is (supposed to be) conveying.[46] The statements above, then, like proverbs, gesture towards the incontrovertible because they appear independent of any merely subjective, and potentially erroneous, input: they are facts, not matters of opinion. They are Delphic utterances. Paradoxically, the more definitive these statements look and sound, the more indeterminate they actually are, for their meanings are applicable to different circumstances and at different times.

   This combination of indeterminacy, figurativeness, and contextual auton-omy within the letters themselves (irrespective of whether they can be said to contain poems) reminds us that we cannot attempt to determine any discus-sion of generic differences according to the presence or absence of meter or the quality and literalness of the language used. Instead, we have to accept that when Dickinson thought she was writing poetry, she changed her habits of inscription from those of her letters. In the letter to Higginson that I discussed previously in this chapter, there is a passage that has been identified by several editors as a poem: it *follows* the biography passage.[47]

> Pass to thy
> Rendezvous of
> Light,
> Pangless except
> for us –
> Who slowly
> ford the
> Mystery
> Which thou
> hast leaped
> across!

> Your Scholar

A material characteristic of poems in Dickinson's handwritten originals is an increase in the frequency of end spaces that do not correspond to paragraph or (prose) sentence breaks; here, such intervals occur after "Light" (7.5 cm), "us" (6.4 cm), and "Mystery" (6.8 cm). Finally, there is a vertical gap of fully 2 cm from "across" to "Your Scholar" that is not typical of letters—the in-creased space is another way in which the poem is distinguished from its environs.

The version to Higginson and its context makes it seem as if the poem were about George Eliot. But recall that an earlier version of the same lines was sent to Susan Dickinson; to her, they would have referred unambiguously to her son Gilbert, as Susan received them shortly after his death on 5 October 1883.[48]

> Pass to thy
> Rendezvous of
> Light,
> Pangless except
> for us –
> Who slowly ford
> the Mystery
> Which thou hast
> leaped across!
>   Emily –

There are some minor adjustments between the versions: "Who slowly ford / the Mystery" (Susan Dickinson), "Who slowly / ford the / Mystery" (Higginson); "Which thou hast / leaped across!" (Susan Dickinson), "Which thou / hast leaped / across!" (Higginson). The end spaces occur in the same places, however: after "Light" (8.2 cm in Susan Dickinson's version, 7.5 cm in Higginson's), "us" (6.3 cm in Susan Dickinson's version, 6.4 cm in Higginson's), and "Mystery" (4.6 cm in Susan Dickinson's version, 6.8 cm in Higginson's). Thus, although "Who slowly ford the Mystery" appears to be delineated differently in the two versions, Dickinson preserves the integrity of the phrase by leaving blank space after "Mystery" to indicate that it is an end word in a metrically defined sequence (that of the line, at the local level, and the stanza, at the next level). Perhaps most critical, however, the words *of the poem* are exactly the same from one communication to another, whereas their prose contexts are entirely different. This extractability is a characteristic of the poetry, not the prose: poetry could be transferred from one environment or context to another, whereas letters (by and large) were not.

One of the accusations that can (legitimately) be leveled at such gestures toward empiricist evidence is that when one isolates a document for discussion, one does so on the basis of its already conforming to the characteristics one wishes to prioritize. That is why, in the case studies which follow, I have attempted to look at Dickinson manuscripts that seem generically ambiguous or problematic: they include portions of writing that have been classified as containing both poems and letters or decisions as to genres have been differently defined by succeeding generations of editors.

III

Writing on the back of a circular printed in red ink and measuring 11.3 × 16.8 cm, advertising *The Children's Crusade* by George Zabriskie Walker, Dickinson composed two drafts, in pencil (sometime around 1872).[49]

> Fly – fly – but as you fly –
> Remember – the second
> pass you by –
> The Second is pursuing
> the Century
> The Century is chasing
> Eternity –   what a
> Ah the Responsibility –
>   Such a Responsibility
>   What a –
> No wonder that the
> little Second flee –
> Out of it's frightened
> way –

> Paradise is no Journey
> because it he is within –
> but for that very cause
> though – it is the
> most Arduous of
> Journeys – because as
> the servant conscientiously
> says at the Door
> we are out –
> always – invariably –

The drafts provide further evidence of how Dickinson sometimes inscribed the same alphabetic characters very differently within the same documents (and often in close physical proximity to each other). Here it is the initial and terminal lowercase *y*'s that are materially divergent: the initial *y* (as in "you") is shaped almost like a Dickinson *s* (with a single reversed curve), whereas the terminal one ("fly") is a single, short, straight stroke. As with the variously rendered *e*'s and *d*'s, the diversity with which Dickinson performed her letter *y* is intriguing but is not intended to influence the contents of those words or sequences of which it is a component. Like the inconsistently executed dash, the *y* is a phenomenon of the handwriting that makes no deliberate contribution to a poem's meaning.

But it is principally the issue of genre that is of concern here. Johnson and Ward numbered the above prose fragments 75 and 99, respectively, and included them in appendix 3 ("Aphorisms") of *Letters*. On the second of these, Franklin concurs that it is a "prose draft" but identifies the first as a poem, to which he assigns the number Fr1244.[50] (William Shurr, in his edition of excavated poems, fails to include any of these, even partially.) The discrepancy tends to confirm what manuscript critics have claimed for some time now: that Dickinson's letters and poems are more difficult to distinguish than the Johnson and Franklin editions always reflect. But one wonders to what extent working drafts may be treated as if they were equivalent to published documents, given that any (especially brief) composition written on a narrow slip or fragment of paper can appear to occupy an intermediate or ambivalent generic position without that being a willed aspect of its composition or projected reception.[51]

The fragments above, however, are physically distinct in their layout: "prose fragment 75" observes patterns that are characteristic of Dickinson's lyrics, which makes it demonstrably the "raw material for a poem."[52] The gaps after "by –" (4.8 cm), "Century" (5.1 cm), "Eternity –" (6.9 cm), and "way –" (6.9 cm) are all consistent with poetic formatting, as are the capitals in rows 2, 4, 6, 8, 11, and 13 (the capitalization of words that appear to be proportionately less significant than others is ordinarily a sign that they head metrical sequences, as with "The," "Ah," and "Out," for instance). There are no such anomalous spaces or inexplicable capitals in the second fragment, "Paradise is no Journey"; almost every line begins with a lowercase word, which indicates that the rows are equivalent to continuous prose and not deliberately separate. Johnson was therefore justified in arranging this cluster as a single unit of prose, just as he was wrong in presenting "Fly – fly – but as you fly" in the same way: its arrangement is that of a poem.

IV

Dickinson wrote to Samuel Bowles around October 1874, shortly after he had paid another of his many visits to Amherst. Bowles had stayed at the Homestead in 1873, and before the Whig Party broke apart in 1854, he publicly supported Edward Dickinson as a conservative of the old school, a man of integrity. In several of her letters to him, Dickinson alludes to the high esteem in which he is held by both her parents: "I think Father and Mother care a great deal for you – and hope you may be well," she wrote about January

1862.[53] The 1874 communication, then, is an elegy for her father (who had passed away earlier that year, on 16 June); it is written in pen on paper measuring 12.7 × 20.4 cm and folded in thirds.[54]

Dear friend.
The Paper
wanders so
I cannot
write my
name on it,
so I give
you Father's
Portrait
instead.

As Summer
into Autumn
slips [page break]
And yet
we sooner
say
"The Summer"
than "the
Autumn", lest
We turn the
Sun away,

And almost
count it an
Affront the
presence to
concede
Of one however
lovely, not
The one [page break]
that we have
loved –

So we evade
the Charge
of Years
On one

> attempting shy
> The Circumvention
> of the Shaft
> Of Life's
> declivity.
>
> Emily

Again, there is much about the handwriting that is inconsistent here but routinely so: the different forms of the letters *d* and *e*, and the crossbars joining the (second and third) ascenders in "Portrait" and (the first and third in) "that" (not to mention the extended stroke through single *t* shapes in "than" and "the"). Such habitual variety is ignored when readers claim that Dickinson's dashes and calligraphy are deliberately crafted in particular poems to convey specific meanings.[55] And a fairly unmistakable in-text transition exists between the prose and the poetry, in the shape of a reference to a prior aesthetic product that the writer is sending as a substitute for a more immediate or personal expression ("I give you Father's Portrait instead"). This division or separation is supplemented materially by the increased vertical gap between the rows of writing (1.5 cm after "instead," unlike the interlineal space of 1 cm or less elsewhere). The spacing is fairly unremarkable until "Portrait" (on the first page), after which there is an interval of 3.7 cm that does not correspond to the end of a sentence, paragraph, or metrical unit but is explained by the word in the next row, "instead," which measures 5.7 cm on its own and clearly would not have fit into the space after "Portrait."

What *is* remarkable about the spacing in the rest of the manuscript is its increased frequency: in addition to the vertical intervals reserved almost exclusively for signaling stanza breaks in Dickinson autographs, certain end-domain blanks function to mark either prose paragraphs or the close of a metrical sequence. In this case, the spaces follow "slips" (at the end of the first page, 6.9 cm), "say" (second page, third row, 9 cm), "concede" (second page, row thirteen, 4.7 cm), "loved" (third page, second row, 6.2 cm), and "Years" (third page, fifth row, 4.7 cm).[56] Clearly, such intervals do not mark the end of paragraphs; they coincide with the completion of metrical entities. Just as clearly, the emergence of capitals that do not correspond to the start of a sentence, the emphasis of a particular word, or a proper name, strongly suggests the regulating presence of nonprosaic limitations in operation at this point.[57] Of course, one could argue that Dickinson felt less comfortable and more formal with Bowles than she did with Susan Dickinson and that the observance of generic distinctions is therefore a function of that formality. But this can be turned around too: the lack of such distinctions in the correspondence with Susan Dickinson is a function of the informality of their relationship and not an indication of an ongoing and mutual experiment at suspending such boundaries. Indeed, if the visual markers relating to poetry in Dickinson's writing increase proportionately to the distance she felt to the reader, might she not then have insisted on preserving and clarifying generic distinctions for an audience she had never met?

V

In 1876, Dickinson sent a message (in pen, on paper measuring 12.7 x 20.5 cm) to Susan Dickinson, a portion of which she would later repeat in a letter to Higginson (in 1877), and in one to Josiah Holland (in 1878), before retaining a copy for her own purposes:[58]

> Sue – this
> is the last
> flower –
>
> To wane
> without
> disparagement
> In a dissembling
> hue
> That will not
> let the Eye
> decide
> If it abide
> or no
> is Sunset's –
> perhaps – only. Emily

One is struck by the double spacing after "flower": 5.8 cm of horizontal space, and 1 cm of vertical (which is twice as large as the average of 5 mm between lines elsewhere). Sufficient room certainly existed for Dickinson to have included "To" on the same plane as "flower," and if the unused space signifies a paragraph break (a shift in theme or mood), one wonders why it is supplemented by the additional move down the page. Such spacing strongly argues that another kind of transition takes place at this point—from prose to poetry. This impression is solidified by the notable spaces after "hue" (8.8 cm), "decide" (5.2 cm), and "no" (6.5 cm), none of which can be explained as having occurred because of there being inadequate room for the next word in the sequence, and none of which coincides with the close of a sentence or paragraph. The gap after "no" is especially significant, because although Dickinson continues the thought of the poem in the prose finale, she still distinguishes it materially from its present application. The poem antecedes and survives the moment of its saying in the letter: it remains set apart—physically and generically—from its epistolary usage.

Such an impression is not weakened by reading the version sent to Higginson, which is substantially the same, except for the prose section:[59]

Is the
Year too
elderly for
your acceptance
of Lowell,
as a slight
symbol of
a Scholar's
Affection?
I designed
"Harold" to
accompany
Emerson, but
Tennyson declines – [page break]
like Browning –
once so rare!
To wane
without
disparagement
In a dissem-
bling hue
That will not
let the Eye
decide
If it abide
or no
is Sunset's,
perhaps – only.
Please re-
member me
with [page break]

Gaps appear after the poem begins: following "hue" (4.1 cm), "decide" (6.2 cm), and "no" (5.8 cm; the nearest space in terms of extent elsewhere in the letter is the 8.3 cm subsequent to "we have / feared he [Austin, ill with malaria] would die" on the last page, which represents a paragraph break). That three such spaces appear in just six rows of writing, whereas only one appears in four pages otherwise, strongly suggests the presence of a different generic entity at that juncture in the message. And it is Dickinson, not her editors, who omits to write on the same row as the end of the poem (after "no"), thus signaling her sense of its separation from the document as a whole. One could go further and point out the difference between the letter's delivery of information (the question of gifts, the greeting to Mrs. Higginson, the report on Austin's sickness, the reference to Helen Hunt Jackson) and the poem's indeterminacy. But the problem with trying to ground any theory of generic distinctions in Dickinson's work on stylistic density is that it does not hold, for so much of the epistolary production is sibylline, has passages of epigrammatic terseness that seem equal to the poetry. There is *some* truth in the distinction (for instance, one does not see surnames in poems, as one does in letters, and one can extrapolate from that particular observation to say that the everyday seldom exists unmodified or transformed in the poems as it can in the prose), but it is not an absolute one, as such critics as Marietta Messmer have compellingly argued.[60] Indeed, my intention is not to speculate as to why Dickinson might have distinguished between genres but simply to observe that she does so.

Early in 1878, Dickinson returned to these words, this time prefacing them again with a letter expressing different concerns (to Josiah Holland, congratulating him on his "repaired health") and with another quatrain:[61]

> But I intrude
> on Sunset, and
> Father and
> Mr Bowles.
> These held their
> Wick above the
> west – [page break]
> Till when the
> Red declined –
> Or how the
> Amber aided it –
> Defied to be
> defined –

> Then waned
> without disparage-
> ment
> In a dissembling
> Hue
> That would not
> let the Eye decide
> Did it abide
> or no –
> Emily.

In *Letters*, Johnson and Ward separate the poem visually from the prose, and Franklin, similarly, pares the lyric from its epistolary context.[62] Unlike the message to Susan Dickinson, however, there is no augmented vertical space after "Bowles," although the horizontal gap of 3.9 cm signals a break of some kind. Nevertheless, the visual design of the text changes at this point: there is an enlarged vertical space of 1.5 cm between "defined" and "Then" (approximately twice the size as normal), following a horizontal space of 4.8 cm after "defined"; these indicate a stanza break, and are more prevalent in Dickinson's poetry than in her prose. In addition, a massive interval of 9.9 cm follows "Hue," and one of 7.1 cm comes after (the dash that follows) "no."

   Finally, Dickinson recorded (probably also in 1878) the second of these stanzas in pencil on a leaf of stationery:[63]

> Then waned
> without disparage-
> ment
> In a dissembling
> hue
> That would not
> let the Eye decide
> Did it abide or
> no –

That portions of lyric writing can be transferred from one document to another and yet remain substantially intact (whereas their prose settings vary, to be ultimately discarded in record copies), shows once again that Dickinson did distinguish between poetry and prose. In letters in which poems are enfolded within the text (rather than included as separate enclosures), explicit verbal references to any change of genre are rare, but the handwriting provides fairly consistent evidence of the emergence and cessation of linguistic entities whose appearance is regulated by principles that are different from or additional to those which govern the movement of prose.[64]

VI

On an unruled bifolium measuring 12.4 × 20.4 cm (and folded by hand in quarters), Dickinson wrote in pencil to Sarah (Mrs. Edward) Tuckerman in 1878; Johnson and Ward, and then Franklin, identify this visually and verbally as a poem in a letter.[65]

> Would it be
> prudent to subject
> an apparitional
> interview to a
> grosser test?
> The Bible
> portentously says
> "that which is [page break]
> Spirit is Spirit."
> Go not too near
> a House of Rose –
> The depredation
> of a Breeze
> Or inundation
> of a Dew
> Alarm it's Walls
> away – [page break]
> Nor try to tie
> the Butterfly,
> Nor climb the
> Bars of Ecstasy –
> In insecurity
> to lie
> Is Joy's insuring
> quality –
> E. Dickinson

Typically, no *immediate* physical difference in the layout of this message accompanies or otherwise announces the shift from the prose section of the letter to the poem (which begins "Go not too near"). It is only at the end of the second page and the space that follows the dash subsequent to "away" that the kind of gap associated with a paragraph or line break appears. Two years later in 1880, when she would receive five poems, Sarah Tuckerman may have been able to recognize the significance of such a break, but in 1878, she was still a comparative novice (the note is thought by Franklin to have been the first of the total of sixteen poems she was to receive, though Johnson and Ward list her as having been sent eight letters previous to 1879). It is certainly possible that Tuckerman may have remained ignorant of the switch until the last page, where at least one space appears that cannot be explained away as a paragraph ending: the 7.2 cm after "lie" appears in the *middle* of a semantic sequence ("In insecurity to lie IS joy's insuring quality") but at the *close* of a metrical segment. And the cluster of end rhymes ("Butterfly," "Ecstasy," "lie," "quality") in addition to the increasingly figurative and ludic language ("tie the Butterfly," "climb the Bars of Ecstasy") would have combined to make the poem's presence difficult to miss at that point in the communication. One wonders, too, if the reference to a "grosser test" of some kind served as an introduction to what followed and whether Tuckerman's cultural competence would have lapsed sufficiently for her not to have detected the presence of regular iambic tetrameter from the second row of the second page onward?

In 1879, Dickinson sent a message next door to the Evergreens, her fifth communication to Susan that year (there would be another two to come), and approximately the two hundred twenty-second of their friendship. On unruled paper measuring 12.8 × 20.4 cm, folded in thirds, she wrote in pencil:[66]

> Susan –
> A little overflowing
> word
> That any, hearing,
> had inferred
> For Ardor or
> for Tears,
> Though Generations [page break]
> [blank page]
> pass away,
> Traditions ripen
> and decay,
> As eloquent
> appears –
>   Emily –

Franklin classifies this as a poem (Fr1501A), Hart and Smith as a letter-poem
(LP215). The material evidence tends to support Franklin's judgment: on the
first page, for instance, there are spaces of 8.3, 3.1, and 4.5 cm after (respec-
tively) "word," "inferred," and "Tears." There is certainly more than enough
room to fit "That" into the space following "word," suggesting that the in-
ducement for transferring to a new line was not physical. By extension, the
sequence "A little overflowing word That any, hearing, had inferred For Ar-
dor or for Tears" can be read as one unit without doing violence to the sense
of the words; the assignment of capitals to (and the pauses before) "That" and
"For" is therefore a function of the grammar of poetry rather than prose. The
continued presence of procedures associated with traditional poetry (where
each line is limited by the predetermined number of its stressed and unstressed
syllables, its boundaries established at the start by a capital and at the end by a
rhyming word or by a word that does not rhyme in an alternating pattern of
rhyming and non-rhyming elements) would seem counterproductive in writ-
ing that is supposed to suspend genres: but those procedures are there.[67]

VII

Dickinson sent another "note to Sarah Tuckerman at the time of the death of
[Professor] Elihu Root, her husband's promising young colleague at Amherst
College, who died 3 December 1880" at the age of thirty-five.[68]

> Dear friend,
>   I thought
> of you, although
> I never saw
> your friend.
> Brother of
> Ophir
> Bright Adieu – [page break]
> Honor, the
> shortest route
> To you –
>   Emily –

Here again, the switch to lyric from epistolary modes is not explicitly intro-
duced; instead, there is the appearance of uppercase letters where one would
not expect them, at least in a letter. The first segment of the note ("I thought
of you, although I never saw your friend.") contains no such capitals; in the

second segment, there are six, one of which ("Brother") coincides with the beginning of a sentence and is therefore unremarkable, but two of which ("Bright," "To") do not and therefore cannot be explained according to the regulating principles of prose. There is also no physical consistency: the word "shortest" begins at the left-hand side of the page but does not receive a capital. What unites "Brother," "Bright," "Honor," and "To" is that each coincides with the beginning of a metrical sequence, and the capitalization is a conventional attribute of such initiation. In addition, a massive space follows "Ophir" (8.2 cm out of the 12 cm available) which cannot be explained away as a paragraph break; the interval signals the end of a metrical unit.[69]

An earlier draft version of (approximately) the same poem, written in pencil on a tiny square of thick brown wrapping paper (measuring 8.2 × 9 cm) is also stored at Amherst College and is thought by Franklin to date to 1878:[70]

> Brother of
> Ingots – Ah
> Peru –
> Empty the
> Hearts that
> purchased
> you –

Unlike the Tuckerman version, which is organized as a four-line unit, this one was clearly recorded as a couplet, though the internal rhyme ("Ingots," "Hearts") means that in theory it could have existed or been composed as a quatrain. The *t* at the beginning of "that" is a fairly unmistakable minuscule, however, and there are gaps in the writing of 4.1 and 4.9 cm after the dashes following "Peru" and "you" that constitute end-domain phenomena: at the time of transcription, then, Dickinson thought of this as a two-line entity.

In addition, a message in the same year from Dickinson to Susan Dickinson has many of the same elements:[71]

> Susan – I dreamed
> of you, last
> night, and send
> a Carnation to
> indorse it –
> Sister of Ophir –
> Ah Peru –
> Subtle the Sum [page break]
> that purchase
> you –

Though not the clearest example of the phenomenon, this message shows one difference between Dickinson's poems and letters—that is, the former sometimes receive multiple performances but remain essentially the same (in terms of underlying structure, if not always in language), whereas few letters were sent to more than one recipient.[72] Typically, the prose sections of the documents currently under discussion are not as similar as the lyric sequences, as was also the case with "To wane without disparagement," which remained fairly consistent from one presentation to another, in the midst of varying prose backdrops.[73] If we isolate the poetry from the prose and put all three versions side by side (as quatrains, for ease of comparison only), one sees a fundamental equivalence: all three have exactly sixteen syllables, for example, and all three have very similar end rhymes (Peru / you; Adieu / you). There are other associations: "Brother / Sister / Brother"; "Ingots / Ophir / Ophir" (ingots being of gold, gold being one of the treasures found in Ophir); as well as the verbal osmosis ("Brother of" in versions 1 and 3; "Ah Peru" in versions 1 and 2; "of Ophir" in versions 2 and 3; "that purchased you / that purchase you" in versions 1 and 2). All these intersecting elements suggest very strongly that we are dealing with different verbal expressions of essentially the same work:[74]

Brother of Ingots – Ah Peru – Empty the Hearts that purchased you –	Sister of Ophir – Ah Peru – Subtle the Sum that purchase you –	Brother of Ophir – Bright Adieu – Honor, the shortest route To you –

By contrast, the prose sections of the two communications differ—the one to Susan Dickinson has eighteen syllables spread over five rows, whereas that to Sarah Tuckerman has fourteen over five:

Dear friend, I thought of you, although I never saw your friend.	Susan – I dreamed of you , last night , and send a Carnation to indorse it –

The *prose* contents are slightly different (with the exception of the first- and second-person pronouns), occasioned by separate events: a dream and the death of a friend's friend. And perhaps this alerts us to a more fundamental difference between poetry and prose as Dickinson practiced it: whereas letters were mostly to historical individuals, poems were largely addressed to a wider (and quite possibly unknown) audience. Of course, it may be that the two genres occasionally overlap; the final version of the poem, for instance, can be thought of as having been adapted for the function of expressing condolence, for suiting a particular reader rather than a readership. And the gender of the subject in the second version is clearly altered to suit Susan. But such emendations are a function of the poem's inclusion *in a letter to a specific person*; broadly speaking, Dickinson avoided such particularities when recording poems in her manuscript anthologies. (And recall that Dickinson's fascicles were not circulated, even to Susan Dickinson, and there are no manuscript books of letters or books of poetry organized according to recipient.) In other words, the distinction generally holds: poems have a certain structural definition that letters do not—sustained metrical patterning in combination with regularly timed rhyme. And this definition manifests itself in consistency across separate versions of the same text and in physical patterns of inscription that are subtly but significantly different from those of prose.[75]

VIII

Among the most striking of the Dickinson autograph fragments are the occasional long and narrow slips of paper on which she composed poems and letters. One of these is believed to date from 1881 and is approximately 38 cm long and 3.6 cm wide: it is a strip of brown wrapping paper, folded in three places, with pencil writing on both sides.[76]

| Cosmopolites without a plea Alight in every Land ~~And of whoever~~ | ~~ask their way~~ – The Compliments of Paradise From these within   <u>those</u> my Hand | Their dappled Journey – to themselves – A compensation fair – gay – |

Without a care –
   Sister
Excuse me
for disturbing
Susan with

fragilities on the
eve of her de
parture – the North
Star is but of a
small fabric
yet it
implies achieves
   much

A comptence
so gay

– Philosophy –
Theology
is their

Knock
and it
shall be
opened

Even a fragment as unusual as this one continues to observe different generic conventions, however: there is 6.2 cm of space from the end of "plea" to a point immediately below the last ascender in "without" in the line above, and 2 cm of space from "Paradise" to a point immediately below the *s* of "Compliments" in the preceding row.[77] There are no such spaces in the prose part of the document, which is a draft message to Susan Dickinson (who was leaving on a trip to Grand Rapids, Michigan; a note was eventually sent on the eve of her departure, 19 October 1882).[78] Once more, the conclusion to be drawn is that generic distinctions manifested themselves as a matter of routine in much of Dickinson's writing, even at the draft stage. It is therefore *theoretically* possible to arrange one of these communicative acts as poetry and the other as prose:

> Cosmopolites without a plea
> Alight in every Land
> The Compliments of Paradise
> From these within my Hand
> Their dappled Journey – to themselves
> A compensation fair –
> Knock and it shall be opened
> is their Theology

Sister
   Excuse me for disturbing Susan with fragilities on the eve of her departure – the North Star is but of a small fabric yet it implies (achieves) much[79]

The first of these reconstructed versions (beginning "Cosmopolites") corresponds to Fr1592 in Franklin's *Poems*. Nevertheless, there are some anomalies: Dickinson begins "is their Theology" with a lowercase *i*; the *abcb* rhyme scheme (Land / Hand) is not sustained by the combination of "fair / Theology," and the meter dissipates in the last two lines (as Franklin reconstitutes them) from regular lines of alternating iambic tetrameter and trimeter.[80] None of this changes the impression of generic differences between the passages beginning "Cosmopolites" and "Sister," not the least of these being the address: is it then wrong to present "Cosmopolites" as a completed poem when Dickinson herself left it as a draft? This document would appear to belong to a category of Dickinson's oeuvre that her editors (excepting Marta Werner) have not always permitted—the unfinished poem. Franklin (and this is especially striking in the reader's edition of 1999) presents "Cosmopolites" as an eight-line lyric (and even his notes do not reflect the complexity of the draft's appearance).[81] Hart and Smith do not include it in *Open Me Carefully*, but their practice tends to the opposite extreme (judging by LP199 and 200): lack of finish is taken as the suspension or rejection of the idea that a poem can be brought to an end, which is to replace one kind of finish (closure, completion, organic unity) with another (open-endedness, deferral, fragmentation). To treat a draft as if it were left deliberately incomplete still implies an overall structure of meaning, rather than alternative semantic sequences that occupy the same physical space. It is to suppose that incompleteness was something that Dickinson worked toward in her composition. But that some poems were left without a decision having been made with reference to variants does not necessarily signify that Dickinson abandoned choice altogether.

IX

Written in pencil on unlined paper, measuring 12.7 × 20.3 cm, and folded in thirds (though clearly not sent, nevertheless), a draft letter to an unidentified recipient (thought by Leyda and Franklin to have been Samuel Bowles the younger) displays the separate material characteristics by which Dickinson distinguished between prose and poetry.[82]

> To ask of
> each that
> gathered Life,
> Oh, where did
> it grow, is
> intuitive.
> That you have
> answered this
> Prince Question
> to your own
> delight, is
> joy to us all –
>
> Lad of Athens,
> faithful be [page break]
> To thyself,
> And Mystery –
> All the rest
> is Perjury –
>
> Please say
> with my ten-

derness to
your Mother,
I shall soon
write her –

E. Dickinson –

Franklin, like Johnson and Ward before him, represents the first and third
portions of this message as prose and the second as poetry (Fr1606B).[83] His
judgment is corroborated by the large interlinear space just before "Lad of
Athens" and immediately subsequent to "is Perjury": whereas in the rest of
the document such spaces average around 1 cm, they increase to (respectively)
1.5 cm and 2.3 cm before and after the poem. It could be argued that vertical
spaces indicate paragraph breaks, but Dickinson's more common procedure
of leaving horizontal terminal space to signal the end of a prose paragraph is
practiced elsewhere here, when she fails to use 5.8 cm of space after "intui-
tive." Dickinson does not normally switch from horizontal to vertical encod-
ing of paragraphs, and thus the appearance of the extra intervals at the begin-
ning and end of the poem is likely more than coincidental and constitutes a
visual form of generic separation. The assignation of capitals to words which
do not follow periods and which bear (comparatively speaking) reduced se-
mantic loads (such as "To" and "And") further hints that a system of conven-
tions other than those associated with prose is in operation from "Lad" and to
"Perjury." In effect, Dickinson's capitals disclose and are formed by the fol-
lowing template, what Wallace Stevens called the "poem of the mind":[84]

Lad of Athens, faithful be
To thyself,
And Mystery –
All the rest is Perjury –

X

Sometime early in 1883, Dickinson began work on Fr1597A, "To see her is a
picture." Four variants are thought to have existed: one (now lost) was tran-
scribed by Susan Dickinson, while another survives as a draft. A third was sent
to Elizabeth Holland; it is made to look as if it was written for her ("May I
present your Portrait to your Sons in Law?").[85] The fourth is believed to have
been meant for Mabel Loomis Todd and is introduced in such a way that it
seems to refer to her daughter, Millicent, then three years old.[86] It is written

in pencil on paper measuring approximately 12.7 × 20.2 cm and folded in
thirds: on the first leaf, about 2.6 cm has been cut away from the top.

Dear friend,
        I dream
of your little
Girl three successive
Nights – I hope
nothing affronts
her –
To see her is
a Picture –
To hear her is
a Tune –
To know her, a
disparagement of
every other Boon –
To know her
not, Affliction – [page break]
To own her for
a Friend
A warmth as near
as if the Sun
Were shining in
your Hand –
Lest she miss
her "Squirrels," I send
her little Playmates
I met in Yesterday's
Storm – the lovely
first that came –
Forever honored
be the Tree whose
Apple winter – worn –
Enticed to Break-
fast from the Sky
Two Gabriels [page break]
Yester Morn –
They registered in
Nature's Book

As Robins, Sire
and Son –
But Angels have
that modest way
To screen them from
renown –

Variants of *both* poems ("To see her is a picture" and [Fr1600] "Forever hon-ored be the tree," as Franklin titles them) were sent to Elizabeth Holland, suggesting once again that Dickinson's poems could be transferred between letters in ways that her prose appears not to have been. The first lines ("I dream of your little Girl three successive Nights – I hope nothing affronts her –") function as an introduction and are followed by 9.3 cm of space. As we have seen, such a gap usually signals some kind of directional shift by Dickin-son—either the appearance of a new paragraph, metrical line, or genre, as here. And as expected, there are gaps—of 3.7 cm and 6.2 cm respectively—after "Picture" and "Tune" that do not seem to have been physically enforced (which is to say that Dickinson did not move her hand farther down the page because she did not have enough room to write the next words—"To," twice). On the next page are similar spaces after "Friend" (followed by 5.5 cm and, in the next line, by "A") and "Hand" (followed by 4.2 cm and, in the next line, by "Lest").

With the resumption of the prose part of the letter, the spaces disappear again; the margins on both side become fairly regular. But when the second poem, "Forever honored be the tree" appears, Dickinson does *not* shift back to her customary way of marking poems: there is no horizontal break (as there was after "nothing affronts her") and no end-domain phenomena (as there was after "Picture," "Tune," "Friend," and "Hand"). There are capitals ("Enticed" and "Two") that are not obviously explicable in prose terms, however, and they suggest two ways in which the poem may be read:

Forever honored be the Tree whose Apple winter – worn –
Enticed to Breakfast from the Sky
Two Gabriels Yester Morn –

or

Forever honored be the Tree whose
Apple winter – worn –
Enticed to Breakfast from the Sky
Two Gabriels Yester Morn –

The first is the version favored by Franklin; the second does not make strict metrical sense but seems potentially justifiable on the grounds that it preserves the rhyme scheme. Johnson and Ward make a third suggestion:[87]

> Forever honored be the Tree
> Whose Apple winter-worn –
> Enticed to Breakfast from the Sky
> Two Gabriels Yester Morn.

This arrangement is the most compelling in terms of systemic regularity: the meter and rhyme become absolutely even, and no violence is done to the spatial logic of the original. But Johnson and Ward seem to have believed either that "whose" was written with an initial capital or that the absence of such a capital was an oversight on Dickinson's part. The question is to what extent such an arrangement can be defended on the grounds of ethics or feasibility. Certainly, both Susan Dickinson's transcript of the poem and the version sent to Holland have "Whose," which strongly indicates that the word was meant to head the second line. But is it safe to assume, then, that Dickinson simply forgot to assign the capital or did so indistinctly, and that the other versions of the poem establish a precedent which this one must follow? Does the version enclosed in the draft letter prove that Dickinson was experimenting with a longer line (disrupting meter and playing with rhyme) or that she was more casual about its inscription (because the reader would recognize the metrical template and make the necessary adjustments; because she was aware that this was a draft and did not have to be precise about its layout; because she lost interest; or because she was not concerned about making the distinction at this stage)?[88]

Intriguingly, the first poem throws up similar challenges, for the combination of initial capitals and end spaces (after "Picture" and "Tune") suggests the following layout:

> To see her is a Picture –
> To hear her is a Tune –
> To know her, a disparagement of every other Boon –

Yet this would appear to contradict the framework of the poem, those scheduled pulses of meter and rhyme that coincide with "Tune" and "Boon":

> To see her is a Picture –
> To hear her is a Tune –

> To know her, a disparagement
> of every other Boon –

On this occasion, both Franklin and Johnson are agreed: the third line ends not with "disparagement" but with "Boon." Franklin is consistent (in this instance), Johnson—given that he was prepared to disarrange "Forever honored be the Tree whose Apple winter – worn"—less so; one wonders why he felt able to change one but not the other, when they are comparable examples.[89]

Another letter from the same period is less problematic. Sent to Joseph K. Chickering and written in pencil on extremely thin paper measuring 13.2 × 20.6 cm, it was folded in quarters:[90]

> Dear friend –
> I had
> hoped to see you,
> but have no
> grace to talk,
> and my own Words
> so chill and
> burn me, that the
> temperature of other
> Minds is too new
> an Awe –
>
> We shun it ere
> it comes,
> Afraid of Joy, [page break]
> Then sue it to
> delay
> And lest it fly,
> Beguile it more
> and more –
> May not this
> be
> Old Suitor Heaven,
> Like our dismay
> at thee?
> Earnestly
> E. Dickinson –

Dickinson quite carefully assigns extra vertical spaces before and after the section beginning "We shun it ere it comes": these spaces are 1.8 cm and 2 cm, respectively, versus 1 cm or less in the rest of the document. And whereas the first rows of writing are similar in length, the rows after "We shun it ere it comes" are more irregular: there is an interval of 6.3 cm after (the comma that follows) "comes," for example. Spaces of 9.4 cm and 11.6 cm (after "delay" and "be," respectively) stand out very strongly when the paper measures only 13.2 cm across to begin with; both these correspond to, and signify, the end of metrically defined sequences. There is no reason why Johnson and Ward, and later Franklin, should not have represented the first sequence of this message as prose and the second as poetry, as Dickinson formatted the two differently herself.

XI

In an 1884 note to Susan, Dickinson grants her sister-in-law permission to use letters addressed to Emily by Samuel Bowles as possible materials for George S. Merriam's proposed biography (the readiness to make these messages available again complicates the theory that Bowles and Dickinson might have been lovers).[91] The document is written in pencil on unlined paper measuring 12.6 × 20.3 cm, and is folded in thirds.

> I felt it no
> betrayal, Dear –
> Go to my Mine
> as to your own,
> only more
> unsparingly –
> I can scarcely
> believe that the
> wondrous Book
> is at last to
> be written, and
> it seems like
> a Memoir of
> the Sun, when
> the Moon is
> gone –
> You remember [page break]
> his swift way
> of wringing and

flinging away
a Theme, and
others picking it
up and gazing[92]
bewildered after
him, and the
prance that
crossed his Eye
at such times
was unrepeatable –
Though the
Great Waters
sleep,
That they are
still the Deep,
We cannot doubt – [page break]
No vacillating
God
Ignited this
Abode
To put it out –

I wish I could
find the
Warrington Words,
but during
my weeks of
faintness, my
Treasures were
misplaced, and
I cannot find
them –

Though Dickinson's correspondence with Susan Dickinson is sometimes taken to be less formal than that with Bowles, she persists in observing generic boundaries even here—in a note sent next door, at a time when (as the words at the end of the quotation reflect) she was gravely, though intermittently, ill. For most of this letter, Dickinson writes from one margin to the other: the exceptions are after "unsparingly" and "gone" (where there are blank intervals measuring 3.8 and 8.3 cm respectively, indicating paragraph breaks). On the second page the spacing and capitalization become erratic (by the standards of prose conventions), starting and ending with that section of the document identified by Franklin as poem Fr1641. Dickinson gives no physical or verbal indication of the switch from prose to poetry, but she organizes the inscription of the poem according to regulations other than those of prose. Thus, "sleep" is followed by a space of 7.9 cm, though it clearly does not correspond to a paragraph break, and there are similar spaces of 9.5 and 7.8 cm after "God" and "Abode." These gaps correspond with and signal the end of a metrical sequence in each case; furthermore, Dickinson inserts a vertical break of 2 cm between the end of the poem ("out") and the resumption of the letter ("I wish I could"). Even as late as 1884, then, and in a note to the woman many have come to regard as her most intimate friend, Dickinson continues to record poetry and prose differently.

Also of interest is the pencil draft of a note (probably, but not certainly) to Otis Lord, written on a very thin and unlined sheet of stationery, measuring 13.2 × 15.2 cm (with rough edges indicating that the paper is no longer whole) and folded in half. It reads:[93]

Sunday –

Second of March,

and the Crow,

and Snow high

as the Spire,

and scarlet

expectations of

things that never

come, because

forever here –

"The Twilight says

to the Turret

if you want

an Existence [page break]

(left margin, reading upward: of injury too innocent)

(right margin, reading upward: when it passed know it To)

As Marta Werner correctly points out in her transcription of the same document, the writing at the left and right margins is fainter than that of the letter and slightly less finished looking; it might belong to the composition of the poems on the other side (only one of which is attended to in what follows):[94]

Circumference
thou Bride
of Awe
Possessing
thou shalt
be
Possessed by
every hallowed
Knight
That bends
a knee to
thee –
dares – to
fears – Covet
thee

re formd to nothi ng but Delig ht which

Whereas the draft letter runs more or less consistently from one margin to the other, its larger end spaces (at the right-hand edge of the text) usually explicable in terms of there being insufficient room for the next word, the draft of the poem operates according to other principles of physical organization.[95] Spaces of 3.2 cm, 6.5 cm, 3.4 cm, and 4.2 cm trail the words "Awe," "be," "Knight," and "thee," respectively—words which have nothing else in common but their placement at the close of metrical units and (in the case of "be" and "thee") their sonic equivalence, itself a function of line endings.

XII

In the last three or four years of her life, the material divisions between poetry and prose in Dickinson's drafts and letters occasionally lapsed, at least with regard to the capitalization of line beginnings. For instance, in 1880 there were twenty-six poems; of these, five include (never more than two) lines that appear from the spacing to be separate or integral but are not assigned an initial capital.[96] Most of these poems remain somewhat unfinished—that is, they include variants. In these poems the failure to capitalize one or two lines may be a consequence of their provisionality, an oversight, or a sign that Dickinson did not always have to tell herself where one line began and another ended. Or perhaps they indicate uncertainty about the status of what is being written—a lack of conviction as to whether they were good enough to be poems. Or they may reflect a slight hesitation (or indifference) as to where line division should take place. Whatever the reason, Dickinson was not as consistent about such matters as she had been during the 1860s and 1870s.

For example; the second draft of a letter to Helen Hunt Jackson, dated to about March 1885 but never sent, incorporates into the prose text two sequences classified as lyrics by Franklin. The second of these is unproblematic and occurs toward the end of the document (on the third page).[97]

> reverse of Bugles –
> Pity me, however,
> I have finished
> Ramona –
> Would that like
> Shakespeare, it
> were just published!
> Knew I how to
> pray, to intercede
> for your Foot
> were intuitive –
> but I am but
> a Pagan.
> Of God we ask
> one favor, that
> we may be for-
> given –
> For what, he is [page break]
> presumed to know –
> The Crime, from
> us, is hidden –
> Immured the whole
> of Life
> Within a magic
> Prison
> We reprimand the
> Happiness
> That too com-
> petes with Heaven –
>
> May I once
> more know,
> and that you
> are saved?

The increased vertical space (from the normal centimeter or less between lines elsewhere to 1.8 cm) after "Heaven" is a characteristic visual gesture on Dickinson's part, indicating the close of the poem and the recommencement of the prose (the final lines are also indented slightly more into the page than the ones that precede them). Such gestures are hers and hers alone; they are not imposed on her posthumously by her editors. And before the poem begins, there is 4.6 cm of space subsequent to the word "Pagan," corresponding (ordinarily) to a paragraph break and in this instance signaling an additional kind of shift.[98] The configurations brought about by the relationship between writing, space, and margins alter during the lyric portion of the letter: there is a visual pause of 8.6 cm after "given" and 7.4 cm, 9 cm, and 6.7 cm of blank space after "Life," "Prison," and "Happiness," respectively. Such interruptions in the writing cannot, logically, represent paragraph breaks (as they would elsewhere in a letter), for there is no clear change of direction or subject (for example) in the sequence "We reprimand the Happiness That too competes with Heaven." Nor does the assignation of the capital to "That" make sense in prose terms: the word does not follow a period or dash, and it has a linking function (as a relative pronoun) rather than a symbolic one (which would constitute another justification for capitalization). Once more, the routine appearance of such distinctions challenges the idea that Dickinson might have suspended generic boundaries by enfolding poems into letters without explicit verbal acknowledgment that she was doing so, for the distinct patterns of material presentation for poetry and prose would still have functioned in effect as indicators of separate generic elements.

But the last years of her production frequently complicate this picture, as shown by the first of the "poems" claimed by Johnson and Ward, and subsequently by Franklin, to be embedded in the Jackson letter:

> tell a Foot –
> Take all away
> from me, but
> leave me Ecstasy,
> And I am
> richer then, than
> all my Fellowmen –
> Is it becoming
> me to dwell
> so wealthily,
> When at my very
> Door are those
> possessing more –
> in abject poverty.
> But the strength
> to perish is some-

times withheld.
That you glance [page break]

Admittedly, some capitals here would not ordinarily be expected in the commission of a prose document—the "And" and "When" that both follow commas, for instance. Those are routine aspects of a poem's appearance in Dickinson's work, as is the space that occurs immediately after "wealthily" (its 4 cm signaling the end of a metrically determined unit). But the 4.8 cm of space after (the dash that follows) "Foot" could theoretically correspond to a paragraph break in a letter or to a pause before the switch from epistolary to lyric modes, and no gap follows "poverty" to assist the reader in recognizing when the poem ends and the prose resumes. (Because this was a draft and Dickinson herself was its first reader, the separation may not have been necessary.) Despite the relative paucity of signals (they *are* there but are not as prolific as in other documents), Johnson and Ward, as well as Franklin, manage to extract the following:[99]

> Take all away from me, but leave me Ecstasy,
> And I am richer then, than all my Fellowmen.
> Is it becoming me to dwell so wealthily,
> When at my very Door are those possessing more –
> in abject poverty.

Of course, modern editors have advantages that contemporaneous readers did not: a textual scholar (and, after her or him, any reader with a variorum edition) can recognize these lines as poetry from the five other variants that exist and use them as a guide. But because Jackson was to receive only this version, she would not have been in a position to compare manuscripts. Had she ever read this text (and there is no evidence that she did), the spacing may have helped her to locate the poem's start (after "Foot") and one line ending (after "wealthily"); the capitals would possibly have alerted her to two line beginnings ("And" and "When": "Is" is explicable grammatically, as the start of a new sentence following a punctuation mark, and "in" starts with a lowercase character). Such prompts may have given Jackson the following impression of the text's formal logic (note that I interpret the mark after "Fellowmen" as a dash; Franklin reads it as a period, as do Johnson and Ward):

> Take all away from me, but leave me Ecstasy,
> And I am richer then, than all my Fellowmen –
> Is it becoming me to dwell so wealthily,
> When at my very Door are those possessing more – in abject poverty.

Alternatively, had Jackson elided material details and read the letter aloud (as nineteenth-century readers often did), the meter and rhyme may have led her in the following direction:

> Take all away from me,
> but leave me Ecstasy,
> And I am richer then,
> than all my Fellowmen –
> Is it becoming me
> to dwell so wealthily,
> When at my very Door
> are those possessing more –
> in abject poverty.

This is closest to Franklin's eight-line version of the first draft of the poem, the original of which was written out in pencil on the reverse portion of an advertising flyer for a January sale: the upper, lower, and right edge of the paper have been cut with scissors and torn in order to create several segments for writing on. This one measures 10.1 × 17.4 cm and is folded in half:[100]

> Take all I
> have away
> But leave
> me Ecstasy
> and I am
> richer then
> than all
> my fellow
> men
> Is it becoming
> me to
> dwell so
> wealthily
> When by my
> very Door
> Are these
> possessing more
> in abject
> poverty –

Franklin chooses to represent this as eight lines, but the spaces (6.5 cm after "men," 4.4 cm after "wealthily," and 3.4 cm after "Door") and capitals ("Take," "But," "Is," "When," and "Are": "and," "than," and "in" are not capitalized, as Franklin acknowledges, though he begins new lines with them in any case) combine to suggest another possibility:

> Take all I have away
> But leave me Ecstasy and I am richer then than all my fellow men
> Is it becoming me to dwell so wealthily
> When by my very Door
> Are these possessing more in abject poverty –

The colossal difficulties faced by Dickinson's editors are nowhere better illustrated than by the following sequences, of which Johnson and Ward print only *one* (corresponding to the second, "published," version sent to Mary and Eben Jenks Loomis on 2 January 1885):[101]

> Dear friends –
> I thought
> as I saw the
> exultant Face
> and the up-
> lifted Letter,
> Take all away
> from me, but
> leave me Ecstasy,
> And I am
> richer then
> Than all my
> Fellow Men –
> Ill it becometh
> me to dwell so
> wealthily [page break]
> When at my very
> Door are those
> possessing more,
> In abject
> poverty –
> And what *is*
> Ecstasy but
> Affection and
> what is Affection
> but the Germ

of the little
Note?
A Letter is a
joy of Earth –
It is denied
the Gods –

Emily,
with love –

Johnson and Ward mistranscribe "Than" as "than," with the result that they (wrongly) produce a five-line version of the poem embedded in this text. Based on the significant capitals ("Take," "And," "Than," "Ill," "When," and "In") and the end spaces (3.8 cm after cm after "Fellow Men," 6.7 cm after "wealthily," and 7.3 cm after "poverty"), Franklin comes closest to approximating Dickinson's practices:[102]

Take all away from me, but leave me Ecstasy,
And I am richer then
Than all my Fellow Men –
Ill it becometh me to dwell so wealthily
When at my very Door are those possessing more,
In abject poverty –

The permutations are endless, but it seems that, editorial divergences and errors aside, Dickinson herself never quite made up her mind about how the lines were best to be organized or presented. One can read her indecision in different ways—as a sign of a dynamic and innovative intelligence attuned to the nuances of meaning afforded by varieties of lineation and deliberately experimenting with them; as an indication that Dickinson was never fully satisfied with the balance of the poem, which she reworked restlessly but fruitlessly to get right; or as a token of a more casual or impressionistic relationship to the lines of this poem (or to their recording in a draft letter) than to others.

XIII

In the same letter to Mary and Eben Jenks Loomis an interval of 8.1 cm follows "Note?," and the communication then closes:

A Letter is a
joy of Earth –

> It is denied
> the Gods –

Is this a two-line poem, as Johnson and Ward, as well as Franklin, believe?[103] Normally, the presence of a capital (in this case, "It") in the middle of a thought would suggest poetry; but when Dickinson came to write the same lines to Charles Clark (in a letter postmarked 19 January 1885), she dropped the initial uppercase letters entirely, writing:

> a Letter is
> a joy of Earth –
> it is denied
> the Gods –

In 1894, Mabel Loomis Todd printed the lines to Clark entirely as prose; in 1958, Johnson and Ward printed the Loomis version (L960) as poetry and the Clark version (L963) as prose.[104] In 1998, Franklin printed both versions as poems, indenting them differently from their prose contexts. Franklin proceeds on the assumption that a verbal sequence which is repeated in separate contexts and which is inscribed on at least one occasion as a poem must remain a poem even in circumstances when it is not formatted as such. Johnson and Ward allow themselves to be persuaded less by verbal recurrence and more by the differing forms of material presentation: since Dickinson omitted to assign uppercase letters in the Clark version, she was clearly not interested in having this sequence acknowledged as poetry, and they follow suit.

However one decides such issues (and each argument has its different merits), the distinctive aggregate of physical tendencies associated with the different genres of Dickinson's writing no longer seems as rigorously or as decisively applied during the 1880s (though one should also allow for the possibility that Dickinson changed her mind with respect to certain writings or that portions of writing could function equally well in different environments). Since these separate characteristics often operate as the only signposts to point readers in the direction of being able to distinguish prose from poetry, what does their failure to appear mean for this "late, brief, scene of Dickinson's writings?"[105]

For some critics, such inconsistency is innovative and improvisational and shows Dickinson slowly and deliberately moving away from standard forms (metrical lines, quatrains, finished versions) and toward embracing uniquely open ways of organization—splitting words and lines, varying stanza length, leaving variants on the page (as if they were part of the poem's formal apparatus), and rejecting traditional distinctions between genres.[106] The manuscripts are seen as embodying a principle of "choosing not choosing"—the suspension of conventional end-oriented writing practices. Dickinson, we are told, increasingly left textual choices to her readers.[107]

But is "choosing not choosing" the only scenario available for explaining the failure to distinguish between poetry and prose in some of the late correspondence? The emotional aftermath of Dickinson's bereavements (especially that of Gilbert, who died in October 1883, but starting with her father in 1874, Samuel Bowles in 1878, Josiah Holland in 1881, Charles Wadsworth in 1882, her mother in the same year, and Judge Lord in 1884); her own illness (diagnosed by her physician as having begun in late 1883 and identified by Norbert Hirschhorn and Polly Longsworth as severe primary hypertension); Susan Dickinson's illnesses in 1884 and 1885; and the terminal marital strain between Susan and Austin Dickinson in the same years—all took their toll.[108] In addition, there was a clear quantitative waning of Dickinson's creative energies: instead of the periods of greatest productivity (227 poems in 1862, 295 in 1863, and 229 in 1865), the highest numbers were 48 in 1871 and 42 in 1877 and 1884. This falling off was eventually accompanied by a cessation in the fascicle form of bookkeeping, the last one of which was collated (but not bound) in 1875.[109] If the fascicles represent completion, the setting aside of poetic documents that Dickinson regarded as finished, does her abandonment of this procedure represent a rejection of the ideals of poetic closure, the switch to a new principle of openness and multiplicity? (Which begs the further questions: do Dickinson's texts have to exist in a draft, unfinished, state for them to be regarded as indeterminate, and is indeterminacy a precondition of good poetry by Dickinson?) Is it not also possible that one of the ways in which the diminution of creative energies manifested itself (apart from the obvious reduction in production) was a weakened capacity to bring poems to a close?[110] Certainly, Dickinson would not have been the first (or last) writer to have been too tired at the end of her life to cope with the daily burden of authorship—not writing alone, but the business of revising and refining (especially since a great deal of her creative energies went into comforting others, such as Susan Dickinson). Henry James was another; Percy Lubbock reported that not "long before his death he confessed that at last he found himself too much exhausted for the 'wear and tear of discrimination.' "[111]

In an 1862 letter to Higginson, Dickinson wrote, "The Mind is so near itself – it cannot see, distinctly – and I have none to ask."[112] In her next letter, she echoed that thought and repeated her concern with being able to discriminate: "While my thought is undressed – I can make the distinction, but when I put them in the Gown – they look alike, and numb." In a subsequent letter, she writes "I had no Monarch in my life, and cannot rule myself, and when I try to organise – my little Force explodes – and leaves me bare and charred –."

It is sometimes thought that these lines are ironic or in some way posed—that Dickinson is saying that she is not interested in being organized or that the claim to disability is a masquerade deployed to disarm Higginson, by appealing to his sense of chivalry. Certainly, the sequence of excerpts from the first letter demonstrates a consistent strategy in her relations with Higginson. Whether or not she was genuine, she often told him of the difficulty of making editorial decisions about her own work and of assessing it critically. For contemporary critics (including myself), the gender aspect of this relationship unsettles, for it reflects the conventional hierarchy between men and women in the nineteenth century. To take Dickinson literally is somehow to fix her within an unequal relation of power, which is why many of us are tempted to describe the petitioning in these letters as a performance. But accepting that Dickinson may have encouraged Higginson to comment on her works is not the same as accepting the legitimacy of a gendered dynamic of power: Dickinson could have genuinely sought and received assistance without that in itself being an argument against the potentially oppressive nature of that intervention.

But what if we were to take Dickinson at her word: what if she really did want and need direction and evaluative judgment, even judgment so tentative with regard to her form that it helped to define through negation what was innovative and daring about her work? For 1862 was the same year in which, during a now celebrated flurry of notes, Dickinson sought and received advice from Susan Dickinson, her most important correspondent, on different versions of "Safe in their Alabaster Chambers." It is absolutely within the bounds of possibility that she would eventually have decided that any pressure to make decisions about final versions derived from outside the self and had more to do with social constructions of art than with the aesthetic process itself. But the lack of closure in the late works may also have been so frustrating or difficult that it took up increasing amounts of what appears in hindsight to have been a decreased imaginative drive: fewer poems took up more time, creating a law of diminishing returns that made writing less fulfilling or satisfying than before. Far from being a release, a source of joy, the number of manuscripts left in abeyance may show that not being able to finish, to close, placed a further strain on Dickinson's imaginative energies. "To great writers," wrote Walter Benjamin, "finished works weigh lighter than those fragments on which they work throughout their lives."[113]

Historically, poetry has involved a measure of selection in arriving at a presentable text. Although Dickinson may have wanted to reject such expectations in composing her own work (may even have succeeded in doing so, at least after 1875), one is obligated, in the absence of explicit evidence to the contrary, to consider alternative structures of explanation. For it is also possible that Dickinson *did* operate with similar paradigms of formal closure (or that she had sporadic doubts about any opposing view of poetry as process, as embodied fragmentation), which made the later works sites of great, unresolvable conflict and tension. If some aspects of the late manuscripts remained intractable, obstinate, refractory to Dickinson, we sanitize the discord they may once have occasioned when we translate them into elements of a fully deliberate and engaged poetic. By extension, we do Dickinson an injustice by failing to consider all the possible explanations—including the bodily—for why she might have marked "A letter is a joy of earth" as a poem in one letter but not another.

This brings us to another aspect of *Webster's* definition of a letter as "a communication made by visible characters from one person to another at a distance," and it has to do with what impact the reception of a letter may have had on its meaning. A person receiving a poem from Dickinson would theoretically be free to make crucial judgments as to its status and its connection to her or him. These judgments would not necessarily have to converge with Dickinson's own intentions, and there is no unambiguous evidence of any contemporaneous reader of a Dickinson letter reflecting on the permeability of generic boundaries when a poem was included within a letter without any explicit reference being made to the enclosure. In other words, the poem's capacity to unsettle generic boundaries would depend to some extent on the ability of the reader-recipient to process this challenge or to respond to it in the proper way.

The genre of any piece of writing is intimately related to the form of its distribution or reception: words enclosed in an envelope and addressed to a historical personage will normally be treated with more flexibility than are printed products, which is to say that one can include drawings, physical changes in the direction of the handwriting, and passages of poetry and of "poetic" writing without this inclusion necessarily disrupting the reader's sense of generic propriety and without these innovations being understood to have implications for literature generally. Moreover, the kinds of material signals given by Dickinson's forms of inscription do not support the idea that she was attempting to defamiliarize received certainties about generic boundaries: even when Dickinson does not separate the poem physically (as an enclosure on a separate page) from the rest of the letter, there will often be a noticeable shift in the physical appearance of the letter which accompanies and effectively announces the change of genre. In other words, the inclusion of a poem in a letter does not necessarily promote a generically transgressive kind of writing.

Nor does it always indicate that the recipient of the poem was its subject, addressee, or implied reader. That the same Dickinson poem could be sent to multiple recipients, whereas letters never were, suggests a difference between poems and epistolary prose that has less to do with some mysterious and inherent quality (the essence of poetry being somehow superior to the essence of prose) and more to do with different uses or functions—not what one is and the other is not but what one does and to whom it is addressed.[114] Conventionally, letters are written with a definite individual in mind, whereas a lyric (at least potentially) addresses a wider audience—not one reader but a readership.[115] One of the differences between a letter and a poem is that the former is intended to operate within a specific relation, whereas this relation is more diffuse in literature. (There is perhaps no better illustration of this difference than when Dickinson complains to Elizabeth Holland in late 1866 about having received a letter that was addressed to both her and Lavinia: "A mutual plum is not a plum," she writes, then continues, "Send no union letters.")[116] Letters and poems have slightly different social functions, then: that a poem is sent in or as a letter does not stop it from being a poem. Instead, the enfolding of lyric writing within epistolary contexts may be understood as a very specific and specialized form of publication or usage—but not a final alignment of a poem's meanings.[117]

Jonathan Culler makes a useful comment about letters and the social network in which they take place. The letter, he writes, "is directly inscribed in a communicative circuit and depends on external contexts whose relevance we cannot deny even if we are ignorant of them. The 'I' of the letter is an empirical individual, as is the 'You' whom it addresses; it was written at a particular time and in a situation to which it refers; and to interpret the letter is to adduce those contexts so as to read it as a specific temporal and individual act."[118] The act of enfolding a poem in a letter might, in theory, relate the poem more definitely to the individual receiving it, and some poems by Dickinson do reflect on the nature of her friendship with an individual and may not transcend that friendship. By contrast, poems can and do address several people at the same time. For example, if we take Walter Raleigh's "If all the world and love were young," we can identify a number of different, but not exclusive, audiences: an imagined reader/listener within the text; Christopher Marlowe, to whose poem "Come live with me and be my love" this one replies; the circle of friends who read the poem in manuscript; and those who read the poem outside the circle. Though including a poem in a letter may appear to close down the number of readerly strata, the poem can still be read in different contexts of reception, especially since evidence indicates that Dickinson sent poems to individuals *and* collected them in fascicles, which were never shown and which appear to have been designed with a wider readership in mind. One might compare the poem to a greeting card: there is a standard message, usually in verse, to which a handwritten salutation and signature are appended.

The card is then delivered and read, and although the core verse is not in itself occasioned by the individual relationships within which it is actualized or performed, it is given significance within that relationship by having been chosen and sent by one person (usually on the grounds that it is relevant in some way to that relationship or its recipient) and received by another, and thus personalized. But the card predates and survives its specific usage, in the same way that the majority of Dickinson's lyrics precede and outlive the circumstances of their occasional distribution in letters.

Literature emerges from identifiable historical and biographical contexts, but it also transcends them in ways that letters do not have to.[119] Letters derive much of their significance from being written by "one person"; authors spend much of their time persuading us that they are *not* the speaker or subject of the work—that the "I" is (presumably or possibly) a persona. "When I state myself, as the Representative of the Verse – it does not mean – me – but a supposed person," writes Dickinson to Higginson.[120] And when she first writes to him, she asks, "Are you too deeply occupied to say if my Verse is alive," not whether her epistolary style needed surgery. Although she sent "Safe in their Alabaster Chambers" to Susan and made changes to it at her request, there is no record of her ever having asked for similar comments about a letter. Thus, while I accept that "This is my letter to the World" is *written* by the historical character known as Emily Dickinson, I would also contend that it is not necessarily *spoken* by her. Or, to put it another way, some of the information that I might expect from a private letter is missing from the poem, including the most important part, the contents of the message. Indeed, the poem's success (to me) lies in the tension between its status as a personal document (Emily Dickinson unburdening herself to the world) and a fictive or imagined one (Emily Dickinson pretending to be someone who unburdens herself), between the promise of intimacy and its postponement. The author of a poem may acknowledge that the work is hers (Dickinson almost invariably signs poems sent to Susan), but she can distance herself from its contents more easily than she can from the contents of a letter; fiction always enables the writer to exercise a displacement of personality, a kind of anonymity. As we saw in the earlier chapter on Bowles, Dickinson appears several times to introduce a poem in the middle of a letter, thus signaling the difference. Her reference to the "Psalmist's sonnet," for example, may be partly a joke (perhaps a private one), but it is also a disguise, a suggestion that the poem's speaker is not to be confused with her.

Though I assume there to be a difference between Dickinson's poems and letters, that difference is not qualitative. Theoretical speculations notwithstanding, there is no simple answer to Marta Werner's question about poems and letters—for four paragraphs of epistolary prose will form a rule (of subject matter, of style, of rhythm) that the fifth one will break. Instead, the distinction has something to do with Dickinson's own methods of presentation, which are subtly but consistently modified at those points which coincide with the initiation of a poem within a letter. A series of strictly material coordinates helps readers to recognize the change, and amounts to generic separation: not only meter and rhyme, but also the sustained use of meter and rhyme accompanied by the deployment of nonessential capitals, as well as the presence of redundant horizontal spaces and vertical intervals that correspond to lines and stanzas, not to sentences and paragraphs. Dickinson's habits of presentation or layout change when she writes poems, showing that she at least continued to make a distinction between epistolary and lyric procedures of organization. We may never know exactly why she did so, but we are obliged to acknowledge that she did. But perhaps one of the reasons more recent readers have become slightly skeptical about such differences is, first, that the demarcation is not as graphically compact, tidy, and dramatic as in printed editions of her correspondence and, second, that the use of meter and rhyme is in itself remarkably varied. And it is toward such splendid and structured polyphony that I turn in the chapters that follow.

CHAPTER FIVE

"The Ear is the Last Face"

The Manuscript as Archive of Rhythm and Rhyme

The material is one thing, the poetry another.

—F. R. Leavis, *The Common Pursuit*

If all the contents of a poet's waste-basket were taken out and printed, and issued in a volume, one result would be that the things which he had disowned would be read by many to whom the great things he had written would be unknown.

—Alfred, Lord Tennyson

THE KINDS of letters that were delivered to private and family boxes in nineteenth-century Amherst varied considerably in terms of size and contents. At the beginning of the century, letters were often folded, with the noninscribed side of the paper facing outward, then sealed with wax, to form an envelope. These could be fairly standard in size (8 × 12.5 cm in the case of a letter from Pelham, Massachusetts, to the "Overseers of [the] Poor Farm, Wilbraham, Ma," dated 4 December 1843; 8 × 13 cm in the case of a letter from Newark, New Jersey, to Ithamar Conkey in Pelham, dated 17 December 1816).[1] In the case of a bifolium (a sheet of paper folded during manufacture to make two leaves, or four pages for writing), such as that sent by Caleb H. Rice from Amherst to Uriel Montague in Westborough, dated 19 March 1846 and measuring 20.2 cm wide and 25.5 cm high, only the first (outer) page is written on, and it is then folded twice vertically and twice horizontally to form an envelope from the last (outer) page, measuring 12.8 cm wide and 7.5 cm high.[2] Of four writing surfaces, then, two remained unused, which was not entirely uncommon, given that the largest proportion of correspondence, then as now, were business letters. As the century progressed, stamps and separate envelopes became more widespread (a collection of nineteenth-century envelopes at the Jones Library of Amherst, for instance, includes samples that are 6.5 × 11.5 cm, 6.5 × 10.5 cm, 7 × 13 cm, 7 × 10.8 cm, 7.5 × 10.5 cm, and 8 × 14 cm), while stationery became more uniformly smaller: much of the paper used by Dickinson for the fascicles was between 12 and 13 cm wide and between 20 and 21 cm high.[3] Advertising circulars and handbills also found their way into postboxes, such as those for "Doctor Speer's Chemical OPO-DELDOC" (17 × 26 cm) and "Wakefield's HAND CORN PLANTER" (16.4 × 30 cm), among others.[4]

Advertising flyers were usually printed on only one side of the paper, leaving the other side blank. Here is a detail from one:

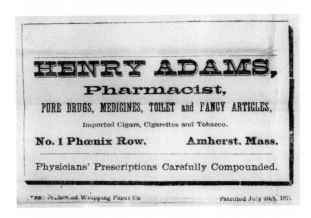

Emily Dickinson, famously, recycled such unused spaces during the initial composition of her poems and letters. Draft poems and letters appeared on abandoned letters; advertising circulars and flyers (for books, sales, etc.); bills for the delivery of milk; concert programs; the torn corners of magazines; dust jackets; the insides of slit envelopes (ordinary and telegram) and on envelope flaps; the flyleaves of books; the margins from book pages, legal forms, and magazines; stationery (quadrille, nonruled, and ruled); notebook leaves; pink paper bills; meeting programs; bits of wrappers (from shops and from products) and strips of wrapping paper (white and brown). Even a one-page letter would have no writing on the reverse side, leaving lots of room for the self-administered dictation of initial ideas and images.

Many of Dickinson's drafts were composed on scraps of paper (and nor was she the only one to use paper so: in 1857, her friend Joseph Lyman, short of paper, "expounded an envelope that had just come from Emily and used it to write his fiancée").[5] Dickinson's "His Mind like Fabrics of the East" is written on two fragments of stationery (one cream and blue-ruled, the other gray-ruled) pinned together.[6] "His Mansion in the Pool" is a pencil draft (on blue-ruled stationery) with trial lines and words for other poems attached to it on a pinned fragment of heavier stationery. "How happy is the little stone" is a pencil draft written on two fragments (the first blue-ruled, with part of a letter from George Montague on the verso; the second a slip of watermarked sta-

tionery) that were pinned together. A pencil draft of "I noticed People disap-
peared" is written on two pinned stationery fragments. The pencil draft of
"Summer – we all have seen" is composed on a leaf of stationery, with alter-
natives on a fragment of quadrille stationery; these were pinned together.
"Tell as a Marksman – were forgotten" is written on two leaves of stationery
pinned together: one blue-ruled, the other monogrammed (with a capital *T*)
and with a false start ("My Dear Sir") by someone else.[7] "The Clover's simple
Fame" is a pencil draft with alternatives, composed on two pinned fragments
of stationery (blue-ruled and watermarked "A PIRIE + SONS" 1862).[8] "The
Gentian has a parched Corolla" exists as a pencil draft, with alternatives, on
two fragments that were attached by pin: one, a blue-ruled sheet with a note
from Austin on the verso, and the other, also blue-ruled with an embossment
and an address by Lavinia on the verso. "The Infinite a sudden Guest" is a
pencil copy on two pinned fragments of stationery (one watermarked "A PIRIE
+ SONS," the other quadrille). The informality of such drafts (they are pinned,
not sewn together) is confirmed by incidental details—the presence of trial
signatures in pencil and ink, for instance (as in autographs 216, 242, 254, 255,
259, 302, and 502 at Amherst College).

Nor was Dickinson the only nineteenth-century poet to organize her drafts
in such a manner. Coleridge's notebooks include one that is made of eight
small scraps of paper that are pinned together and another two where the
pages (measuring 2.5 by 4.5 inches) are sewn together with crochet cotton.[9]
Hallam Tennyson's *Memoirs* runs to ten manuscript volumes; roughly "fas-
tened to the foolscap pages with ordinary dressmaker's pins is an approxi-
mately chronological sequence of family records, unpublished poems, corre-
spondence, hand-copied commentaries on Tennyson and his work from both
published and unpublished sources, and cuttings and tear-sheets from news-
papers and magazines."[10] Some of John Clare's correspondence began as
drafts written on scraps of paper.[11] Thomas Hardy is known to have had a
drawer of drafts, notes, and fragments, which he would revise and expand into
poems, letters, or reviews, according to request. Notebooks contained epithets
that could be worked up into lyrics or something larger.[12] And Marcel Proust,
who wrote at night (as Dickinson also appears to have done, judging from the
internal evidence of letters), often used little slips of paper, *paperoles* and *bec-
quets*, at various stages of the composition process.[13] The papers of Susan
Dickinson are full of clippings and drawings, and those of Otis Lord contain
sketches improvised on (among other things) envelopes, specimens of station-
ery, Orders for the Day for the House of Representatives, and an act of the
Boston Wesleyan Association.[14]

Among the more interesting of these drafts, according to recent commen-
tators, are those inscribed on envelopes, such as Fr1405, "Long Years apart

– can make no," which was written around 1876 on the inside of a split enve-
lope that had been addressed to "Miss Vinnie Dickinson."[15]

The image above shows an alternative for the third and fourth lines of
the poem ("The absence of the Witch does not / Invalidate the spell"). The
hyphen or dash between "In" and "validates" is necessitated by the edges
of the envelope intervening to cause a gap between those sections of the
word, and is a reflex gesture: it indicates that the segments are meant to be
linked, not separated (for all the other gaps in the same portion of the sur-
face writing indicate such separation—"Who [gap] says," for example—
meaning that the introduction of a dash for the same purpose would be su-
perfluous). This fragment is intriguing, then, because it echoes the proce-
dure elsewhere in Dickinson's writings whereby word splits that are
brought about by material circumstances (such as arriving at the edge of the
page before the word is completed) are *usually* signaled as accidental by a
hyphen or dash being attached to the first section of the word, as in
"acclima- / ted" (in Fr1423) or "accommo- / date" (in Fr671; of the ap-
proximately 205 examples of simple word division, about 26—roughly 10
percent—are not marked with dashes).[16] Yet again, the physical evidence of
Dickinson's handwriting would seem to contradict the thesis that word di-
visions in her poetry were deliberate.

Envelopes and envelope flaps have attracted a great deal of critical attention
in the past decade. In a lecture on the importance of Dickinson's manuscripts,
given at Amherst College in 1999, Ellen Louise Hart circulated a transcription
of the holograph for Fr1292 (A 252), in which she included the outline of the
section of envelope on which it was written. The original is triangular in
shape, approximately 11.5 cm in length at the top, and then tapering to a
corner at the bottom:

> In   this   short   Life
> that only lasts an hour
> merely
> How much – how
> little – is
> within our
> power

On the handout that accompanied the lecture, Hart wrote: "This had to be removed from the envelope. This was a 'writing surface' selected for its dimensions and angles."[17] And she went on to point out that the flap was torn along one side (where it had been separated from the rest of the envelope) and along the edges that come together to form the inverted "V" of the top (where the adhesive or sealing agent is normally affixed). The implication of the first part of this statement is that the removal was aesthetically motivated and related to this specific poem (as opposed to a standard practice whereby spare pieces of paper were set aside for general use); in this case, the flap was taken from the envelope with the purpose of providing a fit base for the poem's contents. But nineteenth-century envelopes, much like our own, came in a variety of shapes and sizes and could be opened in just as many ways. Some did not come with the adhesive already applied, and had to be glued shut by the writer after the letter was written and inserted; others were glued during the process of manufacture and had to be moistened to be closed. The quality of glue varied too: the stronger the bond, the more likely that there would be tearing of some kind during opening. Weaker adhesive meant that the letter would open easily and leave no marks. Recipients could open letters by inserting a sharp instrument underneath the rear flap and slitting along the top; a sharp knife would leave a fairly even edge, whereas a blunt letter-opener or even a finger would leave an erratic edge. To give specific examples, an envelope addressed in 1877 by Mary W. Mitchell to Ellen T. Emerson, Concord, Massachussets, and stamped "Ploughkeepsie, 28 April, 6 pm," is ripped along the top edge, very unevenly, and to such an extent that there is a vertical tear on the rear flap.[18] An envelope addressed by Ralph Waldo Emerson to John Haskins, Esq., Concord, and dated 25 September 1849 is mostly intact, a portion of the rear flap having been cut with small scissors near the bottom to release it from the seal.[19]

In the case of A 252 (Fr1292), it is difficult to reconstruct the chronology of its opening. The manuscript original (at Amherst College) shows that the envelope had adhesive applied during the process of manufacture which left marks of approximately 3.65 cm at each side of the flap as it slants toward the bottom and then intersects. Portions of the paper beneath this bonded surface are very thin and ragged; clearly, some paper remained stuck to the envelope, either during the process of opening the original letter or removing the flap for later use.

Hart makes a single path of intention out of a much more complicated and perhaps accidental process. Her flap is carefully selected and then crafted to create a diminishing sense of space, a closing down of options, that reflects the poem's theme exactly. But the poem is short, and the surviving material evidence seems to indicate that Dickinson saved all kinds of scraps and fragments—including envelope flaps—for small bursts of inspiration. "Society for me my misery" (Fr1195A) is written on such a flap, for instance, as is "The vastest earthly Day" (Fr1323A).[20] One wonders, then, if the paper's dimensions are tailored to this poem in particular, or if it would have been useful for a *kind* of writing, either a phase in the process of composition or a more diminutive type of poetry. One wonders, too, if the shape is as deliberate as Hart makes it out to be. Depending on the quality of the glue, the pressure with which the flap was closed, and the care and method of opening, the edge could have been quite irregular.

A relationship between the removal of a flap and the inscription of a poem presupposes a greater degree of careful deliberation than the flaps themselves provide evidence for. It is always possible that flaps were convenient for casual notes to friends—in other words, that their usefulness for Dickinson lay in matters of size and informality (or usage, not mimesis). In an interview from the 1930s, Gertrude Graves, the daughter of Dickinson's cousin John, recalled that "Cousin Emily sent him one of her little three-cornered notes with a beautiful sprig of white jasmine."[21] Speculation aside, we can say with some certainty that Dickinson saved used envelopes for composing or recording revisions—many of her drafts survive in this form, showing that envelopes and parts of envelopes were regarded as spare paper and not to be wasted. "Had we known the Ton she bore" (Fr1185A; about 1870) is written on the inside of an envelope, which has been completely opened out to provide a larger surface area on which to write. In this instance, the flap had been removed, presumably because it was too uneven to write on or because Dickinson wanted to preserve it for smaller acts of recording.[22] "Oh Sumptuous moment" (Fr1186A; about 1870) is written on the inside of an envelope addressed to "Mrs Helen Hunt."[23] "Look back on Time" (Fr1251; about 1872) is written on an envelope fragment, with a missing flap.[24] "As old as Woe" (Fr1259; about 1872) is similarly inscribed on an inner envelope, with no flap. "I never hear that one is dead" (Fr1325; about 1874) is written in pencil on both sides of an envelope incompletely addressed by Lavinia: again, the flap is missing. "Had we our senses" (Fr1310; about 1873) however, has its flap attached: it is intact, and even.[25] "Long Years apart" (Fr1405; about 1876) is written on both sides of an envelope addressed to "Miss Vinnie Dickinson."[26] "It came his turn to beg" (Fr1519; about 1880) is written on the inside of a Western Union telegram addressed to "Vinnie Dickinson / Care Judge Lord."[27] "On that specific Pillow" (Fr1554; about 1881) is partly written on the inside of an envelope, which is fixed with a pin to a scrap of paper to create two clean surfaces.[28] "Pompless no life" (Fr1594B; about 1882) is composed on an envelope addressed by Otis Lord to "Misses Emily and Vinnie Dickinson."[29] This list illustrates that people other than Dickinson saved paper on her behalf; it also suggests that the condition and shape of the paper was not necessarily of her own doing. Additionally, none of these examples exhibit the kind of organic connection Hart claims for "In this short Life"—that between what is written and the shape of the space in which it is written.

What is troubling, finally, about the organicist argument is how much it appears to close down the poem's options. In a sense, the meaning of the poem is modified by its shape: what it may be construed as saying is that we have some power as long as we are alive, but that power and life diminish as the poem (and time) advances. With the print version (Fr1292), the poem is more open:

> In this short Life that only lasts an hour
> How much – how little – is within our power

The couplet already has that sense of brevity which Dickinson wants to communicate; but unlike the envelope variant, it maintains a sense of dynamic balance: "hour" (with its connotations of transience) is brought into contact and conflict with "power" (an important word that slightly mitigates the negative implications of the sequence of "much" and "little"). Whereas the envelope suggests a rapidly diminishing set of options, the couplet allows for other, unstated, opportunities beyond the end of the poem's—and the speaker's—life.

Comments made at the 1999 conference of the Emily Dickinson International Society at Mount Holyoke appeared to underscore the hypothesis of an organic relationship between the substance or subject of certain pieces of writing by Dickinson, the form of their inscription, and the particular paper on which they appear. Ellen Hart, again, argued that the draft variant identified by Franklin as Fr1350B, "The Mushroom is the Elf of Plants," was best understood in the context of its original appearance: it was written in pencil inside "a yellow envelope, set on point so that the physical measure increases then diminishes in length."[30] Such an argument is difficult to prove or disprove: ultimately, it depends rather arbitrarily on whether the reader can accept that the shape of the paper resembles (in abstract or mimetic form) that of a mushroom, or the physical process of a mushroom's growth, and whether such appearances make the poem any more interesting. Hart went on to contend that Franklin had no good reason to standardize the lines of the poem in his 1998 *Poems of Emily Dickinson*. At the same time, Hart left unclear why the variant should *not* have been standardized, making no attempt to explain the specific difference autograph presentation might have made to our understanding.[31]

The poem Fr1350 exists in six separate editions, three of which are partial and one lost. Hart's preference is for version B, which has eight lines and seems to have been a draft (the final version has twenty lines). If B is simply a trial effort, either an attempt at working out the first two quatrains or all that remains of a much larger draft (of sixteen or perhaps twenty lines), how does this influence our understanding of the form of its inscription? And if the angle of inscription is deliberate, in what way? Is it to suggest a mushroom, or to provide more continuous space for writing? For this envelope has had its flap removed, which creates a long and shallow "V" shape along the top: had Dickinson written horizontally along this surface, her writing would have been broken by the gap left by the missing flap. Turned on its side, it was possible to write without interruption. In another instance, "I never hear that one is dead" (Fr1325), written on both sides of an envelope where the flap is still attached, Dickinson positioned the surface on its side, placing the flap to her left in order to write on it:

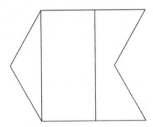

The variants on the reverse side, where there is no flap, are similarly inscribed: written with the flap pointing upward, they would have been broken by the shallow, inverted *V*-shaped opening at the bottom.[32]

A draft of "Summer laid her simple Hat" (Fr1411A) is also written on the inside of an envelope.[33] The flap is still attached, but the envelope has a pattern of slanting lines which intersect with each other to form continuous "X" patterns (rather than "+"). Dickinson uses the lines that are approximately at the same angle as the flap to write on; to read her writing, therefore, one must slant the envelope, as for "The Mushroom is the Elf of Plants." The angle of the writing is determined by the angle of the lines of the paper, however: it is prompted by the material but has no meaning in itself. Indeed, the poem looks very similar to "The Mushroom" except that it ends where the mushroom poem begins—at the angle of the "V" formed by the bottom and lateral edges of the envelope, at the opposite end from the flap. Still another example of writing that is slanted because of the surface dimensions of the inner envelope is "'Twas later when the summer went" (Fr1312).[34] The flap points again to the left: Dickinson positions her writing so that it is parallel with the upper- most edge of the flap and slightly below the area where the glue has been attached. The poem continues at this angle right across the envelope, avoiding a hole where a previously affixed stamp has been cut out, and closing at the opposite end, in bilaterally diminishing space, with:

Winter   came

Yet   that   pa-

thetic Pendulum

m

Keeps

Esoteric

Time.

e

A draft of "We talked with each other about each other" (Fr1506A) is inscribed on another envelope and is written at an angle.[35] Only a fragment of the flap remains attached to the left side: Dickinson begins here, parallel to what remains of the upper edge, and fits in "We / talked with / each other / about each / other," thus making the best possible use of the space available to her.[36] All these examples, such as "The Mushroom is the Elf of Plants," are written at angles, and all have physical reasons for appearing as they do.

Perhaps most crucial, "The Mushroom is the Elf of Plants" is not written on an ordinary postal envelope. On its other side is the printed design of a mortar and pestle, a conventional nineteenth-century emblem for an apothe- cary or druggist. (Pharmacist Henry Adams, of Phoenix Row in Amherst, used a similar symbol.)[37] The envelope paper is slightly thicker than normal, and at one end there are two angled sections of paper that overlap to form a shallow "V" shape. The inner edges of both sit up slightly, especially at the base, and this (together with their thickness) makes them awkward to write across. By setting the envelope on point, Dickinson avoided having to write across these very often; as it is, one can see her avoiding the edges at those junctures where her writing does come close to them (for example, where the two sections meet, when she writes "it [edge] is not / At M [edge] orning"). These features of the paper make it at least feasible that "The Mushroom is the Elf of Plants" is inscribed in such a way to make as much of the page available for physically unobstructed writing as possible. Indeed, the accumulated weight of evidence suggested by the nonsemantic recourse to envelopes generally makes this the more likely of the two scenarios.

Dickinson's eagerness to avoid writing across the edges of specific envelopes can be seen in "The Ditch is dear to the Drunken man" (Fr1679).[38] Dickinson writes on the inside of an envelope addressed to Frank Gilbert (Susan Dickinson's brother) and set on its side with the flap pointing to the right; she writes horizontally up to and including the line "Oblivion bending over him" (which is inscribed as two rows, with the break after "bending"). The paper was then repositioned, with a triangular section at the left side of the base, furthest away from the flap (now pointing up) serving for the last line ("And Honor leagues away"). The triangle on the right was used for variants:

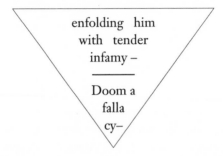

This variation in shape is not meant to affect the poem's meaning: it facilitates the physical act of writing by allowing Dickinson a confined space in which to write without material interruption. Had she written vertically, instead of at an angle, she would have had to write across the edges of the two sections.

I

At one level, the claim that the shape of a piece of paper is designed to have an impact on its meaning seems to demonstrate an extreme kind of formalism—a belief that every detail of a poem's presentational modes is appropriate to its contents.[39] The motivation behind such assumptions is nonetheless unimpeachably genuine: it exists as a scrupulously scholarly reaction against repeated historical misrepresentations of Emily Dickinson's writings. But what if the notion that Dickinson's poems and her manuscripts are one and the same with respect to their material details continues rather than combats such misrepresentations? In what follows, I want to assess the merits of different theories of editing poetry, not by looking at the history of a particular poem's appearances in the world (as in the opening chapter) but by applying such theories to a single autograph. In doing so, I want to provide the reader with a rubric for independently approaching Dickinson's manuscripts: the purpose is to explore the feasibility or usefulness of distinguishing between the inadvertences and substantives of material presentation. The arguments rehearsed and examined here are further intended to form a theoretical and methodological basis for the chapter that follows, in which I look at the metrical characteristics of poems in a single sequence, Fascicle 20, which I have chosen because it was collated around the autumn of 1862 when Dickinson would have been at the height of her poetic maturity and powers; it is thought that the period from 1862 through 1865 coincided with her largest creative enterprise and output.[40]

The poem I will discuss here is Fr1265 (A 479), "Through what transports of Patience," which exists in a variety of different editorial treatments. Like the documents examined at the beginning of this chapter, Dickinson wrote this rough pencil draft on the inside of a partial envelope, addressed by Judge Otis Lord to "Miss Emily Dickinson, / Care Hon. Edward Dickinson, / Amherst, – / Mass." (the line represented here as a dash after Amherst begins as early as the letter *r*, and extends through the *s* and the crossbar of the *t* and then beyond the word, curling back and below on itself slightly at the end). The envelope measures approximately 13.9 cm in width and 8 cm in height; it has a three-cent stamp in the upper left corner of the addressed side and is postmarked "SALEM / NOV / 10 / MASS." When slit open, a small portion of the bottom reverse side of the envelope remained attached to the addressed side. Dickinson then turned the slit envelope around and on its side (so that it became 8 cm in width, and the stamp would be on the reverse side of the upper right corner of the paper on which she wrote). For ease of cross-reference, I have added numbers to the rows of the manuscript:

1. Through what
2. transports of
3. Patience
4. I reached the
5. stolid Bliss
6. To breathe my
7. Blank without
8. thee
9. Attest me this
10. and this –
11. By that bleak

12. Exultation
13. I won as
14. near as this
15. Thy privilege
16. of dying
17. Abbreviate me
18. this
19. Remit me this
20. And this

The following is a copy of Franklin's version, Fr1265, together with his editorial apparatus for the poem (where he records the line division of the original, as well as variants and other features):

> Through what transports of Patience
> I reached the stolid Bliss
> To breathe my Blank without thee
> Attest me this and this –
> By that bleak exultation
> I won as near as this
> Thy privilege of dying
> Abbreviate me this

4] Remit me this and this   6 this] *the i over another letter, perhaps* <i>

Division 1 what | 1 of | 2 the | 3 my | 3 without | 4 me this |
5 bleak | 6 won as | privilege | 8 me | *alt* 4 me this |

Distinguishing between upper- and lowercase letters in Dickinson's manuscripts is necessary given that, as the handwriting continuously evinces, she assigned capitals to words at the beginning of a verse, or poetic, line; it is also a notoriously difficult task. In Franklin's 1998 print edition of the poem, for instance, he represents "exultation" in row 12 with an initial lowercase vowel, when it seems closer to a capital (it looks like a slightly tilted Σ shape). Comparison with other letters in this document alone is not helpful—there are no other words that begin with *e* or *E*, and none of the miniscule *e* shapes elsewhere in the poem are inscribed in any way resembling a capital. Arguing from the evidence of this specific original in isolation would thus lead to the conclusion that the *e* at the beginning of "exultation / Exultation" was meant to be capitalized—and Marta Werner understandably transcribes it thus in her version of the poem in *Emily Dickinson's Open Folios*. But in defense of

Franklin—and Johnson before him—Dickinson casually switched back and forth between closed (*e*) and open (*ε*) shapes for lowercase initial letters, such that capitalization is supremely difficult to judge. Indeed, the problems of the handwriting are well illustrated by the different editorial versions of this poem: Werner and Franklin disagree about the *T/t* at the start of row 6 in the autograph (Werner reads it as being lowercase) and transcribe the three-letter word in row 13 differently too (Werner sees "now," Franklin "won").[41] In the manuscript, there appears to be a pattern whereby the horizontal stroke in a capital *T* extends an equal or similar distance on either side from the vertical stroke. With the minuscule *t*, the horizontal stroke is situated slightly higher on the vertical one and is placed mainly on the right-hand side (at times, as with "transports" in row 2 and "the" in row 4, the horizontal stroke fails to intersect with the vertical at all).

Such considerations are significant to the extent that they help us to gauge the accuracy of Franklin's design, which alters an eighteen-row original to an eight-line poem in the variorum.[42] If we proceed from the assumption that Dickinson's assignation of capitals is not entirely arbitrary, then we can conjecture from the manuscript that rows 2, 5, 8, 10, 14, 16, and 18 might not represent autonomous and integral lines (since Dickinson did not assign them capitals). We can thus reconfigure the rows of the autograph so that words beginning in uppercase coincide with line beginnings, and words in uniform lowercase are enfolded within the previous line:

1. Through what transports of
2. Patience
3. I reached the stolid Bliss
4. To breathe my
5. Blank without thee
6. Attest me this and this –
7. By that bleak
8. Exultation
9. I won as near as this
10. Thy privilege of dying
11. Abbreviate me this

The extent to which this arrangement can be said to be satisfactory lies in its demonstrated consistency in the use of capitals (with the exception of "Bliss" in the third line). In addition, a pattern of rhyme emerges, or begins to emerge: in the first nine verses, there is an instance of rhyme every third line. The fact that the final rhyme occurs only two lines after the penultimate one may be taken as an intensification of the speaker's emotional state: the rhyme accelerates as her response to the experiences described becomes more desperate, insistent, or urgent.

Yet, aspects of the poem remain puzzling. The isolation of the words "Patience" and "Exultation" seems acceptable on the grounds that it heightens their impact, but one wonders, then, why "Bliss" did not receive a similar emphasis. Or, to put it another way, if "Bliss" is initially capitalized for reasons of emphasis, then it follows that "Patience" and "Exultation" (and perhaps "Blank") may be capitalized for similar reasons—to signal prominence and not lineal separation. Furthermore, the physical division of "bleak" and "Exultation" seems to lessen the effect of combining words with such contrary associations in the first place. Part of Dickinson's genius, it seems to me, is phrasal: one remembers not just single words (such as "circumference") but unusual or strikingly innovative verbal sequences, such as "transports of Patience" or "privilege of dying." What exactly is the logic, one might then ask, of the first of these sequences being fractured at a different point from the other? Grammatically speaking, the two phrases are very similar, though "dying" is not a noun but a verb that is also made into a noun by the gerund (the process is called "nominalization"). The line intersections have distinct repercussions, however: in the first, "transports of / Patience," the functional head or center of the phrase, that is, the preposition "of," is separated from its lexical head or center, "Patience." In the second, "Thy privilege / of dying," the functional and lexical heads are kept together. The first sequence is ungrammatical: the preposition has no function unless it is connected to the noun. Of course, the separation may be determined by aesthetic factors, but that is not the issue; the issue is that the physical transcription of two similar types of phrase is not consistent. And this inconsistency suggests that either Dickinson was experimenting at very minute lexical and graphic levels in her manuscripts or she was indifferent to aspects of lineation at those particular points in her poem.

Perhaps the more pertinent question is what is to be gained aesthetically by the distinct separation of the two phrases. One concedes that the spatial arrangement in the autograph of rows 2 and 3 postpones the disclosure of the noun in a way that might reinforce its meaning, so that the reader is forced to wait, to endure delay. But the effect is also to close down some of the aural possibilities. The progression "transports of Patience" in Franklin's edition of the poem can be spoken as it reads *or* as "transports of [pause] Patience," but if we insist on the legitimacy of Dickinson's layout, then "transports of / Patience" *must* be read as "transports of [pause] Patience."

Arguments about the semantic nuances of different physical arrangements in a sequence of lines will always be subjective, to some extent. But evidence in the handwritten original reminds us that capitalization serves two functions for Dickinson: the marking of a separate line or some kind of semantic high-lighting. If we read through the poem with this distinction in mind, then the possibility arises that rows 2, 5, and 8 may not have been intended to be separate. And if we accept this, then there are at least three ways of under-standing the meaning of the poem's appearances, all apparently valid. The first, which I take to be Hart and Smith's (though perhaps not Werner's) position, is that we regard the manuscript layout as physically and intellectu-ally integral in every respect (meaning that we must reproduce it as it stands). The second is that we think of the system of inscription as indicating a less literal layout closer to the eleven-line edition. The third is that the poem contains a variety of material, metrical, and aural codes that together point to a design which may or may not correspond to the layout of the original. In the instance of this poem, the totality of relations suggested by capitals, rhyme, and meter result in a poem that matches Franklin's understanding of it in almost every respect.

1. Through what transports of Patience
2. I reached the stolid Bliss
3. To breathe my Blank without thee
4. Attest me this and this –
5. By that bleak Exultation
6. I won as near as this
7. Thy privilege of dying
8. Abbreviate me this

The possibility of rhythm or meter in the lyric (the two terms may be under-stood to have related but not identical meanings) is not something that I have touched on as yet. In the manuscript original, only row 9 seems to conform to any metrical pattern (iambic dimeter).[43] Certainly, the poem's graphic design does not correspond to a regular pattern of rhythm: rows 2, 3, and 5, for instance, begin with heavily stressed syllables, while rows 6, 8, 9, and 10 com-mence with very light stresses. The row endings of the autograph do not demonstrate any accentual regularity either: the first four rows all close weakly, but "Bliss" at the end of row 5 is firmly stressed. Meter is intermittent at best in the diplomatic, eleven-line version: iambic trimeter in lines 3 and 6, as well as inclusively in lines 9 to 11.[44] Looking at the version that most closely resembles Franklin's, however, one detects something approximating iambic trimeter in the majority of lines. There is a regular syllabic pattern as well: the lines alternate between seven and six syllables. In other words, a regular pat-tern occurs whereby odd lines appear to be hypermetric, creating what might be thought of as a pleasant metrical variation.[45] Finally, a regular pattern of *abcb* rhyme comes to the surface, which is perhaps most important because rhyme "is used as a structural device in English verse to mark the end of metrical units or lines."[46] The convergence of all these factors (capitalization, number of syllables, meter, and rhyme) strongly suggests the editorial propriety of showing that Dickinson's eighteen-row original was meant to be an eight-line poem.

Of course, metrical consistency does not rule out the possibility that Dickinson might have wanted to complicate this scheme by the poem's visual organization. Poets do use a variety of techniques to interrupt meter: caesura and enjambment, singly or together, create pauses and continuities that prevent a poem from being too monotonous. In theory at least, it seems possible—and certainly acceptable—that Dickinson's graphic arrangements act to disrupt an excessive regularity of rhythm or to record a different kind of rhythm. The layout may also correspond to a notational system for signaling delays in the spoken delivery of the poem. For this theory to work, however, one has to accept that it is a *general* strategy: the poem as a whole reads less predictably because of its visual design. As soon as one begins to read the lineation at the specific level, as an extra dimension of the way in which a line or phrase communicates meaning, then problems begin to emerge. For if I accept in principle that "I reached the" enacts the difficulty of reaching, then what does "I won as" mean? Is this another ironic performance of winning (meaning that the line enacts defeat)? In such a scenario, would "to breathe my / Blank" not constitute a kind of tautology, where the word "Blank" redundantly follows the blank space at the end of the previous line? The problem with the organicist hypothesis that the autograph form actively contributes to its content is one of probability: what is the likelihood of the poem being composed simultaneously as a verbal, metrical, musical, and visual sequence? Is it possible to integrate all these characteristics, and (if so) at what stage (before composition, during it, or afterward at the point of rewriting or recording)?

The idea that the physical lines somehow embody or imitate their own contents either works at every level of a poem's inscription or it does not work at all. One cannot ascribe a meaning to a visual aspect of one row or line and then fail to find any meaning in any of the others. The assumption of a graphic procedure in Dickinson seems counterproductive: one finds lost opportunities, contradictions, and even a lack of sophistication that jar with one's sense of this poet's technical originality. Additionally, so many of the late autographs have short lines that reproducing these desensitizes one to their unconventionality. Reading through Hart and Smith's *Open Me Carefully*, for instance, is initially refreshing in the sense that the poetic versions look different from the regular stanzas of previous print editions. But the novelty soon wears off, so that by Section 3 of the book the short lines have become naturalized to such an extent that they no longer seem especially significant. One kind of standard comes to replace another. As Timothy Steele wrote: "It might be added that if one seeks novelty in mere device, even if genuine novelty be found, this novelty must exhaust itself very quickly." And Steele goes on to quote pinball pioneer Harry Williams, who said that "novelty means one thing—sooner or later you get tired of the novelty of it."[47]

II

Considering the merits of the diplomatic transcription against Franklin's eight-line edition may ultimately be a matter of taste. But when it comes to proximity and thus fidelity, the diplomatic version offered by Marta Werner might seem superior.

> Through   what
> transports   of
> Patience
> I   reached   the
> stolid   Bliss
> to   breathe   my
> Blank   without
> thee
> Attest   me   this
> and   this –
> By   that   bleak
> Exultation
> I   now   as
> near   as   this
> Thy   privilege
> of   dying
> Abbreviate   me
> this
> Remit   me   this
>   and this

Werner uses a slightly larger type size than Franklin, as well as greater spacing between words, in an attempt to represent more accurately the relationship between script and space. (At the same time, Franklin's poem is included in the variorum edition with literally thousands of others, whereas Werner concentrates on what Thomas Johnson called the later fragments. The type choices are informed by practical and economic considerations.) Yet there are inconsistencies. Physically, Dickinson's writing occupies a larger extent of the page than the print transcription suggests, for example. Werner's version increases the distance between the script and its surrounding margins (top, bottom, left, and right). The discrepancy is important in that a greater sense of deliberation is imparted to the line sequence than is evident in the original, where the margins are much closer. In the typographic version, the interval of space after the end of a line makes it look as if the line ending is a matter of choice, a formal arrangement or design. In the manuscript, the rows end pretty much as they arrive at the edge of the torn envelope on which they are written. In other words, the idea of a layout that is partly imposed by the exigencies of the paper, by material and not aesthetic constraints, is more evident in the original than in the "diplomatic" version.

A slightly more accurate transcription of the poem might attempt to record the total relationship of blank space, script, and page size to which I have just referred. It would look something like this:

```
Through          what
transports       of
  Patience
I    reached    the
stolid     Bliss
To  breathe   my
Blank   without
thee
Attest   me   this
and    this—
  By  that  bleak
Exultation
I    won   as
  near     as    this
Thy          privilege
of  dying
Abbreviate        me
this
Remit  me  this
          and      this
```

Including the physical "frame" of the page is important because it gives us a better idea as to which spaces are deliberate and which accidental—or at least allows us to entertain the latter possibility. Without the frame, the reader might think that some other factor determined the folding over of the lines. With the frame, it seems equally possible that the deployment of words per line is related to limitations of space.

The second concern I have with Werner's version is her combination of conventionally horizontal script with an increased initial space in the final row. True, there is an indent in the original that might initially appear to justify such an editorial representation. But the indents in the autograph and print versions are brought about by very different circumstances and have different effects. In the manuscript, the writing begins to slant slightly but noticeably in the last five or six rows, so that the word "Remit" is located lower on the left side of the page than "this" on the right side. As a result, the vacant physical space available for inscribing "and this" is less rectangular and more like a triangle, increasing slightly upward from left to right. Dickinson had less room to work in, and she was forced to move further into the page to record the final variants for the poem. In Werner's print version, the physical constraints are not recorded, though they are visible in the accompanying image of the original: without the image, the indent would carry with it an expressive force. A truer adaptation would take into account the angle of the writing and the outer limits of the material on which it is written, so that one might have a more informed idea of why the last two words advance further into the page than do the previous ones:

```
┌─────────────────────────────────┐
│  Abbreviate    me               │
│  this                           │
│  Remit  me    this              │
│     and this                    │
└─────────────────────────────────┘
```

Werner also regularizes the left side of the poem. Although such an arrangement would normally be uncontroversial, in this instance the row beginning "By that bleak" is approximately 1 cm distant from the left edge of the paper, whereas the equivalent space in the line that physically precedes it ("and this") is only 0.3 cm. A number of reasons may be conjectured for this shift: the particular configuration of the torn envelope Dickinson wrote on meant that she had more space available for nine out of the first ten rows of the autograph than for the last ten. The tenth row seems to have been pivotal in some way: she maintains the left margin, then moves slightly inward for the eleventh row. She may have been responding physically to the adjustment in space, feeling that she had slightly less room to work with. Or she may have felt that she had completed something (a metrical line, perhaps) and could now reposition slightly with the start of another. She may even have been signaling the beginning of a different stanza. Whatever the reason (and there may not have been one), the change in space requires acknowledgment; at least potentially, it suggests that the octet Franklin detects may have been two quatrains.

The particular pattern of visual spaces in a Dickinson autograph is always a valuable indicator of how literally we are meant to understand its graphic arrangement. Looking at the manuscript makes clear that the spaces after the words "Patience" (3.3 cm), "thee" (in row 8, 5.4 cm), "and this –" (row 10, 3.3 cm), "Exultation" (2.7 cm), "dying" (3.5 cm), and "this," (row 18, 6.1 cm) are more substantial than elsewhere. Two of these examples ("thee" and "this" in rows 8 and 18) are additionally interesting because they are the only two occasions in the entire autograph where a row contains less than two syllables. Significantly, *what unites all these shorter rows is that they coincide in each instance with the end of what Franklin judges to be a metrical line*:

> Through what / transports of / **Patience** [3]
> I reached the / stolid Bliss
> To breathe my / Blank without / **thee** [8]
> Attest me this / **and this** – [10]
> By that bleak / **Exultation** [12]
> I won as / near as this
> Thy privilege / **of dying** [16]
> Abbreviate me / **this** [18]

Thus the logic of the blank spaces in the autograph is most likely metrical rather than visual. Dickinson would write more or less from one margin of the page to the other except and until she completed the meter, at which point she would begin a new (physical and metrical) line regardless of whether she had reached the right margin or not. It is this rule that most satisfactorily explains the variations in the poem's spatial pattern.

III

At one level, the claim that Dickinson visually dislocates traditional stanzaic arrangements betrays a dissatisfaction with Dickinson's meter. It is as if critics cannot reconcile a degree of structural regularity with the unpredictability of her contents (though Dickinson's meter is actually much more nuanced and sophisticated than her readers have always given her credit for). There is some disagreement about whether Dickinson's poems reveal a rhythmic regularity in the accented and unaccented relationship of their constituent parts. For some, there is evidence of meter.[48] For others, the alleged meter of the poetry runs counter to the natural stress of the words and is therefore a critical or editorial imposition. By and large, one comes to pre-twentieth-century poetry expecting meter, and because most words and verbal sequences are perceived to have rhythm, perhaps one simply adjusts this rhythm to regularize it. Such a charge is impossible to disprove entirely, but linguistic theories of stress in syllables can help to lessen such fears. Briefly summarized, linguistic theorists of meter argue "that the most important characteristics determining stress patterns are rhythm (i.e., alternating prominence) and sensitivity to inherent syllable (or rhyme) weight."[49] That is, certain syllables are more prominent (heavy, strong, or stressed) than others (light, weak, or unstressed). But in English, the pattern of stress is extremely complex: "patience" and "without" are both disyllabic, but one is "left-headed," or trochaic (the emphasis is on the first syllable), and the other "right-headed," or iambic (the emphasis is on the second syllable). All kinds of reasons exist for why this should be so, one of which is that each word consists of different kinds of component—particular consonants, vowels, or combinations of the two that attract greater or lesser weight because of their duration and the nature of their articulation. A long vowel (such as the second and fourth in "Abbreviate") or diphthong (such as "near") will attract more stress than a short one; a component ending in a consonant will be stronger than one ending in a vowel. In addition, there is the factor of meaning: monosyllabic function words such as "of" and "thee" tend to be light, while lexical words ("reached," "Bliss") are intrinsically heavy.[50] Single-syllable words are changeable, however; the degree of stress they generate or attract may alter according to their placement within a semantic or metrical sequence. In a poem such as Dickinson's, where there are many monosyllabic words and a limited number of syllables per verse, some of the lines can be scanned in more than one way. It is always theoretically possible, therefore, to read metrical sequences even when they do not occur or to privilege a regular rhythm when an irregular one is also detectable.

One can attempt to conduct a metrical experiment, dividing words of two or more syllables according to their stress patterns alone. The words "transports," "Patience," "stolid," "dying," and "privilege" all feature stresses on the initial syllable. The words "without," "Attest," and "Abbreviate" have their stress on the second syllable. If one then goes through the poem and cross-references these with the poem's metrical grid (as I see it), one finds only one apparent discrepancy: "transports" causes a shift from iambic to trochaic meter. But because this inversion or substitution is metrically quite common, and because it fits into the poem's schematic use of duple meter, the discrepancy does not disrupt or contradict the assumption of meter.

My former colleague at the Norwegian University of Science and Technology, Professor Nils-Lennart Johannesson, has developed a small set of beat assignment rules, which, on the basis of word stress, can predict the meter of a verse. Thus, attention to the words of Dickinson's poems primarily as syllabic systems attracting different degrees of rhythmic emphasis leads to interesting results. Johannesson's program, originally intended for the analysis of Middle English poetry, awards beats according to whether a word is identified as monosyllabic (with heavy or light stress, marked as M and m, respectively, in the transcription that follows); di- or polysyllabic (with syllables that carry primary [P] or secondary [S] stress, or are unstressed [U]). One applies his procedures to the first line of Dickinson's poem, "Through what transports of Patience," in this way: "Through" is an unstressed monosyllable, "what" a stressed monosyllable, "transports" a disyllable with a stressed and unstressed syllable, "of" is an unstressed monosyllable, and "Patience" a disyllable with a stressed and an unstressed syllable. Thus the poem opens with three beats, beginning with an iambic foot, then a trochaic one, and then an iambic one.[51] Again, such instances of inversion or functional substitution are not unusual in poetry generally or in Dickinson's poetry in particular (note that in the following, different metrical scenarios are offered for lines 3 and 5).

(1) Through what transports of Patience
    mMPUmPU
    Predicted meter:
    x / / x x / x [/ = beat, x = offbeat]

(2) I reached the stolid Bliss
    mMmPUM
    Predicted meter:
    x / x / x /

(3) To breathe my Blank without thee
    mMmMUPm [this assumes that *thee* is realized as a weak monosyllable]
    Predicted meter:
    x / x / x / x

(3) To breathe my Blank without thee
    mMmMUUM [this assumes that *thee* is a stressed monosyllable]
    Predicted meter:
    x / x / x x /

(4) Attest me this and this –
    UpmMmM
    Predicted meter:
    x / x / x /

(5) By that bleak Exultation
    mMmSUPU [this assumes that *bleak* is realized as a weak monosyllable]

Predicted meter:

x / x \ x / x [\ = beat corresponding to secondary stress]

(5) By that bleak Exultation
mMMSUPU [this assumes that *bleak* is a stressed monosyllable]
Predicted meter:
x / / \ x / x

(6) I won as near as this
mMmMmM
Predicted meter:
x / x / x /

(7) Thy privilege of dying
mPUUmPU
Predicted meter:
x / x {/} x / x [{/} = offbeat promoted to beat between two offbeats]

(8) Abbreviate me this
UPUSmM
Predicted meter:
x / x \ x /

(8) Remit me this and this
UpmMmM
Predicted meter:
x / x / x /

The three-stress line within a quatrain may be seen as part of Dickinson's ongoing extension of, and experiment with, Protestant hymn meter, itself a development of the popular ballad tradition. Of the four principal types of hymn meter, "Through what transports of Patience" most closely resembles hallelujah meter (or measure, sometimes referred to as half meter or measure), in that it has four three-stress lines.[52] The variation between seven and six syllables also echoes the symmetry of the common meter form, where the second and fourth lines are shorter, the omission resulting in a slight metrical pause.

These examples, I hope, show that normal patterns of word stress do not have to be suppressed or distorted when scanning a Dickinson poem. Moreover, scanning does not necessarily impose an extraneous or overdetermined system onto a more flexible original. Meter, in short, does not close down debate: there are different ways of reading lines 3 and 5, for instance, according to the degree of emphasis one chooses to give certain words. But one reason why metrical readings attract skepticism and even hostility is that they appear to transform small variations of stress into something more reified and systematic. For instance, when I read aloud the sequence "Thy privilege of dying," I can hear (without considering the line as verse) that primary emphasis falls on the initial syllable in "dying" and secondary emphasis on the initial syllable of "privilege." There is a very slight emphasis on the end syllable in "privilege," and almost none on the medial syllable ("i" is often dropped in speech, and "lege" contains a very weak vowel). In speech, then, one hears two stresses, whereas the metrical scheme presupposes three—on the grounds that "lege" receives a slighter heavier degree of emphasis than "i" and "of," though still not as much as "priv" and "dy" (perhaps not even as much as "Thy"). The meter of this line, iambic trimeter, or x/x/x/x, may be true to the overall pattern of stressed and unstressed syllables in the line, then, but still seem not to reflect the different grades or degrees of stress which are actualized during speech.

Relations between syllables can be much more subtle and nuanced than a term such as "iambic trimeter" suggests. For although we can attach a high degree of determined regularity to the metrical arrangement of the poem, *reading it aloud* will not result in a monotonous fall and rise of the voice. Strong and weak accents may alternate, but within the separate categories there will be varying levels of strength or weakness. Imagine this as a spectrum, at either end of which are the different accents:

weak   strong

The process of scanning a line has the effect of dividing into "weak" and "strong" syllables that may not be very different ("slightly strong," "slightly weak"). Strong and weak are qualities that emerge differentially, then: a syllable resting between two others may be judged weak because of the strength of the others, and yet be stronger than a syllable elsewhere that is assigned stress because of its position between very weak elements. In performance, too, one modulates the meter according to a variety of factors. Meter exists as a structural principle in poetry, but its actualization by the human voice makes it capable of great variation. Meter does not rule out the possibility of *spoken* improvisation or spontaneity, then. Ironically, one of the justifications for reproducing the angle and duration of dashes, as well as lineation, in autograph originals is that they are thought to exist as a set of cues for enunciation—as a kind of dramatic script. But such a script *increases* the degree of authorial control over the poem's sonic arrangements; it is the opposite of an egalitarian metrical practice. Rather than accepting that the move from written form to spoken performance will allow the reader a greater degree of participation, such a theory of Dickinson's manuscripts seems to show her attempting to *overdetermine* their patterns of sound and sense.[53]

IV

Another useful test case for meter and the status of manuscripts generally is the poem "Two Butterflies went out at Noon" (Fr571). According to Franklin, the first version (A, now lost) was sent to the Norcross cousins in the summer of 1863, while another (B) was recorded in Fascicle 25 about the same time:

> Two Butterflies went out at Noon –
> And waltzed opon a Farm –
> Then stepped straight through the Firmament
> And rested, on a Beam –
>
> And then – together bore away
> Opon a shining Sea –
> Though never yet, in any Port –
> Their coming, mentioned – be –
>
> If spoken by the distant Bird –
> If met in Ether Sea
> By Frigate, or by Merchantman –
> No notice – was – to me –
>
> 12] Report was not – to me –
>
> *Division* 3 through |

A third version (C) dates from 1878, well into the period favored by manuscript critics and believed to have included Dickinson's most experimental work. Millicent Todd Bingham and Mabel Loomis Todd thought it a good example of the difficulties of editing Dickinson and included a facsimile of it in *Bolts of Melody: New Poems of Emily Dickinson*.[54] In the pages that follow, a typographic version of the manuscript is included with frames.[55] What interests me, metrically, are the variants that are written on the verso, which can be ordered thus:

> And then espied Circumference
> Then overtook – Circumference
> (iambic tetrameter)

[recto]

Two Butterflies went
out at Noon
And waltzed opon
a Farm
And then espied
Circumference
And +caught a ride
with him –
Then lost themselves
and found themselves
In +eddies of the sun
Fathoms in <u>missed</u> <u>them</u>
Till Rapture
Peninsula – <u>Gravitation</u> <u>chased</u>
And Both were wrecked
in Noon –
To all surviving Butterflies
Be this +Fatuity
Example – and monition
To entomology –

Marginal (left, vertical): Till Gravitation humbled – ejected them

Marginal (right, vertical): noon – from

And caught a ride with him –
And took a bout with him –
(iambic trimeter)

Then lost themselves and found themselves
Then staked themselves and lost themselves
Then chased themselves and caught themselves
(iambic tetrameter)

In eddies of the sun
In Rapids of the Sun
In Gambols with the sun
In Gambols of the sun
for Frenzy of the sun
for Frenzies of the sun
for gambols of the sun
for antics in the sun
for antics with the sun
(iambic trimeter)

[verso]

+Then overtook – and
took a Bout with him –
+   In Rapids of the Sun
+   missed her footing –
+   Drowned – quenched –
Whelmed – in Noon –
+   this Biography –
Until a Zephyr   flung –
pushed them   spurned
chased –   Then staked
                      themselves and
Until a   lost themselves
  Zephyr scourged   in Gambols
                        of
    them   Till with   the
    And they   Gravitation sun –   Frenzy
    were hurled   zies
    from Noon   for Frenzy
                           of the sun
    Then chased   gambols
    themselves and grumbled foundered antics
                                in
    caught   with the
    themselves   sun –

Till Rapture missed Peninsula
Till Rapture missed her footing
Till Gravitation missed them
Till Gravitation chased them
Till Gravitation foundered
Till Gravitation grumbled
Till Gravitation humbled
Until a Zephyr pushed them
Until a Zephyr chased them
Until a Zephyr flung them
Until a Zephyr spurned them
Until a Zephyr scourged them
(iambic tetrameter and trimeter)

And Both were wrecked in Noon –
And Both were Drowned – in Noon

And Both were Quenched – in Noon
And Both were Whelmed – in Noon –
And they were hurled from noon
ejected them from noon –
(iambic trimeter)

Be this Fatuity
Be this Biography
(iambic trimeter)

Martha Nell Smith refers to the "radical lineations and scatterings of text between, around, at angles as she reworked" the first poem into the second.[56] In other words, what most people would see as draft revisions, Smith interprets as a deliberate aesthetic experiment. Each line, so the argument might go, exists in a relationship of dynamic tension with its related lines; with no absolute preference indicated, the lines exist as variants of each other, rather than existing in a secondary or dependent connection to a single, prior, and primary line. The poem might then be represented in different ways; whereas I have grouped lines in a kind of hierarchical order, one might try this instead:

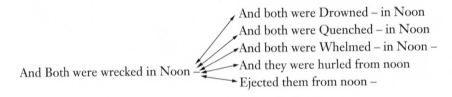

Or alternatively:

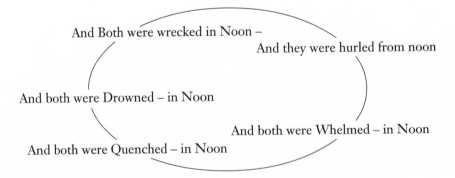

Of course, one could also envisage an electronic alternative whereby the variant readings would be programmed to alternate in random sequences. Because it seems to me that this is one of the implications of foregrounding manuscript editions of Dickinson's poems: since all options are equal in status, we have to read each line in a different order. Traditionally, the semantic direction of the poem, at least for the first reading, is from one line to the next, or [→]

> And then espied Circumference [→]
> And caught a ride with him –

But if the variants have an equal status to the original lines, the semantic direction is much more dynamic and multi-directional, or [↔]

> And then espied Circumference [↔]
> Then overtook – Circumference
> And caught a ride with him – [↔]
> And took a bout with him –

In other words, since Dickinson appears not to have made final choices, but to have embraced a poetics of choosing not choosing, we have to follow suit and weigh all the options in our mind simultaneously as we read. One might protest that a vertical chain of language (rather than a conventionally inscribed horizontal chain) is still a chain: that one is being led in a direction, even if the direction is different from most expectations. The way out of this is to say that Dickinson practiced an egalitarian poetics; she did not exercise choice herself but encouraged the reader to intervene in the text and actively construct the meaning(s) that she or he wanted. In this way we can "perform" different versions of the poem, but the text never becomes the intellectual property of a single being—either the author or the reader. Meaning cannot be said to reside in the writer, the text, or its different audiences. But an aesthetic or moral dilemma arises here. For as soon as I choose which version of the poem I prefer, constructing my own sequences from the diversity of lines available to me, then I begin to do something Dickinson (according to the argument) deliberately shunned: editing, closing down possibilities, advancing one over the many. And if I do the opposite, shuttling back and forth between nonprivileged segues of meaning, then I run the danger of losing the capacity to sustain concentrated interest (and I wonder too if such versions of a poem, shimmering endlessly between poles of meaning, return us to the kinds of self-enclosed artifacts that they were designed to replace). If reading the poems in the order of their chronology in conventional editions leads to a kind of snow blindness, what are the effects of reading such endlessly open manuscripts in clusters? The reproduction of a manuscript layout is seen as refreshing and novel—and it often is. But when presented with an entire collection where the finest nuances of inscription—angle and length of dash; shape of a letter; relation of script to space, word to line, and line to indent—are charged with potential meaning, then such diversity becomes exhausting, at least, for the individual reader. (For the academic or professional reader, of course, they are the opposite: inexhaustible, endless resources of secondary publication.) And when these approaches begin to dominate the way the poems look in the works of critics, they no longer seem novel and refreshing; one form of orthodoxy replaces another.

In almost all the examples of revision that I list above, what remains constant between variants is the meter, which strongly suggests that the meter itself was a much more forceful structural principle in Dickinson's mind than was visual appearance. The one exception to this rule is the progression from "Till Rapture missed Peninsula" to "Till Rapture missed her footing" and the remaining variants (previously listed above). The switch from one instance of iambic tetrameter to eleven of iambic trimeter is the exception that in this case proves the rule: underlying Dickinson's revisions are verbal diversity and metrical regularity. Indeed, the change from tetrameter to trimeter can be thought of as convenient: the rhythm falters because the reader anticipates an extra, stressed syllable, and this frustrated expectation formally mirrors the disequilibrium being described in the line. As one variant suggests, the metrical foot staggers and loses its balance at exactly the same point at which rapture misses her footing. But the point of the revisions as a whole has less to do with such local effects; words are chosen to fit within the metrical pattern (and chosen, too, for their sound, especially in the case of rhyming words). Their selection is based on these needs, and not primarily or only for their sense.

Although in this poem I have posited a potential relation of rhythm and meaning at the extremely local level of the line, such relations may be just as accidental as the congruence of meaning and visual appearance that manuscript critics argue for. What is important is that meter exists as a fairly constant principle governing the choice and order of words in a Dickinson poem. This is not to say that words are chosen to create rhetorical effects—though this may happen from time to time. The metrical consistency of Dickinson's revisions would appear to suggest that, by and large, the form *preceded* the content in most of her writing. The use of meter can be compared to catching a bus or driving a car to work: it is deliberate but not necessarily intentional or meaningful in itself. What is important is where such structures get you, the transportation they offer to a space elsewhere.

V

In "Of Proportion by Situation," chapter 11, book 2, of *The Arte of English Poesie*, George Puttenham wrote: "And I set you downe an occular example: because ye may the better conceiue it. Likewise it so falleth out most times your occular proportion doeth declare the nature of the audible: for if it please the eare well, the same represented by delineation to the view pleaseth the eye well and *è conuerso*: and this is by a naturall *simpathie*, betweene the eare and the eye, and betweene tunes & colours, euen as there is the like betweene the other sences and their obiects of which it apperteineth not here to speake."[57]

And in a manuscript edition of "On First Looking into Chapman's Homer," John Keats made similar drawings:[58]

Much have I travell'd in the Realms of Gold,
   And many goodly States and Kingdoms seen;
   Round many Western islands have I been
Which Bards in fealty to Apollo hold.
Oft of one wide expanse had I been told,
   Which deep-brow'd Homer ruled as his Demesne;
   Yet could I never judge what Men could mean;
Till I heard Chapman speak out loud, and bold :
Then felt I like some Watcher of the Skies
   When a new Planet swims into his Ken;
Or like stout Cortez, when with wond'ring eyes
   He star'd at the Pacific, and all his Men
Look'd at each other with a wild surmise –
   Silent, upon a Peak in Darien –

Visual appearance in Dickinson's work does not have to be taken literally: it exists as the physical manifestation of a pattern of rhythm that may not immediately be discernible to the eye but is to the ear. In the case of the Dickinson poems I have discussed previously, this means seeing the manuscript as being codified through the assignation of capitals at the beginning of, and spaces at the end of, metrical sequences. Within this framework, rhyming words function as braces, connecting pairs of verses within a stanzaic structure of regularly accented words and sonic equivalents. No diagrammatic rendition of this structure exists in Dickinson's hand, but it is there nonetheless:

> Through what transports of Patience
> I reached the stolid Bliss
> To breathe my Blank without thee
> Attest me this and this –
> By that bleak Exultation
> I won as near as this
> Thy privilege of dying
> Abbreviate me this

Here the rhymes occur at regular intervals, as they do in most of Dickinson's poetry: even lines rhyme, odd ones do not. The rhyme is allied to the meter; it indicates the presence of an underlying metrical structure comprised of two-line units. The difference between an eighteen-row diplomatic transcription and the regular print edition of the poem is the difference between surface and depth: on the surface, there are random and intermittent tufts of rhyme at rows 5, 10, 14, and 18; underneath these are the foundations, a blueprint of sonic correspondence which joins lines one and three, lines two and four. Or, put otherwise, lines 1 and 2 and lines 3 and 4 each form a unit, a structure, of two similar halves, whose duration is signaled by the rhyme.

To suggest that Emily Dickinson composed in stanzas (as Franklin did first and as I do now) is not to suppress the materiality of her manuscripts or to reject the claim of her being a graphic poet. It is simply to formulate a different understanding of both. The physicality is asserted by the rhythm and is not exclusively a property of the handwriting. And as for the visual structures, one needs to become more attuned to the invisible links established by patterns of and variations in rhythm and rhyme. The attention currently paid to isolated and fractured words distracts from the architecture of the stanza as a whole, reducing the potential of the poem through focus on its local aspects.[59] For every word that is taken as semantically charged because of its shape or position reflects negatively on those words which are not: they cause them to be invisible, secondary, and help "keep the . . . stanza from being properly seen"— or heard and (not least) *felt*.[60] If anything distinguishes poetry from other genres of literary expression—and explains Dickinson's attraction to the lyric in the great age of women's prose—it is the attention to sound and rhythm as much as sense. It is to those joint forms of stylization and systemization that I turn in the next chapter.

CHAPTER SIX

"Bells whose jingling cooled my Tramp"
Dickinson and Meter

CRITICAL interpretations of the uses to which any writer puts meter are guided by a number of core theories, three of the most important being decorum or propriety, intertextuality, and iconicity. Theories of decorum are perhaps the earliest and the least likely to survive the culture that originated them: Quintilian and Cicero actively disapproved of the use of certain cadences (believing, for example, that the iambic foot was vulgar and suitable only to low themes or subjects) while celebrating others, and both gave very precise advice about the effectiveness of certain metric sequences and combinations.[1] Nonetheless, few critics have gone so far as to suggest that Dickinson chose the forms in which she wrote because they were the *only* fit ones, and fewer still have been taken seriously. Perhaps it is coincidental that a poet so attracted to questions of religious faith would, by and large, employ formal structures that are closely related to hymnal designs. But in "Certayne Notes of Instruction" of 1575, George Gascoigne argued that "the long verse of twelue and fouretene sillables, although it be nou adayes vsed in all Theames, yet in my iudgement it would serue best for Psalmes and Himpnes."[2] And as Johnson also notes, Watts's *Christian Psalmody* and *The Psalms, Hymns and Spiritual Songs* identify the meter of each hymn, and in their introductions "the relative advantage of one meter over another for particular occasions" is discussed.[3] George Whicher pointed out that the preface to Edward Dickinson's copy of *Church Psalmody* stated that a "hymn in long metre generally possesses less vivacity . . . than one in short metre, principally because the stanza in short metre expresses as much of thought and feeling in twenty-six syllables, as the stanza in long metre does in thirty-two. In many instances in this book, hymns in long metre have been changed into common or short metre, by merely disencumbering the lines of their lifeless members."[4] And *The Sabbath Hymn and Tune Book* declared: "As, on the one hand, there is in every high religious experience a fullness of joy which can find a suitable utterance only in the most jubilant strains which musical genius has ever conceived, so, on the other, there is a heart-felt sorrow so deep as to be far beyond the expression of any but the more tender accents, the wailings (it may be) of minor strains."[5]

Whether Dickinson felt hymn forms to be the only ones morally suitable to her interests is debatable, but most critics agree that her recourse to such structures provided a frame of associations within which to work, which brings us to the second of the core theories, that of intertextuality. Metrical code theorists argue that a choice of meter will create a kind of contract with the reader, reminding her or him of previous expressive acts in the same meter. Certain structures will therefore carry contextual information of a very specific nature: hymns, for example, are an inherited media, and by choosing cultural artifacts associated with religious discourse, Dickinson may have aligned herself within a definite tradition of belief. Certainly, the significance of Dickinson's metrical borrowings has been repeatedly understood as expressing either her need or desire for belief or her opposition to religious or patriarchal orthodoxy.[6] In this chapter I do not set out to prove or disprove Dickinson's stance with regard to such arguments. It *may* represent a break with tradition, but it may also extend the concern with faith in slightly different directions. For there is an argument for saying that hymns offer the reader or performer a greater room for maneuver than has always been acknowledged. Although hymns are expressions of faith and worship that are performed publicly and communally, their actual performances are less standardized. They may be understood variously as communicating praise of God, as desiring the faith with which to praise God, as giving thanks that a God exists to be praised, or as giving thanks to God that there exist others to praise him. Though the words are most often sung by groups of people, each person may understand or employ the words differently: in the abstract senses that I have just outlined (for example), or in more particular, immediately personal ways. Hymns may reflect faith and may also serve to encourage and sustain it (and perhaps even to produce its illusion). But they can also be consumed and understood privately, in the home, and even in silence. One should not presume that hymns are simplistically to be related to orthodoxy, then, and Dickinson's lyrics to their more sophisticated revision.[7]

Another way to approach Dickinson's meter is through the theory of sympathetic form—the idea that the manner of a poem's saying is somehow related to its matter. Thus, the 1882 *Elements of Greek Grammar* advised that the "spondaic is used when any thing grave, slow, large, or sad is expressed."[8] More recently, Thomas Johnson interpreted the (mixture of trochaic, iambic, anapestic, and dactylic) rhythms in the second stanza of "Safe in their Alabaster Chambers" as akin to the gentle motion of Mother Nature rocking her children, now "soundlessly asleep." During the 1990s, this iconic aspect received a new twist in the writings of critics attuned to the graphic dimensions of Dickinson's manuscripts. A cluster of scholars has drawn attention to alter-

native or supplementary forms of stylization that were optical rather than
metrical: Ellen Louise Hart claimed that manuscripts displayed "visual strat-
egies," and Susan Howe described letters as "sounds we see. . . . Line breaks
and visual contrapuntal stresses represent an athematic compositional inten-
tion." Martha Nell Smith coined the phrase "visually expressive scriptures"
and usefully summarized some of the guiding principles behind manuscript-
based criticism: "The material record made by Dickinson shows that she be-
gan to focus more and more on the possibilities afforded by the manuscript
page and began to exploit more fully the details of scriptural corporealization—
lineation not bound by patterns and variation of conventional meters, calli-
graphic orthography freed from the regulations of typography, angled marks
of punctuation likewise liberated from the typographical settings of the en-
and em-dash, alternative word choices extricating readers from editorial pre-
determinations, handcrafted units shaped and situated to incorporate (or con-
sciously transform) page design into the work of making meaning."[9]

To take a single example of the kinds of autograph phenomena that have
attracted such intensive scrutiny and speculation, one might look at the fol-
lowing versions of the same opening line (the first standard, the second for-
matted like the autograph):

> Pain – has an Element of Blank –

> Pain – has an Element
> of Blank –

In the view of Jerome McGann, Dickinson deployed the words on the page in
such a way that a blank space coincided with the word "Blank" in the original,
thus enacting a pause that reinforced its meaning.[10] The second of these ver-
sions attempts faithfully to reproduce its visual dimensions: the first (desig-
nated Fr760 by Franklin in the new variorum edition) erases it.[11] Whatever
one thinks about such arguments, they are to be categorized as very interesting
variations on the notion of sympathetic form and therefore legitimate exten-
sions of a long critical tradition whereby rhythmic style is said to complicate,
reflect, or support the contents of a given poem.

In this chapter I pursue various lines of investigation with respect to meter
and its uses, but one of the most consistent will be the intersection of graphic
and aural dimensions of form. Using a limited corpus (the eighteen poems
that comprise Franklin's reconstruction of Fascicle 20 in *Poems of Emily Dick-
inson* [1998]), I want to look at manuscripts, separately and sequentially, in an
effort to define what kinds of regulatory or structural principle they might
embody (graphic, metrical, or both).[12] I will also attempt to chart the ways in
which the manuscript layout of each poem might constitute a series of visual

interventions or initiatives designed to refresh or loosen any possible metrical template (or whether meter provides a background against which visual improvisations are performed). For one of Smith's other observations is that Dickinson's manuscripts disrupt meter for the purposes of variation or emphasis. Again, this is a traditional idea (given a new slant by its attention to the visual): poets who insert different metrical feet at certain points are often complimented for avoiding predictability. Such deviation does not have to be thought of as iconic—though switches from one pattern of meter or rhyme to another have occasionally been thought of as devices for drawing attention to changes in a poem's argument, mood, or setting.

Nevertheless, Dickinson's choices may also have been based on factors I have not yet mentioned: familiarity, pleasure, convenience, or comfort (these factors apply as much to her readers as to herself, of course). Martha England seems relevant: "A lyric poet stores in the recesses of being some idea of form that must be satisfied. That idea is affected by rhythms apprehended within the physical frame. As words and as music, the hymns of Watts became involved with Emily Dickinson's vocal chords, fingers, diaphragm, and lungs very early in life."[13] Such meters were accessible and to some extent fundamental—because they were derived from the tradition of the ballad at least as much as the hymn.[14] And Derek Attridge, among others, has argued that the four-beat structure of ballads and hymns is basic to a greater number of poems in the English language than the more celebrated pentameter (which Dickinson used only occasionally).[15] The motive for choosing this form may be less intellectual (a gesture of dissent or an expression of religious need) than instinctual or essential, for regular rhythm "engages the deepest sources of affective behavior: those neural and muscular periodicities that generate all mental and physical activity."[16]

In addition, hymn meters are quite diverse and capable of being combined in different ways. In *Christian Psalmody* (1821), each hymn is identified as belonging to one of three main kinds of quatrain design—long meter, common meter, and short meter.[17] (In turn, these can be doubled to make eight-line stanzas.)[18] In addition to long meter there is long particular meter (six lines of four beats, or eight syllables, usually iambic tetrameter); as well as common meter, there is common particular meter (a six-line stanza of two successive four-beat lines followed by a three-beat third line, with this pattern then repeated); in addition to short meter, there is short particular meter (a six-line stanza of two three-beat lines followed by a four-beat line, which are then repeated).[19] There are other stanzaic possibilities too: in *The Sabbath Hymn Book* of 1858, the third hymn is classified as 6s and 5s (an eight-line stanza alternating between six- and five-syllable lines); the seventh is 7s (a stanza of repeated seven-syllable lines); and the tenth is L.M.6l (six lines of long meter, or four beats). The variety is, to a modern reader for whom hymn meter is often associated with three or four types only, astonishing: 10s are quatrains of ten-syllable lines (usually iambic pentameter); 11s and 8s are quatrains of alternating eleven- and eight-syllable lines; 6s and 4s combine six- and four-syllable lines; and 7s and 3s have a six-line stanza with five seven-syllable lines closed by a three-syllable line.[20] The list is not exhaustive, but goes a long way toward showing how traditional hymnology might have provided Dickinson with a greater mixture of rhythmical and stanzaic forms and combinations than is always acknowledged.[21] Not the least of the influences related to rhyme: about half of the rhymes in Watts are false, and Dickinson's own looseness in rhyming is therefore an extension of his tradition and not (as it is often formulated) necessarily an attempt at undercutting it formally.[22]

Lastly (but perhaps most obvious), meter functions as a genre marker, a kind of signal to the reader that a certain "set of expectations" is to be engaged. Such generic codification "offer[s] an important way of framing texts which assists comprehension. Genre knowledge orientates competent readers of the genre towards appropriate attitudes, assumptions, and expectations about a text which are useful in making sense of it."[23] What if meter exists primarily as an identification signal, a set of pulses that functions *generally* to induce and sustain a state of attentiveness, a feeling of imaginative preparedness? What if Dickinson's choice of verse forms has to do with fluency: having grown up with these forms, she found it easy or meaningful to work within (and against) their constraints? What if meter provides the intersubjective, conventional organizational costume that liberates performance? Meter would then function in an aggregate way to slow down the process of reading, promoting a kind of focus that is not ordinarily required of prose, but without necessarily being manipulated to create definite semantic effects at any particular local level. Just as important, reasonably predictable rhythmical sequences function as a kind of signature, a formal DNA, that creates a sense of identity, of familiarity and continuity, within which the writer can improvise expressively.

Meter and rhyme are like the fixed lines that define the limits of any sporting arena; what is performed within those lines, however, is capable of almost infinite variety and experimentation. When looking at Dickinson's use of meter, then, I am interested in some aspects of its usage more than others—there will be very little discussion, for example, of what implications the choice of hymn forms might have in terms of Dickinson's faith or skepticism. My main task, as I see it, is to describe what kinds of meter Dickinson deploys, the extent to which she varies or repeats graphic or metrical patterns within and across a single fascicle sequence, and what those patterns might mean. Dickinson's heritage, I have suggested, offered her relatively flexible and various models of metrical organization in the shape of hymnbooks: her education cemented that process. Her *Greek Grammar* included a section on versification, defining "simple feet of two syllables" (spondee, pyrrhic, trochee, and iambus), "simple feet of three syllables" (dactyl, anapæst, tribrach, molossus, amphibrach, amphimacer, bacchius, and antibacchius); as well as compound feet and the normal subtypes of simple feet (iambic monometer, dimeter, trimeter, tetrameter, pentameter, etc.). Illustrative examples were offered in English, making them theoretically applicable; in addition, nineteenth-century metrical theorists disagreed as to whether Greek and Latin forms of scansion could be made to work in English.[24] Meter was important in the nineteenth century: its forms and effects were discussed and debated, but not everyone agreed on what it was. It is therefore a mistake to paint meter as a massive backdrop of orthodoxy against which Dickinson's practices exhibit a total freedom and flexibility: newspaper reviewers notwithstanding, there was greater uncertainty about metrical rules and applications than our century is always able to recognize.

The eighteen poems listed by Ralph W. Franklin as comprising Fascicle 20 are copied in pen on cream laid paper (measuring approximately 12.5×21.3 cm) that is blue-ruled and embossed on the upper left corner ("G & T" within a decorated horizontal oval).[25] The fascicle is made from five groups of paper, each corresponding to a sheet folded during manufacture to make two leaves (or four pages): one leaf is missing, and the fourth page is often not ruled. In what follows, the chapter is divided into sections corresponding to each of the five groupings in the fascicle, designated (following the Harvard numbering) H 62 to H 66, respectively. The poem numbers are those given in Franklin (1998):

1. H 62: (Fr396) "I took one Draught of Life"; (Fr397) "A train went through a burial gate"; (Fr398) "The Morning after Wo"; (Fr399) "Departed – to the Judgment"

2. H 63: (Fr400) "I think the Hemlock likes to stand"; (Fr401C) "Dare you see a Soul at the 'White Heat'?"; (Fr402) "To hear an Oriole sing"; (Fr403B) "I reason, Earth is short"

3. H 64: (Fr404) "To put this World down, like a Bundle"; (Fr405) "Although I put away his life"; (Fr406) "Over and over, like a Tune"

4. H 65: (Fr407A) "One need not be a chamber – to be Haunted"; (Fr408A) "Like Some Old fashioned Miracle"; (Fr409A) "The Soul selects her own Society"

5. H 66: (Fr410) "How sick – to wait – in any place – but thine"; (Fr411) "Mine – by the Right of the White Election!"; (Fr412) "She lay as if at play"; (Fr413) "Heaven is so far of the Mind"

For reasons of space, the poems will not be discussed in equal depth, and some will be classified very briefly. The purpose of the chapter is to tease out what kinds of metrical designs Dickinson used across the fascicle as a whole, which in turn may yield some insights into her methods of composition.

I

The manuscript page on which the first two poems in the fascicle sequence, "I took one Draught of Life" (Fr396) and "A train went through a burial gate" (Fr397), were written is lost; each lyric therefore exists solely in transcript. Both have two quatrains rhyming *abcb*: the first is predominantly iambic trimeter with one line (the seventh) extending to tetrameter; the second has alternating lines of iambic tetrameter and trimeter. (It also appears to have an *abab* rhyme in the first stanza, but this is not repeated in the second and may therefore have been accidental.) According to hymnal doxologies, the first poem corresponds to half meter and the second to common meter.

Like the second, the third poem, "The Morning after Wo" (Fr398) employs a stanza of two successive lines of iambic trimeter followed by tetrameter and then trimeter again.

> The Morning after Wo –
> 'Tis frequently the Way –
> Surpasses all that rose before –
> For utter Jubilee –
>
> As Nature did not Care –
> And piled her Blossoms on –
> The further to parade a Joy
> Her Victim stared opon –
>
> The Birds declaim their Tunes –
> Pronouncing every word
> Like Hammers – Did they
> know they fell
> Like Litanies of Lead –
>
> On here and there – a creature –
> They'd modify the Glee
> To fit some Crucifixal Clef –
> Some key of Calvary –

The initial indentation is caused by the boss, and is a routine and nonsignificant characteristic of many other Dickinson manuscripts. And there are clear visual demarcations between the four stanzas (Dickinson skips a line in each instance). But the third stanza runs over five lines rather than four, and given that stanzaic variation also occurs elsewhere (both in the fascicle and in the work as a whole), it merits close attention. There are three factors to be taken into account when judging its shape: the design established by the other stanzas, the relationship of upper- and lowercase letters, and the pattern of blank marginal spaces between end words and the right edge of the page. Taken together, these provide a template with which to judge the third stanza's status. The fact that "know" begins with a lowercase letter and that the biggest end space on the page (6 cm) occurs immediately after "fell" strongly suggests that "Like Hammers—Did they / know they fell" is written over two physical rows but constitutes a single metrical unit of writing.[26] The other stanzas have a rough *abcb* rhyme scheme and alternating lines of iambic tetrameter and trimeter, such that adjusting the five rows to four lines would also bring them into line with this pattern. The only other explanation would be the iconic one: Dickinson wanted to enact the process of falling at the point that her speaker describes it. Or she wanted to isolate and emphasize "know they fell," slowing down the meter at that point by writing it over two rows rather than one. In other words, the visual deployment of the language at that point may supplement its rhythmic effects, though one might ask why Dickinson chose to isolate that phrase rather than any other (it is hardly the most memorable of the poem's parts or the one with the greatest impact).

Like the first poem, the fourth in the sequence uses mainly iambic trimeter and *abcb* rhyme, thus approximating half meter.[27] Again, however, the manuscript of Fr399, "Departed – to the Judgment," looks very different from the printed version:

> Departed – to the Judgment –
> A Mighty – Afternoon –
> Great Clouds – like Ushers –
> leaning –
> Creation – looking on –
>
> The Flesh – Surrendered –
> Cancelled –
> The Bodiless – begun –
> Two Worlds – like Audiences –
> disperse –
> And leave the Soul – alone –

Applying the same technique as before, it is possible to argue that since "leaning" and "disperse" very clearly begin with lowercase letters and are immediately followed by large domain-end phenomena (blank intervals of 8.5 and 7.9

cm, respectively), they may be regarded as belonging to the previous row.[28] That is, they are separated from what precedes them by physical exigencies (not having any room to write at those particular junctures) and not semantic or aesthetic ones. Again, this explanation does not absolutely preclude the possibility of iconic choices having motivated the isolation of both words, although "leaning" on its own does not lean any more distinctly that "leaning" at the close of a metrical line. (The argument has more merit when applied to "disperse," for separating the word might indeed be said to dramatize such an action.)[29]

Other tendencies coincide with instances of physical run-on lines (which are not to be confused with enjambment), at least in this poem. They almost all seem to occur in lines that are quantifiably longer in some way—either metrically/syllabically ("Two Worlds – like Audiences – disperse") or in terms of how many letters they total ("Great Clouds – like Ushers – leaning"; "The Flesh – Surrendered – Cancelled").[30] Dickinson does not (in this fascicle at least) experiment with the graphic layout of sequences that are shorter—physically and comparatively. One's instinct is to ask why, if she really were playing with the arrangement of the words on the page, she avoided doing so with briefer strings of words. There is more than one answer to that question: the more reduced the verbal succession, the more attention it might be said to receive (because of being spread across fewer elements). The size of paper and script is another factor; when Atossa Frost Stone writes by hand, she fits approximately nine to ten words of prose and between five and six words of poetry onto 16.4 cm of paper.[31] As we saw in previous chapters, Dickinson often uses paper of similar dimensions, but—from the 1860s on—fits only three to four words per line on average onto the page. Given that her most popular metrical form appears to have been iambic tetrameter, or eight unstressed and stressed syllables, the metrical contract was not likely to have been fulfilled by three or four words alone. Under such circumstances, it would have been physically difficult for lines of poetry to be written consistently on the same horizontal axis—and that is why they frequently run over. Lines of trimeter and dimeter, by contrast, are relatively easy to fit into one horizontal component of paper.

In addition, given that run-on segments are often single words ("leaning," "Cancelled," "disperse") and that the argument for their isolation is one of intellectual emphasis, it still seems strange that Dickinson never chose to isolate single words in shorter sequences. And why is the isolation always at the close of a sequence rather than at the beginning? Why is "leaning," in other words, a more suitable candidate for segregation than "Creation" or "The Flesh"? When looking at the patterns of visual design, both within and across individual poems, anomalies, exceptions, and inconsistencies occur if one assigns iconic or formal motives to their segregation. But accepting that run-on occurs at a much-increased rate when the line takes up more physical space surely makes it more likely that it is a product of material and not graphic priorities.

The final point has to do with the poem's variants: "placing" for "leaning" in line 3; "Shifted" for "Cancelled" in line 5; "dissolve," "withdraw," and "retire" for "disperse" in line 7. Though the last examples are synonymous, the first two are not—or at least not directly or obviously so. But what all the variants have in common with the words they might have replaced is their metrical structure, which suggests once more that meter was a decisive factor in the organization of this and any other poem.

II

The fifth poem in the fascicle, Fr400, "I think the Hemlock likes to stand," is closest to common meter, reverting as it does to alternating sequences of iambic tetrameter and trimeter (in Franklin's version), with a very loose rhyme pattern of *abcb*. Again, the manuscript appears divergent from this pattern:

> I think the Hemlock
> likes to stand
> Opon a Marge of Snow –
> It suits his own Austerity –
> And satisfies an awe
>
> That men, must slake in
> Wilderness –
> And in the Desert – cloy –
> An instinct for the Hoar, the
> Bald –
> Lapland's – nescessity [*sic*] –
>
> The Hemlock's nature thrives –
> on cold –
> The Gnash of Northern winds
> Is sweetest nutriment – to him –
> His best Norwegian Wines –
>
> To satin Races – he is nought –
> But children on the Don, [page break]
> Beneath his Tabernacles, play,
> And Dnieper Wrestlers, run.

Like the poem before it, this one opens with an indent that is caused by the boss in the upper-left corner, the raised edges of which Dickinson avoided writing on, here as elsewhere, generally speaking.[32] As with all the other poems in the fascicle, clear graphic divisions exist between stanzas, a feature that also occurs in the letters but most often when there is a poem enclosed or enfolded within it. Once again, there are noticeable end spaces that disrupt the abstract visual pattern of the poem's inscription: 5.6 cm after "stand," 7.6 cm after "Wilderness," 9.4 cm after "Bald," and 8.6 cm after "cold." Again, too, one finds inconsistencies in looking for any pattern of willed designation behind such partitions: why "on cold" but not "Snow," for instance? And why write "Bald" alone: to suspend its literal meaning when that meaning has already been suspended by the assignation of a capital letter, Dickinson's conventional way of indicating nonconventional or additional significance? True, the capitals may work the other way—to indicate that the words were meant to stand alone (for one of the other functions of the capital is to mark the commencement of a metrical line). At which point one wonders: did Dickinson isolate "wilderness" and "bald" because she wanted to emphasize those words, and did she then assign capitals to them to signal that their isolation was deliberate? Or did she assign capitals to isolate them, and then isolate them further by writing them on separate lines (in which case there is a double emphasis, rendering them more important than almost any other word in the entire poem)? Or are they words that receive emphasis through being capitalized (like "Hemlock," "Marge," "Snow," "Austerity") and are then placed on a separate row because they could not fit into the space remaining in the previous row?

It seems to me that this last scenario is the most convincing. Both "likes to stand" and "on cold" definitely belong to the previous row of writing and are meant to complete it, because they begin with words with initial lowercase letters. When joined together with what preceded them, both segments add up to the first lines of stanzas in which lines 1 and 3 are composed in iambic tetrameter. And this makes it more likely that "Wilderness" and "Bald" contain the final stresses necessary for the completion of iambic tetrameter sequences begun by "That men, must slake in" and "An instinct for the Hoar, the." One can push this slightly further by pointing out that run-on does not occur in the even lines of quatrains, which range in length from five ("Upon a Marge of Snow") to two words ("Lapland's – nescessity"). The longer the line, then, and the greater the quantity of words it takes to fulfill the metrical contract, the greater the likelihood of run-on taking place. Thus, the odd lines in the quatrain range from seven to four words: when there are six or seven words, or eight syllables ("I think the Hemlock likes to stand"; "That men, must slake in Wilderness"; "An instinct for the Hoar, the Bald"; "The Hemlock's nature thrives – on cold"), there is run-on. Of course, there are variables here: "To satin Races – he is nought" has six words and does *not* carry over, but in this instance "satin" and "Races" take up only 1.4 cm and 1.6 cm of space, respectively, whereas "Hemlock" (another bisyllabic word in the opening row) takes up 4 cm. And there are other ways of reading such information: Dickinson might not have liked long lines, for instance, and therefore broke them up on the page. But if so, why did she bother to use tetrameter at all if she began to strain at the leash somewhere around the third foot? Why not just write in trimeter and dimeter? Better still, why not just abandon meter altogether? And, again, if one accepts the idea that Dickinson began to experiment visually with the arrangement of the words on the page, why did she invariably limit such experiments to the final portions of the line and never to the start?

The next poem in the fascicle sequence, Fr401C, "Dare you see a Soul at the 'White Heat'?," is one of the most celebrated in the Dickinson canon:

> Dare you see a Soul at the
> "White Heat"?
> Then crouch within the door –
> Red – is the Fire's common tint –
> But when the quickened Ore
>
> Has sated Flame's conditions –
> She quivers from the Forge
> Without a color, but the Light
> Of unanointed Blaze –
>
> Least Village, boasts it's Black-
> smith –
> Whose Anvil's even ring
> Stands symbol for the finer Forge
> That soundless tugs – within – [page break]
>
> Refining these impatient Ores
> With Hammer, and with Blaze
> Until the designated Light
> Repudiate the Forge –

Metrically speaking, what fascinates about the poem is that the framework of beats is quite regular (stanzas 2 and 3 both have 3, 3, 4, and 3 beats; stanzas 1 and 4 have 5, 4, 3, and 4 and 4, 3, 4, and 3, respectively) but that within these parameters the actual meter is quite volatile in terms of foot deployment. The opening line is one of the most challenging of Dickinson's many strong opening lines: it begins with three trochaic feet, their path altered slightly by the intrusion of an unstressed syllable (creating a pyrrhic effect of two unstressed syllables) and a spondee. Line 3 is similarly varied: it has a trochee, an iamb, a trochee, and a single stressed syllable. But both lines 2 and 4 are fairly regular iambic trimeter.

The poem has a number of physical features in common with others, both in Fascicle 20 and elsewhere—the extended cross-stroke that joins the two ascenders in the words "tint," "Without," and "impatient," to take one element. The quotation marks both slant in the same direction, with the second one positioned above and minimally in front of the final *t* in "Heat"; conventionally they are supposed to go in opposite directions (as they are inscribed in the 1852 edition of Ik Marvel's *Reveries of a Bachelor*).[33] Granted, one could create a scenario of intent with which to explain this: the ferocity of the "Heat" is such that Dickinson wanted to represent it visually as breaking free from the constraints of the quotation marks. But such an iconic argument works only if one ignores the consistency with which quotation marks are similarly assigned elsewhere in poems that have nothing to do with heat—physical or creative. The problem with approaching aspects of Dickinson's handwriting as examples of sympathetic form, I am persuaded, is that it isolates a casual and routine aspect of Dickinson's manuscripts as a whole and then ascribes a particular meaning to that instance. And, by extension, if Dickinson was sufficiently indifferent to the physical placement and direction of her punctuation marks, what does that mean for other phenomena such as her dashes (like the one after "within" that slants slightly downward)?

Another aspect of the autograph original that has attracted comment is the word division in the third stanza, which is seen as having an iconic dimension, though it is, thankfully, not that "Black- / smith" recorded in segments over two lines catches the essence of being a blacksmith better than the word written as a single physical entity. Instead, Paul Crumbley suggests the following: "Breaking 'blacksmith' into two words on separate lines, for instance, contrasts 'Black' with the brilliance of forge and heated ore, while the 'smith' portion connotes the anonymity of a common profession and surname; the result exposes the blacksmith's aim to repudiate, while significantly diminishing his power to do so. The reader is forced to consider whether as poet the blacksmith is an artist or a wordsmith."[34] I concede the feasibility of Crumbley's point—and admire the intelligence and imagination with which he arrives at it. Certainly, the division of the word may be perceived as slowing it down at that point, drawing it out to a contemptuous, semi-repulsed pronunciation that seems quite in keeping with Dickinson's generally dismissive com-

ments about working-class people. Of course, other readings are simultane-
ously possible: emphasizing "black" might racialize the smith in contrast to
the "white" speaker, for instance, transforming him into an undistinguished
body whose main purpose is to define through opposition the greater spiritual
purity of the writer. Or perhaps it is a just a racist joke, a pun: even the smallest
of villages has its black (African American) Smith (person's surname). Never-
theless, one cannot escape the possibility that Dickinson split the word be-
cause she ran out of room: in which case, we are like Matthiessen (in *American
Renaissance*), who praised Melville for a felicitous description ("the soiled fish
of the sea") without knowing that it was a printer's error (for "coiled"). Just as
tellingly, though, neither of these readings absolutely requires a word division
in order to be made: the stress on "Blacksmith" favors one syllable over the
other and provides opportunities for speculation similar to those just outlined.
The difference is that, for Crumbley at least, the "unusual punctuation, word
variants, irregular lines," and (though he does not list it) word division have
the effect of foregrounding the poem as linguistic raw material, which fits
conveniently with its subject matter. The autograph's lack of finish reflects its
theme, bringing us back to theories of iconicity, albeit visual ones. Presuma-
bly, then, the autographs as a whole were left deliberately incomplete because
Dickinson wanted to defamiliarize language—to disrupt its flow and draw
attention to how it manufactures an image of experience rather than providing
a window through which to view it.[35]

For Crumbley, then, it is important that Dickinson's editors respect her
wishes when it comes to lineation; thus, "White Heat" should be placed on a
line of its own, because its words are then isolated and made into "special
subjects of inquiry."[36] But he also claims that "Dare," the speaker's first word,
"cautions the reader preparatory to a potentially unsettling encounter"; one
wonders, then, why that word was not similarly segregated. If the logic of
physical isolation is that it increases the rate of inquiry, then "smith" should
receive more attention than "Black." Or perhaps it is the other way: since
Crumbley pays equal attention to "Black-" and "smith," then the definite
pronoun prior to "White Heat" should be carefully attended to as well—
certainly, the horizontal stroke with which Dickinson crosses the *t* in "the" is
more emphatic than elsewhere. But if "White Heat" is indeed a special (dis-
tinctive, exceptional) field of inquiry, does that mean "Dare you see a Soul at
the" is comparatively less special? What adjustments of significance begin to
operate, and at what ratio of adjustment, when two elements of a poem receive
visual emphasis and the rest do not?[37]

Could Dickinson have fit the 4.5 cm of "White Heat" into the 0.4 cm of
space remaining after she had written "Dare you see a Soul at the"? Anticipat-
ing such objections, McGann says that it "does no good to argue, as some

might, that these odd lineations are unintentional—the result of Dickinson finding herself at the right edge of the page, and so folding her lines over. Her manuscripts show that she could preserve the integrity of the metrical unit if she wanted."[38] But one would be more convinced by his (and Crumbley's) arguments if Dickinson regularly had a quantity of space available at the end of a row but chose nonetheless to shift (or split) a word or verbal sequence measuring equivalently less than that space to the next row. That this generally does not happen in Dickinson's poems seems to me to be decisive evidence that such events are not semantically directed, however haunted critics may be by such a possibility.[39]

I suggested earlier in this chapter that responding to Dickinson's autographs as graphically composed documents might silence aspects of their arrangement as a cluster of sounds and rhythmical pulses. In this case, for instance, "White Heat" is regarded as being isolated when it is already metrically salient by virtue of being the closing foot in the poem's only five-beat line. And since "Blacksmith" is a two-syllable word that receives emphasis principally on the first syllable, its graphic dislocation seems redundant—close to a kind of rhetorical tautology. I believe that the virtue of a metrical rather than an ocular response is that "White Heat" is not given preferential treatment but remains as the culminating element in a relentless surge of equal parts that together constitute an aggressive but integral opening line. (By extension, "Blacksmith" would not be singled out from many others as the poem's pivotal noun.) In addition, a visual arrangement would produce a slight pause after "the" (equivalent to a commercial break in poetic terms), whereas the logic of the meter is one of continuous acceleration: the line drives over "at the" and lands with a double bang of the fist on "White Heat."

There are a number of final points to make with regard to the document's material attributes. Though much has been made of Dickinson's refusal to differentiate between poetry and prose, she here assigns capitals that are grammatically redundant and semantically unlikely.[40] Traditionally, capitals are deployed to signal the start of a prose sentence, as Dickinson does. And she also uses capitals to indicate that a word is charged with a more than normal significance. But when Dickinson writes poetry, it becomes evident that filler words—words that have a comparatively minor function such as "Then," "But," and "That"—are capitalized when they coincide with the commencement of a metrical unit, a line of verse. These kinds of generically specific procedures of capitalization do not appear in Dickinson's prose.[41]

Even the most cursory survey of Dickinson's handwriting reveals inconsistencies that are worth pondering. Again, as we also saw in previous chapters, Dickinson employs two different forms of the lowercase *e* here—closed, and open like the capital (ε). And there are different forms of "the" in the first and third rows of writing: the first "the" is formed by separate letters, the first two of which are joined at the top by a cross-stroke. The second "the" is written cursively: the three letters are linked or combined at the bottom, and the cross-stroke misses the ascender of the *t* and intersects with the *h*. "The" continues to be written interchangeably until 1874, and occasionally beyond that. Dickinson's alternative for "She," "it," is written in separate letters: later, the same two letters are joined in "it's Blacksmith." With one exception, the *d* in this poem is consistently inscribed with one stroke, the ascender curving back to the left. But the next poem in the fascicle, "To hear an Oriole sing," features another form, written with two strokes of the pen, with the circular part and the ascender separate.[42] The cumulative impression of this and other samples of the handwriting is that Dickinson was quite varied in the way that she inscribed certain characters, and combinations of characters, of the alphabet. And if Dickinson was so casual about the way in which she inscribed the same letters and words, what does that mean for other phenomena such as her dashes—or for the idea that words and letters convey meanings (or comment on their own inability to do so)?

The points about quotation marks (slanting in the same direction) and differently inscribed alphabetic characters (the open and closed minuscule *e*) as well as combinations of characters (*th* crossed and *th* with only the *h* crossed: *Th* written separately and *Th* joined), can again be made about the next poem in the sequence, Fr402:[43]

> To hear an Oriole sing
> May be a common thing –
> Or only a divine.
>
> It is not of the Bird
> Who sings the same, unheard,
> As unto Crowd –
>
> The Fashion of the Ear
> Attireth that it hear
> In Dun, or fair –
>
> So whether it be Rune –
> Or whether it be none
> Is of within. [page break]
>
> The "Tune is in the Tree –"
> The Skeptic – showeth me –
> "No Sir! In Thee!"

This is one of the most significant poems in the fascicle, precisely because it is unexceptional in its graphic rendering (though the quotation marks in the final stanza slant in the same direction). There is no instance of the fragmented lineation that manuscripts sometimes display, which can be related to its predominantly three-stress structure (with two lines of iambic trimeter followed by a third of either trimeter or dimeter). In other words, the choice of the shorter meter means that each line is much less likely to exceed the horizontal physical space allocated to it on the ruled paper. And since short lines included within poems otherwise exhibiting longer metrical sequences do not run over either, we seem to approach a rule in this autograph sequence: lines with three beats or less do not carry over because they fit within the physical margins of the page. The other poem in the fascicle that is limited to alternating three- and two-beat lines is Fr412, "She lay as if at play," which has no line splits either.[44] And this increases the likelihood that carryover lines or line splits are a result of material factors (how many words can fit into a line) rather than aesthetic ones (division being assigned for semantic purposes).

Given Dickinson's metrical volatility, both across and within poems, one needs to be very careful about adjusting the appearance of a manuscript poem to suit a perception of its rhythm. An obvious example is Fr403: one variant (B), the eighth poem in the fascicle, is quite regular, but an earlier variant (A), sent to Susan, perhaps in 1862, is very different in layout:[45]

> I reason –
>   Earth is short –
> And Anguish – absolute –
> And many – hurt –
> But, <u>What of that?</u>
>   I reason –
>   We should
>   <u>die</u> –
> The <u>best</u> – Vitality
> Could not <u>excel Decay</u> –
> But – <u>What of that?</u>
>   I reason –
>   That in "Heaven" –
> <u>Somehow</u> – it will be <u>even</u> –
> Some <u>new Equation</u> – given –
> But – <u>What of that!</u>

Like some other manuscripts, there is a (very faint) embossment in the upper left-hand corner of the paper; the opening word ("I") touches on it only slightly (approximately one millimeter). This may explain why Dickinson indented the first line, but her common practice elsewhere would have been to fit as much of the rest of that line (assuming it was integral) onto the same row, carrying over to the initial space of the next row and leaving an end space afterward to signal that it was completed. She does not do so here, which strongly suggests that the division is a considered one. And there are no obvious physical blemishes, tears, embossments or even watermarks (the paper is wove, not laid) that might have caused Dickinson to arrange the rest of the poem as she does. The paper was folded twice, immediately below the first two of the choral lines (that is, beneath rows 5 and 11), and sent as a note. Because the writing occupies almost the full extent of the page, it is possible that this particular underlining might have recorded stanzaic division, which could not otherwise have been indicated by a vertical interval in such limited space. The indentation of "I reason" could also be a form of verse paragraphing, but Dickinson has plenty of room to include at least parts of "Earth is short," "We should <u>die</u>," and "That in 'Heaven'" with the repeated initial phrase, so such an explanation seems extremely implausible. Taken together, the evidence supports the contention that Dickinson was playing with space in this version of the poem.

In his edition of the poem, Franklin represents the underlined words in italics, omits the dash that appears after the second "But" (in row 11), and enfolds the verb "*die*" within the previous line.[46] He consistently capitalizes "What" (as I have), though it is only in the second example, and to a less obvious degree the third one, that the *W* seems larger than its surrounding characters.[47] In one edition of these lines, Martha Nell Smith lowercases "what" and retains Dickinson's underlining, though she represents it as continuous ("<u>what of that</u>" rather than "<u>what</u> <u>of</u> <u>that</u>").[48] In the electronic edition at the Dickinson Electronic Archives, the middle "What" of the three phrases is assigned an initial capital.[49] The effect seems to be one of absolute fidelity to the autograph original: the editors do not assign capitals but simply report what is there, which is why they have a capital for the middle query but not for the first and third. In fact, Hart and Smith are correct in saying that the middle capital is the clearest one in terms of comparative dimension. But although the *W*'s in two of the three examples of that word are not clearly distinguishable in size from the letters that surround them, they are rounded, whereas in "somehow," "will," and "new," the *w* is inscribed more narrowly and sharply. Thus Smith, and later Smith and Hart, seem to have taken into consideration only the relative size of the letters, rather than their different shapes, which is a typical weakness in their editorial methods. In other words, Hart and Smith refuse to assign capitals where letters are not clearly differentiated in extent from others in a sequence, in order to eschew the kinds of editorial intervention which they see as intrusive. But in focusing so much on single alphabetic characters and failing to see underlying patterns of inscription, they overcompensate. That the same phrase is repeated three times makes the idea of some consistency in the assigning of capitals not only legitimate but desirable.

> The insouciant refrain dismisses the sorrows of life in stanza one and the sorrows of death in stanza two; this is all within the tradition of *contemptus mundi*, where it is combined with the affirmation that such sorrows are inconsequential in the face of heavenly salvation. A reader familiar with the tradition is led to expect a conclusive shift to some such affirmation, which the first three lines of the last stanza, with their reference to heaven's "new Equation," seem to modify, probably from a question into an answer. The mere repetition of the refrain, without modification, is an ironic surprise, a blend of acid skepticism and devil-may-care puckishness.[50]

This poem depends very much on a tension between reiterated and nonreiterated, predictable and nonconventional, statements and values. It is the repeated elements that are nonconventional: the changing stanzas embrace standard Christian stances on the afterlife. It is therefore not unreasonable to suppose that Dickinson might have wanted to use capitals to reinforce the consistently repeated phrases.

Something of the same problem emerges in attitudes to underlining in the poem. Since Dickinson underlines single words elsewhere in the poem ("best," "somehow," "even"), one is inclined to follow her example and do the same for sequences of words where there is underlining ("excel Decay" or "excel Decay"; "new Equation" or "new Equation"; "What of that" or "*What of that*"). In their edition of the poem for *Open Me Carefully*, Hart and Smith do just that: they write "what of that?" for the first instance of the repeated line.[51] For the next instance, however, they write "What of that?", which seems to correspond to the specificities of Dickinson's script where "of" is not underlined, though the line underneath "What" almost reaches it. But in trying to remain literally true to an apparent aspect of the original, Hart and Smith distort another: the physical gap between "What" and "of" in *their* text becomes larger than in the other two instances. In Dickinson's autograph, there is no such change: the space remains fairly constant, at about one centimeter. By extension, Hart and Smith underline the question mark and exclamation mark at the ends of (respectively) the second and third query but do not do so for the first question mark. In the original, the underlining does not extend as far as the punctuation in any of the three instances. My objection is not so much to the policy as to its application, in this case. Hart and Smith produce a version that looks closer to the original in many ways, but the kind of attention they pay to minor details actually rebounds on them, for their edition of the poem imposes standards that they themselves then fail to live up to. In addition, they confer a greater degree of deliberation to an aspect of the handwriting than is invited, merited, or necessary: that Dickinson wanted "What of that" underlined seems obvious, and the conventions used to signal this (single words underlined or italicized, or the phrase in its entirety) would not seem to matter much (had there been a triple underlining, which cannot be represented by italics, one could argue for a more exact reproduction). Again, it helps to understand that Dickinson was similarly inexact in her underlining elsewhere and that she was not unique in this. Margie Dodge's handwritten "Journal" (1885–86) provides a useful context for underlining practices. On the second page, for example, she writes "<u>te</u>a" and "<u>po</u>t" in close succession: in the first example, the first letter is not underlined, and in the second the third letter is not underlined. On the twelfth page, "<u>mounted</u> photographs" is written in such a way that the underlining does not extend to the *t* of the first word. On page 34, "<u>schoon</u>er" is only partially underlined.[52] This is not to suggest that Dickinson underlined in exactly the same way as Dodge but rather that underlining performed by hand is often casually and imprecisely applied, without there being any specific meaning attached to that imprecision.

"How finely we argue upon mistaken facts," exclaims Tristram Shandy.[53] A reading of this poem that pays attention to the minutiae of its inscription as Hart and Smith represent them will stray beyond plausibility into unfounded conjecture. Even reading the standard print edition will not distort the original to this extent. Representing the emphasis in "what of that" by underlining the words separately or together, or by italicizing them, will not distort the original either. The significance of the frame ("I reason"; "But, <u>What</u> of <u>that</u>?") means that some kind of typographic consistency is allowable. Certainly, there is an echo here of some Platonic dialogues. But writing "<u>What</u> of <u>that</u>?" *does* distort, because it gives the impression that Dickinson wanted to convey a particular nuance of meaning by the change of inscription at that point. It draws attention away from the poem as a whole and toward minor but nonconstituent aspects of its inscription. Indeed, one cannot rule out the possibility that the length of lines underneath words was determined by other physical factors: the movement of the hand, for instance, or the stability of the page on the table. In addition, the manuscript is written in ink, and the pen Dickinson used may have performed in different ways according to the angle, force, and duration of its contact with the paper. Elsewhere in the poem, even the inscription of lines under single words is not always continuous. It may even be that Dickinson did not pay particular or careful attention to the extent of the underlining because it was incidental or obvious in its meaning to her.

Similar conclusions may be drawn about the physical isolation of the verb "die"; since there are single words in the poem that are also accentuated through typographic emphasis but not lineation, it seems possible that "die" was not necessarily meant to occupy a line on its own. It already receives special significance from its metrical emphasis, underlining, and placement at the end of the phrase; the idea that it needs a line on its own seems somewhat like overkill. This is not to contest the argument that "the staggered placement of words on sixteen lines arrests the reader's attention and slows the process of perusal to a halting pace."[54] But it is overstating the case to say that this kind of arrangement breaks free from conventional paradigms of reading (or, by the same token, writing). By its very nature, poetry slows down the process of reading and demands that we concentrate more than we (ordinarily) do with prose. The restlessness of the meter also reinforces that effect. The first stanza starts with successive lines of iambic trimeter followed by lines of iambic dimeter—but the pattern has already been altered in the second stanza, which has three lines of trimeter followed by one. The final stanza seems not so much restless in this respect as uncertain, tentative, incomplete, which is achieved by the simple addition of an extra syllable. Instead of six syllables for every three stresses, there are seven in the first three units of the stanza (counting "I reason – / That in 'Heaven' " as one), with the final syllable unstressed in each instance. The result is a faltering, a falling off, a weakening of the kind of clipped attempt at restraint or control suggested by the masculine ending of the first two stanzas.

There is no question but that Dickinson wanted to segregate the phrase "I reason" in the version she sent to Susan Dickinson and that such visual separation was unusual in the context of her poetry generally. So too was the amount of underlining. It is possible that both these features are not so much (or only) textual experiments as they are related to a specific phase of Dickinson's historical relationship with Susan. The underlining suggests insistence as well as emphasis: either the promotion of a certain theological or intellectual viewpoint, its ironization, or a deliberate stressing of words that formed part of a recurrent dialogue between Dickinson and her sister-in-law at this point. (The other possibility is that Dickinson wanted to disguise the poem's irreverent, skeptical use of rhyme clusters.)

But at a slightly later juncture, in the same year, Dickinson recorded the same poem in Fascicle 20, this time without the line breaks. Franklin designates it as Fr403B:[55]

I reason, Earth is short –
And Anguish – absolute –
And many hurt,
But, what of that?

I reason, we could die –
The best Vitality
Cannot excel Decay,
But, what of that?

I reason, that in Heaven –
Somehow, it will be even –
Some new Equation, given –
But, what of that?

Accepting as absolute the chronology of two poems written in the same year and within a few months or perhaps weeks of each other would be unwise; basing an argument on such a chronology would be foolish in the extreme. But one cannot resist a question: if Dickinson *did* record version B after version A, does this show her moving away from graphic effects, dismissing them as unnecessary or (to use a word that she was not familiar with) gimmicky? Or are the differences between the two versions to do with questions of audience: one (A) personal, the other (B), public? Or is it that Dickinson felt herself able to experiment more with Susan Dickinson because—as Smith and others have rightly pointed out—their correspondence was less formal, more relaxed? Did Dickinson feel the need to guide Susan Dickinson through the poem to a greater extent than she would have others? Or was she experimenting with genre—arranging a poem as if it were a kind of letter? I find no easy answers to such questions. But it is surely significant that Dickinson eschewed visual arrangements in her own archive copy of the poem. Instead, she restored its sonic periodicities: the insistent, compelling, but dissonant rhymes of short-absolute-hurt, die-vitality-decay, and (especially) heaven-even-given. It is the play between the poem's relentless form—its repetitive pulse of rhyme, meter, and refrain—and its ostensibly orthodox contents that makes the poem great.

III

The first poem of the third sheet (H 64) in Fascicle 20 is "To put this World down, like a Bundle" (Fr404), which Franklin dates to autumn 1862.

> To put this World down,
> like a Bundle –
> And walk steady, away,
> Requires Energy – possibly Agony –
> 'Tis the Scarlet way
>
> Trodden with straight renunciation
> By the Son of God –
> Later, his faint Confederates
> Justify the Road –
>
> Flavors of that old Crucifixion –
> Filaments of Bloom, Pontius Pilate
> sowed –
> Strong Clusters, from Barabbas'
> Tomb –
>
> Sacrament, Saints partook before us –
> Patent, every drop,
> With the Brand of the Gentile Drinker
> Who indorsed the Cup – [end of page]

Yet again, the print edition of the poem appears at first reading to deviate from the original: Franklin records the opening line break in his notes on the poem but does not reproduce it. But the break can be read differently, as a willed arrangement. Dickinson could be illustrating her first statement in two ways—through the simile (like a bundle), and through the lowering of the line, which mirrors the lowering of the bundle (or suggests heaviness). Alternatively, the break may simply function to slow the reader down—to impede her or his momentum and enforce a greater level of attention to the poem as a whole. This section of the line, the argument might run, receives more focus because Dickinson wants to ironize or complicate the simile; the world is not a mere bundle, and it is not easily discarded or forgotten.

One runs into problems with such a reading, not because it is unacceptable or unimaginable but because it so inconsistently applied. It is not so much the grammatical aspect (highlighting a phrase, then a noun, and finally a verb) or even the inconsistency in itself; for not knowing when a word or verbal sequence will be highlighted might be thought of as a very successful strategy for keeping readers alert. It is more that only three elements in the poem receive this kind of emphasis, and the attention drawn to them is disproportionate to their significance within the poem as a totality.

The other point is that highlighting "like a Bundle," "sowed," and "Tomb" is not only redundant—they receive a degree of emphasis already from their position within the structures of rhythm and rhyme that the poem embodies—but unnecessarily distracting as well. For the true innovation of this poem is metrical and stanzaic: Dickinson switches from successive quatrains to a tercet and back again. In a later poem in the same fascicle, "How sick – to wait – in any place – but thine" (Fr410), she also begins with a quatrain and then adjusts the next stanzas to three and five lines respectively. And although the quatrain, here as elsewhere, is the dominant form, within those limits Dickinson deploys iambic, trochaic, dactylic, and anapestic feet in a variety of combinations. Those variations do not have to be seen as efforts to match form with content, however they might function generically to keep the reader unsettled and vigilant. Rather, they show that Dickinson was prepared to loosen her metrical forms without abandoning them totally; clearly, contents or word selection took precedence over matters of rhythm and rhyme, with the latter providing a frame or template within which to work.

To return to the present example: the poem's first line is iambic tetrameter but ends with an unstressed syllable (this presumes that "To put this World down, like a Bundle" is one unit). The second has three beats, with one middle trochaic foot flanked by two iambs. The third begins with an iamb, and then has three successive dactyls. The fourth is predominantly trochaic. The second stanza begins with a trochaic foot, followed by successive iambs (the final syllable being unstressed). The next line is trochaic, the third begins with a trochee and is followed by successive iambic feet, and the final line is trochaic.

Depending on how it is pronounced, the third stanza begins with a dactylic foot followed either by successive iambs or (more probably) a pyrrhic foot, two spondees, and an iamb (with an unstressed final syllable). The next line begins with a dactyl, an iamb, and then three trochees, the last one of which is truncated. The final line is iambic. The fourth stanza begins with a dactyl, followed by three successive trochees; the next line has three trochees, though it also possible to read a trochaic, dactylic, and trochaic foot (the final one being typically truncated). The third line can be read as having two anapests and an iambic foot, or as two trochaic feet followed by two iambic ones (and an unstressed final syllable). The final line is trochaic.

Breaking up the rhythm of the poem with graphic or visual deviations would seem to depend on an assumption of metrical regularity (or monotony) for it to be effective; that this poem is metrically unpredictable to begin with suggests that such interventions are unnecessary or misunderstood. And again, Dickinson's cultural experience as well as specific elements of her education would have supplied theoretical and practical precedents for such flexibility: her Greek grammar stated that a "complete verse is called *acatalectic* . . . A

verse, of which the last foot is deficient, is called *catalectic*."[56] Dropping sylla-
bles at the beginning and end of metrical sequences was absolutely acceptable
formal behavior, in other words—however much Dickinson's actualization of
such practices remains uniquely hers.

One thing is certain: interpreting spaces in autographs as equivalent to
domain-end phenomena is never contradicted by the physical evidence on the
page. For example: if one reads the 5.6 cm interval after "Bundle" as an indi-
cator that the phrase belongs to and completes the previous row of writing,
and adjusts it accordingly, the rhyme scheme and number of beats per line are
brought into alignment with the next stanzas:

> To put this World down, like a Bundle –
> And walk steady, away,
> Requires Energy – possibly Agony –
> 'Tis the Scarlet way
>
> Trodden with straight renunciation
> By the Son of God –
> Later, his faint Confederates
> Justify the Road –

But in the third stanza, this pattern is altered: the patterns of rhythm and
rhyme demand a four-line structure [a], but the material evidence suggests
something entirely different and structurally unexpected [b]. For Dickinson
could have fit "Filaments of Bloom, Pontius Pilate sowed" onto separate lines,
whereas "sowed" and "Tomb" could not have fit onto the same row as the
writing preceding them:

> [a]
> Flavors of that old Crucifixion –
> Filaments of Bloom,
> Pontius Pilate sowed –
> Strong Clusters, from Barabbas' Tomb –
>
> [b]
> Flavors of that old Crucifixion –
> Filaments of Bloom, Pontius Pilate sowed –
> Strong Clusters, from Barabbas' Tomb –

Dickinson could override structural imperatives when the occasion de-
manded; perhaps she felt that the momentum or direction of the reading

would have linked "Pontius Pilate sowed" semantically to the following se-
quence ("Strong Clusters") rather than "Filaments of Bloom." Whatever the
reason, factors related to meter and rhyme do not always take priority when
editing the manuscripts; they need to be correlated with and corroborated by
the available material data.

    The next poem in the sequence, and the tenth in the fascicle as a whole, is
Fr405:

> Although I put away his life –
> An Ornament too grand
> For Forehead low as mine, to wear,
> This might have been the Hand
>
> That sowed the flower, he preferred –
> Or smoothed a homely pain,
> Or pushed the pebble from his
> path –
> Or played his chosen tune –
>
> On Lute the least – the latest –
> But just his ear could know
> That whatsoe'er delighted it,
> I never would let go –
>
> The foot to bear his errand –
> A little Boot I know –
> Would leap abroad like Antelope –
> With just the grant to do – [page break]
>
> His weariest Commandment –
> A sweeter to obey,
> Than "Hide and Seek" –
> Or skip to Flutes –
> Or all Day, chase the Bee –
>
> Your Servant, Sir, will weary –
> The Surgeon, will not come –
> The World, will have it's own – to do –
> The Dust, will vex your Fame –

The Cold will force your tightest
door
Some Febuary Day,
But say my Apron bring the
sticks
To make your Cottage gay –

That I may take that promise
To Paradise, with me –
To teach the Angels, avarice, [page break]
You, Sir, taught first – to me.

The basic pattern in the poem is four-line stanzas alternating between iambic
tetrameter and trimeter lines, where the even-numbered lines have three
stresses (or in Attridge's theory, a mute fourth beat). Five stanzas out of eight
deviate from the basic iambic pattern in that the first line in each lacks a final
beat (or replaces a two-syllable final foot with a single secondary stress). And
in the fifth stanza Dickinson seems to have broken up the basic pattern, turn-
ing the normally four-beat third line into two lines of iambic dimeter.[57]

Visually, however, the poem is even more varied: out of eight stanzas, two
have five rows (the second and fifth) and one six (the seventh). One fails to see
a repeated pattern here, unless it is one of randomly interrupting the stanzaic
design in order to increase or maintain the level of concentration being given
to the poem as a whole. In other words, Dickinson might be seen as adjusting
the temporal experience of the poem's structure in such a way that it never
becomes predictable, and consequently never allowing the reader to settle or
feel comfortable. Again, such a premise is absolutely legitimate, given that
meter is one technique among many that a writer such as Dickinson can use
to encourage the kinds of attention its subtlety requires. But one of the (ad-
mittedly minor) concerns that I have with such an argument is that only three
out of the poem's approximately one hundred and seventy-seven words are
then seen as worthy of emphasis. Is there is a particular weight of resonance
(biographical, social, cultural) to the words "path," "door," and "sticks" that
the other words were unable of carrying?

The second problem with critical readings attentive to autograph layout is
the implicit assumption that certain aspects of the poem's material inscription
are *always* potentially significant (line breaks) while others are *never* so (page
breaks). Thus, Dickinson's inscription of the line "But say my Apron bring

the / sticks" is important, but "To teach the Angels, avarice, // You, Sir, taught first – to me" is not. But who decides when one potentially meaningful inadvertence is deliberate and another, equally accidental and equally capable of meaning, is not? For it is possible to ascribe meaning to both moments. The first break delays the speaker's identification of what she is going to carry across the doorjamb, creating suspense. But the page break has exactly the same effect: it delays the ending of the poem by transferring it, or so the argument might go, to another page, thereby creating suspense again and introducing enough of a span in time for the speaker to bring a wholly new note into the poem at that point.

Manuscript critics do not take page breaks seriously, however, even though such an approach clearly fits in with the assumption that manuscripts are "handcrafted units shaped and situated to incorporate (or consciously transform) page design into the work of making meaning."[58] And as I have discussed, although critics regularly uncover meaning in the physical extent and direction of the dash, they ignore the implications of the idiosyncratically recorded quotation marks. Thus, the fact that the dashes subsequent to "preferred" (second stanza, first line) and "latest" (in the first line of the third) decline sharply and abruptly is part of a deliberate textual apparatus, whereas the repeated upper-left to lower-right slant of the quotation marks framing "Hide and Seek" is not. Yet it seems to me that the latter practice has potential consequences for our understanding of the former: the casualness or quirkiness in the inscription of the one should warn us against reading too much into variations in the other.

"Over and over, like a Tune" (Fr406) is the eleventh poem in Fascicle 20:

> Over and over, like a Tune –
> The Recollection plays –
> Drums off the Phantom
> Battlements
> Cornets of Paradise –
>
> Snatches, from Baptized
> Generations –
> Cadences too grand
> But for the Justified
> Processions
> At the Lord's Right hand.

Given that hymnal doxologies are syllabically defined from time to time, there is a temptation to classify this as 8s and 6s—except that, in the second stanza, the syllabic distribution shifts to 9 and 5. Perhaps the adjustment makes no difference; what stays constant is the total of fourteen syllables per two lines, which is a classic form. What also remains constant, however, is the meter, which is not always iambic (there are trochaic substitutions, as well as switches to trochaic meter generally) but which has consistently alternating lines of tetrameter and trimeter. Though one is skeptical of claims that Dickinson's use of hymn meter (in this instance common) uniformly complicates Christian belief, this poem seems to raise the possibility: the references to a "Tune," "Snatches" (of music), and "cadences" make that evident. Without wanting to speculate too much into the exact relationship of form and content, the switching back and forth between trochaic and iambic feet—though not unusual in Dickinson's work generally—can be seen to oppose the more regular rhythms of church singing. But this reading is not a certain one: Dickinson may also be trying to give the memory a dignity and status that is equal to baptism, election, and sainthood—without necessarily being equivalent to them. In that case, the echoes of common meter and the use of religious vocabulary would imply an experience or event of comparable weight and significance. The correspondence may also be closer than a modern, agnostic mind can be comfortable with, however: it is not impossible that the poem might record a conventional—though self-conferred—sense of being among the chosen.

Yet, from the material point of view, the poem seems to confirm the more general tendency in the fascicle as a whole, which is that short metrical lines do not carry over. Whereas eight and nine syllables, or four actualized metrical feet, can create a surplus that has to be accommodated by the next section of horizontal space on the page, five and six syllables, or three metrical feet, fit comfortably within the margins of the page. The more one reads the autographs in this fascicle, and the autographs in general, the more one sees that graphic disruption is an occasional consequence of physical dimension—the extent of the page, the size of the handwriting, and the length of the metrical line. No other explanation so consistently accounts for such deviations.

IV

"One need not be a chamber—to be Haunted" (Fr407A) is the twelfth poem in Fascicle 20, and the first one recorded in the fourth of the five sheets that the booklet is constructed from (H 65).

> One need not be a chamber –
> to be Haunted –
> One need not be a House –

The Brain – has Corridors
surpassing
Material Place –

Far safer of a Midnight –
meeting
External Ghost –
Than an Interior – confronting –
That cooler – Host –

Far safer, through an Abbey –
gallop –
The Stones a'chase –
Than Moonless – One's A'self
    encounter –
In lonesome place – [page break]

Ourself – behind Ourself –
Concealed –
Should startle – most –
Assassin – hid in Our Apart-
    ment –
Be Horror's least –

The Prudent – carries a
Revolver –
He bolts the Door –
O'erlooking a Superior Spectre –
More near –

As I pointed out in chapter 2, the word "Apartment" in this poem is a match-less example of sympathetic visual form: it embodies the very experience of separation or compartmentalization it purports to describe. But I also noted that in L874, Dickinson writes: "Thank Sister / with love, and / reserve an Apart- / ment for two / Cocks in the / Cocks / Thanksgiving plan- / ning –."[59] Reading the first example (the split in the poem) in the light of the second (the splits in the letter), it is clearly impossible to rule out their being acciden-tal: in the case of Fr407A Dickinson did not have sufficient room on the fourth line of her ruled page to complete the word "Apartment," and thus the non-deliberate aspect of its inscription can never absolutely be dismissed.[60]

Still, this poem's atmosphere of terror lends itself to the kinds of dramatic notes that the isolation of certain words suggest. Like a ghost story, the autograph version of the poem can be seen as an exercise in timing: certain phrases or words are delayed by the lineation so that their eventual delivery can be more thrilling. Take the first lines of the stanzas, for example:

1. One need not be a chamber –
   to be Haunted –
2. Far safer of a Midnight –
   meeting
3. Far safer, through an Abbey –
   gallop –
4. Ourself – behind Ourself –
   Concealed –
5. The Prudent – carries a
   Revolver –

Splitting the line heightens the excitement, one might contend, exactly equivalent to the convention in films whereby an actor enters a darkened and apparently empty room at the same time as the music or the camera angle indicates or anticipates a malevolent presence. Yet there are inconsistencies here—minor ones, perhaps, subjective ones almost certainly. First, the line split seems unnecessary in the first four of the five cases, since the dashes already have the function of enacting a delay. (In the fifth example, there is no dash because that line is less scary: it represents a lull, the first note in an ascending tension, and not its highest point.) Second, one observes that in examples 2 and 3, the theatrical elements ("Midnight" and "Abbey") are introduced *before* the break, which weakens the argument for seeing such dislocations as part of a more dramatic apparatus. Again, if the fracturing is for purposes of rhythmical variation, the dashes already bring about such fragmentation very effectively. If the splits are for emphasis, then the elements that are emphasized do not always appear capable of bearing the additional weight of significance assigned to them: "gallop" in particular is not the most promising subject for increased levels of scrutiny. And the shift in the proportion of attention paid to separate elements appears at times to upset the balance of the line: I see "Ourself – behind Ourself – Concealed –" as a single unit, whereas "Ourself – behind Ourself – / Concealed –" is a less effective and more stagy conjunction of two temporal units.[61]

The next poem in the sequence, Fr408A, is another example of how fairly innocuous material characteristics can, if given too much attention, get in the way of the poem proper:[62]

> Like Some Old fashioned
> Miracle –
> When Summertime is done –
> Seems Summer's Recollection – |
> And the affairs of June –
>
> As +infinite Tradition – as
> Cinderella's Bays –
> Or Little John – of Lincoln –
> Green –
> Or Blue Beard's Galleries
>
> Her Bees – have an illusive Hum –
> Her Blossoms – like a Dream
> Elate us – till we almost weep –
> So +plausible – they seem –
>
> Her +Memory – like Strains – enchant –
> Tho' +Orchestra +be dumb –
> The Violin – in Baize – replaced –
> And Ear, and Heaven – numb –

(marginal note, written vertically): + exquisite + Bagatelles —

The attraction of the newest forms of publishing Dickinson—both electronic and editions that claim to allow her to speak for the first time—is their newness. Instead of row after row of uniformly patterned quatrains, manuscript editions of the poems are undeniably more varied, since they include words that are inscribed upside down and—as in this case—vertically along the margin. But as Dickinson said (in Fr1180), "Not anything is stale so long / As Yesterday's Surprise."[63] One becomes quickly desensitized to the new disposition, in other words, so that one starts to anticipate and normalize it, lessening its innovativeness. Unless, that is, one concentrates more than usual and allows oneself to be confronted by the visual isolation of the words "Miracle" and "Green" in Fr408A and to worry at their meaning. But does such isolation make the word any more meaningful than its inclusion in the poem might demand of us anyway? Are we meant to think that this procedure increases the significance of the word "Miracle" beyond, for instance, the three definitions supplied in *Webster's*?[64] Does "Lincoln – / Green" make Lincoln any greener or the color more intense, or is it meant to make us think that the Little John in question is from a Lincoln Green different than the place commonly signified by that appellation? And given that such isolation would, if deliberate, demand a greater level of attention than other, medial, forms of emphasis such as underlining, what is it about the adjective "Green" that is more significant or is meant to have a greater impact than the adjective "Blue"? And what implications for the theory of deliberate word splitting does the insertion of the dash between "Lincoln" and "Green" have, when it is clearly a conventional signal that the words belong together and are not meant to be separate, autonomous integers of meaning? In paying attention to such local details, one tries to second-guess the motives behind their supposed deliberateness, wandering further and further away from the poem as a whole. Hoyt N. Duggan, writing about the noninterventionalist approach to editing the works of the *Pearl* poet, claimed that such a method predictably foregrounded the material document at the expense of the literary text. "The result," he continued, "has been increased fidelity to the MANUSCRIPT and infidelity to the POEM."[65]

V

"A very large proportion of her poems," Thomas Johnson wrote about Dickinson's use of hymn forms, "are in Common Meter." And Martha England agreed: "Emily Dickinson used C[ommon] M[eter] most frequently."[66] If that is the case, then Fr409A is triply unusual: it opens with a line of iambic pentameter; it switches between lines of four and two beats, then four beats and one, rather than (the more common) four and three; and it rhymes *abab*, then *aaaa*, rather than *abcb*.[67]

> The Soul selects her own Society –
> Then – shuts the Door –
> To her divine Majority –
> Present no more –
>
> Unmoved – she notes the Chariots – pausing –
> At her low Gate –
> Unmoved – an Emperor be kneeling
> Opon her Mat –
>
> I've known her – from an ample
> nation –
> Choose One –
> Then – close the Valves of
>   her attention –
> Like Stone –

The metrical arrangement of "The Soul selects her own Society" is atypical, and therefore more than usually motivated: there is a shifting dynamic between odd lines, which are long, and even lines, which are short. This alternating sequence is made more dramatic in the last stanza, where the even lines are reduced from iambic dimeter to monometer. This change is deliberate: a poem that deals with competing impulses of closure and openness can be said to enact that struggle by sequentially expanding and tightening the meter. Especially at the end, there is a sense of shutting down that echoes the poem's theme, or represents its choices in a starker way: the repeated rhymes (centered on the *n*, a palatal affricate) can suggest finality or the diminishment of time left in which to make a decision.

But the manuscript version of the poem—if taken literally—does something else in the last stanza. Its emphasis—semantic and rhythmical—is on the word "nation," whereas the conventionally rendered stress is more relational, contrasting the nine-syllable line containing the phrase "ample nation" with the two-syllable line containing the word "One." That contrast, and its effectiveness, is dissipated if one considers the isolation of "nation" to be deliberate; instead, one bisyllabic cluster limply follows and duplicates another. The lyric architecture falls apart; even the (comparatively) unusual rhyme becomes a rather unconvincing *abbcbb*, rather than the *aaaa* that Dickinson very carefully set up. There is no better example of how an alleged visual rhythm disrupts the balance of the original and silences its sonic and structured effects. For those effects depend on variation from but also within a repeated pattern: the last stanza essentially repeats the polarities of the first two in a more extreme way.

VI

The fifth and final sheet that comprises Fascicle 20 (H 66) contains four poems; "How sick – to wait – in any place – but thine" (Fr410) is the first of these.

> How sick – to wait – in any
> place – but thine –
> I knew last night – when
> someone tried to twine –
> Thinking – perhaps – that
> I looked tired – or alone –
> Or breaking – almost – with
> unspoken pain –

And I turned – ducal –
That right – was thine –
One port – suffices – for a
Brig – like *mine* –

Our's be the tossing – wild
though the sea –
Rather than a mooring –
unshared by thee.
Our's be the Cargo – *unladen – here* –
Rather than the *"spicy isles –"*
And thou – not there – [page break]

Commenting on Franklin's version of the poem, where it is organized into
three stanzas of 4, 3, and 5 lines (respectively), Judy Jo Small has described the
rhyme scheme of "sea/thee" as a rare instance (for Dickinson) of an end-
stopped couplet.[68] But the autograph version shows traces of an earlier and
more conventional structure of rhyme, enabling us to attempt an archaeolog-
ical reconstruction of what the poem may have looked like during the first
stages of its construction.

How sick – to wait –
[I]n any place – but thine –
I knew last night – when
[S]omeone tried to twine –

Thinking – perhaps – that
I looked tired – or alone –
Or breaking – almost – with
[U]nspoken pain –

And I turned – ducal –
That right – was thine –
One port – suffices –
[F]or a Brig – like *mine* –

Our's be the tossing –
[W]ild though the sea –
Rather than a mooring –
[U]nshared by thee.

> Our's be the Cargo –
> [U]*nladen – here –*
> Rather than the *"spicy isles –"*
> And thou – not there –

The tight, clipped rhythm (mainly iambic dimeter and trimeter) seems to suggest the massive emotional forces that it is designed to dam up; but for reasons that can only be guessed at, Dickinson decided that the combination of meter and rhyme was inappropriate (too pat, perhaps?). Instead, she seems to have joined the first two stanzas to fashion a longer sequence that re-creates the heroic couplet (iambic pentameter and rhyming couplets), as well as the virtues of restraint and control it was meant to embody. The effect is stunning: the thirteen dashes powerfully convey the battle between surface form and emotional depths, energies that are then unleashed in the second stanza, which explodes the longer line into smaller fragments, returning to tetrameter in the emphatic, determined declaration of "*One port* – suffices – for a Brig like *mine*." The third stanza, by contrast, turns wistful and wishful at the same time: dactyls and trochees are deployed to create a rolling motion in its first and third lines, before Dickinson switches to the disrupted and discordant rhythm for the sequences beginning "Rather." Perhaps the larger point to make, however, is that Dickinson *did* experiment with the length of lines in order to fashion new stanzaic forms. To focus on the physical arrangement of single words and lines on the page is to miss the highly innovative structural intelligence at work both in this poem, and in the next (Fr411):

> Mine – by the Right of
> the White Election!
> Mine – by the Royal Seal!
> Mine – by the sign in
> the Scarlet prison –
> Bars – cannot conceal!
>
> Mine – here – in Vision – and
> in Veto!
> Mine – by the Grave's Repeal –
> Titled – Confirmed –
> Delirious Charter!
> Mine – long as Ages steal!

———

One of the (many) striking features of this poem is the deft manipulation of its meter, which is deployed in such a way that the accents coincide emphatically with the capitalized words in the opening three lines. In each instance, Dickinson opens with a dactylic foot; the effect—not of the foot itself but of its repetition—is one of conviction, insistence, and resolve. The poem is de-clarative rather than descriptive, and it uses rhythm to underscore the unim-peachable certainty of its claims. And as Small points out, rhyme is a signifi-cant agent in supporting this series of proclamations: "Both stanzas are built on the same end rhyme (*Seal/conceal/Repeal/steal*), and the first pair of these are identical in sound (an instance of *rime riche*). There are two internal rhymes (*Right/White*, and *Mine/Sign*), and six lines begin with the repeated *Mine*. All the rhyme words contain high-front vowels, *i* and *e*, and, with an added ripple of alliteration throughout, the total effect is of noisy excess. Expertly, the lyric uses statement and sound to express a mood of wildly confident exultation. Everything about it contributes to a tone of self-assertion that is *Delirious* and slightly shrill. Rhyme is crucial in producing that tone."[69] The problem with the manuscript version of the poem, if its lineation is regarded as willed, is that the metrical effect—accumulative, relentless, point-edly repeated—is dissipated. Instead of an insistent opening line, we get a tentative one, which hovers nervously on the brink of a justification ("Mine by the Right of" what?) and introduces it too late, and apologetically. The effect is not a grand finale but curtain-failure: the speaker freezes on stage and forgets both her cue and her lines at a crucial moment. Frankly, such a sce-nario might not be entirely unwelcome, for this poem does not really invite us to join in so much as to sit back and wonder at what it is that drives the speaker on. But this is not a lyric tête-à-tête (like "I'm Nobody! Who are you?"): it is in-your-face, a dare that allows for the possibility of no counter-dare, a finger-in-the-chest shout of freedom and independence.

Though it begins with a fairly common trochaic substitution, "Heaven is so far of the Mind" (Fr413) closes the fascicle with two quatrains of common meter, rhyming *abcb*:

> Heaven is so far of the
> Mind
> That were the Mind dissolved –
> The Site – of it – by Architect
> Could not again be proved –
>
> 'Tis Vast – as our Capacity –
> As fair – as our idea –
> To Him of adequate
> desire
> No further 'tis, than Here –

The autograph and print editions of the poem differ in two details: in the former, "Mind" and "desire" are written separately from the lines that they would appear to complete. Since these words are not part of a rhyming sequence, one might argue that their isolation should not be amended. But Dickinson's rhyme structures rely on odd lines being dissonant and on even lines forming a congruence of sound; if this structural regularity is disrupted or delayed, the timing of the poem is slightly thrown. And, again, one wonders at the possible redundancy in isolating words that already receive such strong emphasis from their position as the final accented units in the longest elements of the poem's metrical pattern (with "Mind" already highlighted by being capitalized). Moreover, why is "desire" chosen for such emphasis and not "Here," "idea," or "dissolved"? Though a manuscript reading of such a poem cannot be discounted absolutely, the spaces of 10.3 cm and 9.6 cm subsequent to "Mind" and "desire" make most sense as indications that those words belong to the preceding row of writing in each case.

VII

While the first generation of editors sought to regularize Dickinson within nineteenth-century cultural modalities of grammar, meter, and sound, the most recent seeks to domesticate her within modernist and postmodernist paradigms of fragmentation, incompleteness—and sight. At one level, the attention to Dickinson's graphic forms is a legacy of modernism's interest in the optical and rhythmical (as opposed to the traditionally metrical) stylization of poetry. Typically, modernist poets organized lines of verse according to phrasal segments (based on breath length or the normal syntactic laws of language) or visual divisions that were motivated by intellectual or aesthetic procedures. The traditional form of arranging the majority of Dickinson's stanzas in quatrains is regarded as an editorial imposition that in many cases fails to correspond with the facts of autograph originals. Such arrangements are associated with conformity, conservatism, and restriction. The manuscripts are seen as *visually* disrupting such forms and are associated with liberation, originality, and spontaneity.[70]

To insist that the appearance of a dash, word, line, verse unit, or poem means something is to foreground the visual over the aural. Of course, the angle and duration of a dash *can* be reproduced during speech delivery (as matters of register and inflexion), as can the splitting of a word or its postponed enunciation because of its isolation from other lines. But all this suggests that physicality in Dickinson's work is locally focused, related to significance at particular points and visually directed, rather than—as with meter—general, related to the activation of generic expectations and experienced as a series of beats. One is to do with content and message and foregrounds the specific aspects of a poem's inscription: not how it appears, but what its appearance means. The other is to do with rhythm as something *general* that can be apprehended by the ear and the body: "The apprehension of rhythm involves a richly complex combination of imagination, learned behavior, physical or quasi-physical activity, a mental and physical predisposition or readiness to interpret certain cues the right way, a process of self-correction, adjustment, and confirmation, and rapid learning. To be more precise, rhythm is principally a *physical experience*, either in the sense of a bodily movement or of an imaginary readiness for or recreation of bodily movement; but it is made possible in part by a degree of *mental focusing, expectation, readiness, conscious recognition*, and *will*."[71]

One of the consequences of the graphic approach to the manuscripts is that the significance of sound in her writing generally has to be underplayed. Meter exists as a *dead* structure that is then fractured and rearranged to create vital alternatives. But most of Dickinson's improvisations appear to have been sound related rather than visual (her herbarium, for instance, is quite conventionally organized). At least two of her friends have commented on her piano playing as experimental. In an interview with the *Boston Globe*, the daughter of John L. Graves explains that he used to stay overnight with Emily and Lavinia if both parents were absent. "Often, during these visits to the Dickinson relatives, father would be awakened from his sleep by heavenly music. Emily would explain in the morning, 'I can improvise better at night.'"[72] And in a letter to Susan Dickinson, Kate Anthon remembered "Emily with her dog, & Lantern! often at the piano playing weird and beautiful melodies, all from her own inspiration."[73]

In addition, Dickinson—and her contemporaries—read literature aloud. There are a number of references in *Letters* to such a practice: in L304, to Louise Norcross, Dickinson herself says (though not of her own work), "I read them in the garret, and the rafters wept."[74] To Elizabeth Holland she reports in L721 that "Mother and Vinnie wept – I read it to both at their request." And in another letter (L901) to the same recipient during Holland's illness, she instructs her to "Ask some kind Voice to read to you."[75] Dickinson's early biographers emphasized the same practices: "As Emily became more frail, Lavinia spent hours in reading to her. Sometimes it was Shakespeare, the Brownings, Ruskin or the Revelations. Dante was also a favorite author. Emily was very fond of Miss Lavinia's way of presenting a character. 'Vinnie, if ministers knew how to read as you do, they would impress their audience beyond repeal.' Emily was herself a most charming reader. It was done with great simplicity and naturalness, with an earnest desire to express the exact conception of the author, without any thought of herself, or the impression her reading was sure to make."[76] Susan Dickinson is known to have read poems aloud to guests, and nor was she the only one: in "Annals of the Evergreens," she reports how Samuel Bowles declaimed poems that had been sent to him as editor of the *Republican*.[77] Interestingly, on a manuscript addressed to "Mr Bowles" and sent about 1861, Dickinson wrote:[78]

> The Juggler's *Hat*
> her Country is –
> The Mountain Gorse –
> the *Bee's* –

On the verso, Mary Bowles, Samuel's wife and a Dickinson correspondent in her own right, noted: "I trust you will not read all these aloud in one evening. I do not think reading aloud is good for you. It tires you too much, both your voice and head."[79] It stretches credibility too far, perhaps, to think that Mary's note on Dickinson's original *refers* to that original specifically—or to a private collection of Dickinson's poems that Samuel may have enjoyed declaiming to himself. But there are valuable lessons here, nonetheless; pointers to an informality in nineteenth-century middle-class recycling of epistolary materials, as well as indications of how poetry was appreciated in performance—even privately. All these things suggest that Dickinson's correspondents, her handpicked audience, might have understood her autograph poems in very different ways from today's readership. There is no record of any of her friends ever formulating a sense that the manuscript poem's appearance might have influenced its meaning, for example.

Indeed, Frances Norcross was compelled to write to Higginson after having read a poem aloud to a friend, obviously feeling that it should be included in a subsequent edition of Dickinson's work: "I am impelled to send you my cousin's poem on the Mushroom . . . and also this gem about a Spider. I remember that you said you had not seen the first, and as I was reading it to a friend yesterday, I felt so much impressed with its weirdness and originality, that I felt you ought to see it at once."[80] The poem referred to here (though not the same variant) is "The mushroom is the Elf of Plants" (Fr1350D); Ellen Hart contends that another version (A 416) is more profoundly understood in the context of its original appearance (it was written in pencil inside "a yellow envelope, set on point so that the physical measure increases then diminishes in length").[81] One wonders, then, if some things do get lost in the transformation from the nineteenth-century emphasis on the auditory to the twentieth-century triumph of the ocular.[82] Attention to Dickinson's autographs as visual artifacts is not always reconcilable with their status as scripts for reading: if variants, for example, are designed to shimmer equally and visually between poles of endless possibility, how are they to be vocalized? Did Dickinson think of her late fragments and unfinished works as scripts for a choral performance? For if poems were read aloud not only by Dickinson's contemporaries but by herself, then the variants would have had to be articulated sequentially and the sequence itself structured by some kind of principle or preference.

Fascicle 20 shows evidence of a similarly experimental attitude to rhythm. Keeping in mind that long meter describes a quatrain of four beats per line; common meter a quatrain of alternating four and three beats per line; short meter a quatrain of three beats in the first, second, and fourth lines and four in the third; and half meter a quatrain of three beats per line, one emerges with the following information about Fascicle 20: Fr396, "I took one Draught of Life," has two quatrains: the first is half meter, the second short, rhyming *abcb*. Fr397, "A train went through a burial gate," has two quatrains of common meter, rhyming *abab* and *abcb* (respectively). Fr398, "The Morning after Wo," has four quatrains of short meter, rhyming (mainly) *abcb*. Fr399, "Departed – to the Judgment," has two quatrains of half meter, rhyming *abcb*.[83]

Fr400, "I think the Hemlock likes to stand," has four quatrains of common meter, rhyming *abcb*. Fr401C, "Dare you see a Soul at the 'White Heat'?" has four quatrains: the outer quatrains (one and four) are approximately common meter (with the opening line stretched to five beats), while the inner quatrains (two and three) have short meter. The rhyme scheme is (at times a very loose) *abcb*: in stanzas two and four, the rhyming words change places ("Forge" and "Blaze," "Blaze" and "Forge"), and in the first they are practically identical ("*door*" and "quickene*d Ore*" or "vivi*d Ore*": emphasis added—"vivid" is the variant). Fr402, "To hear an Oriole sing," has five tercets, mainly two lines of iambic trimeter and a third of dimeter, rhyming *aaa*. Fr403B, "I reason, Earth is short," has three quatrains, with two lines of iambic trimeter and two of dimeter in the first stanza, switching to three of trimeter and one of dimeter in the next two, rhyming (loosely) *aaab*; the final line is a refrain.

Fr404, "To put this World down, like a Bundle," has four stanzas: one, two, and four are quatrains, while three has been altered to make a tercet. The quatrains all have very loose common meter, rhyming *abcb*: the tercet was composed in the same way, but with lines two and three combined to make a five-beat line.[84] Fr405, "Although I put away his life," has quatrains of common meter and short meter, rhyming *abcb*, with the fifth quatrain altered to make five lines.[85] Fr406, "Over and over, like a Tune," has two quatrains of common meter, rhyming *abcb*.

Fr407A, "One need not be a chamber – to be Haunted" has five quatrains, alternating between four beats and two or three beats and rhyming *abcb*.[86] Fr408A, "Like Some Old fashioned Miracle," has four quatrains of predominantly common meter, rhyming *abcb*. Fr409A, "The Soul selects her own Society," has three quatrains, alternating between lines of four and two beats; the last quatrain moves between four and one, and the rhyme scheme is *abcb*.[87]

Fr410, "How sick – to wait – in any place – but thine," begins with three successive pentameter lines and a fourth tetrameter, after which the meter in the two remaining three- and five-line quatrains is deliberately fractured for a variety of effects, as I describe above. Fr411, "Mine – by the Right of the White Election!" uses common meter only in a very loose or irregular sense (lines of four beats followed by lines of three, rhyming *abcb*), but its meter is dactylic and (mainly) trochaic rather than iambic. (The first line of the second stanza seems like a perfectly regular trochaic tetrameter with a stressed syllable at the start. Dickinson also divided line 3 into two, making successive lines of dimeter in order to facilitate a pause after "Confirmed" that makes the statement more emphatic and joyous.) Fr412, "She lay as if at play," is closest to half meter (quatrain sequences of three-beat lines), but the last line consistently uses iambic dimeter rather than trimeter. The unusual rhyme scheme consists of rhyming couplets (*aabb*). Fr413, "Heaven is so far of the Mind," uses fairly regular common meter, rhyming *abcb*.

What this tells us is perhaps something that was already known but recently forgotten: Dickinson wrote most often in hymn meters, and both meter and rhyme were primary structural elements in her process of composition.[88] At the same time, her use of those meters is not any more monotonous than the drumbeat that secures the base for some of the best-known and innovative rock music of our own age.[89] One is reminded of a television and cinema advertisement for Phillips stereo equipment, in which the scene opens at night in an urban high-rise setting. Music is being played, and it has an insistent, regular beat. The camera then moves in and out of apartments that are situated close to the musical source: in one, a man lies between sleep and waking, his toe tapping; in another, a baby sucks; in a third, a couple make love; in a fourth, there is the sound of breathing.[90] All these events coincide in rhythm with the music: when it is switched off, the characters are disturbed—the child wails, the man wakes, the couple are interrupted. Rhythm is an essential aspect of human life, and it corresponds to something basic within and outside us: our heartbeat, the movement of the lungs, and the way that we walk, as well as the change from day to night and from season to season. Such a perception of rhythm (as something physical, produced by and felt in the body as much as the mind) coincides with some of Dickinson's core statements about reading poetry and her practice of declaiming her own work and that of others and has therefore informed much of the writing in this chapter.[91] Emphasizing the rhythm of the eye over the rhythms of the ear in reading Dickinson's poems is, I am persuaded, equivalent to switching off the music: what's left is silence.

CHAPTER SEVEN

Toward a Culture of Measurement
in Manuscript Study

A work is never completed except by some accident such as weariness, satisfaction, the need to deliver, or death.

Paul Valéry, "Recollection"

REPORTS OF the death of the author, like the celebrated story of the newspaper obituary read at breakfast by the deceased, may be regarded as premature. For theoretical debates about the status and role of the author and the usefulness or otherwise of a concept such as intention in identifying the site of meaning or meanings in literary works continue to arise at crucial points in the history and practice of critical and editorial activity. Though problematic and contentious, they have a stubborn force as mechanisms for discussing literature, as well as its interpretations. And they might even apply, under certain conditions, to the works of writers who are celebrated for their complexity and indeterminacy. "All men say 'What' to me," wrote Dickinson, but men were not the only ones she succeeded in confusing—Helen Hunt Jackson, famously, was another.[1]

Dickinson seems to recognize that meaning is not a *fiat* and that more often than not words do not mean what, or do not mean all that, they might have been intended to mean. At the level of a particular *poem's* contents, of course, this is not a problem—or is not thought to be a problem by those of us who believe that part of the pleasure of literary texts is that they often cannot be reduced to a single meaning, and may not have been composed with a single meaning in mind. Furthermore, intention, even so far as its recovery is feasible or even desirable, may not be used as a *sole* criterion for appreciating a work of literature and may not even always be used as a *leading* criterion.[2] William K. Wimsatt and Monroe C. Beardsley, for example, argued that although "the designing intellect" might be the *cause* of a poem, it should not be taken as the *standard* "by which the critic is to judge the worth of the poem's performance."[3] One accepts, too, Theodore Redpath's contention that "a poem may mean something different from what the poet intended it to mean, may mean less than the poet intended it to mean, may mean more than [she] intended it to mean; may perhaps sometimes mean substantially what [she] intended."[4] (And in her statements about the messages carried by flowers, Dickinson appears to have been confronted with the realization that not every reader can recover the meanings she wills or recover the correct ones.)[5] Dickinson's manuscripts bequeath to posterity not only editorial challenges; they also ask the present generation of readers whether it is possible or worthwhile to distinguish between "meaning" and "significance," between "motive" and "intention," when attempting to formulate an understanding of the creative process.[6]

It was the American critic E. D. Hirsch who made this classic distinction between what a poem is for the writer (its "meaning") and what it does to the reader or what the reader does to it (its "significance"). Hirsch allowed that a text is capable of generating different interpretations at different times but argued that the original one formulated by the writer has the most authority: "Meaning is the determinate representation of a text for an interpreter. An interpreted text is always taken to represent something, but that something can always be related to something else. Significance is meaning-as-related-to-something-else. If an interpreter did not conceive a text's meaning to be there as an occasion for contemplation or application, he would have nothing to think or talk about. Its thereness, its self-identity from one moment to the next, allows it to be contemplated. Thus, while meaning is a principle of stability in an interpretation, significance embraces a principle of change."[7] At times, meaning and significance may overlap, as when an historical love poem will be associated by a contemporary reader with a period in the person's life when he or she was in love. Love and grief are emotions that may be experienced differently by different people, according to their age, education, gender, nationality, personality, and system of values, and depending on where and when they live. But they nonetheless have a universal aspect that enables readers to approach very closely to the original motive for writing, even if it is in the distant past. Such experiences may be differently apprehended by writer and reader, but they are one of the reasons why good literature seems able to survive the scene of its saying or, as Paul Ricouer puts it, why the "text's career escapes the finite horizon lived by its author."[8] (Experience is not the only key, of course; to employ a word is to suggest a fairly limited set of meanings that are assigned by convention and historical usage to that word, a usage that can be recovered with varying degrees of accuracy in the future or by the continuity of the word's point of reference.) By extension, a reader may also be able to see things of which the author may be unaware but which nonetheless contribute to the poem's fascination—and perhaps even to its intention. These factors come into play when we discuss in detail the appearance of Emily Dickinson's manuscripts, which seem very different from their print editions—closer to the diversities of H.D. and Ezra Pound, the "free-verse mimesis" of Williams, or e. e. cummings's "play with the visual structure of letters."[9] Viewed through the lenses of such technical innovation and experiment, Dickinson's autographs might seem to demonstrate a visually and metrically proleptic form of textual inscription. As Judith Farr puts it, "the danger is that in this, as in other matters, we may ascribe to Emily Dickinson a premonitory iconoclasm that was not actually hers."[10] One could say that these features constitute a valid part of a handwritten poem's significance for a twenty-first-century reader, though not necessarily a premeditated aspect of its meaning.

In the nineteenth century, debates about who controlled the meanings of a text, and where those meanings were lodged, took one form in a series of lawsuits featuring a number of authors, publishers, and translators. In 1853, Harriet Beecher Stowe and her husband filed a case in the United States Third Circuit Court of Appeals against F. W. Thomas, who had translated *Uncle Tom's Cabin* into German and published it without having sought permission from, or given payment to, the author. In his ruling, Judge Robert Grier found that Stowe's *words* were covered by the 1831 Copyright Act but not her *ideas*: "The author's conceptions have become the common property of his readers, who cannot be deprived of the use of them, or their right to communicate them to others clothed in their own language, by lecture or by treatise. The claim of literary property, therefore, after publication, cannot be in the ideas, sentiments or the creations of the imagination of the poet or novelist, as disserved from the language, idiom, style or the outward semblance and exhibition of them."[11] Grier's summary opposes what has become a widely accepted position in literary theory today: that ideas cannot be separated from the language used to communicate them. Nevertheless, issues of copyright continued to be debated in nineteenth-century America; crucial amendments to the first U.S. Copyright Act of 1790 were voted on in 1856 and 1865, and Dickinson's contribution to the debate resulted in one of her most celebrated poems, Fr788, "Publication – is the Auction / Of the Mind of Man," a deeply conservative work which establishes a strict hierarchy of property in the composition of literary works:[12]

> Thought belong to Him who gave it –
> Then – to Him Who bear
> It's Corporeal illustration

Dickinson's speaker seems—in this poem at least—to suggest that meaning is propelled and only made possible by intention, by a first cause that lies outside the realm of the material (either the world or the word). Thought precedes language, and any linguistic manifestations of the first or new idea remain the property of the creator. She walks a fine line here: language is secondary to thought in the process of creation (and therefore potentially independent of it), but the embodiment and expression of a specific and unique thought or series of thoughts—in whatever form—relates to that thought as an egg to its fertilization, or a servant to her or his master. History, in the shape of the Bible (inspired by God but written through many men), offered religious sanction for such an idea: as a bishop in the reign of James I explained, the "first royal author is the King of Kings – God himself, who doth so many things for our imitation."[13] And in the same way that the Divine Author gives life (and perhaps even imaginative ideas) to humans, the human author—the genius or originator—passes these meanings on to the reader, who "bears" but does not own or originate them (to "bear a weight or burden" as a servant or slave carries her or his sovereign's goods; there may also be a pun on the bear, or animal, which furthers the distinction between body and mind in the poem).[14] Thought appears to be separate from its actualization through physical signs, in the same way that the body is animated by the spirit but only temporarily affixed to it. The grand-daughter, daughter, and sister of lawyers has her spokesperson offer an emphatic counter to Grier's ruling: "the claim of literary property" *ought to be* "in the ideas, sentiments or the creations of the imagination of the poet," and such ownership should extend to the expression of those ideas, in whatever "language, idiom or style." In this much, she could find secular philosophical precedent in Locke's familiar passage from the *Two Treatises on Government* (1690): "Though the Earth, and all inferior Creatures be common to all Men, yet every Man has a *Property* in his own *Person*. This no Body has any Right to but himself. The *Labour* of his Body, and the *Work* of his Hands, we may say, are properly his. Whatsoever then he removes out of the State that Nature hath provided, and left it in, he hath mixed his *Labour* with, and joyned it to something that is his own, and thereby makes it his *Property*."[15]

The language of private ownership figures large in Dickinson's pronouncements on her writing: "Lest you meet my Snake and suppose I deceive it was robbed of me," she writes to Higginson of the publication of Fr1096A, "A narrow fellow in the grass," in the *Springfield Daily Republican* of 14 February 1866 (an episode that is discussed earlier in this book).[16] And fully twelve years would pass between the second—and final—appearance of "The Snake" in the *Springfield Weekly Republican* of 17 February 1866 and the (anonymous but sanctioned) publication of another Dickinson poem, Fr112, "Success is counted sweetest," in *A Masque of Poets* (1878).[17] Such a substantial gap (after a period in 1864 when five poems were published, out of a total of only ten ever to appear in her lifetime) suggests that Dickinson was intent on reasserting the exclusive rights to her literary estate, at least during her lifetime.

It was Susan Dickinson who almost certainly supplied Samuel Bowles at the *Republican* with either the original or a transcript of "A narrow fellow in the grass," and on 8 February 1891, five years after Dickinson's death (and only a few weeks after the release of *Poems of Emily Dickinson*), she approached another editor, William Hayes Ward at the *Independent*, with the offer of a "poem on the Martyrs" (Fr187A, "Through the strait pass of suffering").

> Magazines and newspapers are now eager for anything of Emily's, but I should prefer the Independent to them all as I rate it's literary merit most highly. I enclose the poem on the Martyrs – clean and crisp as rock crystal to me. If you will print it for a money compensation I should be glad and will reserve others for you which have never been seen – Scribners gave me $15. for "Renunciation" printed in August [1890]. I do not care for barter and am no "Shylock" but some price is fair – I suppose – I would like this confidential as the sister is quite jealous of my treasures – I was to have compiled the Poems – but as I moved slowly, dreading publicity for us all, she was angry and a year ago took them from me. All I have are mine – given me by my dear Emily while living so I can in honor do with them as I please.[18]

But when Lavinia Dickinson found out that the *Independent* had published two of her sister's poems, on 12 March 1891, without her knowledge or prior permission, she made her objections known in writing: "I wish simply to say that my sister gave her poems to me, all of them, as I can prove, if necessary; and that although copies of them have been given at different times to different persons, they have been so given simply for private perusal, or reading to others, and not to pass the property in them, which is mine.[19] There were misapprehensions on both sides. Lavinia (or, to be more accurate, Lavinia and Mabel Loomis Todd) seems to have underestimated how many poems and letters Susan Dickinson had received during Dickinson's lifetime, fearing instead that Susan had appropriated many of the manuscripts loaned to her by Lavinia in the period after Dickinson's death (on the understanding that Susan would edit them for publication). Susan Dickinson appears to have equated possession of manuscripts with ownership—understandably (because the ones that she retained had been sent to her personally and were often "yellow and faded with time") but mistakenly (since the new copyright law of 1891 stated that every "person who shall print or publish any manuscript whatever without the consent of the author or proprietor first obtained shall be liable to the author or proprietor for all damages occasioned by such injury").[20]

Posthumous publications of Dickinson took place during a period of re-form in copyright regulation, especially in the United States. The Chace Act was passed in 1891 and constituted the first major international copyright law to be implemented by the U.S. Government. Previous to that act, American authors had been protected by a number of laws that derived their origin from British common-law practice and statutory laws. Under the English system, the author had a common-law ownership of her or his work until publication, after which it was a statutory right, protected by the Statute of Anne (dating to 1710). The U.S. Constitution contained similar statutes in 1790. In 1831, when Dickinson was barely a year old, the law held that copyright belonged to the author (if alive) for twenty-eight years or to her or his immediate family for fourteen years; in 1870, the copyright belonged to the author (if alive) and to her or his immediate family both for twenty-eight years.[21]

Slightly more than a decade before her death and not long after the death of her father and the incapacitation through illness of her mother, Dickinson was moved to arrange her last will and testament, which was "signed, sealed, published and declared" on 19 October 1875 and which named Lavinia the sole executor of her estate: "I give devise and bequeath to my only sister Lavinia N. Dickinson all my estate, real and personal, to have and to hold the same to her and her heirs, and assigns forever."[22] After Dickinson's death, Roberts Brothers held the copyright of the 1890, 1891, and 1896 editions of her poems, under a contract with and for Lavinia. The publication of Dickinson poems by Susan Dickinson through *Scribner's* in 1890 and the *Independent* in 1891 therefore represented a legal infringement of Lavinia's copyright, though perhaps not a moral transgression. By extension, Millicent Todd Bingham had no obvious legal or technical right to bequeath Dickinson autographs in her possession to Amherst College, since they were not hers to give in the first place: they belonged to Lavinia (1886–99), to Martha Dickinson Bianchi (1899–1943), and then to Alfred Leete Hampson (who died in 1952 but passed the manuscripts in his custodianship to the Houghton Library of Harvard University in May 1950 by way of a grant from Gilbert Montague).[23] Again, Mabel Loomis Todd's publication of the *Letters of Emily Dickinson* (1931) and Millicent Todd Bingham's publication with her mother of *Bolts of Melody* (1945) "were illegal invasions of the Dickinson family rights. These rights were legally passed to Harvard as a part of [Gilbert Montague's purchase and presentation of Dickinson family papers]."[24]

Theoretical discussions about what literature might mean, as well as how it was meant to convey those meanings, often mesh in interesting ways with competing claims about who owns the legal and moral rights (which are not always seen as synonymous) to publish and to speak on behalf of Emily Dickinson. Not long after Mary Landis Hampson was writing to ask Gilbert Montague if she still had the power to prevent Dickinson biographer George Frisbie Whicher from ever becoming one of her editors, Roland Barthes was beginning to formulate his theories of "the death of the author," claiming that to "give a text an Author is to impose a limit on that text, to furnish it with a final signified, to close the writing."[25] That is, the wife of the former executor of the Dickinson estate was attempting to close down the right to represent Dickinson's texts at a point in history when literary theorists were beginning to favor the idea of "the *scriptible*, open text whose meaning is infinitely deferred because its form can never be settled or effectively engaged."[26] Intriguingly, *both* impulses—the assumption of a moral prerogative to act on behalf of the historical person with regard to her textual transmission and the interpretive right to liberate the meaning of those texts from the Writer in a generalized sense (as a locus of authority for her or his meanings)—are reconciled in manuscript-based approaches to understanding Dickinson's work.[27] For such critics, the unfinished state of many of Dickinson's manuscripts—when there are no choices indicated for word variants, for instance—is a kind of deliberate self-sacrifice, a generous and proleptically postmodernist abnegation of the author's traditional right to impose choices on the reader. In this instance, the author's death (in the sense of the surrender of the right to control meaning) is something that the author willed while still alive. This is slightly different from the *actual* death of the author, however, where it might be thought that the writer's permanent withdrawal from the world prevents readers from ever having recourse to her wishes and thus opens the text to a variety of readings that must remain forever unsanctioned. For manuscript critics, Dickinson's incomplete autographs are not accidents of mood, health, disinterest, or even the interruption of death, but a deliberate strategy, a poetic, implicit in her refusal to publish while alive: the Author is dead; long live the author.

The idea that Dickinson abdicated her lyric monarchy, often refusing to decide which word or phrase she wanted, has clear implications for editors as well as readers. If it is true that she effaced herself and allowed the reader to contribute to the process of forming meaning and even the particulars of the text itself, then it follows that editors are obliged to do no less. Recent textual mappings of Dickinson's landscape therefore attempt to foreground as many of their handwritten deviations from straightforward linear script as possible, not only including information about the direction of the handwriting and dashes but also reproducing them, for example, and thereby allowing the reader to decide whether irregularities were deliberately expressive devices. Such gestures can be seen as democratically enlarging the territory within which choice might be exercised, then, or as prompting the reader to find intentions for manuscript features that may well be casual—and thus placing a greater burden of responsibility on the reader than is necessary (for example, by representing a blank space at the start of a line of poetry but failing to supply information about the placement of an embossment on the paper that coincides with that blank space and explains its necessity; the editorial nonintervention thus forces the reader to come up with alternative explanations for the initial space). At an abstract level, such approaches are admirably inclusive; at another, they may also represent what D. C. Greetham describes as a kind of editorial death-wish, "the futile pretense that no critical decisions are necessary in editing critical texts and that . . . computer programs can protect the editor from having to think."[28]

An example of the equation in Dickinson studies of the death of the author as the last will and testament of the author herself is offered by Sharon Cameron, according to whom "Dickinson frequently appears to be understanding variants not as substitutions, but as additions, as parts of the poem."[29] In support of her interpretation, Cameron quotes the final stanza from Fr319 "Of Bronze – and Blaze." The excerpt under discussion appears in Fascicle 13 as follows:

> My Splendors , are Menagerie –
> But their Competeless Show
> Will entertain   the Centuries
>   When I , am   long   ago ,
> +An   Island in   dishonored
>   Grass –
> Whom none but Daisies, know –
>   Beetles –
> + Some –   _____

This is how Cameron represents the same lines:

> My Splendors, are Menagerie –
> But their Competeless Show
> Will entertain the Centuries
> When I, am long ago,
> [An/Some –] Island in dishonored Grass –
> Whom none but [Daisies,/Beetles –] know.

Cameron's point is that since Dickinson left no verbal or graphic indication as to a preference for "Some" over "An," or "Beetles" over "Daisies," the words exist not as elements that have to be chosen between but as "non-exclusive alternatives."[30] Another argument (though not one sanctioned by Cameron) would be to say that "Of Bronze – and Blaze" is not one poem but *four*, with each performance differing according to the particularities of its combined "variants" (the first version has "An" and "Daisies"; the second, "An" and "Beetles"; the third, "Some" and "Daisies"; and the fourth, "Some" and "Beetles"). This is a comparatively mild example of the idea in some Dickinson circles that variants create new works: G. Thomas Tanselle reports that " 'Those fair – fictitious People,' has twenty-six variants that fit eleven places, amounting to 7,680 poems."[31] And D. C. Greetham, reporting Tanselle's observations in a separate article, asks: "Leaving aside the practical question of who would be willing to publish or read 7,680 'poems', it becomes clear that the implications of [such a method of creating works from variants] are destabilizing, not only of the 'traditional notion of a single best text' . . . but of any text at all."[32]

Nevertheless, Cameron's edited version of the final stanza from "Of Bronze – and Blaze" shifts its physical particulars (albeit openly) and therefore crucially distorts its semantic trajectories; in the original, there is no laterally sequential inscription such as "An Some," for instance.[33] Rather, Dickinson inserts a cross in front of "An" and then writes "Some –" (or perhaps even "some –") below it, but with an interval of two rows of handwriting and an interval of space between them. For a nonnegotiable and dynamic relationship of semantic parity to exist between "An" and "Some," one has to overlook the implications of that interval. Stricty speaking, Cameron is correct in saying that Dickinson did not *physically support her choice* of "An" by crossing "Some" out; but that means in effect that Dickinson did not exercise the option which "Some" might have represented to her. An analogy would be with a soccer team, which fields eleven players, with a number of substitutes on the sidelines, the latter to be used only in the event of a tactical change being decided on or a first-choice player incurring injury or loss of form. The substitutes may be part of the squad from which the team is chosen, but they are not part of the team that starts the match. In the same way, the variants in Dickinson's poem are (in the case of this autograph at least) outside the frame of the poem as it is enacted on the page: their potential existed to be invoked, but never was. Since Dickinson did not cancel her primary selections, they retain their active status: "Some" and "Beetles" are usable but unused elements of the poem's secondary apparatus—not the poem that Dickinson wrote but the poem or poems that she might have written. Indeed, Cameron seems to recognize this implicitly when she says that the "metrics of the poem insist that we choose among the variants (in that the metrical scheme can accommodate one but not two of the variants)."[34]

Whether one agrees with Cameron or not, it seems at least tenable that Dickinson scholars attempt to bring about a reconciliation between author-based and author-free approaches to the text and that this reconciliation is anchored in a view of the manuscripts as willfully abandoned (and not, say, interrupted by death). Susan Howe, for one, has described line breaks, blank spaces, marks, crosses, and dashes in Dickinson's autographs as elements in a "visual intentionality."[35] Although Martha Nell Smith and others never use the word "intention" except to disavow it (or to discover it lurking uncon-sciously in the work of others), it is clear that at some level they see Dickin-son's manuscript practice as similarly intentional—for example, by claiming that Dickinson's correspondence with Susan Dickinson reveals a greater "comfort level" in the materials of its inscription and distribution than does that with Bowles, thereby implying that Dickinson behaved more naturally, more like herself, with Susan and that those autographs are therefore closer to the "real" her.[36] Or, to put it another way; although these critics do not always contend (as Hart did with "biographied") that Dickinson imposes a particular meaning by employing a specific graphic effect at any point, it is clear that they see such an effect as being deliberate or strategic. Dickinson did not always and everywhere intend *a* meaning or *the* meaning by (for ex-ample) her line breaks, but she did intend them to be *meaningful*.[37] Even as such readers reject intention as a criterion for evaluating literary meaning and excellence, however, it sometimes exists as an unspoken assumption in their formulations of a work's *appearances*.[38] For if one insists on the integrity of Dickinson's autograph layout at every level, one works from the position that autographs may include features that are nonaccidental—that exist as signs or elements in an apparatus of intentional structure.[39]

A number of questions suggest themselves at this stage. What identifiable physical evidence exists for claiming that Dickinson's manuscript letters and poems reflect an intention, what Wimsatt and Beardsley called a "design or plan in the author's mind"?[40] To what extent may the particulars of Dickin-son's autograph layout be attributable to matters of private, literary, or epis-tolary convention or preference, or to physical exigency, rather than design? Can material indications move us with any degree of certainty toward the position that Dickinson's autograph layout represents a poetics of abandon-ment?[41] Under discussion here are primarily the *forms* of Dickinson's work, not its *contents*: it might be appropriate to ask if it is possible or even useful to describe a stanza or poetic type—indeed *any* form—as embodying a single (or any) intention. To what degree can intention be said to exist in creative cir-cumstances where the stanza or poem is inherited or preexistent—a familiar or traditional form such as (in Dickinson's case) the ballad or hymnal stanza? For not all such choices are acts with determinate meanings: they can be random, accidental, related to mood or fancy, and not at all to a fully consid-ered intention.[42] As I argued in the preceding chapter on meter, Dickinson's choice of genre may be motivated by factors such as familiarity, convenience, modishness (for the start of the nineteenth century brought a renewal of interest in forms such as the ballad and hymn), and flexibility of rhythm and rhyme—and not necessarily with the aim of conveying a philosophical or emotional position (such as faith or skepticism).[43] In addition, precisely be-cause hymn forms have doxologies—conventionally agreed-upon systems of norms and limits—they can be used by the textual critic to classify Dickinson's poems as belonging, with a greater or lesser degree of fidelity, to certain forms, without having to speculate on the significance of those choices at any degree of actualization. As G. Thomas Tanselle argued, intention may be irrelevant in such circumstances in any case: in his view, the "fact that Emily Dickinson did not 'intend' publication does not alter the basic nature of the material."[44] Manuscript critics, however, argue for a much greater degree of positioning or direction in such matters, with the graphic properties of alpha-betic characters, dashes, lines, and word breaks manipulated to create demon-strable semantic possibilities. And since Dickinson (so the argument contin-ues) rejected publication in her lifetime in order to preserve these innovations for a future audience better able to accept and to understand them, it would appear that some level of intention is assumed as guiding their deployment.

The accuracy of such arguments is difficult to settle when the object of discussion is a creative work, for it is a convention of much interpretative criticism that literature is characterized by its capacity to provoke great num-bers and diversities of response, not all of which will be semantically reconcil-able and very few of which can be dismissed as wrong. But what if the manu-script is a material object, a piece of paper with visual notations that exist primarily as elements of a sign system (writing) but which also displays other physical patterns that encode information as to the object's form, including the status and significance of its constituent parts, as well as its genre? "Books themselves," writes Tanselle, "are works of graphic art and may be studied as such; but a large majority of them are also utilitarian objects that serve to convey written directions for recreating . . . verbal statements (including the ones we call literature)." What if the problem of the manuscripts is one of identification, not interpretation—the erroneous classification of phenomena that "are used as a means of preserving instructions for the repetition of the works" as bearers of meaning, items relating to content and not constitution?[45] The distinction I am describing is usefully illustrated by an episode of Charles Schulz's *Peanuts* cartoon strip (serialized on 14 August 1960), in which three characters look at cloud formations in the sky and respond to them in ways that reflect their personalities and interests. Lucy sees big balls of cotton;

Linus sees, among other things, a map of the British Honduras in the Carib-bean, the profile of (painter and sculptor) Thomas Eakins, and the stoning of Saint Stephen; Charlie Brown sees a "ducky and a horsie."[46] At one level, the characters have a shared understanding of what a cloud is, so that when Lucy invites Linus and Charlie Brown to discuss what they resemble, they are able immediately and unproblematically to identify and focus their attention on the physical object she refers to. The word "cloud" successfully signifies a visible formation in the sky that is made up of gasses. But they then interpret the significance of its appearance in different ways—ways which are difficult to dismiss but which nonetheless do not alter the fact of the cloud's being a cloud. Claims about the graphic potential of Dickinson's manuscripts belong to this secondary process, not of recognition but of creative or associative reading, and they do what Linus, Lucy, and Charlie Brown do not do—confuse appearance with substance, what the autograph poem (or cloud) re-sembles, and what the autograph poem (or cloud) is. It is one thing for a critic to look at an S and think it resembles a wave; such a response is subjective and can hardly be denied. It is another thing entirely to say that the S was shaped to look like a wave and that typography represses that representation; then other criteria of evaluation come into play. For it is the critic's responsibility to cross-check such remarks against the further evidence of poems and letters produced in the same period. For instance, Fr1275B, "The Sea said 'Come' to the Brook," was written about 1872; in the autograph of L392, dated to about 1873, Dickinson writes "Sea" (on the third-last row of the third page) with the capital lying almost horizontal, in the position described by Howe and Smith as suggesting waves. But on the next page, Dickinson writes "Stockings" with a capital S which is so similar in size and flatness as to be identical.[47] What are the implications for theories of optical form in Dickinson that the initial up-percase S is so similar in words with such different meanings? What does it mean that the uppercase S in 1872 and 1873 is often performed with a single stroke, and consists of a slight double curve that slants closer to the horizontal axis than to the vertical—often in a way that makes it indistinguishable from the letter y?

One cannot deny readers the right to take pleasure in the interpretative possibilities afforded by Dickinson's manuscripts and to share this pleasure with others. Indeed, as Michel de Certeau opines, the transformation of the text by its readers is a necessary condition of its surviving the death of the author: "Whether it is a question of newspapers or Proust, the text has a meaning only through its readers; it changes along with them; it is ordered in accord with codes of perception it does not control. It becomes a text only in its relation to the exteriority of the reader, by an interplay of implications and ruses between two sorts of 'expectation' in combination: the expectation that organizes a *readable* space (a literality), and one that organizes a procedure necessary for the *actualization* of the work (a reading)."[48] But as Roger Chartier goes on to specify in his response to de Certeau, the "historian's task is thus to reconstruct the variations that differentiate the *espaces lisibles*—that is, the texts in their discursive and material forms—and those that govern the circumstances of their *effectuation*—that is, the readings, understood as concrete practices and as procedures of interpretation." A historical reconstruction of the manuscripts necessitates other procedures than those of performative ingenuity, brilliant as they often are.[49] As I wrote earlier, attempting to gesture in the direction of likelihood or plausibility in responding to the manuscripts, one requires some hypothesis of objectivity, some more rigorous and precise means of testing insights, that goes beyond the principles of individual pleasure or of postmodernist play. And if one contextualizes Dickinson's manuscripts, as I have above, one finds evidence that complicates and potentially contradicts the conclusions drawn by Hart and Smith. At the same time, one needs to acknowledge that this opposition is limited to conclusions about the local and formal or presentational aspect of such work: that Hart and Smith draw questionable conclusions about specific examples of manuscript practice does not mean that the *larger* practice of making photographic reproductions more easily accessible (electronically or otherwise) to a broader audience can be ignored or declared to be invalid. On the contrary, the initiative is a worthy one—and one of the most impressive of the many editorial projects associated with the promotion of Dickinson's poetry. It is mainly the identification of the codes governing the appearances of those manuscripts that is unconvincing. The point to make, however, is that rigorous and sustained cross-referencing provides us with a set of procedures, a critical apparatus, by which to measure the extent to which contemporary critical approaches to Dickinson's autograph procedures can accurately be formulated as corresponding to the poet's own purposes. The chapter that follows, then, is built on the assumption that contextualization is one method of attempting to move beyond the subjective, and that doing so is desirable. But to achieve historical perspective, one has to take into account the various levels of Dickinson's work, both poetic and epistolary, as well as manuscript practices generally in the nineteenth century, both literary and nonliterary.

Given that Emily Dickinson left no explicit instructions on how her poems were to be presented (if at all) after her death, one might ask if any objective means of identifying her wishes in this regard might reasonably be attempted, much less established and agreed on. In tentatively proposing an affirmative answer to this dilemma, I turn first to poems that Dickinson copied in her own handwriting but did not herself compose: in 1876, for instance, she made a copy of the second and third stanzas of George Herbert's "Mattens." Mixed in with her own manuscripts, it was printed as hers in Millicent Todd Bingham's *Bolts of Melody*, then correctly identified in *Emily Dickinson: A Revelation*. Franklin published it as a poem erroneously attributed to Dickinson.[50] Its usefulness to those who debate procedures for editing Dickinson lies in our being able to compare the published original that Dickinson used (in the *Springfield Daily Republican*) with her copy, which provides valuable insights into her methods of transcription. In most cases, one works backward from the autograph to the idea of the poem that Dickinson might have had at the time of composition—from the object on the page to an approximation of the object in the mind. In this instance, one can adopt the same procedure and then calibrate one's findings with a definite object that exists independently of her in the material world. Which is to say that Dickinson's copies of poems that predate and do not originate with her can be used to construct an independent apparatus for testing hypotheses about her own manuscripts. It is as near as we can ever approach to an empirical evaluation of any such findings in these matters.

This is how Dickinson rendered "Mattens," in pencil on two sides of a single scrap of graph paper measuring 11.8 cm in width and 8.2 cm in height (the vertical space between the stanzas is hers):[51]

> My God – what is a Heart,
> Silver – or Gold – or
> precious stone –
> Or Star – or Rainbow –
> or a part
> Of all these things – or
> all of them in one?
>
> My God – what is a Heart –

> That thou should'st it so
> eye and woo
> Pouring opon it all thy
> art
> As if that thou had'st
> nothing else to do –

Throughout this book, I have argued that separate verbal sequences that are not initialized by a capital letter, and that are followed by proportionately significant amounts of end space, are to be considered as belonging to the row of writing that precedes them. By extension, sequences that are begun with a capital usually correspond to the start of a line of metrical verse. Although there are moments of initial uncertainty (is "Silver" then the first word of a new line or one of the words Dickinson charges with additional significance by assigning a capital to it?), this hypothesis can be applied to the first stanza of the manuscript above, with the following results:[52]

> [Capital] My God – what is a Heart,
> [Capital] Silver – or Gold – or
> [no capital] precious stone – [significant end space]
> [Capital] Or Star – or Rainbow –
> [no capital] or a part [significant end space]
> [Capital] Of all these things – or
> [no capital] all of them in one?

This version, in turn, gestures strongly in the direction of the following:[53]

> My God – what is a Heart,
> Silver – or Gold – or precious stone –
> Or Star – or Rainbow – or a part
> Of all these things – or all of them in one?

In the *Springfield Daily Republican* of Saturday, 28 October 1876, at the end of an article of extracts on "Christian thought," an untitled version of Herbert's poem, featuring only the second, third, and fifth stanzas, was printed (only the relevant stanzas are reproduced here, for ease of comparison):

> My God, what is a heart?
>   Silver, or gold, or precious stone,
> Or star, or rainbow, or a part
>   Of all these things, or all of them in one?
>
> My God, what is a heart?
>   That thou should'st it so eye and woo,
> Pouring upon it all thy art,
>   As if that thou hadst nothing else to do?

Dickinson's version of the second of these stanzas amounts to the following:

My God – what is a Heart –
That thou should'st it so eye and woo
Pouring opon it all thy art
As if that thou had'st nothing else to do –

That Dickinson replaces standard punctuation—mostly commas—with dashes suggests that Brita Lindberg-Seyersted was correct in claiming that the dash and the comma were virtually interchangeable.[54] One also notices that Dickinson automatically and characteristically assigns capitals to words she deemed additionally significant (usually nouns). But what fascinates in the comparison between the poems is the nature of the relationship between the lineation in the printed version and Dickinson's transcription, for the totality of relations between upper- and lowercase letters, as well as end spaces, would strongly suggest that the seven rows of writing in Dickinson's autograph are equivalent to four metrical lines. That such a reconstruction then exactly matches Herbert's second stanza as it appeared in the *Republican* seems to offer compelling evidence that Dickinson would not have regarded her lineation in as fixed a way as manuscript scholars would have us believe. The *Republican* edition would appear to corroborate the findings in earlier chapters of this book: Dickinson's autographs are not to be taken literally with regard to their layout but should be seen as having been shaped and regulated by a number of physical factors, including page length and size of handwriting, in addition to meter and rhyme.[55]

Another sequence of writing provides what Christopher Ricks calls "a proximity that verges upon identity" with a non-Dickinson original—and the existence of the latter provides a set of parameters by which to judge the accuracy of our impressions about Dickinson's autograph appearances.[56] Here is the Dickinson poem, sent to Susan Dickinson in 1882:[57]

Now I lay
thee down to
Sleep –
I pray the Lord
thy Dust to
keep –
And if thou
live before
thou wake –
I pray the
Lord thy
Soul to make –

Again, the substantial white spaces after (the dashes that follow) "Sleep" and "keep" are the familiar markers that accompany line endings. Additional domain-end phenomena are provided by the rhyming words, which, when taken in conjunction with the line-initial capitals ("Now" in row 1, "I" in rows 4 and 10, "And" in row 7) makes it reasonable to suppose that the twelve rows of handwriting correspond to and represent four lines of verse organized as rhyming couplets—which is exactly how Franklin (and Johnson before him) represents them.[58]

> Now I lay thee down to Sleep –
> I pray the Lord thy Dust to keep –
> And if thou live before thou wake –
> I pray the Lord thy Soul to make –

Of course, any reconstruction of these lines is made less complicated by the fact that what Johnson calls a "mock-elegy" is based on a children's bedtime prayer from the *New England Primer* (1777): the pronouns are altered, as well as two of the verbs, but the model is sufficiently similar to enable close comparison.[59]

> Now I lay me down to take my sleep,
> I pray the Lord my Soul to keep,
> If I should die before I wake,
> I pray the Lord my soul to take.[60]

Indeed, the lines were sufficiently familiar for Bianchi, in *Life and Letters*, to have mistakenly or automatically remembered and transcribed the third line as "If thou *should* live before thou wake," the "should" bringing the 1882 copy closer to the 1777 original.[61]

A slightly less satisfactory or reliable comparative model of Dickinson's writing procedures was recorded, Franklin notes, in 1884, when she incorrectly reproduced the first two lines of Algernon Swinburne's "Tristram of Lyonesse" on the verso of a tablet of Home Insurance paper.[62]

> Love first and
> last of all things
> made
> Of which this
> living world is
> but the shade

If we annotate this according to the procedures that I have discussed in this book, we come up with the following:

> [Capital] Love first and
> [no capital] last of all things
> [no capital] made [end space]
> [Capital] Of which this
> [no capital] living world is
> [no capital] but the shade

Or:

> Love first and last of all things made
> Of which this living world is but the shade

The lines are symmetrically iambic and rhyme; they also correspond approximately to Swinburne's own arrangement of the same lines, even though the words themselves differ at some points:[63]

> Love, that is first and last of all things made,
> The light that has the living world for shade,

Though the two versions differ in respect to some verbal particulars, they are identical in terms of layout—or at least identical in terms of what Dickinson's layout *means*. The multiple physical details of Dickinson's autographs indicate a fairly consistent blueprint; that a few are independently confirmed by the architecture of documents not authored by Dickinson corroborates the many. The codes in Dickinson's script show that manuscript design is regulated by principles of meter and rhyme, and not by prerogatives of visual patterning.

I

The objection that could justly be raised to the examples quoted above is that they constitute literary works, and one could imagine a scenario whereby Dickinson rearranged these on the page as an experiment, so as to see what kinds of improvements might be effected by a visually oriented deployment of the lines. The same point can be made about graphic variations in the lineation of different versions of the same Dickinson poem in which the language remains fairly constant otherwise: it is not (the argument might go) that "Oh Shadow on / the Grass" and "Oh Shadow / on the Grass" amount to basically the same thing ("Oh Shadow on the Grass") but that the differently positioned split represents an experimentation with the nuances of line division and placement.[64] It is not that Dickinson wrote the first on paper measuring 12.4 cm in width and ran out of space after the third word (the words being large, and the spaces between them, substantial) but that she spaced the writing in such a way that only three words were placed in the opening line.[65] The merits of such arguments are difficult to weigh, for the line breaks of a poem (like its contents) can be interpreted in completely different ways—ways that are simultaneously legitimate but cannot ultimately be proved or disproved, partly because there appears to be no decisive evidence outside the text (in the shape of authorial comment, direct or reported) to authenticate one view over the other, and partly because the discourse of proof is not a traditional element in evaluating aesthetic judgments of literary works.

But other indications of the status of Dickinson's line breaks and blank spaces exist separately in examples of her handwriting that do not constitute poetry but have implications for poetry nonetheless. Among these are envelopes addressed by Dickinson and salutations at the head of letters. Dickinson's letters were often addressed by friends or family—George Montague and Lavinia Dickinson, for example. Those addressed by Dickinson herself are fairly unremarkable, as shown in the following:

Judge Lord –
    Court House –
        Boston –
	C. H. Clark
	361 – Degraw St –
	    Brooklyn –
	        Long Island

The first of these is 13.3 cm wide and 7.1 cm high: the second 14 cm by 7.8 cm.[66] In the first, Dickinson indents the second and third lines (respectively) 3.7 cm and 5.5 cm from the left edge of the envelope; in the second, the third and fourth lines are indented 2.1 cm and 4.6 cm from the left edge. Again, there is nothing spectacularly unusual or striking about these forms of inscription. But in 1884 and 1885, Dickinson addressed the following envelopes to Eben Loomis, father of Mabel Loomis Todd:

Eben J. Loomis –
1413 – College
Hill Terrace –
    Washington –
        D . C .
	Eben J. Loomis –
	1413, College Hill
	Terrace –
	    Washington.
	        D – C –

The 1884 envelope is similar in size to the others we have just looked at: 14 cm wide and 7.9 cm high.[67] The 1885 envelope is the same size: 14 × 7.9 cm.[68] Where they differ from the previous instances is in the inscription of the second line, the postal address, which is written across two rows. In both cases, Dickinson did not have (or did not leave herself) sufficient room to include "1413, College Hill Terrace –" on the same line, so she completed it on the next available portion of space and then moved further down the envelope when she began another portion of the address. In other words, "1413, College Hill Terrace –" is one unit of meaning, whose inscription across two rows is an accidental property of the small surface of writing and the size of the handwriting. Moreover, Dickinson uses the same convention as the autograph poems to indicate that a word is not deliberately isolated: "Hill Terrace" and "Terrace" are obviously not separate and integral but constituent elements of the address (the street name and residence number) which commences on the previous row and which they continue and complete.

A letter addressed to Mabel Loomis Todd (A 781) provides further clues as to the significance of Dickinson's spacing:

> Brother and Sister's
> Friend –
>   "Sweet   Land
>   of   Liberty" is a

The common salutation at the head of a conventional letter might read "Dear friend" or "Dear [name]." In this instance, Dickinson ran out of space before she could complete the (unusually long and clearly distancing) heading, and it carries over and is concluded on the next horizontal portion of blank paper. Having finished it, she skips the remaining 7.6 cm of space available to her, moves her hand farther down the page, and begins the letter with her familiar initial indent, thus indicating that "Brother and Sister's Friend" constitutes a single unit. The procedure is, of course, exactly the same as in the poems: the refusal to use up all the available horizontal space after a word or phrase means that what is written above that word or phrase is a part of it—its incipient part, no less.

Finally, although Dickinson splits the Eben Loomis address at different points on the same-sized envelope ("1413 College / Hill Terrace" and "1413 College Hill / Terrace"; punctuation omitted), they amount to the same thing: "1413 College Hill Terrace." If we compare this to, say, the five separate versions that exist of the first stanza of Fr1372, interesting and valuable parallels arise, which help point us in the direction of a greater understanding of the totality of the author's inclinations toward her poem's appearance.

A Dew sufficed itself	A Dew sufficed itself	A Dew sufficed itself –	A Dew sufficed itself	A Dew sufficed itself –
And satisfied a Leaf	And satisfied a Leaf	And satisfied a Leaf – *felt*	And satisfied a Leaf –	And satisfied a Leaf
And thought, how vast a Destiny –	And thought "How vast a Destiny"!	And thought "How vast a Destiny"!	And thought "how vast a destiny" –	And felt "How vast a Destiny" –
How trivial is Life.	"How trivial is Life"!	"How trivial is Life"!	"How trivial is Life"!	"How trivial is Life"!

Notice that although the first two *physical* rows thrice appear as "A Dew sufficed / itself" and twice as "A Dew / sufficed itself," each time Dickinson is careful not to interrupt the *metrical* unit (the two rows *in all five examples* add up to the trimeter of "A Dew sufficed itself"). Granted, it may be that Dickinson never made up her mind which version she preferred; perhaps, as Sharon Cameron puts it, she chose not to choose, or moved restlessly and dynamically, between these poles. But it is just as likely that she regarded such deviation as incidental and minor so long as the line's coherence (metrical and semantic) was maintained. Where some critics detect visual improvisation and intricacies of adjustment, one can also perceive selective indifference and remarkable consistency: in successive versions of the poem, one sees repeatedly that the logic of its different appearances is governed by the presence of metrical pattern. And this perception is further supported by the relationship of upper- and lowercase letters: "And satisfied / a Leaf", for example, can be presented as "And satisfied a Leaf" without compromising Dickinson's purposes (because the minuscule *a* indicates that it does not signal the beginning of a new verse).[69] Note too that the poem employs an *abcb* rhyme scheme, which has a crucial signifying power. If we maintain the autograph arrangement where the stanzas are nine, eight, seven, and eight rows long (respectively), this pattern is dissipated—or at least functions more blandly across physical intervals of space that are greater and less stable than in the print version.

II

Another example of how Dickinson's writing is not to be mistaken as the literal embodiment of her wishes with respect to lineation can be found in her transcription of the final line of the first verse paragraph of Emerson's poem "The Snow Storm." In its entirety, the original line reads as "In a tumultuous privacy of storm." In a draft note from around 1884, Dickinson reproduces a portion of the same sequence as:[70]

> " Tumultuous
>   privacy
>   of Storm "

The paper on which this is written measures 11.7 cm across; the word "Tumultuous" takes up (together with its quotation mark) 8.2 cm of this space, or approximately 70 percent of the horizontal writing surface. By extension, "privacy" takes up 6.3 cm (or about 53 percent), and "of Storm"—with its closing quotation marks—9.6 cm (or about 82 percent) of the surface area. Clearly, Dickinson did not think of these three rows of writing as three separate lines: they constitute one sequence excerpted from a single line of verse. But another possible explanation is that Dickinson deliberately rearranged the line across three rows for the purposes of an improved pacing that creates an increased emotive force. One needs to acknowledge that although the rearrangement may be seen as more dramatically propelling the words at the reader, this is not proof in itself that Dickinson designed it to be that way. That twenty-first-century readers may legitimately perceive the lineation of Dickinson's manuscripts to have a greater aesthetic appeal or impact than their regularization in the standard editions of Johnson, Johnson and Ward, and Franklin is not in itself sufficient argument for believing that such arrangements originated with or would have been approved by Dickinson.

Mention of Emerson brings us to another contentious and related aspect of Dickinson's editing—the choice of formatting for paragraphs in her correspondence. Ellen Hart argues the case: "First, Dickinson did not visually separate prose and poetry in her letters. Her prose lines and the lines of a poem are similar in length, she did not consistently divide poetry from prose through spacing, and she did not vary margins. A standard prose format for the letters results in visual inaccuracies, such as Johnson's paragraphing: Dickinson did not use indentation to indicate paragraphs. Second, the relationship between poetry and prose is so complex in Dickinson's writing that lineating poetry but not prose sets up artificial genre distinctions."[71] As we have seen, however, Dickinson does "visually separate prose and poetry in her letters" because the margins vary much more in the latter than they do in the former. And Hart is also less than fully accurate when she claims that "Dickinson did not use indentation to indicate paragraphs." True, Dickinson did not always indent at the *beginning* of paragraphs in letters, but she used a reverse form of indentation at the *close* of the previous paragraph. Although Hart criticizes

Thomas H. Johnson for effectively imposing paragraphs on Dickinson's epistolary documents in his and Theodora Ward's *Letters*, he was actually quite conservative about such formatting. For example, in Johnson and Ward's version of a letter to Samuel Bowles (numbered 205 and dated early April 1859), paragraphs are assigned after the words "feet!," "Springfield!," "years," "more," and "ashamed."[72] This action is justifiable because, on the manuscript, a greater interval of space exists between those words and the right-hand edge of the paper than for other words at the end of a line, which generally and consistently come to within a centimeter of the edge. The words that Johnson and Ward judge as indicating a shift of paragraph are distant from the right side of the paper by (respectively) 4, 3.2, 5.2, 2.5, and 2.3 centimeters. Now, these measurements are approximate because they are taken from photocopies, but they are nonetheless different enough from the normal pattern of end-word spacing to stand out visually. However, in the final paragraph of the letter as Johnson and Ward transcribe it, there is a distance in the manuscript of roughly two centimeters from the end of the word "pencil" to the right edge of the paper, indicating the possibility that Dickinson was closing a paragraph at that point. Johnson and Ward merge this sentence with the next one, making one paragraph where, arguably, there should be two. My point is less to quibble with their choice than to show—and there are countless examples of this—that Johnson and Ward were very careful about their editing of Dickinson's paragraphs and not at all as willful as Hart appears to suggest: they were guided by the visual evidence on the page and not by a sense of stylistic propriety.

In addition, when Hart makes her comments about paragraph indents, she overlooks evidence about manuscript epistolary practice generally in the nineteenth century. In Ralph Waldo Emerson's famous letter (dated Concord, Massachusetts, 21 July 1855) to Walt Whitman, paragraph changes are also indicated by there being unused space at the end of a line—space that is nevertheless sufficient to include the first word or words of the next. So in Emerson's manuscript, in the sequence "I find / the courage of *treatment*, / which so delights us, / and which large perception / only can inspire," the first four of the five end words reach close to the edge of the paper, but there is space left after "inspire," indicating that the sequence "I greet you at the be –" marks a new paragraph (though it is not conventionally indented).[73] Emerson writes of Whitman's poetry, "It has the best merits, / namely, of fortifying / & encouraging." The last words of the first two lines reach much closer to the right edge of the paper than "encouraging" does, indicating that the next phrase, "I did not know" (which is again not indented), constitutes the start of a different paragraph.

In a separate but related case, Emma Spaulding Bryant uses similar techniques of inscription to those of Dickinson in letter to her husband, John

Emory Bryant: rather than indenting at the beginning of a paragraph, she leaves space at the end of the preceding one. The letter in question, dated "Cleveland, July 25, 1873," proceeds thus:[74]

> My Darling.
>   Do you query how
> it happens that I am writing you
> from this place?
> I had not time to write the day
> before I left Wakeman.
> Yesterday morning Lucy and I came
> here and brought baby with us –

Bryant—like Dickinson—maintains a fairly consistent left-side margin, indicating paragraph division instead through the same kind of reverse indentation described above; as a consequence, it is relatively easy to see that there are paragraph shifts after "place?" and "Wakeman." (In addition, Bryant ran out of space on the verso of the second folium but ended by writing vertically along the left-hand margin of the first recto. She wrote, "I wish you were with me daily and I do very much hope to be quite well and [continuing vertically] strong when you see me at Christmas.")

    The codes for paragraphing in handwritten documents were more various in the nineteenth century than is sometimes supposed. Some of them correspond exactly to print procedures: in her journal for 1836, Sarah Hammond uses conventional paragraphing, for example.[75] Others do not: in her letters, Jane Carlyle (wife of Thomas) often displays a "tendency to leave space at the end of a sentence to indicate the end of a paragraph without indenting her next sentence for the beginning of a new paragraph."[76] Similarly, in a letter from Annie Fields to Mrs. Laura Johnson, dated Boston, 28 April 1870, the writer does not use the space available to her at the end of a line in order to indicate paragraph closure, but she also fails to indent at the beginning of the new sequence, thus:[77]

> [page two]
> Infinite is god because he is oldest
> and knows most. [7.6 cm of space follows; the paper is 13.6 cm wide]
> We are impatient of too much introspection. What

> [page two]
> Our intellect is not a gift but
> the Presence of God. [6.5 cm of space follows]
> I did not take notes, he spoke about 30 minutes

[page three]
done to the gentle mind by the presence of
the Hero. [9.9 cm of space follows]
The best study of metaphysics is physics.

[page three]
still further results. [6.6 cm of ensuing space]
There is no stop; all is pulsation, undulation

The first page of Amanda Corey Edmond's journal (1844) has three para-
graphs marked by two end spaces only—a procedure for marking paragraphs
that is repeated throughout the 139 pages of this handwritten text:[78]

board. Moderate breezes and fine weather. [7.3 cm of space, out of
    20.4 cm]
After a pleasant sail out of the harbor, we came more immediately
    [page edge]
                        . . . I silently and earnestly com-
mitted myself and my beloved companions to the kind care of Him
    who is
God of the Sea as well as the land. [9.5 cm]
But the novelty of the voyage, the appearance of the noble ship
    whose [page edge]

The 1839 journal of Elizabeth (Lizzie) Sedgwick demonstrates the variety
of conventions available to the nineteenth-century manuscript writer: she em-
ploys conventional paragraphing almost exclusively but sometimes omits to
use all the horizontal space available to her on the page and begins instead on
the next line, without indenting initially.[79] A handwritten letter from Richard
Whately, archbishop of Dublin, in pen on nonruled paper measuring 11.3 ×
18.1 cm, reads as follows:[80]

Palace
13Octr 1854
The Archbishop wishes Miss
Dix to have access to the
Richmond Lunatic Asylum,
& to Swift's Hospital, & to
be shown whatever may

interest her. [6 cm of space]
She has much experience &
eminent skill, in what relates
to such institutions,
                    R o Dublin

Confusion arises when one looks for the uniform and repetitive procedures of initial indentation associated with print and then fails to find them, or finds them only sporadically, in Dickinson's letters. In printed texts, new paragraphs are always indicated by their being further distant from the margin on the left side of the page than the rest of the writing. Dickinson's letters differ in that they rarely employ initial indentation. But to compare a printed page with a handwritten page and to deduce from this that Dickinson did not assign paragraphs at all or in the same way is to commit a categorical error. Autographs have a wide array of conventions by which paragraphs can be signaled, but that does not alter the fact that paragraphs are indicated. Emily Dickinson's most common procedure for paragraph marking involves her neglecting to use all the horizontal space available to her at specific points on her manuscript page, and those spaces—which can be substantial—always coincide with the closure of a paragraph. That is, in most letters the lines generally and consistently come to within a centimeter of the right edge of the paper; a paragraph close is indicated by there being a greater interval of space between the final word in a sequence and the right-hand edge of the paper than is strictly necessary.

Within nineteenth-century literary culture, then, there are codes or assumptions that readers understood without having to be alerted explicitly to their presence—and these codes, which are variously manifested, apply to poetry as well as to prose.[81] For example, reasons of economy or house style meant that print editions of poetry sometimes divided pages into two columns of print. Although this enabled more writing to be fit onto the page, it often meant that *single* lines of verse had to be arranged spatially and physically as *double* rows of text. Separate editions of Longfellow's "The Wreck of the Hesperus" afford straightforward examples of this practice: the first quotation shows how each stanza in the poem consisted of four lines of alternating tetrameter and trimeter, rhyming *abcb*.

"O father! I hear the sound of guns,
    O say, what may it be?"
"Some ship in distress, that cannot live
    In such an angry sea!"[82]

But in a subsequent edition, where the columns are narrower, the same stanza is arranged like this:

> "O father! I hear the sound of
> guns,
> O say, what may it be?"
> "Some ship in distress, that cannot
> live
> In such an angry sea!"[83]

Clearly, we are not meant to change our reading in response to such typographical variation: the single words in lines 2 and 5 are written with small letters and are indented to signal that their isolation does not make a formal or graphic contribution to the poem's meaning. Here, as elsewhere, the increased space *before* the word "guns," in conjunction with the blank space *after* it, exemplifies a convention indicating that the word belongs to the line immediately preceding it.[84]

Autograph poetry in the nineteenth century is similar to autograph prose in that domain-end phenomena (the close of a line, a break between stanzas) are recorded in a variety of ways, though they amount to the same thing: whether by introducing a physical space or drawing a line to do so, one is still recording a stanzaic interval. The same can be said of instances of runover that are imposed for reasons of material extent, as can be shown in one of Sarah Orne Jewett's handwritten drafts for "To my father," the original of which is housed at the Houghton Library of Harvard and which begins thus:[85]

> When in the quiet house I sat alone
> Sometimes I heard your footfall
> drawing near

At the end of the second row of writing, Jewett clearly decided that the 2.5 cm of space remaining to her were insufficient to complete the line, and she continued in the space below, indenting the phrase "drawing near" 8.9 cm further into the page than the other words with which she began separate lines. A second draft of the poem records (substantially) the same sequence thus:[86]

> When in the quiet house I sat alone
> Sometimes I heard your footfall coming
> near

Again, Jewett found herself running out of room at the right edge of the page and shifted her writing down a level to complete her line. This time, "near" is indented 10.1 cm further into the page. But in a (handstitched) commonplace book made up of "selections from the standard poets" in her own hand (and dated September–December 1860), Jewett recorded such runover lines in two ways: below the incomplete line, or above it—but always indented an average 9 cm further into the page than the other writing.[87]

What emerges from close comparison of Dickinson's autographs with those of her contemporaries is that she indents, like them, but in reverse: exactly as with her procedure for marking prose paragraphs, she leaves terminal and not initial space. In other words, had Dickinson written the lines above, she would have recorded the runover thus:

> When in the quiet house I sat alone
> Sometimes I heard your footfall coming
> near

The systems are essentially mirror images of each other: her contemporaries leave room *at the start* of component elements that are not intentionally separate from what precedes them, beginning these with small letters, whereas Dickinson also begins such entities with small letters but then leaves room *afterward* to indicate that they are not separate by design. The modes of physical inscription are different, but the phenomena they record are exactly the same. And Dickinson's method of transcription is uncommon but not unprecedented. The manuscript of Christopher Smart's *Jubilate Agno* (written between 1758 and 1763) is a case in point: most of the lines in one part begin with the word "Let," most of those in the other with the word "For." Reproduced in a publication of the Houghton Library, Fragment A of the autograph poem shows that Smart recorded runon lines in the same way as Dickinson, beginning them (usually) with a lowercase letter (or an uppercase letter that was demanded by the nature of the word, such as "Lord" or "God"), positioning them at the same left-hand margin of the page as all other lines, but then leaving subsequent space to indicate that they were not integrally separate from the row that immediately preceded them.[88]

A final example of referential consistency across differing systems of demarcation is provided by Fr796D, "The Wind begun to rock the Grass," the autograph fair copy of which had been believed lost until 2001, at which time it was released from a private collection and put up for sale by the Skinner Auction Gallery.[89] Until then, it had been "represented in a transcript (BPL 121–126)" by Mary Thacher Higginson.[90] Higginson's transcript corresponds word for word with the recovered manuscript, which is written in ink on paper watermarked "A. Pirie & Son / 1871" and measuring 12.7 × 20.3 cm (per page; the size of the unfolded sheet is double this), which is correct for that type of paper, a sheet of which Franklin describes in *The Manuscript Books of Emily Dickinson*.[91] The handwriting is right for about 1873, when the copy was sent to Thomas Wentworth Higginson; it was compared with Fr1299 "Dominion lasts until obtained," which Franklin believes to have been sent to Higginson at about the same time.

Fr796C was a revised version of the poem, made by Dickinson in about 1873. Copied from this revised version, Fr796D was sent to T. W. Higginson; the line breaks are different (in what follows, only the first two stanzas are presented, for ease of subsequent reference and comparison).

> The Wind
> begun to rock
> the Grass
> With threatening
> tunes and low –
> He flung
> a Menace at
> the Earth –
> A Menace at
> the Sky –
>
> The Leaves
> unhooked
> themselves
> from Trees
> And started
> all abroad –
> The Dust
> did scoop
> itself like
> Hands
> And throw
> away the Road.

As with most of Dickinson's manuscripts in the 1870s and 1880s, there is a very small ratio of words per row.[92] But what is remarkable is how faithful Mary Thacher Higginson is to the original (there follow the first two stanzas of the transcript):

> The Wind begun to rock
>   the Grass
> With threatening tunes
>   and low –
> He flung a Menace at
>   the Earth –
> A Menace at the Sky –
>
> The Leaves unhooked
>   themselves from trees
> And started all abroad,
> The Dust did scoop
>   itself like Hands
> And throw away the Road.

Higginson preserves Dickinson's capitals and dashes: she mistakes the dash subsequent to "abroad" for a comma and begins "Trees" with a minuscule rather than an uppercase character. But these are clearly misinterpretations— and (given the relative inexperience of the copyist and the ambiguities of Dickinson's late hand) understandable ones: it is clear from the document as a whole that no attempt was made at correcting punctuation or capitalization on the grounds of grammar or taste. It is not too much of an exaggeration to say that Mary Thacher Higginson's record is the single best example of a nineteenth-century rendering of a Dickinson poem by someone other than the poet herself.

What is truly valuable about the document, however, is the extent to which it confirms once again how nineteenth-century readers, *including the poet herself*, understood the layout of Dickinson's autographs. Take the final stanza, for example: here is the original, annotated to clarify line-initial and line-end phenomena.

> [Initial capital] That held
> the Dams
> had parted
> hold [end space]
> [Initial capital] The Waters
> Wrecked the
> Sky[end space]
> [Initial capital] But overlooked
> my Father's
> House – [end space]
> [Initial capital] Just quartering a
> tree – [end space]

Here is Higginson's copy:

> That held the Dams had
>   parted hold
> The Waters Wrecked the
>   Sky
> But overlooked my Father's
>   House,
> Just quartering a tree.

Plainly, Higginson correctly understood that although "That held / the Dams / had parted / hold" took up *four* material rows of writing, these corresponded to *one* line of metrical verse, which she herself then proceed to record across *two* material rows of space. (She also seems to have intuited that the capitalized *W* and *S* at the beginning of "Wrecked" and "Sky" had no significance for the poem's lineation.) Moreover, she marks runover lines that are imposed for reasons of insufficient space by indenting them initially and not assigning them uppercase characters, unless this is called for by emphasis or grammar. That her system differs from that of Dickinson does not alter the fact that they describe essentially the same phenomena.

III

The knowledge, insight, or experience that a writer or reader contemporaneous with Dickinson may have had is not always transferable, relevant, or useful for attempting to evaluate the significance of the originals. At times, however, historical practice and contemporary disposition appear to coincide: modern readers who are understandably apprehensive about the history of Dickinson's distribution through print often gesture toward historical and authorial precedent for their views by invoking a variety of comments made by Susan Dickinson in the years after Emily Dickinson's death. "Susan writes Ward with authority," we are told, and her lifelong correspondence and domestic proximity with the poet makes her a "a hidden authority."[93] Particular attention has been paid to the following passage from an 1891 letter to William Hayes Ward: "I think if you do not feel that your own literary taste is compromised by it I would rather the three verses of the 'Martyrs' should be published if any. I shall not be annoyed if you decide not to publish at all. I should have said <u>printed</u>."[94] The distinction Dickinson's sister-in-law makes here is taken by manuscript critics to imply a careful separation between the limited circulation of handwritten documents (publish) and the typographic representation and subsequent mass distribution of said documents (print). Such a distinction is not unthinkable, though it would be easier to accept if Ward had initiated the correspondence, pressing Susan Dickinson (against her will, so one imagines) to supply more of Emily Dickinson's manuscripts for regularization and misrepresentation in a medium that she is alleged to have rejected. But such is not the case; as we have seen, it was Susan Dickinson who first approached Ward, in writing, on 8 February 1891. It makes little sense to believe that she would have taken the initiative of submitting one of her sister-in-law's poems for inclusion in a newspaper while secretly hoping that the editors would turn it down on the grounds that typographic reproduction would make invisible aspects of the handwriting that were essential to its understanding—though that seems to be what manuscript scholars would have us believe.[95] The distinction made on Susan Dickinson's behalf (and by extension, on Emily Dickinson's behalf, since Susan is transformed into a literary executor manqué) makes even less sense when one considers that Susan herself had written (in December 1890) to T. W. Higginson:

> I planned to give my winter, with my daughter's aid, to the arrangement of a vol. to be printed at my own expense sometime during the year, subject to your approval of course, with an introduction also by yourself, to make the setting perfect. The volume would have been rather more full, and varied, than yours as I should have used many bits of her prose – passages from her letters quite surpassing the correspondence of Gunderodi[e] with Bettine – quaint bits to my children &c &c. Of course I should have forestalled criticism by only printing them. I have been held back from arranging them to be published the past years by your verdict of "un-presentable."[96]

It seems more likely from the aggregate of Susan Dickinson's use of the words that her differentiation between printing and publishing involves different kinds of production and circulation rather than a nonreconcilable opposition between the technologies of inscription ("manuscript or type").[97] Such a conclusion depends at least in part on our knowing that the *Independent* was a prominent and conservative New York weekly that supported domestic and foreign missionary work, as well as American imperialist policies (Ward, famously, attacked Mark Twain for his opposition to imperialist doctrines). Daniel Lombardo tells us that in the mid-1860s, more Amherst people subscribed to the "*Independent* (117 subscriptions), than any other magazine"; founded in 1848 as a Congregationalist journal by Henry Chandler but later expanded to include topics of literary and special interest, its editors included Henry Ward Beecher (1861–64) as well as Ward (1868–1916).[98] The nature of the *Independent* provides us with an insight into Susan Dickinson's afterthought about publication: the *Independent* was subscribed to, not put out for general sale, and would therefore reach a select audience; it had "literary merit" and was morally unimpeachable and would therefore provide the right kind of setting for a poet and an agent who were not by any means political radicals and who shied away from publicity. Moreover, the distinction Susan invokes was a common one in the nineteenth century—the kind that the Reverend Perkins K. Clark (pastor of the First Congregational Church in South Deerfield) referred to in 1859 when he mentioned pamphlets "received occasionally through the mails, marked '*Not published, but printed for private circulation.*'"[99] In other words, there are different kinds and stages of publication: one is limited (both in terms of the number of materials that were printed and in the number of individuals able to read them), refined, to do with discernment and quality; the other is mass scale, often sensational or common, and to do with quantity and profit.

In the same letter to Ward, Susan Dickinson reports that "Mr. Dickinson thinks as Col. Higginson and Niles are to bring out another vol. of the poems, it is not best or fair to them to print many. I do not feel in any way bound to them, but will of course defer to his wish in the matter." With characteristic (and admirable) autonomy, Susan did *not* defer to Austin, for the *Independent* of 12 March published "Two Lyrics by the Late Emily Dickinson" ("Just lost, when I was saved" as "Called Back," and "Through the strait pass of suffering" as "The Martyrs"). In defiance of her husband, she had in fact sent Ward another of Dickinson's manuscripts to go with the first, but Austin Dickinson's objections must nevertheless have been sufficiently pressing for her to feel the necessity of pointing out that the "money part is of little value any way" (and the dismissal of money is an important marker of class as well).[100] The distinction between "print" and "publish" is not a consistent one in Susan Dickinson's usage (she seems to employ them interchangeably in the rest of the correspondence) but is related at that particular point to the competing pressures she was under in the inaugural phase of Dickinson's posthumous literary career: the desire to be associated with, and contribute to, Dickinson's publication, accompanied by the necessity of defending herself from charges of financial self-interest and publicity seeking, or from competitive interference with the Higginson, Todd, and Lavinia Dickinson axis.

In a postscript to a letter of 14 March 1891, Susan Dickinson writes: "It just occurs to me that you may not care to print more after this sort of injunction of Miss Dickinson's."[101] Despite her bravura ("I shall never yield a line in my possession to [Lavinia]" she writes to Ward on 23 March 1891, going on to characterize her sister-in-law as "very foolish in her talk of Law"), Susan Dickinson appears to have been unsettled—and understandably frustrated—by her lack of entitlement in the matter of Dickinson poems sent to her: she never again submitted poems for publication.[102] But if she never got to oversee a public edition of Dickinson's writings, some of her comments have sometimes been misconstrued as the basis for an archaeology of what her edition might have contained and looked like (albeit on the not unreasonable assumption that her closeness to Dickinson would have enabled her to construct an edition of the poems and letters that was more accurate and authoritative than those of Higginson and Todd). Again, there is a biographical and editorial osmosis at work here; Smith claims that "had Susan helped produce the earliest volumes of Emily Dickinson's works, our patterns of reading would have been decidedly altered," and then goes on to speculate on what "the costs to Dickinson's readers have been of the first and then many of the subsequent literary institutions diminishing this primary relationship of hers."[103] At one level, any publications of Dickinson's poetry and letters that arrange them according to the conventional parameters of line, stanza, and paragraph (such as the Harvard editions), are regarded as "subsequent literary institutions" that are seen as the illegitimate descendants of the first, corrupt versions supervised by Higginson and Todd.[104] At another level, the heirs of Susan Dickinson's editorial procedures (as these are excavated from her correspondence) are the rightful disseminators of her tradition: Susan's statement to Ward about her plan to write an article "with illustrations of [Dickinson's] own" is developed into a full-fledged graphic manifesto that eventually sees the light of day as *Open Me Carefully*.[105]

Instead, one of the striking things about viewing Dickinson's manuscripts in the expectation that they will yield drawings or a graphic handwriting is precisely their comparative absence. At Amherst College, by contrast, some of the papers of Susan Dickinson (to Mabel Loomis Todd, before their enmity) and Otis Lord are full of playful doodles: in Susan Dickinson's case these are scribbled images or pasted illustrations from books and magazines; in Lord's case, page after page of caricatures and cartoons ("Member from Sanford attempting to sit on <u>three</u> stools"; "Surprise of Mr Sheppard at the attempt to liken lawyers to anacondas"; " '<u>Oh mighty pens</u>': a rather serious illustration of a piece of classic music").[106] Susan Hale, a contemporary of Dickinson's, has drawings in many of her letters, such as those of 9 June and 19 June 1858, to her sister Lucretia, for instance.[107] A letter of 19 June 1860 to the same sister has a section (on the bottom right-hand corner of the third page) where she writes "Couldn't make [drawing of head] or [drawing of tail]"; another from 8 July 1863 (again to Lucretia) has a drawing of a spider, web, and fly (toward the upper right-hand corner of the fourth page).[108] Compared with these, Dickinson's contribution to the informal visual arts seems paltry. There is the sketch of a tombstone on a message to John L. Graves.[109] L144 (to Austin) has a drawing of a chimney with smoke above the embossed image of the Capitol, with a wild-haired man approaching it who is labeled "Member from the 10th."[110] L214 has a clipped image ("Young TIMOTHY, Learnt Sin to fly") from the *New England Primer* attached, and poems Fr48 and Fr125 have clipped pasted images (of a bird and little Nell from *The Old Curiosity Shop*, respectively), though when Fr125 came to be recorded in Fascicle 6, no images were appended.[111] The letter and both poems are from 1859; more significant, all are to Susan Dickinson. Since Susan's practice, judging by those of her communications that survive, was often to include drawings and clippings in her letters, it seems that Dickinson (as she did in other ways with other correspondents) was emulating her friend and adapting her style to suit her preferences. This may also explain why Susan, in her 1891 letter to Ward, wrote that she planned an article "with illustrations of [Dickinson's] own": such an approach reflected *her own* taste for the visual or for texts that included illustrations (such as the friendship books of the 1800s).[112]

Nevertheless, Emily Dickinson quite clearly had time and opportunity, two of the three primary components of premeditation, for the commission of a language attuned to pictorial dimensions; only the motive appears to have been missing. In an 1846 letter to Abiah Root, for example, Dickinson described her visit to a Chinese museum in Boston, finishing a long paragraph with this: "The Writing Master is constantly occupied in writing the names of visitors who request it upon cards in the Chinese language—for which he charges 12½ cts. apiece. He never fails to give his card besides to the person[s] who wish it. I obtained one of his cards for Viny & myself & I consider them very precious. Are you still in Norwich & attending to music. I am not now taking lessons but I expect to when I return home."[113] And replying in 1885 to Helen Hunt Jackson's statement in a letter that her house in California included a window that "looked straight off towards Japan," Dickinson fashioned two draft letters with the following:[114]

> That you compass "Japan" before you you [*sic*] breakfast, not in the least surprises me, clogged only with the Music, like the Wheels of Birds.

> That you glance at Japan as you breakfast, not in the least surprises me, thronged only with Music, like the Decks of Birds.

The period of time that passed between these letters was a crucial one in the history of political and cultural relations between the United States, China, and Japan. In July 1853, the American expedition to Japan headed by Commodore Matthew Perry began a process that set in motion a tremendous surge of interest in Japanese and Chinese culture—and not least in their forms of writing. Walt Whitman reported on the arrival of the first Japanese delegation to the United States in 1860 for the *New York Times*. A series of articles and lectures helped to increase interest: Lyman Abbott's "Pictures of Japanese" (in the *Harper's* of August 1869) and Bayard Taylor's "Between Europe and Asia" (*Atlantic Monthly*, January 1865) and "Sights In and Around Yedo" (*Scribner's*, 1871) are sporadic but relevant examples, since the Dickinsons subscribed to all three magazines. In 1876 there was a Japanese pavilion at the Centennial Exposition in Philadephia, and two years later Ernest Fenellosa, of Salem, Massachusetts, and Harvard, was invited to teach philosophy at the Imperial University of Tokyo. Closer to home, William S. Clark traveled to Japan in 1876, returning in 1877; he lived not far from the Dickinson Homestead on Main Street. This accumulation of interest in Asian culture would eventually lead to literary movements such as Imagism at the beginning of the twentieth century and to a preoccupation with the relationship between verbal and visual signs that helped bring about the experiments of e.e. cummings, the Concrete poets, and today's fascination with the visual. In short, the conditions that were necessary to bring about a shift in cultural preoccupations, with increasing levels of attention paid to the potential contribution of the visual aspects of script to poetry, were present in Dickinson's lifetime, and it would not be cheating chronology to claim her as a legitimate forerunner of such movements—if one can find references made by her to such an interest.

Emily Dickinson had almost forty years in which to develop or express a sustained interest in the graphic or visual aspects of language as a creative and communicative medium. But there is no evidence that she ever did: she makes no comment on what Chinese looks like in the earlier of the two letter excerpts quoted above, and she declines the opportunity to comment on Japanese forms of (linguistic or pictorial) expression in the later drafts to Jackson.[115] Instead, in what I take to be characteristic and defining responses to areas of cultural stimulation, she moves quickly away in both quotations from visual to sonic forms of stylization, from "glance" to "music." And indeed Dickinson *was* a musician (her improvisations on the piano were locally celebrated), and her preferred genre of poetic expression was a literary re-creation of a musical form, the hymn; it was Austin Dickinson who cultivated a taste for the pictorial, becoming a collector of paintings in the years after his marriage.[116]

Nevertheless, Dickinson is typical of many nineteenth-century writers in thinking that documents associated personally with someone who interested them were "very precious"; many of her comments on other writers take the form of inquiries about the availability of biographies, for instance, and she collected images of poets rather than pictures generally. Although Martha Nell Smith has dismissed "the misguided reverence (in search of originary moments) for manuscripts" at the same time as she promotes these as the primary sites of Dickinson's poetic innovations, such fascination was a legitimate aspect of a manuscript's value to a nineteenth-century audience.[117] In "The Work of Art in the Age of Mechanical Reproduction," Walter Benjamin coins the term "aura" to suggest some of the properties that are associated with original works of art, and his point applies as much to Dickinson's day as it did to Benjamin's, or to our own.[118] Witness John Updike, for example: "I myself find other writers' drafts and worksheets fascinating; one draws closer, bending over (say) Keats' first version of 'Ode to a Nightingale' in the British Museum, to the sacred flame, the furnace of mental concentration was still ductile and yielding to blows of the pen. But inspecting such material is (like most science) a form of prying; we should not forget that what we glimpse here is the long and winding middle of a human process whose end is a *published thing*—shiny, fragrant, infinitely distributable—and whose beginning is the belief on the author's part that he or she has something to say, *something to deliver*."[119]

In 1852, Harriet Beecher Stowe wrote a note (catalogued as to Mary Ann Cockell Milman but perhaps addressed to her husband, Henry Hart Milman, who is the author of the verse referred to, line 1454 from *The Fall of Jerusalem*), in which she included the following request:[120]

> – Would the writer
> be so kind as to give
> me in his own hand the
> lines commencing
> "It matters little at what
> hour o' the day."

Clearly, there was a particular mystique attached to the presence of the writer in the nineteenth century. After Dickinson's death, Susan Dickinson tore off the signature at the close of L1025 "to give a begging friend," and she probably gave that from L586 away to another (Johnson and Ward report that the lower portion of the sheet is missing).[121] And the photostat of the letter "Dear Sue – With the exception of Shakespeare" shows a tear on the bottom half of the original; it seems likely that this section, large enough for the customarily appended signature, was removed to serve as another gift.[122] Autographs were important generally in nineteenth-century culture: H. C. Pease collected the signatures and best wishes of friends and family in his (mass-produced) "autograph album" of the 1860s, as did Sarah Gates (in a book of the same design), Kate P. Kingman (during the 1870s), and others.[123] Dickinson's signature (or one of them at least: "Emily E. Dickinson") is included in an autograph album that belonged to Harriet C. Haile.[124] Later, Martha Dickinson Bianchi pasted the manuscript of Fr817A, the last stanza of "This Consciousness that is aware," into her copy of *The Single Hound* (1914).

And as Paul Crumbley has pointed out, part of the fascination of the manuscript of "Dare you see a Soul at the 'White Heat'?" is that one gets to hold and see a handwritten composition about composition and thus to come closer to the scene of inspiration, of "the sacred flame, the furnace of mental concentration." Although there is an undeniable magic, a charge, associated with such things (they are objects that derive their meaningfulness from their direct and unmediated association with the person who wrote them), there is no record of their being attended to by Dickinson as exercises in the relation of visual form to contents. "You must tell mother that I was delighted to see her handwriting once more" the young Dickinson wrote in November 1847, and her delight is in direct proportion to the source of the handwriting, not a product of her belief that Emily Norcross Dickinson had alerted her to the possible contribution handwriting might have made to the graphic dimensions of linguistic communication.[125]

Indeed, Dickinson's indifference to the importance of her own handwriting in the production of her meanings can be gauged from her response to the following request from Helen Hunt Jackson in 1878 (a year in which Dickinson's experiments with visual form would have been at their most advanced, if manuscript critics are to be believed): "Would it be of any use to ask you once more for one or two of your poems, to come out in the volume of 'no name' poetry which is to be published before long by Roberts Bros.? If you will give me permission I will copy them – sending them in my own handwriting – and promise never to tell any one, not even the publishers, whose the poems are. Could you not bear this much of publicity?"[126] Jackson's last question (about publicity) matches Susan Dickinson's comments (in her obituary for the poet and in a letter of December 1890 to Higginson) about the poet's concern for privacy, suggesting that it was the personal aspect of fame, not the technology of the book, that Emily Dickinson objected to in her lifetime.[127] Such an impression is not weakened by Dickinson's apparent acquiescence to Jackson's invitation to anonymous publication; she even thanked Thomas Niles for having received from him a copy of the edition in which her poem appeared.[128]

Perhaps most crucial, however, is the episode referred to in an earlier chapter when (after a visit in 1877) Dickinson offered Samuel Bowles a choice between "Theophilus" and "Junius."[129] For the edition of *The Letters of Junius* which Dickinson refers to here contains "Fac – Similes of hand writings of Gentlemen whose names have been mentioned as the Author of the Letters."[130] Six different specimens of handwritten notes are reproduced for the purposes of comparison. The practice of printing books with facsimiles goes back to the late seventeenth century, with a good example being Mabillon's *De Re Diplomatica*, the seminal work on paleography, with engraved illustrations of inscriptions and ancient manuscripts. Until lithography and finally photolithography took over, engraving continued to be the main method for reproducing facsimile illustrations. But the books that Emily Dickinson would have been familiar with and could have provided a model for facsimile publication of the poems would have been writing books such as *Towndrow's Guide to Calligraphy* and *The Original Duntonian System of Rapid Writing*.[131] Scores of such penmanship manuals were produced in early- and mid-nineteenth-century New England, consisting of page after page of what looked like handwritten text. They were either engraved or lithographed and produced cheaply for a wide market. If Dickinson wanted her poetry to be represented in as close a way as possible to her own handwritten versions, nineteenth-century technology was equal to the task. Her years at the Amherst Academy (1841–47) would have provided her with countless examples of how easily handwriting could be reproduced. That Dickinson never once alluded to such a desire reinforces the collective impression that it was not the mechanical shortcomings of the publishing industry, the medium of print itself, that she found problematic about publication.[132]

IV

In another cartoon by Charles Schulz, Rerun Van Pelt looks at the horizon and wonders if the cloud he sees there resembles "a pirate ship or a Zamboni" (a Zamboni is a machine for resurfacing ice during hockey games and skating exhibitions).[133] As Hans-Georg Gadamer puts it, meaning "is always partly determined also by the historical situation of the interpreter and hence by the totality of the objective course of history."[134] Or to put it another way, Rerun sees a Zamboni because the machine has been invented by the time he is born and because he has either witnessed a skating rink or played on one—these are forms of social recreation that provide him with a set of references for making sense of what he sees in the world. His perception of the Zamboni in the sky above the lake he gazes across is at least in part understandable by his location in geographic space and (personal and historical) time. The younger brother of Lucy and Linus Van Pelt, he is still at the age where pirate ships are an important part of his culture or worldview. He gazes across a lake: in northern climates, lakes freeze in the winter and are skated on, which may explain the association with the Zamboni.

But does understanding or enjoying the Schulz cartoon depend on knowing what a Zamboni is? An impromptu survey in an Amherst street revealed that most people *did* know what the name referred to. Those who were not familiar with the term guessed from the cartoon that it might have been a machine, a toy, a kind of food, a musical instrument, or a member of the Zamboni family. Two things strike one about the cartoon: first, the use of the term presupposes that Schulz could take it for granted that most of his readers were familiar with the reference; second, an accurate understanding of the cartoon is dependent on this knowledge—as might also be our enjoyment (one of the respondents who did not understand the reference thought that the cartoon was probably cute but frustratingly obscure). In the case of Dickinson's manuscripts, one wonders which characteristics are equivalent to the Zamboni and which are the same as the pirate ship: that is, what assumptions might Dickinson have had with regard to how her audience would have processed the visual signals present in her autographs, and what kinds of information—if any—does a modern audience require to compensate for the absence of such assumptions in contemporary culture? Not unexpectedly, neither the *Concordance to the Poems of Emily Dickinson* nor the *Concordance to the Letters of Emily Dickinson* includes the word "Zamboni" (Frank J. Zamboni was not born until 1901, and the machine he invented to resurface ice was not put into commercial use before 1949), though "pirate" appears twice in the former (both times in Fr1568, "Sweet Pirate of the Heart") and twice in the latter (the note to Sarah Tuckerman in which the only edition of "Sweet Pirate of the Heart" was enclosed).[135] What Dickinson actually wrote, in pencil on unruled paper measuring 12.6 cm across and 20.2 cm down, follows:[136]

Dear   friend,
        The Gray
Afternoon – the
sweet knock, and
the ebbing voice
of the Boys are
a pictorial Memory –
and then the
Little Bins and
the Purple Kernels –
'twas like the
Larder   of   a
Doll –
To the inditing
Heart we wish
no sigh had come –

Sweet   Pirate
of the Heart,
Not   Pirate
of the Sea –
What wrecketh
thee?
Some   Spice's
Mutiny –
Some   Attar's
perfidy?
Confide   in
me –
        Emily –

Unlike the prose section of this document, which has only one final space (9.3 cm after "Doll," or about 74 percent of the available surface, indicating the close of a paragraph), the poem has three spaces: 8.8 cm after "thee," 7.4 cm after "Mutiny," and 5.6 cm after "perfidy" (or about 70 percent, 59 percent, and 44 percent, respectively, of the lateral area of writing; all measurements are taken from the punctuation marks that follow these words to the right edge of the paper, and all indicate metrically defined line endings). Unlike the prose section (conveniently but accidentally limited to the first page of this bifolium), which has three connecting dashes, all of which are followed by words written entirely in lowercase letters, the poem has two such dashes that are followed by words that begin in uppercase, indicating the presence of a different or supplementary grammar to that of prose.[137] For example, Dickinson follows "Some Spice's Mutiny" with a dash, and the next phrase "Some Attar's perfidy" with a question mark: "Some Spice's Mutiny" is therefore not a grammatically separate unit or Dickinson would have assigned it a question mark of its own ("Some Spice's Mutiny? / Some Attar's perfidy?").[138] The combination of line-initial capitals, domain-end phenomena, and rhyme accumulate to suggest the following design:

> Sweet Pirate of the Heart,
> Not Pirate of the Sea –
> What wrecketh thee?
> Some Spice's Mutiny –
> Some Attar's perfidy?
> Confide in me –

Believing that the layout of "Sweet Pirate of the Heart" is literally the same as its appearance on the page is equivalent to looking for the word "Zamboni" in Dickinson's poems and letters: it is to impose a view of the poem inflected by modern cultural and technological realities on a very different medium of expression. Such an approach dissipates the careful and clearly playful rhyme (conceivably designed to be read out as a cluster of pleasing sounds to the orphaned Esty nephews who delivered the New Year's gift that Dickinson here acknowledges), transforming "Heart / Sea / thee / Mutiny / perfidy / me" to "Pirate / Heart / Pirate / Sea / wrecketh / thee / Spice's / Mutiny / Attar's / perfidy / in / me." The aggregate of material details validates the judgment that Dickinson wrote twelve rows of script but six lines of verse; the totality of relations between alphabetic characters written in the upper- or lowercase, rows of writing, blank spaces, the dimension of the lettering and the size of the paper—these are the coordinates that help us map the exact contours of Dickinson's lines, stanzas, and (in the case of lyrics enfolded within the text of letters) poems.

"All artifacts are important as the principal class of evidence for reconstructing what human beings were doing and thinking in the past," and Dickinson's are no different in that respect.[139] But the aggregate of material particulars that constitute a Dickinson manuscript has not yet managed to stimulate consensus among her readers as to their true significance. It is a commonplace of Dickinson criticism that there can never be an authoritative edition of her poetry, either in complete or compiled form, on the grounds that Dickinson herself recorded no absolutely unambiguous statement as to how her work was to be presented. Some critics take this one step further: since Dickinson did not publish in the conventional sense of having her poetry printed and circulated in bound texts, we should not do so either.[140] But this is to confuse biographical (What did Dickinson do with her manuscripts?) with textual evidence (What do the manuscripts tell us about the logic of their own visual appearances and forms of organization?). We can perhaps never hope for a *text* that matches all Dickinson's wishes as an author, but we can perhaps move toward accepting the possibility of an authoritative *edition*—a useful distinction that Fredson Bowers made in one of his last essays:

> The term "definitive text" has been roundly criticized—and justly in many cases—as a concept impossible to formulate in practice. For my purposes there is no point in splitting hairs. Depending upon the document to be edited and the method adopted, the ideal is not always impossible to achieve; but we may agree that especially when multiple authority is involved, or a single text is faulty in some respects, two editors may legitimately differ about the treatment of details and possibly even of fundamentals. Hence to label each as a definitive text of a given work, in any precise sense of the word, would certainly be an anomaly. The term "definitive edition" is another matter, however. A definitive scholarly edition is created from various interlocking parts in which the text composes only one element even though it is the central one.[141]

As we have seen, the material features of Dickinson's manuscripts point toward a consistent application of flexible, sophisticated, but fairly traditional structures of rhyme and rhythm. And although a great many of the later manuscripts in particular were left "in a state of incompletion," including many in the fascicles and sets, it is still the case that "when Dickinson went 'public' with a copy to friends, she would produce a fair copy, all alternates resolved."[142]

The materiality of Emily Dickinson's manuscripts helps locate them in historical practices (of handwriting, of chirographic direction, for instance) even as her contents appear to evade them, and such practices provide invaluable contexts for understanding what their appearances might mean. These factors relate most obviously to the local aspects of Dickinson's presentation, but there is also the further matter of their organization or collation. Again, the physical evidence helps, as Ralph Franklin more than anyone else—in a little-known essay on the fascicles from 1983—has tried to bring to our attention.

> Other aspects of their preparation argue against the fascicles as units constructed on some aesthetic principle. Dickinson used individual sheets of two leaves, not quires of leaves as in a notebook. If she had selected poems and arranged them into a meaningful order and then copied them onto fascicle sheets, the poems would have fallen across the four-page sheets without regard to spatial constraints. Instead we see her fitting poems to space. Her short poems (under eight lines), for example, would have appeared at various places on pages, but almost all were placed at the bottom to fill in after the preceding poem. Her longer poems, those taking three or four pages, would have started on any of the four pages of a Dickinson sheet if they had been part of a prior order (or, for that matter, if they had been randomly selected out of the mass before her). But almost all (19 of 22) began on the first page of a sheet, a point at which, conscious of the limits of her sheets, she knew there would be space to complete such a poem. Twice she began on the second page, once misjudging and running off the sheet onto an extra leaf. Once she began on the third page, also overrunning the limits of the sheet. None of the longer poems began on the fourth page. This pattern would not occur unless, working with the sheet as her unit, Dickinson had been fitting poems to space.[143]

Notwithstanding Franklin's compelling objections (which are admirably free of speculation as to intentions; he reads the physical evidence only), scholars have continued to seek patterns of coherence within and across fascicles.[144] The question remains: how should one organize Dickinson's nearly eighteen hundred poems for readerly consumption in ways that do not compromise the record of her own procedures? It is known, for example, that Dickinson collected approximately eight hundred poems in bound and three hundred more in unbound collections. It is known further that Dickinson distributed approximately six hundred poems to forty correspondents.[145] At one level, then, we could be forgiven for thinking that editions of poetry which follow the order of the fascicles and sets do not compromise Dickinson's methods of selection and compilation. At another level, editions of poetry and letters based on notes sent to individual correspondents would appear not to compromise Dickinson's forms of distribution. Whether they compromise her intentions is another matter entirely. Since we cannot claim to know Dickinson's intentions and since intentionalism in itself is a suspect way of attempting to edit and interpret poems, such a consideration may be irrelevant or inappropriate.

Except that the logic of the fascicles and of the correspondence potentially cancel each other out: for poems sent in letters appear not to depend on fascicle contexts to be understood, and poems included in fascicles appear not to depend on information about historical individuals to be understood.

For example, if we cross-reference the poems sent by mail to Samuel Bowles, Susan Dickinson, Thomas Higginson, Elizabeth Holland, and Louise and Frances Norcross, Susan Dickinson received more than any other. But there was occasional overlapping: Samuel Bowles and Susan Dickinson received three of the same poems (186, 187, 288); Susan Dickinson and Higginson received about thirty of the same (112, 124, 291, 321, 325, 334, 418, 501, 579, 594, 606, 935, 966, 1216, 1227, 1239, 1242, 1267, 1275, 1357, 1369, 1386, 1388, 1394, 1416, 1538, 1574, 1596, 1624, 1626); Susan Dickinson and the Hollands received three (4, 1356, 1563); and Susan Dickinson and the Norcross sisters shared eleven (18, 283, 442, 572, 744, 787, 1120, 1130, 1163, 1166, 1353). Susan Dickinson, Bowles, and Higginson received the same poem once (804), as did Susan Dickinson, Higginson, and the Hollands (796); Susan Dickinson, Higginson, and the Norcross sisters shared the same poem twice (819, 1570). Thus, when we read that Dickinson sent 497 poems to these five recipients (with the Norcrosses tabulated as a single entity), 51 of these were shared—about one in every ten, which makes a slight but important difference. That is, while Dickinson deliberately chose and sometimes altered poems with a particular reader in mind, she was not averse to having more than one recipient for certain poems: about 20 percent of the poems Susan Dickinson read were also read by others. And such a poem as Fr816A, "I could not drink it, Sue," written in 1864 and seeming to invite a definitively biographical perspective, was altered to "I could not drink it, Sweet" when it came to be recorded in Set 5, about early 1865.[146] The first version, written in pencil on nonruled paper measuring 9.9 cm across by 15.2 cm down (with "PARIS" embossed within a horizontal oval, and three folds), is written thus:[147]

> I could not drink
> it , Sue ,
> Till you had tasted
> first –
> Though cooler than
> the Water – was
> The Thoughtfulness of
> Thirst –
>   Emily –

When Dickinson came to record it a short time afterward in one of the unbound packets or sets, she wrote it on the bottom portion of lightly ruled paper measuring 12.9 cm across by 20.4 cm down, managing to fit each line between the three extra centimeters of the page, thus:[148]

> I could not drink it, Sweet,
> Till You had tasted first,
> Though cooler than the Water was
> The Thoughtfulness of Thirst.

By extension, few of the 252 poems thought by Franklin to have been sent to Susan Dickinson reconstitute the sequence of their arrangement in the fascicles. Almost all were sent singly: Fr3 (sent in 1853) is also placed in Fascicle 1, as are the poems Franklin numbers 11, 18, and 24 (sent in 1858: they are 27, 18, and 4 in the fascicle) and 16 (sent in 1859). Fr5 (sent in 1858) is from Fascicle 2, as are the poems Franklin numbers 42, 43, and 44 (sent in the same year; they are 1, 2, and 3 in the fascicle) and 61 (sent in 1859). From Fascicle 5, Susan received nine poems: 99, 105, 106, 110, 112, 115, 117, 120, and 121 (in 1860). In the order of their fascicle sequence, these are 10, 21, 22, 1, 3, 6, 15, 18, and 19. This is a high number: there are twenty-five poems in Fascicle 5, and nine represents 36 percent of that figure. But only four of those (21 and 22, 18 and 19) exist in any exact sequence to each other (and then only as pairs). In other words, if the sequence of the poems is a narrative one, as critics have suggested at intermittent periods of Dickinson's historical reception, then Susan Dickinson would not have been able to follow this narrative in any great detail. The larger point is surely that Dickinson does not seem to have felt that a proper understanding of her poems depended on their being read in the sequence of their collation within and across fascicles. On the other hand, that Dickinson placed most of the poems sent to Susan in fascicles or sets (while she was constructing them, up to late 1864 in the case of the former and through 1865 in the case of the latter, before continuing again from 1871 to 1875) without always alluding to her name strongly suggests that for the majority of these poems, even if biographical contexts are a conjectural aspect of their composition, such contexts are not a significant factor in the poems' subsequent distribution or interpretation.

Therefore, we should be wary of uncritically accepting editions that are anchored in either the fascicles or the correspondence—not because they are wrong but because they have interpretative implications that are not unambiguously supported by the documentary evidence. (And interpretations that build on those editions—or their assumption—may be similarly skewed.) Poems read in the sequence of their placement within and across fascicles, for instance, become like the fixed points of a constellation: we are encouraged to draw lines between elements that may well be related by no more than the accident of their physical and temporal proximity.[149] Similarly, poems read in the sequence of their placement within and across a particular correspondence are all too easily related to the particularities of a relationship, without there being conclusive evidence that they permanently comment on or reflect those particularities.[150] It gets worse: Dickinson collected poems in fascicles and circulated poems in correspondence, but she did not collate correspondences or distribute fascicles. In other words, even if she sent poems to Susan Dickinson every day for decades, Dickinson did not collect them in a separate pastebook titled "The Book of Emily and Susan" (or even in a workbox for that matter). And although she circulated a great many poems during her lifetime and asked occasional advice of Susan Dickinson and Higginson, no record exists of her having distributed or asked similar advice about *sequences* of poems. Finally, although there is ample evidence of Dickinson's having revised individual poems in her possession, often leaving alternative readings, no such evidence exists of poems regularly being sent with variants or of extensive fascicle revision—with significant adjustments being made to the order and contents of a fascicle. Which brings us back to square one: methods of presenting poems grounded in fascicles or in correspondence are not at odds with Dickinson's habits, but they are not unproblematically corroborated by them either.

The history of Fr1096, "A narrow Fellow in the Grass," and its distribution usefully shows how different editions subtly transform its formal appearances and local contexts and thereby provide us with a set of signposts that point us in the direction of particular trajectories of meaning. But Dickinson's own practices—sometime enclosing the same poem in a letter and in a fascicle—suggest that it is still legitimate on occasion to abstract poems from their use-in-correspondence, from their fascicle sequence(s), or from the often unknown circumstances of their composition. Though in this book I set out to demonstrate that the poetry may legitimately be appreciated in contexts other than those of its first material presentation, clearly this need not constitute an either-or situation. Readings which do or do not associate a particular poem with its initial material forms and with the circumstances of its composition and epistolary use will enable different possibilities of meaning (for Dickinson, it might be added, as well as for the reader), and these different possibilities can justifiably be indulged by the same person at different times. Or to put it another way, Dickinson's poems are gravitational centers whose orbits sometimes bring them into contact with other satellites and sites of meaning—but such alignments do not prevent their further passage or ultimately define and detain them. And the accumulated evidence of poems, fascicles, and correspondence is that the arrangement in Franklin's *Poems of Emily Dickinson* (1998) constitutes the best single edition that has hitherto been published, in terms of fidelity to the originals at the levels of form and collation and in terms of best representing, at this point in time, the collective interests of the author, the reader, the researcher, and the teacher. It is therefore that text which most of us should refer to in our conversations about Dickinson, private or professional.

It may be that the drive to present Dickinson's manuscripts in apparently unmediated electronic forms accompanied by diplomatic transcriptions is as much a function of our historical moment as, say, Mabel Loomis Todd's efforts at altering Dickinson's rhymes. In this case, the impulse exists because there is an audience whose members require forms of presentation other than the neat stanzas of the nineteenth century; because there is a perception of serious and sustained inaccuracies in the history of Dickinson's editing and transmission by others; and because the software and technology are now available for the quick reproduction and transmission of the originals in digital form. But it may also be that such a presentation represents a corruption of the originals that is similar to Todd's. Such an idea may seem oxymoronic (for the computer screen is regarded as a transparent window onto the world of the autographs and not a machine that represents them), but I put it forward for consideration because regarding the physical layout of a Dickinson autograph as fully integral suppresses the kinds of signals it may be construed as supplying about the significance of its appearance. If the information compiled in this book is accurate, then the publication of diplomatic transcriptions amounts to a serious distortion of Dickinson's practices equivalent only to the tampering evident in the very early editions of her work. It is reasonable to say that details of Dickinson's calligraphy are "lost to us in printed transcriptions," but it does not follow that such a loss is a serious obstacle to the appreciation of "her poetic practice."[151] It is true to say that since Dickinson did not publish in her lifetime, her "pencil or pen was her printing press and her calligraphic orthography her typeface," but there is no evidence to support the assertion that she did not publish *because she wanted* her "pencil or pen [to be her only] printing press and her calligraphic orthography [to be her only] typeface."[152] And as Tanselle puts it, whether "or not Emily Dickinson's manuscripts were specifically 'intended' for publication is really beside the point; the important matter is that they are manuscripts of poems not prepared for publication."[153]

This is not to say that Emily Dickinson did not resist print or publication for other reasons, however. Such resistance may have been primarily ideological, grounded in an antipathy to the power of the cultural market, or to the increasingly intrusive and cultish publicity attached to the personality of the author. It was certainly influenced in part by the recognition that punctuation was something that often had to be negotiated with publishers, with changes sometimes introduced even after corrected proofs were delivered. Dickinson may have felt anxious about her ability to control an aspect of her production that had vital implications for how her work was to be understood, she may simply have been unmotivated by that aspect of conventional literary distribution, or she may have felt that other people would be in a better position to make judgments about such matters. But although the claim that Dickinson's manuscripts have a design element cannot absolutely be dismissed on aesthetic grounds, it seems unsustainable on the textual evidence. The function of her lettering, lineation, and spacing gestures in the direction of a much more conventional and informal appreciation of poetic layout than has been suggested more recently. Invaluable as the manuscripts undoubtedly are, they need to be approached with a concentrated attention to their remoteness from our own time, in an effort to describe "those documents by every means available, internal and external, and thereby instruct their readers in how to read, in how to go about recreating—as each reader must—the intangible works represented by the texts of the documents."[154] Being aware that reading a manuscript at the beginning of the twenty-first century may not be the same as reading it in the nineteenth century is an important means to descriptive accuracy as well as a moral and intellectual exercise: it reminds us of the difference—the interesting difference—of the historical (for surely one of the fascinations of older literature of any kind is precisely its difference from our own). Emily Dickinson's autograph lyrics continue to speak powerfully to the present, but they travel immense distances from a foreign country called the past, and we would do well to accept that some of their accents may be alien from our own.[155]

Postscript
"Where the Meanings, are"

IN 1998, SUZANNE JUHASZ asked (in an essay that deserves more attention than it has hitherto received): "As teachers and scholars, we find ourselves with a problem and a responsibility. What qualifies, then, as a Dickinson poem? And how can we take responsibility for the text we are using?"[1] In this book I have attempted to move in the direction of partially answering the first of these questions, in the process suggesting that (to paraphrase Robert Lowell) we are charged with a responsibility "to give / each figure in the photograph / [its proper] name."[2] Of course, most Dickinson critics are able to make balanced and informed judgments as to what kind of edition is most appropriate to the purposes of their inquiry: Marta Werner's splendid work in the field of drafts and fragments is a continuously outstanding example. In practice, however, not all of those who choose diplomatic transcriptions of Dickinson autographs are able to relate their choice of text to the contents or communicative strategies of the poems they discuss, and fewer still do so from the perspective of familiarity with the originals. Witness, for example, Adam Frank's otherwise fascinating article "Emily Dickinson and Photography," in which he uses a diplomatic version of Fr337 ("Of nearness to her sundered Things"), a regularized version of Fr901 ("The Soul's distinct connection") with only some of Franklin's editorial apparatus appended, and then a regularized version of Fr450 ("The Outer – from the Inner") with no textual apparatus at all (even though the original features some different line breaks, a word division, and a page break).[3] Frank's article typifies the occasional confusion of the contemporary critic who feels that manuscript-based arrangements of the poetry are now de rigueur. For instance, in his rendering of Fr901 he includes information about variants, but not line division, then places (the wrong kinds of) variant markers *after* words rather than before them (as with "Exhibits," "Flash," and "Click"), in one case moving the cross that marks the variant from the start of a line ("+Not yet suspected") to after the verb ("Not yet suspected†"), thus unintentionally but misleadingly giving the initial impression that it is the verb ("suspected") and not the phrase ("Not yet suspected") that Dickinson had in mind a variant for. Thus, in offering an apparently noninterventional version of the poem, Frank alters it in slight but inconsistent (and textually unsanctioned) ways or makes assumptions about

what information needs to be conveyed to the reader and what does not—
Frank neglects to let the reader know that Dickinson did not use square brack-
ets, for example, and that she wrote something like this:

> \+ Developes + still unsus –
> pected + Fork + Bolt –

She did not (as he appears to claim) write as follows:

> † Exhibits] Developes
> † Not yet susected] still unsuspected † Flash] Fork
> † Click-] Bolt-

(The typo "susected" appears in the article, not the original.) What seems to
me to be unfortunate about Frank's article is, first, that his inconsistent adop-
tion of texts shifts the focus away from what he has to say about the poems,
which is cogent and valuable, and, second, that his article does not require
such attention to manuscript details in the first place, since his approach is
largely thematic and historical and since the texts he discusses are not edito-
rially challenging. And because he has not *seen* the manuscripts themselves,
one wonders what basis he has for discriminating (internally) between which
of their features are pertinent and which not or (more generally) why one
poem merits literal transcription and others do not. By extension, when Paul
Crumbley (in his excellent *Inflections of the Pen*) identifies sixteen varieties of
dash in Dickinson's handwritten lyrics, one anticipates an explanation as to
why a specific kind of dash was inserted at a particular juncture in a poem's
inscription and what difference that application might make to the meaning
of a word, a phrase, a line, or a poem. In other words, if the dashes are so
rigorously distinguished from one another, then each should have a consistent
role or effect, the parameters of which its deployment ought to reveal. Instead,
Crumbley concentrates (rightly, and often brilliantly) on the generalized ef-
fect of Dickinson's dash (which he claims is a "direct challenge to the primacy
of a single unified voice," though he has no problems identifying at least three
such voices, those of the Child, the Bride, and the Queen).[4] Crumbley's ar-
gument would work just as well if it proceeded from an edition of the poems
(or letters, for that matter) which uses a standardized form of the dash, for he
claims that the function of the dash is strategic rather than local: his insistence
on careful manuscript differentiation distracts attention from his larger point
about the dialogic quality of Dickinson's writing.

Crumbley and (to a lesser degree, because he used editions of manuscripts rather than originals) Frank are, like the majority of professional scholars who write on Dickinson, more than capable of justifying their choices when called upon to do so. But there are many more readers and students who do not have access to the autographs, except in reproduced and ideologically mediated ways (one does not instantly find electronic editions of particular poems on the Web but has to pass through various levels of organization which explain the necessity of being there first), and who therefore depend on editors and teachers for guidance. Looking at electronic reproductions of Dickinson's manuscripts is the final stage of a long process that began with *interpretations* about the appearances of Dickinson's texts—interpretations that go beyond the rationale of the archive. Questions arise, then: Does the task of editing inevitably involves choices? Is choosing impossible to avoid in re-creating Dickinson's poetry for a reading audience? What criteria exist for determining which decisions are the most accurate and responsible, and which edition or editions offer the best aggregate examples of attempts at fulfilling those criteria?[5]

In my own case, my search for answers to these questions began after reading what I consider to be one of the best books ever written on the poet, Martha Nell Smith's *Rowing in Eden: Rereading Emily Dickinson*. Smith challenged the reader, thrillingly and with an irresistible combination of originality and impeccable scholarship, to rethink the established tradition of Dickinson as a private poet who did not publish; critiqued (and hopefully dismissed) prejudices about Susan Dickinson; approached Dickinson's writings not chronologically but according to correspondent; and argued that the relation between the manuscripts and their edited versions was akin to that of writing and translation. Inspired by her example, I set out in 1996 to write an article on Dickinson's correspondence with Higginson, with the goal of extending the findings of Smith and Jerome McGann by applying them to a different corpus from the one with which Smith and Ellen Louise Hart were then engaged, and which would eventually be completed as *Open Me Carefully*. But reading the autographs in the Rare Books and Manuscripts division of the Boston Public Library turned out to be a frustrating experience; again and again, I was struck by how expectations about Dickinson's lettering, word division, paragraphing, and generic distinctions were not sustained. I kept seeing, for example, that the margins established by Dickinson handwriting on the right-hand side of the paper she wrote on in her letters changed in a way that coincided each time with the body of a poem. Eventually I began to measure and chart these variations to find out if they were optical illusions (caused by my recognition of the poems enclosed in the text, for example) or physical facts that corresponded either to innovations in the way of organizing lyrics or to identifiable literary conventions. And again and again I found that most of Thomas H. Johnson's recordings of manuscript poems and letters were accurate to their spirit, to their formatting codes, to the relationship of writing and paper as evidence of inherited and consistent formal principles being applied within quantifiable material constraints, and not to a priori assumptions about how poems and letters should look. On the other hand, the opposite seemed to be the case with transcriptions that aspired toward greater fidelity, as we saw earlier with the recording of blank spaces that are explicable in physical terms but raised to the status of rhetorical signs in diplomatic transcriptions. By and large, for example, Emily Dickinson did not use initial indentation to signal the beginning of a new paragraph. There are occasional exceptions: the letter beginning "I hav'nt any paper, dear," has a paragraph ("*You* may tell") on the fourth page of the manuscript which starts approximately one centimeter further into the page than the rest of the writing on the left-hand side.[6] Such anomalies are sometimes the result of a material feature of the paper: again, in the letter beginning "Sister / Ned is safe," the paper is embossed, and there are partial blank spaces at the top of pages 2, 3, and 4, where Dickinson avoids writing on the raised edges left by the stamp.[7] And Dickinson's normal practice of using reverse final indentation, indicating the close of a paragraph by not continuing to write even when there was lateral space available for doing so, can be awkward to repeat in print: a typed paragraph may come so close to the right margin that it would simply blend with the next. To circumvent this, Johnson and Ward deploy standard paragraphing, signaling the start of a new unit by setting its first line back from the left-hand margin of writing. Hart and Smith replace horizontal indentation with a vertical alternative: whereas the vertical gap between continuous lines of prose is ordinarily around three or four millimeters in their edition, this widens to approximately six between the last line of one paragraph and the first line of the next. The short-term advantage is that they avoid initially indented paragraphs, but this solution has no sanction in Dickinson's texts: in the majority of manuscript letters, there is no increase in the proportion of vertical space between *paragraphs* compared with space between *lines* in paragraphs. What Hart and Smith do is a necessity of print editions and only superficially different from the methods used by Johnson and Ward; in substance, they are the same.

Which brings us yet again to the heart of the matter: a conventional and a diplomatic edition of the same poem will involve almost exactly the same number of editorial decisions, but these decisions will not be made equally visible. For example, here are two versions of the same opening stanza:[8]

My Life had stood – a Loaded Gun –   My Life had stood – a
In Corners – till a Day   Loaded Gun –
The Owner passed – identified –   In Corners – till a Day
And carried Me away –   The Owner passed – identified –
                                             And carried Me away –

The first version is Franklin's, and although he has been criticized in some circles for including information about line breaks at the bottom of his page (where he notes in this instance that there is a division after "a" in the first line of the autograph), on the grounds that it seems to contradict his stated position that midline breaks are generally caused by aspects of the artifact, he openly records such emendations where manuscript critics do not (on the grounds that they apparently do not believe that they alter the layout of the text). The second of these is clearly more like the five-row original, which is not the same as saying that it involves fewer interventions—the interventions are different only in being less obvious. For the first version *seems* to intervene at more points but may do so less, whereas the manuscript edition seems to intervene at fewer points but may do so more (for it ignores the collective import of writing and space which suggests that the first two rows of the autograph are one line). It is not necessarily that one approach is intrinsically better than the other, but that, at parallel moments, *both* arrangements involve decisions (the turnover is nondeliberate, the turnover is deliberate); only one seems to acknowledge this openly. Conventional and diplomatic editions are thus mirror-images of each other: both editions involve equal amounts of interpretation, but only the former lays bare its critical nature at the local level.[9] And only the former attends to the *totality* of relationships between lettering, rows, spaces, and paper, which intersect to reveal a set of governing principles, a template that gives shape to their alignment on the page—such as line-initial capitals and blank spaces that function as codes, indicating (respectively) the beginning and end of metrical lines. Like underlining and italics in most software programs or the layout of a page on the Web, the capitals and spaces in Dickinson's manuscripts are effects of preexistent codes (in this case, sociocultural). We see the traces of these codes through their visible effects: the physical arrangement of the manuscript is determined by a combination of material factors and nonphysical conventions. When I marked the presence of such instructions earlier in square brackets, I was effectively doing what my word-processing software does when one selects "Reveal Codes": revealing the kinds of formatting directives that make the page look the way it does.

The first stanza we just considered is from one of Dickinson's best-known and difficult poems: it dates to late 1863, it was collated as the ninth poem in Fascicle 34, and the sum total of its specific appearances is best charted in reproduction by Franklin.[10]

> My Life had stood – a Loaded Gun –
> In Corners – till a Day
> The Owner passed – identified –
> And carried Me away –
>
> And now We roam in Sovreign Woods –
> And now We hunt the Doe –
> And every time I speak for Him
> The Mountains straight reply –
>
> And do I smile, such cordial light
> Opon the Valley glow –
> It is as a Vesuvian face
> Had let it's pleasure through –
>
> And when at Night – Our good Day done –
> I guard My Master's Head –
> 'Tis better than the Eider Duck's
> Deep Pillow – to have shared –
>
> To foe of His – I'm deadly foe –
> None stir the second time –
> On whom I lay a Yellow Eye –
> Or an emphatic Thumb –
>
> Though I than He – may longer live
> He longer must – than I –
> For I have but the power to kill,
> Without – the power to die –

5 in] the –   16 Deep] low   18 stir] harm   23 power] art

Division 1 a | 5 in | 7 speak | 9 such | 13 Our | 13 done – ‖
15 Eider Duck's] Eider – | Duck's   17 deadly | 19 Yellow | 21 may |
23 power |

The poem continues to attract attention more than a century after its composition, not all of it approbatory (Habegger reports that "many readers have been dissatisfied with the way the poem ends").[11] It received perhaps its most brilliant exegetical performance of recent times in Susan Howe's *My Emily Dickinson*; it was Howe who first posited a slave as one of the poem's possible referents (the others being a soul finding God, a soul finding herself, a poet "born into voice by idealizing a precursor," Dickinson herself, the American continent, the savage source of American myth, the "United States in the grip of violence," a "white woman taken captive by Indians," an "unmarried woman . . . waiting to be chosen," and a "frontiersman's gun").[12] The idea that the story of Nat Turner's insurrection may have partially inspired the poem makes superb sense: convinced of his having been ordained at an early age by God; prompted to violence by voices and by visions that included the appearance of a spirit, drops of blood in the fields, and an eclipse of the sun; and eventually surrounded by militia and by state and federal troops in South Hampton County, Virginia, Turner would almost certainly have realized that he would never be able or allowed to die naturally (he was executed in 1831).[13] But Howe's other suggestions have their separate appeal; artists have often externalized their talents as gifts bestowed upon them by a muse that ultimately transcends their lives. The idea that the poem might be spoken by a woman who is about to marry or has already married seems slightly less convincing or obvious. The sequence about *not* sharing the Master's pillow seems, if not to discount that possibility entirely (many nineteenth-century middle-class women, including Harriet Beecher Stowe and Edith Wharton, had separate beds or bedrooms from their husbands), at least to introduce a distinction between the role of the poem's protagonist and that of a wife.[14]

Howe reads the poem, legitimately and insightfully, as it were about someone who is both particular (Emily Dickinson, Catherine Earnshaw, Nat Turner) and representative (woman-artist, bride, slave), whereas I am more interested in what the poem tells us about the object or person who narrates it. The approaches are not necessarily mutually exclusive; the poem still creates the sense of a consciousness that is so incapable of thinking of itself in terms of agency that it conceives of ability, achievement, action, attractiveness, initiative, skill, and usefulness as elements that originate outside the self. One concedes the force and feasibility of Howe's intuitions here: the poem is a powerful meditation on disenfranchisement, and what it does to those disenfranchised, who have to imagine power as something invested in them rather than intrinsically derived. What Dickinson seems interested in representing in this dramatic monologue is the way in which a culture of dependency creates a skewed way of seeing the self and the world. But the ethnically and sexually oppressed are not the only ones who fit the description offered by the poem; the early Puritan settlers often described instances of their own individual and communal resourcefulness as acts of divine intervention, and religious election in the seventeenth and eighteenth centuries was believed to be a state of grace that only God could initiate. The intolerance, militancy, and persecution that sometimes accompanied the sense of being chosen make the poem apply equally well to Puritan self-righteousness, bigotry, and sectarianism as to the denied rights of single women, Native Americans, people of color, and women artists.

So far, I have delayed mentioning the most obvious possibility: that the poem is about a gun (or at least that it is spoken by a gun; what it is about may be another matter entirely, of course). What complicates this idea is principally the first line, which seems to establish an intriguing equation between the life of a speaker and the utilitarian career of a firearm; the narrative of the gun and what it does, it then follows, must relate point by point to a sequence of events in a human life. But what if the poem functions as a kind of negative or reverse allegory—what if it describes not what a life (or life generally) is like, but what a life is *not* like, the qualities that make human life distinct from that of a thing, an object, a tool? What if the poem uses its speaker to identify everything that the writer is not—a sort of "There but by the Grace of God (or good luck or whatever), go I?" What if this is another "nobody" poem, this time spoken by "somebody"? Or, more simply still, what if this is one of twin poems that take as their subject the encroachment of trade, of industrial technology, on the physical and social landscape of Western Massachusetts (the other being Fr383, "I like to see it lap the Miles"), and both of which end by emphasizing the limitations or weaknesses of apparently all-powerful machines? The train is tamed at the close of Fr383; the gun (or the mind and body as tools of a cause) is seen as deadly but utterly dependent on another being to actualize it. (And the master figure remains frighteningly indistinct; his motives are utterly unfathomable.)

Pistols are named in the Massachusetts state industrial census of 1837 as being manufactured in Amherst. Henry A. Morrill, Silas Mosman Jr., and Charles Blair secured a contract for the production of "bowie-knife pistols" in that year (and a report was written on them in the 30 August issue of the *Boston Courier*).[15] Outside Amherst, the Sharps rifle was invented in 1848, though the largest period of its production did not begin until 1860 (only a few hundred were produced prior to that; in 1861, fifty-eight hundred carbines were made by the Sharps Rifle Company alone).[16] The Colt company produced seventy-five thousand pistols and would have made many more if its factory in Hartford, Connecticut, had not burned down in February 1864.[17] And newspapers such as the *Hampshire and Franklin Express* that the Dickinsons subscribed to carried advertisements for pistols and rifles. The Roper Repeating Rifle Company operated in Amherst between the years 1866 and 1868, partly under the auspices of local industrialists H. D. Fearing and Henry F. Hills, and it

employed thirty skilled mechanics at a location near the railway station on
Main Street. Though it was too late to count as a factor in the writing of the
poem, it is an important part of the general context of weapons manufac-
ture in western Massachusetts which, like the train, had caught Dickinson's
attention.[18]

The middle decades of the nineteenth century were a time of great inno-
vation and progress in the history of firearms: though flintlocks were still in
use, a variety of percussion weapons had also been invented and refined. These
would have been either muzzle-loading or breech-loading single-shot pistols,
six-shot revolvers, or long guns (rifles and shotguns): in the countryside
around Amherst, where deer were certainly hunted but small game (including
squirrels, partridge, and wild turkey) was the usual quarry, a muzzle-loading
shotgun with birdshot, accurate within a range of a hundred yards or so, would
have been the gun Dickinson was most likely to have heard or seen (if she saw
any; there are no weapons in the inventories of the Homestead or the Ever-
greens, only a small toy rifle that is thought to have belonged to her nephew
Edward, "Ned").[19] Nevertheless, although some of the poem is taken up with
a narrative of the gun's usage (hunting, shooting, protecting), the terms used
to describe it are human: it speaks and smiles, possesses a yellow eye, and has
a thumb. The latter is typical of the poem's structural manipulation of human
and humane terms for nonhuman and inhumane objects and actions: the
thumb referred to is the exposed spring-loaded hammer of the firearm, which
initiates the firing cycle when it is cocked and which strikes a sealed copper
cap, thus igniting the gunpowder (usually fulminate of mercury) that ejects
the ball or bullet through the barrel. The hammer of the gun resembles the
human thumb but is also connected to it metonymically: it is the thumb of the
person who carries the gun which presses down on its spur to lock it into
place, thus priming the trigger for discharging.[20] In a breech-loading rifle, the
thumb is used to open the breech, to insert the cartridge into the barrel, and
to close the breech; before firing, the hand is held in such a position that the
thumb points toward the muzzle (and thus in the direction of the object being
shot at). The upright rear sight is also adjusted with the thumb of the right
hand, until the target is brought into line with the top of the front sight.
Though it seems most likely that the firearm referred to in the poem is a
muzzle-loading percussion shoulder arm (such as a shotgun), it being the
weapon of choice for the hunters of small game, Dickinson may also have had
in mind a single-action revolver, the firing sequence of which requires the
hammer to be cocked by the thumb. (An advertising flyer of the 1850s shows
a Colt repeating pistol with its hammer drawn back in readiness to strike; it is
also accompanied by scenes of battle, on land and sea, and hunting.)[21] It is also
possible that the thumb referred to is figurative in another way: it might

signify either a thumblike object (the ball or cartridge) or the act of suppressing or dominating.[22]

A notable feature of the poem is its diction, then, which confers positive and occasionally chivalric terms on acts that have devastating consequences: the noise made after firing is defined as a speech-act that the mountains immediately reply to (again suggesting the second element in a polite dialogue rather than a passive echo brought about by a series of merely physical factors). The jet of flame that accompanies the explosion of gasses during firing is described as a smile that illuminates the valley; the effect is out of proportion to both the extent of the flash and to the intent of the projectile it is designed to propel. In addition, there is a deliberately benign and smug pun involving "cordial" and "cordite": the word "cordial" suggests the codes of polite discourse but also "cordite," associated in the popular imagination with the mixture of elements contained in the propellant charge or detonating powder that, ignited, fires the ball or shot. And "pleasure"—signifying both enjoyment and approbation—seems a strange word to use in connection with wounding or killing (the enjoyment might be sadistic, but worse is the possibility that it is not, that it involves no ethical or philosophical judgment whatsoever; "good" is defined as unquestioning obedience to a powerful figure from whom one derives one's own ideological or moral purpose and raison d'être). What unites all of these terms is that they apply a vocabulary derived from the ideals of civilized and perhaps courtly behavior to more violent and destructive realities. Far from being a poem about the oppressed alone, then, "My Life had stood – a Loaded Gun" seems to apply equally well, at least in parts, to the duplicities or blindness of the oppressor, much like Melville's description in *The Confidence Man* of the Indian hater who embodies all of the values (of treachery, cunning, savagery) that he attributes (and seeks to eradicate through extermination) to others.[23]

The accumulated force of these separate references is the suggestion of a human presence behind the story (and thus the sense that it is allegorical or even autobiographical), but they are also understandable as symptomatic of the gun's delusion that it has a constructive and approved impact on the environment around it.[24] Or, to put it another way, although there is no doubt that one of the poem's fascinations is the suspicion that it is allegorical without the exact knowledge of who or what the allegory refers to, it is also possible that Dickinson marshals this sequence of human characteristics ironically or obliquely, to highlight opposing qualities (of speech, joy, generosity) that weaponry, nineteenth-century industrial technology, political activism, or militarism cannot bestow. This possibility seems especially strong in the last stanza (which is sometimes seen as compromising the poem but which the entire poem may well be little more than a vehicle for delivering): human beings have the ability to die naturally, while tools or the components of a machine (physical or political) do not. Such a message hardly seems like a triumph for ordinary humanity, and Dickinson's strategy in the poem may well have been to make it more palatable. At one level, it may only be that death—and more particularly the knowledge of one's transience or vulnerability—allows some human beings to appreciate beauty more keenly, or to sympathize with others, or to desire a relationship with nature that does not involve devastation. At another, Dickinson plays a clever game whereby the gun (or the tool in a wider sense) advances its own longevity first but then concedes the necessity of the master outliving it; as their continued presence in museums testifies, many kinds of implements survive the immediate time of their use and usefulness, but tools do not have the possibility of eternal life, to which death is the necessary conduit. Seen in a loosely religious context, death is a kind of power that is unique to particular classes of men and woman—even men and women who in life are vulnerable to the terrible power of firearms. Again, Dickinson seems to be suggesting that the weapon (or the person as weapon) overestimates its supremacy: the longevity of a gun is not the immortality that is at least potentially available—as a fact, or as a desire, a wish, a hope—to the humans it sometimes outlives.

In a way, Dickinson prepares us for this reversal in the fourth stanza, where the gun guards the master's head but cannot join her or him, either through physical proximity in bed or through the shared capacity to dream and imagine. The prefiguring is simultaneously comical and sensuous (though some critics have speculated on the weapon's phallic associations, the joke is at least in part that a gun cannot enable what a penis or a vagina obviously can—to die in the Elizabethan sense, or to experience sexual orgasm): the speaker boasts that its task as guardian is better than sharing an "Eider Duck's / Deep Pillow." In the United States, the main way of acquiring such feathers in the nineteenth century was to shoot the bird (and thus drive the species toward extinction), and again Dickinson asks us to meditate on the position that it is always better to be a victor than a victim, something or someone who shoots rather than something or someone who is shot. On the other hand, the exclusion from the master's bed is not simply bodily: it is an exclusion from the world of sleep, dreams (and the imagination generally), comfort, and love. Rather than identify her life with that of the gun, then, Dickinson may have used it as Browning used the character of the duke in "My Last Duchess": to disclose, unwittingly through direct speech, weakness and impropriety in the ostensible profession of power.

The poem is utterly consistent and merciless in exposing the deficiencies that belie the speaker's acceptance of its role: the self-satisfied and banal sonorities of "Our good Day done"; the attempt to compensate for the realities of inferiority (though exiled from the comfortable bed, the speaker claims that it would not have it otherwise); and the wonderfully closed, circular, and strained logic of to "foe of His – I'm deadly foe," where the speaker once more defines its merits negatively and oppositionally (not as the champion but as the enemy of its master's enemies). And there are further echoes of "I like to see it lap the Miles" in the relentless and simplistic repetition of "And" in stanzas one and two: it appears four times in four lines, and is then echoed at the start of the third and fourth stanzas. Dickinson uses the conjunction to create the impression of a consciousness fully caught up in action, in doing, in the moment (a kind of latter-day *Natural Born Killer*): only at the last is there a sense of conceptual and abstract thought introduced with the subjunctive and the hint of another perspective on the events and acts that the poem relates.

The names of those critics who have offered interpretations of "My Life had stood – a Loaded Gun" read like a *Who's Who* of Dickinson scholars: a partial list includes Charles Anderson, Paula Bennett, Sharon Cameron, Joanne Feit Diehl, Joanne Dobson, Albert Gelpi, Sandra Gilbert and Susan Gubar, Alfred Habegger, Roland Hagenbüchle, Susan Howe, Thomas H. Johnson, Karl Keller, Helen McNeill, Cristanne Miller, Barbara Mossberg, Rebecca Patterson, Vivianne Pollak, David Porter, Adrienne Rich, Richard Sewall, Robert Weisbuch, and Shira Wolosky.[25] The point of this coda is not to compete with such interpretations, or even to complement them (for already the number of interpretations seems sufficient and their conclusions valid and valuable), but to suggest that the future of Dickinson studies depends a great deal on the early settlement of debates about the logic of her manuscript appearances.

For what united all these critics is that they shared a common point of reference (the 1955 *Poems* and the 1958 *Letters*) that enabled a close attention to the particularities of the *work*; putting "the manuscripts themselves at the center of critical attention" encourages instead an attention to the particularities of the *text*.[26] Scholars must often devote long periods of time to the intensive, not to say obsessive, study of details and fragments—of that which is peripheral to, or a necessary prerequisite to, the reading of the literary work as literary work. This is right and proper: it is how advances in knowledge are made. But such scholarly endeavor, even if originally conceived as a means to an end, can easily become for the scholar an end in itself. The study of Dickinson's manuscripts has been and remains an interesting prelude to, or accompaniment of, the reading of her letters and poems. But it is a means, not an end: the end is the reading of Emily Dickinson's letters and poems.[27]

NOTES

PROLOGUE: *Emily Has Left the Building*

Epigraph: Walter Benjamin, "The Work of Art in the Age of Mechanical Reproduction," in *Illuninations*, ed. Hannah Arendt, trans. Harry Zohn (New York: Shocken, 1968), 220.

1. "Notes & Queries," *Emily Dickinson International Society Bulletin* 13, no. 1 (2001) [henceforth *EDIS Bulletin*]: 21. The new center was to be located at "the rear ell of the house, originally the kitchen, pantry, laundry room, and privy." Such a construction is undoubtedly necessary, and I do not see it as compromising the dignity of Dickinson's former home or her work.

2. Martha Dickinson Bianchi, Last Will and Testament, Amherst, Mass., 15 November 1938, 1. A true copy of the document (made at the Registry of Probate of Hampshire County at Northampton on 18 February 1944) is housed at the Special Collections Room of the Jones Library at Amherst. Nonetheless, letters from Alfred Leete Hampson and Mary Landis Hampson refer to a letter from Martha Bianchi in which she expressed her desire to have the house saved for posterity. See "Correspondence concerning Emily Dickinson Papers," bMS AM 1923, Houghton Library, Harvard College Library, Harvard University, Cambridge, Mass.

3. Gregory Farmer, " 'That the House be Taken Down to the Cellar': How the Evergreens Was Saved," *EDIS Bulletin* 13, no. 1 (2001): 11. Another possibility is suggested by a letter from Helen S. Mitchell to Mary Hampson, who inherited the Evergreens after her husband's death. It reads, in part: "The Amherst Housing Authority, of which I am a member, have been considering possible sites for thirty housing units for elderly citizens of Amherst . . . One of the sites which we would like to consider is your property [the Evergreens] . . . of course, you would receive a fair price for the property." Helen S. Mitchell to Mary Landis Hampson, 26 May 1959, bMS Am 1923 (7), Houghton Library, Harvard College Library, Harvard University. A letter of 29 May 1959, from Hampson to Gilbert Montague (who had bought the Dickinson manuscripts owned by Alfred Hampson and bequeathed them to Harvard) expresses her alarm: "Apparently the Housing Commission in Massachusetts is very powerful, and it seems one is powerless against them, if they wish to take a certain property." But on 4 June, Hampson reported that after a meeting with Helen Mitchell, the Commission "removed [the Evergreens] from the list of possible sites for the housing development." Nonetheless, she admitted: "that letter out of the blue was a frightening thing"—and it made her own ambivalence about the future of the house all the more keenly felt. Hampson wanted to preserve the Evergreens as a memorial to the Dickinson family, and Martha Dickinson Bianchi in particular: but she was also afraid that it might fall into the wrong hands, so to speak.

4. Farmer's article makes it clear that Bianchi wanted to have a Dickinson memorial located at the Evergreens, and that she would not therefore have disapproved of its usage as a museum. Farmer, " 'That the House be Taken Down to the Cellar'," 11.

5. But there is a certain irony to this: a woman who spent much of her life regulat-

ing the exposure of her person and poetry to other people (including friends) finds herself caught up in a cult of the personality, familiarly referred to as "Emily" and not Emily Dickinson or Dickinson. For example, in Ellen Louise Hart and Martha Nell Smith's *Open Me Carefully*: "Loo and Fanny, Emily's cousins, are arriving in Amherst for a visit. The poem that Emily includes here was printed in the *Springfield Daily Republican* on February 14, 1866. It is possible that Emily now sends Susan the poem to replace the copy that Susan sent to the newspaper. From this letter-poem, it is clear that the two women are seeing each other face-to-face. In a letter postmarked March 17, 1866, Emily worried that Higginson would come across the poem in the *Republican* and think that she had been duplicitous concerning her intentions not 'to print.' " Hart and Smith, eds., *Open Me Carefully: Emily Dickinson's Intimate Letters to Susan Huntington Dickinson* (Ashfield: Paris Press, 1998), 174.

6. Martha Nell Smith, "Corporealizations of Dickinson and Interpretive Machines," in *The Iconic Page in Manuscript, Print, and Digital Culture*, ed. George Bornstein and Theresa Lynn Tinkle (Ann Arbor: University of Michigan Press, 1998), 203.

7. At one level, familiarity reflects the sense that Dickinson's lyrics appear to speak directly and immediately to the reader, long after her death. At another, it seems critically naïve and repeats the practice of Archibald MacLeish and others which Suzanne Juhasz, rightly, criticized as patronizing in her preface to *Feminist Critics Read Emily Dickinson* (Bloomington: Indiana University Press, 1983). For a more theoretical discussion of the same issue, see Robert McClure Smith's excellent *The Seductions of Emily Dickinson* (Tuscaloosa: University of Alabama Press, 1996).

8. J. Hillis Miller, *Black Holes* (Stanford: Stanford University Press, 1999), 441.

9. David Leon Higdon, " 'Complete but Uncorrected': The Typescript of Conrad's *Under Western Eyes*," in *Joseph Conrad's "Under Western Eyes": Beginnings, Revisions, Final Form*, ed. David R. Smith (Hamden: Archon Books, 1991), 88.

10. Although Dickinson's sister Lavinia claimed to have found Dickinson's poems, Margaret Maher, according to partial readings of court depositions and an anecdote by Martha Dickinson Bianchi, said that she kept them in her trunk. The available evidence seems to contradict the Margaret Maher scenario. In the trial documents, Maher claimed that Dickinson kept her manuscripts in Maher's trunk. The description she gave, however, was of the fascicles, little volumes of several sheets, tied up with string, containing twelve or fourteen poems—probably those which Lavinia claimed to have found and which Mabel Loomis Todd copied for the first volume of Dickinson's poems released in 1890. Even if Maher were correct, there does not appear to be any strong evidence that she had the loose (non-fascicle or set) poems. In cross-examination, indeed, Maher admitted that she had never read any of Emily Dickinson's poems in her own handwriting.

Many contradictory statements were made about the discovery of Emily Dickinson's manuscripts. At a trial over disputed rights to Dickinson land, Lavinia Dickinson claimed to have discovered them all at one time, though to Mabel Loomis Todd, who received them in several installments, they appeared to be new discoveries. In early 1891 Susan Gilbert Dickinson said that she had had the manuscripts until early 1890. If these general outlines are true, it would suggest that Lavinia Dickinson found all of the manuscripts and delivered most or all of them to Susan Gilbert Dickinson on the understanding that the latter would edit them with a view to publication. When Susan Dickinson failed to do this quickly enough, Lavinia reclaimed them, and for a time—down to about the beginning of 1890—had manuscripts in the hands of both Susan Dickinson and Mabel Loomis Todd. Todd first saw a box with about seven hundred, largely composed of fascicles and sets, from which *Poems by Emily Dickinson*, First Series (1890) was drawn. These were followed in the fall and winter of 1890–91 by additional poems, some of them also described as in a box. At any one moment, Todd seems always to have thought that what had passed into/through her hands was everything and proceeded in the summer of 1891 to index it all, only to record the receipt of yet more only days after she had finished indexing. It would appear that there was either one cache that was released to Mabel Loomis Todd in parts or multiple discoveries, so released to her. Because Susan Gilbert Dickinson herself says she had manuscripts until about the beginning of 1890, Lavinia Dickinson would have had reason to minimize the division to Todd. My thanks to Ralph W. Franklin for his clarification of these issues.

11. Norman Holmes Pearson, "Problems of Literary Executorship," *Studies in Bibliography* 5 (1952–53): 5.

12. The bureau was identified as Dickinson's by Martha Dickinson Bianchi, in *The Life and Letters of Emily Dickinson* (Boston: Houghton Mifflin, 1924), 102. In *Emily Dickinson Face to Face*, she discusses "little packages tied with all sorts of cotton strings for hinges"—the fascicles, in other words (59–60). Otherwise, there were "copies of poems sent her friends, variants and fragments found lying loosely in boxes and drawers." See *Emily Dickinson Face to Face: Unpublished Letters with Notes and Reminiscences* (Boston: Houghton Mifflin, 1932), 59. In a letter of 17 February 1891, to Mrs. C. S. Mack, Lavinia claimed that the poems had been found in a locked box. Quoted in Thomas H. Johnson, ed., *The Poems of Emily Dickinson* (Cambridge: Harvard University Press, Belknap Press, 1955), 1:xxxix. It is not known if these statements are mutually supporting (i.e., that the locked box was found inside the mahogany bureau) or refer to different finds (a box of fascicles and a bureau of loose poems, or vice versa), or if they are contradictory versions of the same find (which may have been in a box, a bureau, or both).

13. Nineteenth-century conduct books stressed that it was the responsibility of a lady to destroy written materials belonging to her. The fact that Dickinson did not suggests either that Maher's story was untrue or that she had confused one group of Dickinson's writings (her storehouse of scraps and fragments) with another (the bound fascicles and sets that she described during the trial).

14. There may be times when casual readers can be said to have fewer obligations to the writer than professional scholars and editors, who are charged with a responsibility—even a duty—to recognize the absolute alterity of the materials in their care. As a reader, for example, I can take personal pleasure in looking at copies of Dickinson's worksheets; as an editor or professional reader, I have concerns that may or may not turn out to coincide with such pleasures.

15. The quotation is from the introduction to Hart and Smith's *Open Me Carefully*, xix. As I will argue, the emphasis on Dickinson's manuscripts may be a function of technological advances in the media of textual reproduction in combination with modernist and postmodernist experiments with visual form. It may also involve an attempt to control Dickinson's writings, to regulate them according to contemporary stylistic preferences, much as the first editors glossed her rhythm and rhyme. Nicholas Jacobs, commenting on the role of the scribe in relation to authorial documents, makes some

observations that are relevant to Dickinson's editing: he claims that alteration "involves an assertion of personality at the expense of someone or something else. In the case of our scribe, the existence of the author and a text independent of himself were subconsciously perceived as a threat to his own autonomy. In altering the text he was reasserting his control over an intractable object and, in so doing, reasserting his own personal dignity. Modern critics who attempt to separate the meaning of a text from its author's intention may fairly be charged with doing exactly the same thing. The phenomenon may be characterized, unkindly, as a mild panic in face of the otherness of the other, or, more charitably . . . as the reemergence of a stifled creative impulse." Jacobs, "Regression to the Commonplace in Some Vernacular Textual Traditions," in *Crux and Controversy in Middle English Textual Criticism*, ed. A. J. Minnis and Charlotte Brewer (Cambridge: D. S. Brewer, 1992), 65. The points seem especially compelling with regard to Bianchi, Bingham, Susan Dickinson, Higginson, and Todd.

16. A 853, Special Collections, Frost Library, Amherst College. Henceforth, all references prefixed by A and followed by a number are to originals at Amherst College.

17. Of course, even if one settles for a consistent mode of presentation—to be faithful to every detail of inscription on the page, there is still the problem of organization. For instance, if "Flowers are so enticing" is a poem or letter-poem, should it be organized as a single unit of meaning, arranged chronologically with nearly two thousand others; according to who received it (many of Dickinson's approximately forty correspondents were sent letters and poems—but not this one); or in the sequence of its collation by the poet herself (Dickinson collected about eight hundred in packets of one kind or another: what happens to those that were not so gathered)?

18. Thomas H. Johnson and Theodora Ward, eds., *The Letters of Emily Dickinson* (Cambridge: Harvard University Press, Belknap Press, 1958) [henceforth *Letters*], 3: 923.

19. That is, Dickinson may not have operated with such distinctions, or she may not have yet decided if the sequence would form part of a poem or a letter.

20. Ralph W. Franklin, *The Editing of Emily Dickinson: A Reconsideration* (Madison: University of Wisconsin Press, 1967), 130, 132.

21. For a generation of scholars, the unfinished state of Dickinson's late manuscripts—when there are no choices indicated for word-variants, for instance—crucially anticipates and validates the postmodernist idea that the author is not in control (or abnegates control) of meaning. Rather than deciding which word or phrase she wanted, or even indicating a preference, in other words, Dickinson consciously left such decisions up to her audience—effacing herself and allowing the reader to contribute actively to the process of forming meaning. The death of Emily Dickinson the writer is therefore very convenient for any interpretive approach founded on the idea that the figurative death of the author is the means by which interpretive emancipation is brought about. And yet, many of Dickinson's pronouncements on poetry—and even her withholding of poems from a general audience—may be read as equating literature with private property (as in the statement that "Thought belong to Him who gave it," from Fr788, "Publication – is the Auction / Of the Mind of Man"). Equally, the failure to indicate preference may reflect Dickinson's absolute confidence in her ability to exercise control over her own literary materials: because she decided who saw which poems and when, she could assume that there was no need to indicate choice when the drafts were to remain unread. Specification would only have been necessary if the documents were to be released to others.

22. At the time of writing, there are multiple editions of Dickinson's work. The older versions include the *Poems by Emily Dickinson* series edited by Mabel Loomis Todd and Thomas Wentworth Higginson (three volumes published in 1890, 1891, and 1896), as well as Todd's edition of *Letters by Emily Dickinson* (1894). In this century, there have been *The Single Hound: Poems of a Lifetime by Emily Dickinson* (1914), *The Complete Poems of Emily Dickinson* (1924), *Life and Letters of Emily Dickinson* (1924), *Further Poems of Emily Dickinson* (1929), *Emily Dickinson Face to Face: Unpublished Letters with Notes and Reminiscences* (1932), *Unpublished Poems of Emily Dickinson* (1935), and *Poems by Emily Dickinson* (1937), all edited by Martha Dickinson Bianchi. There is Millicent Todd Bingham's *Bolts of Melody: New Poems of Emily Dickinson* (1945). In 1955, Thomas Johnson published the three-volume variorum *The Poems of Emily Dickinson*. More recently, Ralph Franklin edited *The Manuscript Books of Emily Dickinson* (1981) and the now standard variorum *Poems of Emily Dickinson* (1998). William Shurr's *New Poems of Emily Dickinson* appeared in 1993, Marta Werner's *Emily Dickinson's Open Folios* in 1995, and Ellen Hart and Martha Nell Smith's *Open Me Carefully* in 1998.

23. One of the first was Ellen Louise Hart, in "The Elizabeth Whitney Putnam Manuscripts and New Strategies for Editing Emily Dickinson's Letters," *Emily Dickinson Journal* 4, no. 1 (1995): 44–74.

24. Chronological sequencing, on the other hand, might be seen as encouraging biographical speculation.

25. Among the foremost interpretations based on the fascicles are Dorothy Huff Oberhaus, *Emily Dickinson's Fascicles: Method and Meaning* (University Park: Pennsylvania State University Press, 1995); Martha Lindblom O'Keefe, *This Edifice: Studies in the Structure of the Fascicles of the Poetry of Emily Dickinson* (Maryland: Mrs. John A. O'Keefe, 1986); and William Shurr, *The Marriage of Emily Dickinson: A Study of the Fascicles* (Lexington: The University of Kentucky Press, 1983).

26. See also Aífe Murray's "send me something drawen / on paper" in *How2*, 1, no. 3 (2000). Murray argues that the originals show that Dickinson "was often caught in the midst of domestic labors, when the muse suggested an idea." Accessed online on 23 May 2001 at <http://www.scc.rutgers.edu/however/vi_3_2000/current/readings/murray.html>.

27. *Letters*, 1:80–81; A 640.

28. Melanie Hubbard, "Dickinson's Advertising Flyers: Theorizing Materiality and the Work of Reading," *Emily Dickinson Journal* 7, no. 1 (1998): 35.

29. Ibid., 27.

30. *Letters*, 3:875. The original is at the Special Collections of the Frost Library, Amherst College.

31. An important, and prior, transcription of this poem is in Marta Werner's excellent *Emily Dickinson's Open Folios: Scenes of Reading, Surfaces of Writing* (Michigan: University of Michigan Press, 1995), n.p. Werner offers a photograph of the original as well as a print transcription that includes vertical and horizontal writing. The punctuation is added by hand; since I am not persuaded that the direction and length of the dashes are especially significant in Dickinson's writings, I am satisfied that mechanical reproduction does not compromise Dickinson's style.

32. *Letters*, 3:919–20. The original is at the Special Collections of the Frost Library, Amherst College.

33. It seems to me that there is much to be gained by the Johnson and Ward "version": a sense of momentum that comes with the rhythm of prose, for example,

which reminds us that Dickinson was a prolific and immensely gifted epistolary per-
former. A potential irony in any theory advancing Dickinson as a generically trans-
gressive artist is that in practice this results in visual arrangements of the letters that
have the effect of privileging their apparently poetic aspects. In other words, rather
than experimenting with the boundaries between the two genres, the effect of retaining
Dickinson's manuscript line spacing gives the impression of converting prose ("Ned
will ask his Cousin's perusal of this 'Scarlet Letter,' whose postage is a Solstice") into
the semblance of poetry. And it seems to me that to do so reduces the potential for free
intervention in those texts, for although it is relatively straightforward to sense the
poetry in prose (as William Shurr once did, to take an extreme example), it is much
more complicated for readers to perform the reverse operation. William H. Shurr, ed.,
New Poems of Emily Dickinson (Chapel Hill: University of Carolina Press, 1993).

    34. A 94-1/2; Johnson, *Poems*, 3:885–86; Ralph W. Franklin, ed., *The Poems of Emily
Dickinson* (Cambridge: Harvard University Press, Belknap Press, 1998), 3:1209–10.

    35. The standard editions of the poem represent "But it can / silence you" as one
metrical line: the logic of manuscript criticism is that the division after "can" should be
respected, making this two lines.

    36. Franklin, *Poems*, 3:1209–10. Like Johnson, I read the final punctuation mark as
a dash; Franklin reads it as a period.

    37. Certainly, the traditional quatrain and octet presentation does not misrepresent
such appearances visually any more than a diplomatic transcription in type (that pre-
serves the integrity of Dickinson's line breaks) does. For the diplomatic version im-
poses a very different relationship of lettering to page, making the poems look long
and thin when in manuscript they do not have this appearance at all. The phrase
"diplomatic transcription" was introduced to recent Dickinson editorial debates by
Ellen Louise Hart, and refers to "line for line print translations of poems and letters
that attempt to represent the manuscripts as accurately as possible, with a detailed
apparatus describing features that do not translate into script." See Hart, "The Eliza-
beth Whitney Putnam Manuscripts and New Strategies for Editing Dickinson's Let-
ters," *Emily Dickinson Journal* 4, no. 1 (1995): 72. Of course, the term "diplomatic
transcription" has a long history of usage within textual scholarship generally.

    38. Ralph Franklin, ed., *Manuscript Books of Emily Dickinson* (Cambridge: Harvard
University Press, Belknap Press, 1981), 2:1376, 1356.

    39. Camilla Wergeland to Jonas Collett, Manuscripts Division, NBO Brevs. 4a:
70, National Library of Oslo. A print transcript of the letter is included in Leiv
Amundsen, ed., *Camilla Collett: Før Brylluppet: Brevveksling med P. J. Collett og andre*
(Oslo: Gyldendal Norsk Forlag, 1983), 159–61. Camilla Collett (1813–95), writer and
women's rights advocate, is regarded as one of the first important Norwegian woman
novelists of the nineteenth century. She was very well educated and came from the
upper middle class of Norwegian society. Her social circumstances, in other words,
make her comparable to Dickinson.

    40. Jane Austen, *Emma* (1815; rpt., London: J. M. Dent & Sons, 1958), 135. Mrs.
Carlyle's quotation is from the seventh definition of "cross v," in the *Oxford English
Dictionary*, 2:115.

    41. A letter from Elizabeth Blackwell to Baroness Anne Isabella Milbanke Byron
concerning women's rights and the education of women physicians, dated 4 March
1851, includes normal horizontal writing in addition to vertical writing in the left
and top margins. The manuscript is in the Blackwell Family Papers, 1759–1960

(bulk 1845–90, 0320T), Library of Congress, Washington, D.C. It is available online at <http://lcweb2.loc.gov/cgi-bin/ampage?collId=mcc&fileName=065/page.db&recNum=0&itemLink=r?ammem/mcc:@field(DOCID+@lit(mcc/065))>, and was accessed 10 December 1999. The final page of a letter (written on unruled fine family stationery) from Alf Collett to his mother, Camilla Collett, dated 6 December 1871, includes four physical lines of writing running from top to bottom in the right hand margin and a final line running top to bottom in the left margin. The size of the writing is significantly different: cramped and small in the right margin, generously spaced and large in the left. The manuscript is in the Manuscripts Department, Brevs. 4:22a, National Library of Oslo. Again, these habits of epistolary inscription appear to have been fairly consistent and casual among the well educated. The practice appears to have survived the nineteenth century: observe the ending of Dodie Smith's dramatic adaptation of her novel *I Capture the Castle*, where Cassandra says, "Only the margin left to write on now" (London: Samuel French, 1952), 84.

42. Private Collection. My thanks to Polly Longsworth for drawing these letters to my attention, and making them available to me.

43. See Deirdre Le Faye, ed., *Jane Austen's Letters*, 3d ed. (Oxford: Oxford University Press, 1995). Austen often crosses letters (using script that is first horizontal, then vertical), writes upside down in the top margins, and sometimes reverses the page and writes upside down between the lines that she had already written.

44. The letter is from 4 October 1841, in Helen Hunt Jackson Letters (1840–45), Mss. Coll., Special Collections, Jones Library, Amherst. I am grateful to Kate Boyle for her generous research assistance and photocopying of relevant materials.

45. Helen Fiske Jackson, A. L. S. from Hadley, Mass., to Rebecca Snell, 7 October 1841, Miscellaneous Manuscripts, drawer 4, Archives and Special Collections, Amherst College. In other words, the force of the convention that vertical writing represented overflow was so powerful that any deviation from that assumption required an explicit statement to that effect. In Dickinson's case, the absence of any such statement suggests that the vertical writing in her manuscripts is not a significant graphic element of their composition—it is related to economies of space, not semantics.

46. Williams, Byron Hartley (1844–1922), Correspondence; Field, Julia K. (1829–90), Correspondence, 1860–1861; Burgess, Ruth Payne, Correspondence 1871–1889, all in Mss. Coll., Special Collections, Jones Library, Amherst.

47. The vertical lines are from "The Sea of Faith" onward. Ashley Collection, A17f2r, British Museum, London. From a photostat in S. O. A. Ullmann, "Dating through Calligraphy: The Example of 'Dover Beach,'" *Studies in Bibliography* 26 (1973): 22.

48. Kristin Herron, "Finding 'Freedom': Researching Emily Dickinson's Bedroom," *EDIS Bulletin* 13, no. 1 (2001): 8.

49. Ibid., 8, 9.

CHAPTER ONE *Packaging Emily: Dickinson in Books*

Epigraph: Melinda T. Koyanis, Director of Intellectual Property, Harvard University Press, quoted in "Scholar Gets Versed in Copyright Law," *Springfield Union News*, 18 December 1995, A5. Her statement was in response to Professor Phillip Stambovsky's request for permission to publish an edition of Dickinson's poems that he had edited directly from the original handwritten manuscripts. The request was refused, in part on the grounds that Ralph Franklin was still in the process of preparing a new edition of the *Poems of Emily Dickinson*, which appeared in 1998. According to the Associated Press article, "Harvard wants to hold off licensing other Dickinson texts until Franklin's is complete."

1. The description is based on an article by Patrick Dilger, in *Inside Albertus: The News of Albertus Magnus College*, Spring–Summer 1996, 1, 4.

2. For the most concise summary of recent trends, see the welcoming remarks and general site of the Dickinson Editing Collective at http://jefferson.village.virginia.edu/dickinson/. Although I take issue with some of the collective's findings, I think that the electronic archives of Dickinson's work on this site are an invaluable scholarly resource and that they have inspired and challenged a great many readers.

3. The wording of this sentence is based on a verbal statement given by Barbara Hanrahan, then editor-in-chief of the University of North Carolina Press, to a reporter and quoted in Dilger, *Inside Albertus*, 4. On 6 May 1950, Alfred Leete Hampson (heir to the Dickinson estate), the President and Fellows of Harvard College, and the Rosenbach Foundation, represented by William McCarthy, were parties to an indenture and bill of sale by which the President and Fellows of Harvard College acquired the manuscripts, other unpublished materials, and literary rights of Emily Dickinson. Clause 10 of that agreement clearly states: "Purchaser [the President and Fellows of Harvard College] is to have sole right to grant or refuse permission to reprint selections from material covered by assignment of copyrights hereunder and to establish fees for such publication." Letter of 1 November 1955 from Mary Landis Hampson to Arthur H. Thornhill (bMS Am 1923 [8], Houghton Library, Harvard College Library, Harvard University).

4. Quoted in Dilger, *Inside Albertus*, 1. One wonders to what extent a translation of Dickinson's autographs into print differs in status from translation into a different language entirely. For instance, the poem "It's easy to invent a Life" has five dashes in the first stanza: a German translation authorized by Harvard University Press replaces these with a single dash, a colon, a comma, and a period (none of which are sanctioned by the original). Is there a discrepancy between allowing this adjustment and refusing Stambovsky's? Hans Bernhard Schiff, *Ich bin niemand: Bost auch du niemand?* (Düsseldorf: Verlag der Handzeichen, 1983), 60.

5. Quoted in Dilger, *Inside Albertus*, 4.

6. Melinda T. Koyanis, quoted in ibid.

7. Ellen Louise Hart and Martha Nell Smith, *Open Me Carefully: Emily Dickinson's Intimate Letters to Susan Huntington Dickinson* (Ashfield: Paris Press, 1998). But there was also some inconsistency in the Harvard line: in 1995, Marta Werner had been allowed to publish her outstanding edition of some of Dickinson's late drafts and fragments, which included diplomatic transcripts. It is possible that the press granted permission on the (mistaken) grounds that Werner's edition had no direct implications for Dickinson's other poems and letters. See Marta L. Werner, ed., *Emily Dickinson's Open Folios: Scenes of Reading, Surfaces of Writing* (Ann Arbor: University of Michigan Press, 1995). Henceforth, all references prefixed by LP are to letter-poems in Hart and Smith, *Open Me Carefully*.

8. Ralph W. Franklin, ed., *The Poems of Emily Dickinson* (Cambridge: Harvard University Press, Belknap Press, 1998), 1:374. The poem is dated by Franklin to 1862. Henceforth, all references prefixed by Fr are to poems in this volume.

9. The other way that Dickinson signaled the nonintentional segregation of se-

quences of writing was through the deployment of blank space. There are two major blank spaces in the portion of the autograph under discussion, and these coincide with line endings: this means that such gaps or intervals signal the limit of metrically defined sequences of writing. In other words, when Dickinson runs out of space during the recording of a line of verse (but before completing the line), she moves down the page and writes what is left of it, at which point she moves automatically down the page again to the beginning of the next line. The result is that her lyric manuscripts have more of these grammatically redundant blank spaces than does her prose (where they signify the end of a paragraph). There will be more on this as the book progresses.

10. Thomas H. Johnson, ed., *The Poems of Emily Dickinson* (Cambridge: Harvard University Press, Belknap Press, 1955); Franklin, ed., *Poems of Emily Dickinson*; Thomas H. Johnson, ed., *The Complete Poems of Emily Dickinson* (Boston: Little, Brown and Company, 1960); Ralph W. Franklin, ed., *The Poems of Emily Dickinson*, reading edition (Cambridge: Harvard University Press, Belknap Press, 1999). Henceforth, all references prefixed by J are to poems in the Johnson (1955) edition.

11. Ralph W. Franklin, ed., *The Manuscript Books of Emily Dickinson* (Cambridge: Harvard University Press, Belknap Press, 1981).

12. Thomas H. Johnson, ed., *Final Harvest: Emily Dickinson's Poems* (Boston: Little, Brown and Company, 1961); Peter Washington, ed., *Dickinson: Poems* (New York: Alfred A. Knopf, 1993); *The Selected Poems of Emily Dickinson* (New York: Modern Library, 1996); *The Selected Poems of Emily Dickinson*, intro. by Billy Collins (New York: Modern Library, 2000). *Dickinson: Poems* is part of the Everyman's Library Pocket Series and is based on the Johnson edition, though like Todd and Higginson it organizes the poems according to themes—in this case, curiously, "The Poet's Art," "The Works of Love," and "Death and Resurrection." This is a partial list; alternatives include Peter Siegenthaler, ed., *Emily Dickinson: Collected Poems* (Philadelphia: Running Press, 1999); Johanna Brownwell, ed., *Poems: Emily Dickinson* (New York: Knopf, 1993). Both are based on the Todd-Higginson editions. *The Essential Dickinson*, selected and intro. by Joyce Carol Oates (Hopewell: Ecco Press, 1996); *Emily Dickinson: A Collection of Poems*, contributing ed. Marcia Peoples Halio (Fort Worth: Harcourt Brace College, 1998); Gregory C. Aaron, ed., *Emily Dickinson: Selected Poems* (Philadelphia: Running Press, 1990); *Selected Poetry of Emily Dickinson* (New York: Doubleday, 1997).

13. Johnson and Ward, eds., *Letters of Emily Dickinson* (1958; reprint, Cambridge: Harvard University Press, Belknap Press, 1996); Thomas H. Johnson, ed., *Emily Dickinson: Selected Letters* (Cambridge: Harvard University Press, Belknap Press, 1971). Henceforth, all references prefixed by L are to letters in the Johnson and Ward (1958) edition.

14. For the DEA, see ⟨http://jefferson.village.virginia.edu/dickinson/⟩.

15. Interestingly, the problems under discussion here have been played out repeatedly during the historical transmission of Dickinson's texts. Mary Landis Hampson wrote in 1956 that it was important to publish a one-volume edition of Dickinson's poems for "college students and lovers of American poetry" (Letter of 16 October 1956 to Arthur Thornhill, president of Little, Brown and Company, bMS Am 1923 [12], Houghton Library, Harvard College Library, Harvard University). At the same time, in several letters from June 1952, Hampson expresses her desire to prevent George Whicher from ever editing an edition of the manuscripts (ibid., bMS Am 1923 [6]). In 1953 she wrote again: "After what Whicher has written about Martha and her

family, and Emily's family, I think tarring and feathering would be too good for him" (Letter of 15 October 1953 to Gilbert Montague, bMS Am 1923 [7], in ibid.).

16. LP18, 48–50.

17. L154, 1:283–85; Ms Am 1118.4 (L19), Houghton Library, Harvard College Library, Harvard University. All references are to the manuscript original.

18. LP138, 163 (late 1860s); Fr1130C, 2:983 (1866). Hart and Smith read "to the Sun" as "To the Sun," as does Johnson (J1136, 2:797). Franklin reads "Mountain" as "mountain."

19. LP153, 178–79 (early 1870s); Fr796B, 2:749–50 (1866); Ms Am 1118.3 (356), Houghton Library, Harvard College Library, Harvard University. All references are to the manuscript original.

20. This version is from *Manuscript Books of Emily Dickinson*, 2:1137–39.

21. Thomas Wentworth Higginson and Mabel Loomis Todd, eds., *Poems by Emily Dickinson*, Second Series (Boston: Roberts Brothers, 1891), 142.

22. ⟨http://www.library.utoronto.ca/utel/rp/poems/dickn33c.html⟩ (accessed 18 March 2002). The Toronto version differs slightly in that it has no raised "A" at the beginning, and it does not put "narrow" in small capitals. There is no space after "rides" and before the semicolon in the second line, and the em dash in the third line is represented by two hyphens.

23. The 1891 edition continues to be accessible in 2002. Its genuine value is to scholars interested in historical editions of Dickinson's work.

24. Janine Barchas argues that the many dashes in the first edition of Sarah Fielding's *David Simple* that were removed in the second edition resulted in the loss of a more flexible and innovative form of punctuation. Janine Barchas, *Graphic Design, Print Culture, and the Eighteenth-Century Novel* (Cambridge: Cambridge University Press, 2003). But as Thomas Keymer points out: "Sarah Fielding shared the standard assumption that punctuation was for compositors to fix. As she wrote to Richardson about a later work, 'I am very apt when I write to be too careless about . . . Stops, but I suppose that will naturally be set right in the printing.' " And he continues: "Probably the first-edition dashes do indeed reflect the look of Sarah's manuscript, though there widely varying styles (broken and unbroken, and of different lengths) will have been dictated by the pieces to hand and the space to be filled when any given line was set in type." Thomas Keymer, "Keep the Clutter." *Times Literary Supplement*, 12 December 2003, 30.

25. D. C. Greetham, "Challenges of Theory and Practice in the Editing of Hoccleve's *Regement of Princes*," in *Manuscripts and Texts: Editorial Problems in Later Middle English Literature*, ed. Derek Pearsall (Cambridge: D. S. Brewer, 1987), 61.

26. D. C. Greetham, *Theories of the Text* (Oxford: Oxford University Press, 1999), 170.

27. Charles Goodrich Whiting, "The Literary Wayside," *Springfield Republican*, 16 November 1890, 4. Quoted in Willis J. Buckingham, *Emily Dickinson's Reception in the 1890s: A Documentary History* (Pittsburgh: University of Pittsburgh Press, 1989), 16.

28. The first quotation is from an anonymous 1890 review of Dickinson's poetry, quoted in Buckingham, *Emily Dickinson's Reception in the 1890s*, 10. The second quotation is from Tim Morris, "The Franklin Edition of Dickinson: Is That All There Is?" *Emily Dickinson Journal*, 8, no. 2 (1999): 1.

29. Of course, original reviewers were responding to Dickinson herself—or so they thought, whereas contemporary critics are disappointed by editions of the poetry

which in their view do not adequately reflect the range of her formal innovations—or so they think.

30. Though I have limited my comments to literary and social history, the upheaval from two major world wars and the Vietnam conflict also has obvious bearings on forms of creative expression and reception.

31. The subtitle of Martha Nell Smith's magnificent first book—one of the best ever written on Dickinson—is significant in this instance, since it shifts the attention to the rights of the reader (and since it foregrounds the relationship between Dickinson and Susan Gilbert Dickinson): the full title is *Rowing in Eden: Rereading Emily Dickinson* (Austin: University of Texas Press, 1992).

32. Martha Nell Smith, "The Poet as Cartoonist," in *Comic Power in Emily Dickinson*, ed. Suzanne Juhasz, Cristanne Miller, and Martha Nell Smith (Austin: University of Texas Press, 1993), 81. The quotation is, "Instead, by mixing media—illustrations from a popular novel with linguistic descriptions of broken-hearted, barefooted, and angelic figures common in popular poetry—Dickinson also mixes tones and in doing so reminds audiences that no singleminded or singlehearted response to a subject is enough." The audience in this case was Susan Dickinson.

33. The number in the fascicles came to over eight hundred poems, and these were supplemented by "a good many fascicle sheets that had never been bound. These unbound groups, called sets following the terminology of *The Manuscript Books of Emily Dickinson* (1981), brought the total to over eleven hundred" (Franklin, introduction to *Poems of Emily Dickinson*, 1:7).

34. Ironically, Johnson's dating strengthened the impression that fascicles were deliberate arrangements. To take the example of Set 6C (discussed later in the chapter): Franklin listed it (in the *Manuscript Books*) as containing twenty-two poems. The first eight were thought by Johnson to have been written around 1864; the next three around 1865, and the final eleven around 1866. Because Dickinson wrote many more poems during these years, it would have seemed that she was selecting poems from different periods and allocating them deliberately to separate fascicles and sets—in other words, according to principles that were not related to the accident of their composition at the same time. In *Poems* (1998), Franklin identifies all twenty-two lyrics in Set 6C as having been completed in 1866. Only two (811, "There is a June when Corn is cut," and 501, "The Robin is the One") were begun earlier; but the variants in 6C (811B and 501C) were finally transcribed in 1866. His revised dating makes the archival logic of organization an equally plausible rationale as the aesthetic one.

35. Franklin, *Manuscript Books of Emily Dickinson*, ix. Early reviewers considered Dickinson's unconventional use of rhyme, grammar, and rhythm as a by-product of her nonpublication: an anonymous reviewer in the *Boston Home Journal* wrote in 1890 that "she penned her poetic inspirations simply for her own gratification and pleasure, with no thought of seeking poetic fame in print." For many contemporary critics and editors, the opposite is the case: Dickinson chose not to publish (or was prevented from doing so) in order to protect the integrity and autonomy of her formal innovations. Quoted in Buckingham, *Dickinson's Reception in the 1890s*, 22.

36. Or, to quote Sharon Cameron (first) and Ralph Franklin (second), was she "choosing not choosing" or was it that "one need not make a choice until one needed to make a choice"? Sharon Cameron, *Choosing Not Choosing: Dickinson's Fascicles* (Chicago: University of Chicago Press, 1992), and Ralph W. Franklin, ed., *Poems of Emily Dickinson*, reading edition, 3.

37. This practice amends received opinion that Dickinson remained unknown and unpublished during her lifetime. As Martha Nell Smith and others have pointed out, such a notion depends on our accepting that publication is first and foremost an industrial activity. See Smith's *Rowing in Eden*.

38. Hart and Smith, *Open Me Carefully*, xix.

39. Roger Chartier, *Readers, Authors, and Libraries in Europe between the Fourteenth and Eighteenth Centuries*, translated from the French by Lydia G. Cochrane (Cambridge: Polity Press, 1994), 3.

40. And none of the grandeur of Shelley in front of Mont Blanc, Wordsworth in the Lake District as a child, or Blake before the Tyger. For male writers, the physical scale of Creation suggests the grandeur of the Creator—the proof of his power, that frightens but also consoles (for if he can build mountains, he can surely save men). For Dickinson, typically, that after-moment of consolation is absent. There are questions but no obvious answers. In that sense, the poem seems to anticipate an almost existential sense of utter isolation in an indifferent universe—with the Zero close to Munch's scream (itself dominated by the circular shape of the mouth forming the scream).

41. The exception is Martha Dickinson Bianchi and Alfred Leete Hampson's prematurely titled *The Complete Poems of Emily Dickinson* (Boston: Little, Brown, 1924).

42. J986, *Poems of Emily Dickinson* (1955), 2:711–12; L378, *Letters*, 2:498–99.

43. Fr1096, *Poems of Emily Dickinson* (1998), 2:951–55; LP147, *Open Me Carefully*, 172–74.

44. L316, to T. W. Higginson, early 1866, *Letters*, 2:450. The *Republican*'s mistake of ending the third line with a question mark was repeated in Bianchi and Hampson's *Complete Poems of Emily Dickinson*.

45. Tom Paulin, *Minotaur: Poetry and the Nation State* (Cambridge: Harvard University Press, 1992), 103.

46. The problem with such a judgment is that it presupposes absolute congruence between the lost manuscript sent to the *Republican* and the version recorded in the fascicles.

47. Nor does she object to the misrepresentation of her handwritten letters by typeset ones.

48. The version is from Franklin, *Manuscript Books of Emily Dickinson*, 2:1137–39. In Franklin's *Poems of Emily Dickinson*, it is Fr1096B.

49. Ms Am 1118.5 (B193), Houghton Library, Harvard College Library, Harvard University. All references are to the manuscript original. The writing is on a single sheet that has been folded to make two pages: the resultant pages measure 10.7 cm in width and 16.6 cm in height, and the writing is in ink.

50. Readers will, I trust, forgive the collapse of time for purposes of argument: the C version had not been written at the time Dickinson protested the alteration made to the earlier version, but my point is still a valid one—namely, that Dickinson did not (at 1872) consider the line arrangements to be unimpeachable.

51. The measurements are taken from the original at Amherst College and are my own; there is no embossment, though there are elsewhere in the fascicle (A 88–13/14). Franklin describes the paper as cream with a blue rule, wove stationery, measuring 203 by 126 mm (*Manuscript Books of Emily Dickinson*, 2:1137–39). The photographic reproduction measures 210 by 124 mm, and any distortion is therefore both minimal and consistent: the difference in breadth is 2 mm, which is the same for the breadth of space under discussion.

52. Though it is not unambiguously evident in the first stanza, the poem has a rhyme scheme—*abcb*, which again suggests that this is a four-line stanza. Rhyme, of course, has two functions: to support the meter and to create patterns of sound. The emphasis in manuscript criticism up to now has been on the visual aspects of the poetry; it is not yet clear how this relates to the aural.

53. A number of writers have seen the poem primarily as a description of the snake's movement, among them Amy Lowell, *Poetry and Poets: Chapters* (Boston: Houghton Mifflin Co., 1930), 103–4, and Walter Blair, Theodore Hornberger, and Randall Stewart, eds., *The Literature of the United States* (Chicago: Scott, Foresman and Co., 1947), 2:749. Neither had access to the manuscripts, and neither therefore refers to the shape of the Z. The significance of the script is important, however, only if one subscribes to the theory that Dickinson's handwriting was occasionally used as an additional mimetic or rhetorical device or if one believes that the poem is primarily descriptive.

54. Fr843 is Ms Am 1118.3 (180), Houghton Library, Harvard College Library, Harvard University; Fr900 is Ms Am 1118.3 (175). All references are to the manuscript originals.

55. This does not mean having to look at every letter of the alphabet in every year of Dickinson's career as a writer. It involves nothing more difficult or extensive than judging the shape of a letter against its production in a single year, for example.

56. Just as important, the later version sent to Susan Dickinson changes the original punctuation, replacing the dash after "him" with a question mark and thus attempting to clear up an unintentional lack of clarity that had been revealed by the version printed in the *Republican*. Far from seeing Dickinson as blindly rejecting all editorial versions of her manuscripts, this change seems to show her responding actively to other (mis)readings of her text. The insertion of the question mark after "him" makes it clear that the speaker does not know whether the reader has encountered such a snake before, whereas the *Republican*'s question mark (after "did you not") suggests that the speaker *does* know for certain that the reader has met the snake. In a version of the same line without any question mark, the meaning could encompass either position.

57. Such is the argument in Dorothy Huff Oberhaus, *Emily Dickinson's Fascicles: Method and Meaning* (University Park: Pennsylvania State University Press, 1995). Oberhaus attends to the fascicles, however, and not the sets; hence she does not consider "A narrow Fellow in the Grass." The other major consideration of image clusters and their relationships in the fascicles is Martha Lindblom O'Keefe, *This Edifice: Studies in the Structure of the Fascicles of the Poetry of Emily Dickinson* (Maryland: Mrs. John A. O'Keefe, 1986). It too stops at the fortieth fascicle.

58. Quickly paraphrased, 1094 states that friends and lovers we formerly cared for deeply often mean little or nothing to us in later years; 1095 declares that the spectacle of the sun rising daily is so impressive that it makes other worldly events and achievements minor in comparison; 1096 is ostensibly the record of a phobia: snakes frightened the speaker as a child, and continue to do so today; 1097 suggests that ashes are all that remains of great heat and light: they should be respected because of the energy that was once there and that is now elsewhere, albeit in an unknown place.

59. The assignation of roman numerals is by Todd and Higginson.

60. Joyce Carol Oates, "Soul at the White Heat: The Romance of Emily Dickinson's Poetry," *Critical Inquiry* 13 (Summer 1987): 806.

61. That is one of the implications of the statement in Oberhaus, where she de-

scribes how "in the process of grappling with these elliptical poems [reading the fascicles] one discovers beneath their surface multiplicity a deep structural and thematic unity" (Oberhaus, *Emily Dickinson's Fascicles*, 3). Cameron makes a similar plea for the centrality of the fascicles and comes off with very different conclusions (in *Choosing Not Choosing*). One finds a Christian paradigm, the other a postmodernist one.

62. Nina Baym, general ed., et al., *The Norton Anthology of American Literature*, 5th ed. (New York: W. W. Norton, 1998).

63. Paul Lauter, general ed., et al., *The Heath Anthology of American Literature*, 4th ed. (Lexington: D. C. Heath, 2002).

64. Smith describes *Open Me Carefully* as "powerful witness to a lesbian passion" in Philip Weiss, "Beethoven's Hair Tells All," *New York Times Magazine*, 29 November 1988, 114. The danger I report is also the advantage: one sees more clearly Susan's importance to Dickinson. And one acknowledges that part of the book's significance is revisionist, as it successfully challenges the long accepted myth that Dickinson was hostile to Susan and that few of her poems were circulated during her lifetime. At the same time, it goes too far in the other direction, or at least, isolating the correspondence has the effect of making the relationship more reciprocal and intense than the historical evidence would suggest. It is still not clear that the Dickinson Editing Collective (DEA), which wants to arrange all Dickinson's correspondence according to recipients, would produce something as valuable as any collected edition where one sees more clearly the variety of styles and modes of address Dickinson practiced and therefore has a more contextualized idea of a correspondent's significance to the writer.

65. LP146 and LP148, *Open Me Carefully*, 171–72, 174–76. The evidence in both cases seems to be that Susan Dickinson marked the verso of the manuscripts with an *x*, though this may have been done after Emily Dickinson's death when Susan Dickinson was preparing a selection of her poems for publication. Hart and Smith often interpret folds as evidence that poems were written and then passed on as notes between the two women. Franklin remarks that 1167 might have been sent to Susan, but does not substantiate.

66. Some readers have misconstrued a letter of 1876, in which Helen Hunt Jackson mentioned to Dickinson that "I have a little manuscript volume with a few of your verses in it," as proof that the latter distributed manuscript miscellanies, but Jackson is almost certainly referring to anthologies of her own where she transcribed favorite poems, including ones sent to her privately (L444a, *Letters*, 2:545). Similarly, the earlier note to Henry Emmons in 1854, where Dickinson politely inquires after "two little volumes of mine which I thought Emily lent you" does not constitute evidence of more extensive transmission of her fascicles. The volumes may simply have been books that Emily Fowler had borrowed; they may also have contained poems that she compiled, rather than composed. At any rate, there are no consistent references to suggest that Dickinson thought of her fascicles as integral to the understanding of poems included within them (L150, *Letters*, 1:280).

67. Even in the Heath selection, which includes a proportionately exaggerated ratio of one poem received by Susan out of every three Dickinson wrote, the total still comes to 23 out of 74. In other words, Dickinson was relatively careful about the number of poems she forwarded to individual correspondents and did not make them aware of fascicle contexts.

68. For this information see Joel Myerson, *Emily Dickinson: A Descriptive Bibliography* (Pittsburgh: University of Pittsburgh Press, 1984), 4–5.

69. The bibliographic information in Myerson makes it clear that this is Binding A; Binding B has gold-stamped writing on the cover (ibid., 3). Confusion results because the covers of the *Poems*, first series, differed according to the edition, issue, and binding. See also appendix 3 in Millicent Todd Bingham, *Ancestors' Brocades: The Literary Début of Emily Dickinson* (New York: Harper and Brothers, 1945), 412–13, for a partial list of the early editions, with descriptions of their covers and prices.

70. At the end of an unpublished interview by Charles W. Moore (the typed original of which is at Yale), Mabel Loomis Todd draws his attention to some Indian pipes in the next room: "By a strange coincidence, a friend sent them to me for Christmas. They are like a whitish clay pipe with the nodding bowl in the air and the end of the stem thrust in the ground. This ghost-flower held a fascination over Emily. It is almost passing belief that the Indian Pipe is related on one side of its family to the colorful azaleas, the rapturous rhododendrons, the laurel, the bonnie heather; and on the other to the colorless wintergreen. In some ways, this phantom of the forest that Emily loved so much, was typical of her. Both the flower and the poet chose to stand in the silence of solitary places. In their battle with heredity and environment, each became another 'flower' from that of its ancestors. Vastly different. The wraith dropped its green robe and garish colors. The poet and flower quit the sunny spots. Sought the deep, dark shade and lonely places. Each was content to be an apparition, removed from its gay kind. But each, nevertheless, came to have a witching, compelling, original fascination of its own. For each was nothing if not original." Charles W. Moore, "An Astronomer Discovers a Star," December 1930, 17–18, unpublished manuscript, Millicent Todd Bingham Collection, 496F, Yale University Archives. The date is conjectural: Moore describes interviewing Todd a "few days after" 10 December 1930 in Cocoa Nut Grove, Florida. Todd several times denies the idea that Dickinson's seclusion was a consequence of a failed love affair. In Bingham's *Ancestors' Brocades*, Thomas Niles is quoted as justifying the silver design of Indian pipes on the grounds that it looked "modest and unobtrusive." And Todd is quoted as adding; "The gray, white and silver of the first edition thus, by happy intuition, expressed somewhat of Emily's 'cool and nun-like personality,' as one of her critics afterwards (perhaps mistakenly) described her." Bingham claimed that the "dainty binding [was] devised partly with this symbolism in mind, [and] partly in the hope of beguiling Christmas shoppers into buying the book for the beauty of its cover" (69 n. 17).

71. Thomas Wentworth Higginson, preface to *Poems by Emily Dickinson* (1890), reprinted in *Poems (1890–1896) by Emily Dickinson: A Facsimile Reproduction of the Original Volumes Issued in 1890, 1891, and 1896 with an Introduction*, ed. George Monteiro (Gainesville: Scholar's Facsimiles & Reprints, 1967), v–vi.

72. Dickinson herself worked the same theme in Fr534, "How many Flowers fail in Wood." Interestingly, the Indian pipe is also known popularly as "the corpse plant" (on the grounds that it feeds off decayed organic matter): the relationship of Dickinson's poetry to death was described in 1864, when she admitted that she "sang off charnel steps" (L298, *Letters*, 2:436). The Indian pipe (Monotropa uniflora) is quite small (often around 7.5 cm) and obtains nourishment from fungi associated with tree roots: it is therefore quite reclusive in itself. John W. Thieret, revising author, *National Audubon Society Field Guide to North American Wildflowers: Eastern Region* (New York: Alfred A. Knopf, 2001), 637–38. I was fortunate enough to see Indian pipes myself in August 2001, "in Prof Tyler's woods" behind and above the Homestead, where Dickinson hid to watch the coming of the train to Amherst in 1852 (L127, *Letters*, 1:254).

73. Alexander Young, "Boston Letter," *Critic*, n.s. 14, 11 October 1890, 183–84, reprinted in Buckingham, *Dickinson's Reception in the 1890s*, 9. The received wisdom of Dickinson's nonpublication has effectively been challenged in more recent years, especially—and importantly—by Martha Nell Smith in *Rowing in Eden*. Dickinson sent poems to Helen Hunt Jackson, Thomas Wentworth Higginson, Thomas Niles (editor at Roberts Bros.), Samuel Bowles (editor of the *Springfield Republican*), and Josiah Holland (editor of *Scribner's*). Susan Dickinson read Emily's poems to guests; it has recently been suggested that her cousins Louise and Frances Norcross may have read them at literary gatherings in Concord as well.

74. Later critics such as William Dean Howells would attempt to identify Dickinson's poetry as evidence of a legitimate and autonomous literary tradition in the United States, whereas the British critic Andrew Lang responded in terms that negatively replicated the book's visual association of Dickinson with original and aboriginal talent: "I cannot go nearly so far as Mr. Howells, because if poetry is to exist at all, it really must have form and grammar, and must rhyme when it professes to rhyme. The wisdom of the ages and the nature of man insist on so much. We may be told that Democracy does not care, any more than the Emperor did, for grammar. But even if Democracy overleaps itself and lands in savagery again, I believe that our savage successors will, though unconsciously, make their poems grammatical. Savages do not use bad grammar in their own conversation or in their artless compositions. That is a fault of defective civilizations" (Buckingham, *Emily Dickinson's Reception in the 1890s*, 122).

75. Young, "Boston Letter," in ibid., 9.

76. The "extraordinary grasp and insight revealed in these poems . . . make any little violation of poetic rule seem of no account," wrote another anonymous reviewer, in "Books and Authors," *Boston Home Journal*, n.s. 4, 22 November 22 1890, 10, reprinted in Buckingham, *Emily Dickinson's Reception in the 1890s*, 23.

77. Monteiro, *Poems (1890–1896)*, 142–43.

78. The *Republican* edition altered the meaning of the lines from "If you didn't see the snake initially, its sudden appearance could be quite frightening" to "You have met the snake before, haven't you?" The Todd-Higginson alteration is not quite as decisive.

79. In a letter of 1910 to J. B. Pinker, Joseph Conrad asked: "What do you think of the title to give the book? Would Under Western Eyes do at all—or something of the kind? A title pertains to the publishing part of the business." Since Dickinson did not publish, the argument might go, she did not have to think of titles, and this position differs slightly from arguing that she was opposed to titles as a rule. One of the interesting aspects of her comments to Higginson was that she referred to the poem as "my Snake" and not as the poem of mine that was wrongly entitled "The Snake." See Frederick R. Karl and Laurence Davies, eds., *The Collected Letters of Joseph Conrad* (Cambridge: Cambridge University Press, 1990), 4:319. My thanks to Jeremy Hawthorn for drawing this letter to my attention.

80. Johnson, *Poems of Emily Dickinson*, 2:711–13; and Johnson and Ward, *Letters of Emily Dickinson*, 2:498–99.

81. The reader's edition also has a book-jacket with a photograph of white flowers on the cover. Franklin, *Poems of Emily Dickinson*, reading edition.

82. The original manuscript is Ms Am 1118.5 (B 193), Houghton Library, Harvard College Library, Harvard University.

83. Hart and Smith, *Open Me Carefully*, xxv.

84. One of the most intriguing of the poem's material aspects is the end spacing for the first stanza: there is 3.1 cm after "Grass," as one would expect, but then 3.6 cm after "met him?" which is unusual, given that other versions of the poem record the line break *later*, after "Did you not." Either Dickinson wanted a new arrangement ("You may have met him? / Did you not"), or she was going out of her way to show Susan that a question mark should not have been appended to "Did you not," as it was in the *Springfield Republican* edition. Which begs the question; did Susan send Bowles (or the *Republican*) Dickinson's first copy of "A narrow fellow in the grass," or did Susan send Susan's own transcript of it, one in which she had mistakenly or deliberately inserted a question mark?

85. James Guthrie, "Near Rhymes and Reason: Style and Personality in Dickinson's Poetry," in *Approaches to Teaching Dickinson's Poetry*, ed. Robin Riley Fast and Christine Mack Gordon (New York: Modern Language Association of America, 1989), 70–77.

86. As mentioned before, the number-title HB 193 corresponds to the number assigned by the Houghton Library at Harvard, where the original is housed (as Ms Am 1118.5 [B193]). The image of Ms Am 1118.5 (B193) is stored at <http://www.iath.virginia.edu/dickinson/working/hb193.htm> (accessed 28 January 2002).

87. In the autograph, "further on" measures 7.5 cm, and there is a space of 1.5 cm between the words; there is a space of 1 cm after "on." "Boggy Acre" measures 10.4 cm, and there is a space of 1.5 cm between the words: there is a space of 7 mm after "acre." "cool for Corn" measures 11 cm and there is a space of 1 cm between the first and second words, and 1.1 cm between the second and third words; there is a space of 5 mm after "Corn." Ms Am 1118.5 (B193). All references are to the manuscript original.

88. To take a few examples of closed (e) and open (ᴇ) versions of the same lowercase letter: Dickinson writes "difference," "Spaᴄᴇ," "Presenᴄᴇ," "A narrow Fᴇllow," "His notice," and so forth. (The ᴇ in these instances records occurrences of the open minuscule *e* shape and not an attempt to reproduce the character exactly.)

89. Nevertheless, the reader (or viewer) is not told why attempts at reproducing the extent and direction of the dash are important, whereas variations in the lettering are not.

90. The examples of the intersecting cross-strokes are random; these are not the only ones.

91. G. Thomas Tanselle, "Commentary: Not the Real Thing," *Times Literary Supplement*, 24 August 2001, 14.

92. Thomas J. Johnson, "Establishing a Text: The Emily Dickinson Papers," *Studies in Bibliography* 5 (1952–53): 26.

93. Ibid., 28.

94. Whether or not the original is "the real thing" is another question. It is my contention that the relation between the physical objects known as Dickinson's manuscripts and the verbal works in which editors such as Franklin represent them is much closer than the linguistic representations of the manuscripts on the Web.

95. Quoted in Dilger, *Inside Albertus*, 4.

96. For instance, at the opening plenary of the 1999 EDIS conference at Mount Holyoke, Marjorie Perloff's understanding of Dickinson's poetry was subjected to critique on the grounds that she had not looked at manuscript versions of the poems

she discussed. And in e-mail discussion groups, assessments about the appearance of manuscripts and the meanings of those appearances have been dismissed on the grounds that it was assumed photocopies had been used. The question then arises: are digital copies fully adequate to the originals? In an article on the rationale of digital archives, Smith points out that "if readers cannot see the marks [on Dickinson's manuscripts], they cannot decide whether Dickinson intended anything by them." And she goes on to say that electronic editions allow readers to "decide for themselves whether those marks mean anything poetically and whether Dickinson intended the meanings readers find." The assumption here appears to be that electronic versions *are* fully acceptable substitutes for the originals, and that they should become the basis for critical discussion. Martha Nell Smith, "Electronic Resources on Emily Dickinson," *EDIS Bulletin* 12, no. 2 (2000): 13, 26. All quotations are from page 26.

97. J. Hillis Miller, *Black Holes* (Stanford: Stanford University Press, 1999), 491.

98. Hart, "The Elizabeth Whitney Putnam Manuscripts and New Strategies for Editing Emily Dickinson," 68.

99. <http://jefferson.village.virginia.edu/dickinson/classroom/Spring99/edition/Franklin/f-dis.htm> (accessed 26 March 2002).

100. The first version is A 678 in the Special Collections, Frost Library, Amherst College; the second is Ms Am 1118.3 (361) at the Houghton Library, Harvard College Library, Harvard University. All references are to the manuscript originals.

101. Ms Am 1118.3 (361), Houghton Library, Harvard College Library, Harvard University, Fr194B, *Poems*, 1:228–29. All references are to the manuscript original.

102. What follows is my own transcript of A 678. Johnson fails to italicize "Here's" in the prose part of the message. Otherwise, his version is the same as Franklin's. See L250, *Letters*, 2:394.

103. The paper for the version sent to Susan Dickinson is similarly embossed "PARIS" in the left hand corner of the bifolium (one sheet, two pages, four leaves). The second leaf is left blank. The paper is unruled and folded in quarters; it measures approximately 9.9 cm in width and 15.3 cm in height. The writing is in ink.

104. The version of the poem sent to Susan Dickinson is reproduced by Hart and Smith as LP120 in *Open Me Carefully*, 151.

105. In the second version of the poem, Ms Am 1118.3 (361), the pattern is the same: the first two rows of writing extend to near the right edge of the paper, but not the third, which leaves an interval of 4.4 cm. In short, the sequence "The Wife without the Sign" is one unit. The same argument can be extended to other places on the page: rows seven and eight, "Royal, all but the / Crown" (followed by an end space of 6.1 cm), is one unit, as is "Betrothed, without / the Swoon" (followed by an end space of 4.1 cm). In places where Dickinson shortens the line—"Gold – to Gold," "In a Day," "Tri Victory"—Franklin (and Johnson before him) reflect and respect this. There is no doubt that Dickinson used short lines from time to time, as here; the question is where and how she did so. (I use the term "row" to refer to a physical line of writing in an autograph; "line" or "verse" refers to a single line of meter.)

106. Jeremy Hawthorn, *A Glossary of Contemporary Literary Theory*, 4th ed. (London: Edward Arnold, 2000), 312.

107. Vygotsky cites "the declaration of love between Kitty and Levin by means of initial letters" in *Anna Karenina* as showing "clearly that when the thoughts of the speakers are the same, the role of speech is reduced to a minimum." The point can also

be made about shared cultural assumptions: in tight social circles with personal contact, where an interest in literature is taken for granted, no formal introduction is required for a poem in a letter. See Lev Vygotsky, *Thought and Language*, ed. and trans. Alex Kozulin (Cambridge: MIT Press, 1986), 237 and 239.

108. It is not that the deliberate exploitation of the visual properties of language in order to create semantic effects was unknown in Dickinson's day, or before. But it would have been sufficiently out of the ordinary that one would think that she would have wanted to make her usage clear in some way. The lack of an explicit commentary on such a dimension to her creative enterprise may derive from an assumption that it was unnecessary or redundant—because taken for granted—or because no such dimension existed as a conscious or consistent part of her work.

109. L187, *Letters*, 2:333. The letter dates to about 1858 and is to an unknown recipient (the so-called Master).

110. L61, to Emily Fowler Ford, about 1851, in *Letters*, 1:154.

111. Dominic Strinati, *An Introduction to Theories of Popular Culture* (London: Routledge, 1995), 125. And he goes on to say, "The roses may also be sent as a joke, an insult, a sign of gratitude, and so on. They may indicate passion on the part of the sender but repulsion on the part of the receiver; they may signify family relations between grandparents and grandchildren rather than relations between lovers, and so on."

112. Graham Hough, "An Eighth Type of Ambiguity," in *On Literary Intention: Critical Essays*, ed. David Newton-de Molina (Edinburgh: Edinburgh University Press, 1976), 240.

113. In the later version to Susan Dickinson, the first *d* is made with two strokes of the pen, while the one at end of "conferred" is made with a single stroke. The open *e* is closer to the Greek sigma: thus in the later version "BΣtrothed" becomes "BΣtrothΣd," "conferred" is written "conferrΣd," "Degree" is written "DΣgree."

114. There is a practical dimensions to the these questions: which of the editions of "Title divine is mine" is most reliable? Martha Dickinson Bianchi offers one transcript (of the version sent to Susan Dickinson) that is twenty-one lines long. For the first eight lines, she seems to follow the manuscript, but then represents "Betrothed, without the / Swoon" as one line, "Betrothed, without the Swoon." This seems inconsistent, but it turns out that she allows "The Wife without / the Sign" to remain divided in two because she misreads "the" as "The" (and thus thinks that the capital indicates the beginning of a line). In fact, the lowercase *t* is quite distinct from the uppercase one that begins the poem and the previous line but identical to the one that begins "the Swoon." In short, Bianchi's edition is a careless one and can safely be discounted. See Bianchi, *The Life and Letters of Emily Dickinson* (Boston: Houghton Mifflin, 1924), 49–50. By extension, Hart and Smith accurately transcribe the minuscule characters that initialize "the sign" and "the Swoon," but they assign separate lines to these sequences, making them the only ones in their twenty-two-line version that begin with small letters. As both phrases begin in lowercase, occupy single rows (respectively, rows three and ten), and are followed by end spaces (4.4 cm and 4.1 cm), all indicating that they belong to the sequence preceding them, one can also proceed from the assumption that their version is unreliable, at least at those particular instances. See Hart and Smith, *Open Me Carefully*, 151–52.

115. Fr194, *Poems of Emily Dickinson*, 1:228–29.

CHAPTER TWO *Getting Nearer, Knowing Less: Emily Dickinson's*
Correspondence with Susan Gilbert Dickinson

The chapter title refers to F1433C, "But Susan is a stranger yet," which includes the lines: "That those who know her know her less / The nearer her they get" (*Poems*, 3: 1255). The poem is dated around 1877 and therefore represents a reasonably late summary of Dickinson's attitude to the sister-in-law she loved and admired but never fully understood. A later encomium, L757, "With the exception of Shakespeare, you have told me of more knowledge than any one living – To say that sincerely is strange praise," is characteristic (*Letters*, 3:733). Since Shakespeare was available only through his works, Dickinson seems to be suggesting that Susan has provided her with a massive array of materials for creative development—everything from love to hate, compassion to anger, friendship to indifference. One can see why this might have been seen as strange praise; Dickinson is effectively saying that Susan Dickinson's complexity and depth are equal to all of the volumes of Shakespeare. She is like every character in not just one play but all of them. This praise is warm but also slightly mystified, and Richard B. Sewall was surely right to say that Dickinson was implying "a Shakespearian range of temperament and qualities" (Sewall, *The Life of Emily Dickinson* [New York: Farrar, Straus and Giroux, 1974], 1:199).

1. For the most concise summary of recent trends, see the welcoming remarks and general site of the Dickinson Editing Collective at <http://jefferson.village.virginia .edu/dickinson/>. Although I take issue with some of their findings, the electronic archives of Dickinson's work on this site are an invaluable scholarly resource which have inspired and challenged a great many readers.

2. According to Johnson's estimates, there are no letters for 1856, 1857, 1863, and 1867 (*The Letters of Emily Dickinson*, ed. Thomas H. Johnson and Theodora Ward [Cambridge: Harvard University Press, Belknap Press, 1986], 3:964–65). Franklin notes no poems in 1850–52, 1855–57, 1868, 1874, and 1885–86 (*The Poems of Emily Dickinson*, ed. Ralph W. Franklin [Cambridge: Harvard University Press, Belknap Press, 1998], 3:1549–50. In other words, the only years when Susan did not receive anything were in 1856 and 1857, and there may have been letters that were lost or destroyed. It is Alfred Habegger who dates the first letter to late February 1851: see his *My Wars Are Laid Away in Books* (New York: Random House, 2001), 268, 694.

3. Ralph W. Franklin, *The Editing of Emily Dickinson: A Reconsideration* (Madison: University of Wisconsin Press, 1967), 120.

4. Appendix 3, *Letters*, 3:964–65; Appendix 7, *Poems*, 3:1549–50. Franklin also includes poems near the end of his edition that exist only in transcript by Susan Dickinson, and one therefore needs to consider the possibility that the originals of these were sent over the period of their long friendship; Franklin numbers these 1689–1746. In other words, the figure he gives for 252 poems may conceivably be adjusted upward to about 309. Many of Susan Dickinson's transcripts are included among the Dickinson papers at the Houghton Library of Harvard (bMs Am 1118.95, box 12). These were catalogued by Martha Dickinson Bianchi as "Poems Selected by SHD for typing." The handwriting seems to date to the late 1880s or early 1890s, at least based on comparison between the transcripts and letters written by Susan Dickinson to William Hayes Ward in 1891 (MS L.s. 8 February, 14 March, 23 March 1891, Amy Lowell Collection, Houghton Library, Harvard College Library, Harvard University). There are broad similarities between upper- and lowercase *a* characters in the letters and transcripts, as

well as the uppercase *G* and *D*, and the lowercase *p* (these being characters that are quite striking and more straightforward to compare). That the transcripts appear to have been made after Dickinson's death does not rule out the possibility that they were sent before that.

5. Franklin also thought that no poems were sent in 1874. The reasons for the lack of correspondence in the mid-1850s may be related to Susan's marriage to Austin Dickinson; presumably, there was more personal contact. Hart and Smith, in *Open Me Carefully*, challenge the notion that any interruption occurred in the correspondence, either in the 1850s or in the last two years before Dickinson died (*Open Me Carefully: Emily Dickinson's Intimate Letters to Susan Huntington Dickinson* [Ashfield: Paris Press, 1998]). Since much of the dating is necessarily provisional, the accuracy of Franklin's estimates, those of Johnson and Ward, and the challenge of Hart and Smith are difficult to assess. The number of poems thought to have been sent to Susan is based on Franklin's estimate; I have not included those which exist only in transcripts by Susan and whose holographs are missing. It is possible that these poems were first read and transcribed by Susan after Dickinson's death and that the originals were then destroyed. It should be kept in mind that the Norcross sisters burned all their correspondence from their cousin, after (carefully edited) copies were made of them. Had Susan Dickinson or Mabel Loomis Todd destroyed manuscripts after copying them, they would only have been acting in accordance with the conventions of the day.

6. Letters are only necessary in times of absence; the higher rate of poems seems to suggest regular contact (and thus no need to send letters, which are full of the everyday happenings that are otherwise covered face to face).

7. Franklin estimates 1863, 1865, and 1862 as (in diminishing order) the years of her highest literary production, generally. The year 1862 was formerly thought (by Johnson) as her most productive. The numbers never reach the heights of 1860, however, when Susan was sent twenty out of fifty-four poems—a massive 37 percent.

8. In other words, even though Dickinson was said to have been unhappy with Susan's giving Samuel Bowles a copy of "A narrow fellow in the grass" (which appeared in the *Republican* of February 1866), there is no evidence that she began to withhold poems in retaliation. The percentages remain fairly constant.

9. In 1874, there were no poems sent (out of 38 written); in 1875, 7 out of 34 (around 20.6 percent); in 1876, 4 out of 31 (12.9 percent); in 1877, 4 out of 42 (9.5 percent); in 1878, 3 out of 23 (13 percent); in 1879, 7 out of 35 (20 percent); in 1880, 3 out of 26 (11.5 percent); in 1881, 1 out of 25 (4 percent); in 1882, 5 out of 27 (18.5 percent); in 1883, 8 out of 34 (23.5 percent); in 1884, 8 out of 42 (19 percent). There are no poems for 1885 and 1886. Given that the dating of these documents is tentative, the ratio of poems sent to poems written remains impressively stable; though there are years when the numbers fall (1874 and 1882), these do not establish a precedent in the way that they do with Bowles, for instance.

10. It is entirely possible that Emily Dickinson might have been romantically attracted to Susan and that the attachment had an erotic aspect to it. Arguments against such a view cannot easily be predicated on Susan Dickinson's alleged indifference, for her letters to Emily have not survived. But Dickinson's correspondence with Otis Lord (from 1878 onward), as well as the Master letters and some of her remarks about Wadsworth, suggests an equal intensity (though perhaps not an intensity equally or daily sustained) to those about Susan Dickinson. And middle-class nineteenth-century women often adopted a language of love in their letters to each other. If sexual procliv-

ities have to be named, then chances are that Dickinson was not exclusively lesbian or heterosexual: she could have been bisexual, without necessarily being aware of it. For more on this, see Martha Ackmann's superb review essay on *Open Me Carefully* in the *Emily Dickinson Journal* 8, no. 2 (1999): 111–13. The argument that Dickinson's letters were censored to cover up her passionate love for Susan has been most recently refuted by Alfred Habegger, who in examining a printer's copy of *Letters* (1894) found that Dickinson's brother Austin blue-penciled even the most innocuous references to his family. Those erasures that are legible show nothing erotic; the obliteration is consistent with Austin's desire not to have his own family in the public eye. See *My Wars Are Laid Away in Books*, 303.

11. Hart and Smith, *Open Me Carefully*, xvi.

12. The tentativeness need not be related to Emily's relationship to Susan; by 1850, Dickinson was already aware that the strength of her attachment to other friends could not always be reciprocated. L38, 1:101–2, Ms Am 1118.5 (B131), Houghton Library, Harvard College Library, Harvard University. All references are to the manuscript original. I employ italics rather than the underlining of the original. Johnson transcribes "tho' " as "tho," which is certainly feasible.

13. Fr41, 1:93.

14. Nor was Dickinson alone in using idiosyncratically inscribed dashes. Three manuscript drafts of the poem "A Bird's Song in the Morning" by Sarah Orne Jewett, for instance, exhibit such tendencies. In the second draft, line 1, the word "Spring –" is written at an angle sloping down from left to right, as is the dash. In line 7, the word "end –" has a dash that is horizontal and squiggly. In the third draft, line 1, "Spring –" is written normally, but the dash slopes upwards, from left to right, at a steep angle. In line 7, after "End –," the dash is similar—it angles sharply upward, from left to right. Ms Am 1743 23 (2), Houghton Library, Harvard College Library, Harvard University. All references are to the manuscript originals.

15. Charles R. Anderson, *Emily Dickinson's Poetry: Stairway of Surprise* (New York: Holt, Rinehart and Winston, 1960), 305; Edith Perry Stamm, "Emily Dickinson: Poetry and Punctuation," *Saturday Review*, 30 March, 1963, 26–27, 74.

16. Stamm, "Emily Dickinson," 27.

17. Ebenezer Porter, *The Rhetorical Reader; Consisting of Instructions for Regulating the Voice, with a Rhetorical Notation* (New York: Mark H. Newman, 1835). Porter's system of emphasis places an accent above the syllable of any word that is to be pronounced in a particular way, whereas Dickinson's records a dash subsequent to the word. Dickinson's system would seem less focused, then, because the reader does not receive her or his signal while the work is being read (the signal postdates the encounter with the word), and the reader still has to work out which syllable (in a word with two or more syllables) requires attention.

18. In other words, it is not clear that dashes can fulfill the function of punctuation integers and pronunciation indicators at the same time. They are not necessarily compatible systems.

19. Theodora Ward, "Poetry and Punctuation," in "Letters to the Editor," *Saturday Review*, 27 April 1963, 25.

20. Ward, "Poetry and Punctuation," *Saturday Review*, 27 April 1963, 25.

21. In response, Edith Perry Stamm claimed that the punctuation of the Dickinson manuscripts had more nuances than Ward allowed for and that her practice continued in the letters as well ("The Punctuation Problem," *Saturday Review*, 25 May 1963, 23).

Her remarks were more extensively outlined in Edith Wylder, *The Last Face: Emily Dickinson's Manuscripts* (Albuquerque: University of New Mexico Press, 1971).

22. The penciled "Prof Tuckerman" is written in Dickinson's hand on a piece of paper measuring 12.7 × 2.9 cm which is carefully torn along the upper and one lateral edge and folded approximately in half. On the reverse side is a draft of "Ferocious as a Bee without a wing." The mark that follows Tuckerman angles sharply upwards, another example of the physical diversity with which Dickinson inscribed her dashes. A 184, Special Collections, Frost Library, Amherst College. All references are to the manuscript original.

23. The Holland envelope is included in the document catalogued as ibid., A 20. All references are to the manuscript original.

24. The envelopes to Mrs. Todd are (respectively) included in the documents catalogued as A 782, A 777, and A 785, in ibid. All references are to the manuscript originals.

25. The envelope to "Mr Chickering" is included with the document catalogued as A 798, in ibid. (though the dash represented as an accent at the end of the address is situated much lower on the line than indicated here). The previous envelope in the collection, A 797, has the same phenomenon: dots that are like dashes (measuring 0.3 mm each) and a third stroke (0.2 mm) that is either a period or a dash. All references are to the manuscript originals.

26. L558, 2:614; Fr1479, 3:1293. The date was supplied by the recipient, who endorsed the manuscript; Johnson and Ward, and Franklin, confirm it by the handwriting. A 34, Special Collections, Frost Library, Amherst College. All references are to the manuscript original.

27. Atossa Frost Stone, Manuscript Journal (1817–28), Rare Books and Manuscripts, Smith College, Northampton; Solomon B. Ingram, Solomon B. Ingram's / Book Amherst Octr 1827, Special Collections, Jones Library, Amherst; Elizabeth Barrett Browning, ANS (October 1856), Misc. Manuscripts, Archives and Special Collections, Amherst College; Kathleen Coburn, "Editing the Coleridge Notebooks," in *Editing Texts of the Romantic Period*, ed. John D. Baird (Toronto: A. M. Hakkert, 1972), 11.

28. Of course, such information can still be valuable in other ways: as a sign of the author's education, her attitude to the English language in America, her pronunciation, and so on.

29. Simon Nowell-Smith, "Authors, Editors, and Publishers," in *Editor, Author, and Publisher: Papers Given at the Editorial Conference, University of Toronto, 1968*, ed. William J. Howard (Toronto: University of Toronto Press, 1969), 21.

30. Charles Richard Sanders, "Editing the Carlyle Letters," in *Editing Nineteenth-Century Texts: Papers Given at the Editorial Conference, University of Toronto, November 1966*, ed. John M. Robson (Toronto: University of Toronto Press, 1967), 88.

31. Brita Lindberg, "Emily Dickinson's Punctuation," *Studia Neophilologica* 37 (1965): 327–59; Brita Lindberg-Seyersted, *The Voice of the Poet: Aspects of Style in the Poetry of Emily Dickinson* (Cambridge: Harvard University Press, 1968), 180–96.

32. Lindberg-Seyersted, *Voice of the Poet*, 196.

33. In other words, Lindberg-Seyersted's dismissal of Stamm is valid, but her suggestion that the dashes mark different rhythmical units may be little better.

34. One of the striking features of manuscript drafts to "Master"—for instance, A 828—is that the writing is neat and frequently cursive, and the dashes are also fairly

regular. But at different points the dashes are either sharply vertical or otherwise volatile in placement. The sequence "you have felt the Horizon" has its dash almost vertical and just below the *o* in Horizon, for instance; after "Have you the little Chest" and "Could you come to New England," the dashes are sharply angled downward and below the line of writing. For those dashes to function rhetorically, they would have to match the sentiment being expressed (and the dash after New England contrarily suggests that the speaker would be disappointed if he or she fulfilled her wishes), and the recipient would have to be sufficiently familiar with their usage to be able, first, to distinguish non-meaningful (regular) from meaningful (irregular) usage and, second, to interpret correctly the significance of those dashes deliberately deployed. It seems more reasonable to suppose that the uniformity of Dickinson's handwriting and the occasional disparities of dash inscription and placement mean that dashes were less important to her or that she was hesitant about where to place them sometimes (because of lack of space or other factors), or that some dashes were added during a second or third reading.

35. Fr318B, 1:336 (about 1865), Ms Am 1118.3 (312), Houghton Library, Harvard College Library, Harvard University. Henceforth, all references beginning "Ms Am" are from the Houghton Library. Though the poem was sent to Susan Dickinson, Hart and Smith do not include it in *Open Me Carefully*.

36. Fr549A, 2:551 (summer 1863); Ms Am 1118.3 (346). Again, the poem is not included in *Open Me Carefully*.

37. Lack of space prevents a more thorough analysis of contemporaneous examples, but similarities exist between Dickinson's word breaks and those of other nineteenth-century writers. For example, an undated letter from Andrew Duncan (1773–1832) to Dorothea Lynde Dix, written in pen on nonruled paper measuring 12.3 × 18.6 cm, reads: "My Dear Miss Dix / I find that Hugh Miller / & his family are so far recover– / –ed as to see strangers– / He is to receive my friend / Miss Borthwich with an / English gentleman tomor / – row at 2. to go over his / course of geological speci– / –mens – I said to Miss / B. that I would mention / this to you – as it is best / to meet a man in / his element." Ms Am 1838.2 (3); all references are to the manuscript original. Interestingly, Duncan uses only dashes for punctuation: a letter from Adelaide Proctor (1825–64) to Dorothea Lynde Dix is similar in that she uses only dashes for punctuation (Ms Am 1838.2 [7]; all references are to the manuscript original). In her Diary (20 September 1876–8 October 1877), Abigail May Alcott uses dashes almost exclusively for punctuation (Ms Am 1817.2 [15]; all references are to the manuscript original). Sarah S. Hammond's "Journal of a Tour from Boston to Virginia and back" (1836), in which she uses conventional paragraphing and extremely regular and neat cursive writing, combines ordinary punctuation with dashes—that is, she will write a comma or a period and then add a dash to both. As her Journal develops, her dashes vary in length; sometimes they are doubled (– – [MS Am 1609]; all references are to the manuscript original). In a (undated) letter from William Wordsworth to Dorothea Dix, the British poet uses two commas, five dashes, and (at the end of the letter) one period (Ms Am 1838.2 [12]; all references are to the manuscript original). Dashes seem to have been a much more widespread, diverse, and routine phenomenon in handwritten documents than scholars always seem to allow for when they discuss their deployment in Dickinson's letters.

38. LP1, autumn/winter 1850, 7–8; L38, December 1850, 1:101–2. Johnson and Ward omit "Thursday noon." Hart and Smith do not indent the first paragraph. Both

editions correctly assign new paragraphs after "alone" (which has a space of approximately 4 cm after it). Neither edition includes the page break, which occurs after "Columbarium" (pp. 1–2).

39. LP2, 9 October 1851, 8–10; L56, 9 October 1851, 1:143–45. Johnson and Ward omit "Thursday evening." Hart and Smith do not indent the first paragraph. Both editions correctly assign new paragraphs after "sailing on," "shining now," "than the first?," "lives of our's," "to do," and "vacant places" (which have spaces after them of approximately 4 cm, 2.1 cm, 2 cm, 3.3 cm, 5 cm, and 5.7 cm, respectively). Neither edition includes the page breaks, which occur after "and I told you" (pp. 1–2), "makes me" (pp. 2–3) and "to have them" (pp. 3–4).

40. L70, 21 January 1852, 1:168–69. Johnson and Ward omit "Wednesday noon –." They correctly assign new paragraphs after "two" and "pass away" (which have spaces after them of approximately 3.4 cm and 4.4 cm, respectively). They do not indicate page breaks, which occur after "Susie you would" (pp. 1–2), "too!" (pp. 2–3), and "subject" (pp. 3–4). Written vertically on the left margin of the first page is "Love, much love!" (Johnson and Ward omit the underlining and represent the writing as a postscript).

41. LP3, February 1852, 10–13; L73, 6 February 1852, 1:175–76. Johnson and Ward omit "Friday forenoon." Hart and Smith do not indent the first paragraph. Both editions correctly assign new paragraphs after "you.," "no!," "refused.," "sad –," and "frightful" (which have spaces after them of approximately 3.2 cm, 5 cm, 2.3 cm, 1.7 cm, and 3.5 cm, respectively). Neither edition includes the page breaks, which occur after "hand as the only" (pp. 1–2), "faintly – and" (pp. 2–3), and *ugly things* (pp. 3–4). Hart and Smith assign an additional paragraph break after "scare little children" and before "Dont *you* run, Susie dear," where there is an interval of approximately 2.2 cm. Johnson and Ward clearly felt that there was semantic continuity here (in the idea of frightening); Hart and Smith believe that there is a switch from a mock-serious description of Dickinson's feelings about herself to a direct address. Both arguments have their merits, and the physical space after "children" is larger than at least one other end marker and almost equal to another. My own preference is for Hart and Smith's interpretation, on the grounds that Dickinson disrupts continuity elsewhere in this phase of the letter (paragraphs 3 and 4, both focusing on Lavinia Dickinson, referred to as Vinnie).

42. LP4, about February 1852, 13–14; L74, about February 1852, 1:177. Johnson and Ward omit "Wednesday morn." Hart and Smith do not indent the first paragraph. Both editions correctly assign a new paragraph after "I shall be!" (which has a space after it of approximately 3.5 cm). Neither edition includes the page breaks, which occur after "love me more if" (pp. 1–2) and "wear out if they" (pp. 2–3). Hart and Smith correctly note that "Vinnie's love – Mother's –" is written upside down on the first page, though they fail to specify the positioning (it is in the top margin). They also note that "Love to Hattie from us all. Dear Mattie is almost well" appears in the margin of the third page but fail to specify that the first sentence appears in the left margin, and is written vertically, while the second appears in the right margin and is also vertical. Johnson and Ward include all these as postscripts. Since Hart and Smith do not supply full information as to placement and direction, their additional notes are of little use. They also appear to contradict their view that Dickinson began visual experiments toward the end of the 1850s—that is, if visual experiments began then, there is no need to represent the letter's graphic attributes. If they began earlier (or might have

begun earlier), then all the details of the letter's appearances should not be noted but faithfully represented.

43. LP5, about February 1852, 14–19; L77, about February 1852, 1:181–84. Johnson and Ward omit "Sunday morning –." Hart and Smith do not indent the first paragraph. Both editions correctly assign new paragraphs after "for us!" and "injure you" (which have spaces after them of approximately 10.4 and 5.3 cm, on the first and second pages respectively). Neither edition includes the page breaks, which occur after "terrestial – no" (pp. 1–2), "*alone.*" (pp. 2–3), and "wonder –" (pp. 3–4: what follows is "ful you are"). Hart and Smith provide two additional paragraphs, after "because you know!" and "*alone.*" The first is followed by a space of only 1.7 cm, the second by a page break; both are therefore debatable. Hart and Smith correctly note that "Susie, what shall I do . . . *respect* for him!" is written upside down on the first page, and "And when shall I . . . *ever!*" is written in the margin of the first page (though they fail to specify that it is written on the left margin and that the writing goes from the bottom of the page to the top). By extension, we are told on which page the remaining three paragraphs are to be found, but not their exact placement on the page. In *Letters*, Johnson and Ward include the paragraphs as postscripts, beginning with "Susie" and ending with "Who loves you most . . . Emilie –" (page 4, left margin, bottom to top). Again, they are the more methodologically consistent, for they regard physical placement as inessential information. Hart and Smith imply that such information is relevant but fail to supply every detail about placement, thereby distinguishing between potentially meaningful and merely incidental details. Marginal placement appears to belong to the former category; direction and lateral specifics to the latter.

44. LP6, 5 April 1852, 19–23; L85, 5 April 1852, 1:193–96; Johnson and Ward omit "Monday morning –." Hart and Smith do not indent the first paragraph. Both editions correctly assign new paragraphs after "*sorrow.*" (p. 1, 5.9 cm), "working" (p. 2, 2.0 cm), "forevermore!" (p. 2, 2.8 cm), "me!" (p. 2, 4.4 cm), "away!" (p. 2, 4.0 cm), "*more.*" (p. 2, 3.5 cm), "out!" (p. 3, 8.8 cm), "Plantains?" (p. 3, 2.8 cm), "small" (p. 4, 4.1 cm), and "good" (p. 4, 3.1 cm). Neither edition includes the page breaks, which occur after "care –" (pp. 1–2), "know" (pp. 2–3), and "hardly know" (pp. 3–4). Hart and Smith record the placement of the paragraphs that follow the signature; Johnson and Ward record them as postscripts, but join the statement written upside down on the first page ("Father's sister . . . crape.") with that written on the left margin ("A great deal of love . . . *note.*") to form one single paragraph. They are certainly separate, however, and in previous transcriptions marginalia were assigned the status of independent paragraphs by Johnson and Ward: this instance seems inconsistent on their part. Hart and Smith reproduce the marginal writing on pages two and three as *separate*, and their notes intervene as follows: "Austin comes home on Wednesday, but he'll only stay two days, so I fancy [note on page placement] we shant go sugaring, as 'we did last year.' *Last year* is gone, Susie – did you ever think of *that*?" Obviously, such breaks are imposed by the amount of space Dickinson had available on the page and are not semantic phenomena. Like all Dickinson's marginalia at this stage of her career, such material properties can be safely ignored. I will return to consider whether or not such details *become* important; for now, I hope that the evidence presented so far strongly suggests that it is mostly paragraph identification that is problematic in the letters during the 1850s.

45. L88, late April 1852, 1:201–3.

46. L92, about May 1852, 1:208–9.

47. L93, early June 1852, 1:209–11.

48. L94, 1 June 1852, 1:211–12.

49. L96, 27 June 1852, 1:215–16.

50. L97, early December 1852, 1:216–17.

51. The twenty-five letters are written on approximately thirty-nine pages, though many of these are left partially unused.

52. LP102, 1864, 130–31; L288, about 1864, 2:430; LP144, autumn 1869, 168–70; L333, autumn 1869, 2:464.

53. LP5, 14–19; L77, 1:181–84. LP103, 131–33; L294, 2:434. The second letter is chosen because of its length: Dickinson was receiving eye treatment in Cambridge and was therefore writing letters rather than short notes to Susan and the rest of her family. A number of critics, David Porter among them, have pointed out that her eye problems may have forced her to change her handwriting, producing larger alphabetical characters and intervocalic spaces. Porter, review essay on *New Poems by Emily Dickinson*, by William Shurr, *Emily Dickinson Journal* 4, no. 1 (1995): 127.

54. The poems (sent to Sue) are "Of all the Sounds" (Fr334, 1863, 1:359–60: "wor- / king"); "The One who could repeat the Summer day" (Fr549A, 1863, 2:551: "repro- / duce"); "I send two Sunsets" (Fr557A, 1863, 2:557: "compe- / tition"); "The Soul's Superior instants" (Fr630A, 1863, 2:620–21: "as- / cended"); "No Other can reduce" (Fr738B, 1865, 2:669–70: "Con- / sequence"); "Bloom opon the Mountain" (Fr787B, 1863, 2:740, "dis- / appear" and "expan- / ding"); "All I may – if small" (Fr799A, 1864, 2:755: "muni- / ficence); "To be alive, is power" (Fr876B, 1864, 2:817: "Fin- / itude"); "The Overtakelessness of Those" (Fr894B, 1865, 2:831: "accomp- / lished").

55. Fr787B, 1863, 2:740.

56. Fr1253A, about 1872, 2:1080–81; A 339. Not represented in this transcription is the mark (a comma) below and to the right of the *n* of "Perdition."

57. My thanks to John Lancaster, curator of special collections at Frost Library, Amherst College, for independently confirming these measurements in an e-mail from 2000. My original measurements, taken from a photostat at the Houghton Library, were 0.6 cm, 0.3 cm, and 0.4 cm. In other words, there were no substantial differences.

58. Fr407A, 1:430–31; Ms Am 1118.5 (B67). LP239, late November 1883, 248–49; L874, late November 1883, 3:803. All references are to the manuscript original. Johnson and Ward cut out the second reference to "cocks," though it may be a rare visual-verbal joke.

59. Ms Am 1118.3 (350). All references are to the manuscript original. Fr630A, 2: 620–21; LP87, 120.

60. Fr796A, 2:749.

61. Ms Am 1118.5 (B98); L226, 2:369. All references are to the manuscript original.

62. Ms Am 1118.5 (B125); L239, 2:381; LP65, 102; Fr188A, 1:223. Franklin italicizes the question mark, Johnson (J220, 1:158) does not. The original underlining ends before the question mark.

63. The prose version is in Martha Dickinson Bianchi, *Emily Dickinson Face to Face: Unpublished Letters with Notes and Reminiscences* (Boston: Houghton Mifflin, 1932), 255.

64. A 635, Special Collections, Frost Library, Amherst College.

65. Fr285A, 1:303.

66. Letters in women's literature have often functioned formally as a means of

mediating between private and public discourses—one thinks immediately of Fanny Burney's *Evelina* (1778), Susanna Rowson's *Charlotte Temple* (1791), or (more recently) Alice Walker's *The Color Purple* (1982) and Ana Castillo's *The Mixquiahuala Letters* (1986). At some level, Dickinson used her correspondence to promote her poetry in ways that did not compromise her apparently intense need for privacy. To some extent, also, Dickinson's epistolary distribution can be seen as a singular response to the cultural market and to wider political phenomena, or as one indication of a historical crisis in the relations between lyric poet and literary audience. So the letter-poems may not represent a challenge to generic conventions so much as a familiar technique of disguising publication.

67. Ralph W. Franklin, *The Manuscript Books of Emily Dickinson* (Cambridge: Harvard University Press, Belknap Press, 1981), 2:859–60. Ms Am 1118.3 (123). All references are to the manuscript original.

68. One is inclined to think that many of the poems or portions of poems reproduced by Dickinson in her notes and letters do acquire additional meanings or directions that are dependent on personal relationships; they may even derive many of those meanings from the relationship in the first place. Some of these meanings are clearly local and contingent. (For an exemplary reading of this kind, see Habegger's interpretation of Fr1368B in *My Wars Are Laid Away in Books*, 557.) But Dickinson seems not to have wanted to invoke these when recording them for posterity.

69. Ms Am 1118.3 (315); Fr940A, 2:864. All references are to the manuscript original. The isolation of "far," which is placed at the halfway point of the poem, at the end of a metrical line and segregated by anterior and posterior dashes, shows that Dickinson could manipulate punctuation and placement within a rhythmical system and stanzaic structure, without having to rely on visual special effects. Dickinson's sense of architecture is easy to miss: in this case, the parallels ("So," "What," "What" / "So," "That" / "Thy") are a kind of chiasmus. The poem seeks to convert distance and infrequency into closeness, in a way that is reminiscent of paragraph 4 in L272 to Samuel Bowles (*Letters*, 2: 416).

70. Martha Dickinson Bianchi, *The Single Hound: Poems of a Lifetime* (Boston: Little, Brown and Company, 1915), 138.

71. L336, 2:465; LP137, 162; A.N.S. [1871?], Mortimer Rare Book Room, William Allan Neilson Library, Smith College. All references are to the manuscript original.

72. In row 1, the lowercase *e* letters are regular; in row 2, they look more like capitals. Row 3 reverts to regular lowercase; rows 4 and 7 are like capitals.

73. Hale, Lucretia Peabody, to Edward Everett Hale, 11 June 1855, Folder 51-1, Sophia Smith Collection, Smith College, Northampton.

74. This is also how Franklin arranges the poem (Fr893, 2:830).

75. Ms Am 1118.5 (B20); L334, 2:464; LP134, 161. All references are to the manuscript original. In *Open Me Carefully*, the tiny indentation at the beginning, which is in part a consequence of the embossment, is distorted into a paragraph indent. In fact, the writing slopes minimally, so that the margin formed by the initial letters is slightly angled from upper right to lower left; only at "we" does the margin shift inward a bit.

76. Fr1279, 2:1105–8.

77. William Shurr, *New Poems of Emily Dickinson* (Chapel Hill: University of North Carolina Press, 1993), 24.

78. Note on LP134, 285.

79. L350, 2:478; Fr1158B, 2:1006; LP149, 176. Johnson dates the writing to 1870, Franklin to 1869, Hart and Smith to the 1870s. Hart and Smith believe this to be "a revision of a portion of a letter-poem sent to Susan in the late 1860s" (*Open Me Carefully*, 176).

80. Ms Am 1118.5 (B23); Fr1158A, 2:1006. All references are to the manuscript original.

81. Ms Am 1118.5 (B33); Fr1191, 2:1032. All references are to the manuscript original. In the Franklin edition, "Holiday" is incorrectly transcribed or printed as "holiday."

82. L581, 2:631; L660, 3:672.

83. Sewall wrongly intimates that Dickinson moved from addressing her sister-in-law as "Dollie" and "Sue" to "Susan": she ceased to use "Dollie" after 1862 but continued to use "Sue" up to and including 1886, by Johnson's reckoning. Cynthia Mac-Kenzie notes the "Dollie" of L42, 1:112 (1851), but working with the letters as Johnson defines them, she omits other examples, among them the 1862 poem F285A, "The Love a Child can show – below," which Franklin notes was addressed to Susan but never sent (*Poems*, 1:303). Hart and Smith include this as if it were sent, though they note that it remained unfolded, one of the signs that it may not have been delivered. The entry for "Sue" counts 168 instances, some of which are the verb, not the name. But there are also "Sue's" and bracketed names, which amount to another 18 examples. And however formal the letters sometimes seem, this is not to suggest emotional coldness where there quite clearly was none: Dickinson and Susan seem to have met each other face to face quite regularly, so that the correspondence would let Dickinson say things she may have been unable to do otherwise. See Cynthia MacKenzie, *Concordance to the Letters of Emily Dickinson* (Boulder: University of Colorado Press, 2000). Marietta Messmer, in her excellent *A Vice for Voices*, records the many examples of adulation in early letters to Susan, but omits to mention that Dickinson included very similar remarks in messages to Samuel Bowles (portraying Susan, Lavinia, and herself as communicants at the church of Sam, so to speak). It might have been interesting to see what points of convergence, if any, existed between such similar, but differently addressed, religious and amorous hyperbole and what implications such rhetorical strategies might have for our understanding of the relationship with either. See Marietta Messmer, *A Vice for Voices: Reading Emily Dickinson's Correspondence* (Amherst: University of Massachusetts Press, 2001), 87.

84. "Immortality" is an exception, almost certainly because the *l* that intervenes between the first and second *t* would have to be crossed as well.

85. Hart and Smith, *Open Me Carefully*, xxiv.

86. Ibid., note on LP9, 273.

87. Ibid., notes on LP32 (p. 276), LP43 (p. 277), LP74 (p. 280), LP37 (p. 276), and LP13 (p. 274).

88. Miller's other comment on the debate about the dash is also pertinent: "Unfortunately a critical commitment to the object of the poem itself does not protect the poetry from being distorted to fit an extraneous frame of reference." See Ruth Miller, *The Poetry of Emily Dickinson* (Middletown: Wesleyan University Press, 1968), 35.

89. Hart and Smith, *Open Me Carefully*, xxiii.

90. Smith, *Rowing in Eden: Rereading Emily Dickinson* (Austin: University of Texas Press, 1992), 65. Smith was, and is, a pioneering scholar, and her response has to be seen in its original context—as the first move in a new but not yet fully formulated

direction in Dickinson criticism. The reason so many examples of the crossed *t* are provided here is not to deny the legitimacy of Smith's first and local reaction but to suggest that Dickinson's habits of handwriting in this and other instances are common and consistent enough not to call for any special explanation. Only a thorough documentation of the *t* can enable us to see how easy but misleading it is to read interpretive implications into Dickinson's chirographic behaviors.

91. All examples are from Ms Am 1118.4 (L15); L70, 21 January 1852, 1:168–69.

92. Ms Am 1118.4 (L16); L102, 24 February 1853, 1:220–21; LP13, 39–41; the joined "together" is on row 7 of the first autograph page, "thought" on row 14 of the second. Ms Am 1118.4 (L8); L103, 5 March 1853, 1:223–24; LP14, 41–43: "thought" is on row 13 of the first page.

93. Ms Am 1118.4 (L6); L176, 27 November / 3 December 1854, 1:310–12; LP 19, 51–53: both words occur on page 3, row 21.

94. A 21, Special Collections, Frost Library, Amherst College; L243, December 1861, 2:383–84. Both words occur on the first autograph page, rows 1 and 16 respectively. The Reverend Dwight had been a minister at Amherst First Church.

95. Ms Am 1118.5 (B44); L258, early 1862, 2:400–401; LP70, 105–7. The word "taught" is the first in the second row of text on the first manuscript page.

96. Ms Am 1118.5 (B31); L303, early 1865?, 2:440. There is only one page: "Thank Sue, but / not Tonight. / Further nights. / Emily." Johnson and Ward read "Tonight" as "tonight."

97. Ms Am 1118.3 (339); Fr974B, 2:884–85. The words occur on rows 6 and 7 of the first (autograph) page.

98. A 201, Special Collections, Frost Library, Amherst College; Fr1185, 2:1028 (row 7) and A 202, Fr1310, 3:1131 (row 6). A 439, Fr1171B, 2:1014 ("Strategist" is located on the third row of the first page).

99. Ms Am 1118.5 (B193); L378, autumn 1872, 2:498–99; LP 147, 172–74. The words occur towards the end of the letter, on the third and fourth pages, rows 15 and 6, respectively.

100. Ms Am 1118.2 (35a); Fr1453B, 3:1270. There are five words joined this way on the first autograph page, and one ("that") on the second. Ms Am 1118.3 (358); Fr1486A, 3:1300 ("that" is in row 4, page 2). A 799, Special Collections, Frost Library, Amherst College; L786, 3:750. A second note to the same recipient has "substantiate" in the eighth row of the first page (A 806, Special Collections, Frost Library, Amherst College). Ms Am 1118.5 (B 119); L853, 3:790; LP227, 237 (the word occurs on row 6 of the first page). Ms Am 1118.3 (294); Fr1596B, 3:1396–97; LP231, 239–41 ("temerity" is in row 11, second autograph page).

101. The habit is not limited to fair copies either. A draft of "Facts by our side are never sudden" (A 179) has a cross-stroke over the word "portentous" that begins above the initial *o* and ends just after the final *s* (Special Collections, Frost Library, Amherst College: all references are to the manuscript original).

102. The manuscript is at the John Hay Library of Brown University, Providence, Rhode Island.

103. All these manuscripts are from the Special Collections of the Jones Library, Amherst.

104. Dr. Seymour L. Rudman Collection, Special Collections, Jones Library, Amherst. At the time of writing (December 2001), the collection had not yet been catalogued. Interestingly, given the disagreement as to Dickinson's use of paragraphing,

an 1836 letter from Hannah Whitemore of Pelham to Isiah Pepper leaves space after "he is gone or not" and begins a new paragraph but has no initial indentation. Dickinson uses the same format.

105. Special Collections, Jones Library, Amherst. On the first page, the stroke after the *t* in "Charlestown" continues to the *n*. In "attempt" the stroke commences from the second ascender only and on to the *p*. On page 99, "constantly" is written so that both ascenders are joined with a single cross-stroke. On page 199, "continues" has a stroke above and after the ascender, and to the *e*.

106. Ibid.

107. Margie R. Dodge, Journal (1885–86), 2, 12, Rare Books and Manuscripts, Neilson Library, Smith College, Northampton.

108. Ms Am 1118.5 (B184); L364, 2:489–90; LP158, 181–82. Elements of this communication coincide with Fr1202, 2:1041.

109. Of the eleven spaces, three are page breaks, and two are arguable. The space after "live," row 10 of the first page, is 1.7 cm, and the word that follows it, "No" occupies 1.5 cm of space. When one adds the approximately 0.5 cm of space that separates words from each other, then it seems possible that this space may not correspond to a change of paragraph. The second arguable example is "superstitious" in line 23: it is followed by 3.5 cm, but the next word ("Chickens") takes up 5.8 cm, and it is therefore certain that this does not represent the close of a paragraph. Despite these doubts, and the fact that "Fluency" (the final word on the third page of the manuscript) quite clearly joins with "abroad" (the first word on the fourth page), I have counted these as examples of significant spacing. The number in the prose section still amounts to only one in every four; without these, it would be one in every five.

110. Ms Am 1118.5 (B54); Fr1416A, 3:1235; L480, 2:569; LP194, 214. Hart and Smith have the "Emily" signature on the same line as "perhaps – only," when it is slightly lower, and squeezed into the remaining space.

111. Ms. Am. 1093 (87), Boston Public Library, Rare Books and Manuscripts; Fr1416B, 3:1235; L486, 2, 571–72. In the version sent to Dr. Holland (Ms Am 1118.2 [H46]; Fr1416C, 3: 1235–36; L544, 2:605–6) Dickinson left 6.8 cm after "no."

112. Ms Am 1118.5 (B62); Fr1433C, 3:1255; L530, 2:598; LP196, 215–16.

113. A point first made to me by Alfred Habegger.

114. Photostat of Ms Am 1118:5 (B2); Fr5, 1:61–62; L757, 3:733; LP229, 238–39. The original is missing.

115. There are exceptions. In Ms Am 1118.5 (B66) there is a vertical split, but no indication of poetry. The manuscript corresponds to L1025, 3:894 and LP252, 261–62, written at a time when Dickinson was seriously ill. The incongruity may therefore be attributable to other factors.

116. Ms Am 1118.5 (B79); Fr1624B, 3:1423–24; L868, 3:799; LP234, 242–44. All references are to the manuscript original. The letter and the poem within it are evidence of Dickinson's generosity, but also of her own inexhaustible grief at Gilbert's death.

117. Bianchi rearranged some of these lines as a quatrain: "His life was like a bugle / That winds itself away: / His elegy an echo, / His requiem ecstasy." One sympathizes with the impulse: the lines are metrical, and they rhyme. But the spacing and uppercase letters in the original do not reflect a desire to have this acknowledged as a poem. Bianchi also suggests that the sequence "Dawn and meridian in one. Wherefore would he wait, wronged only of night, which he left for us?" should be read as "Dawn and

meridian in one, wherefore would he wait, wronged only of night, which he left for us?" The capital at the start of "wherefore" is not absolutely clear, and the arrangement seems right: there is an end space of 7 cm after "requiem ecstasy" that unequivocally represents a paragraph break, and "Dawn and meridian in one" appears otherwise incomplete. See Martha Dickinson Bianchi, *The Life and Letters of Emily Dickinson* (Boston: Houghton Mifflin Company, 1924), 85.

118. Not even William Shurr, in *New Poems of Emily Dickinson*, includes these lines, though he does have three-line sequences among the poems he excavates from letters.

119. Ms Am 1118.5 (B88); Fr1638B, 3:1437; L910, 3:829.

120. Ms Am 1118.5 (B90); Fr1658, 3:1452; L912, 3:830; LP246, 256.

121. Habegger goes on to contest the idea that "the entire communication is a poem, that we must retain ED's lineation, and that the message is erotic" (*My Wars Are Laid Away in Books*, 738 n. 619).

122. L912, 3:830; Fr1658, 3:1452.

123. Ms Am 1118.5 (B106); L911, 3:830; LP 245, 256.

124. Ms Am 1118.5 (B73); Fr3A, 1:57; L105, 1:226; LP15, 44. Hart and Smith mention in their notes on the poem that after "Comrade," the dash "points up to the right, heightening the excited, exclamatory tone of the heading's command" (*Open Me Carefully*, 274 n. 15). If the inscription was significant, then it should have been represented in the poem and not relegated to a footnote. If it was not significant, then it should not have been mentioned.

125. Notes to L105, 1:226. I find Johnson and Ward's argument unconvincing. The first paragraph of L103 in *Letters* (1:222), is instructive: "I know dear Susie is busy, or she would not forget her lone little Emilie, who wrote her just as soon as she'd gone to Manchester, and has waited so patiently till she can wait no more, and the credulous little heart, fond even tho' forsaken, will get it's big black inkstand, and tell her once again how well it loves her." In the same letter she asks: "Why dont you write me, Darling" (1:223). L106 to Austin Dickinson states, "I have heard once from Susie – not much tho' " (1:228). And Lavinia Dickinson reported that Susan Dickinson's silence "made E. very unhappy & me vexed" (quoted in *My Wars Are Laid Away in Books*, 304). To infer from Fr3A (1:57) that Dickinson was trying to promote a joint literary enterprise is to take Dickinson out of context; having sent three letters to Susan without reply, she was encouraging a note in return.

126. Notes to LP15, 274.

127. A 82-7/8, Special Collections, Frost Library, Amherst College; Fr3B, 1:57; *Manuscript Books of Emily Dickinson*, 1:17. The same omission can be observed for other poems (Fr194, 202, and 227, for example): as a rule, Dickinson did not include introductory or framing remarks in her fascicles. And this in turn suggests that, first, she *did* operate with genre distinctions and, second, that the original biographical context (if and when it existed) was *not* something she felt it was necessary to preserve. Franklin reads "west" as "West."

128. bMs Am 1118.95, box 12 (ST 23), Houghton Library, Harvard College Library, Harvard University.

129. Ibid. (ST 24).

130. A 655, Special Collections, Frost Library, Amherst College; Fr123A, 1:158.

131. Of course, we enter difficult territory here. Is Susan Dickinson an unreliable guide because she also ignored the capitalization, punctuation, and lack of titling, in which case her view of the lineation is also suspect? Or did Susan Dickinson know that such characteristics of the autographs were a consequence of their unpublished state,

and therefore disposable? There are other possibilities: Susan was correct about the lineation but wrong about the capitals and dashes, for instance. But such a view is inconsistent in its application and impossible to verify. The point to make, surely, is that if Hart and Smith are correct in seeing Susan as a uniquely positioned reader and potential editor, then her procedures of transcription appear to contradict theirs. And if those procedures were wrong, then what does that say about Susan's taste and accuracy as critic, reader, and writer during Dickinson's lifetime? For Susan's poetry is utterly conventional in comparison with Dickinson's; the latter may have inspired the former, but she does not appear to have influenced her successfully.

132. Ms Am 1118.3 (333); Fr1293, 3:1122; LP142, 167

133. In *Emily Dickinson: Monarch of Perception* (Amherst: University of Massachusetts Press, 2000), I argued that Dickinson ignored Susan's conclusion that the poem did not need a second stanza, recording three variants in her fascicles. After the poem was published in the *Republican*, Dickinson sent a different version of it to Higginson, clearly distancing herself from the printed version, which had been Susan's preference.

134. One excerpt is erroneously identified: Fr888A is not a draft but the last stanza of " 'Twould ease a butterfly" (*Poems*, 2:826), and it follows Dickinson's practice of occasionally sending parts of poems to Susan rather than the full version. The wider import of such selection is that Dickinson carefully regulated what kinds of materials she sent to particular correspondents, modulating and from time to time effectively censoring portions that might have been misconstrued. The drawback of arranging an edition of letters according to their recipient is that one misses its rhetorical or adapted aspects.

135. Martha Dickinson Bianchi, *Emily Dickinson Face to Face*, n.p. The photograph is inserted between page 260 and page 261. The draft is also reproduced verbally on page 259.

136. Fr1354, 3:1174–75.

137. Ms Am 1118.3 (244); LP199, 217–18; Fr1365, 3:1185–86. Ms Am 1118.3 (338); LP200, 219; Fr1423, 3:1242–43.

138. Bianchi, *The Single Hound*, x.

139. A 741, which survives in three partial sheets and is a fair copy draft in pencil, has pinholes, suggesting that either Dickinson used pins to keep loose sheets together during the process of composition or (posthumously) her editors did. Special Collections, Frost Library, Amherst College.

140. Which is to say that it is slightly longer at the top than at the bottom and that one end of the slip is angled. Ibid., A 440. A facsimile of the same document is included in Marta Werner, *Emily Dickinson's Open Folios: Scenes of Reading, Scenes of Writing* (Ann Arbor: University of Michigan Press, 1995), n.p. Werner includes a transcript of the letter in an unknown hand (Franklin thinks that of Millicent Todd Bingham), but she appears to identify it as having been written by Dickinson, which seems unlikely. Bingham worked with the Lord materials for her *Emily Dickinson: A Revelation* (1954). Comparison with the handwriting in a 1956 letter from Bingham (in Washington, D.C.) to Mr. Charles Green, director of the Jones Library, Amherst, and dated 8 February 1956 shows that Franklin was correct. The habit of using the cross-stroke on the ascender of a *t* to join two words ("the Bible" in the transcript, "to go" and "the sorting" in the letter) is the same in both documents, as is the inscription of other alphabetic characters. The letter is in the Special Collections, Jones Library, catalogued under E. D. Todd, Mabel Loomis, Typewriter Correspondence.

141. A 359, Special Collections, Frost Library, Amherst College. A facsimile of the

original is in Werner, *Open Folios*. The paper was originally blue ruled, and this fragment derives from either the top or bottom section (where there is an interval of unruled white space). Dickinson wrote against the rule, in pencil. The word at the top of the paper that is cut almost in half seems to be "the."

142. A 193, Special Collections, Frost Library, Amherst College (both drafts). A facsimile of the original is in Werner, *Open Folios*.

143. A 734 and A 736, Special Collections, Frost Library, Amherst College. A facsimile of the original is in Werner, *Open Folios*. Dickinson moved through rough drafts to fair copies, which were the final stage before a letter was written and sent.

144. A 738 and A 739, Special Collections, Frost Library, Amherst College. A facsimile of the original is in Werner, *Open Folios*.

145. A 827 ("Dear Master / I am ill – / but grieving more / that you are ill") is folded in quarters. Another so-called Master draft, A 828, written in pen on blue-lined stationery, but with pencil revisions, is folded in thirds. A 829, another draft, is folded in half. A 830, thought by Jay Leyda (who prepared guide sheets for the Dickinson materials donated to Amherst College by Bingham) to have been a discarded draft to Mrs. Ellen (Richard) Mather, reads in its entirety: "Dear friend, / Accept this / spotless Supper / Though Midsummer"; it is folded in thirds. The contention that Dickinson folded documents before she wrote on them (to avoid folding the writing) is not borne out by this communication: the *S* in "Supper" intersects the top fold.

146. The white dress formerly on display at the Dickinson Homestead has a pocket that measures approximately 13.9 cm wide by 14.7 cm high. These measurements are for the fabric part of the pocket, excluding the trim. Clearly, any draft that measured 29.8 cm in breadth would not have fitted into such a space without folding. Most of Dickinson's letters and poems were written on narrower paper, however, anything from 9 or 10 cm (approximately) to just over 20 cm. Although the smaller range of width measurements would have fitted into the pocket without folding, this depended very much on how close the fit *and* how high the paper was: anything taller than 14 cm would have had to be folded, for example. (A 689, written in ink on unruled paper, measured 10.1 × 16 cm: A 697, written in pencil on unruled paper, measured 9.9 × 15.2 cm; A 706, written in pencil on squared paper, measured 11.8 × 18.5 cm.) And if Dickinson placed papers elsewhere on her person—in her sleeves, for instance—she would have had to fold them. All originals are at Special Collections, Frost Library, Amherst College.

147. Saying, for example, "that it was Susan who swaddled Emily's body for burial" is inaccurate; Bianchi (who is credited as the source of this information) observes that Susan requested a white flannel robe for her sister-in-law, which was prepared for and placed on the body by Eunice R. Powell. It is in Hart and Smith's *Open Me Carefully* that this remark is made and then (incorrectly) attributed to Bianchi in *Face to Face* (p. 265; the source is given as "*FF* 61" on p. 295). What Bianchi quotes there is a letter from Powell: "Your mother came to me when Miss Emily died and said, 'When we come into the world we are wrapped in soft, white flannel, and I think it fitting that we leave that way.' So I made a robe of the softest, finest flannel and personally put it on your Aunt Emily" (*Emily Dickinson Face to Face*, 61). Again, no evidence exists for the claim that throughout "Emily's final illness, Susan is her constant caretaker" (Hart and Smith, *Open Me Carefully*, 263). The note on this document cites Bianchi for its source (*Emily Dickinson Face to Face*, 269), but she makes no such statement at that point, writing instead that as "Emily grew increasingly frail—oftenest in her own room—the

little messages still continued from her to her chosen 'Sister,' confidante, and enduring refuge" (268–69). It was Lavinia who nursed her sister; even Austin seems to have sat with her, occasionally reporting back to Susan on her condition. Mrs. Jameson writes in her diary that "her sister's watchfulness and loving care have kept her a year longer than we supposed possible." In Jay Leyda, *The Years and Hours of Emily Dickinson*, 2: 471. The point is not to deny Susan Dickinson her considerable due but to acknowledge its precise nature, for she continued to care for Dickinson in her own way: a "delicate and strange" supper is acknowledged, and Lavinia is described entering "with the Sea" just when Dickinson was writing "Susan fronts on the Gulf Stream" (L1025 and L1028, 3:894, 895). Another note begins "How lovely every Solace," suggesting gratitude for another act of kindness: the next states "Thank you, dear Sue – for every solace" (L1029 and L1030, 3:895). Hart and Smith quote Bianchi as saying that her mother was "under a shadow of apprehension about Aunt Emily" and that the children "carried the little notes back and forth as we always had." The first seems more accurate than the claim of nursing; the second seems to confirm the impression that the women wrote but did not actually see each other (*Open Me Carefully*, 263).

148. Hart and Smith, *Open Me Carefully*, xxv.

149. Todd herself writes: "Now that Emily's *Poems* are actually out, and my name on the title-page, [Sue and her progeny] rage more than ever. *Why* is a mystery to me for they had the entire box of Emily's mss. over there for nearly two years after she died, and Vinnie's urging them all the time, even with fierce insistence, to do something about getting them published. But Susan is afflicted with an unconquerable laziness, and she kept saying she would, & she would perhaps until Vinnie was wild. At last she announced that she thought nothing had better be done about it, they would never sell – there was not enough money to get them out – the public would not care for them, & so on – in short she gave it up" (Polly Longsworth, *Austin and Mabel: The Amherst Affair & Love Letters of Austin Dickinson and Mabel Loomis Todd* [New York: Farrar, Straus and Giroux, 1984], 294–95). Much of this is suspect, filtered as it was first through Lavinia and then through Todd herself, who as Austin's lover was not likely to side with his wife. For unconquerable laziness, one should—at least in this instance—read an inability or unwillingness to finish the job: Susan Dickinson's doubts seem related to financing and reception rather than doubt as to the merits of the poems. But some of the comments ring true because they overlap with Susan Dickinson's thoughts about a private volume, which would have had to be funded by someone within the family and would have had a limited circulation. Unpleasant and threatening letters from Ned to Lavinia at the time when *Letters* was published (1894) make it clear that Susan *was* furious that Todd was editing Dickinson's works, for a complex array of reasons.

150. Mabel Loomis Todd, ed., *The Letters of Emily Dickinson* (Boston: Roberts Brothers, 1894).

151. The same point can be made of Martha Dickinson Bianchi's inclusion of "Safe in their Alabaster Chambers" in her *Life and Letters of Emily Dickinson*. Rather than attempting to challenge generic boundaries, Bianchi's presentation of the poem's variants in the context of an epistolary exchange between Susan and Emily about the second stanza is an attempt at promoting her mother's importance. The exchange between Emily and Susan is useful and interesting because it challenges the negative views of relations between the two women *and* shows us Dickinson responding to other opinions of her work (and not writing in isolation). But reproducing the poem in this

context does not provide us with an image of generic heterogeneity; rather, it situates the significance of the text within the nexus of relations between two historical individuals.

152. By all accounts, Lavinia Dickinson destroyed Emily's collection of letters, and quickly regretted having done so. And in *Emily Dickinson Face to Face*, Bianchi wrote; "In accordance with Aunt Emily's request, my mother before her own death destroyed such letters as she considered confidential" (176).

153. Ibid., 177. Bianchi meant that Susan was not given the opportunity to do so, but it cuts both ways: Susan survived Emily by several decades and could have written something more substantial had she been motivated to do so.

CHAPTER THREE   *"Because I could not say it – I fixed it in the Verse":*
Dickinson and Samuel Bowles

The chapter title is from A 679, L251, 2:394–95. The letter A followed by a space and number refers to manuscripts at Special Collections, Frost Library, Amherst College.

1. L189, 2:334–35. Johnson and Ward dated the letter to June 1858. This date was revised by Myra Himelhoch and Rebecca Patterson to summer 1859 in "The Dating of Emily Dickinson's Letters to the Bowles Family, 1858–1862," *Emily Dickinson Bulletin* 5, no. 20 (March 1972): 2. Bowles lived from 1826 to 1878; his wife, Mary, from 1827 to 1893. When it became clear toward the end of 1877 that Bowles was dying, Dickinson widened the circle of her correspondents to include Maria Whitney, a distant relation of Mary's whom Bowles had befriended while undergoing a cure at the Hydropathic Institute in Northampton between October and November of 1861. According to Johnson and Ward, Whitney "spent much time with members of the Bowles family in their home and on their travels, especially during the sixties and seventies. Like the Bowleses she saw a good deal of Austin and Susan Dickinson, and thus knew ED." See Thomas H. Johnson and Theodora Ward, eds., *The Letters of Emily Dickinson* (Cambridge: Harvard University Press, Belknap Press, 1958), 3:957. The correspondence with the Bowles circle therefore survived his death. After that, Dickinson continued to write to Mary (seven letters from 1878 to 1881, three in the year of his death), to Samuel Bowles Jr. (twelve letters from 1879 to 1885, five in the final year of her correspondence with him), and to Maria Whitney (seventeen letters from 1877 to 1886, five in the year of Bowles's death).

2. Johnson and Ward list thirty-five letters thought to have been sent to Bowles: 189, 193, 205, 219, 220, 223, 229, 241, 242, 247, 249, 250, 251, 252, 256, 257, 259, 266, 272, 275, 276, 277, 283, 284, 299, 300, 341, 415, 420, 438, 465, 466, 489, 505, 515. Franklin estimates there to have been forty poems; he excludes nine previously believed to have been sent to Bowles. Dickinson occasionally broke her own rule about letters addressed to more than one person, in letters to the Hollands and to the Norcross sisters, Louise and Frances.

3. There are scattered references to commencement in Dickinson's letters to him.

4. The experiment involved trying out "mowing machines" and took place on 30 June 1858. It was reported in the *Republican* the following day. "Annals of the Evergreens," manuscript page 2, Ms Am 1118.95, box 9. My thanks to Alfred Habegger for drawing the significance of this passage to my attention. His extensive and valuable discussion of the Bowles friendship includes this information in *My Wars Are Laid Away in Books* (New York: Random House, 2001), 376.

5. Richard B. Sewall, *The Life of Emily Dickinson* (New York: Farrar, Straus and Giroux, 1974), 468. There are 163 letters, written between 1858 and 1878, the year that Bowles died. To put things into perspective, Dickinson sent about 200 letters to Susan Dickinson and only 35 to Samuel Bowles. Her first letter to him was sent in the summer of 1859; Habegger points out that the generally accepted date for the first draft of the Master letter was spring 1858 (*My Wars Are Laid Away in Books*, 376). All this makes it extremely unlikely that he was "Master" or that she even loved him. The Bowles letter to Dickinson is discussed by Habegger in ibid., 571–72, 731.

6. Theodora Ward's statement is a useful one: "The place that Samuel Bowles filled in the life of Emily Dickinson cannot be clearly defined, though the high value he held for her is plainly seen in all she wrote to him and about him. The nature of their relation remains as elusive as her friendship with Higginson was categorical" (Ward, *The Capsule of the Mind: Chapters in the Life of Emily Dickinson* [Cambridge: Harvard University Press, Belknap Press, 1961], 150). But even then, too much can be—and has been—read into that "elusive" quality.

7. Jay Leyda, *The Years and Hours of Emily Dickinson* (New Haven: Yale University Press, 1960), 2:35. Tellingly, Bowles does not write directly to Dickinson: more often than not, he seems to have sent greetings to her via Susan and Austin Dickinson.

8. George S. Merriam, *The Life and Times of Samuel Bowles* (New York: Century Co., 1885), 2:79. Kate Anthon also referred to "celestial evenings in the library" of the Evergreens. Catharine Scott Turner Anthon to Susan Dickinson, 6 September [?], bMS Am 1118.95 (box 9, Dickinson Family Papers, Houghton Library, Harvard College Library, Harvard University).

9. See Habegger, *My Wars Are Laid Away in Books*, 448, 644–45, 720.

10. L241, 2:382 (October 1861, as Johnson and Ward number and date it), records an occasion when Bowles visited and she felt unable to, or decided not to, see him. L277, 2:419–20, records another. In both cases Dickinson explains that she did not reject him personally. In the first, she was preoccupied and did not want to bother him at a time when (according to her) he needed "light – and air" (because he was recovering from illness). In the second she claims "I gave my part that they might have the more." Both letters reflect the shared or extended nature of the connection: Bowles was someone Dickinson met in a group, with Austin, Susan, and Lavinia Dickinson. The later assertions by Lavinia and Austin that Dickinson's withdrawal was not unusual are borne out in this instance; they both thought that she had behaved badly, not compulsively (in part because this was their first visit from Bowles after his trip to Europe).

11. L223, early August 1860, 2:366. Dickinson mentions "Mrs Fry and Miss Nightingale" and fears that she is now "Mrs Jim Crow." She asks Bowles to forgive his little "Bob o' Lincoln again!" "Mrs Fry" was Elizabeth Gurney Fry, who worked for prison reform: she died in 1845. "Bob o' Lincoln" is a pun on the name of the bobolink, one of Dickinson's favorite birds: in her first (extant) letter to the Bowleses, Dickinson refers to "brooks that sang like Bobolinks," suggesting that what attracted her to them was their interest in nature and music. In this context, the name functions as a typically comic and self-deprecating reference to herself: the "o' Lincoln" may also be a kind of invented Irish name. Jim Crow was a stock figure from nineteenth-century popular culture; a clown in blackface, he represented a caricature of African Americans in minstrel shows from the 1830s onward. Dickinson uses ethnic stereotypes to suggest her own silliness, while reminding Bowles that, like these figures, her buffoonery is an

impersonation manipulated for the purposes of dramatic entertainment. Interestingly, Bowles was politically more progressive on women's issues than Dickinson herself.

12. According to the notes in *Letters*, Stearns was killed at Newbern in North Carolina, on 14 March 1862. Austin Dickinson's stunned repetition of the news, "Frazer is killed," is reported by his sister as "Two or three words of lead," a word that also appears in Fr398, which describes the emotional aftermath of a death (L256, 2:398–99; *Poems*, 1:422). Habegger points out that in the same letter she asks, "And would you be kinder than sometimes – and put the name – on – too," which suggests that he was forwarding mail from her to someone else and disguising the origin of the correspondence by addressing it in his own hand (*My Wars Are Laid Away in Books*, 443): he feels that Austin's name is used as cover throughout the letter. Note that Dickinson spelled Frazar with an *e* ("Frazer").

13. L284, 2:426.

14. Southampton, 21[?] October 1861. Quoted in Leyda, *Years and Hours of Emily Dickinson*, 2:35.

15. L259, 2:402, is dated early April 1862 by Johnson and Ward. Himelhoch places it more convincingly at the end of March, when Bowles had canceled another visit and before Susan and Austin Dickinson were believed to have visited him in the first week of April (Himelhoch, "The Dating of Emily Dickinson's Letters," 12–13). This portion of the letter corresponds to A 681a in the original (the third page of four, at Special Collections, Frost Library, Amherst College). There are no irregular spaces that would suggest paragraphs, except after "hand –," where the quotation ends; it is followed by 6 cm of space and clearly marks the end of a paragraph.

16. See L193, 2:339.

17. Susan Dickinson, to Higginson, 4 January 1891, quoted in Millicent Todd Bingham, *Ancestors' Brocades: The Literary Début of Emily Dickinson* (New York: Harper and Brothers, 1945), 92.

18. L247, 2:390; L189, 2:334; L205, 2:352.

19. Johnson and Ward supply a list of letters organized by recipient and year; Bowles is in *Letters*, 3:961. Correcting the list on the basis of Habegger's summary (in *My Wars Are Laid Away in Books*, 644–45), one emerges with the following chronology: 189, 193, 205 (1859); 223 (1860); 219, 220, 229, 241, 242, 250, 251, 252, 299, 300 (1861); 247, 249, 256, 257, 259, 266, 272, 275, 276, 277, 283 (1862); 284 (1863); 415, 420, 465 (1874); 438 (1875); 466 (1876); 489, 505, 515 (1877). L341 (1870) was probably not sent.

20. The fact that L341 was not sent does not fully disqualify it from being a letter, of course. The impulse to write to Bowles was still there in that year.

21. Critics do not always confine themselves to the individual relationship between Bowles and Dickinson for possible answers to these questions. According to Cynthia Griffin Wolff there were strains between the Bowles and Dickinson *families* because Mary was jealous of Samuel's friendship with Susan Dickinson. However, Bowles's letter to his daughter Sallie in November 1869 gives no hint of any rift: "I ran up to Amherst Friday afternoon via Northampton and back Saturday morning, making a pleasant little visit with the Dickinsons." Cynthia Griffin Wolff, *Emily Dickinson* (New York: Alfred A. Knopf, 1986), 392; Merriam, *The Life and Times of Samuel Bowles*, 2: 150.

22. Himelhoch and Patterson, "The Dating of Emily Dickinson's Letters," 7–8.

23. A 692; L219, 2:363; Fr227A 1:251. The layout here is *not* based on the manu-

script, except with regard to punctuation and capitalization, which differ between Franklin and Johnson. Franklin records line division correctly as occurring at line 1 after "wrestled," line 3 after "smiling," line 5 after "passing," and line 7 after "still."

24. L216, 2:361.

25. Ms Am 1118.5 (B162); L306, 2:441. About March 1865. Johnson and Ward argue that "tropes involving water are especially predominant in messages written during the period that ED was under treatment for her eyes." They also correctly identify the capital in the sequence "dear, If I."

26. L207, 2:354.

27. The dating is from Himelhoch and Patterson, "The Dating of Emily Dickinson's Letters," 2, and Habegger, *My Wars Are Laid Away in Books*, 644. Johnson and Ward had dated the letter to the same year, but from early April.

28. A 675, L247, 2:390. But there are other manuscript letters made of one sheet folded to make two leaves (A 691, A 698, and A 707, for example), where the second page is left blank and Dickinson resumes writing on the third, without this being remarkable. So it may well be that Dickinson played with the idea that Bowles would mistake the unused page for indifference on her part and made more of it than we should (as an example of a more extensive and strategic approach to visual organization).

29. A 689. Written in ink on unruled paper, measuring 10.1 × 16 cm, the poem was folded as for a recipient, but not sent. Franklin makes two errors in his transcription: he mistakes a *c* for a *w* in "What *c*ould it hinder so" (emphasis added) and inserts a dash between "to" and "say?" The dash is in fact the impression of another dash made on the other side of the paper—the second one in the sequence "Tell Him – no – you." This dash is located 0.8 cm from the top of the page, and approximately 2.05 cm from the right edge of the paper.

30. *The Young Lady's Own Book: A Manual of Intellectual Improvement and Moral Development* (Philadelphia: John Locken, 1841), 111.

31. The quotation from Theodora Ward reads in full: "The time and place in which [Samuel Bowles] lived favored such relations, for women of his class were beginning to assert their individuality, and at the same time were protected by the accepted view that human beings were made of separate elements that could be designated as 'carnal' and 'spiritual.' Women of the type who interested him—intellectual, articulate, yet possessing feminine charm—simply lived above suspicion. Even a little light flirtation was permissible, since the absolute barriers were recognized on both sides." See Ward, *Capsule of the Mind*, 147.

32. Judith Farr, *The Passion of Emily Dickinson* (Cambridge: Harvard University Press, 1992), 188.

33. Merriam, *Life and Times of Samuel Bowles*, 1:210.

34. L189, 2:334; Merriam, *Life and Times of Samuel Bowles*, 2:79.

35. Himelhoch and Patterson, "The Dating of Emily Dickinson's Letters," 8. The *Emily Dickinson Bulletin*, edited and published by Frederick L. Morey, is not to be confused with the *Bulletin* of the Emily Dickinson International Society. Habegger confirms the dating independently, in *My Wars Are Laid Away in Books*, appendix 5, 644.

36. L223, 2:366; L189, 2:334. See also Martha Nell Smith, *Rowing in Eden: Rereading Emily Dickinson* (Austin: University of Texas Press, 1992), who argues that the Master letters may have been sent to Susan Dickinson or that at the least Dickinson

self-consciously adopted the culturally constructed position of a "woman" toward another person whom she genders as a "man."

37. In L189, he and Mary are "Friends" (2:334); in 193, 219, 220, 223, 242, 252, 257, 272, 299, and 505 he is "Mr Bowles"; in 205 he is "Friend" and "Sir" (2:351); in 241 he is "Swiveller"; in 229, 247, 249, 251, 256, 259, 266, 275, 276, 277, 300, 416, 420, 438, 489, and 515 he is "friend."

38. Himelhoch and Patterson, "The Dating of Emily Dickinson's Letters," 2.

39. A 645; L189, 2:334–35. Written on one sheet, folded to make two leaves. The paper measures approximately 10 cm in width and 16 cm in height and is embossed "PARIS".

40. The phrase "You should find us all at the gate" in this letter (to take one instance of a refrain in the letters to Bowles) is repeated in L247, where she writes, "Only three weeks more to wait at the Gate!" Dickinson self-consciously pictures herself in the terms of sentimental domesticity, though there is no reason to doubt the sincerity of her feelings.

41. The words are taken from A 697 (Fr949A, 2:869).

42. L193, 2:338 ("estate" and "gold"); L205, 2:352, and L438, 2:540 ("gems").

43. L275, 2:418; L415, 2:527.

44. In "Annals of the Evergreens," manuscript page 5, Susan Dickinson reports Bowles as saying, "You know I found the Brownings through you." And she described him as just about to sail for Europe on his first trip, where "the only books I take, are the Bible and Aurora Leigh" (Ms Am 1118.95, box 9).

45. For the Habegger reference, see *My Wars Are Laid Away in Books*, 385–86. Jasper is also a precious stone (a red, yellow, or brown quartz). There may also be a reference to the character from Dickens's unfinished *Edwin Drood* (1870); the reference to the Rose at the beginning of the letter may have associations with Rosa Budd, the principal female character in the novel. Bowles must also have known his scripture in ways that contemporary readers do not: Cephas was the name given to the apostle Peter by Jesus. It means "rock": the name "Peter" derives from the Latin "petra." The New Testament character Apollos was from Alexandria in Egypt. About A.D. 56 he came to Ephesus, where he began to teach in the synagogue "the things concerning Jesus, being acquainted only with the baptism of John." See Acts 18:24–28. In Corinth, he taught the Bible and was a skilled preacher; a schism developed in the church between those who followed him and those who followed Paul. See 1 Corinthians 16:12. The quotation seems to be a shorthand way of referring to contemporaneous theological disputes. The final biblical allusion is from 1 Corinthians 3:21–22: "Therefore let no man glory in men. For all things are yours."

46. L241, 2:382. Or, to put it another way, they relate mostly through books and letters or as performative characters in a fiction of their own making. The marchioness is a devoted carer who saves Swiveller's life; in many letters, Dickinson acts as a kind of therapist, a verbal nurse, for a man who was often ill.

47. L242, 2:382–83; in Shakespeare's play, Helena pursues Bertram, and devises a plan that traps him into marrying her. L249, 2:393; "The Prisoner of Chillon" by George Gordon Byron, Lord Byron, first appeared in 1816 and was based on events in the life of François Bonivard (1493–1570), who was imprisoned underground in the castle of Chillon (Switzerland) from 1532 until he was released in 1536. L275, 2:418; Henry Howard, Earl of Surrey, was born in 1517, in Hunsdon, Hertfordshire, and was executed for alleged treason on 13 January 1547 in London; together with Sir Thomas

Wyatt (1503–42), a self-acknowledged influence, he is credited with having introduced and translated forms of Italian poetry which would become very important in English writing. L300, 2:437–38; Dickinson is offering Bowles a copy of Browning's *Dramatis Personae*. He had turned down a copy of the Brontë sisters' poems (offered in L299).

48. L205, 2:351–52; *The Book of Common Prayer* (Cambridge: Cambridge University Press, 1961), 29. The phrase derives from the following lines: "He [Jesus Christ] suffered and the third day he rose again, and ascended into heaven. And he shall come again to judge both the quick and the dead." In later translations, the line reads as "the living and the dead." The phrase is also mentioned in Acts 10:42 and 1 Peter 4:5.

49. L241, 2:382, and L261, 2:404. There is also a reference to "palms" in L196 (2: 342), which is characteristically whimsical, but the "Palm" in L242 (2:383) is much more serious, even mystical: the inference seems to be that wrens too will enter Heaven, but Dickinson referred to herself as "small, like the Wren" (L268, 2:411). The reference to the Virgin Mary at the end is typical of Dickinson's idolatry with regard to friends: Mary becomes a kind of quasi-sacred mother figure, partly because she was often pregnant. Such references show that Dickinson was often more sensitive to other people's problems than she is often given credit for.

50. This is not a phenomenon limited to the Bowles correspondence. A manuscript note to Susan Phelps, dated 1860, is a random example of the same feature and looked as follows: "When thou goest through / the Waters, I will / go with thee / Emilie –." A.N.S., 8 May 1860, Mortimer Rare Book Room, William Allan Neilson Library, Smith College.

51. Strangely, however, this aspect of manuscript inscription has not received any attention. In A 688, the manuscript of Fr600B ("Her – 'last Poems' "), the quotation marks around "last Poems" both slant in the same direction (from bottom left to top right). And in A 691, the manuscript in which Fr193A (" 'Speech' – is a prank of *Parliament*") is embedded, both *"Speech"* and *"Tears"* have quotation marks that run in the same direction (the quotation marks are missing from Franklin's edition: see *Poems*, 1: 226–27). I mention this because manuscript critics do not in practice behave as if all the material details of a manuscript are significant, which is to say that they, too, operate with the assumption that some aspects are accidental or idiosyncratic and some are not. What one would like to know is the principle that allows readers to ascribe meaning to a dash that is acutely angled but to ignore another punctuation sign that seems equally unconventional.

52. Other examples of quotation marks that both slant in the same direction are included in A 649 (L205), A 660 (Fr202A), A 671 (L241), A 674 (Fr225A), A 667 (L229), A 678 (Fr194A), A 703 (L420), and A 796 (Fr208A)—and the list is not exhaustive. But in A 709 (L515), the quotation marks for "Theophilus" both slant upper left to lower right, while the ones on "Cephas" are both the opposite, lower left to upper right. In the same letter, Dickinson puts conventional quotation marks around "Rascal" on the last leaf. And in A 680 (L256), Dickinson twice repeats the phrase "Frazer is killed": the first is inscribed conventionally, the second with only a closing quotation mark. Such casual variation from the norm should make us hesitate about assigning meaning to variation in the inscription of other marks, such as the dash. Indeed, in A 680a (L256), Dickinson begins the third row with, "He cares for you – when." The dash is written slightly in front of and below the "when," even though it is clear that Dickinson could have inscribed it normally and then squeezed "when" in on the same row or moved it to the next. Since no semantic imperative was at work

here, one guesses that the dash might have been added later, during a first reading of the freshly composed letter, when "you" and "when" had already been placed too close together for a clear dash to be inserted between them. And one therefore wonders how many of Dickinson's other errant dashes (those which are slanted, curtailed, or placed at unusual positions with relation to the lettering elsewhere on the paper) similarly postdate the first writing of a poem or letter.

53. Smith, *Rowing in Eden*, 65. Smith has consistently denied that she imputed a mimetic intent to Dickinson's lettering, and a later reference includes the observation that letters shaped to look like waves have an antimimetic and comic purpose (85). But for her point to be conceded, the lettering still has to be seen as crafted in such a way as to resemble waves (which *then* becomes a joke about the absurd lengths to which mimetic discourse goes in an effort to describe its subject).

54. A 796; L252, 2:395; Fr208A, 1:239. About early 1861. "Whippowil" (row 2), "Whose" (row 4), "Whose" (row 6), and "Whose" (row 12) in the original are all written with the curved uppercase *W* that Smith refers to. The *W* in the second row, first page, of A 680 (L256) is similarly described. The letters are unremarkable by Dickinson's own standards, in other words, and should not be deemed a significant part of a poem or letter's formal apparatus. Theodora Ward thought that the capital *W* was "rounded at the base until . . . late January 1875, when the first pointed W appears" (*Emily Dickinson's Letters to Dr. and Mrs. Josiah Gilbert Holland*, 242).

55. A 698, Fr803A, 2:758; A 646, L193, 2:338–39; A 660, L220, 2:364; A 671, L241, 2:382; A 674, Fr255A, 1:275; A 675, L247, 2:390; A 678, Fr194A, 1:228; A 679, L251, 2:394–95; A 680, L256, 2:398–99; A 681, L259, 2:402; A 691, L252, 2:395; A 709, L515, 2:589. All references are to the manuscript originals.

56. A 704, L438, 2:540. All references are to the manuscript original. (The "Peach – before the time" compliment is part of a deft manipulation of seasonal imagery in the correspondence with Bowles. "We reckon – your coming by the Fruit" is another example [L272, 2:416]). See the reference in the previous chapter to "Rare to the Rare," where there are instances of closed and open minuscule *e* shapes in a note to Susan.

57. A 706, L489, 2:574. All references are to the manuscript original. As Ward points out, Dickinson also wrote other letters differently within the same period or even the same document. See her very useful appendix D in *Emily Dickinson's Letters to Dr. and Mrs. Josiah Gilbert Holland*, 239–44.

58. For instance, in Sarah Orne Jewett's Commonplace Book (Ms Am 1743.26 [1] at the Houghton Library, Harvard University), written in the author's own hand, she switches back and forth between the closed *e* and the open ε, though both represent the lowercase *e*. For instance, she writes "Selections from the standard POETS" and "Now John is herε."

59. A 182, Fr1507, 3:1319. All references are to the manuscript original.

60. A 184. All references are to the manuscript original. The draft is of "Ferocious as a Bee without a wing" (Fr1492, 3:1309).

61. A 179, Fr1530, 3:1339. All references are to the manuscript original. In A 182, Dickinson writes "demand" in the final row with an ascender that slopes slightly to the right in the first *d* and then an ascender that curves to the left in the final *d*.

62. Smith, *Rowing in Eden*, 85. The full quotation is: "I contend that her lines neither accidentally spill over (as one might contend for 'Assassin hid in our Apart- / ment') or conform to nineteenth-century print conventions, nor does her handwriting

uncontrollably sprawl." It is not clear from this if Smith is denying or arguing for the thesis that the split "Apartment" was deliberate.

63. A 677, L300, 2:437; A 680, L256, 2:398; A 685, L275, 2:418; A 671, L241, 2: 382. All references are to the manuscript original.

64. A 687, Fr608A, 2:604. All references are to the manuscript original.

65. L272, 2:416.

66. A 684. All references are to the manuscript original.

67. The date is confirmed by Himelhoch and Patterson, "The Dating of Emily Dickinson's Letters," 13.

68. L189, 2:334; L205, 2:351–52.

69. A 675, L247, 2:390. All references are to the manuscript original.

70. A 660, L220, 2:364. Johnson dates the document to 1860; Franklin, who identifies it as Fr202A (1:234), dates it to 1861.

71. Johnson, *Poems* (1955), 1:134, Franklin, *Poems* (1998), 1:234.

72. A 677; L229, 2:371; Fr272A, 1:290. The verb "wore" seems unusual and may be "were," but the vowel is shaped like an *o* and not an *e*, and no attempt has been made to alter it.

73. L300, 2:438.

74. Ibid., 2:437–38. The new date is Habegger's (*My Wars Are Laid Away in Books*, 645).

75. Johnson follows "sleigh" with a period, though it seems more like a dash (L229, 2:371). On the other hand, Johnson correctly transcribes "Liquors": though the initial capital is unmistakable, Franklin's edition of the poems represents it as "liquors" (Fr272, 2:290).

76. According to Sewall, "In the winter or early Spring of 1861, an arduous trip to Amherst by sleigh during a heavy snowstorm left Bowles with a chill and the severe sciatica that sent him to Dr. Denniston's in Northampton that fall." (Sciatica is a neuralgia of the hip and thigh; also pain in the sciatic nerve, the largest in the human body, from the pelvis to the thigh.) This is the first of many references to illness: despite her reported satire of Florence Nightingale elsewhere, Dickinson could play the soothing nurse when she felt she needed to (Sewall, *Life of Emily Dickinson*, 481). Leyda refers to the same incident (*Years and Hours*, 2:25). Apart from being ill often, Bowles had a passion for fast horses, one that he shared with Austin Dickinson: "He had no eye for the 'points' of a horse; he knew when an animal served his turn, and that was all he cared for. He did not establish any personal understanding with his steed, but handled it according to his mood. 'He was fonder of reckless driving,' said William Collins, 'than any man I ever knew.' Not seldom he would come to the stable of an afternoon, jaded and silent, take a good horse with William the driver, and speed over the dozen miles of pleasant country road to Mount Vision, a spot on the western slope of the Wilbraham hills, commanding a very wide and noble prospect. Scarcely a word would be said, till, stopping on the brow of the hill, and having looked for a few minutes over the calm uplifting scene, he would say to his appreciative companion, 'William, that's good!'—then quietly jog home" (Merriam, *Life and Times of Samuel Bowles*, 78).

77. A 698; Fr803A, 2:758. The poem is not included in Johnson and Ward's *Letters*.

78. Or to put it another way, understanding the nature of the reference to Herschel (the surname of two astronomers, William and John, the first of whom discovered Uranus) or to Mercury is more relevant to understanding the poem than knowing that

it was sent to Bowles. Biographers would disagree, of course: when dealing with a poet who did not publish in the conventional sense, autobiographical considerations may come into play as we interpret. For such an approach to Fr803A, see Habegger, *My Wars Are Laid Away in Books*, 449. Habegger's redating of the letters leads him to believe that Dickinson stopped writing to Bowles for about a decade, further weakening the argument that he could have been the Master.

79. The poems are (with F for fascicle, S for set): Fr9 (F1); Fr60 (F2); Fr97 (F5); Fr187 (F36); Fr202, Fr208, Fr209, and Fr 253 (F10); Fr226, Fr227, Fr230, and Fr237 (F9); Fr255 and Fr258 (F11); Fr197 (F12); Fr374 (F18); Fr478 (F22); Fr608 (F26); Fr635 (F31); Fr803 (S5); Fr804 (S6a); Fr949 (S7); and Fr1383 (S14).

80. Although she circulated a great many poems during her lifetime and asked occasional advice of Susan Dickinson and Higginson, there is no record of her having distributed or asked similar advice about *sequences* of poems. Finally, although there is ample evidence of Dickinson's having revised individual poems in her possession, often leaving alternative readings, no such evidence exists of poems regularly being sent with variants or extensive fascicle revision, with significant adjustments being made to the order and contents of a fascicle.

81. A 697; Fr949A, 2:869. The document is not in *Letters*. It is written in pencil on unruled paper measuring 9.9 × 15.2 cm, embossed with an oval sign inscribed "PARIS".

82. Mabel Loomis Todd, *The Letters of Emily Dickinson* (Boston: Roberts Brothers, 1894), 1: 208. Todd uses capitals only at the start of each line, omits the comma after "comes" and "departs," and replaces the dash after "Light" and "Freight" with a period. She changes " 'Tis Heavy, and 'tis Light" to " 'T is heavy, and 't is light." Martha Dickinson Bianchi, *The Life and Letters of Emily Dickinson* (Boston: Houghton Mifflin, 1924), 236. Bianchi uses capitals only at the start of each line, omits the commas after "comes" and "departs," and replaces the dash after "Light" and "Freight" with a period. Bianchi's version, in other words, seems to be lifted from Todd's and does not necessarily or independently corroborate Todd's choices.

83. Set 7, A 86-7/8 (Special Collections, Frost Library, Amherst College); Fr949B, 2:870.

84. Ms Am 1118.3 (263); L341, 2:560: Fr1173A, 2:1015–16. About 1870.

85. Interestingly, the note may never have been sent, for it was found among Dickinson's papers after her death; either that or it was a draft, or Bowles received it and forgot to bring it with him after he left the Evergreens. Of course, if it *was* unsent, then to some extent the poem's last lines and the history of its nontransmission coincide: the speaker could or would not express her emotions for this man, and the poet refused to send him poems. Again, there may be no strictly psychological reason for the speaker's reluctance to join the chorus of praise. Certain cultural and social imperatives might have prevented an unmarried woman from expressing love or admiration for a married man: one of them may have been precisely that her *admiration might have been mistaken for love*. In addition, it is not simply the case that the speaker is *unable* to express her feelings for the subject: it may be that she *will* not, because her feelings toward him are more complicated, even ambivalent.

86. A 709; Fr1432B, 3:1252; L515, 2:589–90.

87. In the *Boston Sunday Globe*, 12 January 1930, 41. The note enclosed the quotation, "I, Jesus, send mine angel." Graves was the daughter of John L. Graves, a cousin of the Dickinson girls.

88. According to Sewall, "Theophilus" refers to Theophilus Parsons (*Life of Emily*

Dickinson, 510). In the Harvard list of Dickinson family books is a *Memoir of Theophilus Parsons* (Boston: Ticknor and Fields, 1859), by his son, also Theophilus Parsons; the book has the signatures of Edward and Lavinia Dickinson. Theophilus Parsons (Junior) was born 17 May 1797 and died on 26 January 1882. A professor at Harvard Law School, he wrote on the constitutionality of the South's secession and penned memoirs both of himself and of his father, as well as essays on religion. Crucially, he was one of Austin's teachers at Harvard Law School (see *My Wars Are Laid Away in Books*, 695). The "Junius" refers to *The Letters of Junius* (New York: Leavitt & Company, 1851). Junius was reputed to be Sir Philip Francis (1740–1818), author of a series of political letters that appeared in London's *Public Advertiser* newspaper between 1769 and 1771. These letters, from an insider, caused great uproar and consternation within the English government and led to their publisher, Henry Sampson Woodfall (a former schoolfellow of Francis's), being tried for sedition. James Boswell mentions "Junius" several times in his biography of Johnson (Boswell, *The Life of Samuel Johnson* [London: Hutchinson & Co, 1906], 333, 426). Woodfall brought out a separate edition of the letters in 1772, and his son George, a three-volume edition in 1812. The Dickinson edition is signed with a presentation from Edward to Austin, 16 April 1859. It was often the custom in the nineteenth century to give away some of the deceased's belongings to close friends and family, to preserve his memory. *The Dictionary of National Biography: From the Earliest Times to 1900* (Oxford: Oxford University Press, 1913), 611–620.

89. A 706, A 706a, "Dear friend, You have / the most / triumphant Face / out of / Paradise – / probably because / you are there / constantly," includes the poem "Ourselves – we do inter – with sweet derision" (Fr1449, 3:1267). Written on squared paper (measuring approximately 11.8 × 18.5 cm), in pencil, it averages about two words per row: it might therefore seem difficult to say where the letter ends and the poem begins. The words are not inscribed cursively, and large spaces occur between the words, which in themselves take up a large amount of room. For instance, in the sequence "the Dust – who," "the" measures 1.3 cm, "Dust" 3.4 cm, and "who" 1.8 cm: the spaces between them come to about 3.7 cm. Clearly, there is little room for maneuver. Nonetheless, when the poem begins, Dickinson writes "Ourselves" 1.6 cm in from the left edge of the paper; immediately after "Religion" follows a massive and (in this document) unprecedented interval of 7 cm, corresponding to the end of a metrical line. This is not a paragraph closure, because "the Balm of that Religion" is clearly completed by "That doubts – as fervently as it believes" (L489, 2:574). Once more, even in cramped conditions, spaces appear that do not correspond to prose writing.

90. A 679; L251, 2:394–95; Fr187B, 1:221–22. All references are to the manuscript original.

CHAPTER FOUR *The Way I read a Letter's – this": Dickinson and Genre*

Epigraphs: Marta L. Werner, *Emily Dickinson's Open Folios: Scenes of Reading, Surfaces of Writing* (Ann Arbor: University of Michigan Press, 1995), 35; Noah Webster, *An American Dictionary of the English Language* (Amherst: J. S. and C. Adams, 1844), 2:49, 316.

1. Carpenter & Morehouse, *The History of the Town of Amherst, Massachusetts* (Amherst: Carpenter & Morehouse, 1896), 332.

2. General Services Administration of the National Archives and Records, Wash-

ington, D.C., to Mr. Charles Green, librarian of the Jones Library, 28 January 1955, in Folder "Amherst—Postmasters," in Special Collections, Jones Library, Amherst. The postmasters were James Watson, 1 January 1806; Joseph Watson, 1 January 1807; Rufus Kellogg, 21 November 1809; Jay White, 26 April 1824; Hezekiah W. Strong, 20 April 1825; Samuel C. Carter, 30 March 1842; Seth Nims, 9 May 1845; Samuel C. Carter, 29 May 1849; Seth Nims, 3 June 1853; Lucius M. Boltwood, 17 June 1861; Jairus M. Skinner, 15 August 1874; John Jameson, 20 December 1876; Orson G. Couch, 30 March 1885; Byron H. Williams, 9 August 1898. The letter in which Nims is referred to is L16, 21 October 1847, 1:48–49: "Well, I dreamed a dream & Lo!!! Father had failed & mother said that 'our rye field which she & I planted, was mortgaged to Seth Nims.' I hope it is not true but do write soon & tell me for you know 'I should expire with mortification' to have our rye field mortgaged, to say nothing of it's falling into the merciless hands of a loco!!!" A "loco-foco" was a Massachusetts Whig term for a Democrat; Nims was postmaster during the presidencies of Polk (1845–49), Pierce, and Buchanan (1853–61).

3. Alfred Habegger, *My Wars Are Laid Away in Books* (New York: Random House, 2001), 20–21.

4. Carpenter & Morehouse, *History of the Town of Amherst*, 332.

5. Letter from Seth Nims, microfilm, Special Collections, Jones Library, Amherst. Quotation from Carpenter & Morehouse, *History of the Town of Amherst*, 333.

6. L130, to Austin Dickinson, 1 July 1853. In Thomas H. Johnson and Theodora Ward, eds., *The Letters of Emily Dickinson* (Cambridge: Harvard University Press, Belknap Press, 1958), 1:260. Henceforth, all references prefixed by L are to letters in this edition.

7. Folder on "Amherst – Post Office, List of box-holders, 1861," Special Collections, Jones Library, Amherst. Daniel Lombardo identifies Dickinson's box number as 207, but his source is slightly later (between 1862 and 1866); box numbers clearly must have changed. See *Tales of Amherst: A Look Back* (Amherst: Jones Library, 1986), 100–102.

8. Cynthia MacKenzie, ed., *Concordance to the Letters of Emily Dickinson* (Boulder: University Press of Colorado, 2000), 408–11.

9. "Special Collections Finding Aid: Emily Dickinson," in Special Collections, Jones Library, Amherst.

10. The manuscripts are assigned numbers: 80–95 correspond to fascicles; 96–540 are unbound poems and fragments; 541–1012 are letters, drafts, and prose fragments.

11. Thomas H. Johnson, *The Poems of Emily Dickinson* (Cambridge: Harvard University Press, Belknap Press, 1955), 2:711–13; Johnson and Ward, *Letters*, 2:498–99. Henceforth, all references prefixed by J are to poems in the Johnson edition of the poems.

12. L972, 3:864; William Shurr, *New Poems of Emily Dickinson* (Chapel Hill: University of North Carolina Press, 1993), 35.

13. Ellen Louise Hart, "The Elizabeth Whitney Putnam Manuscripts and New Strategies for Editing Emily Dickinson's Letters," *Emily Dickinson Journal* 4, no. 1 (1995): 44–74.

14. L247, 2:390.

15. L252, 2:395, and A 691; L505, 2:584, and A 707; Fr 600, 2:597, and A 688. Henceforth, all references prefixed by A are to manuscript originals at Special Collections, Frost Library, Amherst College; all references prefixed by Fr are to poems in

Ralph W. Franklin, ed., *The Poems of Emily Dickinson* (Cambridge: Harvard University Press, Belknap Press, 1998).

16. L972, to T. W. Higginson, February 1885, 3:863–64.

17. One of the first to publish correspondence according to recipient was Theodora Ward, *Letters to Dr. and Mrs. Josiah Gilbert Holland* (Cambridge: Harvard University Press, 1951). Ward was the granddaughter of the Hollands. Ralph W. Franklin also released *The Master Letters of Emily Dickinson* (Amherst: Amherst College Press, 1986). Susan Dickinson always claimed that her edition would have included poems and letters; in that sense, Smith and Hart are fulfilling her promise.

18. Ms Am 1093 (111), Department of Rare Books and Manuscripts, Boston Public Library.

19. Hart and Smith include such details in *Open Me Carefully*. But the size of the paper is not mentioned, which is the crucial omission.

20. L790, 3 December 1882, 3:753; Shurr, *New Poems of Emily Dickinson*, 58.

21. Marta L. Werner, *Emily Dickinson's Open Folios: Scenes of Reading, Surfaces of Writing* (Ann Arbor: University of Michigan Press, 1995). The pages in this part of Werner's book are not numbered; they correspond to A 749c, A 749d, and A 749e, in the section entitled "Open Folios: An Experimental Edition of Emily Dickinson's Drafts and Fragments."

22. Ibid., 55.

23. Ibid., 24 (figure 15).

24. An unfortunate consequence of such an emphasis on the visual is that a reader who is blind would be unable to register some of the foremost aspects of the poem's apparatus of meaning. (As technology advances, of course, such side effects may be overcome.)

25. Hart and Smith, *Open Me Carefully*, xxv.

26. Ibid., 174.

27. To recap: "A narrow fellow in the grass" exists in three copies, one lost. The earliest of these, Fr1096B in Franklin's edition of the poems, is estimated as having been recorded around 1865 and was collected in a booklet of the poet's own making. A later version (Fr1096C), transcribed around 1872, was again sent to Susan, perhaps to replace the first one or to clear up any misunderstanding about the punctuation (2: 953).

28. Poetry and prose are traditionally divided on the basis of, first, what is written about and, second, how they are written. In other words, they are thought to have different subject matters or themes, and poetry is linguistically denser and more compressed than prose. Such distinctions are difficult to sustain in Dickinson's work.

29. A 686, "Dear friend / I cannot see you," is L276, 2:419; A 687, "So glad we are," is Fr608A, 2:604–05.

30. All the spaces coincide with the end of longer metrical sequences—lines of iambic tetrameter, in this instance.

31. Shurr, *New Poems of Emily Dickinson*, 2.

32. Jane Austen, *Jane Austen's Letters*, ed. Deirdre Le Faye (Oxford: Oxford University Press, 1995), 68.

33. L468, 2:558; Ms D56 7, Special Collections, Frost Library, Amherst College.

34. Demetrius, *On Style*, ed. and trans. W. Rhys Roberts (Cambridge: Cambridge University Press, 1902), sections 223–24.

35. L177, 2:315; Ms Am 1118.4 (L1), Houghton Library, Harvard College Li-

brary, Harvard University. Johnson and Ward omit Dickinson's date ("Sabbath Day"). In demanding communications from others, Dickinson often specified that she sought "a long letter" rather than just a letter (interestingly, Jane Austen seems to have complained that letters from men differed from those by women in being too short).

36. L190, 2:335–36. Johnson and Ward do not include Dickinson's date ("Friday night"): my estimate includes this and the signature, and is based on the manuscript original in Special Collections, Jones Library, Amherst.

37. L310, 2:444; Ms Am 1118.5 (B1). The paper is embossed with a Roman female head. The minuscule *e* is open (ε), and the dash after "Emily" slants upward from lower left to upper right—but so too does the symbol above the *i* in the name ("Emíly"). Henceforth, all references prefixed by Ms Am are to originals at Houghton Library, Harvard College Library, Harvard University, unless otherwise indicated.

38. L392, 2:508; Ms Am 1118.5 (B150). The letter is written in pen, on paper that is unruled, folded into thirds, and watermarked "A Pirie & Sons / 1870." Johnson and Ward fail to assign a paragraph after "which went," though the 7.6 cm of space clearly demands it. The rest of the page continues (after the 5 cm of space subsequent to "one"): "Vinnie drank / your Coffee / and has looked / like you / since, which / is nearly a [page break] comfort." That wonderfully dry observation of personal social ritual with named individuals is rare in Dickinson's poetry. The dash after "Emily" slants downward from upper left to lower right, but, again, so does the symbol above the *i* in the name ("Emìly").

39. L584, 2:631; Ms Am 1118.5 (B50). The paper measures 12.8 × 11.8 cm, and the note is written in pencil on paper that is not ruled, is folded in half, and bears the watermark "[Wes]ton's [Li]nen 76." Again, the dash after "Emily" slants upward from lower left to upper right, as does the symbol above the *i* in the name ("Emíly"). Johnson and Ward mistakenly represent "contest" as "Contest." The word "capitulates" is followed by a dash in this representation, but it may very well be a period.

40. L869, 3:800; Ms Am 1118.4 (L50). The paper is folded in thirds, is unruled, and has a watermarked date (1881). The writing, in pencil, reads: "Perhaps the / dear, grieved / Heart would / open to a / flower, which / blesses unre- / quested, and / serves without / a Sound – / Emily –."

41. Note that the dash which closes this note is curved (~). But the envelope that accompanies the note has the same dash: it reads "Mrs Cooper~." The variety of dashes written on envelopes is compelling evidence that such diversity elsewhere is not a significant or signifying element of Dickinson's formal apparatus.

42. The definition of "verse-epistle" is taken from *The New Princeton Encyclopedia of Poetry and Poetics*, ed. Alex Preminger and T. V. F. Brogan (Princeton, N.J.: Princeton University Press, 1993), 1351. It may well be that Susan Dickinson was thinking of the tradition of the verse-epistle when she coined her term "letter-poem."

43. Austen's letter-poem (to Francis Austen, 26 *July* 1809) begins, "My dearest Frank, I wish you joy / Of Mary's safety with a Boy, / Whose birth has given little pain / Compared with that of Mary Jane." In *Jane Austen's Letters to Her Sister Cassandra and Others*, ed. R. W. Chapman (Oxford: Oxford University Press, 1952), 264–66. Holmes's begins, "Yes, write, if you want to, there's nothing like trying; / Who knows what a treasure your casket may hold? / I'll show you that rhyming's as easy as lying, / If you'll listen to me while the art I unfold." Holmes, "A Familiar Letter," <http://www.gutenberg.net/etext05/ohp0810.txt> (accessed 4 October 2001).

44. A 249, for example, written on a fragment of stationery watermarked "F. H. D.

& Co." includes "immured in Heaven – what a Cell," "Undertow of the Organ," and "With thanks for my health I send you Anthony's Orchard" on one side, separated by single horizontal strokes, and "Lad of Athens" on the back: the first is a draft line from Fr1628, the second and third parts of notes, and the fourth an early version of Fr1606.

45. Brita Lindberg-Seyersted, *The Voice of the Poet: Aspects of Style in the Poetry of Emily Dickinson* (Cambridge: Harvard University Press, 1968), 29.

46. Fr519, 1:527–28.

47. Ms Am 1093 (111), Boston Public Library, Rare Books and Manuscripts. Fr1624B, 3:1424.

48. Ms Am 1118.5 (B79); L868, 3:799; Fr1624A, 3:1423–24.

49. The first draft is A 186; the paper is folded in quarters. Franklin records this draft as Fr1244, 2:1076; Johnson and Ward define it as "raw material for a poem," but classify it as a prose fragment (henceforth referred to as PF), PF75, 3:923. The second draft is PF99, 3:926. "Paradise is no Journey" is misprinted as "Paradise *in* no Journey" (emphasis added).

50. Franklin, *Poems*, 2:1076.

51. Generic suspension depends to a greater or lesser extent on there being an audience capable of having its expectations unsettled. But there is no evidence that Dickinson's readers had their assumptions about generic discreteness unsettled in the least: they seem to have coped remarkably well.

52. The description, curiously, is from *Letters*, though the editors go on to categorize this as a prose fragment (3:923).

53. A 675a; L247, 2:390. Written in ink, on unruled paper, measuring 10.1 × 16 cm. One sheet, two leaves. Embossed with an ornate rectangular design in which "PARIS" is stamped. In the letter Dickinson asks, "When did the Dark happen?" Bowles had been ill since the year before; in January, his conditioned deteriorated. She also asks, "did you vote upon 'Robert'?" Elizabeth Barrett Browning had died in June of 1861, and Dickinson was suggesting Robert (Browning) as a name for the latest Bowles child, a boy.

54. A 703; F1341C, 3:1159–60; L420, 2:529.

55. For instance, Dickinson writes "PresencE" and "concedE" (the E in this instance signifying the open *e*, rather than the more conventional closed *e* that she also used for lowercase characters), as well as "Evade" (with the ascender on the *d* curving left and the letter made with one continuous stroke) and "declivity" (with the ascender on the *d* going straight and angled slightly to the right and the letter made with two strokes— one looped, the other straight). The diversity is clear but is not a motivated element of the poem's formal apparatus; such diversity reminds us that similar inconsistencies in the writing of the dash also do not amount to willed differentiation for several rhetorical purposes.

56. There are two other spaces that I deemed worth measuring (for they stood out clearly as different in their physical relations to the right edge of the page) but that turned out not to be significant. The penultimate row on the second leaf has 3.1 cm after "not," which is unusually large, but the "the" with which the next row begins takes up 3.5 cm of space and would not have fit into the space remaining in the previous row. Similarly, row 6 of the third page has the sequence "One [*sic*] one" and then 2.3 cm; but the "attempting" that follows measures 7.5 cm and could not possibly have been written on the same row. (Note that I have emended the "One one" in the text.)

57. The anonymous author of a handbook on the etiquette of writing letters claims

with respect to capitals that "all writers agree that every sentence should begin with one, and that proper names and the emphatical words in a sentence, should be distinguished by them" (*American Letter Writer, or the Art of Polite Correspondence* [Brookfield, Mass.: Merriam & Cooke, 1842], xvii).

58. The letter to Susan Dickinson is Ms Am 1118.5 (B54), which is a half sheet torn vertically along the left side and written on one side only, in ink. The paper is unruled and unembossed and measures 12.7 × 20.5 cm. It is folded in quarters, and there is a small paper repair in the lower left corner. L480, 2:569; Fr1416A, 3:1235. Hart and Smith include the message as LP194 (214). Their version disappoints, in part because the book promises more than it delivers by way of material precision. In this case, they represent "perhaps – only. Emily" as one line, in uniform type; the signature is slightly lower, however, and very much smaller than the writing in the rest of the document. Clearly, the scarcity of space at the end of the page forced Dickinson to reduce her name in order to make it fit: and since she habitually writes her name a line further down than anything else in a letter, Hart and Smith would not have compromised her practices by doing the same. As it stands, then, the line misrepresents what Dickinson wrote in ways that Johnson and Ward do not, if only because they remain true to the spirit of what is written, whereas Hart and Smith purport to reproduce its materiality and do not. Hart and Smith also mistranscribe "this / is the last" as "This / is the last."

59. Ms Am 1093 (87), Department of Rare Books and Manuscripts, Boston Public Library. Franklin's edition misidentifies the BPL number as 78. Fr1416B, 3:1235; L486, 2:571.

60. Marianne Messmer, *A Vice for Voices: Reading Emily Dickinson's Correspondence* (Amherst: University of Massachusetts Press, 2001). One could attempt to create a thematic distinction between poetry and prose based on Dickinson's pronouncements on both genres. No poems begin "This was a letter-writer," or "The letter-writers light but lamps," or "I reckon when I count at all, first letter-writers," or "They shut me up in poetry," and so on (though the reason may be metrical more than semantic). Dickinson *did* write "This is my letter to the World," a poem that has often been read as if it referred fairly unproblematically to the body of writing left behind after her death. But as with "Going to – Her! / Happy – Letter," one detects a gap between what the letter says and what is said about letters: between the correspondent and the poet, in other words. The letter writer may promise the "simple News that Nature told," but the poet who reports this speech refused to reveal what the contents of that message might be. And in "Going to – Her," the speaker instructs the letter to say everything that she did not include in the letter—that could not, in fact, be included in a letter. Notwithstanding these objections, it seems to me that distinctions between Dickinson's poetry and prose based on attitude, themes, contents, or linguistic register cannot easily be sustained (except temporally; the early letters are copious and expansive in ways that the early poems are not, for instance). It is true that poems habitually lack the kinds of mundane information that prose typically conveys, but the simplest distinction is the one that Dickinson made—the material one, suggesting that she had expectations about her letters and their response different from what she had about poems. What the difference might have been is not something I am interested in pursuing here; I simply want to register that it exists.

61. Ms Am 1118.2 (46). The letter is written in ink on a single unruled and unembossed sheet, originally 25.4 cm wide by 20.5 cm high. It is folded vertically to make a bifolium, then folded vertically and horizontally to fit into an envelope.

62. L544, 2:605–6; Fr1416C, 3:1236.

63. A 468.

64. For instance, in 1881 Dickinson drew up a draft of "An Antiquated Tree" (Fr1544A), then included a copy of it in a letter to Elizabeth Holland (Fr1544B): the original of *A* is at Amherst College (A 130): *B* is Ms Am 1118.2 (59) at the Houghton Library, Harvard College Library, Harvard University. Dickinson's career is full of poems that are retained as poems only in record copies and then included in letters to others, retaining the lyric formatting.

65. A 34; L558, 2:614; Fr1479, 3:1293. The date was supplied by the recipient, who endorsed the manuscript: Johnson and Ward, as well as Franklin, confirm it by the handwriting.

66. Ms Am 1118.3 (230).

67. Again, it would seem inconsistent that Dickinson begins some lines with capitals and others—that are seen by critics as being deliberately separate—in minuscule.

68. The quotation is from Franklin, *Poems*, 3:1283; he numbers this version of the poem as Fr1462C. Johnson and Ward identify this as L677, *Letters*, 3:682. They assign a period after "friend"; Franklin uses a comma. Given the elongated stroke, Franklin's guess seems correct. But Dickinson elongates the dots above the *i* in "Ophír," "Bríght," and "Adíeu," so that the physical evidence is not decisive in this instance; my intuition is that Johnson and Ward were right. A 41. All references are to the manuscript original.

69. The other possibility is that Dickinson wanted "Ophir" to receive particular attention—proportionately more attention than any other segment of the poem (as it is the only element that has a physical line of its own). Such a possibility, while not unthinkable, seems unlikely: would Dickinson really have wanted additional focus on the Ophir, rather than on the dead man's relationship to Ophir, as in "Brother of Ophir"? And is "Ophir" really more important that "Honor"? And does it make a difference that "Brother" takes up 4.5 cm of space, and "Ophir" only 2.7 cm? The manuscript, incidentally, takes up 12 × 20.3 cm and is written on nonruled (Weston's Linen 1876) paper, in pencil, and folded in thirds (see A 41).

70. A 157.

71. Ms Am 1118.5 (B32). Franklin's edition of Fr1462B fails to record the division after "purchase" (3:1283). Hart and Smith's edition of LP207 misidentifies the final "that" as "That" (223). They also describe the calligraphy as "dramatic" (both in the notes on this document and online at <http://www.emilydickinson.org/working/zhb326.htm> [accessed 5 February 2002]). They identify a possible pun: "you" is "Sou" (i.e., "Sue"), on the grounds that "Emily's 'Y' looks like an 'S'." The *y* in the second and final rows of writing is in lowercase, however (meaning that to read it as a capital *S*, one has to accept, first, that the *y* was modified to look like an *S* and, second, that it does not matter that one is minuscule and the other not). Hart and Smith also note that the final dash is elongated and slopes downward: in fact, it curves downward and then back up, like the ~ shape, ending at the same level as it began because of the small serif on the left.

72. To take a random example, Fr1481, "We knew not that we were to live," exists in two versions that are, verbally, the same, but which have different prose contexts. One (A) was sent to Higginson, the other (B) to Maria Whitney. The first is introduced thus: "Till it has loved – no man or woman can become itself – Of our first Creation we are unconscious." The second is introduced thus: "Though we are each – unknown – to ourself – and each other – 'tis not what Well conferred it, the dying Soldier asks –

it is only the water" (3:1294). Franklin thought the documents were written toward the end of 1878.

73. Note, for instance, that the dashes appear at exactly the same intervals: after the fifth syllable, the eighth, and the sixteenth. And although the third version (the only one actually arranged as a quatrain) has five syllables in the third line and three in the fourth, the total number of syllables is eight, exactly the number of syllables in the second line of versions one and two (which Dickinson arranged as couplets). Structurally, then, the three poems are the same.

74. The largest spaces in the Susan Dickinson edition of the poem occur after "indorse it" (4.65 cm), "Peru" (2.8 cm), and "you" (6.3 cm; all the measurements of Ms Am 1118.5 [B32] are taken after the dashes that follow these phrases and to the right edge of the paper). These coincide with the beginning of the poem, the first line break, and the end.

75. To repeat; sections of prose demonstrate metrical tendencies—but not ones that are sustained over several lines to the extent that they constitute fully rhyming quatrains. When they do so, Dickinson usually marks them as poems.

76. A 160.

77. The decision to measure just below the *t* and *s* in the respective superior lines was taken to establish a consistent margin for all the end words, so as to attempt an evaluation of which lines were shorter than others. The first stroke (to the right of "plea" and the left of "the compliments") that divides this portion of writing on the long narrow strip of paper from the next angles down from the top edge of the paper to a point that is further left of it on the bottom edge; the second stroke (to the right of "compliments" and left of "Journey") angles down from the top edge of the paper to a point that is further right of it on the bottom edge. Using either or both of these as margins against which to define spacing patterns at the end of rows of writing would have produced distorted findings.

78. Johnson and Ward include two drafts of the letter (L774, 3:743). The information about Susan Dickinson's departure to Grand Rapids, Michigan, to attend the marriage of Frank Gilbert's daughter Belle is from the notes to L774. Dickinson draws lines between the different segments of the poem (perhaps because some kind of margin was helpful to its composition), but not in the prose sequence (though here divisions are created by the folds). Another draft, A 636, written on a fragment of envelope (measuring approximately 12.3 cm across and 9.7 cm high) addressed by Judge Lord to "Misses Emily and Vinnie Dickinson / Amherst / Mass." It reads "Excuse / Emily and / her atoms / the North / Star is / of small / fabric / but it / implies / much / presides." The underlined word "yet" is written at an angle adjacent to "implies"— possibly as a variant for "but." Johnson and Ward identify the last word, which is very difficult to read because of the envelope flap crease and the faintness of the pencil, as "besides." But in the two drafts and one version of this note, Dickinson toyed with "denotes," "achieves," and "implies" for the final verb, suggesting the choice was a difficult one: my feeling is that "presides" was yet another variant.

79. Johnson and Ward indent "Excuse me" (as Dickinson did not) and put "achieves" before "implies" (with "implies" in parentheses); in the manuscript, "implies" precedes "achieves."

80. Franklin assumes that "Without a care" is a variant for "without a plea" (in the first line), but the placement of the writing (on the reverse side of the paper, *after* the first part of the poem has been composed) and the sonic similarity of "fair" and "care"

(in a poem where the rhyme falls on every second line) suggest that it could equally have been a variant for the last line ("is their Theology"). Similarly, the sequence "A comp[e]tence so gay" (which is a variant for "A compensation fair") would provide a slightly closer rhyme with "Theology" (or "Philosophy") and may well have been composed with that idea.

81. Franklin, *Poems* (1999): 584, 649.

82. A 713.

83. *Poems*, 3:1410; Franklin transcribes the first section as prose, and omits the third section altogether: the implication, then, is that it too is prose.

84. Wallace Stevens, "Of Modern Poetry," in *Collected Poems of Wallace Stevens* (New York: Alfred Knopf, 1954), 239–40.

85. L802, to Elizabeth Holland, early 1883, 3:760–61.

86. A 767; the manuscript original corresponds in this instance to Fr1597D, the version (believed by Franklin to have been intended) for Mabel Loomis Todd.

87. L809, 3:766–67.

88. The fascinating thing about this manuscript is that Dickinson turned the page over, placed it sideways on the writing surface (thus increasing its horizontal dimensions from 12.7 cm to 20.2 cm), and then returned to the kind of formatting associated with poetry, with additional spaces after "Morn" (8.3 cm), "Book" (7.8 cm), "Son" (9.8 cm), and "renown" (12.3 cm). But what intrigues is that Dickinson does not use all the space available to her on the page; there are spaces of between 5 cm and 6 cm from the end of "in," "Sire," "have," "way," and "from" to the right edge of the page. The two folds in the paper may explain why this is so: these become vertical when the paper is positioned laterally, and the second of these seems to have functioned as a kind of margin or edge for Dickinson. Since she had clearly abandoned the message at this stage (this was going to remain a draft, not a finished letter), it may be that Dickinson was trying to estimate how much paper she needed for a new version of the letter. The fact that the lines of writing turn over when there is no obvious material reason for doing so tends, in this instance at least, to support the possibility that autograph lineation might occasionally have been deliberate.

89. Franklin is not always consistent, though; his reconstruction of Fr1607, "How slow the Wind," begins the second line of this supposed couplet with a small letter ("how late their Feathers be!"; 3:1410). Johnson represents the same as a three-line poem: "How slow the Wind – / how slow the sea – / how late their Feathers be!" (J1571, 3:1083). But if Dickinson failed to format these lines as a poem, they should not be represented thus, meter and rhyme notwithstanding.

90. A 799; Franklin transcribes this as Fr1595 (3:1395), and Johnson and Ward represent it as L798 (3:758). Franklin has a comma after "more," Johnson and Ward a dash. Johnson and Ward seem to me to be correct in this instance.

91. The consoling denial of treachery in the beginning suggests that similar expressions or emotions may have been voiced or made indirectly known by Dickinson in the past, with reference to Susan Dickinson's purloining of some early poems. See Ms Am 1118.5 (B158).

92. Franklin mistranscribes this sequence as "others picking and gazing," instead of "others picking it up and gazing" (3:1439).

93. A 132/133; the draft letter is on A 132, and the draft poems are on A 133 and are divided by a line.

94. Werner, *Emily Dickinson's Open Folios*, n.p., notes for A 132. Werner records

"expectations" as "Expectations," justifiably, on the grounds that the letter which be-
gins the word is written ε. But Dickinson switches back and forth between closed and
open lowercase e characters elsewhere (both here and in the correspondence generally),
so that there is occasion for the permanent suspension of certainty in this instance.
Werner also (wrongly, I believe) records "that bends" rather than "That bends."
Franklin's version has "to Covet thee" (Fr1636A, 3:1434), but this must be a printer's
error: his notes to the poem twice refer to "covet thee" (with a lowercase letter, in
other words). In the same notes, Franklin records "bends a Knee," where Werner
(rightly, I believe) has "bends a knee."

95. The one exception in the prose is the space after "here," which amounts to 3.8
cm. The next word after it is "The," and there probably was enough room to inscribe
it on the same line. Such a break may therefore indicate some kind of transition,
equivalent to a new paragraph.

96. The originals are A 229, A 309, A 310, and A 343. One manuscript is lost, and
exists only as a transcript.

97. A 819; the second poem begins on page A 819b and continues through A 819c.
Franklin identifies "Of God we ask one favor" as Fr1675 (3:1467–68). The writing is
in pencil on nonruled transatlantic paper that is folded in thirds, measuring 13 × 20.6
cm.

98. An earlier draft, A 817, contains some of the same words: it is preceded by "I
am but a / Pagan," with 7.7 cm left before the next lines, "Of God we ask / one favor
[4.3 cm] / That we may / be forgiven [3.7 cm]." The formatting suggests a break
between the prose and poetry and then very clear line divisions.

99. L976 (draft no. 2), 3:866–77; Fr1671E, 3:1464 (L976 has "more,").

100. Fr1671A, 3:1463; A 370.

101. L960, 3:854–55; J1640, 3:1123; A 776. The original envelope still survives:
measuring 14 cm across by 7.7 cm deep, it is stamped on the back, "Washington, Rec'd
Jan 3, 1885"). The paper measures 12.6 × 20.2 cm, is divided in thirds, and unruled.
Dickinson writes in pencil on the first page of a sheet of paper that has been folded
during manufacture to produce two leaves; she then skips the second page and writes
on the third.

102. Fr1671B, 3:1463; A 776. All references are cross-checked with the manuscript
original.

103. J1639, 3:1123; Fr1672A, 3:1466. The poem is also indented separately as two
lines in L960, 3:855.

104. L960, 3:855; L963, 3:857.

105. The quotation is from Werner, Emily Dickinson's Open Folios, 55.

106. By extension, such critics have moved away from explanations of her nonpub-
lication as a consequence of the failure of others (Higginson, Bowles, and Josiah Hol-
land) to encourage her, to seeing it as a deliberate choice made in the interest of
preserving the formal integrity of her texts. Such a move is politically empowering:
Dickinson ceases to be the victim of incompetent but influential male professionals.

107. It seems to me that, if this is true, we have little to complain about if editors
do, then, make choices as to which edition of a poem, stanza, line, phrase, word, or
punctuation mark seem best to them. But a kind of double-bind exists here. For while
the message of textual egalitarianism continues to be preached, anyone who actually
does decide to construct her or his version of a poem is then criticized for going against
Dickinson's wishes and practices. The Dickinson manuscript with its plethora of non-

chosen variants is in essence as closed off and static as a Johnson stanza is thought to have been: its potential exists only as long as we agree not to have preferences. If we choose, we close, we bind. One is reminded of the dancers on Keats's "Ode on a Grecian Urn," their potential frozen forever in art.

108. Norbert Hirschhorn and Polly Longsworth, " 'Medicine Posthumous': A New Look at Emily Dickinson's Medical Conditions," *New England Quarterly* 69 (June 1996): 299–316. For this summary, I am indebted to Habegger's *My Wars Are Laid Away in Books*, 615–25.

109. For an overview of fascicle and set production, see Franklin, *Poems of Emily Dickinson*, 3:1538–41.

110. One of the problems with such a thesis is the use of the word "weak," which is the adjective used in the nineteenth century to describe women ("the weaker sex"). In other words, any focus on a lessening in the capacity to bring poems to a close coincides with sexist evaluations of women's physical and intellectual abilities. To say that Dickinson finished fewer and fewer poems seems like an accusation of failure and frailty, and if the person stating this happens to be male, then the argument is easy to dismiss on political grounds. I hope it is clear, however, that my speculations as to Dickinson's unfinished drafts do not arise out of a sense of some personal deficiency or a perception of lack that is grounded in the presumption of the feebleness (imaginative, intellectual, or physical) of women. There are parallels with Hawthorne's notably (and even compulsively) unfinished later writings.

111. Percy Lubbock, ed., *The Letters of Henry James* (London: Macmillan, 1920), 1:xiv.

112. L260, 15 April 1862; L261, 25 April 1862; L271, August 1862, all to T. W. Higginson.

113. Quoted in J. M. Coetzee, "The Marvels of Walter Benjamin," *New York Review of Books*, January 2001, 28.

114. Thomas H. Johnson elaborates on this in the introduction to the *Letters*: "[Letters] enabled her to control the time and the plane of her relationships. The degree and nature of any intimacy was hers to choose. Henceforth the letters are composed with deliberation, each with the chosen recipient in mind, and it becomes clear that a letter written to Higginson, for instance, could never have been intended for Bowles or anyone else" (*Letters of Emily Dickinson*, 1:xix).

115. Samuel Johnson defines the difference in the 1781 entry on Pope in *Prefaces, Biographical and Critical, to the Works of the English Poets*: "Friendship has no tendency to secure veracity, for by whom can a man so much wish to be thought better than he is as by him whose kindness he desires to gain or keep? Even in writing to the world there is less constraint: the author is not confronted with his reader, and takes his chance of approbation among the different dispositions of mankind; but a letter is addressed to a single mind of which the prejudices and partialities are known, and must therefore please, if not by favouring them, by forbearing to oppose them" (*The Oxford Authors: Samuel Johnson*, ed. Donald Greene [Oxford: Oxford University Press, 1984], 729.

116. L321, 2:455.

117. I don't mean to say that the celebrated indeterminacy of Dickinson's poems is somehow compromised or contaminated by their inclusion in letters, but that letters provide the possibility of a more determinate structure of interpretation than the poems would on their own. (And this structure appears to have been discarded when

Dickinson came to recording final versions of her poems in fascicles and sets and when she sent versions of the same poem to multiple recipients.)

118. Jonathan Culler, *The Pursuit of Signs: Semiotics, Literature, Deconstruction* (London: Routledge and Kegan Paul, 1975), 165.

119. This is not to say that letters—especially Emily Dickinson's letters—cannot survive the scene of their saying; it is to suggest that *they are not obliged to* in quite the same way that literature conventionally is. Even some of Dickinson's letters originate from a historically identifiable individual and circulate within specific relationships at particular times and in definite places: some are dated ("Sunday morning," "Thursday evening"), headed ("Susan," "Dear friend"), and signed ("Emilie," "E. Dickinson," "Emily Dickinson," "Emily," "Your scholar," "Phaeton"), but the variety of the signatures means that one should be wary of simplistically believing that the letters are more transparent than the lyrics. Samuel Johnson offers a useful warning against such temptations: "It has been so long said as to be commonly believed that the true characters of men may be found in their letters, and that he who writes to his friend lays his heart open before him. But the truth is that such were the simple friendships of the *Golden Age*, and are now the friendships only of children. Very few can boast of hearts which they dare lay open to themselves, and of which, by whatever accident exposed, they do not shun a distinct and continued view; and certainly what we hide from ourselves we do not shew to our friends. There is, indeed, no transaction which offers stronger temptations to fallacy and sophistication than epistolary intercourse. In the eagerness of conversation the first emotions of the mind often burst out before they are considered; in the tumult of business interest and passion have their genuine effect; but a friendly letter is a calm and deliberate performance in the cool of leisure, in the stillness of solitude, and surely no man sits down to depreciate by design his own character" (*Oxford Authors: Samuel Johnson*, 729).

120. L268, 2:412; L260, 2:403.

CHAPTER FIVE *"The Ear is the Last Face": The Manuscript as Archive of Rhythm and Rhyme*

Epigraphs: F. R. Leavis, *The Common Pursuit* (Harmondsworth: Penguin, 1966), 88; William Knight, "A Reminiscence of Tennyson," in *Tennyson: Interviews and Recollections*, ed. Norman Page (London: Macmillan, 1983), 265–66.

1. Envelopes and Stamps Folder A, Special Collections, Jones Library, Amherst.

2. Caleb H. Rice to Uriel Montague, 19 March 1846, in Montague, Uriel, Correspondence, Special Collections, Jones Library, Amherst.

3. For a complete list of paper measurements and a full description of stationery types, see Ralph W. Franklin, *The Manuscript Books of Emily Dickinson* (Cambridge: Harvard University Press, Belknap Press, 1981), appendix 5, 2:1411–12. Appendix 3 of the same volume correlates type of paper with the estimated year of fascicle production.

4. In Advertisements, Miscellaneous, Special Collections, Jones Library, Amherst.

5. See Alfred Habegger, *My Wars Are Laid Away in Books: The Life of Emily Dickinson* (New York: Random House, 2001), 347.

6. Fr1471, in *The Poems of Emily Dickinson* (Cambridge: Harvard University Press, Belknap Press, 1998), 3:1288; henceforth, all references prefixed by Fr are to poems in this edition. The manuscript is A 211, Special Collections, Frost Library, Amherst College; henceforth, all references prefixed by A are to manuscript originals in this

collection. Fr1355, 3:1175–76, and A 210, A 210a; Fr1570A, 3:1372–73, and A 222, A 222a; Fr1154A, 3:1003, and A 238; Fr1413, 3:1232, and A 366, A 366b. Fr1414, 3:1234 is written in pencil on an invitation from Dr. and Mrs. William A. Stearns inviting Edward and Emily Norcross Dickinson to call on them (A 220). That Dickinson used scrap paper from other people does not rule out the possibility that she shaped such paper to her own purposes, but it should make us slightly wary: the shape of the fragments may sometimes be someone else's doing.

7. Fr1148, 2:997–98; A 373. Leyda, in his note to the manuscript at Special Collections, Frost Library, Amherst College, asks if the false start might have been made by Mrs. Tuckerman, a correspondent of Dickinson's. In which case, one wonders if Dickinson's friends supplied her with scrap paper, as (for example) her sister Lavinia did.

8. Fr1256, 2:1083–84, A 388 and A 388a; Fr1458, 3:1278–79, A 398 and A 398a; Fr1344, 3:1162, A 401.

9. Kathleen Coburn, "Editing the Coleridge Notebooks," in *Editing Texts of the Romantic Period*, ed. John D. Baird (Toronto: A. M. Hakkert, 1972), 10.

10. Michael Millgate, *Testamentary Acts: Browning, Tennyson, James, Hardy* (Oxford: Clarendon Press, 1992), 51.

11. Mark Storey, " 'Creeping into Print': Editing the Letters of John Clare," in *The Theory and Practice of Text-Editing*, ed. Ian Small and Marcus Walsh (Cambridge: Cambridge University Press, 1991), 62–89.

12. Michael Millgate, *Testamentary Acts*, 130–31.

13. *Paperoles* and *becquets* are synonyms for little scraps of paper—technically the latter are "paste-ins" (see entry 3899 "becquet/béquet" in *Elsevier's Dictionary of Library Science, Information and Documentation*, comp. W. E. Clason [Amsterdam: Elsevier Scientific Publishing Company, 1976], 290). For the information on the "notebooks, proofs, little slips of paper, *paperoles*, and *becquets* that Proust scribbled on in those interminable thousand and one nights in his cork-lined room," see J. Hillis Miller, *Black Holes* (Stanford: Stanford University Press, 1999), 429.

14. Susan Dickinson's materials are A 791–1c in the Special Collections, Frost Library, Amherst College. Otis Lord's are A 761a–z in ibid.

15. A 277. What follows is a partial reproduction only. Franklin omits to note that both "his" and "spell" are underlined—rightly, on the grounds that the lines form a division between this and the next portion of writing ("The embers / of a / Thousand") and do not represent a form of emphasis. See Fr1405, 3:1224–25.

16. The word divisions in Dickinson's writings are listed in appendix 10 of Franklin's *Poems of Emily Dickinson*, 3:1562–66. Among those *not* marked with a dash are "Delig / ht" and "Bu / gles" (Fr1636 and 1655 respectively), "oc / cupant" & "mir / acle" (both Fr1594), and "nothi / ng" (Fr1636). It would be stretching matters considerably to imagine that these represented puns, unless one accepts that "ht" and "ng" are abbreviations or acronyms of one kind or another, in which case one wonders how they connect to "delig" and "nothi," respectively.

17. Ellen Louise Hart, "Editing in Amherst: The History and Mystery of Emily Dickinson's Manuscripts to Susan Dickinson," July 19, 1999, Barnett Reading Room, Special Collections, Frost Library, Amherst College.

18. Mary W. Mitchell to Ellen T. Emerson, manuscript letter dated 27 April, bMs Am 1280.226 (3853), Houghton Library, Harvard College Library, Harvard University. Unless stated otherwise, future references prefixed by bMs Am are to originals at Houghton.

19. Ralph Waldo Emerson, manuscript letter to John Haskins, 25 September 1849, bMs Am 1280.226 (2248).

20. Fr1195A, 2:1037 (about 1871); A 351/352. The full poem reads "Society for me my misery / Since Gift of Thee –." The row-breaks occur after "me" and "of." Also on the same flap are variant lines (7 and 8) for Fr1127B, "Step lightly on this narrow spot" (2:1058), which read: "Or Fame erect/ her siteless Citadel –." Fr1323, 3:1147; A 449. Most of the poem is inscribed on the left hand side of the flap (which is placed physically so that the space decreases as one reads down). "The vastest earthly Day / Is shrunken small / By – shrivelled / dwindled / one Defaulting / Face / Behind / a Pall –." Variants, both vertically and horizontally inscribed, appear on the right. "By" is situated lower than "shriveled"; the dash slants down and left.

21. "A Cousin's Memories of Emily Dickinson: Boston Woman Also Recalls Visit of the Poetess' Sister, Lavinia," in the *Boston Sunday Globe*, 12 January 1930, 41. Gertrude Graves was the daughter of John L. Graves, a cousin of the Dickinson girls. She writes in full: "But I remember a visit made by my father to the Dickinson home, when Cousin Emily sent him one of her little three-cornered notes with a beautiful sprig of white jasmine." It could be that Dickinson used the flaps of envelopes for notes to people in her immediate vicinity, though it is also possible that the note was folded in a way of her own devising. Contemporaneous books of etiquette often refer to a culture of leaving corners on a note; some folds indicated whether or not the sender required a reply. A letter from Dickinson to Susan Phelps, the manuscript of which is at Smith College, is folded at the top in a manner that clearly indicates two corners having been made. These may have been to prevent the enclosed rosebud from falling out, or they may have signaled that no reply was necessary. A.N.S., 8 May 1860, Mortimer Rare Book Room, William Allan Neilson Library, Smith College. A calling card from Mrs. Herbert T. Cowles is folded at the bottom left corner, and a message written in hand states "Thursday, March Twenty-first, Three o'clock." Again, the folding would indicate the necessity or otherwise of reply. E. D., Todd, Mabel Loomis, Miscellaneous Collection, Special Collections, Jones Library, Amherst. Many letters from Frances Anne (Fanny) Kemble to Mary Eliot (Dwight) Parkman are folded in thirds and then folded again in such a way that they form triangles, with the name of Mrs. Parkman in the middle. See the box labeled Ms Am 1639, Houghton Library, Harvard University.

22. Fr1185, 2:1028; A 201.

23. Fr1186, 2:1028–29; A 316. There is very clear stanzaic division between "Now I abundance see" and "Which was to" on the first side (the second begins "famish, then or now –"). Franklin prints the poem as nine lines: it may well have been two quatrains.

24. Fr1251, 2:1080, and A 278; Fr1259, 2:1086–87, and A 139; Fr1325, 3:1148, and A 236. I use only partial versions of titles in this section of writing.

25. Fr1310, 3:1131–32; A 202. Dickinson also used fragments of stationery: "Left in immortal Youth" (Fr1289), "Yesterday is History" (Fr1290), "The Beggar at the Door for Fame" (Fr1291), "The Face we choose to miss" (Fr1293), not to mention Fr1296 (A and B), Fr1297, and Fr1300B (all dating from 1873), all written on stationery fragments. To pick out one of these as especially appropriate to the poem it carries is to ignore the overwhelming logic of Dickinson's fragment usage as a whole: it is an incidental aspect of the poem's significance.

26. Fr1405, 3:1224–25; A 277. The last two lines are written on the outside of the envelope; the first of these on the left side, the last on the right (with the vertical "understand" intersecting with the horizontal "Miss." The "Miss" is from an address, "Miss Vinnie Dickinson," written by Abigail I. Cooper.

27. Fr1519, 3:1328; A 193/194. The legend "Western Union Telegraph Co." has been partly ripped during opening, along the *e*, *l*, *e*, *g*, and *h* of "Telegraph." On the same envelope is another poem, "Glass was the Street – in Tinsel Pearl" (Fr1518).

28. Fr1554, 3:1360; A 317. The first part of the poem is written on the scrap of paper; "To situations / new / The effort / to comprise / it / Is all the / soul can do –" is written on the envelope.

29. Fr1594B, 3:1393–94; A 636.

30. Fr1350B, 3:1166–70; A 416.

31. Hart made these comments during the Roundtable on Editing and Archiving (Panel 8, Session 3, of "Emily Dickinson at Home," the 3rd Emily Dickinson International Society Conference) at Mt. Holyoke College, Saturday, 14 August 1999. Hart may have abbreviated her argument because of pressures of time, of course.

32. There are numerous examples of Dickinson positioning the envelope differently in response to variations in the envelope and to get a satisfactory writing surface. "Without a smile – Without a throe" (Fr1340, 3:1157–58) is written on the inside of an envelope with the flap pointing downwards; "The way Hope builds his House" (Fr1512, 3:1322) is written on an envelope with the flap pointing up. Both originals are at Special Collections, Frost Library, Amherst College: the first was written in 1874 (A 531), the second in 1879 (A 450). The first envelope has had a portion from the top cut with scissors, because the flap has torn off some of the paper it was affixed to (it was addressed to "Mr and Mrs Edward Dickinson"). The second, addressed to "Mrs Edward Dickinson and Family" has only flap and address portion intact.

33. Fr1411A, 3:1228–29; A 364. In 1874, the inside of an envelope split vertically down the middle (and thus with half a flap) was used for "Surprise is like a thrilling – pungent" (Fr1324, 3:1147–48; A 367). The envelope, like A 236 (Fr1325, 3:1148) was addressed by Lavinia Dickinson. Once more, we see Dickinson making use of envelopes written on or received by other members of her family: can we be absolutely certain that she tore all of these papers into the shapes that we see today?

34. Fr1312, 3:1133; A 499.

35. Fr1506A, 3:1317–18; A 514.

36. Another section of the flap is attached to the lower to middle right-hand side of the envelope.

37. Pharmacist Henry Adams's Prescription Book, 1882–1885, Special Collections, Frost Library, Amherst College.

38. Fr1679, 3:1470; A 391.

37. Pharmacist Henry Adams's Prescription Book, 1882–1885, Special Collections, Frost Library, Amherst College.

38. Fr1679, 3:1470; A 391.

39. See <http://jefferson.village.virginia.edu/dickinson/>.

40. See appendix 2 in Franklin, *Poems of Emily Dickinson*, 3:1533. Franklin's breakdown of poems per year has 227 in 1862, 295 in 1863, 98 in 1864, and 229 in 1865. Though the numbers cannot be absolutely accurate (given that they are estimated according to changes in the handwriting only), it still seems a reasonable assumption that the period of time in question was one of her most productive.

41. Marta Werner, *Emily Dickinson's Open Folios: Scenes of Reading, Surfaces of Writing* (Ann Arbor: University of Michigan Press, 1995), 83–84; Franklin, *Poems of Emily Dickinson*, 2:1090–93. Both points are difficult to settle. With respect to "won" versus "now," what clinches the matter for me is that the Dickinson *w* here seems to have five clear strokes (all linked: ascender, descender, ascender, descender, ascender), whereas

the *n* seems to have an ascender, a descender / ascender stroke (where the pencil goes down and then up on the same stroke), and then a single stroke that curves slightly more gently than the more abrupt strokes in the *w*. In other words, "won" is probably the correct reading—though I suspect that Werner is correct in calling the *e* at the beginning of "Exultation" a capital. I should add that I think of Werner's book as first and foremost a rigorous, scholarly, and pioneering attempt at identifying ways in which to transcribe Dickinson drafts; her conclusions may not necessarily have implications for the ways in which we transcribe poems and letters. Werner seems to me to be more descriptive in her orientation toward texts; Hart and Smith are more interpretive.

42. The original has twenty rows, not eighteen. But it is assumed that rows 19 and 20 are variants for 17 and 18 (or vice versa) and that the two pairs (17 and 18, and 19 and 20) echo each other's meanings to such an extent that including both would effectively be to make one redundant.

43. Of course, the absence of meter presupposes the necessity of its presence to begin with; one can always argue that there is no meter in the manuscript version because none was intended.

44. The phrase "diplomatic translation," discussed in a previous chapter, was introduced to Dickinson studies by Ellen Louise Hart in "The Elizabeth Whitney Putnam Manuscripts and New Strategies for Editing Emily Dickinson's Letters," *Emily Dickinson Journal* 4, no. 1 (1995): 72. It refers to a process of editing texts which respects the physical particularities of their manuscript versions. (The *Journal* lists the name in Hart's title as "Elizabeth Putnam Whitney" on its contents page, *v*.)

45. There will be more on this later. The odd line endings of the poem are feminine, or unstressed, which dissipates the otherwise rising meter. It also creates a sense of disappointment or interruption, since there an expected fourth ictus does not materialize.

46. Derek Attridge, *Poetic Rhythm: An Introduction* (Cambridge: Cambridge University Press, 1995), 10. In this case, the "unit" is made up of two lines.

47. Timothy Steele, *Missing Measures: Modern Poetry and the Revolt against Meter* (Fayetteville: University of Arkansas Press, 1990), 73.

48. They include Annie Finch, *The Ghost of Meter: Culture and Prosody in American Free Verse* (Ann Arbor: University of Michigan Press, 1993); Thomas H. Johnson, *Emily Dickinson: An Interpretative Biography* (Cambridge: Harvard University Press, 1955); Brita Lindberg-Seyersted, *The Voice of the Poet: Aspects of Style in the Poetry of Emily Dickinson* (Cambridge: Harvard University Press, 1968); James Olney, *The Language(s) of Poetry: Walt Whitman, Emily Dickinson, Gerard Manley Hopkins* (Athens: University of Georgia Press, 1993); David Porter, *The Art of Emily Dickinson's Early Poetry* (Cambridge: Harvard University Press, 1966); and Judy Jo Small, *Positive as Sound: Emily Dickinson's Rhyme* (Athens: University of Georgia Press, 1990), among others. More recent discussions include Cristanne Miller's presidential address to the annual meeting of the Emily Dickinson International Society (St. Paul, Minn., summer 2000) and Christine Ross's "Uncommon Measures: Emily Dickinson's Subversive Prosody," *Emily Dickinson Journal* 10, no. 1 (2001): 70–98. Miller called for an adjustment of attention from the visual and the modernist to the aural and nineteenth-century lyric conventions.

49. John A. Goldsmith, *Autosegmental and Metrical Phonology* (Oxford: Basil Blackwell, 1990), 171.

50. Nouns, verbs, and adjectives receive primary stress, in other words; prepositions, conjunctions, and adverbs receive much less, if any.

51. Alternatively, "Through what transports of Patience" may be realized as three feet: the first iambic, the second dactylic, and the third trochaic. Such switches from duple meter to triple and back again are quite rare, and because the dominant meter of the poem as a whole seems to be duple (based on two-syllable feet), then it would seem more plausible that the line switches from iambic to trochaic and back again to iambic, with the extrametric syllable at the end typical of the pattern of odd (as opposed to even) line endings in the poem.

52. Hallelujah or half meter/measure usually consists of four lines of iambic tri-meter, or with three stresses. The other types of meter, discussed in the next chapter, are as follows: long meter or measure (four lines with four stresses); common meter or measure (alternating lines of iambic tetrameter and trimeter, or four and three stresses); and short meter or measure (two lines of trimeter, one tetrameter, and a final one of trimeter, or lines of three, four, and three stresses). Thomas Hardy was another who used these forms for some of his poems. "I Look into My Glass" is in short measure, "The Rambler" is in long measure, "Epitaph on a Pessimist" is in common measure, and "At Day-Close in November" is in short measure (though it is not consistently iambic). See David Wright, ed., *Thomas Hardy: Selected Poems* (Harmonds-worth: Penguin, 1978), 289, 219, 249, 216 (respectively).

53. The manuscript appearance of Dickinson's lyrics is not governed solely by the logic of meter and rhyme, for the physical exigency of the page is a clear factor. But if the manuscripts appearances are not governed solely by meter, close attention to the logic of their accumulated material details is persuasive evidence that they were met-rically composed. Additionally, it is remarkable how the grammatical units of the poem coincide with the conventional understanding of its lineal/metrical logic. If one writes the poem out as prose and then divides it according to grammatical segments, the division mirrors the meter:

> Through what transports of Patience [Prepositional phrase, adverbial]
> I reached the stolid Bliss [Main clause]
> To breathe my Blank without thee [Infinitive phrase, adverbial]
> Attest me this and this –
>
> By that bleak Exultation [Prepositional phrase, adverbial]
> I now as near as this
> Thy privilege of dying
> Abbreviate me this

54. Mabel Loomis Todd and Millicent Todd Bingham, eds., *Bolts of Melody: New Poems of Emily Dickinson* (New York: Harper & Brothers, 1945), xx–xxi.

55. A 498.

56. Martha Nell Smith, "Corporealizations of Dickinson and Interpretive Ma-chines," in *The Iconic Page in Manuscript, Print and Digital Culture*, ed. George Born-stein and Theresa Tinkle (Ann Arbor: University of Michigan Press, 1998), 205.

57. George Puttenham, *The Arte of English Poesie* (1589; reprint, Menston, York-shire: Scolar Press, 1968), 70.

58. John Keats, "On First Looking into Chapman's Homer," in *John Keats, Poetry Manuscripts at Harvard: A Facsimile Edition*, ed. Jack Stillinger (Cambridge: Harvard University Press, Belknap Press, 1990), [13].

59. Again, such procedures are damaging to the reception and understanding of a poet who is so fond of the general and the universal.

60. Dennis Taylor, *Hardy's Metres and Victorian Prosody* (Oxford: Oxford University Press, 1988), 189. Taylor also quotes the Puttenham sequence. Much of what I say here and in the next chapter is directly influenced by Taylor's writing.

CHAPTER SIX *"Bells whose jingling cooled my Tramp": Dickinson and Meter*

The chapter title derives from Dickinson's letter of 7 June 1862 to Higginson, when she writes: "I thanked you for the justice – but could not drop the Bells whose jingling cooled my Tramp" (L265, in Thomas H. Johnson and Theodora Ward, eds., *The Letters of Emily Dickinson* [Cambridge: Harvard University Press, Belknap Press, 1958], 2:408). Higginson seems to have urged Dickinson not to underestimate or completely to disregard the importance of meter or rhyme. She goes on to report that he described her "gait" as "spasmodic": the Spasmodic school included P. J. Bailey, Sydney Dobell, Alexander Smith, and other late Romantic, early Victorian minor poets. In an article titled "Sensation Novels," attributed to H. L. Manse, he described poetry of the Spasmodic school being justified by an author who "professes to owe its birth to convulsive throes in the soul of the writer." It was aimed at the nerves, and not the brain (Manse, "Sensation Novels," *Quarterly Review* 113, no. 226 [April 1863]: 482–514). The identification of Higginson's phrase with the Spasmodic school was first made by Gary Lee Stonum, *The Dickinson Sublime* (Madison: University of Wisconsin Press, 1990), 6–7. Henceforth, references prefixed by L are to the Johnson and Ward edition of the *Letters*.

1. "A Specimen of Cadences, for Latin Composition, approved of and recommended by Cicero and Quinctilian," in *Introduction to the Making of Latin*, ed. William Biglow (Salem: Cushing and Appleton, 1809), 216–23.

2. George Gascoigne, quoted in Annie Finch, *The Ghost of Meter: Culture and Prosody in American Free Verse* (Ann Arbor: University of Michigan Press, 1993), 5.

3. Thomas H. Johnson, *Emily Dickinson: An Interpretive Biography* (Cambridge: Harvard University Press, 1955), 85. The edition Edward Dickinson used was Samuel Worcester, *The Psalms, hymns and spiritual songs of the Rev. Isaac Watts: To which are added select hymns from other authors and directions for musical expression*, new ed., the selection enlarged and the indexes greatly improved by Samuel Worcester (Boston: Crocker & Brewster, 1834), Houghton Library, Harvard College Library, Harvard University. Edward's name is stamped in gold on the front board, and his signature on both the front pastedown and the first loose flyleaf directly facing it. There is much discussion in the preface of fitting the tune to the meaning, which Dickinson might have found interesting, as the tune reflects the meter. Worcester quotes the preface to the former editions on p. v: "The effect of public psalmody is often exceedingly marred by a psalm or a hymn being sung to an ill-adapted tune. The leaders of singing choirs are not always persons of good taste and judgment; and the best qualified leader cannot always, at the moment, so fully possess himself of the sentiments of the portion given out, as immediately to recur to a tune well suited to express them. It might, therefore, it was thought, be highly useful to sit down at leisure, and refer each psalm and hymn, not merely to a proper key, but to a suitable tune."

4. George Whicher, *This Was A Poet: A Critical Biography of Emily Dickinson* (New York: Scribner's, 1938), 240–41.

5. Preface to *The Sabbath Hymn and Tune Book, for the Service of Song in the House of the Lord* (New York: Mason & Hamlin, 1865), vi.

6. See Finch, *Ghost of Meter*, 13–30.

7. Which is not to say that she never parodied conventional expectations. As Martha Winburn England points out, "In hymns, certain rhyme words occur in pairs so often that the matching amounts almost to a cliché. Three times in one lyric ([J]409) she tempts the reader to anticipate the rhyme word *grace*, but grace is not pronounced at this Vision of Judgment" (England, *Hymns Unbidden: Donne, Herbert, Blake, Emily Dickinson and the Hymnographers* [Astor: New York Public Library, 1966], 135). My point is that the presence of common meter as a basic structural element does not exist principally as an ironic muscle, waiting constantly to be flexed. The meter is there because she liked it, because it felt comfortable, and because it was adaptable.

8. *Elements of Greek Grammar, Taken Chiefly from the Grammar of Caspar Frederick Hachenberg* (Hartford: Roberts & Burr, 1822), 173; Johnson, *Emily Dickinson*, 108; Susan Howe, *The Birth-mark: Unsettling the Wilderness in American Literary History* (Hanover: Wesleyan University Press, 1993), 139; Ellen Louise Hart, "The Elizabeth Whitney Putnam Manuscripts and New Strategies for Editing Dickinson's Letters," *Emily Dickinson Journal* 4, no. 1 (1995): 44–74.

9. "Visually expressive scriptures" is used twice at the Dickinson Electronic Archives site: in <http://www.jefferson.virginia.village.edu/dickinson/pluge1.html> and <http://www.jefferson.virginia.village.edu/dickinson/archive_description.html> (accessed on 29 August 2001). Martha Nell Smith, "Corporealizations of Dickinson and Interpretive Machines," in *The Iconic Page in Manuscript, Print, and Digital Culture*, ed. George Bornstein and Theresa Tinkle (Ann Arbor: University of Michigan Press, 1998), 196.

10. Jerome McGann, *Black Riders: The Visible Language of Modernism* (Princeton: Princeton University Press, 1993), 28.

11. Such remarks are interesting but difficult to evaluate in terms of accuracy: exactly the same blank space will appear elsewhere in other poems with different subjects, and yet only in this specific instance will it be seen as advancing or supporting a particular idea or perception. In other words, like other kinds of formalism this procedure seems arbitrarily and subjectively applied.

12. Fascicle 20 is chosen in part because others have written about it: Sharon Cameron, *Choosing Not Choosing: Dickinson's Fascicles* (Chicago: University of Chicago Press, 1992); Dorothy Huff Oberhaus, *Emily Dickinson's Fascicles: Method and Meaning* (University Park: University of Pennsylvania Press, 1995); and Martha Lindblom O'Keefe, *This Edifice: Studies in the Structure of the Fascicles of the Poetry of Emily Dickinson* (Maryland: Mrs. John A. O'Keefe, 1986). The point is not to argue against such studies of the fascicle but to acknowledge and (hopefully) to expand on the rich tradition of its discussion. In addition, the fascicle has many examples of what Hart and Smith describe as "the calligraphic design and placement of the text on the page," and is therefore an excellent test case for the validity or otherwise of such a hypothesis (*Open Me Carefully: Emily Dickinson's Intimate Letters to Susan Huntington Dickinson* [Ashfield: Paris Press, 1998], 65).

13. England, *Hymns Unbidden*, 116.

14. Dickinson's *abcb* rhymes are closer to the ballad than (for example) to the hymns of Watts, which are *abab*.

15. For a discussion of Dickinson and patriarchal meter, see Finch, *Ghost of Meter*, 13–30.

16. Derek Attridge, *The Rhythms of English Poetry* (London: Longman, 1982), 300.

17. Samuel Worcester, ed., *Christian Psalmody in Four Parts: Comprising Dr. Watts's Psalms Abridged; Dr Watts's Hymns Abridged; Select Hymns from Other Authors; and Select Harmony* (Boston: Samuel T. Armstrong and Crocker & Brewster, 1821). This is the fifth edition, and it—like the others—was known as *Watts & Select*. In *The Princeton Encyclopedia of Poetry and Poetics*, the fourth kind of meter is half meter (ed. Alex Preminger and T. V. F. Brogan [Princeton: Princeton University Press, 1993], 119). Reading through various historical editions of hymns, I could find only one instance of such a term, which may mean simply that it was not commonly used in New England. Instead, there is a stanza categorized as "h.m.," which corresponds to the definition of half meter in the encyclopedia (a quatrain of three beats per line). But in all the Watts editions, "h.m." is defined either as hallelujah meter, with particular meter as a related form ("p.m." for short, though "particular" also seems to have been a catchall term in some editions). One wonders if this is what Dickinson had in mind when she wrote "Strong Hallelujahs roll" (in Fr373, "This World is not conclusion," in *The Poems of Emily Dickinson*, ed. Ralph W. Franklin [Cambridge: Harvard University Press, Belknap Press, 1998], 1:397. Henceforth, all references prefixed by Fr are to poems in this edition). For examples: *The Psalms of David, Imitated in the Language of the New-Testament, and applied to the Christian State and Worship* (Northampton: William Butler, 1799), 218–19, defines "particular metre" as four lines of three beats and four of two. *The Psalms of David, Imitated in the Language of the New-Testament, and applied to the Christian State and Worship* (Boston: Manning & Loring, 1812), 466–68, describes the same as "hallelujah metre." *The Psalms of David, Imitated in the Language of the New-Testament, and applied to the Christian State and Worship* (Boston: Lincoln and Edmands, 1816), 590–91, also uses "hallelujah metre." *The Psalms of David, Imitated in the Language of the New-Testament, and applied to the Christian State and Worship* (Exeter, N.H.: John Williams, 1819), 265–66, refers to "particular metre." *The Psalms of David, Imitated in the Language of the New Testament, and applied to the Christian State and Worship* (Exeter, N.H.: J. C. Gerrish, 1828), 268–69, *The Psalms of David, Imitated in the Language of the New Testament, and applied to the Christian State and Worship* (Sandbornton, N.H.: D. U. Moulton, 1828), 257–59, both refer to and give many examples of "particular metre."

18. Long meter has four lines of eight syllables, usually arranged as iambic tetrameter; common meter has four lines of alternating eight and six syllables, usually arranged as iambic tetrameter and trimeter (respectively); short meter has two lines of six syllables, a third of four, and a fourth of six, arranged as iambic trimeter (in lines 1, 2, and 4) and tetrameter (in line 3). Hallelujah meter can be defined as a quatrain of six-syllable lines, usually iambic trimester; but in *The Sabbath Hymn Book* it is always four lines of six syllables followed by either (a) two lines of eight (four lines of iambic trimeter followed by two of iambic tetrameter), or (b) four lines of four syllables (four lines of iambic trimeter followed by four of iambic dimeter). See, for example, *The Sabbath Hymn Book: For the Service of Song in the House of the Lord* (New York: Mason Brothers, 1858), nos. 356 and 357, 211–12. The first has four lines of six syllables followed by four lines of four; the second has four lines of six syllables followed by two lines of four syllables. But the four-beat lines are always divided by caesura, as in "With all our powers, Eternal King / Thy name we sing, while faith adores."

19. Johnson lists common, long and short meter and then common and short particular meter (but not long). He also refers to 7s and 6s (quatrains of alternating seven- and six-syllable lines) and sixes. He goes on: "The principal trochaic meters are *Sevens, Eights and Sevens, Eights and Fives, Sevens and Fives, Sixes and Fives,* and *Sixes*.

Of the dactyls, which were arranged principally in *Elevens, Elevens and Tens*, and *Tens and Nines*, Emily Dickinson chose almost exclusively the last named when she chose it as the meter for an entire poem" (Johnson, *Emily Dickinson*, 85).

20. In the "Doxologies" section of another hymnal, two types of long meter are illustrated, along with common meter, short meter, half meter, and 7s. Peculiar meters are then described two pages later: they are 12s; 12, 11; 11s; 10, 11; 11, 10; 8s; 8, 7; 8, 6; 7s; 7, 6; 7, 8; 8s; 6, 8; 6, 5; 6, 4; 5, 6; 5, 6, 9. In *Hymns for Social Worship: Selected from Watts, Doddridge, Newton, Cowper, Steele, and Others* (New York: American Tract Society, 1840), 466–67. The point is that critics who focus only on the "three standard forms" miss that there were many, many more models that Dickinson could choose to emulate and refine as she wished. The irony is that certain structures used by Dickinson, and defined posthumously as deviant and defiant, were quite familiar within the hymn tradition.

21. Just as tangentially interesting, Isaac Watts recommended that students, when reading, write comments and questions: "Make a book, of perhaps 3 or 4 sheets of paper, as it may contain a treasure worth preserving." (I am not claiming that Dickinson read this passage and decided to follow it but that the idea of the manuscript book as archive was not entirely foreign to New England culture.) See Watts, *The Improvement of the Mind*, ed. Joseph Emerson (Boston: James Loring, 1832), 74.

22. Martha England writes: "Watts divided the phonetic spectrum in two parts, apparently, and freely rhymed any dark vowel sound with any other, any light vowel sound with any other. He did not rhyme dark with light vowels, either in vowel rhyme or suspended rhyme, except in a few cases. One is the sibilant; any sibilant seemed to serve in itself as a rhyme without consideration of the preceding vowel sound; thus, he occasionally rhymed peace-pronounce, etc. The long *o* rhymed thus: boast-frost-trust; hope-prop-up; shone-son; stroke-flock; goat-foot; road-clod; groan-dawn. But long or short *o* did not rhyme with *a, e, i*. In vowel rhyme such matchings occur more frequently than in suspended rhyme, but the rule is the same. Any nasal consonant was made equal to any other. He rhymed *m* with *n*, *n* with *nd* and *ng*, and (rarely) *m* with *ng*. *F* and *v* are equivalent. Both he and Emily Dickinson sounded *l* and *r* so lightly that the sounds might be ignored in rhyming. He rhymed thought-not-note-vault-court. Emily Dickinson rhymed dark with light vowel sounds, and accepted many consonants as equivalent that were distinguished by Watts" (England, *Hymns Unbidden*, 129 n. 28). Johnson claims that "Custom decreed exact patterns and exact rhymes in English poetry" but omits to mention that the "supple and varied" rhyme Dickinson favored had in a sense already been approved by Watts (*Emily Dickinson*, 87).

23. Daniel Chandler, "An Introduction to Genre Theory," <http://www.aber.ac .uk/~dgc/intgenre2.html> (accessed 7 April 2000).

24. E. A. Sophocles, *A Greek Grammar for the Use of Learners* (Hartford: H. Huntington, 1838), 265–76. See Carlton Lowenberg, *Emily Dickinson's Textbooks* (Lafayette, Calif.: Carlton Lowenberg, 1986), 94.

25. This information is taken in part from Ralph H. Franklin, *The Manuscript Books of Emily Dickinson* (Cambridge: Harvard University Press, Belknap Press, 1981) 1:434, and from my own measurements of packet 8, Ms Am 1118.3 (61–68) at the Houghton Library, Harvard University. Of the small groups of paper in this packet, only five (62–66) correspond to the fascicle as Franklin describes it. The others have different kinds of paper, with distinct embossments. In what follows, all of the descriptions are based on the manuscript originals.

26. Recall that a capital at the beginning of a row and a large space at the close

constitute domain-initial and domain-end insignia, respectively. The next largest end space on the page is after "Jubilee" (4.1 cm). See Ms Am 1118.3 (61). Henceforth, all references prefixed by Ms Am are to manuscript originals at Houghton Library.

27. The difference is that half meter often—but not always—has two additional lines of tetrameter. Another possible definition would have been 7s, but too many of the lines exceed the total of seven syllables for this to be fully satisfactory.

28. Interestingly, both words are preceded with a cross, Dickinson's indication that there were variant words available for them. In both cases, the variants are written in lowercase. Ms Am 1118.3 (61).

29. And the rhyme of the poem ("Afternoon," "on," "begun," and "alone") occurs at regular intervals (every second line) in the print edition of the poem but is dissipated in the autograph (if taken too literally). Judy Jo Small describes how the "sublime mood here is supported by the ambiguous rhymes, low vowels modulated around one soft consonant." Needless to say, her reading—of this or any other poem where she detects regular rhyme—would be invalidated by a manuscript-based edition of the poems (Small, *Positive as Sound: Emily Dickinson's Rhyme* [Athens: University of Georgia Press, 1990], 137).

30. "Great Clouds . . ." has twenty-eight letters and three dashes; "The Flesh . . ." has twenty-eight letters and three dashes. By contrast, a short sequence such as "Cre- ation – looking on –" has seventeen letters and two dashes. In other words, the longer the line, the more likely it is to have to be written on more than one row, which suggests once more that the logic behind such arrangements is predominantly material.

31. Atossa Frost Stone, "Manuscript Journal" (1817–28), Rare Books and Manu- scripts, William Allan Neilson Library, Smith College, Northampton. The paper is 16.4 cm wide; the left margin for prose is perhaps 1.2 cm and 3.5 cm for poetry.

32. Ms Am 1118.3 (63).

33. Ik Marvel, *Reveries of a Bachelor, or a Book of the Heart* (New York: Charles Scribner, 1852). The edition, which is the same read by Dickinson, is cited as an example that nineteenth-century practice did not differ from contemporary usage. Dickinson varied her habits—most often both sets of quotation marks will slant in a similar direction, but at other times they may be conventionally inscribed, or some- times one set will run in one direction and the next two in another. Ik Marvel was the pseudonym of Donald G. Mitchell (1822–1908).

34. Paul Crumbley, *Inflections of the Pen: Dash and Voice in Emily Dickinson* (Lexing- ton: University Press of Kentucky, 1997), 9.

35. Ibid. Crumbley contrasts the rough manuscript with the more polished 1891 edition by Todd and Higginson. His reasons are legitimate: he wants to show the editorial practices that prevented Dickinson from publishing and the "dominant dis- course she sought to dismantle." Thus the Todd-Higginson edition represents con- formity and normalization, whereas the manuscript embodies heteroglossia.

36. Ibid., 7.

37. By extension, if capitalization, inverted commas, and underlining are Dickin- son's most common designations of emphasis, would arranging the words on the page not make these obsolete?

38. McGann, *Black Riders*, 28.

39. I use the word "haunted" deliberately, because it seems to me that some critics and editors are—perhaps rightly—outraged by the accommodations made by editors in the past and are therefore afraid of making a different set of errors. By not interven-

ing in Dickinson's manuscripts, by reproducing them as fully as possible, they hope to avoid those mistakes.

40. Generally speaking, too, vertical spaces in Dickinson's work correspond to stanza breaks or, sometimes, to generic separation, which is to say that Dickinson will write in prose, jump a line or increase the space to the next piece of writing, and then begin the poem. Vertical spacing in prose letters with no poems is very rare.

41. There is also a degree of overlap between the handwriting in the letters and the poems, an area that has received a great deal of critical attention recently: the autographs have been described as using a "performance script," and letter shapes have been read as if they represented emotional states or physical objects. A great deal has been made of the way that "Tonight" is written in the poem "Wild Nights"—as if it were unusually emphatic and erotically charged. There are similar examples in this poem—the cross-stroke that joins the two ascenders (vertical strokes) in the words "tint," "Without," and "impatient," for instance. But those words, and "tonight" also, are written in exactly the same way in letters—to Austin Dickinson, Higginson, Bowles, women neighbors, and Dickinson's aunts and uncles, and (though not by her) in Edward Dickinson's account books as well as the autograph books, correspondence, and journals and travel diaries of her contemporaries. Cross-strokes are typical in both poems and letter, and should not therefore be regarded as significant; they are certainly decorative, but not the constituent elements of a new graphic apparatus of meaning. But no matter how careful attention to the material particulars of an autograph might be, this does not rule out its being subsumed within larger theoretical and ideological agendas. Or as Ruth Miller once put it, "a critical commitment to the object of the poem itself does not protect the poetry from being distorted to fit an extraneous frame of reference" (Miller, *The Poetry of Emily Dickinson* [Middletown: Wesleyan University Press, 1968], 35).

42. The letter appears at the beginning of "divine" in the third line.

43. These examples are taken from the final three lines of the poem. They can be observed in Franklin, *Manuscript Books*, 1:442. In my case, I consulted the original.

44. The meter is usually two lines of iambic trimeter followed by two of iambic dimeter, with rhyming couplets.

45. The original is Ms Am 1118.3 (274); the print version is Fr403A, 1:427.

46. Representing underlining in italics would have been perfectly acceptable practice, for Dickinson also. In a letter to Higginson (L503, 2:583), she reported how a clergyman had asked " 'Is the Arm of the Lord shortened that it cannot save?' " during a funeral attended by her as a child, and she continues: "He italicized the 'cannot.' " She means that the clergyman gave the word particular stress, but it shows how conventions of distinction in print (italic), speech (stress), and handwriting (underlining) were interchangeable for Dickinson. Dickinson drew from the terminology of print emphasis in a few other letters, and in six poems, suggesting that her imagination was far from repelled by the art of typesetting.

47. Dickinson's uppercasing and lowercasing of individual letters is not a matter of size only: she inscribed them in different ways. Franklin, *Manuscript Books*, 1:427.

48. Martha Nell Smith, "Dickinson's Manuscripts," in *The Emily Dickinson Handbook*, ed. Gudrun Grabher, Roland Hagenbüchle, and Cristanne Miller (Amherst: University of Massachusetts Press, 1999), 125.

49. See <http://jefferson.village.virginia.edu/dickinson/working/h274.htm> (accessed 2 May 2001).

50. Small, *Positive as Sound*, 198.

51. Hart and Smith, *Open Me Carefully*, 107–8.

52. Margie R. Dodge, "Journal" (1885–86), 2, 12, 34. Rare Books and Manuscripts, William Allan Neilson Library, Smith College, Northampton.

53. Laurence Sterne, *The Life and Opinions of Tristram Shandy, Gentleman* (1760; reprint, Gainesville: University of Florida Press, 1978), 1:379. Phutatorius has just uttered the mild oath "Zounds," and those around him speculate wildly about the possible reasons for this, thinking that he is going to attack another character in the room, Yorick. In fact, a hot chestnut has rolled into the man's trousers.

54. Martha Nell Smith, *Rowing in Eden: Rereading Emily Dickinson* (Austin: University of Texas Press, 1992), 67.

55. Interestingly, given the difference of opinion regarding "exultation" and "Exultation" in "Through what transports of Patience," both "excel" and "even" are written with open (*E*) type of letters, though they are clearly lowercase.

56. Sophocles, *Greek Grammar*, 267.

57. The rearrangement is based on the assumption that the *O* at the start of "Or" is uppercase, and that it is assigned the capital because it commences a line of its own.

58. Smith, "Corporealizations of Dickinson and Interpretive Machines," 196. Nor do they assign or uncover meaning in the lines that divide one poem from another, though line shapes within the poem are often discussed as if they were extensions of its rhetorical vocabulary. But one of the implications of the drawn line that divides one poem from another is that Dickinson did operate with notions of completeness and discreteness: the line says that one poem is distinct from the next, that it has boundaries—a clear beginning and ending.

59. LP239, 248–49; L874, 3:803. Franklin reads "Moonless" as "moonless" in Fr407A.

60. One begins to imagine, to attempt to recreate, the procedures by which Dickinson may have deliberately arranged such word splits. Picture, if you will, a line of poetry that you want to split somewhere around the fourth foot: how do you ensure that the word is split at the right place on the page? Would there not, at some stage in the career generally if not the composition in particular, be evidence of the pen overwriting an earlier penciled sketch of the line where Dickinson worked out the proportions of word and space necessary to get the split just right? And surely one would want to experiment a little with which words to split: why do none of Dickinson's drafts have lists of different split words (like the variants)? And if splitting was deliberate, why is it never positioned physically at the beginning or in the middle of a line, but always at the right margin of the paper?

61. And as Small points out, two of three variants have the same metrical pattern, which suggests that the rhythmical makeup of the word was a primary factor in its being chosen (Small, *Positive as Sound*, 193).

62. Fr408A, 1:432. Owing to a printer's error, "Little John" is typed as "little John" in Franklin's edition; the reader should note that only the vertically inscribed alternatives ("exquisite" and "Bagatelles") are included in this transcript ("Memories" and "Review"—above "Memory" and "enchant"—are others, as well as "is"—above "be").

63. Fr1180, 2:1022.

64. "MIR´A-CLE, *n.* [Fr. from L. *miraculum*, from *miror*, to wonder; Arm. *miret*, to hold. See *Marvel*.] 1. Literally, a wonder or wonderful thing; but appropriately, 2. In *theology*, an event or effect contrary to the established constitution and course of

things, or a deviation from the known laws of nature; a supernatural event. *Miracles* can be wrought only by almighty power, as when Christ healed lepers, saying, 'I will, be thou clean;' or calmed the tempest, 'Peace, be still.' . . . 3. Anciently, a spectacle or dramatic representation exhibiting the lives of the saints." See Noah Webster, *An American Dictionary of the English Language* (Amherst, Mass.: J. S. and C. Adams, 1844), 2:134.

65. Hoyt N. Duggan, "Libertine Scribes and Maidenly Editors: Meditations on Textual Criticism and Metrics," in *English Historical Metrics*, ed. C. B McCully and J. J. Anderson (Cambridge: Cambridge University Press, 1996), 223.

66. Johnson, 85–86; England, *Hymns Unbidden*, 130 n. 30.

67. Fr409A, 1:434. Franklin prints "close the Valves," which is questionable. The first *c* is bigger than the other letters in the word, but this is often the case with Dickinson's handwriting (the phrase "an ample nation," for instance, has three words whose initial letters are all bigger than their final ones). Generally speaking, capitals are distinguishable by being inscribed differently (*T* and *t*, *H* and *h*), or (as in the case of *c* and *a*) by being much taller than their minuscule equivalents. In this instance, the editor's decision is accepted because the practice in the rest of the poem is to write verbs that are not line-initial in small letters: thus, "selects," "shuts," "notes," and "kneeling."

68. Small, *Positive as Sound*, 26. Franklin transcribes "someone" as "some one"; I retain the single word because although it is written in cursive with a slight gap between its parts, the gap is minimal, and gaps in cursive writing are not uncommon in Dickinson's script either. The quotation marks around *"spicy isles"* both slant in the same direction, from upper left to lower right. Franklin omits the dash between "Brig" and "like." Note that I employ italics for emphasis here: the underlining for Fr403A was necessary for that discussion only.

69. Small, *Positive as Sound*, 129.

70. If this sounds political, it is because manuscript critics often adopt a discourse of egalitarianism when describing their positions: *Open Me Carefully*, the title of one edition, is remarkable for its combination of sexual, textual, and pluralist associations, none of which are negative but all of which transform the debate about manuscripts into something more than editorial discussion. Indeed, one of the arguments for making electronic images of the manuscripts available on the Web is political, for they then become accessible to a greater number of people. Whether they become accessible to a greater diversity of people is another question, of course; it remains to be seen if the demographic makeup of Dickinson's readership will be significantly altered in terms of class and ethnic background. But the emphasis on the visual dimensions of her work at a time when popular culture emphasizes intensely regular rhythm and rhyme also runs the risk of making Dickinson less accessible rather than more so.

71. Amittai F. Aviram, *Telling Rhythm: Body and Meaning in Poetry* (Ann Arbor: University of Michigan Press, 1994), 87.

72. "A Cousin's Memories of Emily Dickinson: Boston Woman Also Recalls Visit of the Poetess' Sister, Lavinia," *Boston Sunday Globe*, 12 January 1930, 41.

73. Catharine Scott Turner Anthon to Martha Dickinson Bianchi, 8 October 1914, bMS Am 1118.95, box 9, Dickinson Family Papers, Houghton Library, Harvard University.

74. L304, 2:440 (of course, this could mean that Dickinson read the letters silently, but the location [the garret rather than her bedroom], and the "reception" [rafters do

not weep, but personifying them would be redundant if Dickinson had not read the Shakespeare aloud] suggest that Dickinson is referring to declamation); L721, 3:706.

75. L901, 3:824. That Dickinson declaimed her own poems is described in Martha Ackmann, " 'I'm Glad I Finally Surfaced': A Norcross Descendent Remembers Emily Dickinson," *Emily Dickinson Journal*, 5, no. 2 (1996): 120–26.

76. Mary J. Reid, "Julia C. Dorr and Some of her Poet Contemporaries," *Midland Monthly* 3, no. 6 (June 1895): 506. My thanks to Alfred Habegger for bringing this article to my attention.

77. Susan Dickinson recalled "some rare effusion of fine sentiment, over an unpublished poem which he would draw from his pocket, having received it in advance from the fascinated editor. I especially remember two such, 'Pomegranite flowers' by Harriet Prescott, in a number of the Atlantic in the year '61, and a little unpublished poem of Mrs. Browning's which I fear I have lost." In "Annals of the Evergreens," 3; bMS Am 1118.95, box 9, Dickinson Family Papers, Houghton Library, Harvard University.

78. Fr186A, 1:220–21.

79. A 668, Special Collections, Frost Library, Amherst College. The manuscript is written in ink, on stationery embossed "PARIS." All references prefixed by A are to manuscript originals in this collection.

80. Frances Norcross, quoted in Millicent Todd Bingham, *Ancestors' Brocades: The Literary Debut of Emily Dickinson* (New York: Harper and Brothers, 1945), 142.

81. Franklin, notes to Fr1350B, 3:1166.

82. As Gay Wilson Allen wrote, "no matter how the lines are printed on the page, when the poems are read aloud the conventional iambic rhythmical patterns are plainly discernible." His wider comments make it clear that meter is fundamental to Dickinson's sense of a poem's organization and that editorial procedures guided by autograph lineation are suspect. See Gay Wilson Allen, *American Prosody* (New York: American Book Company, 1935), 314.

83. I read the seventh line of Fr399 as having two successive iambic feet, a pyrrhic foot (two unstressed syllables) and a final iamb.

84. The justification for suggesting that the third stanza might have been first composed as a quatrain is the rhyme scheme: "Crucifixion," "Bloom," "sowed," "Tomb" represents the same *abcb* pattern as the rest of the poem. "Filaments of Bloom" is scanned as a dactyl and an iamb in this scheme, rather than the (to my ear) more labored triple trochee which it might also be read as.

85. In either common meter or short meter, the third line has four beats; in this poem, Dickinson divided it into two lines of iambic dimeter instead.

86. The opening line, "One need not be a chamber – to be Haunted," is iambic to begin with, but the sequence "to be Haunted" seems to be stressed mainly on the third syllable ("Haunt"), meaning that its first two syllables are pronounced relatively quickly. The sudden rush and the emphasis on "Haunt" creates a dramatic effect, especially after the pause enacted by the dash and the unstressed final syllable of "chamber."

87. The first line has been read as iambic pentameter (mainly on the grounds that it has ten syllables and is perfectly regular until the final word, "Society"), but it can also be read as iambic tetrameter with a concluding pyrrhic foot. This emphatic, driving beat that is undercut by a weak final foot seems characteristic of the dialectic of the entire poem, which ebbs and flows in its attitude to the speaker's choice.

88. In that sense, George Whicher's advice seems to have been ignored: "May we

hope also that future editors of Emily Dickinson will not print her poems in such a way as to disguise their metrical structure!" And he went on to complain about editions in which single "lines have been broken into two or even three separate lines, false lines formed by joining fragments metrically distinct, stanzas divided in the middle, and the stanzaic basis of entire poems concealed by failure to divide. It is true that Emily had little sense for the visible form of a poem. She sometimes divided or merged lines as her habit of writing in a bold hand on small scraps of paper dictated. She was quite capable of writing a poem 'solid' like prose, merely capitalizing the first word of each line and not always remembering to do that. Since she freely capitalized important words within the line as well, it is often impossible to tell, except by ear, whether an apparent line in manuscript is a true line or not. The tune was in her head, and she was indifferent to its representation on paper. Her editors, however, should not permit themselves to share her indifference" (Whicher, *This Was a Poet*, 239–40).

89. Hers, as Martha England once noted, "differ from eighteenth-century hymns (especially from those by Watts) by their greater metrical freedom, freer use of en-jambment, use of more images with no scriptural source. The voice is that of a lone singer rather than the voice of the congregation assembled" (England, *Hymns Unbid-den*, 119). And Whicher notes, "No one who disregards editorial perversities and reads the poems metrically can avoid the perception that Emily Dickinson was both ortho-dox in her choice of meters, except in a very small number of poems, and skillful in blending the fixed beat of the meter with the free cadences of speech. Her preference was for iambic or trochaic measures and for the four-stress line" (Whicher, *This Was a Poet*, 240).

90. A wonderful variation on this idea takes place in the 1991 French film *Delica-tessen*, co-directed by Jean-Pierre Jeunet and Marc Caro: a couple's lovemaking on a bed with squeaky springs dictates the rhythm of cello playing, wall painting, and knit-ting elsewhere in the house.

91. "If I read a book [and] it makes my whole body so cold no fire ever can warm me I know *that* is poetry. If I feel physically as if the top of my head were taken off, I know *that* is poetry. These are the only way I know it. Is there any other way." Re-ported by Higginson and included in L342a, 2:473–74.

CHAPTER SEVEN   *Toward a Culture of Measurement in Manuscript Study*

The title of this chapter is borrowed from an exhibit at the Houghton Library, Harvard College Library, Harvard University, curated by Bruce Redford and titled "The Mea-sure of Ruins: Dilettanti in the Levant, 1750–1770" (it ran from 5 November 2001 to 26 January 2002). The program for the exhibit opens thus: "What role should imagi-nation play in the recovery of the past? During the middle decades of the eighteenth century, British students of classical antiquity pursued two contrasting approaches to this question. On the one hand, they supported what architectural historians have called a 'culture of measurement,' which stressed the importance of daily investigation and accurate recording. On the other, they cultivated not only the measure but the pleasure of ruins—their power to evoke ancient grandeur, stimulate subjective reverie, and enhance contemporary taste. In Great Britain the most influential supporters of the empirical project were members of the Society of Dilettanti, connoisseurs and collectors who had made the Grand Tour to Italy. Virtuosi of a different stamp, the architect Robert Adam and his many imitators promoted an eclectic vision of the antique—a vision that both reflected and reinforced a vogue for the picturesque." It is not difficult to see current debates about the status of Dickinson's manuscripts as an opposition between attempts at accuracy of observation and recording and attempts at re-creating atmosphere and aura—or between measure and pleasure.

Epigraph: Paul Valéry, "Recollection," in *The Collected Works of Paul Valéry*, ed. Jackson Mathews, trans. David Paul (New Jersey: Princeton University Press, 1971), 1:xvi–xvii.

1. L271, 2:415. Henceforth, all references prefixed by L are to *The Letters of Emily Dickinson*, ed. Thomas H. Johnson and Theodora Ward (Cambridge: Harvard University Press, Belknap Press, 1958). On the occasion of her marriage to William S. Jackson on 22 October 1875, Helen Hunt Jackson received a letter from Dickinson (L444, 2:544) and then asked to have it explained (L444a, 2:544–47).

2. The wording of this passage is taken from Theodor Redpath's "The Meaning of a Poem," in *On Literary Intention*, ed. David Newton-De Molina (Edinburgh: University Press, 1976), 18.

3. William K. Wimsatt and Monroe C. Beardsley, "The Intentional Fallacy," in *The Verbal Icon: Studies in the Meaning of Poetry* (Lexington: University of Kentucky Press, 1954), 4. The description of their argument is taken from Jeremy Hawthorn, *A Glossary of Contemporary Literary Theory* (London: Arnold, 2000), 175. In an obvious sense, Wimsatt and Beardsley were right: one need not accept the opinion of the minor writer who intended to write a major poem (or to say something profound in an interesting way) and thought that he or she had done so.

4. Redpath, "Meaning of a Poem," 18.

5. "You ask me what my flowers said – then they were disobedient – I gave them messages" (L187, 2:333).

6. The first distinction, between "meaning" and "significance," is made by E. D. Hirsch in *Validity in Interpretation* (New Haven: Yale University Press, 1967), 46. The second distinction is offered by Quentin Skinner in "Motives, Intentions, and the Interpretation of Texts," in *On Literary Intention*, ed. Newton-De Molina, 210–21.

7. Hirsch, *Validity in Interpretation*, quoted in Frank Kermode, *Essays on Fiction, 1971–82* (London: Routledge and Kegan Paul, 1983), 204

8. Paul Ricouer, *Interpretation Theory: Discourse and the Surplus of Meaning* (Fort Worth: Texas Christian University Press, 1976), 30.

9. The quotations are from Dennis Taylor, *Hardy's Metres and Victorian Prosody* (Oxford: Oxford University Press, 1988), 191. On the other hand, Dickinson's autographs may represent an extreme and unsuccessful development of the tradition of figured poetry in English literature. At any rate, being given the credit for foreseeing what has largely been a literary cul-de-sac is an ambiguous compliment.

10. Judith Farr, *The Passion of Emily Dickinson* (Cambridge: Harvard University Press, 1992), 374.

11. The quotation from Judge Robert Grier's ruling on *Stowe v. Thomas* is taken from Siva Vaidhyanathan, *Copyrights and Copywrongs: The Rise of Intellectual Property and How It Threatens Creativity* (New York: New York University Press, 2001), 49.

12. Fr788, 2:742. Henceforth, all references prefixed by Fr are to poems as numbered in *The Poems of Emily Dickinson*, ed. Ralph W. Franklin (Cambridge: Harvard University Press, Belknap Press, 1998).

13. Isaak D'Israeli describes how James I had a bishop defend the printing of the king's works, which was thought to have discredited the monarch through association

with a trade. The bishop wrote: "The majesty of kings . . . is not unsuited to a writer of books. . . . The first royal author is the King of Kings – God himself, who doth so many things for our imitation." Quoted in Ian Hamilton, *Keepers of the Flame: Literary Estates and the Rise of Biography* (London: Hutchinson, 1992), 8.

14. Noah Webster, *An American Dictionary of the English Language* (Amherst, Mass.: J. S. and C. Adams, 1844), 1:152–53. Definition 15 is "to bear testimony or witness. This seems to imply *utterance*, like the Latin *fero*, to relate or utter." Dickinson may also be invoking the idea that the writer or reader carries the sign, the emblem, of thought, which originates outside the self.

15. John Locke, *Two Treatises on Government*, ed. Peter Laslett (1690; London: Cambridge University Press, 1967), 305–6.

16. L316, 2:450; to T. W. Higginson, early 1866.

17. Franklin, *Poems*, 3:1532.

18. Susan Huntington Dickinson, A. L. s. to William Hayes Ward, Amherst, Mass., 8 February 1891. Amy Lowell Collection, Houghton Library, Harvard University, quoted in Millicent Todd Bingham, *Ancestors' Brocades: The Literary Debut of Emily Dickinson* (New York: Harper, 1945), 114–15.

19. Lavinia Dickinson, A. L. s. to William Hayes Ward, Amherst, Mass., 20 March 1891, Amy Lowell Collection, Houghton Library, Harvard University. Lavinia Dickinson's signature at the end is written in her usual fashion—scrawling and with a heavier ink and thicker script than the rest of the letter—indicating that the letter was written by someone else and dictated by her; written by someone else, on her behalf, and signed by her; or written by someone else and signed by her at that person's request. Lavinia's letter refers to (and rejects any possibility of) a "pooling of interests": the suggestion "to pool your interests" (with Susan Dickinson) was made by Ward in a letter to Mabel Loomis Todd (dated 13 March 1891), quoted in Bingham, *Ancestors' Brocades*, 116. It therefore seems that Lavinia was writing at Todd's behest. Although Lavinia Dickinson and Mabel Loomis Todd did not write to William Hayes Ward until March, the conflict over who owned copyright on poems by Emily Dickinson that were in Susan Dickinson's possession and who had the right to publish them is already hinted at in the close of the letter (discussed later in this chapter) in which Susan makes the distinction between "print" and "publish": she adds that "Mr. Dickinson thinks as Col. Higginson and Niles are to bring out another vol. of the poems, it is not best, or fair to them to print many. I do not feel bound to them, but will of course defer to his wish in the matter."

20. Thomas Niles to Mabel Loomis Todd, 30 March 1891, quoted in *Ancestors' Brocades*, 119. The "new copyright law" is Niles's phrase, and it refers to the latest of a series of amendments to the earlier U.S. Copyright Act of 1790: amendments were voted on in 1802, 1819, 1831, 1856, 1865, 1875, 1890, and 1897. A new copyright act was brought into force in 1909. See L. Ray Patterson and Stanley W. Lindberg, *The Nature of Copyright: A Law of Users' Rights* (Athens: University of Georgia Press, 1991).

21. The situation today is different, of course. In a 1991 article, Beth Kiley Kinder, then copyright and permissions manager at Harvard University Press, pointed out that anything "published more than 75 years ago is now in the public domain *in the form in which it is was published at that time*. All the new material introduced in Johnson's edition, in particular the variorum *Poems*—corrections, restorations of doctored texts, ED's alternative readings and variant versions, as well as the 41 poems appearing for the first time—is covered by the copyrights to his edition." See Kinder, "To Quote or

Not to Quote? Questions and Answers about the Copyright Status of Dickinson Works," *Emily Dickinson International Society Bulletin* 3, no. 2 (November/December 1991): 1. Does this mean that works that do *not* follow the visual appearance of the Johnson editions are not copyrighted by Harvard University Press, or does Franklin's inclusion of information about line breaks and word divisions in effect secure an extension of the copyright to the manuscript layout? Does the publication of autographs on the Web—for instance, at the Dickinson Electronic Archives site at <www.emilydickinson.org>—mean that arrangements which coincide with print transcriptions made available there have to cede copyright to its editors?

22. Emily Dickinson, "Last Will and Testament," photostat, Special Collections, Jones Library, Amherst. The will mentions "my only and dearly beloved brother William A. Dickinson," her "beloved and honored mother" (not referred to by name), and "my only sister Lavinia N. Dickinson." It was witnessed by Luke Sweetser, Elizabeth Lord, and Margaret Maher. The original is at the Houghton Library, Harvard University.

23. Lavinia Dickinson died in 1899 without leaving a will. At the Hampshire Probate and Family Court in Northampton, box 312, no. 10, docket 5799, there is the "Request of Martha Gilbert Dickinson to be administratrix of her deceased Aunt Lavinia Dickinson's estate, Oct. 2, 1899," and "Appointment of Martha G. Dickinson as administratrix of Lavinia Dickinson's estate, Oct. 3, 1899." A letter dated Amherst, Massachusetts, 1 November 1955, from Mary Hampson to Little, Brown & Co., begins: "On 6 May, 1950, my late husband, Alfred Leete Hampson, the President and Fellows of Harvard College, and the Rosenbach Company [represented by family friend Bill McCarthy] were parties to an agreement entitled an Indenture and Bill of Sale by which the President and Fellows of Harvard College acquired the manuscripts, other unpublished materials, and literary rights of Emily Dickinson which were owned by my husband." Clause 8 of that agreement read as follows: "Owner hereby assigns to Purchaser all literary property and rights of Emily Dickinson and all copyrights in the literary works of Emily Dickinson and all of his rights to sue for infringements thereof, past and future, subject to any valid agreements with publishers. Purchaser agrees that if any literary works are prepared from the material of the Dickinson collection Purchaser will cause publisher of such literary works to pay Owner a customary royalty in accordance with the general practices in the publishing business, and after the death of Owner to pay such royalties to his wife, Mary Landis Hampson, and after the death of both of them to apply such royalties toward the upkeep of the Emily Dickinson Memorial Room." Clause 10 reads: "Purchaser is to have sole right to grant or refuse permission to reprint selections from material covered by assignment of copyrights hereunder and to establish fees for such publication" (bMs Am Box 1923, letter from Mary Landis Hampson, Houghton Library, Harvard University: henceforth, all references prefixed by bMs Am are to originals at Houghton Library). The purchase of Dickinson's manuscripts in the 1950s was as much an aspect of the historical moment as the interest in their graphic potential is of ours. In the 1950s, North America was beginning to recover from the aftermath of the Second World War, and research libraries began to enlarge their collections, often in competition with each other, and usually (as with Dickinson) through private donations rather than through active purchases. At the same time, the "concept of investigating the creative process through every stage in a text from manuscript to print scarcely existed. What Philip Larkin once characterized as the 'magical value' of a . . . writer's manuscripts was always

recognized, but, with a few exceptions, not the 'meaningful' value" (Jenny Stratford, "English Literary Manuscripts in the Twentieth Century," in *The Book Encompassed: Studies in Twentieth-Century Bibliography*, ed. Peter Davison [Cambridge: Cambridge University Press, 1992], 49).

24. Letter of 10 October 1960, a copy of which was forwarded to Mrs. Alfred Hampson, from William McCarthy Jr., curator of the Philip H. & A.S.W. Rosenbach Foundation, 2010 De Lancey Place, Philadelphia, Special Collections, Jones Library, Amherst. In 2002, ownership of Emily Dickinson's originals does not extend to ownership of the copyright; Boston Public Library and Amherst College are two cases in point, for they can allow access to and use of the manuscripts in their possession, but the final say on their reproduction for scholarly purposes rests with Harvard University Press. Houghton Library still retains copyright of the manuscript images; Harvard University Press has had the copyright to the poems since 1955, and to the letters since 1958.

25. Roland Barthes, "The Death of the Author," *Image-Music-Text* (London: Fontana Press, 1977), 147. The essay first appeared in 1968.

26. D. C. Greetham, *Theories of the Text* (Oxford: Oxford University Press, 1999), 322.

27. See "Detailed Description of the Archives," at <http:www.emilydickinson .org/archive_description.html> (accessed 30 April 2002). Members of the Dickinson family are referred to by their first names or nicknames ("Susan," "Mattie," "Ned," and "Gib"), so that a sense of familiarity and even continuity results between the Dickinson family and the Dickinson Electronic Archives.

28. D. C. Greetham, *Textual Scholarship: An Introduction* (New York: Garland Publishing, 1992), 355.

29. Sharon Cameron, "Dickinson's Fascicles," in *The Marks in the Fields: Essays on the Uses of Manuscripts*, ed. Rodney G. Dennis, with Elizabeth Falsey (Cambridge: Houghton Library, 1992), 155.

30. Ms Am 1118.3 (74); Fr319, 1:337; Cameron, "Dickinson's Fascicles," 157.

31. G. Thomas Tanselle, "The Editorial Problem of Final Authorial Intention," *Studies in Bibliography*, 29 (1976): 208. Fr369, 1:393–94.

32. Greetham, *Theories of the Text*, 322.

33. In addition, one notes that Cameron ignores the physical isolation of "Grass." Such a decision is justified, but it is still a decision; Cameron continues to make choices about what is and is not significant about the original (the variants are important, but not the lineation) even while her interpretation develops the idea that Dickinson rejected the making of such choices. In practice, Cameron operates with a hierarchy when it comes to "choosing not choosing": some aspects are intentional, some not. My argument is that if one accepts (implicitly or explicitly) that not all the particulars of the original are important, one also accepts that choices have to be made about which details to include within interpretive discussion or editorial presentation. Reproducing manuscripts does not suspend the exercise of choice—in which case, how does one evaluate which decisions are the right ones?

It is easy to see why more recent critics promote the use of electronic as well as, or rather than, typographic texts: an electronic edition of "Of Bronze – and Blaze" could shimmer dynamically between different performances within the same physical space, for example, in ways that print cannot always manage. The poem's possible versions could be presented synoptically or sequenced in alternative and alternating layers. Of course, as soon as readers offer an interpretation of a poem which is based on a particular textual configuration, then they commit themselves to the principle that such a configuration is more useful or appropriate than others. At least in theory, it might be thought that a belief in the several formations of a poem inherent in an autograph can logically be sustained only by using either photographic reproductions of the original in a textual or electronic form or a diversity of nonhierarchically presented typographic editions. A single typographic image of a manuscript poem (such as the one Cameron offers) is produced with or promotes the assumption that most aspects of an autograph are fully considered and that only transcriptions which follow the original lineation are accurate. Most scholars operate with an assumption that the version of the poem they look at is authentic in some way or more acceptable to them than other versions. In a sense, they frame the poem for the moment of their reading, even if they go on to release it from that frame afterward. Very few critics offer multiple editions of the same poem in their readings; implicitly, they accept a particular design. Even the promotion of a version of a poem with all its variants included represents a commitment to *that* version of the poem as the correct one: offering a version where choices are made as to variants must (according to manuscript logic) represent a contamination of the original, a lessening of its potential.

34. Cameron, "Dickinson's Fascicles," 155.

35. Susan Howe, "Some Notes on Visual Intentionality in Emily Dickinson," <http://www.scc.rutgers.edu/however/print_archive/alertsvol3no4.html#some> (accessed 24 April 2002).

36. The concept of intention is often rejected in Dickinson studies, only to reappear in other guises. In a letter to the *London Review of Books*, for example, Martha Nell Smith writes (on behalf of the Dickinson Editing Collective) that "we do not presume to be recovering Emily Dickinson's intentions nor offering a purer understanding of them" (Smith, *London Review of Books*, 5 October 2000, 4). And in a response to chapters in my *Monarch of Perception*, she states: "Though Mitchell's may be, our critical understanding of authorial intentions is not so simplistic that we assume we can know and recover Dickinson's." In the overview "Electronic Resources on Emily Dickinson" in the *EDIS Bulletin* of November/December 2000, she repeats this stance, attempting to correct two major misconceptions about the work of the DEA: "One is that their editors presume to recover Dickinson's intentions and thus get readers closer to the poet herself. None of the editors are so simplistic in our understanding of authorial intentions that we presume we can recover Dickinson's and then present them in an unadulterated form" (Smith, "Electronic Resources on Emily Dickinson," *Emily Dickinson International Society Bulletin* 12, no. 2 [2000]: 13, 26; all quotations are from page 26). It seems here that Smith does not appear to abandon or dismiss the idea that writers might have intentions; what she contests is the idea that these are recoverable or that her editorial work involves any attempt to do so. At the same time, Smith goes on to say in the same article: "The editors of the electronic archives believe that words attributed to Dickinson and passed down through her Norcross cousins tell us something crucial about intentions." And again: "Gaining an understanding of the intentions of poets and their readers has, then, always been a complicated matter" (Smith, "Electronic Resources," 26). Nevertheless, the drive to reproduce Dickinson's manuscripts in the first place proceeds from an assumption that they contain valuable information about her writing practices, and that (at some level) these might be deliberate. In a 1991 conference on Dickinson, Ellen Louise Hart echoed Susan Howe's concept

of a "visual intentionality" in the manuscripts, arguing that this would serve as a key to an edition of Dickinson's poems and letters to Susan Dickinson (later published as *Open Me Carefully*) (quoted in Marget Sands, "Editing/Publication," *Emily Dickinson International Society Bulletin* 4, no. 2 [November/December 1992]: 14). In the same article, Jeanne Holland notes that "if Dickinson did not intend to print, then the printing of her poetry misrepresents it" (14). The language of manuscript critics often gestures in the direction of intentionalism; at other times it is rejected only to be inferred again from the negation of a word with the opposite meaning. To deny that certain material features of a manuscript might be "accidental," for instance, carries with it the suggestion that such features must be intentional. The validity of exploring intentions is denied, while significant claims are made about "Dickinson's poetic mind at work" in the manuscripts. See Smith, *Rowing in Eden: Rereading Emily Dickinson* (Austin: University of Texas Press, 1992), 69, and Smith, "Corporealizations of Dickinson and Interpretive Machines," *The Iconic Page in Manuscript, Print, and Digital Culture*, ed. George Bornstein and Theresa Tinkle (Ann Arbor: University of Michigan Press, 1998), 202. In other words, Smith is not opposed to intentionalism with regard to autograph poems but to typographic versions: "That conclusions or postulations about Dickinson's final intentions for print need not be drawn does not discount her intentions altogether, for her doubling of this lyric reveals her conscious departure from and interrogation of the predictability of standard poetic forms" (Smith, *Rowing in Eden*, 69).

37. Since Dickinson never oversaw a print edition of her works, is the question of how she might have wanted her writings to be presented left permanently in abeyance? For readers such as Franklin, the lack of authorial intention is a consequence of so many of her texts' remaining unfinished; for others, the lack of intention is a kind of intention—or the abandonment of the concept of textual meaning as the embodiment of an author's final intentions. For every negative, there is a positive: it is not that Dickinson was *denied* the opportunity to print but that she *chose* to work with manuscript forms of inscription and circulation. It is not that she *failed* to produce finished texts in the latter stages of her career but that she *rejected* the very idea of textual completion. What if, it is argued, Dickinson did not want us to go beyond her manuscripts? What if the entire logic of her refusal to publish was an effort at preserving the integrity of her handwritten forms?

38. Thus, it is not that Dickinson *fit* two or three words on the lateral space of her paper but that she *placed* two or three words on the lateral space of her paper.

39. By extension, urging "accuracy" or "diplomacy" in our transcriptions of Dickinson's autographs suggests that their appearance is careful or deliberate, that the split in "apos- / tasy" (to take a previously cited example) is not a felicitous accident but a willed arrangement. But the assumption that the division and arrangement of "apostasy" across two physical lines was deliberately contrived is based partly on a double suppression: of the material relationship between Dickinson's script and the paper she wrote on, and of the conventions of nineteenth-century lettering generally and Dickinson's handwriting in particular. It is not that such knowledge of the physical extent of a page and the handwriting on it permanently discredits the possibility of aesthetic deliberateness, but that such arguments are given a fuller contextualization.

40. Wimsatt and Beardsley, "The Intentional Fallacy," 4.

41. Traditionally, ignoring variants in an unfinished manuscript may be (or has been) justified on the grounds that the writer was an artist of the finished product, a

writer who worked with print publication in mind. What is different about Dickinson
is not her manuscript practice per se, however, but that she remained largely unpubli-
shed in her own lifetime. It is this aspect of her life that leaves open the possibility that
her failure to print was based on an aversion not only to the medium of type itself but
also to the practice of finishing poems, of making choices between first- and second-
order elements, of distinguishing between words and variants. In other words, scratch
at the surface of any manuscript reading of a poem and one finds an appeal to biography
for its justification: it is not that the manuscripts offer absolutely unambiguous evi-
dence of a poetics of abandonment, but that the manuscripts read in the light of one of
several possible scenarios for the poet's decision not to publish combine to suggest
such a possibility. It is not that the death of the author is sufficiently compelling as a
textual theory that it might help liberate us from the necessity of invoking the author's
wishes with regard to her materials, but that the raw materials in combination with
Dickinson's historical and literary segregation makes such an approach the only one
that she personally sanctioned.

42. Or the intention may relate less to the communication of an originating idea
("flowers are like the sun") than—for example, with Keats—an attempt to show that a
particular form can be mastered (though often, as in the case of a sonnet, the choice of
the form may determine the nature of the subject matter), in ways that may not relate
in any obvious manner to the poem's contents. Attempting to demonstrate mastery of
a form can be seen as an intention in itself—and a rather important one. But when
Milton writes a sonnet beginning, "Avenge, O Lord, thy slaughtered saints," much of
the shock effect of the line depends on its divergence from generic expectations, for
the sonnet is principally associated with love. On the one hand, that association acts as
a grid against which to read the poem's shocking central image (of the woman and
child thrown from the mountain); on the other, Milton's rage is contained in and by
the choice of genre—for beneath the disbelief at God's apparent absence on the occa-
sion of the massacre is the constant presence of pattern, design, and purpose, God's
love for man, and man's love for God. Milton sets up a dialogue between generic codes
and content in the poem: he expresses human feelings of anger, even fear, at the
triumph of barbarism and anarchy but situates this within a medium which speaks of
continuing and continual order and love. In that sense, Milton's choice of genre can
be seen as *motivated*. The same may be said of Shelley's "Ode to the West Wind": the
experimentation with a genre long associated with public expressions of support for
the great and the good advances the poem's concern with the necessity of spiritual and
political renewal. By extension, much of the poem's formal aspects reinforce Shelley's
call for change. The combination of masculine and feminine rhyme, for example,
indirectly suggests the necessary conditions for new life. The echo of the sonnet form
in the length of each of the five sections hints at some principle of love, or creative and
positive power, underlying all experience—even the most destructive. And the use of
terza rima resembles the restless, dynamic, and inevitable nature of change. All these
formal features acquire the status of rhetorical effects, signs with definable meanings.

43. For a recent description of the "fascination with the literary recreation of songs,
ballads, hymns refrains and other musical forms," see Yopie Prins, "Victorian Meters,"
in *The Cambridge Companion to Victorian Poetry*, ed. Joseph Bristow (Cambridge: Cam-
bridge University Press, 2000), 89–113.

44. Tanselle, "Final Authorial Intention," 206.

45. G. Thomas Tanselle, *A Description of Descriptive Bibliography* (Washington,
D.C.: Library of Congress, 1992), 11.

46. Charles M. Schulz, *Peanuts Jubilee: My Life and Art with Charlie Brown and Others* (London: Allen Lane, 1975), 51, plate 14. My thanks to Jeremy Hawthorn for bringing this to my attention.

47. Fr1275B, 2:1100; A 432/431. L392, 2:508–9; Ms Am 1118.5 (B150). There is another capital *S* on the sixth page ("Seldoms") that is not quite as horizontal, but again very similar in shape to the *S* in "Sea." Most of the *S* and *Y* characters in Ms Am 1118.5 (B150) are on their sides, proof yet again that the same characters in A 432/431 are not unique. The letters were compared by having one photocopied onto a transparency, and then placed over the other two (separately) for the purposes of comparison. Susan Howe and Martha Nell Smith argue independently of each other that Dickinson's hand-scripted letters occasionally make visual contributions to a poem's meaning, so that in this one instance the *S*'s are said to be shaped like waves and the *T*'s formed to resemble choppy seas. (See Smith, *Rowing in Eden*, 82–85.) In a previous article, I argued that such remarks were insufficiently contextualized: the *S* and *T* characters were shaped in exactly the same way in many other manuscript poems and letters of the same year which had nothing to do with water.

48. Michel de Certeau, *The Practice of Everyday Life*, trans. Steven F. Rendall (Berkeley: University of California Press, 1984), 170–71; Roger Chartier, *The Order of Books: Readers, Authors, and Libraries in Europe between the Fourteenth and Eighteenth Centuries*, trans. Lydia G. Cochrane (Cambridge: Polity Press, 1994), 2.

49. I am not attempting to accuse critics of irresponsibility. If Dickinson did think of her manuscripts as open to a variety of visual patterns, then their approach is justifiable.

50. Millicent Todd Bingham, *Emily Dickinson: A Revelation* (New York: Harper & Brothers, 1954), 108–9; Franklin, *Poems of Emily Dickinson*, 3:1583. There is a mistake in the transcription: a comma is inserted after "My God" in line five, when the manuscript shows a dash.

51. A 890, Special Collections, Frost Library, Amherst College. The right and bottom edges of the paper are torn, neatly, and the paper is ruled vertically and horizontally. Henceforth, all references prefixed by A are to manuscripts at the Special Collections, Frost Library.

52. Ultimately, of course, the uncertainty is resolved by the rhyme scheme. Here are the alternatives:

> My God – what is a Heart, Silver – or Gold – or precious stone –
> Or Star – or Rainbow – or a part
> Of all these things – or all of them in one?

> My God – what is a Heart,
> Silver – or Gold – or precious stone –
> Or Star – or Rainbow – or a part
> Of all these things – or all of them in one?

Herbert's stanza (the second) reveals an *abab* rhyme scheme with equidistant lines; if we accept the first version, the opening line is unwieldy and the "Heart" / "part" rhyme disappears.

53. The alternative view would be that Dickinson transcribed the poem for the purposes of improvement or experimentation, attempting to see if shorter lines, isolated words, and an altered rhyme scheme might produce better or simply different

effects. But Dickinson was an inveterate quoter in her correspondence, and it makes just as much sense to think of these as potential fillers for future messages. They would certainly have been more convenient to carry in her pocket than a copy of the newspaper in which they appeared—less messy too.

54. Brita Lindberg-Seyersted, *The Voice of the Poet: Aspects of Style in the Poetry of Emily Dickinson* (Cambridge: Harvard University Press, 1968), 196.

55. Of course, the counterargument is that Dickinson deliberately revised Herbert's stanzas with a view to improving them. They are imitative exercises, but not copies. Such a view would see the dashes (instead of commas), nouns in capitals (instead of lowercase), and altered lineation as proof of a comprehensive refashioning of the standard original into a freer form. But anomalies still remain: why the lowercase letters at the start of some rows and uppercase at the start of others, for instance? And why continue to use rhyme, a structural device depending on regularity for its function? Moreover, if Dickinson thought it acceptable to change one man's poetry for her own devices, does that mean it is acceptable for us to change hers for ours?

56. Christopher Ricks, "Review of R. W. Franklin's *The Poems of Emily Dickinson*," in *Essays in Criticism* 49, no. 3 (1999): 271.

57. Fr1575, 3:1381; Ms Am 1118.5 (B22).

58. Fr1575, 3:1381. The poem is dated by Franklin—as it was by Johnson before him—to about 1882. The space to the right edge of the paper from the dashes that follow "Sleep" and "keep" are (respectively) 8 cm and 7.8 cm: this is about 64 percent of the paper (a half sheet of unruled laid paper, 12.5 cm wide and 23 cm high, torn along the left edge). The writing is in pencil.

59. J1539, *The Poems of Emily Dickinson*, ed. Thomas H. Johnson (Cambridge: Harvard University Press, Belknap Press, 1955), 3:1060 (henceforth., all references prefixed by J are to poems in this edition). Alfred Habegger reports that Otis Lord recited "the whole of [hymn writer] Isaac Watts's grimmest song" at a dinner given by Susan Dickinson at the Evergreens, and that "Vinnie topped this with a comic rendition of another hymn by Watts." In Habegger, *My Wars Are Laid Away in Books* (New York: Random House, 2001), 585. Perhaps the satire was inspired by Lord and Lavinia Dickinson's usage, or perhaps that kind of ironic adjustment was part of the culture.

60. *The New-England Primer, Improved* (Boston: Edward Draper, 1777), n.p.

61. Martha Dickinson Bianchi, *The Life and Letters of Emily Dickinson* (Boston: Houghton Mifflin Co., 1924), 61.

62. Franklin, *Poems*, 3:1584. The manuscript, A 175b, is at Amherst College. The unruled portion of the paper Dickinson writes on measures 8.2 cm in width and 12.5 cm in height and the writing is in pencil.

63. Algernon Charles Swinburne, *Poems: Selections* (Boston: D. C. Heath, 1905), 5.

64. Fr1237A ("Oh Shadow on / the Grass") and Fr1237B ("Oh Shadow / on the Grass"), 2:1068. The first is dated to about 1871, the second to 1872, well into the conjectured period of Dickinson's experiment with the graphic properties of letter, word and line. The first is Ms Am 1118.3 (205), the second is A 315.

65. Ms Am 1118.3 (205) measures about 12.4 cm across but fits three words to the first row of writing; A 315 is 13.2 cm across, but fits two words to the first row of writing. The first is written in 1871, in ink on cream paper with a blue rule; "Oh" takes up about 2cm of space, and "Shadow," almost five. The second is written in pencil on graph paper; "Oh" takes up about 4 cm of space, and "Shadow," 6.5 cm. In addition, the first row of A 315 is substantially indented (1.8 cm), and Dickinson skips every second of the ruled lines as she moves down the page (in Ms Am 1118.5 [205], she

writes on consecutive lines). Is the spacing deliberate or aesthetic—or a function of changes in the writing implement, the kind of paper, the year, the time of year or day, the poet's mood or some such?

66. The Lord envelope is A 740; the Charles Clark is A 730.

67. A 774. The stamp is in the upper left corner and is affixed horizontally rather than vertically (with the result that the head seems to be lying on its nose, in other words). On the back of the envelope are two postmarks: "CARRIER / NOV/ 20 / 2 PM / 3" and "WASHINGTON REC'D / NOVE/ 20 / 10 AM/ 1884." The writing is in ink.

68. A 776. The stamp is in the upper left corner, and is affixed horizontally rather than vertically. On the back of the envelope are two postmarks: "CARRIER / JAN/ 3 / 2 PM / 9" and "WASHINGTON REC'D / JAN/ 3 / 9 AM/ 1885." The writing is in ink.

69. The one exception to this rule is the sequence "And thought 'How vast a Destiny'," which is represented by two physical lines in versions A and E (as Franklin identifies them) but by a cluster of three lines in B, C, and D. But since the *metrical* line is iambic tetrameter (rather than the trimeter elsewhere), Dickinson may be construed as having allowed herself extra space with which to record the additional syllables.

70. Ralph Waldo Emerson, *Poems* (Boston: Houghton, Mifflin and Company, 1896), 42; A 769.

71. Ellen Louise Hart, "The Elizabeth Whitney Putnam Manuscripts and New Strategies for Editing Emily Dickinson's Letters," *Emily Dickinson Journal* 4, no. 1 (1995): 49.

72. *Letters*, 2:351–52.

73. <http://lcweb2.loc.gov/cgi-bin/query/r?ammem/mcc:@field(DOCID+@lit (mcc/012))> (accessed 10 December 1999). See also the final page of Mary Todd Lincoln's 2 November 1862 autograph letter to her husband Abraham, in which she writes "if you will send the / check by Tuesday, will / be much obliged –," then leaves space before beginning "One line to say that we / are occasionally remembered [etc.]" <http://lcweb2.loc.gov/cgi-bin/query/r?ammem/mcc:@field(DOCID+@lit(mcc/ 032))> (accessed 10 December 1999). Even a cursory search of digitized images on the Internet shows that what is described as unique and meaningful in Dickinson's manuscripts was typical of the century generally.

74. "Emma Spaulding Bryant Letters: An On-line Archival Collection," <http:// scriptorium.lib.duke.edu/bryant//1873-07-25.html> (accessed 3 September 1999).

75. Sarah Hammond, Journal (1836), Ms Am 1609.

76. Charles Richard Sanders, "Editing the Carlyle Letters," in *Editing Nineteenth-Century Texts: Papers Given at the Editorial Conference, University of Toronto, November 1966*, ed. John M. Robson (Toronto: University of Toronto Press, 1967), 88.

77. Annie Fields, letter to Mrs. Johnson, Boston, 28 April 1870, Ms Am 1679. The language of the letter may sound familiar to the student of nineteenth-century literature: Fields is reporting on a series of lectures given by Emerson in Cambridge.

78. Amanda M. Corey Edmond, "Journal of a Tour across the Atlantic, and through England, Scotland, Ireland, France, Germany & Belgium" (1844), 1, Rare Books and Manuscripts, William Alan Neilson Library, Smith College, Northampton. The journal pages measure 20.4 cm wide and 26.8 cm high.

79. Elizabeth Sedgwick, Journal (1839), Ms Am 1670.1.

80. Richard Whately (1787–1863), A. L. s. to the Masters of Swift's Hospital and Richmond Lunatic Asylum, Dublin, 13 October 1854, Ms Am 1838.2 (10).

81. There are all kinds of examples of people in the past having taken for granted

information that people in the present are ignorant of. The Greenfield historian Lucy Cutler Kellogg notes a record that begins: "The first meeting of the Post in its present quarters was held August 7, 1900." The writer assumed that the whereabouts of the post office would be known to her readers, in other words: today, it is not. Kellogg, *History of Greenfield 1900–1929* (Town of Greenfield, Mass., 1931), 1451.

82. Charles Mackay, ed., *A Thousand and One Gems of English Poetry* (London: George Routledge & Sons, 1867), 573.

83. Humphrey Milord, ed., *The Poetical Works of Henry Longsworth Longfellow* (London: Oxford University Press, 1921), 48.

84. That the linear segregation of differentially indented lowercase words was not intended to affect the meaning of the poem does not, however, prohibit readers from appropriating that possibility. It would seem perfectly justifiable to argue that the arrangement of Longfellow's quatrain as six lines exists as a resource for writers of today who are interested in the meaningful potential of writing's graphic dimensions.

85. Sarah Orne Jewett, "To my father," unsigned draft, Ms Am 1743. 23 (1). Written in pen on unlined paper, folded in thirds.

86. Ibid., Ms Am 1743. 23 (2).

87. Sarah Orne Jewett, "Selections from the Standard Poets" (commonplace book), Ms Am 1743. 26 (1). Written in pen on unruled paper, the fifteen pages of poetry are recorded on paper that bears the advertisement of "Dentists' / Fine Gold Foil / Manufactured by / Charles Abbey & Sons / Nos 228 & 230 Pear St / Philadelphia." Autograph books of the day show similar variety in the methods of inscribing runover lines. In that of Sarah Gates (1860–70s), one friend (Lyman Howard) indents the word or phrase approximately one centimeter further into the page than other, whole lines. Another (Clara Bennett) completes the lines in the space immediately above the word at the right edge of the page. See Sarah Gates, Autographs, Special Collections, Jones Library, Amherst. In her journal of 1836 (Ms Am 1609), Sarah Hammond places portions of the line that do not fit into the space available above the line to which the portion belongs, thus:

sprung"

"And, chirping, from the ground the grass-hopper up

Annie Fields, quoted earlier in this chapter, does the same (Ms Am 1679).

88. For an image of the Smart autograph of *Jubilate Agno*, see Dennis, *Marks in the Fields*, 168.

89. If the consignor is to be believed, the fair copy of "The Wind begun to rock the Grass" had been in the same family since the turn of the nineteenth century; the provenance is important, since it would rule out the possibility of any twentieth-century forgers.

90. Notes for Fr796, 2:751. The Boston Public Library (Rare Books and Manuscripts) catalogue number for the Mary Thacher Higginson transcript is Ms Am 1093 (126)a–c ("a" corresponding to the first page, "b" to the second, etc.; Franklin's number corresponds, I believe, to the folder in which this particular manuscript is included).

91. Ralph W. Franklin, ed., *The Manuscript Books of Emily Dickinson* (Cambridge: Harvard University Press, Belknap Press, 1981) 2:1411. Ms Am 1118.5 (B123) is also written on the same kind of paper; it was sent to Susan Dickinson.

92. For the record, the last three stanzas read thus:

The Wagons
quickened
on the Streets –
The Thunder
hurried slow –
The Lightning
showed a
Yellow Beak,
And then
a livid Claw –

The Birds
put up the
Bars to
Nests –
The Cattle
fled to Barns –
Then came
one Drop
of Giant Rain
And then
as if the Hands

That held
the Dams
had parted
hold
The Waters
Wrecked the
Sky
But overlooked
my Father's
House –
Just quartering a
tree –

93. Smith, *Rowing in Eden*, 218, 213.

94. Susan Huntington Dickinson, A. L. s. to William Hayes Ward, Amherst, Mass., 18 February 1891, Amy Lowell Collection, Houghton Library, Harvard, quoted in Bingham, *Ancestors' Brocades*, 115, and in Smith, *Rowing in Eden*, 15.

95. Rather, Susan Dickinson is playing a rather delicate game whereby she initiates the process of publication but tries to be indifferent to the outcome of the request. She is distancing herself from charges of financial self-interest or a desire for publicity and maintaining a sense of social superiority.

96. Susan Dickinson, quoted in Bingham, *Ancestors' Brocades*, 86. Alfred Habegger concurs: "Sue's idea, however, was to print, not publish: believing that 'for all of us women not fame but "Love and home and certainty are best,' " she dreamed of a privately circulated collection of poems and letters" (*My Wars Are Laid Away in Books*, 628). That Susan preferred a limited and selected edition suggests that she wanted to

protect Dickinson's privacy and she believed that not all the poems were worth publishing. When Mabel Loomis Todd edited a third volume of the poems, Edward ("Ned") Dickinson wrote in August 1896 to Lavinia, threatening that she "would be held responsible naturally for any such performance, and would do more to injure any just fame that may belong to Aunt Emily, simply from a literary point of view, than any thing that could be done" (quoted in Polly Longsworth, *Austin and Mabel: The Amherst Affair and Love Letters of Austin Dickinson and Mabel Loomis Todd* [1984; reprint, Amherst: University of Massachusetts Press, 1999], 409).

97. The phrase in quotation marks is Susan Dickinson's and is from the same letter to Higginson. She had told him that the poems would be "marvelous whether in manuscript or type," suggesting that her recognition of their quality did not depend on their acceptance for publication and that whether they were in manuscript or type made no difference to them as poems (that is, type did not distort them).

98. Daniel Lombardo, *Tales of Amherst: A Look Back* (Amherst: Jones Library, 1986), 100. The details about the *Independent*'s history are derived from "Description of the Archives" of the holdings in American publishing history, Department of Rare Books and Special Collections, Princeton University Library.

99. Perkins K. Clark, *Reply to "The Existence of Two Churches in South Deerfield"* (Greenfield: S. S. Eastman & Company, 1859), 4. On the title page of a 1777 edition of *The New England Primer* is "*Printed* by EDWARD DRAPER, at his Printing-Office, in *Newbury-Street*, and Sold by JOHN BOYLE in *Marlborough-Street*." An *Introduction to the Making of Latin* (1809) is "PUBLISHED BY CUSHING & APPLETON" in Salem but printed by "*Joshua Cushing, Printer, Boston*." *New-England Primer*, n.p; William Biglow, *Introduction to the Making of Latin* (Salem: Cushing and Appleton, 1809). These last two are slightly different examples of the distinction under discussion here: there are different stages in the process whereby publication takes place, one involving the submission of a work, its acceptance by an editor, and subsequent inclusion in a newspaper or magazine, and the other involving the mass publication of said newspaper or magazine and its general distribution for economic profit (both that of the publisher and the person submitting the poem). The 1831 *Confessions of Nat Turner* was published by Thomas R. Gray but printed by Lucas and Deaver. In this instance, "published" seems to have meant "written and paid for by" (since Gray was the author of the book, which he claimed to have been dictated to him by Turner while he awaited execution); the printer is the means by which the publication is made available. Again, these are additional factors to be considered when attempting to understand what Susan Dickinson might have meant by her distinction.

100. Susan Huntington Dickinson, A. L. s. to William Hayes Ward, Amherst, Mass., 18 February 1891, Amy Lowell Collection, Houghton Library, Harvard; Sheila T. Clendenning, *Emily Dickinson: A Bibliography 1850–1966* (Ohio: Kent State University Press, 1968), 13.

101. Susan Huntington Dickinson, A. L. s. to William Hayes Ward, Amherst, Mass., 14 March 1891, Amy Lowell Collection, Houghton Library, Harvard.

102. Ibid., 23 March 1891.

103. Smith, *Rowing in Eden*, 218, 220.

104. As we saw in an earlier chapter, Susan Dickinson's transcripts of Emily Dickinson's poems are as conventional and regular as those of Todd and Higginson. She even tells Higginson that most "of your titles [for Dickinson's poems in the 1890 edition] are perfect – a few I don't happen to fancy." Notice that it is not titling in itself

to which Susan Dickinson objects, but particular titles she does not like. Susan Dickinson, in Bingham, *Ancestors' Brocades*, 86.

105. Dickinson to William Hayes Ward, 23 March 1891. The letter is quoted in Bingham, *Ancestors' Brocades*, 118, and in Smith, "The Poet as Cartoonist," in *Comic Power in Emily Dickinson*, ed. Suzanne Juhasz, Cristanne Miller, and Martha Nell Smith (Austin: University of Texas Press, 1993), 69.

106. Susan Dickinson's materials are A 791–1c, and Otis Lord's, A 761a–z, Special Collections, Frost Library, Amherst College. The three images described here correspond to A 761d, A 761i, and A 761k.

107. Susan Hale, letters to Lucretia Peabody Hale, 9, 19 June 1858, folder 61–16, Sophia Smith Collection, William Alan Neilson Library, Smith College, Northampton.

108. Ibid., 19 June 1860 and 3 July 1863.

109. Pencil draft of note to John L. Graves, A 357.

110. L144, 1:275. For an image and description of the same letter, see Martha Nell Smith's excellent "The Poet as Cartoonist" in *Comic Power*, 74–77.

111. L214, 2:359–60, and Ms Am 1118.5 (B114); Fr48, 1:99, and Ms Am 1118.5 (B186); Fr125A, 1:165, and Ms Am 1118.5 (B175). Jack Capps, in *Emily Dickinson's Reading* (Cambridge: Harvard University Press, 1966), 181, reports that three of the illustrations from the Dickinson copy of the *Primer* were removed: those for *C* ("Christ crucify'd, For sinners dy'd"), *T* ("Young TIMOTHY, Learnt Sin to fly") and *X* ("XERXES did die, and so must I"). The lessons: more illustrations may have existed than are extant; the proportion of images used from texts was still quite small; not all these were necessarily used ironically (Dickinson was not in the habit of ridiculing Christ's crucifixion); and not all these were necessarily cut out and used by Dickinson (they may have been taken by others).

112. Dickinson to William Hayes Ward, 23 March 1891. The letter is quoted in Bingham, *Ancestors' Brocades*, 118, and in Smith, "The Poet as Cartoonist," in *Comic Power*, 69. A friendship book, such as *Friendship's Offering: A Christmas, New-Year, and Birthday Present* (Philadelphia: E. H. Butler & Co., 1855), was an anthology that included essays, stories, poems, and pictures.

113. L13 to Abiah Root, Boston, 8 September 1846, 1:37.

114. Draft 1 is L976, 3:866; draft 2 is in *Letters*, 3:867. The quotation from the Jackson letter is from its inclusion as L976a, 3:869. The second of these drafts is A 819: the reference to Japan occurs on the second page of four, written in pencil on transatlantic paper, and folded into thirds. The draft was never sent, reminding us once again that folding is not in itself evidence of transmission or distribution.

115. In his *Manual of Classical Literature*, N. W. Fiske, professor of Latin and Greek languages at Amherst College, described the origins of written language as it emerged through the historical stages of speech, picture writing, or visual imitation (associated with Native Americans), the hieroglyphics of Ancient Egypt, syllable writing (like the Chinese and Cherokee), until the development of an alphabet, most extensively developed with the Greeks and Romans. There is a clearly racial dimension to this: it is Europeans who are associated with the highest forms of language use, and picture writing is a decidedly lower form of expression. In addition, given nineteenth-century debates about the potentially negative effects of the North American physical landscape on the civilization of its inhabitants (a preoccupation announced, for example, in Fenimore Cooper's opening description of the endless North American forests in *The*

Last of the Mohicans), it seems unlikely that Dickinson would want to align herself with precisely the kinds of people and media that critics of American culture saw as debased. N. W. Fiske, *Manual of Classical Literature, from the German of J. J. Eschenburg* (Philadelphia: Key and Biddle, 1836), 11–21.

116. The Evergreens has a Japanese screen in the dining room, and several pieces of Japanese Imari porcelain that Susan Dickinson is likely to have acquired.

117. Smith, *Rowing in Eden*, 252, n. 6.

118. Walter Benjamin, "The Work of Art in the Age of Mechanical Reproduction," in *Illuminations*, ed. Hannah Arendt, trans. Harry Zohn (New York: Shocken, 1968), 217–42.

119. John Updike, "Preface to a Partial Catalogue of My Own Leavings," in *The Art of Adding and the Art of Taking Away: Selections from John Updike's Manuscripts, an Exhibition at the Houghton Library*, by Elizabeth Falsey (Cambridge: Harvard College Library, 1987), 3.

120. Harriet Beecher Stowe, A. L. s. to Mary Ann (Cockell) Milman (1852), n.p., in Miscellaneous Manuscripts, Special Collections, Frost Library, Amherst College. Stowe mentions what an impact the *Fall of Jerusalem* (1820) had on her—the lines in question are spoken by the character Miriam, a convert from Judaism to Christianity: "It matters little at what hour o' the day / The righteous falls asleep; death cannot come / To him untimely who is fit to die." From *The Poetical Works of the Rev. H. H. Milman* (London: John Murray, 1840), 1:66. Stowe, like Dickinson, does not indent the second physical row of a single line of verse further into the page than the first row.

121. L1025, 3:894, and Ms Am 1118.5 (B66). L586, 2:632, and Ms Am 1118.5 (B55).

122. L757, 3:733, and Photostat Ms Am 1118.5 (B2). The manuscript is now missing. The manuscripts were not always as important to Susan during Dickinson's life, though she sometimes read poems she liked to friends and visitors (such as Todd, for instance). The manuscript of Fr1158B, 2:1006 (Ms Am 1118.5 [B 23]), includes a shopping list in Susan Dickinson's handwriting.

123. Sarah Gates, Kate P. Kingman, and H. C. Pease, "Autographs," in Autograph Albums, Clifton Johnson Collection, Special Collections, Jones Library, Amherst. Gates and Pease had autograph books from the same company; called *The Sunbeam Album*, Kingman's was produced in New York by George A. Leavitt during the 1870s and included printed illustrations as well as blank pages for personal dedications and signatures.

124. Archives and Special Collections, Emily Dickinson Collection, Mount Holyoke College Library; Franklin, *Poems*, 2:771.

125. L17, 1:51.

126. L573a, 2:624.

127. Martha Dickinson Bianchi recalls being instructed by her parents to protect her aunt's right to privacy (*Emily Dickinson Face to Face: Unpublished Letters with Notes and Reminiscences* [Boston: Houghton Mifflin, 1932], 50). And in the same book, she recalls her mother alluding to the poem included in *Masque of Poets*: Dickinson went "so white [Susan] regretted the impulse which had led her to express her own thrill in it." Bianchi claims that the poem was "published without permission," though Dickinson's subsequent reaction (no outrage, no refusal to speak to Niles or Jackson) does not bear that out. It seems more likely that if the encounter reported by Bianchi did take place, she misunderstood its import: Dickinson's tension might have related to

her having published without having informed Susan beforehand, despite having previously denied any interest in publication.

128. The letter is missing, but its existence may be inferred from Thomas Niles's reply to her (see *Letters*, 3:626). Had Dickinson been attuned to the relationship between handwriting and meaning, one would have expected resistance to her appearance in *A Masque of Poets*, or at the very least some negative commentary in letters or notes to Higginson, Jackson, Niles, or Susan Dickinson.

129. A 709; F1432B, 3:1252; L515, 2:589.

130. *The Letters of Junius, from the latest London edition, with fac-similes of attributed authors* (New York: Leavitt & Company, 1851).

131. Thomas Towndrow, *Towndrow's Guide to Calligraphy; Being a New and Complete Series of Fine-Hand Copies, Suitably Arranged in Progressive Exercises; Designed for the Easy Attainment of a Bold, Free, Expeditious, and Beautiful Style of Writing* (Salem: Ives and Jewett, 1839); A. R. Dunton and J. V. R. Chapman, *The Original Duntonian System of Rapid Writing, Revised and Improved* (Boston: J. M. Whittemore and Company, 1855).

132. The counterargument, that Dickinson's non-publication is an implicit recognition that publishing institutions and techniques could never properly reproduce the visual aspects of her art, presupposes that the technology of nineteenth-century typography was so limited, so fixed, that it could not have adjusted to the demands of a visually innovative lyric intelligence. And yet even a passing acquaintance with the theories and techniques of print in the 1800s—with specimen books, for instance, or Owen Jones's 1856 *Grammar of Ornament*—shows an industry remarkably attuned to a diversity of visual effects and colors (see the *Specimen of Printing Types and Ornaments from the Type and Stereotype Foundry of John T. White* [New York: No. 45 Gold, Near Fulton-Street, 1843]). Even if one accepts the possibility of Ellen Hart's arguments about "The Mushroom is the Elf of Plants," one wonders why print—which coped with George Herbert's pattern poems—could not have accommodated the alleged design of Dickinson's poems. I am thinking here of "The Altar" and "Easter Wings," pattern poems that were perfectly well represented in early print editions of Herbert's work. The latter, indeed, was arranged vertically, that is, with script running from the top to the bottom of the page (in direction, not extent), where today it is usually presented horizontally.

133. Charles Schultz, "Either a Pirate Ship or a Zamboni," *Peanuts*, syndicated on 30 July 1997.

134. Hans-Georg Gadamer, *Truth and Method*, trans. and ed. Garrett Barden and John Cumming (New York: Continuum, 1975), 263.

135. S. P. Rosenbaum, ed., *A Concordance to the Poems of Emily Dickinson* (Ithaca: Cornell University Press, 1964), 578; Cynthia MacKenzie, ed., *Concordance to the Letters of Emily Dickinson* (Boulder: University Press of Colorado, 2000), 563. The poem is Fr1568, 3:1371; the letter is L745, 3:723. Both Franklin and Johnson and Ward date the poem to January 1882.

136. A 42. The paper is folded in thirds and endorsed (presumably by Tuckerman, since the writing is cursive and in ink) "Emilie Dickinson / Jan 1882." The paper is watermarked "WESTON'S / LINEN / 1876."

137. That is, the prose has a total of five dashes, two of which are terminal (they mark the close of a paragraph and sentence); the poem has three dashes, one of which is terminal (it marks the end of the poem) and the other two of which coincide with

the end of metrically, but not grammatically, defined sequences ("Sweet Pirate of the Heart, Not Pirate of the Sea – What wrecketh thee?" and "Some Spice's Mutiny – Some Attar's perfidy? Confide in me –"). In other words, the capitals that follow "Sea" and "Mutiny" are not explicable in terms of prose; they exist only because they mark the beginning of a line of verse.

138. As Franklin also points out in his editorial apparatus to the poem, "perfidy" was originally followed by a dash; Dickinson then appended a question mark.

139. Tanselle, *Description of Descriptive Bibliography*, 35.

140. The evidence for this is contradictory. The editors of the Dickinson Electronic Archives site claim that they "do not presume to know how [Dickinson] would have preferred her work to be presented to the public (i.e., in print or manuscript)." But the editors' emphasis on the visual aspects of the text and their importance to a deeper understanding of the writings suggests very strongly that print is always going to be an inadequate medium for representing the poetry. The rationale for having a manuscript site contradicts such denials, in other words. And one reacts to the presumption that Dickinson would have approved of any form of widespread publication, for the assumption is that only the *medium* of presentation would have been problematic, and not publication itself. See <http://www.jefferson.virginia.village.edu/dickinson/archive_description.html>

141. Fredson Bowers, "Notes on Theory and Practice in Editing Texts," in *The Book Encompassed: Studies in Twentieth-Century Bibliography*, ed. Peter Davison (Cambridge: Cambridge University Press, 1992), 244.

142. Ralph W. Franklin, "The Emily Dickinson Fascicles," *Studies in Bibliography* 36 (1983): 16.

143. Ibid., 18.

144. As Franklin also points out, human beings have a tenacious and often admirable capacity for finding patterns in random events and signs. One is reminded of William Gaddis's *Carpenter's Gothic*, in which Paul Booth, a Vietnam veteran turned media consultant, tries to explain the latest scheme he is working on to his wife, Elizabeth, by drawing a diagram for her on the blank side of a letter. He thinks the diagram illustrates Senate committees and aspects of the Food for Africa campaign; she sees a kidney, a coastline, and a series of arrows, and another character named McCandless believes it is a child's drawing. Finally, a CIA agent looks at the same document and says, "It's Cressy. I just figured it out. It's the battle of Cressy," referring to the 1396 battle between the French and English armies at Crecy-en-Ponthieu (William Gaddis, *Carpenter's Gothic* [New York: Viking, 1985], 147).

145. Franklin, *Poems of Emily Dickinson: Reading Edition* (Cambridge: Harvard University Press, Belknap Press, 1999), 3.

146. Fr816, 2:770–71.

147. Ms Am 1118.5 (B139).

148. A 91-3/4.

149. As Franklin admits, there *are* fascicles that seem to have common themes or topics: fourteen of the twenty-two poems in packet 82 are about flowers, for instance. But is the relation a planned theme, or does it derive from the poems' having "a single author out of whose particular experience, interests, concerns, and techniques they have emerged" (Franklin, "Emily Dickinson Fascicles," 20)? It is one thing to say that the fascicles have a design that was implemented across many years and forty hand-assembled manuscript books; it is quite another to say that Dickinson often wrote

about flowers. As Richard B. Sewall pointed out: "One difficulty is that almost any random groupings of eighteen or twenty of ED's stronger poems can be shown to have similar coherence, so recurrent are her major themes, images and symbolic structures" (Richard B. Sewall, *The Life of Emily Dickinson* [New York: Farrar, Straus and Giroux, 1974], 2:538, n. 4). Sewall's statement is also quoted by Franklin.

150. For example, Fr1433A, "What mystery pervades a well," includes a line ("But nature is a stranger yet") that Dickinson transcribed as "But Susan is a stranger yet" in a variant (Fr1433C) sent next door in 1877 (3:1254–55). Does this indicate that Susan Dickinson was the original subject of the poem or that Dickinson modified it because the same point applied to her sister-in-law? And if Susan Dickinson was the original, do we accept that the version with the line about her is more authoritative than the one with the line about nature?

151. Smith, *Rowing in Eden*, 16.

152. Ibid.

153. Tanselle, "The Editorial Problem of Final Authorial Intention," 206. Tanselle also writes that Dickinson's "distrust of publication does not obligate an editor to leave her poems unpublished (or to edit them as if they were private papers) any more than an author's 'deathbed' edition obligates an editor to regard previous editions as superseded."

154. Tanselle, *Description of Descriptive Bibliography*, 35.

155. The reference to a foreign country invokes the first line of the prologue to L. P. Hartley's novel *The Go-Between*: "The past is a foreign country: they do things differently there" (Harmondsworth: Penguin, 1958), 7.

POSTSCRIPT *"Where the Meanings, are"*

1. Suzanne Juhasz, "Materiality and the Poet," in *The Emily Dickinson Handbook* (Amherst: University of Massachusetts Press, 1998), 428.

2. Robert Lowell, "Epilogue," in *Day by Day* (New York: Farrar, Straus and Giroux, 1977), 127. The lines read: "We are poor passing facts, / warned by that to give / each figure in the photograph / his living name."

3. Adam Frank, "Emily Dickinson and Photography," *Emily Dickinson Journal* 10, no. 2 (2001): 1–21.

4. Paul Crumbley, *Inflections of the Pen: Dash and Voice in Emily Dickinson* (Lexington: University Press of Kentucky, 1997), 2.

5. The best edition is, by definition, not a perfect one, as Ralph Hanna III has argued in "Producing Manuscripts and Editions." Hanna's concept of "best responsible text" has been a strong influence on this postscript (*Crux and Controversy in Middle English Textual Criticism*, ed. A. J. Minnis and Charlotte Brewer [Suffolk: D. S. Brewer, 1992], 128). He also uses the phrase "best text in aggregate," which seems to have been a principle in Franklin's work as well.

6. L194, 2:339–41; LP29, 74–75.

7. L320, 2:454–55.

8. Fr764, 2:722–23; Ralph W. Franklin, *The Manuscript Books of Emily Dickinson* (Cambridge: Harvard University Press, Belknap Press, 1981), 2:825–26.

9. That is, Franklin records his emendations at the bottom of the poem; Hart and Smith do not, on the grounds that they do not believe that they make emendations. My argument is that they do and that Franklin's edition is superior because it performs

what Ralph Hanna terms "various steps in order to achieve the same variety of display and scrutiny which other modes of critical edition routinely offer" (Hanna, "Producing Manuscripts and Editions," 128).

10. Fr764, 2:722–23.

11. Alfred Habegger, *My Wars Are Laid Away in Books* (New York: Random House, 2001), 501.

12. Susan Howe, *My Emily Dickinson* (Berkeley: North Atlantic Books, 1985), 76–77. I have only one problem with Howe's list: it seems chronological, like an early piece of reader-response criticism, so that the possibilities she mentions for the protagonist are not entirely borne out by the rest of the poem. For instance, the speaker of the poem suggests that it may live longer than the master, which does not seem unproblematically to apply to a relationship between a human and a divine being. Such an objection is not necessarily definitive; adjustments can be made to explain it away. Still, one would have liked to see Howe negotiate the relationship between the first stanza (which unequivocally supports the range of personalities and types offered by Howe) and the final stanza (which does not; which narrows down the range of potential reference or at least makes them less evident than the first). For the section on an unmarried woman, Howe gives as an example Catherine Earnshaw being chosen by "lover-husband-owner" Edgar Linton. Linton does not strike me as a lover in anything more than a technical sense (he is a father), and although he belongs to the landowning class, he is not individually masterful, unlike Heathcliff. In addition, Brontë makes it clear that Catherine is the one who chooses Edgar over Heathcliff. Finally, Elizabeth Gaskell's biography of Charlotte Brontë included the information that Patrick, the father, invariably carried "a loaded pistol about with him. It lay on his dressing table with his watch; with his watch it was put on in the morning" (Gaskell, *The Life of Charlotte Brontë* [Harmondsworth: Penguin, 1975], 90). The biography was first published in London in 1857, and is alluded to in a Dickinson letter of 1876 (L471, 2: 559).

13. Thomas Wentworth Higginson had written on Nat Turner's insurrection: Howe suggests "My Life had stood – a Loaded Gun" "may have been triggered by parts of it" (Howe, *My Emily Dickinson*, 125). The events described in this summary are derived from Thomas R. Gray, *The Confessions of Nat Turner* (Baltimore: Thomas R. Gray, 1831).

14. Or to the role of the wife at the time of the poem's telling: the speaker may be distinguishing between her present state (of widowhood, abandonment, separation) and a married past.

15. George R. Taylor, "The Rise and Decline of Manufactures and Other Matters," in *Essays on Amherst's History*, ed. Theodore P. Greene (Amherst: Vista Trust, 1978), 63. Carpenter & Morehouse, *History of the Town of Amherst, Massachusetts* (Amherst: Carpenter & Morehouse, 1896), 295–97.

16. Harold F. Williams, *Winchester, the Gun that Won the West* (Washington, D.C.: Combat Forces Press, 1952), 5.

17. Michael A. Bellesiles, *Arming America: The Origins of a National Gun Culture* (New York: Alfred A. Knopf, 2000), 417.

18. Roper Rifle Co. Folder, Special Collections, Jones Library, Amherst.

19. I am grateful to Richard Golden, of the Springfield Armory in Massachusetts, and Philip Eckert, of Old Sturbridge Village in Massachusetts, for much of this information. Additional sources include Ellsworth S. Grant, *The Colt Legacy: The Colt Ar-*

mory in Hartford, 1850–1980 (Providence, R.I.: Mowbray, 1982), and Claude Blair, ed., *Pollard's History of Firearms* (New York: Macmillan, 1983). Deer hunters in Massachusetts today are permitted to use only shotguns, on the grounds that these have a more reduced range and are therefore less likely to cause accidental harm to humans (whereas a rifle bullet that misses its target can travel much greater distances and therefore expose more people to risk). For a more amusing description of hunting around Amherst, see Daniel Lombardo, *Tales of Amherst: A Look Back* (Amherst: Jones Library, 1986), 118–19. The hunting season began in September, which might help support the thesis that the poem was written in the latter part of the year. Typically, Dickinson creates a mythic and timeless scene from otherwise very time- and place-specific circumstances.

20. By extension, the yellow eye may be a metonym (the eye that looks through the sight on the gun or that aligns it with the target; mid-century shotguns also had rudimentary front sights, usually a ball or a nub) or a metaphor (the flame that emerges from the circular barrel resembles an eye by virtue of its roundness at that point). The yellow eye also suggests jaundice, or at least a physically and morally unhealthy condition.

21. Grant, *Colt Legacy*, 11.

22. Howe lists suppression as one of the possibilities; Laurence Perrine first mentioned the thumb as bullet in the *Explicator* 21, no. 3 (1962): item 21. The image of a thumb flying through the air seems unintentionally comic, however. In addition, the modern bullet is longer than the kinds of objects shot in the mid-nineteenth century: perhaps Perrine was thinking of those when he speculated on the similarity.

23. The critics who have come closest to this position are Shira Wolosky, *Emily Dickinson: A Voice of War* (New Haven: Yale University Press, 1984), 92–95; Marianne Boruch, "Dickinson Descending," *Georgia Review* 40, no. 4 (Winter 1986): 872–73; and J. Bakker, "Emily Dickinson's Secret," *Dutch Quarterly Review of Anglo-American Letters* 16, no. 4 (1986): 345–46. It is also possible that the poem is a twin of Fr291, "It sifts from Leaden Sieves"—a politically conservative meditation on the disenfranchised as tools of political unrest (1:311–14).

24. The autobiographical element is strengthened by the reference to Vesuvius, which is taken as Dickinson's image for herself as a hidden force. For more on this, see Adrienne Rich, "Vesuvius at Home: The Power of Emily Dickinson," *Parnassus: Poetry in Review* 5, no. 1 (Fall–Winter 1976): 771–73.

25. The list is derived from Joseph Duchac, *The Poems of Emily Dickinson: An Annotated Guide to Commentary Published in English, 1890–1977* (Boston: G. K. Hall, 1979), 327–31, and Duchac, *The Poems of Emily Dickinson: An Annotated Guide to Commentary Published in English, 1978–1989* (New York: G. K. Hall, 1993), 257–62.

26. <http://jefferson.village.virginia.edu/dickinson/archive_description.html> (accessed 29 August 2001).

27. This criticism is not aimed at Marta Werner, who seems to me to be more archival than interpretive in her orientation. I am reluctant to return to the days before 1955, when the transmission by others of Emily Dickinson's writing was carried out through a series of competing and flawed editions that kept her in the public eye but failed to generate the momentum of serious interest that followed Johnson's variorum *Poems of Emily Dickinson*. For that momentum to be regained, we need quickly to reestablish consensus about what constitutes the most reliable single editions of her works, and in 2003 the "best responsible texts" are Ralph W. Franklin's (1998) *Poems*

of Emily Dickinson, and *Letters of Emily Dickinson* edited by Johnson and Theodora Ward. It seems to me that the publication in 1955 and 1958 of scholarly editions of Dickinson's poems and letters goes a long way toward explaining the flowering of interest in her work that led (among other things) to Richard B. Sewall's *Emily Dickinson: A Collection of Critical Essays* (1963) and *The Life of Emily Dickinson* (1974), to David Porter's *The Art of Emily Dickinson's Early Poetry* (1966) and *The Modern Idiom* (1981), to Suzanne Juhasz's *Naked and Fiery Forms* (1976) and *The Undiscovered Continent* (1983), to Cristanne Miller's *Emily Dickinson: A Poet's Grammar* (1987), and not least to the founding of the Emily Dickinson International Society in 1989.

Index of Poems, Letters, and Prose Fragments

Poem numbers (and variant letters) are those of Ralph W. Franklin, *The Poems of Emily Dickinson*, Variorum Edition (Cambridge, Mass.: Harvard University Press, Belknap Press, 1998). (For fascicles and sets, see the main index.) Letters and prose fragments follow the numeration of Thomas H. Johnson and Theodora Ward, *The Letters of Emily Dickinson* (Cambridge, Mass.: Harvard University Press, Belknap Press, 1958). Bracketed manuscript numbers preceded by letters refer to items in the following collections: A: Special Collections, Frost Library, Amherst College; BPL: Department of Rare Books and Manuscripts, Boston Public Library; H: Houghton Library, Harvard College Library; S: Mortimer Rare Book Room, William Allan Neilson Library, Smith College.

Franklin, Ralph W., "The Emily Dickinson Fascicles," 307, 412–13n149

Franklin, Ralph W., *The Manuscript Books of Emily Dickinson*, 6–7, 23, 28–29

Franklin, Ralph W., *The Poems of Emily Dickinson*: and capitalization, 202–3; editorial practices, 42–44, 68–69, 135, 202–5, 317; formatting in, 124, 125, 174; and generic divisions, 116, 184; as point of reference, 311; reception of, 21, 28; and unfinished drafts, 167

Gasciogne, George, 223

gender, 186

genre(s): 131–90; aphorisms, 154; and classification of Dickinson's manuscripts, 4–6, 133–39, 143–44, 153–54; and context, 53; and Dickinson's intent, 6–7, 140, 187, 374n60; and drafts, 142–43, 167–68; epigrams, 73–74, 134, 139–40; generic boundaries in Dickinson's letters, 130, 133–90, 329–30n33, 371n28, 373n51; and historical context, 52, 189, 342–43n107; and manuscript-based criticism, 4, 88, 133, 328n17; and nineteenth-century manuscript conventions, 53–55; proverbs, 150–51; and subject matter, 149, 371n28; verse-epistles, 150. *See also* letter-poems; letters

Graves, Gertrude M., 126, 196, 382n21

Greetham, D. C., 272, 273

guns, in nineteenth-century America, 320–22

Guthrie, James, 45

Habegger, Alfred, 90, 131, 346n10, 361n5

Hampson, Alfred Leete, 1, 270, 325n2, 332n3, 398–99n23

Hampson, Mary Landis, 270–71, 325nn2–3, 333–34n15, 398–99n23

handwriting: and dating of poems, 29, 128; and Dickinson's health, 47, 351n53; and Dickinson's intent, 110, 302–3; and editorial practices, 142–43; in letters and poems, 391n41; and nineteenth-century practice, 61; variations in, 47–48, 64; word forms, 237–38. *See also* commas; dashes; letter-forms; quotation mark(s); underlining

Hardy, Thomas, 193

Hart Ellen, "Editing in Amherst," 194–97

Hart, Ellen, "The Elizabeth Whitney Putnam Manuscripts and New Strategies for Editing Emily Dickinson's Letters": and diplomatic transcription, 384n44; on formatting of letters, 286–87; and generic divisions, 134; and organicist theory, 135–38, 197–98; on visual puns, 134

Hart, Ellen, and Martha Nell Smith, *Open Me Carefully*: and capitalization, 240–41; and Dickinson's intent, 45; and Dickinson's letter-forms, 76–77; editorial practices, 6, 38, 96–97, 135–36, 241–42, 298; on folds, 338n65; formatting in, 43–44, 135, 206–7, 349–50nn42–44, 374n58; and generic divisions, 38, 91, 43, 51, 143; and Harvard University Press, 20; and letter-poem genre, 44, 69, 82, 87–88, 99, 143–44, 149; and organicist theory, 205; and photographic reproductions, 277; representation of spaces, 24–26, 316; and underlining, 241–43; and unfinished drafts, 167–68

Harvard University Press, 19–20, 22, 48, 331–32n

Herbert, George, "Mattens," 277–80

Herron, Kristin, 16

Higdon, David, 2

Higginson, Mary Thacher, 292–95

Higginson, Thomas Wentworth, 32–33, 103, 133, 158, 185–86, 296; poems sent to, 133, 158, 293, 308; relationship with Dickinson, 103, 185–86, 386n. *See also* Todd, Mabel Loomis, and Thomas Wentworth Higginson

Hirsch, E. D., Jr., 266

Hirschhorn, Norbert, 185

Holland, Elizabeth, 169, 171, 188, 261; poems sent to, 308

Holland, Josiah, 159, 185

Howe, Susan, 274, 319–20, 414n12

Hubbard, Melanie, 8

humor, in Dickinson's writings, 105–6, 118, 149, 361–62n11

hymn(s), Protestant: and ballads, 213, 226; meter, 213, 223–24, 226–27, 250–51, 264, 385n52, 388–89nn17–20, 395n89; rhyme, 227, 387n7, 389n22; stanzas, 74–75, 274–75; Watts's hymnals, 223, 226–27, 386n3

hypertext markup language. *See* electronic reproductions

hyphens, and word splits, 194

imagery, Dickinson's: birds, 107; flowers, 3–4, 149; sea, 103–5; seasonal, 366n56; wine, 115

indentation. *See* spaces, horizontal

Independent, The, 295–97

Jackson, Helen (Fiske) Hunt, 15, 265, 299

James, Henry, 185

Jewett, Sarah Orne, 291–92

DOMHNALL MITCHELL is professor of nineteenth-century American literature at the Norwegian University of Science and Technology. He has published articles on Emily Dickinson in *American Literature, Legacy, Nineteenth-Century Literature,* and the *Emily Dickinson Journal* and has chapters on Dickinson in *The Cambridge Companion to Emily Dickinson* (2002) and *Twayne Literary Voices: American Literature in Historical Context, 1820–1870* (2005). Mitchell has been the recipient of a fellowship from the Houghton Library, Harvard University (2000), and the Copeland Fellowship from Amherst College (2002) for his work on Dickinson's manuscripts. He has published two books: *Emily Dickinson: Monarch of Perception* (2000) and (with Paul Goring and Jeremy Hawthorn) *Studying Literature: The Essential Companion* (2001).